NINE MODERN CLASSICS

Other Texts by BARNET, BERMAN, BURTO

Aspects of the Drama: A Handbook
A Dictionary of Literary, Dramatic, and Cinematic Terms Second Edition
An Introduction to Literature: Fiction, Poetry, Drama Fourth Edition
Tragedy and Comedy: An Anthology of Drama
Types of Drama: Plays and Essays

By SYLVAN BARNET

A Short Guide to Writing About Literature Second Edition

Published by LITTLE, BROWN AND COMPANY

SYLVAN BARNET
Tufts University
MORTON BERMAN
Boston University
WILLIAM BURTO
Lowell State College

NINE MODERN CLASSICS

AN ANTHOLOGY OF SHORT NOVELS

LITTLE, BROWN AND COMPANY
Boston

LIBRARY OF CONGRESS CATALOG CARD NO. 72-14218

FIRST PRINTING

Published simultaneously in Canada
by Little, Brown & Company (Canada) Limited

PRINTED IN THE UNITED STATES OF AMERICA

ACKNOWLEDGMENTS

JOSEPH CONRAD

Heart of Darkness is reprinted by permission of J. M. Dent & Sons Ltd. and the Trustees of the Joseph Conrad Estate. Photograph used courtesy of J. M. Dent & Sons Ltd.

FYODOR M. DOSTOEVSKY

Notes from the Underground is reprinted by permission of The Macmillan Company, New York, and William Heinemann Ltd., London, from Fyodor M. Dostoevsky, *White Knights and Other Stories,* translated by Constance Garnett. Printed in Great Britain. Photograph used by permission of Radio Times Hulton Picture Library.

WILLIAM FAULKNER

Old Man is reprinted by permission of Random House, Inc., from William Faulkner, *The Faulkner Reader.* Copyright 1939, renewed 1967 by Mrs. William Faulkner and Mrs. Paul D. Summers. Photograph by Ralph Thompson used courtesy of Random House.

FRANZ KAFKA

The Metamorphosis is reprinted by permission of Schocken Books, Inc., from Franz Kafka, *The Penal Colony.* Copyright © 1948 by Schocken Books, Inc. Photograph used courtesy of Schocken Books, Inc.

THOMAS MANN

Mario and the Magician is reprinted by permission of Alfred A. Knopf, Inc., from Thomas Mann, *Stories of Three Decades,* translated by H. T. Lowe-Porter. Copyright 1931, renewed 1959 by Alfred A. Knopf, Inc. Photograph by by Max Ehlert used by permission of Black Star.

HERMAN MELVILLE

Photograph used by permission of Brown Brothers.

ALEXANDER SOLZHENITSYN

One Day in the Life of Ivan Denisovich is reprinted by permission of Brandt & Brandt. Translation copyright © 1963 by Thomas P. Whitney. Photograph used by permission of Black Star.

LEO N. TOLSTOY

The Death of Ivan Ilych is reprinted by permission from Leo N. Tolstoy, *Ivan Ilych, Hadji Murad and Other Stories,* translated by Louise and Aylmer Maude and published by Oxford University Press. Photograph used by permission of Sovfoto.

JEAN TOOMER

Cane is reprinted by permission of Liveright, Publishers, New York. Copyright © 1951 by Jean Toomer. Photograph used courtesy of Marjorie Content Toomer.

PREFACE

In the House of Fiction there are many mansions, but in college courses in literature the short story usually occupies the royal suite. Doubtless this is because such stories by their brevity lend themselves nicely to classroom analysis, but a steady diet of short stories, with their condensed ironies and illuminations, is a bit thin. Howard Nemerov, in *Poetry and Fiction,* says wickedly: "Short stories amount for the most part to parlor tricks, party favors with built-in snappers, gadgets for inducing recognitions and reversals: a small pump serves to build up the pressure, a tiny trigger releases it, there follow a puff and a flash as freedom and necessity combine; finally a Celluloid doll drops from the muzzle and descends by parachute to the floor."

This collection offers longer works which, as the general introduction tries to suggest, belong to a subdivision of the novel. Most of them, however, can be easily read in a single sitting; and because a reader can remember—at least until the next day—almost everything in a short novel, classroom discussion can be accurate as well as lively.

We have tried to keep the editorial apparatus unobtrusive. Foreign words and obscure allusions are annotated, and we hope readers will find provocative the general introduction and the afterwords to each short novel, all of which bite off more than they chew. The short biographies offer a minimal context, and the glossary at the rear offers definitions of the chief critical terms used in talking about short novels.

Finally, we want to thank Jane Aaron, Charles Christensen, and David Giele of Little, Brown and Company, and the publishers, agents, and translators who granted us permission to use copyrighted material. We are especially grateful to Mrs. Marjorie Content Toomer for her generous cooperation.

S.B.
M.B.
W.B.

CONTENTS

NINE MODERN CLASSICS

FICTION: A GENERAL INTRODUCTION

There is a valuable book called *Understanding Fiction,* but probably most writers would agree that more valuable than *understanding* literature is *experiencing* it. John Keats knew what it was to experience literature: when he read Homer he "felt . . . like some watcher of the skies / When a new planet swims into his ken," and when he sat down to re-read Shakespeare's *King Lear,* he knew that he would "burn through" the play. We often think that literature and life are two entirely different things, but Keats knew that to read a great book is to live intensely. Recently Jorge Luis Borges put the matter quite simply: "I think of reading a book as no less an experience than traveling or falling in love." Even more recently Alexander Solzhenitsyn said, in the speech he would have delivered if the Soviet Union had allowed him to accept the Nobel Prize he won in 1970, "Literature can convey condensed experience from one land to another . . . [enabling] one nation to learn the history of another with such strength of recognition that it seems to have undergone the experience itself." The novels in this book are offered with the hope that readers will respond to them; the editorial apparatus, including this introduction, seeks to help readers to understand these short novels, but the further aim is to deepen or enlarge the readers' experiences of the novels and of themselves.

Let us begin, a bit coldly, by trying to set some limits to the word "novel." It is not easy to define the novel as a literary form. We cannot define it by its subject matter or emotional effect or mode of presentation as we *can* define (for example) tragedy: a serious representation, usually ending with death or a death-like state such as blindness, aiming at arousing pity and fear, presented by impersonators. About the novel we can not say much more than that it is (1) fiction, (2) prose, (3) fairly long (already we are weaseling), (4) usually realistic, often chronicling bourgeois experience. But to number these characteristics is perhaps falsely to imply that one can be scientific in this business of defining the novel. Take the first point, the novel as fiction. In fact, how do we know that a given work is fictional? Novels almost always present themselves as fact. They name names and give dates and avoid the improbable and do all they can to persuade the reader that he is hearing about something that happened. When we pick up a novel, of course, we are prepared for fiction, whereas we may be getting fact or something very close to it. There are, for example, highly autobiographical novels such as D. H. Lawrence's *Sons and Lovers,* James Joyce's *A Portrait of the Artist as a Young Man,* and Alexander Solzhenitsyn's *One Day in the Life of Ivan Denisovich,* books that probably contain a good deal more of what really happened than many political autobiographies which claim to offer the truth. William Styron's *The Confessions of Nat Turner* draws upon history, and in the present collection Melville's *Benito Cereno,* closely based on something that really happened, even includes chunks of historical documents. So it may be better to say that we accept a novel as fiction, whether or not it really is. The second point, the use of prose, is less arguable, but what it means in part is that the novel uses language that sounds rather like the language we use daily, language that is not conspicuously rhythmical or ornate or attractive in itself — though in fact our utterances are not nearly as orderly and as lucid as the novelist's. Moreover, if we read the novel attentively, and not as we read the newspaper at breakfast, we notice that novelists have a fondness for metaphor and other figurative devices that we tend to associate with poetry; certain threads of imagery may run through the book. Their writing remains prose, not poetry, but in these respects their use of language is closer to the poet's than it is to our speech. The novelist gives us the illusion of staying close to our idiom, for he is usually seeking to create a world rather like ours, but his prose is certainly not our talk.

The third point, length, is hopeless. One knows that a novel is longish, but how long is longish, and at what point does a long story become a short novel? The best we can do at the moment is to postpone the matter until the end of this introduction, where there is a brief discussion of the short novel.

The fourth point, realism in the novel, requires and deserves the fullest treatment. The word "novel" is related to the word "news," and news is supposed to be true, real. A novel is news, the story of a happening — and though "story" often implies untruth, it is related to "history," a word that implies truth. In its origins the novel owes much to historical writing and to autobiography and biography (a history of an individual). Novelists may invent their happenings, but they deal with things that closely resemble the stuff of this world; they regularly avoid talking animals, enchanted sleepers, and they even avoid heroes, for our age no longer believes in heroes in the sense of godlike men or men who deserve reverence. When Thackeray subtitled *Vanity Fair* "A Novel without a Hero" he was speaking for most novelists throughout Europe. In Russia, for example, Dostoevsky began *The Brothers Karamazov* thus:

> In beginning the life story of my hero, Alexey Fyodorovich Karamazov, I find myself in somewhat of a quandary. Namely, although I call Alexey Fyodorovich my hero, I myself know that he is by no means a great man, and hence I foresee such unavoidable questions as these: "What is so remarkable about your Alexey Fyodorovich, that you have chosen him as your hero? What has he accomplished? What is he known for, and by whom? Why should I, the reader, spend time learning the facts of his life?"

Heroes in the traditional sense belong to the world of romance, and practitioners have been careful to distinguish novels from romances. Sir Walter Scott, a romancer, writing for the *Encyclopaedia Britannica* in 1823, says that in a romance the interest "turns upon marvellous and uncommon incidents" whereas in the novel "the events are accommodated to the ordinary train of human events, and the modern state of society." Hawthorne, in the preface to his *The House of the Seven Gables* (1851) makes much the same point when he distinguishes between the romance and the novel:

> The latter form of composition is presumed to aim at a very minute fidelity, not merely to the possible, but to the probable and ordinary course of man's experience. The former — while, as a work of art, it must rigidly subject itself to laws, and while it sins unpardonably so far as it may swerve aside from the truth of the human heart — has fairly a right to present that truth under circumstances, to a great extent, of the writer's own choosing or creation.

In short, we customarily get in the novel what Henry James called an "air of reality (solidity of specification)," and this includes a richly detailed sense of place very like places we know and a sense of people very like people we meet. Since the readers of most novels have been members of the middle class, a class that has rarely undervalued itself, novels have usually presented the experiences of middle-class people, and have tended to adopt the middle-class assumption that the subjective experiences of individuals are important and ought to be described in scrupulous detail. And so in novels we get an insistent dwelling on detail, not only detail about states of mind but about clothing, food, livingquarters, etc., and the effect of this is not — as in romance — to convey a sense of the wonderful, but to convey a sense of the real in all of its particularity. (This point is discussed further in the afterword to *The Death of Ivan Ilych,* p. 226.) Let one of our novelists, Thomas Mann, speak about the importance of realism. In a letter he says, "In the final analysis accuracy, 'authenticity,' the striking resemblance to real life, is what always gives us pleasure in art, in the rendering of psychological as well as objective states. . . . Realism is the backbone; it gives a work the ring of truth."

And yet, of course, the mere accurate representation of details — though no easy job — is not enough to hold us and hold us again and again. The details, however abundant, must be selective, chosen by a single mind, and endowed with a significance. George Eliot, in *Adam Bede,* does not claim that she gives an exact picture of reality, but only that she seeks to "give a faithful account of man and things as they have mirrored themselves in my mind." Art, that is, is not merely a representation of reality but a *response* to it. (Here again the novel is related to history, for history, as Henry James says in *The American Scene,* "is never, in any rich sense, the immediate crudity of what 'happens,' but the much finer complexity of what we read into it and think of in connection with it.") The choice of a particular story with all of its particular details — out of all of the possible happenings that flutter about in the world — is of course conditioned by each writer's temperament, but Joseph Conrad was scarcely oversimplifying when he wrote that "the pursuit of happiness . . . is the only theme that can be legitimately developed by the novelist who is the chronicler of the adventures of mankind amongst the dangers of the kingdom of the earth. And the kingdom of this earth itself, the ground upon which his individualities stand, stumble, or die, must enter into his scheme of faithful record." This is finely put and it is true, but we can go further and say, speaking only a little too loosely, that if we stand back from the rich details of the novel, we usually see a slightly ironic presentation of the development from innocence to experience, from insubstantial happiness or self-satisfaction to a somewhat humbled and saving awareness of the way of the world. (In the present volume this motif is readily apparent in Melville's *Benito Cereno,* Tolstoy's *The Death of Ivan Ilych,* Conrad's *Heart of Darkness,* Kafka's *The Metamorphosis,* Toomer's *Cane,* and Mann's *Mario and the Magician,* though of course the treatment in each story is so complex and so rich that no story in any way comes close to "saying the same thing" as another.)

Novelists have, doubtless sincerely, often said that they write simply in order to create something that will please them; "My motto is 'Art for *my* sake,' " D. H. Lawrence said, and Thomas Mann said that a novelist is a man who entertains himself. But we know, too, that novelists no less than other men are endowed with what Dr. Johnson called "that hunger of the imagination which preys incessantly upon life." The flux of experience is not merely perceived but is given a shape by the imagination, and the writer feels a pressure to embody in words and thus to communicate — even if at first only to himself — his sense not only of an experience but of its meaning. The idea that "this must be told" is finely stated by Lady Murasaki in the eleventh-century Japanese novel, *The Tale of Genji.* She has Prince Genji say (in Arthur Waley's eloquent translation),

> The storyteller's own experience of men and things, whether for good or ill — not only what he has passed through himself, but even events which he has only witnessed or been told of — has moved him to an emotion so passionate that he can no longer keep it shut up in his heart. Again and again something in his own life or in that around him will seem to the writer so important that he cannot bear to let it pass into oblivion. There must never come a time, he feels, when men do not know about it.

We do not, of course, have to go to the Far East for this wisdom. One of our novelists, Joseph Conrad, a few years after writing *Heart of Darkness* touched on this matter of the novelist giving us not the world as it is (what is it?) but the world as he has experienced and understood it:

> Every novelist must begin by creating for himself a world, great or little, in which he can honestly believe. This world cannot be made otherwise than in his own image: it is fated to remain individual and a little mysterious, and yet it must resemble something already familiar to the experience, the thoughts and the sensations of his readers. At the heart of fiction, even the least worthy of the name, some sort of truth can be found.

It really is as simple, and as complex, as that; it is also as simple and as complex as Tolstoy's statement that literature is concerned with questions of how men live and should live. The great novelists give us not simply a representation of the buzzing confusion of experience — what William James called mere "weather" — but a representation shaped by an attitude, by a philosophy. This is not the place to talk about such technical terms as "plot," "character," and "motivation," but we can say here that in a work of fiction things all hang together, and we can follow the work because the writer has united scraps of reality with assumptions about or responses to happenings and people. But this unifying vision made up out of assumptions or responses is not something that can be reduced to a simple message, for, as we all now know, the medium — in this case prose fiction — is the message, and the thousands of sentences in the story all play their part in precisely defining the message. Once more we can quote Joseph Conrad, this time describing Marlow, the central character in *Heart of Darkness:*

> The yarns of seamen have a direct simplicity, the whole meaning of which lies within the shell of a cracked nut. But . . . to him the meaning of an episode was not inside like the kernel but outside, enveloping the tale which brought it out only as a glow brings out a haze. . . .

Fictions have meanings, though the meanings cannot be put into a nutshell. And fictions have uses, though not quite of the sort that the convict in Faulkner's *Old Man* thought. This convict had been an avid reader of Westerns, and he thought he could learn from these fictions, apparently so rich in detail, how to rob a train. He was mistaken, but that was partly because the fictions he read were not really based on a vision of how men live and should live. The incidental realistic details — say descriptions of cowboy clothing and of gold watches handed over to robbers — apparently had nothing to do with an understanding of how men — even robbers — really live, though better Westerns might indeed provide assistance in living the life of a robber.

What uses, then, does fiction have? First, we can say that it entertains, and surely anything that brings pleasure to us cannot easily be dismissed. Second, we can say that it gives us a sense of experiences that are not our own; it helps to free us from the prison of the self and lets us share in alien states of mind. This much is obvious and indisputable. But can we not go further, and argue that literature gives us an understanding of life? Need we hold with some theorists that Dostoevsky's *Notes from Underground* (for example) gives us nothing but an extremely detailed picture of a single imaginary person? Can we not say that in literature we discover a vision — we can call it a hypothesis if that sounds more scientific and more impressive — that seems to conform to our experience and that also enlarges or enriches, however minutely, our sense of how men live and should live? And finally, can we not say that although we may already know how they live and should live (though who would claim this knowledge?) literature transforms this intellectual knowledge into something more vital, more penetrating, more deeply felt and more dearly cherished, if only by reassuring us — through its fictions — that our own hopes and fears are not merely our own but are shared by mankind?

A NOTE ON THE SHORT NOVEL

It is probably impossible to define to everyone's satisfaction a novel, and it is surely impossible to define a short novel. E. M. Forster suggested that a novel is at least 50,000 words, i.e., about 100 pages, but if one is willing to settle for 50,000 would one really balk at 49,500? Or at 49,000? Or at 48,000? Still, just as none of us can point to the precise moment when day becomes night but can all tell the difference between day and night, we usually know a novel when we read one, and perhaps we need not greatly fret about whether a given work is a novel, a short novel, or a long story. Yet it is worth mentioning that names other than "short novel" have been applied to works whose length places them between the novel and the short story. That these names are all foreign perhaps indicates not only that the form developed in Europe but also that the form has been relatively neglected by English and American writers and critics. The German term *Novelle* is sometimes used, but German critics restrict it to a work dealing with only one event, and that of an extraordinary nature. The Italian term *novella,* though fairly often used, originally referred to stories as brief as three or four pages, such as many of Boccaccio's, and it seems unreasonable to change the meaning so violently. Nor will "novelette" do; it diminishes or disparages, sounding too much like "starlet" or "kitchenette." *Nouvelle* is perhaps a little better, but despite Henry James's reference to "the shapely *nouvelle*" the word has not been much used.

So let us be content with the term "short novel" and not be dogmatic about length or subject matter. And let us recognize that a writer's vision must find its appropriate form, though he may not know at first what that form will be. When Thomas Mann began *The Magic Mountain,* he thought he was beginning a short novel, but it turned out to be 700 pages. Henry James knew this experience too, for he spoke of "the long stories that had thoroughly meant to be short."

Has a short novel more unity than a novel? (One does not want to say "than a full-length novel," for a short novel is, in its way, full-length too, just as a one-act play is, in the most important sense, a full-length play.) No, any good work of art is fully unified, and size has nothing to do with unity: a good paragraph is as unified as the essay of which it is a part, but its relative brevity does not make it more unified than the essay; an eagle is as unified as an elephant, but no more so. E. M. Forster says in *Aspects of the Novel* that a novel can never achieve the beauty of form that a play can, and Thomas Mann says in a letter that "the coherent and pregnant form" of the short novel "has more durability than the loose, expansive form of the novel," but this assertion seems questionable; it may not be true that (as Mann says) "works of monumental stature . . . are bound occasionally to flag, to lapse into a venerable dullness."

We can, however, say that a short novel in some way or another covers less than a novel: it may cover a shorter time span; it usually deals with fewer characters; and it scarcely can deal with the commonest material of the novel, an enormous sense of the reality of a particular place and social milieu in which several characters develop as they move through many encounters and experiences. Most often a short novel deals with a single situation, especially with an isolated protagonist facing a moral test. But probably the thing that especially distinguishes the short novel from the novel is the way we read it. What the most unflagging novelist cannot achieve is the reader's continuous clear perception of the novel's unity: when the reader reaches the end he no longer holds clearly in his mind the beginning or even the middle. Even if one reads a novel at a single sitting, one cannot keep it all in mind, and of course the reading of most novels is a matter of many days or even weeks or months. When we read novels, we usually read for some random period, stopping when we have to stop, and our day's stint does not necessarily coincide with any formal principle within the book. (That is why the reading of a novel, or anything else, in weekly serial form — where the author determines the units — is a very different experience from reading the same material in a book in snatches of our own choosing and at irregular intervals.) Most short novels, on the other hand, can easily be read in a single sitting (all can be read in a single sitting by a determined or absorbed reader) and so they have an impact quite different from that of a novel.

Efforts to remember everything in a novel are bound to fail, but such efforts can come near to fulfillment with a short novel, and so it is not utterly outrageous to offer as advice to readers of short novels some words of Henry James: "Try to be one of the people on whom nothing is lost."

HERMAN MELVILLE

Herman Melville (1819–1891) was born and died in New York City. Because his family had lost its money, he was set to work as a messenger at the age of thirteen. The years 1839–44 were mainly spent at sea; in 1842 he jumped ship and lived briefly in the Marquesas Islands and in Tahiti. He published *Typee* (based on his experience in the Marquesas) in 1846 and *Omoo* (based on his experience in Tahiti) in 1847; both were moderately popular, but he never again in his lifetime reached a fairly large public. In 1847 too he married, settling first in New York, but in 1850 he bought a farm in Lenox, Massachusetts, and became friendly with Nathaniel Hawthorne. Other significant dates: *Moby-Dick,* 1851; *Pierre,* 1852; "Bartelby," 1853; *Benito Cereno,* 1855; journey to Europe and the Holy Land, 1857; sold farm and returned to New York, 1863; 1866–85 worked as Inspector of Customs in New York, unnoticed by the literary world.

BENITO CERENO

In the year 1799, Captain Amasa Delano, of Duxbury in Massachusetts, commanding a large sealer and general trader, lay at anchor with a valuable cargo in the harbor of St. Maria — a small, desert, uninhabited island toward the southern extremity of the long coast of Chile. There he had touched for water.

On the second day, not long after dawn, while lying in his berth, his mate came below, informing him that a strange sail was coming into the bay. Ships were then not so plenty in those waters as now. He rose, dressed, and went on deck.

The morning was one peculiar to that coast. Everything was mute and calm; everything gray. The sea, though undulated into long roods of swells, seemed fixed, and was sleeked at the surface like waved lead that has cooled and set in the smelter's mold. The sky seemed a gray surtout. Flights of troubled gray fowl, kith and kin with flights of troubled gray vapors among which they were mixed, skimmed low and fitfully over the waters, as swallows over meadows before storms. Shadows present, foreshadowing deeper shadows to come.

To Captain Delano's surprise, the stranger, viewed through the glass, showed no colors, though to do so upon entering a haven, however uninhabited in its shores, where but a single other ship might be lying, was the custom among peaceful seaman of all nations. Considering the lawlessness and loneliness of the spot, and the sort of stories at that day associated with those seas, Captain Delano's surprise might have deepened into some uneasiness had he not been a person of a singularly undistrustful good nature, not liable except on extraordinary and repeated incentives, and hardly then, to indulge in personal alarms any way involving the imputation of malign evil in man. Whether, in view of what humanity is capable, such a trait implies, along with a benevolent heart, more than ordinary quickness and accuracy of intellectual perception, may be left to the wise to determine.

But whatever misgivings might have obtruded on first seeing the stranger would almost, in any seaman's mind, have been dissipated by observing that the ship, in navigating into the harbor, was drawing too near the land, a sunken reef making out off her bow. This seemed to prove her a stranger, indeed, not only to the sealer, but the island; consequently she could be no wonted freebooter on that ocean. With no small interest Captain Delano continued to watch her — a proceeding not much facilitated by the vapors partly mantling the hull, through which the far matin light from her cabin streamed equivocally enough; much like the sun — by this time hemisphered on the rim of the horizon, and, apparently, in company with the strange ship entering the harbor — which, wimpled by the same low, creeping clouds, showed not unlike a Lima intrigante's one sinister eye peering across the Plaza from the Indian loophole of her dusk *saya-y-manta.*[1]

It might have been but a deception of the vapors, but the longer the stranger was watched the more singular appeared her maneuvers. Erelong it seemed hard to decide whether she meant to come in or no — what she wanted, or what she was about. The wind, which had breezed up a little during the night, was now extremely light and baffling, which the more increased the apparent uncertainty of her movements.

Surmising at last that it might be a ship in distress, Captain Delano ordered his whaleboat to be dropped, and, much to the wary opposition of his mate, prepared to board her, and, at the least, pilot her in. On the night previous, a fishing party of the seamen had gone a long distance to some detached rocks out of sight from the sealer, and, an hour or two before daybreak, had returned, having met with no small success. Presuming that the stranger might have been long off soundings, the good captain put several baskets of the fish, for presents, into his boat, and so pulled away. From her continuing too near the sunken reef deeming her in danger, calling to his men he made all haste to apprise those on board of their situation. But, some time ere the boat came up, the wind, light though it was, having shifted, had headed the vessel off, as well as partly broken the vapors from about her.

Upon gaining a less remote view, the ship, when made signally visible on the verge of the leaden-hued swells, with the shreds of fog here and there raggedly furring her, appeared like a whitewashed monastery after a thunderstorm, seen perched upon some dun cliff among the Pyrenees. But it was no purely fanciful resemblance which now, for a moment, almost led Captain Delano to think that nothing less than a shipload of monks was before him. Peering over the bulwarks were what really seemed, in the hazy distance, throngs of dark cowls; while, fitfully revealed through the open portholes, other dark moving figures were dimly descried, as of Black Friars pacing the cloisters.

Upon a still nigher approach, this appearance was modified, and the true

1 [A woman's loose robe covering the head as well as the body. — Editors' note.]

character of the vessel was plain — a Spanish merchantman of the first class, carrying Negro slaves, amongst other valuable freight, from one colonial port to another. A very large, and, in its time, a very fine vessel, such as in those days were at intervals encountered along that main; sometimes superseded Acapulco treasure ships, or retired frigates of the Spanish king's navy, which, like superannuated Italian palaces, still, under a decline of masters, preserved signs of former state.

As the whaleboat drew more and more nigh, the cause of the peculiar pipe-clayed aspect of the stranger was seen in the slovenly neglect pervading her. The spars, ropes, and great part of the bulwarks looked woolly from long unacquaintance with the scraper, tar, and the brush. Her keel seemed laid, her ribs put together, and she launched, from Ezekiel's Valley of Dry Bones.

In the present business in which she was engaged, the ship's general model and rig appeared to have undergone no material change from their original warlike and Froissart pattern. However, no guns were seen.

The tops[2] were large, and were railed about with what had once been octagonal network, all now in sad disrepair. These tops hung overhead like three ruinous aviaries, in one of which was seen perched, on a ratline, a white noddy, a strange fowl so called from its lethargic, somnambulistic character, being frequently caught by hand at sea. Battered and moldy, the castellated forecastle seemed some ancient turret long ago taken by assault, and then left to decay. Toward the stern, two high-raised quarter galleries — the balustrades here and there covered with dry tindery sea moss — opening out from the unoccupied state cabin, whose deadlights, for all the mild weather, were hermetically closed and calked — these tenantless balconies hung over the sea as if it were the grand Venetian canal. But the principal relic of faded grandeur was the ample oval of the shieldlike sternpiece, intricately carved with the arms of Castile and Leon, medallioned about by groups of mythological or symbolical devices, uppermost and central of which was a dark satyr in a mask holding his foot on the prostrate neck of a writhing figure, likewise masked.

Whether the ship had a figurehead, or only a plain beak, was not quite certain, owing to canvas wrapped about that part, either to protect it while undergoing a refurbishing, or else decently to hide its decay. Rudely painted or chalked, as in a sailor freak, along the forward side of a sort of pedestal below the canvas, was the sentence, SEGUID VUESTRO JEFE ("follow your leader"), while upon the tarnished headboards near by appeared, in stately capitals, once gilt, the ship's name *SAN DOMINICK*, each letter streakingly corroded with tricklings of copper-spike rust; while, like mourning weeds, dark festoons of sea grass slimily swept to and fro over the name with every hearselike roll of the hull.

As, at last, the boat was hooked from the bow along toward the gangway

2 [Platforms near the tops of the mainmasts. — Editors' note.]

amidship, its keel, while yet some inches separated from the hull, harshly grated as on a sunken coral reef. It proved a huge bunch of conglobated barnacles adhering below the water to the side like a wen — a token of baffling airs and long calms passed somewhere in those seas.

Climbing the side, the visitor was at once surrounded by a clamorous throng of whites and blacks, but the latter outnumbering the former more than could have been expected, Negro transportation ship as the stranger in port was. But, in one language, and as with one voice, all poured out a common tale of suffering; in which the Negresses, of whom there were not a few, exceeded the others in their dolorous vehemence. The scurvy, together with the fever, had swept off a great part of their number, more especially the Spaniards. Off Cape Horn they had narrowly escaped shipwreck; then, for days together, they had lain tranced without wind; their provisions were low; their water next to none; their lips that moment were baked.

While Captain Delano was thus made the mark of all eager tongues, his one eager glance took in all faces, with every other object about him.

Always upon first boarding a large and populous ship at sea, especially a foreign one, with a nondescript crew such as Lascars[3] or Manila men, the impression varies in a peculiar way from that produced by first entering a strange house with strange inmates in a strange land. Both house and ship — the one by its walls and blinds, the other by its high bulwarks like ramparts — hoard from view their interiors till the last moment, but in the case of the ship there is this addition: that the living spectacle it contains, upon its sudden and complete disclosure, has, in contrast with the blank ocean which zones it, something of the effect of enchantment. The ship seems unreal; these strange costumes, gestures, and faces but a shadowy tableau just emerged from the deep, which directly must receive back what it gave.

Perhaps it was some such influence, as above is attempted to be described, which, in Captain Delano's mind, heightened whatever, upon a staid scrutiny, might have seemed unusual, especially the conspicuous figures of four elderly grizzled Negroes, their heads like black, doddered willow tops, who, in venerable contrast to the tumult below them, were couched, sphinxlike, one on the starboard cathead, another on the larboard, and the remaining pair face to face on the opposite bulwarks above the mainchains. They each had bits of unstranded old junk in their hands, and, with a sort of stoical self-content, were picking the junk into oakum, a small heap of which lay by their sides. They accompanied the task with a continuous, low, monotonous chant, droning and druling away like so many gray-headed bagpipers playing a funeral march.

The quarter-deck rose into an ample elevated poop, upon the forward verge of which, lifted, like the oakum-pickers, some eight feet above the general

3 [East Indian sailors. — Editors' note.]

throng, sat along in a row, separated by regular spaces, the cross-legged figures of six other blacks, each with a rusty hatchet in his hand, which, with a bit of brick and a rag, he was engaged like a scullion in scouring, while between each two was a small stack of hatchets, their rusted edges turned forward awaiting a like operation. Though occasionally the four oakum-pickers would briefly address some person or persons in the crowd below, yet the six hatchet-polishers neither spoke to others nor breathed a whisper among themselves, but sat intent upon their task, except at intervals, when, with the peculiar love in Negroes of uniting industry with pastime, two and two they sideways clashed their hatchets together, like cymbals, with a barbarous din. All six, unlike the generality, had the raw aspect of unsophisticated Africans.

But that first comprehensive glance which took in those ten figures, with scores less conspicuous, rested but an instant upon them, as, impatient of the hubbub of voices, the visitor turned in quest of whomsoever it might be that commanded the ship.

But as if not unwilling to let nature make known her own case among his suffering charge, or else in despair of restraining it for the time, the Spanish captain, a gentlemanly, reserved-looking, and rather young man to a stranger's eye, dressed with singular richness but bearing plain traces of recent sleepless cares and disquietudes, stood passively by, leaning against the mainmast, at one moment casting a dreary, spiritless look upon his excited people, at the next an unhappy glance toward his visitor. By his side stood a black of small stature, in whose rude face, as occasionally, like a shepherd's dog, he mutely turned it up into the Spaniard's, sorrow and affection were equally blended.

Struggling through the throng, the American advanced to the Spaniard, assuring him of his sympathies, and offering to render whatever assistance might be in his power. To which the Spaniard returned for the present but grave and ceremonious acknowledgments, his national formality dusked by the saturnine mood of ill-health.

But losing no time in mere compliments, Captain Delano, returning to the gangway, had his basket of fish brought up, and as the wind still continued light, so that some hours at least must elapse ere the ship could be brought to the anchorage, he bade his men return to the sealer and fetch back as much water as the whaleboat could carry, with whatever soft bread the steward might have, all the remaining pumpkins on board, with a box of sugar and a dozen of his private bottles of cider.

Not many minutes after the boat's pushing off, to the vexation of all, the wind entirely died away, and, the tide turning, began drifting back the ship helplessly seaward. But trusting this would not long last, Captain Delano sought, with good hopes, to cheer up the strangers, feeling no small satisfaction that, with persons in their condition, he could — thanks to his frequent voyages along the Spanish Main — converse with some freedom in their native tongue.

While left alone with them, he was not long in observing some things tending to heighten his first impressions; but surprise was lost in pity, both for the Spaniards and blacks, alike evidently reduced from scarcity of water and provisions, while long-continued suffering seemed to have brought out the less good-natured qualities of the Negroes, besides at the same time impairing the Spaniard's authority over them. But, under the circumstances, precisely this condition of things was to have been anticipated. In armies, navies, cities, or families, in nature herself, nothing more relaxes good order than misery. Still, Captain Delano was not without the idea that had Benito Cereno been a man of greater energy, misrule would hardly have come to the present pass. But the debility, constitutional or induced by hardships bodily and mental, of the Spanish captain was too obvious to be overlooked. A prey to settled dejection, as if long mocked with hope he would not now indulge it even when it had ceased to be a mock, the prospect of that day, or evening at furthest, lying at anchor, with plenty of water for his people, and a brother captain to counsel and befriend, seemed in no perceptible degree to encourage him. His mind appeared unstrung, if not still more seriously affected. Shut up in these oaken walls, chained to one dull round of command whose unconditionality cloyed him, like some hypochrondriac abbott he moved slowly about, at times suddenly pausing, starting, or staring, biting his lip, biting his fingernail, flushing, paling, twitching his beard, with other symptoms of an absent or moody mind. This distempered spirit was lodged, as before hinted, in as distempered a frame. He was rather tall, but seemed never to have been robust, and now with nervous suffering was almost worn to a skeleton. A tendency to some pulmonary complaint appeared to have been lately confirmed. His voice was like that of one with lungs half gone — hoarsely suppressed, a husky whisper. No wonder that, as in this state he tottered about, his private servant apprehensively followed him. Sometimes the Negro gave his master his arm, or took his handkerchief out of his pocket for him; performing these and similiar offices with that affectionate zeal which transmutes into something filial or fraternal acts in themselves but menial, and which has gained for the Negro the repute of making the most pleasing body servant in the world; one, too, whom a master need be on no stiffly superior terms with, but may treat with familiar trust — less a servant than a devoted companion.

Marking the noisy indocility of the blacks in general, as well as what seemed the sullen inefficiency of the whites, it was not without humane satisfaction that Captain Delano witnessed the steady good conduct of Babo.

But the good conduct of Babo, hardly more than the ill-behavior of others, seemed to withdraw the half-lunatic Don Benito from his cloudy languor. Not that such precisely was the impression made by the Spaniard on the mind of his visitor. The Spaniard's individual unrest was, for the present, but noted as a conspicuous feature in the ship's general affliction. Still, Captain Delano was not a little concerned at what he could not help taking for the time to be Don Benito's unfriendly indifference towards himself. The Spaniard's manner, too, conveyed a sort of sour and gloomy disdain, which he seemed at no pains to disguise. But this the American in charity ascribed to the harassing effects of sickness, since, in former instances, he had noted that there are peculiar natures on whom prolonged physical suffering seems to cancel every social instinct of kindness, as if, forced to black bread themselves, they deemed it but equity that each person coming nigh them should, indirectly, by some slight or affront, be made to partake of their fare.

But erelong Captain Delano bethought him that, indulgent as he was at the first in judging the Spaniard, he might not after all have exercised charity enough. At bottom it was Don Benito's reserve which displeased him, but the same reserve was shown towards all but his faithful personal attendant. Even the formal reports which, according to sea usage, were, at stated times, made to him by some petty underling, either a white, mulatto, or black, he hardly had patience enough to listen to without betraying contemptuous aversion. His manner upon such occasions was, in its degree, not unlike that which might be supposed to have been his imperial countryman's, Charles V, just previous to the anchoritish retirement of that monarch from the throne.

This splenetic disrelish of his place was evinced in almost every function pertaining to it. Proud as he was moody, he condescended to no personal mandate. Whatever special orders were necessary, their delivery was delegated to his body servant, who in turn transferred them to their ultimate destination, through runners, alert Spanish boys or slave boys, like pages or pilot fish within easy call continually hovering round Don Benito. So that to have beheld this undemonstrative invalid gliding about, apathetic and mute, no landsman could have dreamed that in him was lodged a dictatorship beyond which, while at sea, there was no earthly appeal.

Thus the Spaniard, regarded in his reserve, seemed the involuntary victim of mental disorder. But, in fact, his reserve might, in some degree, have proceeded from design. If so, then here was evinced the unhealthy climax of that icy though conscientious policy more or less adopted by all commanders of large ships, which, except in signal emergencies, obliterates alike the manifestation of sway with every trace of sociality, transforming the man into a block, or rather into a loaded cannon, which, until there is call for thunder, has nothing to say.

Viewing him in this light, it seemed but a natural token of the perverse habit induced by a long course of such hard self-restraint that, notwithstanding the present condition of his ship, the Spaniard should still persist in a demeanor which, however harmless or, it may be, appropriate, in a well-appointed vessel, such as the *San Dominick* might have been at the outset of the voyage, was anything but judicious now. But the Spaniard, perhaps, thought that it was with captains as with gods: reserve, under all events, must still be their cue. But probably this appearance of slumbering dominion might have been but an attempted disguise to conscious imbecility — not deep policy, but shallow device. But be all this as it might, whether Don Benito's manner was designed or not, the more Captain Delano noted its pervading reserve, the less he felt uneasiness at any particular manifestation of that reserve towards himself.

Neither were his thoughts taken up by the captain alone. Wonted to the quiet orderliness of the sealer's comfortable family of a crew, the noisy confusion of the *San Dominick's* suffering host repeatedly challenged his eye. Some prominent breaches, not only of discipline but of decency, were observed. These Captain Delano could not but ascribe, in the main, to the absence of those subordinate deck officers to whom, along with higher duties, is intrusted what may be styled the police department of a populous ship. True, the old oakum-pickers appeared at times to act the part of monitorial constables to their countrymen, the blacks, but though occasionally succeeding in allaying trifling outbreaks now and then between man and man, they could do little or nothing toward establishing general quiet. The *San Dominick* was in the condition of a transatlantic emigrant ship, among whose multitude of living freight are some individuals, doubtless, as little troublesome as crates and bales, but the friendly remonstrances of such with their ruder companions are of not so much avail as the unfriendly arm of the mate. What the *San Dominick* wanted was, what the emigrant ship has, stern superior officers. But on these decks not so much as a fourth mate was to be seen.

The visitor's curiosity was roused to learn the particulars of those mishaps which had brought about such absenteeism, with its consequences, because, though deriving some inkling of the voyage from the wails which at the first moment had greeted him, yet of the details no clear understanding had been had. The best account would, doubtless, be given by the captain. Yet at first the visitor was loath to ask it, unwilling to provoke some distant rebuff. But, plucking up courage, he at last accosted Don Benito, renewing the expression of his benevolent interest, adding that, did he (Captain Delano) but know the particulars of the ship's misfortunes, he would, perhaps be better able in the end to relieve them. Would Don Benito favor him with the whole story.

Don Benito faltered, then, like some somnambulist suddenly interfered with, vacantly stared at his visitor, and ended by looking down on the deck. He maintained this posture so long that Captain Delano, almost equally disconcerted, and involuntarily almost as rude, turned suddenly from him, walking forward to accost one of the Spanish seamen for the desired information. But he had hardly gone five paces, when, with a sort of eagerness, Don Benito invited him back, regretting his momentary absence of mind, and professing readiness to gratify him.

While most part of the story was being given, the two captains stood on the after part of the main deck, a privileged spot, no one being near but the servant.

"It is now a hundred and ninety days," began the Spaniard, in his husky whisper, "that this ship, well officered and well manned, with several cabin passengers — some fifty Spaniards in all — sailed from Buenos Ayres bound to Lima, with a general cargo, hardware, Paraguay tea and the like — and," pointing forward, "that parcel of Negroes, now not more than a hundred and fifty, as you see, but then numbering over three hundred souls. Off Cape Horn we had heavy gales. In one moment, by night, three of my best officers, with fifteen sailors, were lost, with the mainyard, the spar snapping under them in the slings as they sought, with heavers, to beat down the icy sail. To lighten the hull, the heavier sacks of maté[4] were thrown into the sea, with most of the water pipes lashed on deck at the time. And this last necessity it was, combined with the prolonged detentions afterwards experienced, which eventually brought about our chief causes of suffering. When ——"

Here there was a sudden fainting attack of his cough, brought on, no doubt, by his mental distress. His servant sustained him, and, drawing a cordial from his pocket, placed it to his lips. He a little revived. But, unwilling to leave him unsupported while yet imperfectly restored, the black with one arm still encircled his master, at the same time keeping his eye fixed on his face, as if to watch for the first sign of complete restoration, or relapse, as the event might prove.

The Spaniard proceeded, but brokenly and obscurely, as one in a dream.

— "Oh, my God! rather than pass through what I have, with joy I would have hailed the most terrible gales; but ——"

His cough returned and with increased violence; this subsiding, with reddened lips and closed eyes he fell heavily against his supporter.

"His mind wanders. He was thinking of the plague that followed the gales," plaintively sighed the servant; "my poor, poor master!" wringing one hand, and with the other wiping the mouth. "But be patient, *señor,*" again turning to Captain Delano, "these fits do not last long; master will soon be himself."

Don Benito reviving, went on; but, as this portion of the story was very brokenly delivered, the substance only will here be set down.

It appeared that after the ship had been many days tossed in storms off the

4 [A kind of tea. — Editors' note.]

Cape, the scurvy broke out, carrying off numbers of the whites and blacks. When at last they had worked round into the Pacific, their spars and sails were so damaged, and so inadequately handled by the surviving mariners, most of whom were become invalids, that, unable to lay her northerly course by the wind, which was powerful, the unmanageable ship for successive days and nights was blown northwestward, where the breeze suddenly deserted her, in unknown waters to sultry calms. The absence of the water pipes now proved as fatal to life as before their presence had menaced it. Induced, or at least aggravated, by the more than scanty allowance of water, a malignant fever followed the scurvy, with the excessive heat of the lengthened calm making such short work of it as to sweep away, as by billows, whole families of the Africans, and a yet larger number, proportionally, of the Spaniards, including, by a luckless fatality, every remaining officer on board. Consequently, in the smart west winds eventually following the calm, the already rent sails, having to be simply dropped, not furled, at need, had been gradually reduced to the beggars' rags they were now. To procure substitutes for his lost sailors, as well as supplies of water and sails, the captain, at the earliest opportunity, had made for Baldivia, the southernmost civilized port of Chile and South America, but upon nearing the coast the thick weather had prevented him from so much as sighting that harbor. Since which period, almost without a crew, and almost without canvas and almost without water, and at intervals giving its added dead to the sea, the *San Dominick* had been battledored[5] about by contrary winds, inveigled by currents, or grown weedy in calms. Like a man lost in woods, more than once she had doubled upon her own track.

"But throughout these calamities," huskily continued Don Benito, painfully turning in the half-embrace of his servant, "I have to thank those Negroes you see, who, though to your inexperienced eyes appearing unruly, have, indeed, conducted themselves with less of restlessness than even their owner could have thought possible under such circumstances."

Here he again fell faintly back. Again his mind wandered, but he rallied, and less obscurely proceeded.

"Yes, their owner was quite right in assuring me that no fetters would be needed with his blacks; so that while, as is wont in his transportation, those Negroes have always remained upon deck — not thrust below, as in the Guineamen[6] — they have, also, from the beginning, been freely permitted to range within given bounds at their pleasure."

Once more the faintness returned — his mind roved — but, recovering, he resumed:

5 [Knocked around like a shuttlecock. — Editors' note.]
6 [Ships involved in slave trade with the west African coast of Guinea. — Editors' note.]

"But it is Babo here to whom, under God, I owe not only my own preservation, but likewise to him, chiefly, the merit is due of pacifying his more ignorant brethren, when at intervals tempted to murmurings."

"Ah, master," sighed the black, bowing his face, "don't speak of me; Babo is nothing; what Babo has done was but duty."

"Faithful fellow!" cried Captain Delano. "Don Benito, I envy you such a friend; slave I cannot call him."

As master and man stood before him, the black upholding the white, Captain Delano could not but bethink him of the beauty of that relationship which could present such a spectacle of fidelity on the one hand and confidence on the other. The scene was heightened by the contrast in dress, denoting their relative positions. The Spaniard wore a loose Chile jacket of dark velvet; white small-clothes and stockings, with silver buckles at the knee and instep; a high-crowned sombrero of fine grass; a slender sword, silver mounted, hung from a knot in his sash — the last being an almost invariable adjunct, more for utility than ornament, of a South American gentleman's dress to this hour. Excepting when his occasional nervous contortions brought about disarray, there was a certain precision in his attire curiously at variance with the unsightly disorder around, especially in the belittered ghetto, forward of the mainmast, wholly occupied by the blacks.

The servant wore nothing but wide trousers, apparently, from their coarseness and patches, made out of some old topsail; they were clean, and confined at the waist by a bit of unstranded rope, which, with his composed, deprecatory air at times, made him look something like a begging friar of St. Francis.

However unsuitable for the time and place, at least in the blunt-thinking American's eyes, and however strangely surviving in the midst of all his afflictions, the toilette of Don Benito might not, in fashion at least, have gone beyond the style of the day among South Americans of his class. Though on the present voyage sailing from Buenos Ayres, he had avowed himself a native and resident of Chile, whose inhabitants had not so generally adopted the plain coat and once plebeian pantaloons, but, with a becoming modification, adhered to their provincial costume, picturesque as any in the world. Still, relatively to the pale history of the voyage, and his own pale face, there seemed something so incongruous in the Spaniard's apparel as almost to suggest the image of an invalid courtier tottering about London streets in the time of the plague.

The portion of the narrative which perhaps most excited interest, as well as some surprise, considering the latitudes in question, was the long calms spoken of, and more particularly the ship's so long drifting about. Without communicating the opinion, of course, the American could not but impute at least part of the detentions both to clumsy seamanship and faulty navigation. Eying Don

Benito's small, yellow hands, he easily inferred that the young captain had not got into command at the hawsehole, but the cabin window; and if so, why wonder at incompetence, in youth, sickness, and gentility united?

But, drowning criticism in compassion, after a fresh repetition of his sympathies, Captain Delano, having heard out his story, not only engaged, as in the first place, to see Don Benito and his people supplied in their immediate bodily needs, but, also now further promised to assist him in procuring a large permanent supply of water, as well as some sails and rigging; and, though it would involve no small embarrassment to himself, yet he would spare three of his best seamen for temporary deck officers, so that without delay the ship might proceed to Conception, there fully to refit for Lima, her destined port.

Such generosity was not without its effect, even upon the invalid. His face lighted up; eager and hectic, he met the honest glance of his visitor. With gratitude he seemed overcome.

"This excitement is bad for master," whispered the servant, taking his arm, and with soothing words gently drawing him aside.

When Don Benito returned, the American was pained to observe that his hopefulness, like the sudden kindling in his cheek, was but febrile and transient.

Erelong, with a joyless mien, looking up towards the poop, the host invited his guest to accompany him there, for the benefit of what little breath of wind might be stirring.

As, during the telling of the story, Captain Delano had once or twice started at the occasional cymbaling of the hatchet-polishers, wondering why such an interruption should be allowed, especially in that part of the ship, and in the ears of an invalid; and moreover, as the hatchets had anything but an attractive look, and the handlers of them still less so, it was, therefore, to tell the truth, not without some lurking reluctance, or even shrinking, it may be, that Captain Delano, with apparent complaisance, acquiesced in his host's invitation. The more so since, with an untimely caprice of punctilio, rendered distressing by his cadaverous aspect, Don Benito, with Castilian bows, solemnly insisted upon his guest's preceding him up the ladder leading to the elevation, where, one on each side of the last step, sat for amorial supporters and sentries two of the ominous file. Gingerly enough stepped good Captain Delano between them, and in the instant of leaving them behind, like one running the gantlet, he felt an apprehensive twitch in the calves of his legs.

But when, facing about, he saw the whole file, like so many organ-grinders, still stupidly intent on their work, unmindful of everything beside, he could not but smile at his late fidgety panic.

Presently, while standing with his host looking forward upon the decks below, he was struck by one of those instances of insubordination previously alluded to. Three black boys, with two Spanish boys, were sitting together on the hatches, scraping a rude wooden platter in which some scanty mess had recently been cooked. Suddenly one of the black boys, enraged at a word dropped by one of his white companions, seized a knife, and, though called to forbear by one of the oakum-pickers, struck the lad over the head, inflicting a gash from which blood flowed.

In amazement, Captain Delano inquired what this meant. To which the pale Don Benito dully muttered that it was merely the sport of the lad.

"Pretty serious sport, truly," rejoined Captain Delano. "Had such a thing happened on board the *Bachelor's Delight*, instant punishment would have followed."

At these words the Spaniard turned upon the American one of his sudden, staring, half-lunatic looks, then, relapsing into his torpor, answered, "Doubtless, doubtless, *señor*."

Is it, thought Captain Delano, that this hapless man is one of those paper captains I've known, who by policy wink at what by power they cannot put down? I know no sadder sight than a commander who has little of command but the name.

"I should think, Don Benito," he now said, glancing toward the oakum-picker who had sought to interfere with the boys, "that you would find it advantageous to keep all your blacks employed, especially the younger ones, no matter at what useless task, and no matter what happens to the ship. Why, even with my little band, I find such a course indispensable. I once kept a crew on my quarter-deck thrumming mats for my cabin, when, for three days, I had given up my ship — mats, men, and all — for a speedy loss, owing to the violence of a gale, in which we could do nothing but helplessly drive before it."

"Doubtless, doubtless," muttered Don Benito.

"But," continued Captain Delano, again glancing upon the oakum-pickers and then at the hatchet-polishers, near by, "I see you keep some, at least, of your host employed."

"Yes," was again the vacant response.

"Those old men there, shaking their pows from their pulpits," continued Captain Delano, pointing to the oakum-pickers, "seem to act the part of old dominies to the rest, little heeded as their admonitions are at times. Is this voluntary on their part, Don Benito, or have you appointed them shepherds to your flock of black sheep?"

"What posts they fill, I appointed them," rejoined the Spaniard, in an acrid tone, as if resenting some supposed satiric reflection.

"And these others, these Ashantee conjurers here," continued Captain Delano, rather uneasily eying the brandished steel of the hatchet-polishers, where in spots, it had been brought to a shine, "this seems a curious business they are at, Don Benito?"

"In the gales we met," answered the Spaniard, "what of our general cargo was not thrown overboard was much damaged by the brine. Since coming into calm weather, I have had several cases of knives and hatchets daily brought up for overhauling and cleaning."

"A prudent idea, Don Benito. You are part owner of ship and cargo, I presume; but none of the slaves, perhaps?"

"I am owner of all you see," impatiently returned Don Benito, "except the main company of blacks, who belonged to my late friend, Alexandro Aranda."

As he mentioned this name, his air was heartbroken; his knees shook; his servant supported him.

Thinking he divined the cause of such unusual emotion, to confirm his surmise Captain Delano after a pause said: "And may I ask, Don Benito, whether — since awhile ago you spoke of some cabin passengers — the friend, whose loss so afflicts you, at the outset of the voyage accompanied his blacks?"

"Yes."

"But died of the fever?"

"Died of the fever. Oh, could I but ——"

Again quivering, the Spaniard paused.

"Pardon me," said Captain Delano, lowly, "but I think that, by a sympathetic experience, I conjecture, Don Benito, what it is that gives the keener edge to your grief. It was once my hard fortune to lose, at sea, a dear friend, my own brother, then supercargo. Assured of the welfare of his spirit, its departure I could have borne like a man, but that honest eye, that honest hand — both of which had so often met mine — and that warm heart — all, all — like scraps to the dogs — to throw all to the sharks! It was then I vowed never to have for fellow voyager a man I loved, unless, unbeknown to him, I had provided every requisite, in case of a fatality, for embalming his mortal part for interment on shore. Were your friend's remains now on board this ship, Don Benito, not thus strangely would the mention of his name affect you."

"On board this ship?" echoed the Spaniard. Then, with horrified gestures, as directed against some spector, he unconsciously fell into the ready arms of his attendant, who, with a silent appeal toward Captain Delano, seemed beseeching him not again to broach a theme so unspeakably distressing to his master.

This poor fellow now, thought the pained American, is the victim of that sad superstition which associates goblins with the deserted body of man, as ghosts with an abandoned house. How unlike are we made! What to me, in like case, would have been a solemn satisfaction, the bare suggestion, even, terrifies the Spaniard into this trance. Poor Alexandro Aranda! what would you say could you here see your friend — who on former voyages, when you for months were left behind, has, I dare say, often longed and longed for one peep at you — not transported with terror at the least thought of having you anyway nigh him.

At this moment, with a dreary graveyard toll betokening a flaw, the ship's forecastle bell, smote by one of the grizzled oakum-pickers, proclaimed ten o'clock through the leaden calm, when Captain Delano's attention was caught by the moving figure of a gigantic black emerging from the general crowd below and slowly advancing towards the elevated poop. An iron collar was about his neck, from which depended a chain thrice wound round his body, the terminating links padlocked together at a broad band of iron, his girdle.

"How like a mute Atufal moves," murmured the servant.

The black mounted the steps of the poop, and, like a brave prisoner brought up to receive sentence, stood in unquailing muteness before Don Benito, now recovered from his attack.

At the first glimpse of his approach, Don Benito had started; a resentful shadow swept over his face, and, as with the sudden memory of bootless rage, his white lips glued together.

This is some mulish mutineer, thought Captain Delano, surveying, not without a mixture of admiration, the colossal form of the Negro.

"See, he waits your question, master," said the servant.

Thus reminded, Don Benito, nervously averting his glance as if shunning, by anticipation, some rebellious response, in a disconcerted voice, thus spoke:

"Atufal, will you ask my pardon now?"

The black was silent.

"Again, master," murmured the servant, with bitter upbraiding eying his countryman; "Again, master; he will bend to master yet."

"Answer," said Don Benito, still averting his glance, "say but the one word, *pardon*, and your chains shall be off."

Upon this, the black, slowly raising both arms, let them lifelessly fall, his links clanking, his head bowed; as much as to say, "No, I am content."

"Go," said Don Benito, with inkept and unknown emotion.

Deliberately as he had come, the black obeyed.

"Excuse me, Don Benito," said Captain Delano, "but this scene surprises me; what means it, pray?"

"It means that that Negro alone, of all the band, has given me peculiar cause of offense. I have put him in chains; I ——"

Here he paused; his hand to his head, as if there were a swimming there, or a sudden bewilderment of memory had come over him; but meeting his servant's kindly glance seemed reassured, and proceeded:

"I could not scourge such a form. But I told him he must ask my pardon. As yet he has not. At my command, every two hours he stands before me."

"And how long has this been?"

"Some sixty days."

"And obedient in all else? And respectful?"

"Yes."

"Upon my conscience, then," exclaimed Captain Delano, impulsively, "he has a royal spirit in him, this fellow."

"He may have some right to it," bitterly returned Don Benito, "he says he was king in his own land."

"Yes," said the servant, entering a word, "those slits in Atufal's ears once held wedges of gold; but poor Babo here, in his own land, was only a poor slave; a black man's slave was Babo, who now is the white's."

Somewhat annoyed by these conversational familiarities, Captain Delano turned curiously upon the attendant, then glanced inquiringly at his master; but, as if long wonted to these little informalities, neither master nor man seemed to understand him.

"What, pray, was Atufal's offense, Don Benito?" asked Captain Delano; "if it was not something very serious, take a fool's advice, and, in view of his general docility, as well as in some natural respect for his spirit, remit him his penalty."

"No, no, master never will do that," here murmured the servant to himself, "proud Atufal must first ask master's pardon. The slave there carries the padlock, but master here carries the key."

His attention thus directed, Captain Delano now noticed for the first that, suspended by a slender silken cord from Don Benito's neck, hung a key. At once, from the servant's muttered syllables, divining the key's purpose, he smiled and said: "So, Don Benito — padlock and key — significant symbols, truly."

Biting his lip, Don Benito faltered.

Though the remark of Captain Delano, a man of such native simplicity as to be incapable of satire or irony, had been dropped in playful allusion to the Spaniard's singularly evidenced lordship over the black, yet the hypochondriac seemed some way to have taken it as a malicious reflection upon his confessed inability thus far to break down, at least on a verbal summons, the entrenched will of the slave. Deploring this supposed misconception, yet despairing of correcting it, Captain Delano shifted the subject; but finding his companion more than ever withdrawn, as if still sourly digesting the lees of the presumed affront above mentioned, by and by Captain Delano likewise became less talkative, oppressed, against his own will, by what seemed the secret vindictiveness of the morbidly sensitive Spaniard. But the good sailor, himself of a quite contrary disposition, refrained on his part alike from the appearance as from the feeling of resentment, and if silent, was only so from contagion.

Presently the Spaniard, assisted by his servant, somewhat discourteously crossed over from his guest, a procedure which, sensibly enough, might have been allowed to pass for idle caprice of ill-humor had not master and man, lingering round the corner of the elevated skylight, began whispering together in low voices. This was unpleasing. And more: the moody air of the Spaniard, which at times had not been without a sort of valetudinarian stateliness, now seemed anything but dignified, while the menial familiarity of the servant lost its original charm of simple-hearted attachment.

In his embarrassment, the visitor turned his face to the other side of the ship. By so doing, his glance accidentally fell on a young Spanish sailor, a coil of rope in his hand, just stepped from the deck to the first round of the mizzen rigging. Perhaps the man would not have been particularly noticed were it not that, during his ascent to one of the yards, he, with a sort of covert intentness, kept his eye fixed on Captain Delano, from whom, presently, it passed, as if by a natural sequence, to the two whisperers.

His own attention thus redirected to that quarter, Captain Delano gave a slight start. From something in Don Benito's manner just then, it seemed as if the visitor had, at least partly, been the subject of the withdrawn consultation going on — a conjecture as little agreeable to the guest as it was flattering to the host.

The singular alternations of courtesy and ill-breeding in the Spanish captain were unaccountable, except on one of two suppositions — innocent lunacy, or wicked imposture.

But the first idea, though it might naturally have occurred to an indifferent observer, and, in some respect, had not hitherto been wholly a stranger to Captain Delano's mind, yet, now that, in an incipient way, he began to regard the stranger's conduct something in the light of an intentional affront, of course the idea of lunacy was virtually vacated. But if not a lunatic, what then? Under the circumstances, would a gentleman, nay, any honest boor, act the part now acted by his host? The man was an impostor. Some low-born adventurer, masquerading as an oceanic grandee, yet so ignorant of the first requisites of mere gentlemanhood as to be betrayed into the present remarkable indecorum. That strange ceremoniousness, too, at other times evinced, seemed not uncharacteristic of one playing a part above his real level. Benito Cereno — Don Benito Cereno — a sounding name. One, too, at that period, not unknown, in the surname, to supercargoes and sea captains trading along the Spanish Main, as belonging to one of the most enterprising and extensive mercantile families in all those provinces, several members of it having titles; a sort of Castilian Rothschild, with a noble brother, or cousin, in every great trading town of South America. The alleged Don Benito was in early manhood, about twenty-nine or thirty. To assume a sort of roving cadetship in the maritime affairs of such a house, what more likely scheme for a young knave of talent and spirit? But the Spaniard was a pale invalid. Never mind. For even to the degree of simulating mortal disease, the craft of some tricksters had been known to attain. To think that, under the aspect of infantile weakness, the most savage energies might be couched — those velvets of the Spaniard but the silky paw to his fangs.

From no train of thought did these fancies come; not from within, but from without; suddenly, too, and in one throng, like hoarfrost, yet as soon to vanish, as the mild sun of Captain Delano's good nature regained its meridian.

Glancing over once more towards his host — whose side face, revealed above the skylight, was now turned towards him — he was struck by the profile, whose clearness of cut was refined by the thinness incident to ill-health, as well as ennobled about the chin by the beard. Away with suspicion. He was a true offshoot of a true hidalgo Cereno.

Relieved by these and other better thoughts, the visitor, lightly humming a tune, now began indifferently pacing the poop, so as not to betray to Don Benito that he had at all mistrusted incivility, much less duplicity; for such mistrust would yet be proved illusory, and by the event, though, for the present, the circumstance which had provoked that distrust remained unexplained. But when that little mystery should have been cleared up, Captain Delano thought he might extremely regret it did he allow Don Benito to become aware that he had indulged in ungenerous surmises. In short, to the Spaniard's black-letter text, it was best, for a while, to leave open margin.

Presently, his pale face twitching and overcast, the Spaniard, still supported by his attendant, moved over towards his guest, when, with even more than his usual embarrassment, and a strange sort of intriguing intonation in his husky whisper, the following conversation began:

"*Señor,* may I ask how long you have lain at this isle?"

"Oh, but a day or two, Don Benito."

"And from what port are you last?"

"Canton."

"And there, *señor,* you exchanged your sealskins for teas and silks, I think you said?"

"Yes. Silks, mostly."

"And the balance you took in specie, perhaps?"

Captain Delano, fidgeting a little, answered, "Yes; some silver; not a very great deal, though."

"Ah — well. May I ask how many men have you, *señor?*"

Captain Delano slightly started, but answered, "About five-and-twenty, all told."

"And at present, *señor,* all on board, I suppose?"

"All on board, Don Benito," replied the Captain, now with satisfaction.

"And will be tonight, *señor?*"

At this last question, following so many pertinacious ones, for the soul of him Captain Delano could not but look very earnestly at the questioner, who, instead of meeting the glance, with every token of craven discomposure dropped his eyes to the deck; presenting an unworthy contrast to his servant, who, just then, was kneeling at his feet, adjusting a loose shoe buckle, his disengaged face meantime, with humble curiosity, turned openly up into his master's downcast one.

The Spaniard, still with a guilty shuffle, repeated his question:

"And — and will be tonight, *señor?*"

"Yes, for aught I know," returned Captain Delano — "but nay," rallying himself into fearless truth, "some of them talked of going off on another fishing party about midnight."

"Your ships generally go — go more or less armed, I believe, *señor?*"

"Oh, a six-pounder or two, in case of emergency," was the intrepidly indifferent reply, "with a small stock of muskets, sealing spears, and cutlasses, you know."

As he thus responded, Captain Delano again glanced at Don Benito, but the latter's eyes were averted, while, abruptly and awkwardly shifting the subject, he made some peevish allusion to the calm, and then, without apology, once more, with his attendant, withdrew to the opposite bulwarks, where the whispering was resumed.

At this moment, and ere Captain Delano could cast a cool thought upon what had just passed, the young Spanish sailor before mentioned was seen descending from the rigging. In act of stooping over to spring inboard to the deck, his voluminous, unconfined frock, or shirt, of coarse woolen, much spotted with tar, opened out far down the chest, revealing a soiled undergarment of what seemed the finest linen, edged, about the neck, with a narrow blue ribbon, sadly faded and worn. At this moment the young sailor's eye was again fixed on the whisperers, and Captain Delano thought he observed a lurking significance in it, as if silent signs, of some Freemason sort, had that instant been interchanged.

This once more impelled his own glance in the direction of Don Benito, and, as before, he could not but infer that himself formed the subject of the conference. He paused. The sound of the hatchet-polishing fell on his ears. He cast another swift side look at the two. They had the air of conspirators. In connection with the late questionings, and the incident of the young sailor, these things now begat such return of involuntary suspicion that the singular guilelessness of the American could not endure it. Plucking up a gay and humorous expression, he crossed over to the two rapidly, saying: "Ha, Don Benito, your black here seems high in your trust, a sort of privy councilor, in fact."

Upon this, the servant looked up with a good-natured grin, but the master started as from a venomous bite. It was a moment or two before the Spaniard sufficiently recovered himself to reply; which he did, at last, with cold constraint: "Yes, *señor*, I have trust in Babo."

Here Babo, changing his previous grin of mere animal humor into an intelligent smile, not ungratefully eyed his master.

Finding that the Spaniard now stood silent and reserved, as if involuntarily, or purposely giving hint that his guest's proximity was inconvenient just then, Captain Delano, unwilling to appear uncivil even to incivility itself, made some trivial remark and moved off, again and again turning over in his mind the mysterious demeanor of Don Benito Cereno.

He had descended from the poop, and, wrapped in thought, was passing near a dark hatchway leading down into the steerage, when, perceiving motion there, he looked to see what moved. The same instant there was a sparkle in the shadowy hatchway and he saw one of the Spanish sailors, prowling there, hurriedly placing his hand in the bosom of his frock, as if hiding something. Before the man could have been certain who it was that was passing, he slunk below out of sight. But enough was seen of him to make it sure that he was the same young sailor before noticed in the rigging.

What was that which so sparkled? thought Captain Delano. It was no lamp — no match — no live coal. Could it have been a jewel? But how come sailors with jewels? — or with silk-trimmed undershirts either? Has he been robbing the trunks of the dead cabin passengers? But if so he would hardly wear one of the stolen articles on board ship here. Ah, ah — if, now, that was indeed, a secret sign I saw passing between this suspicious fellow and his captain awhile since; if I could only be certain that, in my uneasiness, my senses did not deceive me, then ——

Here, passing from one suspicious thing to another, his mind revolved the strange questions put to him concerning his ship.

By a curious coincidence, as each point was recalled, the black wizards of Ashantee would strike up with their hatchets, as in ominous comment on the white stranger's thoughts. Pressed by such enigmas and portents, it would have been almost against nature had not, even into the least distrustful heart, some ugly misgivings obtruded.

Observing the ship, now helplessly fallen into a current, with enchanted sails drifting with increased rapidity seaward, and noting that, from a lately intercepted projection of the land, the sealer was hidden, the stout mariner began to quake at thoughts which he barely durst confess to himself. Above all, he began to feel a ghostly dread of Don Benito. And yet, when he roused himself, dilated his chest, felt himself strong on his legs, and coolly considered it — what did all these phantoms amount to?

Had the Spaniard any sinister scheme, it must have reference not so much to him (Captain Delano) as to his ship (the *Bachelor's Delight*). Hence the present drifting away of the one ship from the other, instead of favoring any such possible scheme, was, for the time at least, opposed to it. Clearly any suspicion combining such contradictions must need be delusive. Beside, was it not absurd to think of a vessel in distress — a vessel by sickness almost dismanned of her crew — a vessel whose inmates were parched for water — was it not a thousand times absurd that such a craft should, at present, be of a piratical character; or her commander, either for himself or those under him, cherish any desire but for speedy relief and refreshment? But, then, might not general distress, and thirst in particular, be affected? And might not that same undiminished Spanish crew, alleged to have perished off to a remnant, be at that very moment lurking in the hold? On heartbroken pretense of entreating a cup of cold water, fiends in human form had got into lonely dwellings, nor retired until a dark deed had been done. And among the Malay pirates it was no unusual thing to lure ships after them into their treacherous harbors, or entice boarders from a declared enemy at sea, by the spectacle of thinly manned or vacant decks, beneath which prowled a hundred spears with yellow arms ready to upthrust them through the mats. Not that Captain Delano had entirely credited such things. He had heard of them — and now, as stories, they recurred. The present destination of the ship was the anchorage. There she would be near his own vessel. Upon gaining that vicinity, might not the *San Dominick*, like a slumbering volcano, suddenly let loose energies now hid?

He recalled the Spaniard's manner while telling his story. There was a gloomy hesitancy and subterfuge about it. It was just the manner of one making up his tale for evil purposes, as he goes. But if that story was not true, what was the truth? That the ship had unlawfully come into the Spaniard's possession? But in many of its details, especially in reference to the more calamitous parts, such as the fatalities among the seamen, the consequent prolonged beating about, the past sufferings from obstinate calms and still continued suffering from thirst; in all these points, as well as others, Don Benito's story had corroborated not only the wailing ejaculations of the indiscriminate multitude, white and black, but likewise — what seemed impossible to be counterfeit — by the very expression and play of every human feature which Captain Delano saw. If Don Benito's story was throughout an invention, then every soul on board, down to the youngest Negress, was his carefully drilled recruit in the plot: an incredible inference. And yet, if there was ground for mistrusting his veracity, that inference was a legitimate one.

But those questions of the Spaniard. There, indeed, one might pause. Did they not seem put with much the same object with which the burglar or assassin, by daytime, reconnoiters the walls of a house? But, with ill purposes to solicit such information openly of the chief person endangered, and so, in effect, setting him on his guard — how unlikely a procedure was that? Absurd, then, to suppose that those questions had been prompted by evil designs. Thus, the same conduct which in this instance had raised the alarm, served to dispel it. In short, scarce any suspicion or uneasiness, however apparently reasonable at the time, which was not now with equal apparent reason dismissed.

At last he began to laugh at his former forebodings, and laugh at the strange ship for, in its aspect, someway siding with them, as it were; and laugh, too, at the odd-looking blacks, particularly those old scissors-grinders, the Ashantees; and those bed-ridden old knitting women, the oakum-pickers; and almost at the dark Spaniard himself, the central hobgoblin of all.

For the rest, whatever in a serious way seemed enigmatical was now good-naturedly explained away by the thought that, for the most part, the poor invalid scarcely knew what he was about; either sulking in black vapors, or putting idle questions without sense or object. Evidently, for the present the man was not fit to be intrusted with the ship. On some benevolent plea withdrawing the command from him, Captain Delano would yet have to send her to Conception, in charge of his second mate, a worthy person and good navigator — a plan not more convenient for the *San Dominick* than for Don Benito; for, relieved from all anxiety, keeping wholly to his cabin, the sick man, under the good nursing of his servant, would, probably, by the end of the passage, be in a measure restored to health, and with that he should also be restored to authority.

Such were the American's thoughts. They were tranquilizing. There was a difference between the idea of Don Benito's darkly preordaining Captain Delano's fate and Captain Delano's lightly arranging Don Benito's. Nevertheless, it was not without something of relief that the good seaman presently perceived his whaleboat in the distance. Its absence had been prolonged by unexpected detention at the sealer's side, as well as its returning trip lengthened by the continual recession of the goal.

The advancing speck was observed by the blacks. Their shouts attracted the attention of Don Benito, who, with a return of courtesy approaching Captain Delano, expressed satisfaction at the coming of some supplies, slight and temporary as they must necessarily prove.

Captain Delano responded, but while doing so, his attention was drawn to something passing on the deck below: among the crowd climbing the landward bulwarks, anxiously watching the coming boat, two blacks, to all appearances accidentally incommoded by one of the sailors, violently pushed him aside, which the sailor someway resenting, they dashed him to the deck, despite the earnest cries of the oakum-pickers.

"Don Benito," said Captain Delano quickly, "do you see what is going on there? Look!"

But, seized by his cough, the Spaniard staggered, with both hands to his face, on the point of falling. Captain Delano would have supported him, but the servant was more alert, who, with one hand sustaining his master, with the other applied the cordial. Don Benito restored, the black withdrew his support, slipping aside a little, but dutifully remaining within call of a whisper. Such discretion was here evinced as quite wiped away, in the visitor's eyes, any blemish of impropriety which might have attached to the attendant from the indecorous conferences before mentioned, showing, too, that if the servant were to blame it might be more the master's fault than his own, since, when left to himself, he could conduct thus well.

His glance called away from the spectacle of disorder to the more pleasing one before him, Captain Delano could not avoid again congratulating his host upon possessing such a servant, who, though perhaps a little too forward now and then, must upon the whole be invaluable to one in the invalid's situation.

"Tell me, Don Benito," he added, with a smile — "I should like to have your man here myself — what will you take for him? Would fifty doubloons be any object?"

"Master wouldn't part with Babo for a thousand doubloons," murmured the black, overhearing the offer, and taking it in earnest, and, with the strange vanity of a faithful slave appreciated by his master, scorning to hear so paltry a valuation put upon him by a stranger. But Don Benito, apparently hardly yet completely restored, and again interrupted by his cough, made but some broken reply.

Soon his physical distress became so great, affecting his mind, too, apparently, that, as if to screen the sad spectacle, the servant gently conducted his master below.

Left to himself, the American, to while away the time till his boat should arrive, would have pleasantly accosted some one of the few Spanish seamen he saw, but recalling something that Don Benito had said touching their ill conduct, he refrained, as a shipmaster indisposed to countenance cowardice or unfaithfulness in seamen.

While, with these thoughts, standing with eye directed forward towards that handful of sailors, suddenly he thought that one or two of them returned the glance and with a sort of meaning. He rubbed his eyes and looked again, but again seemed to see the same thing. Under a new form, but more obscure than any previous one, the old suspicions recurred, but, in the absence of Don Benito, with less of panic than before. Despite the bad account given of the sailors, Captain Delano resolved forthwith to accost one of them. Descending the poop, he made his way through the blacks, his movement drawing a queer cry from the oakum-pickers, prompted by whom, the Negroes, twitching each other aside, divided before him, but, as if curious to see what was the object of this deliberate visit to their ghetto, closing in behind in tolerable order, followed the white stranger up. His progress thus proclaimed as by mounted kings-at-arms, and escorted as by a Kaffir guard of honor, Captain Delano, assuming a good-humored, off-handed air, continued to advance; now and then saying a blithe word to the Negroes, and his eye curiously surveying the white faces, here and there sparsely mixed in with the blacks, like stray white pawns venturously involved in the ranks of the chessmen opposed.

While thinking which of them to select for his purpose, he chanced to observe a sailor seated on the deck engaged in tarring the strap of a large block, a circle of blacks squatted round him inquisitively eying the process.

The mean employment of the man was in contrast with something superior in his figure. His hand, black with continually thrusting it into the tarpot held for him by a Negro, seemed not naturally allied to his face, a face which would have been a very fine one but for its haggardness. Whether this haggardness had aught to do with criminality could not be determined, since, as intense heat and cold, though unlike, produce like sensations, so innocence and guilt, when, through casual association with mental pain stamping any visible impress, use one seal — a hacked one.

Not again that this reflection occurred to Captain Delano at the time, charitable man as he was. Rather another idea. Because observing so singular a haggardness combined with a dark eye, averted as in trouble and shame, and then again recalling Don Benito's confessed ill opinion of his crew, insensible, he was operated upon by certain general notions which, while disconnecting pain and abashment from virtue, invariably link them with vice.

If, indeed, there be any wickedness on board this ship, thought Captain Delano, be sure that man there has fouled his hand in it, even as now he fouls it in the pitch. I don't like to accost him. I will speak to this other, this old Jack here on the windlass.

He advanced to an old Barcelona tar, in ragged red breeches and dirty nightcap, cheeks trenched and bronzed, whiskers dense as thorn hedges. Seated between two sleepy-looking Africans, this mariner, like his younger shipmate, was employed upon some rigging — splicing a cable — the sleepy-looking blacks performing the inferior function of holding the outer parts of the ropes for him.

Upon Captain Delano's approach, the man at once hung his head below its previous level; the one necessary for business. It appeared as if he desired to be thought absorbed with more than common fidelity in his task. Being addressed, he glanced up, but with what seemed a furtive, diffident air, which sat strangely enough on his weather-beaten visage, much as if a grizzly bear, instead of growling and biting, should simper and cast sheep's eyes. He was asked several questions concerning the voyage — questions purposely referring to several particulars in Don Benito's narrative, not previously corroborated by those impulsive cries greeting the visitor on first coming on board. The questions were briefly answered, confirming all that remained to be confirmed of the story. The Negroes about the windlass joined in with the old sailor, but, as they became talkative, he by degrees became mute, and at length quite glum, seemed morosely unwilling to answer more questions, and yet, all the while, this ursine air was somehow mixed with his sheepish one.

Despairing of getting into unembarrassed talk with such a centaur, Captain Delano, after glancing round for a more promising countenance but seeing none, spoke pleasantly to the blacks to make way for him, and so, amid various grins and grimaces, returned to the poop, feeling a little strange at first, he could hardly tell why, but upon the whole with regained confidence in Benito Cereno.

How plainly, thought he, did that old whiskerando yonder betray a consciousness of ill desert. No doubt when he saw me coming he dreaded lest I, apprised by his captain of the crew's general misbehavior, came with sharp words for him, and so down with his head. And yet — and yet, now that I think of it, that very old fellow, if I err not, was one of those who seemed so earnestly eying me here awhile since. Ah, these currents spin one's head round almost as much as they do the ship. Ha, there now's a pleasant sort of sunny sight; quite sociable, too.

His attention had been drawn to a slumbering Negress, partly disclosed through the lacework of some rigging, lying, with youthful limbs carelessly disposed, under the lee of the bulwarks, like a doe in the shade of a woodland rock. Sprawling at her lapped breasts was her wide-awake fawn, stark naked, its black little body half lifted from the deck, crosswise with its dam's; its hands, like two paws, clambering upon her; its mouth and nose ineffectually rooting to get at the mark; and meantime giving a vexatious half-grunt, blending with the composed snore of the Negress.

The uncommon vigor of the child at length roused the mother. She started up, at a distance facing Captain Delano. But as if not at all concerned at the attitude in which she had been caught, delightedly she caught the child up, with maternal transports, covering it with kisses.

There's naked nature, now, pure tenderness and love, thought Captain Delano, well pleased.

This incident prompted him to remark the other Negresses more particularly than before. He was gratified with their manners: like most uncivilized women, they seemed at once tender of heart and tough of constitution, equally ready to die for their infants or fight for them. Unsophisticated as leopardesses, loving as doves. Ah! thought Captain Delano, these, perhaps, are some of the very women whom Ledyard saw in Africa, and gave such a noble account of.

These natural sights somehow insensibly deepened his confidence and ease. At last he looked to see how his boat was getting on, but it was still pretty remote. He turned to see if Don Benito had returned, but he had not.

To change the scene, as well as to please himself with a leisurely observation of the coming boat, stepping over into the mizzen-chains, he clambered his way into the starboard quarter-gallery — one of those abandoned Venetian-looking water balconies previously mentioned — retreats cut off from the deck. As his foot pressed the half-damp, half-dry sea mosses matting the place, and a chance phantom cat's-paw — an islet of breeze, unheralded, unfollowed — as this ghostly cat's-paw came fanning his cheek; as his glance fell upon the row of small, round, deadlights — all closed like coppered eyes of the coffined — and the state-cabin door, once connecting with the gallery, even as the deadlights had once looked out upon it, but now calked fast like a sarcophagus lid; and to a purple-black, tarred-over, panel, threshold, and post; and he bethought him of the time when that state cabin and this state balcony had heard the voices of the Spanish king's officers, and the forms of the Lima viceroy's daughters had perhaps leaned where he stood — as these and other images flitted through his mind as the cat's-paw through the calm, gradually he felt rising a dreamy inquietude, like that of one who alone on the prairie feels unrest from the repose of the noon.

He leaned against the carved balustrade, again looking off toward his boat, but found his eye falling upon the ribbon grass, trailing along the ship's water line, straight as a border of green box, and parterres of seaweed, broad ovals and crescents, floating nigh and far, with what seemed long formal alleys between, crossing the terraces of swells, and sweeping round as if leading to the grottoes below. And overhanging all was the balustrade by his arm, which, partly stained with pitch and partly embossed with moss, seemed the charred ruin of some summerhouse in a grand garden long running to waste.

Trying to break one charm, he was but becharmed anew. Though upon the wide sea, he seemed in some far inland country, prisoner in some deserted château, left to stare at empty grounds and peer out at vague roads where never wagon or wayfarer passed.

But these enchantments were a little disenchanted as his eye fell on the corroded mainchains. Of an ancient style, massy and rusty in link, shackle, and bolt, they seemed even more fit for the ship's present business than the one for which she had been built.

Presently he thought something moved nigh the chains. He rubbed his eyes, and looked hard. Groves of rigging were about the chains; and there, peering from behind a great stay, like an Indian from behind a hemlock, a Spanish sailor, a marlinespike in his hand, was seen, who made what seemed an imperfect gesture towards the balcony, but immediately, as if alarmed by some advancing step along the deck within, vanished into the recesses of the hempen forest like a poacher.

What meant this? Something the man had sought to communicate, unbeknown to anyone, even to his captain. Did the secret involve aught unfavorable to his captain? Were those previous misgivings of Captain Delano's about to be verified? Or, in his haunted mood at the moment, had some random, unintentional motion of the man, while busy with the stay as if repairing it, been mistaken for a significant beckoning?

Not unbewildered, again he gazed off for his boat. But it was temporarily hidden by a rocky spur of the isle. As with some eagerness he bent forward, watching for the first shooting view of its beak, the balustrade gave way before him like charcoal. Had he not clutched an outreaching rope he would have fallen into the sea. The crash, though feeble, and the fall, though hollow, of the rotten fragments, must have been overheard. He glanced up. With sober curiosity peering down upon him was one of the old oakum-pickers, slipped from his perch to an outside boom, while below the old Negro, and, invisible to him, reconnoitering from a porthole like a fox from the mouth of its den, crouched the Spanish sailor again. From something suddenly suggested by the man's air, the mad idea now darted into Captain Delano's mind that Don Benito's plea of indisposition, in withdrawing below, was but a pretense: that he was engaged there maturing his plot, of which the sailor, by some means gaining an inkling, had a mind to warn the stranger against, incited, it may be, by gratitude for a kind word on first boarding the ship. Was it from foreseeing some possible interference like this that Don Benito had, beforehand, given such a bad character of his sailors, while praising the Negroes, though, indeed, the former seemed as docile as the latter the contrary? The whites, too, by nature, were the shrewder race. A man with some evil design, would he not be likely to speak well of that stupidity which was blind to his depravity, and malign that intelligence from which it might not be hidden? Not unlikely, perhaps. But if the whites had dark secrets concerning Don Benito, could then Don Benito be any way in complicity with the blacks? But they were too stupid. Besides, who ever heard of a white so far a renegade as to apostatize from his very species almost, by leaguing in against it with Negroes? These difficulties recalled former ones. Lost in their mazes, Captain Delano, who had now regained the deck, was uneasily advancing along it when he observed a new face; an aged sailor seated cross-legged near the main hatchway. His skin was shrunk up with wrinkles like a pelican's empty pouch, his hair frosted, his countenance grave and composed. His hands were full of ropes, which he was working into a large knot. Some blacks were about him obligingly dipping the strands for him, here and there, as the exigencies of the operation demanded.

Captain Delano crossed over to him and stood in silence surveying the knot, his mind, by a not uncongenial transition, passing from its own entanglements to those of the hemp. For intricacy, such a knot he had never seen in an American ship, nor indeed any other. The old man looked like an Egyptian priest making Gordian knots for the temple of Ammon. The knot seemed a combination of double-bowline-knot, treble-crown-knot, back-handed-well-knot, knot-in-and-out-knot, and jamming knot.

At last, puzzled to comprehend the meaning of such a knot, Captain Delano addressed the knotter: "What are you knotting there, my man?"

"The knot," was the brief reply, without looking up.

"So it seems; but what is it for?"

"For someone else to undo," muttered back the old man, plying his fingers harder than ever, the knot being now nearly completed.

While Captain Delano stood watching him, suddenly the old man threw the knot towards him, saying in broken English — the first heard in the ship — something to this effect: "Undo it, cut it, quick." It was said lowly, but with such condensation of rapidity, that the long, slow words in Spanish, which had preceded and followed, almost operated as covers to the brief English between.

For a moment, knot in hand, and knot in head, Captain Delano stood mute, while, without further heeding him, the old man was now intent upon other ropes. Presently there was a slight stir behind Captain Delano. Turning, he saw the chained Negro, Atufal, standing quietly there. The next moment the old sailor rose, muttering, and, followed by his subordinate Negroes, removed to the forward part of the ship, where in the crowd he disappeared.

An elderly Negro, in a clout like an infant's, and with a pepper-and-salt head and a kind of attorney air, now approached Captain Delano. In tolerable Spanish, and with a good-natured, knowing wink, he informed him that the old knotter was simple-witted, but harmless, often playing his odd tricks. The Negro concluded by begging the knot, for of course the stranger would not care to be troubled with it. Unconsciously, it was handed to him. With a sort of *congé*,[7] the Negro received it, and, turning his back, ferreted into it like a detective custom-house officer after smuggled laces. Soon, with some African words equivalent to pshaw, he tossed the knot overboard.

All this is very queer, thought Captain Delano, with a qualmish sort of emotion; but, as one feeling incipient seasickness, he strove, by ignoring the

7 [A bow or a curtsy. — Editors' note.]

symptoms, to get rid of the malady. Once more he looked off for his boat. To his delight, it was now again in view, leaving the rocky spur astern.

The sensation here experienced, after at first relieving his uneasiness, with unforeseen efficacy soon began to remove it. The less distant sight of that well-known boat — showing it, not as before, half blended with the haze but with outline defined, so that its individuality, like a man's, was manifest; that boat, *Rover* by name, which, though now in strange seas, had often pressed the beach of Captain Delano's home, and, brought to its threshold for repairs, had familiarly lain there, as a Newfoundland dog; the sight of that household boat evoked a thousand trustful associations, which, contrasted with previous suspicions, filled him not only with lightsome confidence, but somehow with half humorous self-reproaches at his former lack of it.

"What, I, Amasa Delano — Jack of the Beach, as they called me when a lad — I, Amasa, the same that, duck-satchel in hand, used to paddle along the waterside to the schoolhouse made from the old hulk — I, little Jack of the Beach, that used to go berrying with cousin Nat and the rest — I to be murdered here at the ends of the earth on board a haunted pirate ship by a horrible Spaniard? Too nonsensical to think of! Who would murder Amasa Delano? His conscience is clean. There is someone above. Fie, fie, Jack of the Beach! you are a child indeed; a child of the second childhood, old boy; you are beginning to dote and drool, I'm afraid."

Light of heart and foot, he stepped aft, and there was met by Don Benito's servant, who, with a pleasing expression responsive to his own present feelings, informed him that his master had recovered from the effects of his coughing fit, and had just ordered him to go present his compliments to his good guest, Don Amasa, and say that he (Don Benito) would soon have the happiness to rejoin him.

There now, do you mark that? again thought Captain Delano, walking the poop. What a donkey I was. This kind gentleman who here sends me his kind compliments, he, but ten minutes ago, dark-lantern in hand, was dodging round some old grindstone in the hold, sharpening a hatchet for me, I thought. Well, well; these long calms have a morbid effect on the mind, I've often heard, though I never believed it before. Ha! glancing towards the boat, there's *Rover,* a good dog, a white bone in her mouth. A pretty big bone though, seems to me. — What? Yes, she has fallen afoul of the bubbling tide rip there. It sets her the other way, too, for the time. Patience.

It was now about noon, though, from the grayness of everything, it seemed to be getting towards dusk.

The calm was confirmed. In the far distance, away from the influence of land, the leaden ocean seemed laid out and leaded up, its course finished, soul gone, defunct. But the current from landward, where the ship was, increased, silently sweeping her further and further towards the tranced waters beyond.

Still, from his knowledge of those latitudes, cherishing hopes of a breeze, and a fair and fresh one, at any moment, Captain Delano, despite present prospects, buoyantly counted upon bringing the *San Dominick* safely to anchor ere night. The distance swept over was nothing, since, with a good wind, ten minutes' sailing would retrace more than sixty minutes' drifting. Meantime, one moment turning to mark *Rover* fighting the tide rip and the next to see Don Benito approaching, he continued walking the poop.

Gradually he felt a vexation arising from the delay of his boat; this soon merged into uneasiness, and at last — his eye falling continually, as from a stage box into the pit, upon the strange crowd before and below him, and by and by recognizing there the face, now composed to indifference, of the Spanish sailor who had seemed to beckon from the mainchains — something of his old trepidations returned.

Ah, thought he, gravely enough, this is like the ague: because it went off, it follows not that it won't come back.

Though ashamed of the relapse, he could not altogether subdue it; and so, exerting his good nature to the utmost, insensibly he came to a compromise.

Yes, this is a strange craft, a strange history, too, and strange folks on board. But — nothing more.

By way of keeping his mind out of mischief till the boat should arrive, he tried to occupy it with turning over and over, in a purely speculative sort of way, some lesser peculiarities of the captain and crew. Among others, four curious points recurred:

First, the affair of the Spanish lad assailed with a knife by the slave boy; an act winked at by Don Benito. Second, the tyranny in Don Benito's treatment of Atufal, the black, as if a child should lead a bull of the Nile by the ring in his nose. Third, the trampling of the sailor by the two Negroes, a piece of insolence passed over without so much as a reprimand. Fourth, the cringing submission to their master of all the ship's underlings, mostly blacks, as if by the least inadvertence they feared to draw down his despotic displeasure.

Coupling these points, they seemed somewhat contradictory. But what then, thought Captain Delano, glancing towards his now nearing boat — what then? Why, Don Benito is a very capricious commander. But he is not the first of the sort I have seen, though it's true he rather exceeds any other. But as a nation — continued he in his reveries — these Spaniards are all an odd set; the very word Spaniard has a curious, conspirator, Guy-Fawkish twang to it. And yet I dare say Spaniards in the main are as good folks as any in Duxbury, Massachusetts. Ah good! At last *Rover* has come.

As, with its welcome freight, the boat touched the side, the oakum-pickers, with venerable gestures, sought to restrain the blacks, who, at the sight of three gurried[8] water casks in its bottom and a pile of wilted pumpkins in its bow, hung over the bulwarks in disorderly raptures.

Don Benito, with his servant, now appeared, his coming, perhaps, hastened by hearing the noise. Of him Captain Delano sought permission to serve out the water, so that all might share alike, and none injure themselves by unfair excess. But sensible, and, on Don Benito's account, kind as this offer was, it was received with what seemed impatience; as if aware that he lacked energy as a commander, Don Benito, with the true jealousy of weakness, resented as an affront any interference. So, at least, Captain Delano inferred.

In another moment the casks were being hoisted in, when some of the eager Negroes accidentally jostled Captain Delano where he stood by the gangway, so that, unmindful of Don Benito, yielding to the impulse of the moment, with good-natured authority he bade the black stand back, to enforce his words making use of a half-mirthful, half-menacing gesture. Instantly the blacks paused, just where they were, each Negro and Negress suspended in his or her posture, exactly as the word had found them — for a few seconds continuing so — while, as between the responsive posts of a telegraph, an unknown syllable ran from man to man among the perched oakum-pickers. While the visitor's attention was fixed by this scene, suddenly the hachet-polishers half rose, and a rapid cry came from Don Benito.

Thinking that at the signal of the Spaniard he was about to be massacred, Captain Delano would have sprung for his boat, but paused, as the oakum-pickers, dropping down into the crowd with earnest exclamations, forced every white and every Negro back, at the same moment, with gestures friendly and familiar, almost jocose, bidding him, in substance, not be a fool. Simultaneously the hatchet-polishers resumed their seats, quietly as so many tailors, and at once, as if nothing had happened, the work of hoisting in the casks was resumed, white and blacks singing at the tackle.

Captain Delano glanced towards Don Benito. As he saw his meager form in the act of recovering itself from reclining in the servant's arms, into which the agitated invalid had fallen, he could not but marvel at the panic by which himself had been surprised, on the darting supposition that such a commander, who, upon a legitimate occasion, so trivial too, as it now appeared, could lose all self-command, was, with energetic iniquity, going to bring about his murder.

The casks being on deck, Captain Delano was handed a number of jars and cups by one of the steward's aids, who, in the name of his captain, entreated him to do as he had proposed — dole out the water. He complied, with republican

8 [Garbage-splashed. — Editors' note.]

impartiality as to this republican element, which always seeks one level, serving the oldest white no better than the youngest black, excepting, indeed, poor Don Benito, whose condition, if not rank, demanded an extra allowance. To him, in the first place, Captain Delano presented a fair pitcher of the fluid, but, thirsting as he was for it, the Spaniard quaffed not a drop until after several grave bows and salutes, a reciprocation of courtesies which the sight-loving Africans hailed with clapping of hands.

Two of the less wilted pumpkins being reserved for the cabin table, the residue were minced up on the spot for the general regalement. But the soft bread, sugar, and bottled cider Captain Delano would have given the whites alone, and in chief Don Benito, but the latter objected; which disinterestedness not a little pleased the American; and so mouthfuls all around were given alike to whites and blacks, excepting one bottle of cider, which Babo insisted upon setting aside for his master.

Here it may be observed that as, on the first visit of the boat, the American had not permitted his men to board the ship, neither did he now, being unwilling to add to the confusion of the decks.

Not uninfluenced by the peculiar good humor at present prevailing, and for the time oblivious of any but benevolent thought, Captain Delano, who from recent indications counted upon a breeze within an hour or two at furthest, dispatched the boat back to the sealer, with orders for all the hands that could be spared immediately to set about rafting casks to the watering place and filling them. Likewise he bade word be carried to his chief officer that if, against present expectation, the ship was not brought to anchor by sunset, he need be under no concern; for as there was to be a full moon that night, he (Captain Delano) would remain on board ready to play the pilot, come the wind soon or late.

As the two Captains stood together observing the departing boat — the servant, as it happened, having just spied a spot on his master's velvet sleeve, and silently engaged rubbing it out — the American expressed his regrets that the *San Dominick* had no boats, none, at least, but the unseaworthy old hulk of the longboat, which, warped as a camel's skeleton in the desert and almost as bleached, lay pot-wise inverted amidships, one side a little tipped, furnishing a subterraneous sort of den for family groups of the blacks, mostly women and small children, who, squatting on old mats below, or perched above in the dark dome on the elevated seats, were descried, some distance within, like a social circle of bats sheltering in some friendly cave, at intervals, ebon flights of naked boys and girls three or four years old darting in and out of the den's mouth.

"Had you three or four boats now, Don Benito," said Captain Delano, "I think that, by tugging at the oars, your Negroes here might help along matters some. Did you sail from port without boats, Don Benito?"

"They were stove in the gales, *señor.*"

"That was bad. Many men, too, you lost then. Boats and men. Those must have been hard gales, Don Benito."

"Past all speech," cringed the Spaniard.

"Tell me, Don Benito," continued his companion with increased interest, "tell me, were these gales immediately off the pitch of Cape Horn?"

"Cape Horn? — who spoke of Cape Horn?"

"Yourself did, when giving me an account of your voyage," answered Captain Delano, with almost equal astonishment at this eating of his own words, even as he ever seemed eating his own heart, on the part of the Spaniard. "You yourself, Don Benito, spoke of Cape Horn," he emphatically repeated.

The Spaniard turned, in a sort of stooping posture, pausing an instant as one about to make a plunging exchange of elements, as from air to water.

At this moment a messenger boy, a white, hurried by, in the regular performance of his function carrying the last expired half-hour forward to the forecastle from the cabin timepiece, to have it struck at the ship's large bell.

"Master," said the servant, discontinuing his work on the coat sleeve and addressing the rapt Spaniard with a sort of timid apprehensiveness, as one charged with a duty the discharge of which, it was foreseen, would prove irksome to the very person who had imposed it and for whose benefit it was intended, "master told me never mind where he was, or how engaged, always to remind him, to a minute, when shaving-time comes. Miguel has gone to strike the half-hour afternoon. It is *now,* master. Will master go into the cuddy?"

"Ah — yes," answered the Spaniard, starting, as from dreams into realities, then, turning upon Captain Delano, he said that erelong he would resume the conversation.

"Then if master means to talk more to Don Amasa," said the servant, "why not let Don Amasa sit by master in the cuddy, and master can talk, and Don Amasa can listen, while Babo here lathers and strops."

"Yes," said Captain Delano, not unpleased with this sociable plan, "yes, Don Benito, unless you had rather not, I will go with you."

"Be it so, *señor.*"

As the three passed aft, the American could not but think it another strange instance of his host's capriciousness, this being shaved with such uncommon punctuality in the middle of the day. But he deemed it more than likely that the servant's anxious fidelity had something to do with the matter, inasmuch as the timely interruption served to rally his master from the mood which had evidently been coming upon him.

The place called the cuddy was a light deck cabin formed by the poop, a sort of attic to the large cabin below. Part of it had formerly been the quarters of the officers, but since their death all the partitionings had been thrown down and the whole interior converted into one spacious and airy marine hall; for absence of fine furniture and picturesque disarray of odd appurtenances, somewhat answering to the wide, cluttered hall of some eccentric bachelor squire in the country, who hangs his shooting jacket and tobacco pouch on deer antlers, and keeps his fishing rod, tongs, and walking stick in the same corner.

The similitude was heightened, if not originally suggested, by glimpses of the surrounding sea, since, in one aspect, the country and the ocean seem cousins-german.

The floor of the cuddy was matted. Overhead, four or five old muskets were stuck into horizontal holes along the beams. On one side was a claw-footed old table lashed to the deck, a thumbed missal on it, and over it, a small, meager crucifix attached to the bulkhead. Under the table lay a dented cutlass or two with a hacked harpoon, among some melancholy old rigging, like a heap of poor friars' girdles. There were also two long, sharp-ribbed settees of Malacca cane, black with age, and uncomfortable to look at as inquisitors' racks, with a large, misshapen armchair, which, furnished with a rude barber's crotch at the back, working with a screw, seemed some grotesque engine of torment. A flag locker was in one corner, open, exposing various colored buntings, some rolled up, others half unrolled, still others tumbled. Opposite was a cumbrous washstand of black mahogany, all of one block, with a pedestal like a font, and over it a railed shelf, containing combs, brushes, and other implements of the toilet. A torn hammock of stained grass swung near, the sheets tossed, and the pillow wrinkled up like a brow, as if whoever slept here slept but illy, with alternate visitations of sad thoughts and bad dreams.

The further extremity of the cuddy, overhanging the ship's stern, was pierced with three openings, windows or portholes, according as men or cannon might peer, socially or unsocially, out of them. At present neither men nor cannon were seen, though huge ringbolts and other rusty iron fixtures of the woodwork hinted of twenty-four-pounders.

Glancing towards the hammock as he entered, Captain Delano said, "You sleep here, Don Benito?"

"Yes, *señor*, since we got into mild weather."

"This seems a sort of dormitory, sitting room, sail loft, chapel, armory, and private closet all together, Don Benito," added Captain Delano, looking round.

"Yes, *señor;* events have not been favorable to much order in my arrangements."

Here the servant, napkin on arm, made a motion as if waiting his master's good pleasure. Don Benito signified his readiness, when, seating him in the Malacca armchair, and for the guest's convenience drawing opposite one of the settees, the servant commenced operations by throwing back his master's collar and loosening his cravat.

There is something in the Negro which, in a peculiar way, fits him for avocations about one's person. Most Negroes are natural valets and hairdressers, taking to the comb and brush congenially as to the castinets, and flourishing them apparently with almost equal satisfaction. There is, too, a smooth tact about them in this employment, with a marvelous, noiseless, gliding briskness, not ungraceful in its way, singularly pleasing to behold, and still more so to be the manipulated subject of. And above all is the great gift of good humor. Not the mere grin or laugh is here meant. Those were unsuitable. But a certain easy cheerfulness, harmonious in every glance and gesture, as though God had set the whole Negro to some pleasant tune.

When to this is added the docility arising from the unaspiring contentment of a limited mind, and that susceptibility of blind attachment sometimes inhering in indisputable inferiors, one readily perceives why those hypochondriacs, Johnson and Byron — it may be, something like the hypochondriac Benito Cereno — took to their hearts, almost to the exclusion of the entire white race, their servingmen, the Negroes, Barber and Fletcher. But if there be that in the Negro which exempts him from the inflicted sourness of the morbid or cynical mind, how, in his most prepossessing aspects, must he appear to a benevolent one? When at ease with respect to exterior things, Captain Delano's nature was not only benign, but familiarly and humorously so. At home, he had often taken rare satisfaction in sitting in his door, watching some free man of color at his work or play. If on a voyage he chanced to have a black sailor, invariably he was on chatty and half-gamesome terms with him. In fact, like most men of a good, blithe heart, Captain Delano took to Negroes, not philanthropically, but genially, just as other men to Newfoundland dogs.

Hitherto, the circumstances in which he found the *San Dominick* had repressed the tendency. But in the cuddy, relieved from his former uneasiness, and, for various reasons, more sociably inclined than at any previous period of the day, and seeing the colored servant, napkin on arm, so debonair about his master, in a business so familiar as that of shaving too, all his old weakness for Negroes returned.

Among other things, he was amused with an odd instance of the African love of bright colors and fine shows, in the black's informally taking from the flag locker a great piece of bunting of all hues and lavishly tucking it under his master's chin for an apron.

The mode of shaving among the Spaniards is a little different from what it is with other nations. They have a basin, specifically called a barber's basin, which on one side is scooped out, so as accurately to receive the chin, against which it is closely held in lathering, which is done, not with a brush, but with soap dipped in the water of the basin and rubbed on the face.

In the present instance salt water was used for lack of better, and the parts lathered were only the upper lip and low down under the throat, all the rest being cultivated beard.

The preliminaries being somewhat novel to Captain Delano, he sat curiously eying them, so that no conversation took place, nor, for the present, did Don Benito appear disposed to renew any.

Setting down his basin, the Negro searched among the razors, as for the sharpest, and, having found it, gave it an additional edge by expertly stropping it on the firm, smooth, oily skin of his open palm; he then made a gesture as if to begin, but midway stood suspended for an instant, one hand elevating the razor, the other professionally dabbling among the bubbling suds on the Spaniard's lank neck. Not unaffected by the close sight of the gleaming steel, Don Benito nervously shuddered; his usual ghastliness was heightened by the lather, which lather, again, was intensified in its hue by the contrasting sootiness of the Negro's body. Altogether the scene was somewhat peculiar, at least to Captain Delano, nor, as he saw the two thus postured, could he resist the vagary that in the black he saw a headsman, and in the white a man at the block. But this was one of those antic conceits, appearing and vanishing in a breath, from which, perhaps, the best-regulated mind is not always free.

Meantime the agitation of the Spaniard had a little loosened the bunting from around him, so that one broad fold swept curtainlike over the chair arm to the floor, revealing, amid a profusion of armorial bars and ground colors — black, blue, and yellow — a closed castle in a blood-red field diagonal with a lion rampant in a white.

"The castle and the lion," exclaimed Captain Delano — "why, Don Benito, this is the flag of Spain you use here. It's well it's only I, and not the King, that sees this," he added, with a smile, "but" — turning towards the black — "it's all one, I suppose, so the colors be gay"; which playful remark did not fail somewhat to tickle the Negro.

"Now, master," he said, readjusting the flag, and pressing the head gently further back into the crotch of the chair, "now, master," and the steel glanced nigh the throat.

Again Don Benito faintly shuddered.

"You must not shake so, master. See, Don Amasa, master always shakes when I shave him. And yet master knows I never yet have drawn blood, though it's true if master will shake so I may some of these times. Now master," he continued. "And now, Don Amasa, please go on with your talk about the gale, and all that; master can hear, and, between times, master can answer."

"Ah yes, these gales," said Captain Delano; "but the more I think of your voyage, Don Benito, the more I wonder, not at the gales, terrible as they must have been, but at the disastrous interval following them. For here, by your account, have you been these two months and more getting from Cape Horn to St. Maria, a distance which I myself, with a good wind, have sailed in a few days. True, you had calms, and long ones, but to be becalmed for two months, that is, at least, unusual. Why, Don Benito, had almost any other gentleman told me such a story, I should have been half disposed to a little incredulity."

Here an involuntary expression came over the Spaniard, similar to that just before on the deck, and whether it was the start he gave, or a sudden gawky roll of the hull in the calm, or a momentary unsteadiness of the servant's hand, however it was, just then the razor drew blood, spots of which stained the creamy lather under the throat; immediately the black barber drew back his steel, and, remaining in his professional attitude, back to Captain Delano, and face to Don Benito, held up the trickling razor, saying, with a sort of half humorous sorrow, "See, master — you shook so — here's Babo's first blood."

No sword drawn before James the First of England, no assassination in that timid king's presence, could have produced a more terrified aspect than was now presented by Don Benito.

Poor fellow, thought Captain Delano, so nervous he can't even bear the sight of barber's blood; and this unstrung, sick man, is it credible that I should have imagined he meant to spill all my blood, who can't endure the sight of one little drop of his own? Surely, Amasa Delano, you have been beside yourself this day. Tell it not when you get home, sappy Amasa. Well, well, he looks like a murderer, doesn't he? More like as if himself were to be done for. Well, well, this day's experience shall be a good lesson.

Meantime, while these things were running through the honest seaman's mind, the servant had taken the napkin from his arm, and to Don Benito had said — "But answer Don Amasa, please, master, while I wipe this ugly stuff off the razor, and strop it again."

As he said the words, his face was turned half round, so as to be alike visible to the Spaniard and the American, and seemed, by its expression, to hint that he was desirous, by getting his master to go on with the conversation, considerately to withdraw his attention from the recent annoying accident. As if glad to snatch the offered relief, Don Benito resumed, rehearsing to Captain Delano that, not only were the calms of unusual duration, but the ship had fallen in with obstinate currents, and other things he added, some of which were but repetitions of former statements, to explain how it came to pass that the passage from Cape Horn to St. Maria had been so exceedingly long, now and then mingling with his words incidental praises, less qualified than before, to the blacks, for their general good conduct. These particulars were not given consecutively, the servant, at convenient times, using his razor, and so, between the intervals of shaving, the story and panegyric went on with more than usual huskiness.

To Captain Delano's imagination, now again not wholly at rest, there was something so hollow in the Spaniard's manner, with apparently some reciprocal hollowness in the servant's dusky comment of silence, that the idea flashed across him that possibly master and man, for some unknown purpose, were acting out, both in word and deed, nay, to the very tremor of Don Benito's limbs, some juggling play before him. Neither did the suspicion of collusion lack apparent support, from the fact of those whispered conferences before mentioned. But then, what could be the object of enacting this play of the barber before him? At last, regarding the notion as a whimsey, insensibly suggested, perhaps, by the theatrical aspect of Don Benito in his harlequin ensign, Captain Delano speedily banished it.

The shaving over, the servant bestirred himself with a small bottle of scented waters, pouring a few drops on the head, and then diligently rubbing, the vehemence of the exercise causing the muscles of his face to twitch rather strangely.

His next operation was with comb, scissors, and brush, going round and round, smoothing a curl here, clipping an unruly whisker hair there, giving a graceful sweep to the temple lock, with other impromptu touches evincing the hand of a master, while, like any resigned gentleman in barber's hands, Don Benito bore all much less uneasily, at least, than he had done the razoring; indeed, he sat so pale and rigid now that the Negro seemed a Nubian sculptor finishing off a white statue head.

All being over at last, the standard of Spain removed, tumbled up, and tossed back into the flag locker, the Negro's warm breath blowing away any stray hair which might have lodged down his master's neck, collar and cravat readjusted, a speck of lint whisked off the velvet lapel — all this being done, backing off a little space, and pausing with an expression of subdued self-complacency, the servant for a moment surveyed his master, as, in toilette at least, the creature of his own tasteful hands.

Captain Delano playfully complimented him upon his achievement, at the same time congratulating Don Benito.

But neither sweet waters, nor shampooing, nor fidelity, nor sociality, delighted the Spaniard. Seeing him relapsing into forbidding gloom, and still remaining seated, Captain Delano, thinking that his presence was undesired just then, withdrew, on pretense of seeing whether, as he had prophesied, any signs of a breeze were visible.

Walking forward to the mainmast, he stood awhile thinking over the scene, and not without some undefined misgivings, when he heard a noise near the cuddy, and, turning, saw the Negro, his hand to his cheek. Advancing, Captain Delano perceived that the cheek was bleeding. He was about to ask the cause, when the Negro's wailing soliloquy enlightened him.

"Ah, when will master get better from his sickness; only the sour heart that sour sickness breeds made him serve Babo so, cutting Babo with the razor because, only by accident, Babo had given master one little scratch, and for the first time in so many a day, too. Ah, ah, ah," holding his hand to his face.

Is it possible, thought Captain Delano; was it to wreak in private his Spanish spite against this poor friend of his that Don Benito, by his sullen manner, impelled me to withdraw? Ah this slavery breeds ugly passions in man. — Poor fellow!

He was about to speak in sympathy to the Negro, but with a timid reluctance he now re-entered the cuddy.

Presently master and man came forth, Don Benito leaning on his servant as if nothing had happened.

But a sort of love quarrel, after all, thought Captain Delano.

He accosted Don Benito, and they slowly walked together. They had gone but a few paces, when the steward — a tall, rajah-looking mulatto, Orientally set off with a pagoda turban formed by three or four Madras handkerchiefs wound about his head, tier on tier — approaching with a saalam, announced lunch in the cabin.

On their way thither, the two captains were preceded by the mulatto, who, turning round as he advanced, with continual smiles and bows, ushered them on, a display of elegance which quite completed the insignificance of the small bareheaded Babo, who, as if not unconscious of inferiority, eyed askance the graceful steward. But, in part, Captain Delano imputed his jealous watchfulness to that peculiar feeling which the full-blooded African entertains for the adulterated one. As for the steward, his manner, if not bespeaking much dignity of self-respect, yet evidenced his extreme desire to please, which is doubly meritorious, as at once Christian and Chesterfieldian.[9]

Captain Delano observed with interest that while the complexion of the mulatto was hybrid, his physiognomy was European — classically so.

"Don Benito," whispered he, "I am glad to see this usher-of-the-golden-rod of yours; the sight refutes an ugly remark once made to me by a Barbados planter, that when a mulatto has a regular European face, look out for him; he is a devil. But see, your steward here has features more regular than King George's of England, and yet there he nods, and bows, and smiles, a king, indeed — the king of kind hearts and polite fellows. What a pleasant voice he has, too."

"He has, *señor*."

9 [Courteous. — Editors' note.]

"But tell me, has he not, so far as you have known him, always proved a good, worthy fellow?" said Captain Delano, pausing, while with a final genuflexion the steward disappeared into the cabin; "come, for the reason just mentioned, I am curious to know."

"Francesco is a good man," somewhat sluggishly responded Don Benito, like a phlegmatic appreciator, who would neither find fault nor flatter.

"Ah, I thought so. For it were strange indeed, and not very creditable to us whiteskins, if a little of our blood mixed with the African's should, far from improving the latter's quality, have the sad effect of pouring vitriolic acid into black broth — improving the hue, perhaps, but not the wholesomeness."

"Doubtless, doubtless, *señor*, but" — glancing at Babo — "not to speak of Negroes, your planter's remark I have heard applied to the Spanish and Indian intermixtures in our provinces. But I know nothing about the matter," he listlessly added.

And here they entered the cabin.

The lunch was a frugal one. Some of Captain Delano's fresh fish and pumpkins, biscuit and salt beef, the reserved bottle of cider, and the *San Dominick*'s last bottle of Canary.

As they entered, Francesco, with two or three colored aids, was hovering over the table giving the last adjustments. Upon perceiving their master they withdrew, Francesco making a smiling *congé*, and the Spaniard, without condescending to notice it, fastidiously remarking to his companion that he relished not superfluous attendance.

Without companions, host and guest sat down, like a childless married couple, at opposite ends of the table, Don Benito waving Captain Delano to his place, and, weak as he was, insisting upon that gentleman being seated before himself.

The Negro placed a rug under Don Benito's feet, and a cushion behind his back, and then stood behind, not his master's chair, but Captain Delano's. At first, this a little surprised the latter. But it was soon evident that, in taking his position, the black was still true to his master, since by facing him he could the more readily anticipate his slightest want.

"This is an uncommonly intelligent fellow of yours, Don Benito," whispered Captain Delano across the table.

"You say true, *señor*."

During the repast, the guest again reverted to parts of Don Benito's story, begging further particulars here and there. He inquired how it was that the scurvy and fever should have committed such wholesale havoc upon the whites, while destroying less than half of the blacks. As if this question reproduced the whole scene of plague before the Spaniard's eyes, miserably reminding him of his solitude in a cabin where before he had had so many friends and officers round him, his hand shook, his face became hueless, broken words escaped; but directly the same memory of the past seemed replaced by insane terrors of the present. With starting eyes he stared before him at vacancy. For nothing was to be seen but the hand of his servant pushing the Canary over towards him. At length a few sips served partially to restore him. He made random reference to the different constitution of races, enabling one to offer more resistance to certain maladies than another. The thought was new to his companion.

Presently Captain Delano, intending to say something to his host concerning the pecuniary part of the business he had undertaken for him, especially — since he was strictly accountable to his owners — with reference to the new suit of sails, and other things of that sort, and naturally preferring to conduct such affairs in private, was desirous that the servant should withdraw, imagining that Don Benito for a few minutes could dispense with his attendance. He, however, waited awhile, thinking that, as the conversation proceeded, Don Benito, without being prompted, would perceive the propriety of the step.

But it was otherwise. At last catching his host's eye, Captain Delano, with a slight backward gesture of his thumb, whispered, "Don Benito, pardon me, but there is an interference with the full expression of what I have to say to you."

Upon this the Spaniard changed countenance, which was imputed to his resenting the hint, as in some way a reflection upon his servant. After a moment's pause, he assured his guest that the black's remaining with them could be of no disservice; because since losing his officers he had made Babo (whose original office, it now appeared, had been captain of the slaves) not only his constant attendant and companion, but in all things his confidant.

After this, nothing more could be said; though indeed Captain Delano could hardly avoid some little tinge of irritation upon being left ungratified in so inconsiderable a wish, by one, too, for whom he intended such solid services. But it is only his querulousness, thought he, and so, filling his glass, he proceeded to business.

The price of the sails and other matters was fixed upon. But while this was being done, the American observed that, though his original offer of assistance had been hailed with hectic animation, yet now when it was reduced to a business transaction, indifference and apathy were betrayed. Don Benito, in fact, appeared to submit to hearing the details more out of regard to common propriety than from any impression that weighty benefit to himself and his voyage was involved.

Soon his manner became still more reserved. The effort was vain to seek to draw him into social talk. Gnawed by his splenetic mood, he sat twitching his beard, while to little purpose the hand of his servant, mute as that on the wall, slowly pushed over the Canary.

Lunch being over, they sat down on the cushioned transom, the servant placing a pillow behind his master. The long continuance of the calm had now affected the atmosphere. Don Benito sighed heavily, as if for breath.

"Why not adjourn to the cuddy," said Captain Delano; "there is more air there." But the host sat silent and motionless.

Meantime his servant knelt before him with a large fan of feathers. And Francesco, coming in on tiptoes, handed the Negro a little cup of aromatic waters, with which at intervals he chafed his master's brow, smoothing the hair along the temples as a nurse does a child's. He spoke no word. He only rested his eye on his master's, as if, amid all Don Benito's distress, a little to refresh his spirit by the silent sight of fidelity.

Presently the ship's bell sounded two o'clock, and through the cabin windows a slight rippling of the sea was discerned, and from the desired direction.

"There," exclaimed Captain Delano, "I told you so, Don Benito, look!"

He had risen to his feet, speaking in a very animated tone, with a view the more to rouse his companion. But though the crimson curtain of the stern window near him that moment fluttered against his pale cheek, Don Benito seemed to have even less welcome for the breeze than the calm.

Poor fellow, thought Captain Delano, bitter experience has taught him that one ripple does not make a wind, any more than one swallow a summer. But he is mistaken for once. I will get his ship in for him, and prove it.

Briefly alluding to his weak condition, he urged his host to remain quietly where he was, since he (Captain Delano) would with pleasure take upon himself the responsibility of making the best use of the wind.

Upon gaining the deck, Captain Delano started at the unexpected figure of Atufal, monumentally fixed at the threshold, like one of those sculptured porters of black marble guarding the porches of Egyptian tombs.

But this time the start was, perhaps, purely physical. Atufal's presence, singularly attesting docility even in sullenness, was contrasted with that of the hatchet-polishers, who in patience evinced their industry; while both spectacles showed that, lax as Don Benito's general authority might be, still, whenever he chose to exert it, no man so savage or colossal but must, more or less, bow.

Snatching a trumpet which hung from the bulwarks, with a free step Captain Delano advanced to the forward edge of the poop, issuing his orders in his best Spanish. The few sailors and many Negroes, all equally pleased, obediently set about heading the ship towards the harbor.

While giving some directions about setting a lower stun-sail, suddenly Captain Delano heard a voice faithfully repeating his orders. Turning, he saw Babo, now for the time acting, under the pilot, his original part of captain of the slaves. This assistance proved valuable. Tattered sails and warped yards were soon brought into some trim. And no brace or halyard was pulled but to the blithe songs of the inspirited Negroes.

Good fellows, thought Captain Delano, a little training would make fine sailors of them. Why see, the very women pull and sing too. These must be some of those Ashantee Negresses that make such capital soldiers, I've heard. But who's at the helm? I must have a good hand there.

He went to see.

The *San Dominick* steered with a cumbrous tiller, with large horizontal pulleys attached. At each pulley end stood a subordinate black, and between them, at the tillerhead, the responsible post, a Spanish seaman, whose countenance evinced his due share in the general hopefulness and confidence at the coming of the breeze.

He proved the same man who had behaved with so shamefaced an air on the windlass.

"Ah — it is you, my man," exclaimed Captain Delano — "well, no more sheep's-eyes now; look straight forward and keep the ship so. Good hand, I trust? And want to get into the harbor, don't you?"

The man assented with an inward chuckle, grasping the tillerhead firmly. Upon this, unperceived by the American, the two blacks eyed the sailor intently.

Finding all right at the helm, the pilot went forward to the forecastle to see how matters stood there.

The ship now had way enough to breast the current. With the approach of evening, the breeze would be sure to freshen.

Having done all that was needed for the present, Captain Delano, giving his last orders to the sailors, turned aft to report affairs to Don Benito in the cabin, perhaps additionally incited to rejoin him by the hope of snatching a moment's private chat while the servant was engaged upon deck.

From opposite sides, there were, beneath the poop, two approaches to the cabin, one further forward than the other, and consequently communicating with a longer passage. Marking the servant still above, Captain Delano, taking the nighest entrance — the one last named, and at whose porch Atufal still stood — hurried on his way, till, arrived at the cabin threshold, he paused an instant, a little to recover from his eagerness. Then, with the words of his intended business upon his lips, he entered. As he advanced toward the seated Spaniard, he heard another footstep, keeping time with his. From the opposite door, a salver in hand, the servant was likewise advancing.

"Confound the faithful fellow," thought Captain Delano; "what a vexatious coincidence."

Possibly the vexation might have been something different, were it not for the brisk confidence inspired by the breeze. But even as it was he felt a slight twinge, from a sudden indefinite association in his mind of Babo with Atufal.

"Don Benito," said he, "I give you joy; the breeze will hold, and will increase. By the way, your tall man and timepiece, Atufal, stands without. By your order, of course?"

Don Benito recoiled, as if at some bland satirical touch delivered with such adroit garnish of apparent good breeding as to present no handle for retort.

He is like one flayed alive, thought Captain Delano; where may one touch him without causing a shrink?

The servant moved before his master, adjusting a cushion; recalled to civility, the Spaniard stiffly replied: "You are right. The slave appears where you saw him, according to my command, which is that if at the given hour I am below he must take his stand and abide my coming."

"Ah now, pardon me, but that is treating the poor fellow like an ex-king indeed. Ah, Don Benito," smiling, "for all the license you permit in some things, I fear lest, at bottom, you are a bitter hard master."

Again Don Benito shrank, and this time, as the good sailor thought, from a genuine twinge of his conscience.

Again conversation became constrained. In vain Captain Delano called attention to the now perceptible motion of the keel gently cleaving the sea; with lackluster eye, Don Benito returned words few and reserved.

By and by, the wind having steadily risen, and still blowing right into the harbor, bore the *San Dominick* swiftly on. Rounding a point of land, the sealer at distance came into open view.

Meantime Captain Delano had again repaired to the deck, remaining there some time. Having at last altered the ship's course so as to give the reef a wide berth, he returned for a few moments below.

I will cheer up my poor friend this time, thought he.

"Better and better, Don Benito," he cried as he blithely re-entered: "there will soon be an end to your cares, at least for a while. For when, after a long, sad voyage, you know, the anchor drops into the haven, all its vast weight seems lifted from the captain's heart. We are getting on famously, Don Benito. My ship is in sight. Look through this side light here; there she is, all a-taunt-o![10] The *Bachelor's Delight*, my good friend. Ah, how this wind braces one up. Come, you must take a cup of coffee with me this evening. My old steward will give you as fine a cup as ever any sultan tasted. What say you, Don Benito, will you?"

At first, the Spaniard glanced feverishly up, casting a longing look towards the sealer, while, with mute concern his servant gazed into his face. Suddenly

10 [Fully rigged. — Editors' note.]

the old ague of coldness returned, and dropping back to his cushions he was silent.

"You do not answer. Come, all day you have been my host; would you have hospitality all on one side?"

"I cannot go," was the response.

"'What? it will not fatigue you. The ships will lie together as near as they can without swinging foul. It will be little more than stepping from deck to deck, which is but as from room to room. Come, come, you must not refuse me."

"I cannot go," decisively and repulsively repeated Don Benito.

Renouncing all but the last appearance of courtesy, with a sort of cadaverous sullenness, and biting his thin nails to the quick, he glanced, almost glared, at his guest, as if impatient that a stranger's presence should interfere with the full indulgence of his morbid hour. Meantime the sound of the parted waters came more and more gurglingly and merrily in at the windows; as reproaching him for his dark spleen, as telling him that, sulk as he might, and go mad with it, nature cared not a jot, since whose fault was it, pray?

But the foul mood was now at its depth, as the fair wind at its height.

There was something in the man so far beyond any mere unsociality or sourness previously evinced that even the forbearing good nature of his guest could no longer endure it. Wholly at a loss to account for such demeanor, and deeming sickness with eccentricity, however extreme, no adequate excuse, well satisfied, too, that nothing in his own conduct could justify it, Captain Delano's pride began to be roused. Himself became reserved. But all seemed one to the Spaniard. Quitting him, therefore, Captain Delano once more went to the deck.

The ship was now within less than two miles of the sealer. The whaleboat was seen darting over the interval.

To be brief, the two vessels, thanks to the pilot's skill, erelong in neighborly style lay anchored together.

Before returning to his own vessel, Captain Delano had intended communicating to Don Benito the smaller details of the proposed services to be rendered. But as it was, unwilling anew to subject himself to rebuffs, he resolved, now that he had seen the *San Dominick* safely moored, immediately to quit her, without further allusion to hospitality or business. Indefinitely postponing his ulterior plans, he would regulate his future actions according to future circumstances. His boat was ready to receive him; but his host still tarried below. Well, thought Captain Delano, if he has little breeding, the more need to show mine. He descended to the cabin to bid a ceremonious, and, it may be, tacitly rebukeful adieu. But to his great satisfaction, Don Benito, as if he began to feel the weight of that treatment with which his slighted guest had, not indecorously, retaliated upon him, now, supported by his servant, rose to his feet, and grasping Captain

Delano's hand, stood tremulous, too much agitated to speak. But the good augury hence drawn was suddenly dashed by his resuming all his previous reserve with augmented gloom, as, with half-averted eyes, he silently reseated himself on his cushions. With a corresponding return of his own chilled feelings, Captain Delano bowed and withdrew.

He was hardly midway in the narrow corridor, dim as a tunnel, leading from the cabin to the stairs, when a sound, as of the tolling for execution in some jail-yard, fell on his ears. It was the echo of the ship's flawed bell striking the hour, drearily reverberated in this subterranean vault. Instantly, by a fatality not to be withstood, his mind, responsive to the portent, swarmed with superstitious suspicions. He paused. In images far swifter than these sentences, the minutest details of all his former distrusts swept through him.

Hitherto, credulous good nature had been too ready to furnish excuses for reasonable fears. Why was the Spaniard, so superfluously punctilious at times, now heedless of common propriety in not accompanying to the side his departing guest? Did indisposition forbid? Indisposition had not forbidden more irksome exertion that day. His last equivocal demeanor recurred. He had risen to his feet, grasped his guest's hand, motioned toward his hat; then, in an instant, all was eclipsed in sinister muteness and gloom. Did this imply one brief repentant relenting at the final moment from some iniquitous plot, followed by remorseless return to it? His last glance seemed to express a calamitous yet acquiescent farewell to Captain Delano forever. Why decline the invitation to visit the sealer that evening? Or was the Spaniard less hardened than the Jew, who refrained not from supping at the board of him whom the same night he meant to betray? What imported all those daylong enigmas and contradictions, except they were intended to mystify, preliminary to some stealthy blow? Atufal, the pretended rebel but punctual shadow, that moment lurked by the threshold without. He seemed a sentry, and more. Who, by his own confession, had stationed him there? Was the Negro now lying in wait?

The Spaniard behind — his creature before: to rush from darkness to light was the involuntary choice.

The next moment, with clenched jaw and hand, he passed Atufal, and stood unharmed in the light. As he saw his trim ship lying peacefully at anchor and almost within ordinary call; as he saw his household boat, with familiar faces in it, patiently rising and falling on the short waves by the *San Dominick*'s side; and then, glancing about the decks where he stood, saw the oakum-pickers still gravely plying their fingers, and heard the low, buzzing whistle and industrious hum of the hatchet-polishers still bestirring themselves over their endless occupation; and more than all, as he saw the benign aspect of nature taking her innocent repose in the evening, the screened sun in the quiet camp of the west shining out like the mild light from Abraham's tent — as charmed eye and ear took in all these, with the chained figure of the black, clenched jaw and hand relaxed. Once again he smiled at the phantoms which had mocked him, and felt something like a tinge of remorse that, by harboring them even for a moment, he should by implication have betrayed an atheist doubt of the ever-watchful Providence above.

There was a few minutes' delay, while, in obedience to his orders, the boat was being hooked along to the gangway. During this interval, a sort of saddened satisfaction stole over Captain Delano at thinking of the kindly offices he had that day discharged for a stranger. Ah, thought he, after good actions one's conscience is never ungrateful, however much so the benefited party may be.

Presently his foot, in the first act of descent into the boat, pressed the first round of the side ladder, his face presented inward upon the deck. In the same moment he heard his name courteously sounded, and, to his pleased surprise, saw Don Benito advancing — an unwonted energy in his air, as if, at the last moment, intent upon making amends for his recent discourtesy. With instinctive good feeling, Captain Delano, withdrawing his foot, turned and reciprocally advanced. As he did so, the Spaniard's nervous eagerness increased, but his vital energy failed, so that, the better to support him, the servant, placing his master's hand on his naked shoulder, and gently holding it there, formed himself into a sort of crutch.

When the two captains met, the Spaniard again fervently took the hand of the American, at the same time casting an earnest glance into his eyes, but, as before, too much overcome to speak.

I have done him wrong, self-reproachfully thought Captain Delano; his apparent coldness has deceived me; in no instance has he meant to offend.

Meantime, as if fearful that the continuance of the scene might too much unstring his master, the servant seemed anxious to terminate it. And so, still presenting himself as a crutch, and walking between the two captains, he advanced with them towards the gangway; while still, as if full of kindly contrition, Don Benito would not let go the hand of Captain Delano but retained it in his, across the black's body.

Soon they were standing by the side, looking over into the boat, whose crew turned up their curious eyes. Waiting a moment for the Spaniard to relinquish his hold, the now embarrassed Captain Delano lifted his foot to overstep the threshold of the open gangway, but still Don Benito would not let go his hand. And yet, with an agitated tone, he said, "I can go no further; here I must bid you adieu. Adieu, my dear, dear Don Amasa. Go — go!" suddenly tearing his hand loose, "go, and God guard you better than me, my best friend."

Not unaffected, Captain Delano would now have lingered, but, catching the meekly admonitory eye of the servant, with a hasty farewell he descended into his boat, followed by the continual adieus of Don Benito, standing rooted in the gangway.

Seating himself in the stern, Captain Delano, making a last salute, ordered the boat shoved off. The crew had their oars on end. The bowsmen pushed the boat a sufficient distance for the oars to be lengthwise dropped. The instant that was done, Don Benito sprang over the bulwarks, falling at the feet of Captain Delano; at the same time calling towards his ship, but in tones so frenzied that none in the boat could understand him. But, as if not equally obtuse, three sailors, from three different and distant parts of the ship, splashed into the sea, swimming after their captain, as if intent upon his rescue.

The dismayed officer of the boat eagerly asked what this meant. To which Captain Delano, turning a disdainful smile upon the unaccountable Spaniard, answered that, for his part, he neither knew nor cared; but it seemed as if Don Benito had taken it into his head to produce the impression among his people that the boat wanted to kidnap him. "Or else — give way for your lives," he wildly added, starting at a clattering hubbub in the ship, above which rang the tocsin of the hatchet-polishers, and seizing Don Benito by the throat he added, "this plotting pirate means murder!" Here, in apparent verification of the words, the servant, a dagger in his hand, was seen on the rail overhead, poised, in the act of leaping, as if with desperate fidelity to befriend his master to the last; while, seemingly to aid the black, the three white sailors were trying to clamber into the hampered bow. Meantime, the whole host of Negroes, as if inflamed at the sight of their jeopardized captain, impended in one sooty avalanche over the bulwarks.

All this, with what preceded and what followed, occurred with such involutions of rapidity that past, present, and future seemed one.

Seeing the Negro coming, Captain Delano had flung the Spaniard aside, almost in the very act of clutching him, and, by the unconscious recoil shifting his place, with arms thrown up so promptly grappled the servant in his descent, that with dagger presented at Captain Delano's heart, the black seemed of purpose to have leaped there as to his mark. But the weapon was wrenched away, and the assailant dashed down into the bottom of the boat, which now, with disentangled oars, began to speed through the sea.

At this juncture, the left hand of Captain Delano, on one side, again clutched the half-reclined Don Benito, heedless that he was in a speechless faint, while his right foot, on the other side, ground the prostrate Negro, and his right arm pressed for added speed on the after oar, his eye bent forward, encouraging his men to their utmost.

But here the officer of the boat, who had at last succeeded in beating off the towing sailors, and was now, with face turned aft, assisting the bowsman at his oar, suddenly called to Captain Delano to see what the black was about, while a

Portuguese oarsman shouted to him to give heed to what the Spaniard was saying.

Glancing down at his feet, Captain Delano saw the free hand of the servant aiming with a second dagger — a small one, before concealed in his wool — with this he was snakishly writhing up from the boat's bottom at the heart of his master, his countenance lividly vindictive, expressing the centered purpose of his soul; while the Spaniard, half-choked, was vainly shrinking away, with husky words, incoherent to all but the Portuguese.

That moment, across the long-benighted mind of Captain Delano, a flash of revelation swept, illuminating, in unanticipated clearness, his host's whole mysterious demeanor, with every enigmatic event of the day, as well as the entire past voyage of the *San Dominick*. He smote Babo's hand down, but his own heart smote him harder. With infinite pity he withdrew his hold from Don Benito. Not Captain Delano, but Don Benito, the black, in leaping into the boat, had intended to stab.

Both the black's hands were held, as, glancing up towards the *San Dominick*, Captain Delano, now with scales dropped from his eyes, saw the Negroes, not in misrule, not in tumult, not as if frantically concerned for Don Benito, but, with mask torn away, flourishing hatchets and knives in ferocious piratical revolt. Like delirious black dervishes, the six Ashantees danced on the poop. Prevented by their foes from springing into the water, the Spanish boys were hurrying up to the topmost spars, while such of the few Spanish sailors not already in the sea, less alert, were descried, helplessly mixed in, on deck with the blacks.

Meantime Captain Delano hailed his own vessel, ordering the ports up, and the guns run out. But by this time the cable of the *San Dominick* had been cut, and the fag end, in lashing out, whipped away the canvas shroud about the beak, suddenly revealing, as the bleached hull swung round towards the open ocean, death for the figurehead, in a human skeleton, chalky comment on the chalked words below, FOLLOW YOUR LEADER.

At the sight, Don Benito, covering his face, wailed out: " 'Tis he, Aranda! my murdered, unburied friend!"

Upon reaching the sealer, calling for ropes, Captain Delano bound the Negro, who made no resistance, and had him hoisted to the deck. He would then have assisted the now almost helpless Don Benito up the side; but Don Benito, wan as he was, refused to move, or be moved, until the Negro should have been first put below out of view. When, presently assured that it was done, he no more shrank from the ascent.

The boat was immediately dispatched back to pick up the three swimming sailors. Meantime, the guns were in readiness, though, owing to the *San Dominick* having glided somewhat astern of the sealer, only the aftermost one could be brought to bear. With this, they fired six times, thinking to cripple the fugitive ship by bringing down her spars, but only a few inconsiderable ropes were shot away. Soon the ship was beyond the gun's range, steering broad out of the bay, the blacks thickly clustering round the bowsprit, one moment with taunting cries towards the whites, the next with upthrown gestures hailing the now dusky moors of ocean — cawing crows escaped from the hand of the fowler.

The first impulse was to slip the cables and give chase. But, upon second thoughts, to pursue with whaleboat and yawl seemed more promising.

Upon inquiring of Don Benito what firearms they had on board the *San Dominick,* Captain Delano was answered that they had none that could be used, because, in the earlier stages of the mutiny, a cabin passenger, since dead, had secretly put out of order the locks of what few muskets there were. But with all his remaining strength Don Benito entreated the Americans not to give chase, either with ship or boat, for the Negroes had already proved themselves such desperadoes that, in case of a present assault, nothing but a total massacre of the whites could be looked for. But, regarding this warning as coming from one whose spirit had been crushed by misery, the American did not give up his design.

The boats were got ready and armed. Captain Delano ordered his men into them. He was going himself when Don Benito grasped his arm.

"What! have you saved my life, *señor,* and are you now going to throw away your own?"

The officers also, for reasons connected with their interests and those of the voyage, and a duty owing to the owners, strongly objected against their commander's going. Weighing their remonstrances a moment, Captain Delano felt bound to remain; appointing his chief mate — an athletic and resolute man, who had been a privateer's-man — to head the party. The more to encourage the sailors, they were told that the Spanish captain considered his ship good as lost; that she and her cargo, including some gold and silver, were worth more than a thousand doubloons. Take her, and no small part should be theirs. The sailors replied with a shout.

The fugitives had now almost gained an offing. It was nearly night, but the moon was rising. After hard, prolonged pulling, the boats came up on the ship's quarters, at a suitable distance laying upon their oars to discharge their muskets. Having no bullets to return, the Negroes sent their yells. But upon the second volley, Indianlike, they hurtled their hatchets. One took off a sailor's fingers. Another struck the whaleboat's bow, cutting off the rope there, and remaining stuck in the gunwale like a woodman's ax. Snatching it, quivering, from its lodgment, the mate hurled it back. The returned gauntlet now stuck in the ship's broken quarter-gallery, and so remained.

The Negroes giving too hot a reception, the whites kept a more respectful distance. Hovering now just out of reach of the hurtling hatchets, they, with a view to the close encounter which must soon come, sought to decoy the blacks into entirely disarming themselves of their most murderous weapons in a hand-to-hand fight, by foolishly flinging them, as missiles, short of the mark, into the sea. But, erelong perceiving the stratagem, the Negroes desisted, though not before many of them had to replace their lost hatchets with handspikes, an exchange which, as counted upon, proved, in the end, favorable to the assailants.

Meantime, with a strong wind the ship still clove the water, the boats alternately falling behind and pulling up to discharge fresh volleys.

The fire was mostly directed towards the stern, since there, chiefly, the Negroes at present were clustering. But to kill or maim the Negroes was not the object. To take them, with the ship, was the object. To do it, the ship must be boarded, which could not be done by boats while she was sailing so fast.

A thought now struck the mate. Observing the Spanish boys still aloft, high as they could get, he called to them to descend to the yards, and cut adrift the sails. It was done. About this time, owing to causes hereafter to be shown, two Spaniards, in the dress of sailors and conspicuously showing themselves, were killed, not by volleys, but by deliberate marksman's shots; while, as it afterwards appeared, by one of the general discharges Atufal, the black, and the Spaniard at the helm likewise were killed. What, now, with the loss of the sails and loss of leaders, the ship became unmanageable to the Negroes.

With creaking masts, she came heavily round to the wind, the prow slowly swinging into view of the boats, its skeleton gleaming in the horizontal moonlight and casting a gigantic ribbed shadow upon the water. One extended arm of the ghost seemed beckoning the whites to avenge it.

"Follow your leader!" cried the mate; and, one on each bow, the boats boarded. Sealing-spears and cutlasses crossed hatchets and handspikes. Huddled upon the longboat amidships, the Negresses raised a wailing chant, whose chorus was the clash of the steel.

For a time, the attack wavered, the Negroes wedging themselves to beat it back, the half-repelled sailors, as yet unable to gain a footing, fighting as troopers in the saddle, one leg sideways flung over the bulwark and one without, plying their cutlasses like carters' whips. But in vain. They were almost overborne, when, rallying themselves into a squad as one man, with a huzzah they sprang inboard, where, entangled, they involuntarily separated again. For a few breaths' space there was a vague, muffled, inner sound, as of submerged swordfish rushing hither and thither through shoals of blackfish. Soon, in a reunited band, and joined by the Spanish seamen, the whites came to the surface, irresistibly driving the Negroes toward the stern. But a barricade of casks and sacks, from side to side, had been thrown up by the mainmast. Here the Negroes faced about, and though scorning peace or truce, yet fain would have had respite. But, without pause overleaping the barrier, the unflagging sailors again closed. Exhausted, the blacks now fought in despair. Their red tongues lolled, wolflike, from their black mouths. But the pale sailors' teeth were set; not a word was spoken, and, in five minutes more, the ship was won.

Nearly a score of the Negroes were killed. Exclusive of those by the balls, many were mangled; their wounds — mostly inflicted by the long-edged sealing-spears, resembling those shaven ones of the English at Preston Pans, made by the poled scythes of the Highlanders. On the other side, none were killed, though several were wounded, some severely, including the mate. The surviving Negroes were temporarily secured, and the ship, towed back into the harbor at midnight, once more lay anchored.

Omitting the incidents and arrangements ensuing, suffice it that, after two days spent in refitting, the ships sailed in company for Conception, in Chile, and thence for Lima, in Peru; where, before the viceregal courts, the whole affair, from the beginning, underwent investigation.

Though, midway on the passage, the ill-fated Spaniard, relaxed from constraint, showed some signs of regaining health with free-will, yet, agreeably to his own foreboding, shortly before arriving at Lima, he relapsed, finally becoming so reduced as to be carried ashore in arms. Hearing of his story and plight, one of the many religious institutions of the City of Kings opened an hospitable refuge to him, where both physician and priest were his nurses, and a member of the order volunteered to be his one special guardian and consoler, by night and by day.

The following extracts, translated from one of the official Spanish documents, will, it is hoped, shed light on the preceding narrative, as well as, in the first place, reveal the true port of departure and true history of the *San Dominick*'s voyage, down to the time of her touching at the island of St. Maria.

But ere the extracts come it may be well to preface them with a remark.

The document selected, from among many others, for partial translation, contains the deposition of Benito Cereno, the first taken in the case. Some disclosures therein were at the time held dubious, for both learned and natural reasons. The tribunal inclined to the opinion that the deponent, not undisturbed in his mind by recent events, raved of some things which could never have happened. But subsequent depositions of the surviving sailors, bearing out the revelations of their captain in several of the strangest particulars, gave credence to the rest. So that the tribunal, in its final decision, rested its capital sentences upon statements which, had they lacked confirmation, it would have deemed it but duty to reject.

I, DON JOSÉ DE ABOS AND PADILLA, His Majesty's Notary for the Royal Revenue, and Register of this Province, and Notary Public of the Holy Crusade of this Bishopric, etc.

Do certify and declare, as much as is requisite in law, that, in the criminal cause commenced the twenty-fourth of the month of September, in the year seventeen hundred and ninety-nine, against the Negroes of the ship *San Dominick*, the following declaration before me was made:

Declaration of the first witness, DON BENITO CERENO.

The same day, and month, and year, His Honor, Doctor Juan Martínez de Rozas, Councilor of the Royal Audience of this Kingdom, and learned in the law of this Intendency, ordered the captain of the ship *San Dominick*, Don Benito Cereno, to appear, which he did in his litter, attended by the monk Infelez, of whom he received the oath, which he took by God, our Lord, and a sign of the Cross, under which he promised to tell the truth of whatever he should know and should be asked; and being interrogated agreeably to the tenor of the act commencing the process, he said that, on the twentieth of May last, he set sail with his ship from the port of Valparaiso, bound to that of Callao, loaded with the produce of the country beside thirty cases of hardware and one hundred and sixty blacks of both sexes, mostly belonging to Don Alexandro Aranda, gentleman, of the city of Mendoza; that the crew of the ship consisted of thirty-six men beside the persons who went as passengers; that the Negroes were in part as follows:

[*Here, in the original, follows a list of some fifty names, descriptions, and ages, compiled from certain recovered documents of Aranda's, and also from recollections of the deponent, from which portions only are extracted.*][11]

— One, from about eighteen to nineteen years, named José, and this was the man that waited upon his master, Don Alexandro, and who speaks well the Spanish, having served him four or five years; * * * a mulatto, named Francesco, the cabin steward, of a good person and voice, having sung in the Valparaiso churches, native of the province of Buenos Ayres, aged about thirty-five years. * * * A smart Negro, named Dago, who had been for many years a gravedigger among the

11 [The bracketed and italicized passages are Melville's, as are the asterisks later. — Editors' note.]

Spaniards, aged forty-six years. * * * Four old Negroes, born in Africa, from sixty to seventy, but sound, calkers by trade, whose names are as follows: the first was named Muri, and he was killed (as was also his son named Diamelo); the second, Nacta; the third, Yola, likewise killed; the fourth, Ghofan; and six full-grown Negroes, aged from thirty to forty-five, all raw, and born among the Ashantees — Matiluqui, Yan, Lecbe, Mapenda, Yambaio, Akim; four of whom were killed; * * * a powerful Negro named Atufal, who being supposed to have been a chief in Africa, his owner set great store by him. * * * And a small Negro of Senegal, but some years among the Spaniards, aged about thirty, which Negro's name was Babo; * * * that he does not remember the names of the others, but that still expecting the residue of Don Alexandro's papers will be found, will then take due account of them all, and remit to the court; * * * and thirty-nine women and children of all ages.

[*The catalogue over, the deposition goes on*]

* * * That all the Negroes slept upon deck, as is customary in this navigation, and none wore fetters, because the owner, his friend Aranda, told him that they were all tractable; * * * that on the seventh day after leaving port, at three o'clock in the morning, all the Spaniards being asleep except the two officers on the watch, who were the boatswain, Juan Robles, and the carpenter, Juan Bautista Gayete, and the helmsman and his boy, the Negroes revolted suddenly, wounded dangerously the boatswain and the carpenter, and successively killed eighteen men of those who were sleeping upon deck, some with handspikes and hatchets, and others by throwing them alive overboard, after tying them; that of the Spaniards upon deck they left about seven, as he thinks, alive and tied, to maneuver the ship, and three or four more, who hid themselves, remained also alive. Although in the act of revolt the Negroes made themselves masters of the hatchway, six or seven wounded went through it to the cockpit, without any hindrance on their part; that during the act of revolt the mate and another person, whose name he does not recollect, attempted to come up through the hatchway, but, being quickly wounded, were obliged to return to the cabin; that the deponent resolved at break of day to come up the companionway, where the Negro Babo was, being the ringleader, and Atufal, who assisted him, and having spoken to them, exhorted them to cease committing such atrocities, asking them, at the same time what they wanted and intended to do, offering, himself, to obey their commands; that notwithstanding

this, they threw, in his presence, three men, alive and tied, overboard; that they told the deponent to come up and that they would not kill him; which having done, the Negro Babo asked him whether there were in those seas any Negro countries where they might be carried, and he answered them, No; that the Negro Babo afterwards told him to carry them to Senegal, or to the neighboring islands of St. Nicholas, and he answered that this was impossible on account of the great distance, the necessity involved of rounding Cape Horn, the bad condition of the vessel, the want of provisions, sails, and water; but that the Negro Babo replied to him he must carry them in anyway, that they would do and conform themselves to everything the deponent should require as to eating and drinking; that after a long conference, being absolutely compelled to please them, for they threatened to kill all the whites if they were not, at all events, carried to Senegal, he told them that what was most wanting for the voyage was water, that they would go near the coast to take it, and thence they would proceed on their course; that the Negro Babo agreed to it, and the deponent steered towards the intermediate ports, hoping to meet some Spanish or foreign vessel that would save them; that within ten or eleven days they saw the land, and continued their course by it in the vicinity of Nasca; that the deponent observed that the Negroes were now restless and mutinous because he did not effect the taking in of water, the Negro Babo having required, with threats, that it should be done, without fail, the following day; he told him he saw plainly that the coast was steep, and the rivers designated in the maps were not to be found, with other reasons suitable to the circumstances, that the best way would be to go to the island of Santa Maria, where they might water easily, it being a solitary island, as the foreigners did; that the deponent did not go to Pisco, that was near, nor make any other port of the coast, because the Negro Babo had intimated to him several times that he would kill all the whites the very moment he should perceive any city, town, or settlement of any kind on the shores to which they should be carried; that having determined to go to the island of Santa Maria, as the deponent had planned, for the purpose of trying whether, on the passage or near the island itself, they could find any vessel that should favor them, or whether he could escape from it in a boat to the neighboring coast of Arruco, to adopt the necessary means he immediately changed his course, steering for the island; that the Negroes Babo and Atufal held daily conferences, in which they discussed what was necessary for their design of returning to Senegal, whether they were to kill all the Spaniards, and particularly the deponent; that eight days after parting from the coast of Nasca, the deponent being on the watch a little after daybreak, and soon after the Negroes had their meeting, the Negro Babo came to the place where the deponent was and told him that he had determined to kill his master, Don Alexandro Aranda, both because he and his companions could not otherwise be sure of their liberty, and that, to keep the seamen in subjection, he wanted to prepare a warning of what road they should be made to take did they or any of them oppose him, and that, by means of the death of Don Alexandro, that warning would best be given, but that what this last meant the deponent did not at the time comprehend, nor could not, further than that the death of Don Alexandro was intended; and moreover the Negro Babo proposed to the deponent to call the mate Raneds, who was sleeping in the cabin, before the thing was done, for fear, as the deponent understood it, that the mate, who was a good navigator, should be killed with Don Alexandro and the rest; that the deponent, who was the friend from youth of Don Alexandro, prayed and conjured, but all was useless, for the Negro Babo answered him that the thing could not be prevented, and that all the Spaniards risked their death if they should attempt to frustrate his will in this matter or any other; that, in this conflict, the deponent called the mate, Raneds, who was forced to go apart, and immediately the Negro Babo commanded the Ashantee Martinqui and the Ashantee Lecbe to go and commit the murder; that those two went down with hatchets to the berth of Don Alexandro, that, yet half alive and mangled, they dragged him on deck; that they were going to throw him overboard in that state, but the Negro Babo stopped them, bidding the murder be completed on the deck before him, which was done, when, by his orders, the body was carried below, forward; that nothing more was seen of it by the deponent for three days; * * * that Don Alonzo Sidonia, an old man, long resident at Valparaiso, and lately appointed to a civil office in Peru, whither he had taken passage, was at the time sleeping in the berth opposite Don Alexandro's; that awakening at his cries, surprised by them, and at the sight of the Negroes with their bloody hatchets in their hands, he threw himself into the sea through a window which was near him, and was drowned, without it being in the power of the deponent to assist or take him up; * * * that a short time after killing Aranda, they brought upon deck his german-cousin, of middle-age, Don Francisco Masa, of Mendoza, and the young Don Joaquín, Marqués de Aramboalaza, then lately from Spain, with his Spanish servant Ponce, and the three young clerks of Aranda, José

Mozairi, Lorenzo Bargas, and Hermenegildo Gandix, all of Cádiz; that Don Joaquín and Hermenegildo Gandix, the Negro Babo, for purposes hereafter to appear, preserved alive, but Don Francisco Masa, José Mozairi, and Lorenzo Bargas, with Ponce the servant, beside the boatswain, Juan Robles, the boatswain's mates, Manuel Viscaya and Roderigo Hurta, and four of the sailors the Negro Babo ordered to be thrown alive into the sea, although they made no resistance nor begged for anything else but mercy; that the boatswain, Juan Robles, who knew how to swim, kept the longest above water, making acts of contrition, and, in the last words he uttered, charged this deponent to cause mass to be said for his soul to our Lady of Succor; * * * that, during the three days which followed, the deponent, uncertain what fate had befallen the remains of Don Alexandro, frequently asked the Negro Babo where they were, and, if still on board, whether they were to be preserved for interment ashore, entreating him so to order it; that the Negro Babo answered nothing till the fourth day, when, at sunrise, the deponent coming on deck, the Negro Babo showed him a skeleton, which had been substituted for the ship's proper figurehead — the image of Christopher Colón, the discoverer of the New World; that the Negro Babo asked him whose skeleton that was, and whether, from its whiteness, he should not think it a white's, that, upon discovering his face, the Negro Babo, coming close, said words to this effect: "Keep faith with the blacks from here to Senegal, or you shall in spirit, as now in body, follow your leader," pointing to the prow; * * * that the same morning the Negro Babo took by succession each Spaniard forward, and asked him whose skeleton that was, and whether, from its whiteness, he should not think it a white's; that each Spaniard covered his face; that then to each the Negro Babo repeated the words in the first place said to the deponent; * * * that they (the Spaniards), being then assembled aft, the Negro Babo harangued them, saying that he had now done all; that the deponent (as navigator for the Negroes) might pursue his course, warning him and all of them that they should, soul and body, go the way of Don Alexandro if he saw them (the Spaniards) speak or plot anything against them (the Negroes) — a threat which was repeated every day; that, before the events last mentioned, they had tied the cook to throw him overboard, for it is not known what thing they heard him speak, but finally the Negro Babo spared his life, at the request of the deponent; that a few days after, the deponent, endeavoring not to omit any means to preserve the lives of the remaining whites, spoke to the Negroes of peace and tranquillity, and agreed to draw up a paper, signed by the deponent and the sailors who could write, as also by the Negro Babo, for himself and all the blacks, in which the deponent obliged himself to carry them to Senegal, and they not to kill any more, and he formally to make over to them the ship, with the cargo, with which they were for that time satisfied and quieted. * * * But the next day, the more surely to guard against the sailors' escape, the Negro Babo commanded all the boats to be destroyed but the longboat, which was unseaworthy, and another, a cutter in good condition, which, knowing it would yet be wanted for towing the water casks, he had it lowered down into the hold.

* * * * * * *

[*Various particulars of the prolonged and perplexed navigation ensuing here follow, with incidents of a calamitous calm, from which portion one passage is extracted, to wit:*]

— That on the fifth day of the calm, all on board suffering much from the heat and want of water, and five having died in fits, and mad, the Negroes became irritable, and for a chance gesture, which they deemed suspicious — though it was harmless — made by the mate, Raneds, to the deponent in the act of handing a quadrant, they killed him; but that for this they afterwards were sorry, the mate being the only remaining navigator on board, except the deponent.

* * * * * * *

— That omitting other events which daily happened, and which can only serve uselessly to recall past misfortunes and conflicts, after seventy-three days' navigation, reckoned from the time they sailed from Nasca, during which they navigated under a scanty allowance of water, and were afflicted with the calms before mentioned, they at last arrived at the island of Santa Maria, on the seventeenth of the month of August, at about six o'clock in the afternoon, at which hour they cast anchor very near the American ship *Bachelor's Delight*, which lay in the same bay, commanded by the generous Captain Amasa Delano; but at six o'clock in the morning they had already descried the port, and the Negroes became uneasy, as soon as at distance they saw the ship, not having expected to see one there; that the Negro Babo pacified them, assuring them that no fear need be had; that straightway he ordered the figure on the bow to be covered with canvas, as for repairs, and had the decks a little set in order; that for a time the Negro Babo and the Negro Atufal conferred; that the Negro Atufal was for sailing away but the Negro Babo would not, and, by himself, cast about what to do; that at last he came to the deponent, proposing to him to say and do all that the deponent declares to have said and done to the American captain; * * * * * * * that the Negro Babo warned him that if he varied in the least, or uttered any word, or gave any look that should give the least intimation of the past events or present state, he would instantly kill him, with all his companions, showing a dagger which he carried hid, saying something which, as he understood it, meant that that dagger would be alert as his eye; that the Negro Babo then announced the plan to all his companions, which pleased them; that he then, the better to disguise the truth, devised many expedients, in some of them uniting deceit and defense; that of this sort was the device of the Six Ashantees before named, who were his bravoes; that them he stationed on the break of the poop, as if to clean certain hatchets (in cases, which were part of the cargo), but in reality to use them, and distribute them at need, and at a given word he told them; that, among other devices, was the device of presenting Atufal, his right-hand man, as chained, though in a moment the chains could be dropped; that in every particular he informed the deponent what part he was expected to enact in every device, and what story he was to tell on every occasion, always threatening him with instant death if he varied in the least: that, conscious that many of the Negroes would be turbulent, the Negro Babo appointed the four aged Negroes, who were calkers, to keep what domestic order they could on the decks; that again and again he harangued the Spaniards and his companions, informing them of his intent and of his devices, and of the invented story that this deponent was to tell, charging them lest any of them varied from that story; that these arrangements were made and matured during the interval of two or three hours between their first sighting the ship and the arrival on board of Captain Amasa Delano; that this happened about half-past seven o'clock in the morning, Captain Amasa Delano coming in his boat, and all gladly receiving him; that the deponent, as well as he could force himself, acting then the part of principal owner and a free captain of the ship, told Captain Amasa Delano, when called upon, that he came from Buenos Ayres, bound to Lima, with three hundred Negroes; that off Cape Horn, and in a subsequent fever, many Negroes had died; that also, by similar casualties, all the sea officers and the greatest part of the crew had died.

* * * * * * *

[*And so the deposition goes on, circumstantially recounting the fictitious story dictated to the deponent by Babo, and through the deponent imposed upon Captain Delano, and also recounting the friendly offers of Captain Delano, with other things, but all of which is here omitted. After the fictitious story, etc., the deposition proceeds:*]

* * * * * * *

— that the generous Captain Amasa Delano remained on board all the day, till he left the ship anchored at six o'clock in the evening, deponent speaking to him always of his pretended misfortunes, under the forementioned principles, without having had it in his power to tell a single word or give him the least hint, that he might know the truth and state of things, because the Negro Babo, performing the office of an officious servant with all the appearance of submission of the humble slave, did not leave the deponent one moment; that this was in order to observe the deponent's actions and words, for the Negro Babo understands well the Spanish, and besides, there were thereabout some others who were constantly on the watch, and likewise understood the Spanish; * * * that upon one occasion, while deponent was standing on the deck conversing with Amasa Delano, by a secret sign the Negro Babo drew him (the deponent) aside, the act appearing as if originating with the deponent; that then, he being drawn aside, the Negro Babo proposed to him to gain from Amasa Delano full particulars about his ship, and crew, and arms; that the deponent asked "For what?" that, the Negro Babo answered he might conceive; that, grieved at the prospect of what might overtake the generous Captain Amasa Delano, the deponent at first refused to ask the desired questions, and used every argument to induce the Negro Babo to give up this new design; that the Negro Babo showed the point of his dagger; that after the information had been obtained the Negro Babo again drew him aside, telling him that that very night he (the deponent) would be captain of two ships, instead of one, for that, great part of the American's ship's crew being to be absent fishing, the six Ashantees, without anyone else, would easily take it; that at this time he said other things to the same purpose; that no entreaties availed; that, before Amasa Delano's coming on board, no hint had been given touching the capture of the American ship; that to prevent this project the deponent was powerless; * * * — that in some things his memory is confused, he cannot distinctly recall every event; * * * — that as soon as they had cast anchor at six of the clock in the evening, as has before been stated, the American captain took leave, to return to his vessel; that upon a sudden impulse, which the deponent believes to have come from God and his angels, he, after the farewell had been said, followed the generous Captain Amasa Delano as far as the gunwale, where he stayed, under pretense of taking leave, until Amasa Delano should have been seated in his boat; that, on shoving off, the deponent sprang from the gunwale into the boat, and fell into it, he knows not how, God guarding him; that —

* * * * * * *

[Here, in the original, follows the account of what further happened at the escape, and how the San Dominick *was retaken, and of the passage to the coast; including in the recital many expressions of "eternal gratitude" to the "generous Captain Amasa Delano." The deposition then proceeds with recapitulatory remarks, and a partial renumeration of the Negroes, making record of their individual part in the past events, with a view to furnishing, according to command of the court, the data whereon to found the criminal sentences to be pronounced. From this portion is the following;]*

— That he believes that all the Negroes, though not in the first place knowing to the design of revolt, when it was accomplished, approved it. * * * That the Negro José, eighteen years old, and in the personal service of Don Alexandro, was the one who communicated the information to the Negro Babo about the state of things in the cabin, before the revolt; that this is known, because, in the preceding midnight, he used to come from his berth, which was under his master's, in the cabin, to the deck where the ringleader and his associates were, and had secret conversations with the Negro Babo, in which he was several times seen by the mate; that, one night, the mate drove him away twice; * * * that this same Negro José was the one who, without being commanded to do so by the Negro Babo, as Lecbe and Martinqui were, stabbed his master, Don Alexandro, after he had been dragged half-lifeless to the deck; * * * that the mulatto steward, Francesco, was of the first band of revolters, that he was, in all things, the creature and tool of the Negro Babo; that, to make his court, he, just before a repast in the cabin, proposed to the Negro Babo poisoning a dish for the generous Captain Amasa Delano; this is known and believed, because the Negroes have said it; but that the Negro Babo, having another design, forbade Francesco; * * * that the Ashantee Lecbe was one of the worst of them, for that, on the day the ship was retaken, he assisted in the defense of her with a hatchet in each hand, with one of which he wounded in the breast the chief mate of Amasa Delano, in the first act of boarding; this all knew; that, in sight of the deponent, Lecbe struck with a hatchet, Don Francisco Masa, when, by the Negro Babo's orders, he was carrying him to throw him overboard alive, beside participating in the murder, before mentioned, of Don Alexandro Aranda and others of the cabin passengers; that, owing to the fury with which the Ashantees fought in the engagement with the boats, but this Lecbe and Yan survived; that Yan was bad as Lecbe; that Yan was the man who, by Babo's command, willingly prepared the skeleton of Don Alexandro, in a way the Negroes afterwards told the deponent, but which he, so long as reason is left him, can never divulge; that Yan and Lecbe were the two who, in a calm by night, riveted the skeleton to the bow; this also the Negroes told him; that the Negro Babo was he who traced the inscription below it; that the Negro Babo was the plotter from first to last; he ordered every murder, and was the helm and keel of the revolt; that Atufal was his lieutenant in all, but Atufal with his own hand committed no murder, nor did the Negro Babo; * * * that Atufal was shot, being killed in the fight with the boats, ere boarding; * * * that the Negresses, of age, were knowing to the revolt, and testified themselves satisfied at the death of their master, Don Alexandro; that, had the Negroes not restrained them, they would have tortured to death, instead of simply killing, the Spaniards slain by command of the Negro Babo; that the Negresses used their utmost influence to have the deponent made away with; that, in the various acts of murder, they sang songs and danced — not gaily, but solemnly, and before the engagement with the boats, as well as during the action, they sang melancholy songs to the Negroes, and that this melancholy tone was more inflaming than a different one would have been, and was so intended; that all this is believed, because the Negroes have said it. * * * — that of the thirty-six men of the crew, exclusive of the passengers (all of whom are now dead), which the deponent had knowledge of, six only remained alive, with four cabin boys and ship boys, not included with the crew; * * * — that the Negroes broke an arm of one of the cabin boys and gave him strokes with hatchets.

[Then follow various random disclosures referring to various periods of time. The following are extracted;]

— That during the presence of Captain Amasa Delano on board, some attempts were made by the sailors, and one by Hermenegildo Gandix, to convey hints to him of the true state of affairs, but that these attempts were ineffectual, owing to fear of incurring death, and, furthermore, owing to the devices which offered contradictions to the true state of affairs, as well as owing to the generosity and piety of Amasa Delano incapable of sounding such wickedness; * * * that Luys Galgo, a sailor about sixty years of age, and formerly of the king's navy, was one of those who sought to convey tokens to Captain Amasa Delano; but his intent, though undiscovered, being suspected, he was, on a pretense, made to retire out of sight, and at last into the hold, and there was made away with. This the Negroes have since said; * * * that one of the ship boys feeling, from Captain Amasa Delano's presence, some hopes of release, and not having enough prudence, dropped some chance word respecting his expectations, which being overheard and understood by a slave boy with whom he was eating at the time, the latter struck him on the head with a knife, inflicting a bad wound, but of which the boy is now healing; that likewise, not long before the ship was brought to anchor, one of the seamen steering at the time endangered himself by letting the blacks remark some expression in his countenance, arising from a cause similar to the above, but this sailor, by his heedful after conduct, escaped; * * * that these statements are made to show the court that from the beginning to the end of the revolt it was impossible for the deponent and his men to act otherwise than they did; * * * — that the third clerk, Hermenegildo Gandix, who before had been forced to live among the seamen, wearing a seaman's habit, and in all respects appearing to be one for the time, he, Gandix, was killed by a musket ball fired through mistake from the boats before boarding; having in his fright run up the mizzen rigging, calling to the boats — "don't board," lest upon their boarding the Negroes should kill him; that this inducing the Americans to believe he some way favored the cause of the Negroes, they fired two balls at him, so that he fell wounded from the rigging, and was drowned in the sea; * * * — that the young Don Joaquín Marqués de Aramboalaza, like Hermenegildo Gandix, the third clerk, was degraded to the office and appearance of a common seaman; that upon one occasion when Don Joaquín shrank, the Negro Babo commanded the Ashantee Lecbe to take tar and heat it, and pour it upon Don Joaquín's hands; * * * — that Don Joaquín was killed owing to another mistake of the Americans, but one impossible to be avoided, as, upon the approach of the boats, Don Joaquín, with a hatchet tied edge out and upright to his hand, was made by the Negroes to appear on the bulwarks; whereupon, seen with arms in his hands and in a questionable attitude, he was shot for a renegade seaman; * * * — that on the person of Don Joaquín was found secreted a jewel, which, by papers that were discovered, proved to have been meant for the shrine of our Lady of Mercy in Lima, a votive offering, beforehand prepared and guarded, to attest his gratitude when he should have landed in Peru, his last destination, for the safe conclusion of his entire voyage from Spain, * * * — that the jewel, with the other effects of the late Don Joaquín, is in the custody of the brethren of the Hospital de Sacerdotes, awaiting the disposition of the honorable court; * * * — that, owing to the condition of the deponent, as well as the haste in which the boats departed for the attack, the Americans were not forewarned that there were, among the apparent crew, a passenger and one of the clerks disguised by the Negro Babo; * * * — that, beside the Negroes killed in the action, some were killed after the capture and reanchoring at night, when shackled to the ringbolts on deck; that these deaths were committed by the sailors, ere they could be prevented. That so soon as informed of it, Captain Amasa Delano used all his authority, and in particular with his own hand struck down Martínez Gola, who having found a razor in the pocket of an old jacket of his which one of the shackled Negroes had on, was aiming it at the Negro's throat; that the noble Captain Amasa Delano also wrenched from the hand of Bartholomew Barlo a dagger, secreted at the time of the massacre of the whites, with which he was in the act of stabbing a shackled Negro, who, the same day, with another Negro, had thrown him down and jumped upon him; * * * — that, for all the events, befalling through so long a time, during which the ship was in the hands of the Negro Babo, he cannot here give account, but that what he has said is the most substantial of what occurs to him at present, and is the truth under the oath which he has taken; which declaration he affirmed and ratified, after hearing it read to him.

He said that he is twenty-nine years of age, and broken in body and mind; that when finally dismissed by the court, he shall not return home to Chile but betake himself to the monastery on Mount Agonia without; and signed with his honor, and crossed himself, and, for the time, departed as he came, in his litter, with the monk Infelez, to the Hospital de Sacerdotes.

BENITO CERENO.

DOCTOR ROZAS.

If the deposition have served as the key to fit into the lock of the complications which precede it, then, as a vault whose door has been flung back, the *San Dominick*'s hull lies open today.

Hitherto the nature of this narrative, besides rendering the intricacies in the beginning unavoidable, has more or less required that many things, instead of being set down in the order of occurrence, should be retrospectively or irregularly given; this last is the case with the following passages, which will conclude the account:

During the long, mild voyage to Lima, there was, as before hinted, a period during which the sufferer a little recovered his health, or, at least in some degree, his tranquillity. Ere the decided relapse which came, the two captains had many cordial conversations — their fraternal unreserve in singular contrast with former withdrawments.

Again and again it was repeated how hard it had been to enact the part forced on the Spaniard by Babo.

"Ah, my dear friend," Don Benito once said, "at those very times when you thought me so morose and ungrateful, nay, when, as you now admit, you half thought me plotting your murder, at those very times my heart was frozen; I could not look at you, thinking of what, both on board this ship and your own, hung, from other hands, over my kind benefactor. And as God lives, Don Amasa, I know not whether desire for my own safety alone could have nerved me to that leap into your boat, had it not been for the thought that, did you, unenlightened, return to your ship, you, my best friend, with all who might be with you, stolen upon that night in your hammocks, would never in this world have wakened again. Do but think how you walked this deck, how you sat in this cabin, every inch of ground mined into honeycombs under you. Had I dropped the least hint, made the least advance towards an understanding between us, death, explosive death — yours as mine — would have ended the scene."

"True, true," cried Captain Delano, starting, "you have saved my life, Don Benito, more than I yours; saved it, too, against my knowledge and will."

"Nay, my friend," rejoined the Spaniard, courteous even to the point of religion, "God charmed your life, but you saved mine. To think of some things you did — those smilings and chattings, rash pointings and gesturings. For less than these, they slew my mate, Raneds; but you had the Prince of Heaven's safe conduct through all ambuscades."

"Yes, all is owing to Providence, I know: but the temper of my mind that morning was more than commonly pleasant, while the sight of so much suffering, more apparent than real, added to my good-nature, compassion, and charity, happily interweaving the three. Had it been otherwise, doubtless, as you hint, some of my interferences might have ended, unhappily enough. Besides, those feelings I spoke of enabled me to get the better of momentary distrust, at times when acuteness might have cost me my life, without saving another's. Only at the end did my suspicions get the better of me, and you know how wide of the mark they then proved."

"Wide, indeed," said Don Benito, sadly; "you were with me all day; stood with me, sat with me, talked with me, looked at me, ate with me, drank with me; and yet, your last act was to clutch for a monster, not only an innocent man, but the most pitiable of all men. To such degree may malign machinations and deceptions impose. So far may even the best man err in judging the conduct of one with the recesses of whose condition he is not acquainted. But you were forced to it, and you were in time undeceived. Would that, in both respects, it was so ever, and with all men."

"You generalize, Don Benito; and mournfully enough. But the past is passed; why moralize upon it? Forget it. See, yon bright sun has forgotten it all, and the blue sea, and the blue sky; these have turned over new leaves."

"Because they have no memory," he dejectedly replied; "because they are not human."

"But these mild trades[12] that now fan your cheek, do they not come with a human-like healing to you? Warm friends, steadfast friends are the trades."

"With their steadfastness they but waft me to my tomb, *señor*," was the foreboding response.

"You are saved," cried Captain Delano, more and more astonished and pained; "you are saved: what has cast such a shadow upon you?"

"The Negro."

There was silence, while the moody man sat, slowly and unconsciously gathering his mantle about him, as if it were a pall.

There was no more conversation that day.

But if the Spaniard's melancholy sometimes ended in muteness upon topics

12 [Trade winds. — Editors' note.]

like the above, there were others upon which he never spoke at all; on which, indeed, all his old reserves were piled. Pass over the worst, and, only to elucidate, let an item or two of these be cited. The dress, so precise and costly, worn by him on the day whose events have been narrated, had not willingly been put on. And that silver-mounted sword, apparent symbol of despotic command, was not, indeed, a sword, but the ghost of one. The scabbard, artificially stiffened, was empty.

As for the black — whose brain, not body, had schemed and led the revolt, with the plot — his slight frame, inadequate to that which it held, had at once yielded to the superior muscular strength of his captor, in the boat. Seeing all was over, he uttered no sound, and could not be forced to. His aspect seemed to say: since I cannot do deeds, I will not speak words. Put in irons in the hold with the rest, he was carried to Lima. During the passage, Don Benito did not visit him. Nor then, nor at any time after, would he look at him. Before the tribunal he refused. When pressed by the judges he fainted. On the testimony of the sailors alone rested the legal identity of Babo.

Some months after, dragged to the gibbet at the tail of a mule, the black met his voiceless end. The body was burned to ashes; but for many days, the head, that hive of subtlety, fixed on a pole in the Plaza, met, unabashed, the gazes of the whites, and across the Plaza looked towards St. Bartholomew's church, in whose vaults slept then, as now, the recovered bones of Aranda, and across the Rimac bridge looked towards the monastery, on Mount Agonia without; where, three months after being dismissed by the court, Benito Cereno, borne on the bier, did, indeed, follow his leader.

AFTERWORD

Writers, not surprisingly, are often moved to write about what they have read. Melville found the gist of the story of *Benito Cereno* in the eighteenth chapter of Amasa Delano's *A Narrative of Voyages and Travels in the Northern and Southern Hemispheres* (1817). In this chapter Delano, an American sea captain, tells of his encounter in 1805 with a Spanish ship whose slaves had taken possession of the ship and had forced the Spanish captain to pretend that he was still in command so that the slaves could at night capture Delano's ship. When Delano was returning to his ship, however, the Spanish captain leaped into Delano's boat and explained the true situation. Delano's men boarded the Spanish ship, subdued the blacks, and delivered them to a court which sentenced several to death. Delano's simply told factual account, which includes legal documents of the testimony, also details his wranglings with the Spanish captain, who had promised Delano half of the value of the ship and the cargo and then sought to evade his part of the bargain.

Although Delano thus devotes a substantial amount of space to matters that Melville ignores, Delano's account is less than half as long as Melville's. Which means that Melville is taking what he wishes from Delano — a strange experience — and making it into something of his own. This was his usual practice: he told Hawthorne that he liked to have "a skeleton of actual reality to build about with fulness and veins and beauty." The question is, What was he building? First, he was building a good story. We all know that some people can tell stories — even about what happened on the way to work yesterday — better than other people. Doubtless, even if Melville simply had wanted to tell Delano's story exactly as Delano saw it, including the wrangle over salvage rights, Melville could have told it more interestingly than Delano. But in fact Melville must have wanted to tell a story of his own, for he not only suppressed parts of Delano's story, but he also made substantial changes and additions. Benito Cereno's character is, of course, changed, by omitting all reference to his later unprincipled behavior. Babo's role is greatly enlarged; in the source, he is not Cereno's constant companion (Babo's son has that role), he does not leap into the boat after Cereno and menace him with a dagger — in fact it is Cereno who later cruelly stabs a fettered black with a dagger, and Babo never comes to trial, for he is killed when the Americans, aware of the true state of things, board the Spanish ship and fetter the mutinous blacks. Melville omits Delano's reference to the judicial execution of other blacks, but dwells on the invented execution of Babo, thereby further emphasizing Babo's role. These examples, admittedly not chosen at random, suggest that Melville is concerned not with what happened (such was Delano's concern) but with telling a story that has an inner coherence and that adds up to something.

We read the story and enjoy it, and if it is really a good story and if we have read it with interest, we come back to it, to savor it again and to savor it more fully. What we find in a story, of course, partly depends on what we bring to it: in chapter 99 of *Moby-Dick* Captain Ahab sees a gold coin as an emblem of his own firmness, but one of the mates sees it only as purchasing power: "at two cents the cigar, that's nine hundred and sixty cigars."

Now, when we read any story about blacks, we probably read it differently from the way our great-grandparents did. Although whites ought not to congratulate themselves on their openmindedness, it is probably true that most are less racist than their ancestors of a century ago. For one thing, they have less misinformation on which to base their responses: no longer holding a sort of pseudo-Darwinian view that blacks represent mankind at a lower stage of evolution than whites, they are less likely to believe that blacks retain a savagery (or lustfulness or indolence or whatever) outgrown by whites in the evolutionary process. But if to this small degree they are sophisticated, in another respect they are at a disadvantage: their sensibilities are now so guilty, so insecure, that they may be too easily disturbed by any story in which a black behaves wickedly; confronted with a villainous black they quickly justify his actions by calling attention to the injustice "the system" perpetrates on him, and they tend to forget that he is a character in a particular story, living not in our world but in the world the author put him in. All this is by way of saying that it is probably very difficult for us, white or black, to enjoy and deeply experience Melville's story, which in part shows black people acting savagely. We can easily say that enslaved people can scarcely be expected to act lovingly, but the troublesome fact is that Melville nowhere in *Benito Cereno* suggests that the institution of slavery is responsible for black cruelty. (He might easily have done so; during his youth the Supreme Court had decided, in the internationally famous *Amistad* affair, in which black slaves killed a Spanish captain and sailed to New York and freedom, that blacks in quest of their freedom might legitimately kill those who enslaved them.) Melville does nothing to justify the actions of the blacks, and so the depiction of blacks in *Benito Cereno* must offend any reader who believes that a story gives a fairly close transcription of the author's views of all details of daily reality.

If the blacks in this story are — as simply as that — Melville's ideas of what black men are, we can say that Melville has not much to tell us about men. Of course, we at first see the blacks through Delano's eyes, not Melville's: they seem to be a simple bunch, cheerful, fond of bright colors, affectionate, given to giggling, endowed with "a certain easy cheerfulness, harmonious in every glance and gesture, as though God had set the whole Negro to some pleasant tune." True, Delano looks on one black, Atufal, with "admiration," perceiving "a royal spirit in him," but even this compliment is based entirely on Atufal's physical appearance, and today we can see the racist implications in such praise of bodily excellence. (Cf. "Negroes have a natural sense of rhythm.") Much of the story, however, turns on the idea that the blacks are not what they seem to Delano, a point brilliantly illustrated in the scene where Babo is shaving Cereno. "Among other things, [Delano] was amused with an odd instance of the African love of bright colors and fine shows, in the black's informally taking from the flag locker a great piece of bunting of all hues and lavishly tucking it under his master's chin for an apron." But we soon learn that the apparently affectionate and simple Babo is not demonstrating a fondness for bright colors and is not dutifully shaving his master; he is cunningly taking the opportunity to insult the Spanish flag and to torture Cereno.

Surely part of the story is about Delano's shifts of mind, his intermittent suspicions and moments of "dreamy inquietude," whereby he occasionally moves from "a singularly undistrustful good nature" to some little awareness of "malign evil in man." But he is a man of the New World, and reality is hard to fathom, and he never fully grasps Cereno's perception of evil. Near the end of the story, aware that appearances have deceived, but still unshaken by his new awareness, Delano seeks to cheer up the pensive Don Benito by saying that "the past is passed," and that "yon bright sun has forgotten it all, and the blue sea, and the blue sky." But Don Benito, perhaps with an Old World sense of guilt and of tragedy, will not be cheered: he points out that the bright sun and the blue sea and sky are undisturbed "because they have no memory" and "are not human." Delano persists, saying, "You are saved, . . . you are saved: what has cast such a shadow upon you?" The answer is two words: "The Negro," that is, Don Benito's understanding of Babo. In the simplest view, then, "the Negro" is an embodiment of the "malign evil," perception of which has a small effect on Delano but which utterly disables Benito Cereno.

Let us trust that Melville was not saying that blacks are the embodiment of evil. Let us trust that his characters can both be themselves (e.g., Babo is Babo, a particular black in a particular story) and can radiate suggestions, but that these suggestions are *not* literally about superficially similar people in the real world. A black in fiction may be a richly detailed individual and he may also suggest "malign evil" without sanctioning us to believe that the blacks we encounter in our daily life embody "malign evil." Surely it is clear that in so far as Babo comes to "stand for" anything beyond an individual in a story, it is not blacks in general, but a mysterious unappeasable evil that lurks beneath a surface of affability. (He thus resembles Shakespeare's Iago in *Othello;* especially when we compare the captured Babo's refusal to speak with Iago's "from this time forth I never will speak word." Their silence is their victory; their captors can punish their bodies but they remain mysterious and in their way they defeat their captors.) It is Benito Cereno's full perception (apparently scarcely available to the hearty American activist Delano) of this mysterious evil that unnerves him, drives him into a monastery after his rescue (Melville's addition to his source), and causes him to die before he is thirty. His ship's motto was "Follow your leader," but the ship's original leader, a figurehead of the adventurous and optimistic Christopher Columbus, had been replaced by the rebellious slaves with the skeleton of Don Alexandro Aranda, Cereno's friend who innocently had thought that the slaves could be trusted unfettered. The last paragraph of the story, summarizing the deaths of Babo and Benito, makes tolerably clear the enduring destructive power that Babo embodies and Aranda and Benito came to experience:

Some months after, dragged to the gibbet at the tail of a mule, the

> black met his voiceless end. The body was burned to ashes; but for many days, the head, that hive of subtlety, fixed on a pole in the Plaza, met, unabashed, the gazes of the whites, and across the Plaza looked towards St. Bartholomew's church, in whose vaults slept then, as now, the recovered bones of Aranda, and across the Rimac bridge looked towards the monastery, on Mount Agonia without; where, three months after being dismissed by the court, Benito Cereno, borne on the bier, did, indeed, follow his leader.

Surely no one can hear any accent of racism in this passage, but it may be well to conclude with a passage on blackness that Melville wrote a few years before *Benito Cereno*. Reviewing his friend Hawthorne's *Mosses from an Old Manse* (but we can think of Melville himself and his own *Benito Cereno*) in which he found both sunlight and blackness, he wrote: "Certain it is . . . that this great power of blackness in him derives its force from its appeals to that Calvinistic sense of Innate Depravity and Original Sin, from whose visitations, in some shape or other, no deeply thinking mind is always and wholly free."

FYODOR M. DOSTOEVSKY

Fyodor Mikhailovich Dostoevsky (1812–1881) was the son of an impoverished nobleman, a physician who was murdered by his own serfs. Dostoevsky graduated from the St. Petersburg School of Military Engineering, and briefly served in the engineering division of the War Ministry, but in 1844 he resigned in order to devote his life to writing. Between 1846 and 1849 he published some stories and a novel entitled *Poor Folk.* In 1849, accused of radical socialism, he was arrested and sentenced to death. While standing before the firing squad, he was reprieved by Czar Nicholas I and his sentence was reduced to four years of hard labor in Siberia. In Siberia he underwent a political and religious conversion from atheistic socialism, emerging as a defender of the Czar and of the Orthodox Church. After serving his sentence he spent six years as a private in an army post near Mongolia, where he married his first wife and suffered the first of many attacks of epilepsy. Allowed to return to St. Petersburg in 1858, he worked on *The House of the Dead;* this novel, based on his experiences in the Siberian prison, was published in 1862. In 1864, the year that his first wife died (he married again, two years later), *Notes from Underground* was published, followed by a succession of other novels: *Crime and Punishment* in 1866, *The Idiot* in 1868, *The Possessed* in 1871, and *The Brothers Karamazov* in 1880, less than three months before his death.

NOTES FROM UNDERGROUND

Translated by Constance Garnett

PART 1. UNDERGROUND

I

I am a sick man. . . . I am a spiteful man. I am an unattractive man. I believe my liver is diseased. However, I know nothing at all about my disease, and do not know for certain what ails me. I don't consult a doctor for it, and never have, though I have a respect for medicine and doctors. Besides, I am extremely superstitious, sufficiently so to respect medicine, anyway (I am well-educated enough not to be superstitious, but I am superstitious). No, I refuse to consult a doctor from spite. That you probably will not understand. Well, I understand it, though. Of course, I can't explain who it is precisely that I am mortifying in this case by my spite: I am perfectly well aware that I cannot "pay out" the doctors by not consulting them; I know better than any one that by all this I am only injuring myself and no one else. But still, if I don't consult a doctor it is from spite. My liver is bad, well — let it get worse!

I have been going on like that for a long time — twenty years. Now I am forty. I used to be in the government service, but am no longer. I was a spiteful official. I was rude and took pleasure in being so. I did not take bribes, you see, so I was bound to find a recompense in that, at least. (A poor jest, but I will not scratch it out. I wrote it thinking it would sound very witty; but now that I have seen myself that I only wanted to show off in a despicable way, I will not scratch it out on purpose!)

When petitioners used to come for information to the table at which I sat, I

The author of the diary and the diary itself are, of course, imaginary. Nevertheless it is clear that such persons as the writer of these notes not only may, but positively must, exist in our society, when we consider the circumstances in the midst of which our society is formed. I have tried to expose to the view of the public more distinctly than is commonly done one of the characters of the recent past. He is one of the representatives of a generation still living. In this fragment, entitled "Underground," this person introduces himself and his views, and, as it were, tries to explain the causes owing to which he has made his appearance and was bound to make his appearance in our midst. In the second fragment there are added the actual notes of this person concerning certain events in his life. [— Author's note.]

used to grind my teeth at them, and felt intense enjoyment when I succeeded in making anybody unhappy. I almost always did succeed. For the most part they were all timid people — of course, they were petitioners. But of the uppish ones there was one officer in particular I could not endure. He simply would not be humble, and clanked his sword in a disgusting way. I carried on a feud with him for eighteen months over that sword. At last I got the better of him. He left off clanking it. That happened in my youth, though.

But do you know, gentlemen, what was the chief point about my spite? Why, the whole point, the real sting of it lay in the fact that continually, even in the moment of the acutest spleen, I was inwardly conscious with shame that I was not only not a spiteful but not even an embittered man, that I was simply scaring sparrows at random and amusing myself by it. I might foam at the mouth, but bring me a doll to play with, give me a cup of tea with sugar in it, and maybe I should be appeased. I might even be genuinely touched, though probably I should grind my teeth at myself afterwards and lie awake at night with shame for months after. That was my way.

I was lying when I said just now that I was a spiteful official. I was lying from spite. I was simply amusing myself with the petitioners and with the officer, and in reality I never could become spiteful. I was conscious every moment in myself of many, very many elements absolutely opposite to that. I felt them positively swarming in me, these opposite elements. I knew that they had been swarming in me all my life and craving some outlet from me, but I would not let them, would not let them, purposely would not let them come out. They tormented me till I was ashamed: they drove me to convulsions and — sickened me, at last, how they sickened me! Now, are not you fancying, gentlemen, that I am expressing remorse for something now, that I am asking your forgiveness for something? I am sure you are fancying that. . . . However, I assure you I do not care if you are. . . .

It was not only that I could not become spiteful, I did not know how to become anything: neither spiteful nor kind, neither a rascal nor an honest man, neither a hero nor an insect. Now, I am living out my life in my corner, taunting myself with the spiteful and useless consolation that an intelligent man cannot become anything seriously, and it is only the fool who becomes anything. Yes, a man in the nineteenth century must and morally ought to be pre-eminently a characterless creature; a man of character, an active man, is pre-eminently a limited creature. That is my conviction of forty years. I am forty years old now, and you know forty years is a whole lifetime; you know it is extreme old age. To live longer than forty years is bad manners, is vulgar, immoral. Who does live beyond forty? Answer that, sincerely and honestly. I will tell you who do: fools and worthless fellows. I tell all old men that to their face, all these venerable old men, all these silver-haired and reverend seniors! I tell the whole world that to its face. I have a right to say so, for I shall go on living to sixty myself. To seventy! To eighty! . . . Stay, let me take breath. . . .

You imagine no doubt, gentlemen, that I want to amuse you. You are mistaken in that, too. I am by no means such a mirthful person as you imagine, or as you may imagine; however, irritated by all this babble (and I feel that you are irritated) you think fit to ask me who am I — then my answer is, I am a collegiate assessor. I was in the service that I might have something to eat (and solely for that reason), and when last year a distant relation left me six thousand roubles in his will I immediately retired from the service and settled down in my corner. I used to live in this corner before, but now I have settled down in it. My room is a wretched, horrid one in the outskirts of the town. My servant is an old country-woman, ill-natured from stupidity, and, moreover, there is always a nasty smell about her. I am told that the Petersburg climate is bad for me, and that with my small means it is very expensive to live in Petersburg. I know all that better than all these sage and experienced counsellors and monitors. . . . But I am remaining in Petersburg; I am not going away from Petersburg! I am not going away because . . . ech! Why, it is absolutely no matter whether I am going away or not going away.

But what can a decent man speak of with most pleasure?

Answer: Of himself.

Well, so I will talk about myself.

II

I want now to tell you, gentlemen, whether you care to hear it or not, why I could not even become an insect. I tell you solemnly, that I have many times tried to become an insect. But I was not equal even to that. I swear, gentlemen, that to be too conscious is an illness — a real thoroughgoing illness. For man's everyday needs, it would have been quite enough to have the ordinary human consciousness, that is, half or a quarter of the amount which falls to the lot of a cultivated man of our unhappy nineteenth century, especially one who has the fatal ill-luck to inhabit Petersburg, the most theoretical and intentional town on the whole terrestrial globe. (There are intentional and unintentional towns.) It would have been quite enough, for instance, to have the consciousness by which all so-called direct persons and men of action live. I bet you think I am writing all this from affectation, to be witty at the expense of men of action; and what is more, that from ill-bred affectation, I am clanking a sword like my officer. But, gentlemen, whoever can pride himself on his diseases and even swagger over them?

Though, after all, every one does do that; people do pride themselves on their diseases, and I do, may be, more than any one. We will not dispute it; my contention was absurd. But yet I am firmly persuaded that a great deal of consciousness, every sort of consciousness, in fact, is a disease. I stick to that. Let us leave that, too, for a minute. Tell me this: why does it happen that at the very, yes, at the very moments when I am most capable of feeling every refinement of all that is "good and beautiful," as they used to say at one time, it would, as though of design, happen to me not only to feel but to do such ugly things, such that. . . . Well, in short, actions that all, perhaps, commit; but which, as though purposely, occurred to me at the very time when I was most conscious that they ought not to be committed. The more conscious I was of goodness and of all that was "good and beautiful," the more deeply I sank into my mire and the more ready I was to sink in it altogether. But the chief point was that all this was, as it were, not accidental in me, but as though it were bound to be so. It was as though it were my most normal condition, and not in the least disease or depravity, so that at last all desire in me to struggle against this depravity passed. It ended by my almost believing (perhaps actually believing) that this was perhaps my normal condition. But at first, in the beginning, what agonies I endured in that struggle! I did not believe it was the same with other people, and all my life I hid this fact about myself as a secret. I was ashamed (even now, perhaps, I am ashamed): I got to the point of feeling a sort of secret abnormal, despicable enjoyment in returning home to my corner on some disgusting Petersburg night, acutely conscious that that day I had committed a loathsome action again, that what was done could never be undone, and secretly, inwardly gnawing, gnawing at myself for it, tearing and consuming myself till at last the bitterness turned into a sort of shameful accursed sweetness, and at last — into positive real enjoyment! Yes, into enjoyment, into enjoyment! I insist upon that. I have spoken of this because I keep wanting to know for a fact whether other people feel such enjoyment. I will explain: the enjoyment was just from the too intense consciousness of one's own degradation; it was from feeling oneself that one had reached the last barrier, that it was horrible, but that it could not be otherwise; that there was no escape for you; that you never could become a different man; that even if time and faith were still left you to change into something different you would most likely not wish to change; or if you did wish to, even then you would do nothing; because perhaps in reality there was nothing for you to change into.

And the worst of it was, and the root of it all, that it was all in accord with the normal fundamental laws of over-acute consciousness, and with the inertia that was the direct result of those laws, and that consequently one was not only unable to change but could do absolutely nothing. Thus it would follow, as the result of acute consciousness, that one is not to blame in being a scoundrel; as though that were any consolation to the scoundrel once he has come to realize that he actually is a scoundrel. But enough. . . . Ech, I have talked a lot of nonsense, but what have I explained? How is enjoyment in this to be explained? But I will explain it. I will get to the bottom of it! That is why I have taken up my pen. . . .

I, for instance, have a great deal of *amour propre.*[1] I am as suspicious and prone to take offence as a humpback or a dwarf. But upon my word I sometimes have had moments when if I had happened to be slapped in the face I should, perhaps, have been positively glad of it. I say, in earnest, that I should probably have been able to discover even in that a peculiar sort of enjoyment — the enjoyment, of course, of despair; but in despair there are the most intense enjoyments, especially when one is very acutely conscious of the hopelessness of one's position. And when one is slapped in the face — why then the consciousness of being rubbed into a pulp would positively overwhelm one. The worst of it is, look at it which way one will, it still turns out that I was always the most to blame in everything. And what is most humiliating of all, to blame for no fault of my own but, so to say, through the laws of nature. In the first place, to blame because I am cleverer than any of the people surrounding me. (I have always considered myself cleverer than any of the people surrounding me, and sometimes, would you believe it, have been positively ashamed of it. At any rate, I have all my life, as it were, turned my eyes away and never could look people straight in the face.) To blame, finally, because even if I had had magnanimity, I should only have had more suffering from the sense of its uselessness. I should certainly have never been able to do anything from being magnanimous — neither to forgive, for my assailant would perhaps have slapped me from the laws of nature, and one cannot forgive the laws of nature; nor to forget, for even if it were owing to the laws of nature, it is insulting all the same. Finally, even if I had wanted to be anything but magnanimous, had desired on the contrary to revenge myself on my assailant, I could not have revenged myself on any one for anything because I should certainly never have made up my mind to do anything, even if I had been able to. Why should I not have made up my mind? About that in particular I want to say a few words.

III

With people who know how to revenge themselves and to stand up for themselves in general, how is it done? Why, when they are possessed, let us suppose,

1 [Self-esteem. — Editors' note.]

by the feeling of revenge, then for the time there is nothing else but that feeling left in their whole being. Such a gentleman simply dashes straight for his object like an infuriated bull with its horns down, and nothing but a wall will stop him. (By the way: facing the wall, such gentlemen — that is, the "direct" persons and men of action — are genuinely nonplussed. For them a wall is not an evasion, as for us people who think and consequently do nothing; it is not an excuse for turning aside, an excuse for which we are always very glad, though we scarcely believe in it ourselves, as a rule. No, they are nonplussed in all sincerity. The wall has for them something tranquillizing, morally soothing, final — maybe even something mysterious . . . but of the wall later.)

Well, such a direct person I regard as the real normal man, as his tender mother Nature wished to see him when she graciously brought him into being on the earth. I envy such a man till I am green in the face. He is stupid. I am not disputing that, but perhaps the normal man should be stupid, how do you know? Perhaps it is very beautiful, in fact. And I am the more persuaded of that suspicion, if one can call it so, by the fact that if you take, for instance, the antithesis of the normal man, that is, the man of acute consciousness, who has come, of course, not out of the lap of Nature but out of a retort (this is almost mysticism, gentlemen, but I suspect this, too), this retort-made man is sometimes so nonplussed in the presence of his antithesis that with all his exaggerated consciousness he genuinely thinks of himself as a mouse and not a man. It may be an acutely conscious mouse, yet it is a mouse, while the other is a man, and therefore, et caetera, et caetera. And the worst of it is, he himself, his very own self, looks on himself as a mouse; no one asks him to do so; and that is an important point. Now let us look at this mouse in action. Let us suppose, for instance, that it feels insulted, too (and it almost always does feel insulted), and wants to revenge itself, too. There may even be a greater accumulation of spite in it than in *l'homme de la nature et de la vérité.*[2] The base and nasty desire to vent that spite on its assailant rankles perhaps even more nastily in it than in *l'homme de la nature et de la vérité.* For through his innate stupidity the latter looks upon his revenge as justice pure and simple; while in consequence of his acute consciousness the mouse does not believe in the justice of it. To come at last to the deed itself, to the very act of revenge. Apart from the one fundamental nastiness the luckless mouse succeeds in creating around it so many other nastinesses in the form of doubts and questions, adds to the one question so many unsettled questions, that there inevitably works up around it a sort of fatal brew, a stinking mess, made up of its doubts, emotions, and of the contempt spat upon it by the direct men of action who stand solemnly about it as judges

2 [The man of nature and truth. — Editors' note.]

and arbitrators, laughing at it till their healthy sides ache. Of course the only thing left for it is to dismiss all that with a wave of its paw, and, with a smile of assumed contempt in which it does not even itself believe, creep ignominiously into its mouse-hole. There in its nasty, stinking, underground home our insulted, crushed and ridiculed mouse promptly becomes absorbed in cold, malignant and, above all, everlasting spite. For forty years together it will remember its injury down to the smallest, most ignominious details, and every time will add, of itself, details still more ignominious, spitefully teasing and tormenting itself with its own imagination. It will itself be ashamed of its imaginings, but yet it will recall it all, it will go over and over every detail, it will invent unheard-of things against itself, pretending that those things might happen, and will forgive nothing. Maybe it will begin to revenge itself, too, but, as it were, piecemeal, in trivial ways, from behind the stove, incognito, without believing either in its own right to vengeance, or in the success of its revenge, knowing that from all its efforts at revenge it will suffer a hundred times more than he on whom it revenges itself, while he, I daresay, will not even scratch himself. On its death-bed it will recall it all over again, with interest accumulated over all the years and. . . .

But it is just in that cold, abominable half despair, half belief, in that conscious burying oneself alive for grief in the underworld for forty years, in that acutely recognized and yet partly doubtful hopelessness of one's position, in that hell of unsatisfied desires turned inward, in that fever of oscillations, of resolutions determined for ever and repented of again a minute later — that the savour of that strange enjoyment of which I have spoken lies. It is so subtle, so difficult of analysis, that persons who are a little limited, or even simply persons of strong nerves, will not understand a single atom of it. "Possibly," you will add on your own account with a grin, "people will not understand it either who have never received a slap in the face," and in that way you will politely hint to me that I too, perhaps, have had the experience of a slap in the face in my life, and so I speak as one who knows. I bet that you are thinking that. But set your minds at rest, gentlemen, I have not received a slap in the face, though it is absolutely a matter of indifference to me what you may think about it. Possibly, I even regret myself that I have given so few slaps in the face during my life. But enough . . . not another word on that subject of such extreme interest to you.

I will continue calmly concerning persons with strong nerves who do not understand a certain refinement of enjoyment. Though in certain circumstances these gentlemen bellow their loudest like bulls, though this, let us suppose, does them the greatest credit, yet, as I have said already, confronted with the impossible they subside at once. The impossible means the stone wall! What stone wall? Why, of course, the laws of nature, the deductions of natural science, mathematics. As soon as they prove to you, for instance, that you are descended from a monkey, then it is no use scowling, accept it for a fact. When they prove to you that in reality one drop of your own fat must be dearer to you than a hundred thousand of your fellow creatures, and that this conclusion is the final solution of all so-called virtues and duties and all such prejudices and fancies, then you have just to accept it, there is no help for it, for twice two is a law of mathematics. Just try refuting it.

"Upon my word," they will shout at you, "it is no use protesting: it is a case of twice two makes four! Nature does not ask your permission, she has nothing to do with your wishes, and whether you like her laws or dislike them, you are bound to accept her as she is, and consequently all her conclusions. A wall, you see, is a wall . . . and so on, and so on."

Merciful heavens! but what do I care for the laws of nature and arithmetic, when, for some reason, I dislike those laws and the fact that twice two makes four? Of course I cannot break through the wall by battering my head against it if I really have not the strength to knock it down, but I am not going to be reconciled to it simply because it is a stone wall and I have not the strength.

As though such a stone wall really were a consolation, and really did contain some word of conciliation, simply because it is as true as twice two makes four. Oh, absurdity of absurdities! How much better it is to understand it all, to recognize it all, all the impossibilities and the stone wall; not to be reconciled to one of those impossibilities and stone walls if it disgusts you to be reconciled to it; by the way of the most inevitable, logical combinations, to reach the most revolting conclusions on the everlasting theme, that even for the stone wall you are yourself somehow to blame, though again it is as clear as day you are not to blame in the least, and therefore grinding your teeth in silent impotence to sink into luxurious inertia, brooding on the fact that there is no one even for you to feel vindictive against, that you have not, and perhaps never will have, an object for your spite, that it is a sleight-of-hand, a bit of juggling, a card-sharper's trick, that it is simply a mess, no knowing what and no knowing who, but in spite of all these uncertainties and jugglings, still there is an ache in you, and the more you do not know, the worse the ache.

IV

"Ha, ha, ha! You will be finding enjoyment in toothache next," you cry, with a laugh.

"Well? Even in toothache there is enjoyment," I answer. I had toothache for a whole month and I know there is. In that case, of course, people are not spiteful in silence, but moan; but they are not candid moans, they are malignant moans, and the malignancy is the whole point. The enjoyment of the sufferer finds expression in those moans; if he did not feel enjoyment in them he would not moan. It is a good example, gentlemen, and I will develop it. Those moans express in the first place all the aimlessness of your pain, which is so humiliating to your consciousness; the whole legal system of Nature on which you spit disdainfully, of course, but from which you suffer all the same while she does not. They express the consciousness that you have no enemy to punish, but that you have pain; the consciousness that in spite of all possible Vagenheims[3] you are in complete slavery to your teeth; that if some one wishes it, your teeth will leave off aching, and if he does not, they will go on aching another three months; and that finally if you are still contumacious and still protest, all that is left you for your own gratification is to thrash yourself or beat your wall with your fist as hard as you can, and absolutely nothing more. Well, these mortal insults, these jeers on the part of some one unknown, end at last in an enjoyment which sometimes reaches the highest degree of voluptuousness. I ask you, gentlemen, listen sometimes to the moans of an educated man of the nineteenth century suffering from toothache, on the second or third day of the attack, when he is beginning to moan, not as he moaned on the first day, that is, not simply because he has toothache, not just as any coarse peasant, but as a man affected by progress and European civilization, a man who is "divorced from the soil and the national elements," as they express it nowadays. His moans become nasty, disgustingly malignant, and go on for whole days and nights. And of course he knows himself that he is doing himself no sort of good with his moans; he knows better than any one that he is only lacerating and harassing himself and others for nothing; he knows that even the audience before whom he is making his efforts, and his whole family, listen to him with loathing, do not put a ha'porth of faith in him, and inwardly understand that he might moan differently, more simply, without trills and flourishes, and that he is only amusing himself like that from ill-humour, from malignancy. Well, in all these recognitions and disgraces it is that there lies a voluptuous pleasure. As though he would say: "I am worrying you, I am lacerating your hearts, I am keeping every one in the house awake. Well, stay awake then, you, too, feel every minute that I have toothache. I am not a hero to you now, as I tried to seem before, but simply a nasty person, an impostor. Well, so be it, then! I am very glad that you see through me. It is nasty for you to hear my despicable moans: well, let it be nasty; here I will let you have a nastier flourish in a minute. . . ." You do not understand even now, gentlemen? No, it seems our development and our consciousness must go further to understand all the intricacies of this pleasure. You laugh? Delighted. My jests, gentle-

3 [Dentists in Petersburg. — Editors' note.]

men, are of course in bad taste, jerky, involved, lacking self-confidence. But of course that is because I do not respect myself. Can a man of perception respect himself at all?

V

Come, can a man who attempts to find enjoyment in the very feeling of his own degradation possibly have a spark of respect for himself? I am not saying this now from any mawkish kind of remorse. And, indeed, I could never endure saying, "Forgive me, Papa, I won't do it again," not because I am incapable of saying that — on the contrary, perhaps just because I have been too capable of it, and in what a way, too! As though of design I used to get into trouble in cases when I was not to blame in any way. That was the nastiest part of it. At the same time I was genuinely touched and penitent, I used to shed tears and, of course, deceived myself, though I was not acting in the least and there was a sick feeling in my heart at the time. . . . For that one could not blame even the laws of nature, though the laws of nature have continually all my life offended me more than anything. It is loathsome to remember it all, but it was loathsome even then. Of course, a minute or so later I would realize wrathfully that it was all a lie, a revolting lie, an affected lie, that is, all this penitence, this emotion, these vows of reform. You will ask why did I worry myself with such antics: answer, because it was very dull to sit with one's hands folded, and so one began cutting capers. That is really it. Observe yourselves more carefully, gentlemen, then you will understand that it is so. I invented adventures for myself and made up a life, so as at least to live in some way. How many times it has happened to me — well, for instance, to take offence simply on purpose, for nothing; and one knows oneself, of course, that one is offended at nothing, that one is putting it on, but yet one brings oneself, at last, to the point of being really offended. All my life I have had an impulse to play such pranks, so that in the end I could not control it in myself. Another time, twice, in fact, I tried hard to be in love. I suffered, too, gentlemen, I assure you. In the depth of my heart there was no faith in my suffering, only a faint stir of mockery, but yet I did suffer, and in the real, orthodox way; I was jealous, beside myself . . . and it was all from *ennui,* gentlemen, all from *ennui;* inertia overcame me. You know the direct, legitimate fruit of consciousness is inertia, that is, conscious sitting-with-the-hands-folded. I have referred to this already. I repeat, I repeat with emphasis: all "direct" persons and men of action are active just because they are stupid and limited. How explain that? I will tell you: in consequence of their limitation they take immediate and secondary causes for primary ones, and in that way persuade themselves more quickly and easily than other people do that they have found an infallible foundation for their activity, and their minds are at ease and you know that is the chief thing. To begin to act, you know, you must first have your mind completely at ease and no trace of doubt left in it. Why, how am I, for example, to set my mind at rest? Where are the primary causes on which I am to build? Where are my foundations? Where am I to get them from? I exercise myself in reflection, and consequently with me every primary cause at once draws after itself another still more primary, and so on to infinity. That is just the essence of every sort of consciousness and reflection. It must be a case of the laws of nature again. What is the result of it in the end? Why, just the same. Remember I spoke just now of vengeance. (I am sure you did not take it in.) I said that a man revenges himself because he sees justice in it. Therefore he has found a primary cause, that is, justice. And so he is at rest on all sides, and consequently he carries out his revenge calmly and successfully, being persuaded that he is doing a just and honest thing. But I see no justice in it, I find no sort of virtue in it either, and consequently if I attempt to revenge myself, it is only out of spite. Spite, of course, might overcome everything, all my doubts, and so might serve quite successfully in place of a primary cause, precisely because it is not a cause. But what is to be done if I have not even spite (I began with that just now, you know)? In consequence again of those accursed laws of consciousness, anger in me is subject to chemical disintegration. You look into it, the object flies off into air, your reasons evaporate, the criminal is not to be found, the wrong becomes not a wrong but a phantom, something like the toothache, for which no one is to blame, and consequently there is only the same outlet left again — that is, to beat the wall as hard as you can. So you give it up with a wave of the hand because you have not found a fundamental cause. And try letting yourself be carried away by your feelings, blindly, without reflection, without a primary cause, repelling consciousness at least for a time; hate or love, if only not to sit with your hands folded. The day after to-morrow, at the latest, you will begin despising yourself for having knowingly deceived yourself. Result: a soap-bubble and inertia. Oh, gentlemen, do you know, perhaps I consider myself an intelligent man only because all my life I have been able neither to begin nor to finish anything. Granted I am a babbler, a harmless vexatious babbler, like all of us. But what is to be done if the direct and sole vocation of every intelligent man is babble, that is, the intentional pouring of water through a sieve?

VI

Oh, if I had done nothing simply from laziness! Heavens, how I should have respected myself then. I should have respected myself because I should at least have been capable of being lazy; there would at least have been one quality, as it were, positive in me, in which I could have believed myself. Question: What is he? Answer: A sluggard; how very pleasant it would have been to hear that of oneself! It would mean that I was positively defined, it would mean that there was something to say about me. "Sluggard" — why, it is a calling and vocation, it is a career. Do not jest, it is so. I should then be a member of the best club by right, and should find my occupation in continually respecting myself. I knew a gentleman who prided himself all his life on being a connoisseur of Lafitte. He considered this as his positive virtue, and never doubted himself. He died, not simply with a tranquil, but with a triumphant, conscience, and he was quite right, too. Then I should have chosen a career for myself, I should have been a sluggard and a glutton, not a simple one, but, for instance, one with sympathies for everything good and beautiful. How do you like that? I have long had visions of it. That "good and beautiful" weighs heavily on my mind at forty. But that is at forty; then — oh, then it would have been different! I should have found for myself a form of activity in keeping with it, to be precise, drinking to the health of everything "good and beautiful." I should have snatched at every opportunity to drop a tear into my glass and then to drain it to all that is "good and beautiful." I should then have turned everything into the good and the beautiful; in the nastiest, unquestionable trash, I should have sought out the good and the beautiful. I should have exuded tears like a wet sponge. An artist, for instance, paints a picture worthy of Gay. At once I drink to the health of the artist who painted the picture worthy of Gay, because I love all that is "good and beautiful." An author has written *As you will:* at once I drink to the health of "any one you will" because I love all that is "good and beautiful."

I should claim respect for doing so. I should persecute any one who would not show me respect. I should live at ease, I should die with dignity, why, it is charming, perfectly charming! And what a good round belly I should have grown, what a treble chin I should have established, what a ruby nose I should have coloured for myself, so that every one would have said, looking at me: "Here is an asset! Here is something real and solid!" And, say what you like, it is very agreeable to hear such remarks about oneself in this negative age.

VII

But these are all golden dreams. Oh, tell me, who was it first announced, who was it first proclaimed, that man only does nasty things because he does not know his own interests; and that if he were enlightened, if his eyes were opened to his real normal interests, man would at once cease to do nasty things, would at once become good and noble because, being enlightened and understanding his real advantage, he would see his own advantage in the good and nothing else, and we all know that not one man can, consciously, act against his own interests, consequently, so to say, through necessity, he would begin doing good? Oh, the babe! Oh, the pure, innocent child! Why, in the first place, when in all these thousands of years has there been a time when man has acted only from his own interest? What is to be done with the millions of facts that bear witness that men, *consciously,* that is, fully understanding their real interests, have left them in the background and have rushed headlong on another path, to meet peril and danger, compelled to this course by nobody and by nothing, but, as it were, simply disliking the beaten track, and have obstinately, wilfully, struck out another difficult, absurd way, seeking it almost in the darkness. So, I suppose, this obstinacy and perversity were pleasanter to them than any advantage. . . . Advantage! What is advantage?

And will you take it upon yourself to define with perfect accuracy in what the advantage of man consists? And what if it so happens that a man's advantage, *sometimes,* not only may, but even must, consist in his desiring in certain cases what is harmful to himself and not advantageous. And if so, there can be such a case, the whole principle falls into dust. What do you think — are there such cases? You laugh; laugh away, gentlemen, but only answer me: have man's advantages been reckoned up with perfect certainty? Are there not some which not only have not been included but cannot possibly be included under any classification? You see, you gentlemen have, to the best of my knowledge, taken your whole register of human advantages from the averages of statistical figures and politico-economical formulas. Your advantages are prosperity, wealth, freedom, peace — and so on, and so on. So that the man who should, for instance, go openly and knowingly in opposition to all that list would, to your thinking, and indeed mine too, of course, be an obscurantist or an absolute madman: would not he? But, you know, this is what is surprising: why does it so happen that all these statisticians, sages and lovers of humanity, when they reckon up human advantages invariably leave out one? They don't even take it into their reckoning in the form in which it should be taken and the whole reckoning depends upon that. It would be no great matter, they would simply have to take it, this advantage, and add it to the list. But the trouble is, that this strange advantage does not fall under any classification and is not in place in any list. I have a friend for instance. . . . Ech! gentlemen, but of course he is your friend, too; and indeed there is no one, no one, to whom he is not a friend!

When he prepares for any undertaking this gentleman immediately explains to you, elegantly and clearly, exactly how he must act in accordance with the laws of reason and truth. What is more, he will talk to you with excitement and passion of the true normal interests of man; with irony he will upbraid the shortsighted fools who do not understand their own interests, nor the true significance of virtue; and, within a quarter of an hour, without any sudden outside provocation, but simply through something inside him which is stronger than all his interests, he will go off on quite a different tack — that is, act in direct opposition to what he has just been saying about himself, in opposition to the laws of reason, in opposition to his own advantage — in fact, in opposition to everything.... I warn you that my friend is a compound personality, and therefore it is difficult to blame him as an individual. The fact is, gentlemen, it seems there must really exist something that is dearer to almost every man than his greatest advantages, or (not to be illogical) there is a most advantageous advantage (the very one omitted of which we spoke just now) which is more important and more advantageous than all other advantages, for the sake of which a man if necessary is ready to act in opposition to all laws; that is, in opposition to reason, honour, peace, prosperity — in fact, in opposition to all those excellent and useful things if only he can attain that fundamental, most advantageous advantage which is dearer to him than all. "Yes, but it's advantage all the same" you will retort. But excuse me, I'll make the point clear, and it is not a case of playing upon words. What matters is, that this advantage is remarkable from the very fact that it breaks down all our classifications, and continually shatters every system constructed by lovers of mankind for the benefit of mankind. In fact, it upsets everything. But before I mention this advantage to you, I want to compromise myself personally, and therefore I boldly declare that all these fine systems — all these theories for explaining to mankind their real normal interests, in order that inevitably striving to pursue these interests they may at once become good and noble — are, in my opinion, so far, mere logical exercises! Yes, logical exercises. Why, to maintain this theory of the regeneration of mankind by means of the pursuit of his own advantage is to my mind almost the same thing as ... as to affirm, for instance, following Buckle, that through civilization mankind becomes softer, and consequently less bloodthirsty, and less fitted for warfare.

Logically it does seem to follow from his arguments. But man has such a predilection for systems and abstract deductions that he is ready to distort the truth intentionally, he is ready to deny the evidence of his senses only to justify his logic. I take this example because it is the most glaring instance of it. Only look about you: blood is being spilt in streams, and in the merriest way, as though it were champagne. Take the whole of the nineteenth century in which Buckle lived. Take Napoleon — the Great and also the present one. Take North America — the eternal union. Take the farce of Schleswig-Holstein.[4] ... And what is it that civilization softens in us? The only gain of civilization for man-

4 [Allusions to the America Civil War and to Denmark's war with Austria and Prussia. — Editors' note.]

kind is the greater capacity for variety of sensations — and absolutely nothing more. And through the development of this many-sideness man may come to finding enjoyment in bloodshed. In fact, this has already happened to him. Have you noticed that it is the most civilized gentlemen who have been the subtlest slaughterers, to whom the Attilas and Stenka Razins could not hold a candle, and if they are not so conspicuous as the Attilas and Stenka Razins it is simply because they are so often met with, are so ordinary and have become so familiar to us. In any case civilization has made mankind if not more blood-thirsty, at least more vilely, more loathsomely blood-thirsty. In old days he saw justice in bloodshed and with his conscience at peace exterminated those he thought proper. Now we do think bloodshed abominable and yet we engage in this abomination, and with more energy than ever. Which is worse? Decide that for yourselves.

They say that Cleopatra (excuse an instance from Roman history) was fond of sticking gold pins into her slave-girls' breasts and derived gratification from their screams and writhings. You will say that that was in the comparatively barbarous times; that these are barbarous times too, because also, comparatively speaking, pins are stuck in even now; that though man has now learned to see more clearly than in barbarous ages, he is still far from having learnt to act as reason and science would dictate. But yet you are fully convinced that he will be sure to learn when he gets rid of certain old bad habits, and when common sense and science have completely re-educated human nature and turned it in a normal direction. You are confident that then man will cease from *intentional* error and will, so to say, be compelled not to want to set his will against his normal interests. That is not all; then, you say, science itself will teach man (though to my mind it's a superfluous luxury) that he never has really had any caprice or will of his own, and that he himself is something of the nature of a piano-key or the stop of an organ, and that there are, besides, things called the laws of nature; so that everything he does is not done by his willing it, but is done of itself, by the laws of nature. Consequently we have only to discover these laws of nature, and man will no longer have to answer for his actions and life will become exceedingly easy for him. All human actions will then, of course, be tabulated according to these laws, mathematically, like tables of logarithms up to 108,000, and entered in an index; or, better still, there would be published certain edifying works of the nature of encyclopaedic lexicons, in which everything will be so clearly calculated and explained that there will be no more incidents or adventures in the world.

Then — this is all what you say — new economic relations will be established, all ready-made and worked out with mathematical exactitude, so that every possible question will vanish in the twinkling of an eye, simply because every possible answer to it will be provided. Then the "Palace of Crystal"[5] will be built. Then. . . . In fact, those will be halcyon days. Of course there is no guaranteeing (this is my comment) that it will not be, for instance, frightfully dull then (for what will one have to do when everything will be calculated and tabulated?), but on the other hand everything will be extraordinarily rational. Of course boredom may lead you to anything. It is boredom sets one sticking golden pins into people, but all that would not matter. What is bad (this is my comment again) is that I daresay people will be thankful for the gold pins then. Man is stupid, you know, phenomenally stupid; or rather he is not at all stupid, but he is so ungrateful that you could not find another like him in all creation. I, for instance, would not be in the least surprised if all of a sudden, apropos of nothing, in the midst of general prosperity a gentleman with an ignoble, or rather with a reactionary and ironical, countenance were to arise and putting his arms akimbo, say to us all: "I say, gentlemen, hadn't we better kick over the whole show and scatter rationalism to the winds, simply to send these logarithms to the devil, and to enable us to live once more at our own sweet foolish will!" That again would not matter; but what is annoying is that he would be sure to find followers — such is the nature of man. And all that for the most foolish reason, which, one would think, was hardly worth mentioning: that is, that man everywhere and at all times, whoever he may be, has preferred to act as he chose and not in the least as his reason and advantage dictated. And one may choose what is contrary to one's own interests, and sometimes one *positively ought* (that is my idea). One's own free unfettered choice, one's own caprice — however wild it may be, one's own fancy worked up at times to frenzy — is that very "most advantageous advantage" which we have overlooked, which comes under no classification and against which all systems and theories are continually being shattered to atoms. And how do these wiseacres know that man wants a normal, a virtuous choice? What has made them conceive that man must want a rationally advantageous choice? What man wants is simply *independent* choice, whatever that independence may cost and wherever it may lead. And choice, of course, the devil only knows what choice. . . .

VIII

"Ha! ha! ha! But you know there is no such thing as choice in reality, say what you like," you will interpose with a chuckle. "Science has succeeded in so far analyzing man that we know already that choice and what is called freedom of will is nothing else than —— "

5 [The Crystal Palace in London housed the Great Exhibition of 1851, a sort of World's Fair. — Editors' note.]

Stay, gentlemen, I meant to begin with that myself. I confess, I was rather frightened. I was just going to say that the devil only knows what choice depends on, and that perhaps that was a very good thing, but I remembered the teaching of science . . . and pulled myself up. And here you have begun upon it. Indeed, if there really is some day discovered a formula for all our desires and caprices — that is, an explanation of what they depend upon, by what laws they arise, how they develop, what they are aiming at in one case and in another and so on, that is, a real mathematical formula — then, most likely, man will at once cease to feel desire, indeed, he will be certain to. For who would want to choose by rule? Besides, he will at once be transformed from a human being into an organ-stop or something of the sort; for what is a man without desires, without free will and without choice, if not a stop in an organ? What do you think? Let us reckon the chances — can such a thing happen or not?

"H'm!" you decide. "Our choice is usually mistaken from a false view of our advantage. We sometimes choose absolute nonsense because in our foolishness we see in that nonsense the easiest means for attaining a supposed advantage. But when all that is explained and worked out on paper (which is perfectly possible, for it is contemptible and senseless to suppose that some laws of nature man will never understand), then certainly so-called desires will no longer exist. For if a desire should come into conflict with reason we shall then reason and not desire, because it will be impossible retaining our reason to be *senseless* in our desires, and in that way knowingly act against reason and desire to injure ourselves. And as all choice and reasoning can be really calculated — because there will some day be discovered the laws of our so-called free will — so, joking apart, there may one day be something like a table constructed of them, so that we really shall choose in accordance with it. If, for instance, some day they calculate and prove to me that I made a long nose at some one because I could not help making a long nose at him and that I had to do it in that particular way, what *freedom* is left me, especially if I am a learned man and have taken my degree somewhere? Then I should be able to calculate my whole life for thirty years beforehand. In short, if this could be arranged there would be nothing left for us to do; anyway, we should have to understand that. And, in fact, we ought unwearyingly to repeat to ourselves that at such and such a time and in such and such circumstances Nature does not ask our leave; that we have got to take her as she is and not fashion her to suit our fancy, and if we really aspire to formulas and tables of rules, and well, even . . . to the chemical retort, there's no help for it, we must accept the retort too, or else it will be accepted without our consent. . . ."

Yes, but here I come to a stop! Gentlemen, you must excuse me for being over-philosophical; it's the result of forty years underground! Allow me to indulge my fancy. You see, gentlemen, reason is an excellent thing, there's no disputing that, but reason is nothing but reason and satisfies only the rational side of man's nature, while will is a manifestation of the whole life, that is, of the whole human life including reason and all the impulses. And although our life, in this manifestation of it, is often worthless, yet it is life and not simply extracting square roots. Here I, for instance, quite naturally want to live, in order to satisfy all my capacities for life, and not simply my capacity for reasoning, that is, not simply one-twentieth of my capacity for life. What does reason know? Reason only knows what it has succeeded in learning (some things, perhaps, it will never learn; this is a poor comfort, but why not say so frankly?) and human nature acts as a whole, with everything that is in it, consciously or unconsciously, and, even if it goes wrong, it lives. I suspect, gentlemen, that you are looking at me with compassion; you tell me again that an enlightened and developed man, such, in short, as the future man will be, cannot consciously desire anything disadvantageous to himself, that that can be proved mathematically. I thoroughly agree, it can — by mathematics.

But I repeat for the hundredth time, there is one case, one only, when man may consciously, purposely, desire what is injurious to himself, what is stupid, very stupid — simply in order to have the right to desire for himself even what is very stupid and not to be bound by an obligation to desire only what is sensible. Of course, this very stupid thing, this caprice of ours, may be in reality, gentlemen, more advantageous for us than anything else on earth, especially in certain cases. And in particular it may be more advantageous than any advantage even when it does us obvious harm, and contradicts the soundest conclusions of our reason concerning our advantage — for in any circumstances it preserves for us what is most precious and most important — that is, our personality, our individuality. Some, you see, maintain that this really is the most precious thing for mankind; choice can, of course, if it chooses, be in agreement with reason; and especially if this be not abused but kept within bounds. It is profitable and sometimes even praiseworthy. But very often, and even most often, choice is utterly and stubbornly opposed to reason . . . and . . . and . . . do you know that that, too, is profitable, sometimes even praiseworthy? Gentlemen, let us suppose that man is not stupid. (Indeed one cannot refuse to suppose that, if only from the one consideration, that, if man is stupid, then who is wise?) But if he is not stupid, he is monstrously ungrateful! Phenomenally ungrateful. In fact, I believe that the best definition of man is the ungrateful biped. But that is not all, that is not his worst defect; his worst defect is his perpetual moral obliquity, perpetual — from the days of the Flood to the Schleswig-Holstein period.

Moral obliquity and consequently lack of good sense; for it has long been accepted that lack of good sense is due to no other cause than moral obliquity.

Put it to the test and cast your eyes upon the history of mankind. What will you see? Is it a grand spectacle? Grand, if you like. Take the Colossus of Rhodes, for instance, that's worth something. With good reason Mr. Anaevsky[6] testifies of it that some say that it is the work of man's hands, while others maintain that it has been created by Nature herself. Is it many-coloured? It may be it is many-coloured, too: if one takes the dress uniforms, military and civilian, of all peoples in all ages — that alone is worth something, and if you take the undress uniforms you will never get to the end of it; no historian would be equal to the job. Is it monotonous? It may be it's monotonous too: it's fighting and fighting; they are fighting now, they fought first and they fought last — you will admit that it is almost too monotonous. In short, one may say anything about the history of the world — anything that might enter the most disordered imagination.

The only thing one can't say is that it's rational. The very word sticks in one's throat. And, indeed, this is the odd thing that is continually happening: there are continually turning up in life moral and rational persons, sages and lovers of humanity, who make it their object to live all their lives as morally and rationally as possible, to be, so to speak, a light to their neighbours simply in order to show them that it is possible to live morally and rationally in this world. And yet we all know that those very people sooner or later have been false to themselves, playing some queer trick, often a most unseemly one. Now I ask you: what can be expected of man since he is a being endowed with such strange qualities? Shower upon him every earthly blessing, drown him in a sea of happiness, so that nothing but bubbles of bliss can be seen on the surface; give him economic prosperity, such that he should have nothing else to do but sleep, eat cakes and busy himself with the continuation of his species, and even then out of sheer ingratitude, sheer spite, man would play you some nasty trick. He would even risk his cakes and would deliberately desire the most fatal rubbish, the most uneconomical absurdity, simply to introduce into all this positive good sense his fatal fantastic element. It is just his fantastic dreams, his vulgar folly, that he will desire to retain, simply in order to prove to himself — as though that were so necessary — that men still are men and not the keys of a piano, which the laws of nature threaten to control so completely that soon one will be able to desire nothing but by the calendar. And that is not all: even if man really were nothing but a piano-key, even if this were proved to him by natural science and mathematics, even then he would not become reasonable, but would purposely do something perverse out of simple ingratitude, simply to gain his point. And if he does not find means he will contrive destruction and chaos, will contrive sufferings of all sorts, only to gain his point! He will launch

6 [A minor contemporary novelist. — Editors' note.]

a curse upon the world, and as only man can curse (it is his privilege, the primary distinction between him and other animals) it may be by his curse alone he will attain his object — that is, convince himself that he is a man and not a piano-key! If you say that all this, too, can be calculated and tabulated — chaos and darkness and curses, so that the mere possibility of calculating it all beforehand would stop it all, and reason would reassert itself — then man would purposely go mad in order to be rid of reason and gain his point! I believe in it, I answer for it, for the whole work of man really seems to consist in nothing but proving to himself every minute that he is a man and not a piano-key! It may be at the cost of his skin, it may be by cannibalism! And this being so, can one help being tempted to rejoice that it has not yet come off, and that desire still depends on something we don't know?

You will scream at me (that is, if you condescend to do so) that no one is touching my free will, that all they are concerned with is that my will should of itself, of its own free will, coincide with my own normal interests, with the laws of nature and arithmetic.

Good heavens, gentlemen, what sort of free will is left when we come to tabulation and arithmetic, when it will all be a case of twice two makes four? Twice two makes four without my will. As if free will meant that!

IX

Gentlemen, I am joking, and I know myself that my jokes are not brilliant, but you know one can't take everything as a joke. I am, perhaps, jesting against the grain. Gentlemen, I am tormented by questions; answer them for me. You, for instance, want to cure men of their old habits and reform their will in accordance with science and good sense. But how do you know, not only that it is possible, but also that it is *desirable,* to reform man in that way? And what leads you to the conclusion that man's inclinations *need* reforming? In short, how do you know that such a reformation will be a benefit to man? And to go to the root of the matter, why are you so positively convinced that not to act against his real normal interests guaranteed by the conclusions of reason and arithmetic is certainly always advantageous for man and must always be a law for mankind? So far, you know, this is only your supposition. It may be the law of logic, but not the law of humanity. You think, gentlemen, perhaps that I am mad? Allow me to defend myself. I agree that man is pre-eminently a creative animal, predestined to strive consciously for an object and to engage in engineering — that is, incessantly and eternally to make new roads, *wherever they may lead.* But the reason why he wants sometimes to go off at a tangent may just be that he is *predestined* to make the road, and perhaps, too, that however stupid the "direct" practical man may be, the thought sometimes will occur to him that the road almost always does lead *somewhere*, and that the destination it leads to is less important than the process of making it, and that the chief thing is to save the well-conducted child from despising engineering, and so giving way to the fatal idleness, which, as we all know, is the mother of all the vices. Man likes to make roads and to create, that is a fact beyond dispute. But why has he such a passionate love for destruction and chaos also? Tell me that! But on that point I want to say a couple of words myself. May it not be that he loves chaos and destruction (there can be no disputing that he does sometimes love it) because he is instinctively afraid of attaining his object and completing the edifice he is constructing? Who knows, perhaps he only loves that edifice from a distance, and is by no means in love with it at close quarters; perhaps he only loves building it and does not want to live in it, but will leave it, when completed, for the use of *les animaux domestiques* — such as the ants, the sheep, and so on. Now the ants have quite a different taste. They have a marvellous edifice of that pattern which endures for ever — the ant-heap.

With the ant-heap the respectable race of ants began and with the ant-heap they will probably end, which does the greatest credit to their perseverance and good sense. But man is a frivolous and incongruous creature, and perhaps, like a chess-player, loves the process of the game, not the end of it. And who knows (there is no saying with certainty), perhaps the only goal on earth to which mankind is striving lies in this incessant process of attaining, in other words, in life itself, and not in the thing to be attained, which must always be expressed as a formula, as positive as twice two makes four, and such positiveness is not life, gentlemen, but is the beginning of death. Anyway, man has always been afraid of this mathematical certainty, and I am afraid of it now. Granted that man does nothing but seek that mathematical certainty, he traverses oceans, sacrifices his life in the quest, but to succeed, really to find it, he dreads, I assure you. He feels that when he has found it there will be nothing for him to look for. When workmen have finished their work they do at least receive their pay, they go to the tavern, then they are taken to the police-station — and there is occupation for a week. But where can man go? Anyway, one can observe a certain awkwardness about him when he has attained such objects. He loves the process of attaining, but does not quite like to have attained, and that, of course, is very absurd. In fact, man is a comical creature; there seems to be a kind of jest in it all. But yet mathematical certainty is, after all, something insufferable. Twice two makes four seems to me simply a piece of insolence. Twice two makes four is a pert coxcomb who stands with arms akimbo barring your path and spitting. I admit that twice two makes four is an excellent thing, but if we are to give everything its due, twice two makes five is sometimes a very charming thing too.

And why are you so firmly, so triumphantly, convinced that only the normal and the positive — in other words, only what is conducive to welfare — is for the advantage of man? Is not reason in error as regards advantage? Does not man, perhaps, love something besides well-being? Perhaps he is just as fond of suffering? Perhaps suffering is just as great a benefit to him as well-being? Man is sometimes extraordinarily, passionately, in love with suffering, and that is a fact. There is no need to appeal to universal history to prove that; only ask yourself, if you are a man and have lived at all. As far as my personal opinion is concerned, to care only for well-being seems to me positively ill-bred. Whether it's good or bad, it is sometimes very pleasant, too, to smash things. I hold no brief for suffering nor for well-being either. I am standing for . . . my caprice, and for its being guaranteed to me when necessary. Suffering would be out of place in vaudevilles, for instance; I know that. In the "Palace of Crystal" it is unthinkable; suffering means doubt, negation, and what would be the good of a "palace of crystal" if there could be any doubt about it? And yet I think man will never renounce real suffering, that is, destruction and chaos. Why, suffering is the sole origin of consciousness. Though I did lay it down at the beginning that consciousness is the greatest misfortune for man, yet I know man prizes it and would not give it up for any satisfaction. Consciousness, for instance, is infinitely superior to twice two makes four. Once you have mathematical certainty there is nothing left to do or to understand. There will be nothing left but to bottle up your five senses and plunge into contemplation. While if you stick to consciousness, even though the same result is attained, you can at least flog yourself at times, and that will, at any rate, liven you up. Reactionary as it is, corporal punishment is better than nothing.

X

You believe in a palace of crystal that can never be destroyed — a palace at which one will not be able to put out one's tongue or make a long nose on the sly. And perhaps that is just why I am afraid of this edifice that it is of crystal and can never be destroyed and that one cannot put one's tongue out at it even on the sly.

You see, if it were not a palace, but a hen-house, I might creep into it to avoid getting wet, and yet I would not call the hen-house a palace out of gratitude to it for keeping me dry. You laugh and say that in such circumstances a hen-house is as good as a mansion. Yes, I answer, if one had to live simply to keep out of the rain.

But what is to be done if I have taken it into my head that that is not the only object in life, and that if one must live one had better live in a mansion.

That is my choice, my desire. You will only eradicate it when you have changed my preference. Well, do change it, allure me with something else, give me another ideal. But meanwhile I will not take a hen-house for a mansion. The palace of crystal may be an idle dream, it may be that it is inconsistent with the laws of nature and that I have invented it only through my own stupidity, through the old-fashioned irrational habits of my generation. But what does it matter to me that it is inconsistent? That makes no difference since it exists in my desires, or rather exists as long as my desires exist. Perhaps you are laughing again? Laugh away; I will put up with any mockery rather than pretend that I am satisfied when I am hungry. I know, anyway, that I will not be put off with a compromise, with a recurring zero, simply because it is consistent with the laws of nature and actually exists. I will not accept as the crown of my desires a block of buildings with tenements for the poor on a lease of a thousand years, and perhaps with a sign-board of a dentist hanging out. Destroy my desires, eradicate my ideals, show me something better, and I will follow you. You will say, perhaps, that is not worth your trouble; but in that case I can give you the same answer. We are discussing things seriously; but if you won't deign to give me your attention, I will drop your acquaintance. I can retreat into my underground hole.

But while I am alive and have desires I would rather my hand were withered off than bring one brick to such a building! Don't remind me that I have just rejected the palace of crystal for the sole reason that one cannot put out one's tongue at it. I did not say that because I am so fond of putting my tongue out. Perhaps the thing I resented was, that of all your edifices there has not been one at which one could not put out one's tongue. On the contrary, I would let my tongue be cut off out of gratitude if things could be so arranged that I should lose all desire to put it out. It is not my fault that things cannot be so arranged, and that one must be satisfied with model flats. Then why am I made with such desires? Can I have been constructed simply in order to come to the conclusion that all my construction is a cheat? Can this be my whole purpose? I do not believe it.

But do you know what: I am convinced that we underground folk ought to be kept on a curb. Though we may sit forty years underground without speaking, when we do come out into the light of day and break out we talk and talk and talk. . . .

XI

The long and the short of it is, gentlemen, that it is better to do nothing! Better conscious inertia! And so hurrah for underground! Though I have said that I envy the normal man to the last drop of my bile, yet I should not care to be in his place such as he is now (though I shall not cease envying him). No, no; anyway the underground life is more advantageous. There, at any rate, one can. . . . Oh, but even now I am lying! I am lying because I know myself that it is not underground that is better, but something different, quite different, for which I am thirsting, but which I cannot find! Damn underground!

I will tell you another thing that would be better, and that is, if I myself believed in anything of what I have just written. I swear to you, gentlemen, there is not one thing, not one word of what I have written, that I really believe. That is, I believe it, perhaps, but at the same time I feel and suspect that I am lying like a cobbler.

"Then why have you written all this?" you will say to me.

"I ought to put you underground for forty years without anything to do and then come to you in your cellar, to find out what stage you have reached! How can a man be left with nothing to do for forty years?

"Isn't that shameful, isn't that humiliating?" you will say, perhaps, wagging your heads contemptuously. "You thirst for life and try to settle the problems of life by a logical tangle. And how persistent, how insolent are your sallies, and at the same time what a scare you are in! You talk nonsense and are pleased with it; you say impudent things and are in continual alarm and apologizing for them. You declare that you are afraid of nothing and at the same time try to ingratiate yourself in our good opinion. You declare that you are gnashing your teeth and at the same time you try to be witty so as to amuse us. You know that your witticisms are not witty, but you are evidently well satisfied with their literary value. You may, perhaps, have really suffered, but you have no respect for your own suffering. You may have sincerity, but you have no modesty; out of the pettiest vanity you expose your sincerity to publicity and ignominy. You doubtlessly mean to say something, but hide your last word through fear, because you have not the resolution to uttter it, and only have a cowardly impudence. You boast of consciousness, but you are not sure of your ground, for though your mind works, yet your heart is darkened and corrupt, and you cannot have a full, genuine consciousness without a pure heart. And how intrusive you are, how you insist and grimace! Lies, lies, lies!"

Of course I have myself made up all the things you say. That, too, is from underground. I have been for forty years listening to you through a crack under the floor. I have invented them myself, there was nothing else I could invent. It is no wonder that I have learned it by heart and it has taken a literary form. . . .

But can you really be so credulous as to think that I will print all this and give it to you to read too? And another problem: why do I call you "gentlemen," why do I address you as though you really were my readers? Such confessions as I intend to make are never printed nor given to other people to read. Anyway, I am not strong-minded enough for that, and I don't see why I should be. But you see a fancy has occurred to me and I want to realize it at all costs. Let me explain.

Every man has reminiscences which he would not tell to every one, but only to his friends. He has other matters in his mind which he would not reveal even to his friends, but only to himself, and that in secret. But there are other things which a man is afraid to tell even to himself, and every decent man has a number of such things stored away in his mind. The more decent he is, the greater the number of such things in his mind. Anyway, I have only lately determined to remember some of my early adventures. Till now I have always avoided them, even with a certain uneasiness. Now, when I am not only recalling them, but have actually decided to write an account of them, I want to try the experiment whether one can, even with oneself, be perfectly open and not take fright at the whole truth. I will observe, in parenthesis, that Heine says that a true autobiography is almost an impossibility, and that man is bound to lie about himself. He considers that Rousseau certainly told lies about himself in his confessions, and even intentionally lied, out of vanity. I am convinced that Heine is right; I quite understand how sometimes one may, out of sheer vanity, attribute regular crimes to oneself, and indeed I can very well conceive that kind of vanity. But Heine judged of people who made their confessions to the public. I write only for myself, and I wish to declare once and for all that if I write as though I were addressing readers, that is simply because it is easier for me to write in that form. It is a form, an empty form — I shall never have readers. I have made this plain already. . . .

I don't wish to be hampered by any restrictions in the compilation of my notes. I shall not attempt any system or method. I will jot things down as I remember them.

But here, perhaps, some one will catch at the word and ask me: if you really don't reckon on readers, why do you make such compacts with yourself — and on paper too — that is, that you won't attempt any system or method, that you jot things down as you remember them, and so on, and so on? Why are you explaining? Why do you apologize?

Well, there it is, I answer.

There is a whole psychology in all this, though. Perhaps it is simply that I am a coward. And perhaps that I purposely imagine an audience before me in order that I may be more dignified while I write. There are perhaps thousands of reasons. Again, what is my object precisely in writing? If it is not for the benefit of the public why should I not simply recall these incidents in my own mind without putting them on paper?

Quite so; but yet it is more imposing on paper. There is something more impressive in it; I shall be better able to criticize myself and improve my style. Besides, I shall perhaps obtain actual relief from writing. To-day, for instance, I am particularly oppressed by one memory of a distant past. It came back vividly to my mind a few days ago, and has remained haunting me like an annoying tune that one cannot get rid of. And yet I must get rid of it somehow. I have hundreds of such reminiscences; but at times some one stands out from the hundred and oppresses me. For some reason I believe that if I write it down I should get rid of it. Why not try?

Besides, I am bored, and I never have anything to do. Writing will be a sort of work. They say work makes man kind-hearted and honest. Well, here is a chance for me, anyway.

Snow is falling to-day, yellow and dingy. It fell yesterday, too, and a few days ago. I fancy it is the wet snow that has reminded me of that incident which I cannot shake off now. And so let it be a story apropos of the falling snow.

PART 2. APROPOS OF THE WET SNOW

When from dark error's subjugation
My words of passionate exhortation
  Had wrenched thy fainting spirit free;
And writhing prone in thine affliction
Thou didst recall with malediction
  The vice that had encompassed thee:
And when thy slumbering conscience, fretting
  By recollection's torturing flame,
Thou didst reveal the hideous setting
  Of thy life's current ere I came:
When suddenly I saw thee sicken,
  And weeping, hide thine anguished face,
Revolted, maddened, horror-stricken,
  At memories of foul disgrace.

NEKRASSOV
(translated by Juliet Soskice)

I

At that time I was only twenty-four. My life was even then gloomy, ill-regulated, and as solitary as that of a savage. I made friends with no one and positively avoided talking, and buried myself more and more in my hole. At work in the office I never looked at any one, and I was perfectly well aware that my companions looked upon me, not only as a queer fellow, but even looked upon me — I always fancied this — with a sort of loathing. I sometimes wondered why it was that nobody except me fancied that he was looked upon with aversion. One of the clerks had a most repulsive, pock-marked face, which looked positively villainous. I believe I should not have dared to look at any one with such an unsightly countenance. Another had such a very dirty old uniform that there was an unpleasant odour in his proximity. Yet not one of these gentlemen showed the slightest self-consciousness — either about their clothes or their countenance or their character in any way. Neither of them ever imagined that they were looked at with repulsion; if they had imagined it they would not have minded — so long as their superiors did not look at them in that way. It is clear to me now that, owing to my unbounded vanity and to the high standard I set for myself, I often looked at myself with furious discontent, which verged on loathing, and so I inwardly attributed the same feeling to every one. I hated my face, for instance: I thought it disgusting, and even suspected that there was something base in my expression, and so every day when I turned up at the office I tried to behave as independently as possible, and to assume a lofty expression, so that I might not be suspected of being abject. "My face may be ugly," I thought, "but let it be lofty, expressive, and, above all, *extremely* intelligent." But I was positively and painfully certain that it was impossible for my countenance ever to express those qualities. And what was worst of all, I thought it actually stupid-looking, and I would have been quite satisfied if I could have looked intelligent. In fact, I would even have put up with looking base if, at the same time, my face could have been thought strikingly intelligent.

Of course, I hated my fellow-clerks one and all, and I despised them all, yet at the same time I was, as it were, afraid of them. In fact, it happened at times that I thought more highly of them than of myself. It somehow happened quite suddenly that I alternated between despising them and thinking them superior to myself. A cultivated and decent man cannot be vain without setting a fearfully high standard for himself, and without despising and almost hating himself at certain moments. But whether I despised them or thought them superior I dropped my eyes almost every time I met any one. I even made experiments whether I could face So-and-So's looking at me, and I was always the first to drop my eyes. This worried me to distraction. I had a sickly dread, too, of being ridiculous, and so had a slavish passion for the conventional in everything external. I loved to fall into the common rut, and had a whole-hearted terror of any kind of eccentricity in myself. But how could I live up to it? I was morbidly sensitive, as a man of our age should be. They were all stupid, and as like one another as so many sheep. Perhaps I was the only one in the office who fancied that I was a coward and a slave, and I fancied it just because I was more highly developed. But it was not only that I fancied it, it really was so. I was a coward and a slave. I say this without the slightest embarrassment. Every decent man of our age must be a coward and a slave. That is his normal condition. Of that I am firmly persuaded. He is made and constructed to that very end. And not only at the present time owing to some casual circumstances, but always, at all times, a decent man is bound to be a coward and a slave. It is the law of nature for all decent people all over the earth. If any one of them happens to be valiant about something, he need not be comforted nor carried away by that; he would show the white feather just the same before something else. That is how it invariably and inevitably ends. Only donkeys and mules are valiant, and they only till they are pushed up to the wall. It is not worth while to pay attention to them, for they really are of no consequence.

Another circumstance, too, worried me in those days: that there was no one like me and I was unlike any one else. "I am alone and they are *every one*," I thought — and pondered.

From that it is evident that I was still a youngster.

The very opposite sometimes happened. It was loathsome sometimes to go to the office; things reached such a point that I often came home ill. But all at once, apropos of nothing, there would come a phase of skepticism and indifference (everything happened in phases to me), and I would laugh myself at my intolerance and fastidiousness, I would reproach myself with being *romantic*. At one time I was unwilling to speak to any one, while at other times I would not only talk, but go to the length of contemplating making friends with them. All my fastidiousness would suddenly, for no rhyme or reason, vanish. Who knows, perhaps I never had really had it, and it had simply been affected, and got out of books. I have not decided that question even now. Once I quite made friends with them, visited their homes, played preference, drank vodka, talked of promotions. . . . But here let me make a digression.

We Russians, speaking generally, have never had those foolish transcendental "romantics" — German, and still more French — on whom nothing produces any effect; if there were an earthquake, if all France perished at the barricades, they would still be the same, they would not even have the decency to affect a change, but would still go on singing their transcendental songs to the hour of their death, because they are fools. We, in Russia, have no fools; that is well known. That is what distinguishes us from foreign lands. Consequently these transcendental natures are not found amongst us in their pure form. The idea that they are is due to our "realistic" journalists and critics of that day, always on the lookout for Kostanzhoglos and Uncle Pyotr Ivanitches[7] and foolishly ac-

7 [The first is a character in Gogol's *Dead Souls*, the second in Goncharov's *An Ordinary Story*. — Editors' note.]

cepting them as our ideal; they have slandered our romantics, taking them for the same transcendental sort as in Germany or France. On the contrary, the characteristics of our "romantics" are absolutely and directly opposed to the transcendental European type, and no European standard can be applied to them. (Allow me to make use of this word "romantic" — an old-fashioned and much respected word which has done good service and is familiar to all.) The characteristics of our romantics are to understand everything, *to see everything and to see it often incomparably more clearly than our most realistic minds see it;* to refuse to accept anyone or anything, but at the same time not to despise anything; to give way, to yield, from policy; never to lose sight of a useful practical object (such as rent-free quarters at the government expense, pensions, decorations), to keep their eye on that object through all the enthusiasms and volumes of lyrical poems, and at the same time to preserve "the good and the beautiful" inviolate within them to the hour of their death, and to preserve themselves also, incidentally, like some precious jewel wrapped in cotton wool if only for the benefit of "the good and the beautiful." Our "romantic" is a man of great breadth and the greatest rogue of all our rogues, I assure you. . . . I can assure you from experience, indeed. Of course, that is, if he is intelligent. But what am I saying! The romantic is always intelligent, and I only meant to observe that although we have had foolish romantics they don't count, and they were only so because in the flower of their youth they degenerated into Germans, and to preserve their precious jewel more comfortably, settled somewhere out there — by preference in Weimar or the Black Forest.

I, for instance, genuinely despised my official work and did not openly abuse it simply because I was in it myself and got a salary for it. Anyway, take note, I did not openly abuse it. Our romantic would rather go out of his mind — a thing, however, which very rarely happens — than take to open abuse, unless he had some other career in view; and he is never kicked out. At most, they would take him to the lunatic asylum as "the King of Spain" if he should go very mad. But it is only the thin, fair people who go out of their minds in Russia. Innumerable "romantics" attain later in life to considerable rank in the service. Their many-sidedness is remarkable! And what a faculty they have for the most contradictory sensations! I was comforted by this thought even in those days, and I am of the same opinion now. That is why there are so many "broad natures" among us who never lose their ideal even in the depths of degradation; and though they never stir a finger for their ideal, though they are arrant thieves and knaves, yet they tearfully cherish their first ideal and are extraordinarily honest at heart. Yes, it is only among us that the most incorrigible rogue can be absolutely and loftily honest at heart without in the least ceasing to be a rogue. I repeat, our romantics, frequently, become such accomplished rascals (I use the term "rascals" affectionately), suddenly display such a sense of reality and practical knowledge, that their bewildered superiors and the public generally can only ejaculate in amazement.

Their many-sidedness is really amazing, and goodness knows what it may develop into later on, and what the future has in store for us. It is not a poor material! I do not say this from any foolish or boastful patriotism. But I feel sure that you are again imagining that I am joking. Or perhaps it's just the contrary, and you are convinced that I really think so. Anyway, gentlemen, I shall welcome both views as an honour and a special favour. And do forgive my digression.

I did not, of course, maintain friendly relations with my comrades and soon was at loggerheads with them, and in my youth and inexperience I even gave up bowing to them, as though I had cut off all relations. That, however, only happened to me once. As a rule, I was always alone.

In the first place I spent most of my time at home, reading. I tried to stifle all that was continually seething within me by means of external impressions. And the only external means I had was reading. Reading, of course, was a great help — exciting me, giving me pleasure and pain. But at times it bored me fearfully. One longed for movement in spite of everything, and I plunged all at once into dark, underground, loathsome vice of the pettiest kind. My wretched passions were acute, smarting, from my continual, sickly irritability. I had hysterical impulses, with tears and convulsions. I had no resources except reading — that is, there was nothing in my surroundings which I could respect and which attracted me. I was overwhelmed with depression, too; I had an hysterical craving for incongruity and for contrast, and so I took to vice. I have not said all this to justify myself.... But, no! I am lying. I did want to justify myself. I make that little observation for my own benefit, gentlemen. I don't want to lie. I vowed to myself I would not.

And so, furtively, timidly, in solitude, at night, I indulged in filthy vice, with a feeling of shame which never deserted me, even at the most loathsome moments, and which at such moments nearly made me curse. Already even then I had my underground world in my soul. I was fearfully afraid of being seen, of being met, of being recognized. I visited various obscure haunts.

One night as I was passing a tavern I saw through a lighted window some gentlemen fighting with billiard cues, and saw one of them thrown out of the window. At other times I should have felt very much disgusted, but I was in such a mood at the time, that I actually envied the gentleman thrown out of the window — and I envied him so much that I even went into the tavern and into the billiard-room. "Perhaps," I thought, "I'll have a fight, too, and they'll throw me out of the window."

I was not drunk — but what is one to do — depression will drive a man to such a pitch of hysteria? But nothing happened. It seemed that I was not even equal to being thrown out of the window and I went away without having my fight.

An officer put me in my place from the first moment.

I was standing by the billiard-table and in my ignorance blocking up the way, and he wanted to pass; he took me by the shoulders and without a word — without a warning or an explanation — moved me from where I was standing to another spot and passed by as though he had not noticed me. I could have forgiven blows, but I could not forgive his having moved me without noticing me.

Devil knows what I would have given for a real regular quarrel — a more decent, a more *literary* one, so to speak. I had been treated like a fly. This officer was over six foot, while I was a spindly little fellow. But the quarrel was in my hands. I had only to protest and I certainly would have been thrown out of the window. But I changed my mind and preferred to beat a resentful retreat.

I went out of the tavern straight home, confused and troubled, and the next night I went out again with the same lewd intentions, still more furtively, abjectly and miserably than before, as it were, with tears in my eyes — but still I did go out again. Don't imagine, though, it was cowardice made me slink away from the officer: I never have been a coward at heart, though I have always been a coward in action. Don't be in a hurry to laugh — I assure you I can explain it all.

Oh, if only that officer had been one of the sort who would consent to fight a duel! But no, he was one of those gentlemen (alas, long extinct!) who preferred fighting with cues, or, like Gogol's Lieutenant Pirogov, appealing to the police. They did not fight duels and would have thought a duel with a civilian like me an utterly unseemly procedure in any case — and they looked upon the duel altogether as something impossible, something free-thinking and French. But they were quite ready to bully, especially when they were over six foot.

I did not slink away through cowardice, but through an unbounded vanity. I was afraid not of his six foot, not of getting a sound thrashing and being thrown out of the window; I should have had physical courage enough, I assure you; but I had not the moral courage. What I was afraid of was that every one present, from the insolent marker down to the lowest little stinking, pimply clerk in a greasy collar, would jeer at me and fail to understand when I began to protest and to address them in literary language. For of the point of honour — not of honour, but of the point of honour *(point d'honneur)* — one cannot speak among us except in literary language. You can't allude to the "point of honour" in ordinary language. I was fully convinced (the sense of reality, in spite of all my romanticism!) that they would all simply split their sides with laughter, and that the officer would not simply beat me, that is, without insulting me, but would certainly prod me in the back with his knee, kick me round the billiard-table, and only then perhaps have pity and drop me out of the window.

Of course, this trivial incident could not with me end in that. I often met that officer afterwards in the street and noticed him very carefully. I am not quite sure whether he recognized me, I imagine not; I judge from certain signs. But I — I stared at him with spite and hatred and so it went on . . . for several years! My resentment grew even deeper with years. At first I began making stealthy inquiries about this officer. It was difficult for me to do so, for I knew no one. But one day I heard some one shout his surname in the street as I was following him at a distance, as though I were tied to him — and so I learnt his surname. Another time I followed him to his flat, and for ten kopecks learnt from the porter where he lived, on which storey, whether he lived alone or with others, and so on — in fact, everything one could learn from a porter. One morning, though I had never tried my hand with the pen, it suddenly occurred to me to write a satire on this officer in the form of a novel which would unmask his villainy. I wrote the novel with relish. I did unmask his villainy, I even exaggerated it; at first I so altered his surname that it could easily be recognized, but on second thoughts I changed it, and sent the story to the *Otetchestvenniya Zapiski*. But at that time such attacks were not the fashion and my story was not printed. That was a great vexation to me.

Sometimes I was positively choked with resentment. At last I determined to challenge my enemy to a duel. I composed a splendid, charming letter to him, imploring him to apologize to me, and hinting rather plainly at a duel in case of refusal. The letter was so composed that if the officer had had the least understanding of the good and the beautiful he would certainly have flung himself on my neck and have offered me his friendship. And how fine that would have been! How we should have got on together! "He could have shielded me with his higher rank, while I could have improved his mind with my culture, and, well . . . my ideas, and all sorts of things might have happened." Only fancy, this was two years after his insult to me, and my challenge would have been a ridiculous anachronism, in spite of all the ingenuity of my letter in disguising and explaining away the anachronism. But, thank God (to this day I thank the Almighty with tears in my eyes) I did not send the letter to him. Cold shivers run down my back when I think of what might have happened if I had sent it.

And all at once I revenged myself in the simplest way, by a stroke of genius!

A brilliant thought suddenly dawned upon me. Sometimes on holidays I used to stroll along the sunny side of the Nevsky about four o'clock in the afternoon. Though it was hardly a stroll so much as a series of innumerable miseries, humiliations and resentments; but no doubt that was just what I wanted. I used to wriggle along in a most unseemly fashion, like an eel, continually moving aside to make way for generals, for officers of the Guards and the Hussars, or for ladies. At such minutes there used to be a convulsive twinge at my heart, and I used to feel hot all down my back at the mere thought of the wretchedness of my attire, of the wretchedness and abjectness of my little scurrying figure. This was a regular martyrdom, a continual, intolerable humiliation at the thought, which passed into an incessant and direct sensation, that I was a mere fly in the eyes of all this world, a nasty, disgusting fly — more intelligent, more highly developed, more refined in feeling than any of them, of course, but a fly that was continually making way for every one, insulted and injured by every one. Why I inflicted this torture upon myself, why I went to the Nevsky, I don't know. I felt simply drawn there at every possible opportunity.

Already then I began to experience a rush of the enjoyment of which I spoke in the first chapter. After my affair with the officer I felt even more drawn there than before: it was on the Nevsky that I met him most frequently, there I could admire him. He, too, went there chiefly on holidays. He, too, turned out of his path for generals and persons of high rank, and he, too, wriggled between them like an eel; but people like me, or even better dressed than me, he simply walked over; he made straight for them as though there was nothing but empty space before him, and never, under any circumstances, turned aside. I gloated over my resentment watching him and . . . always resentfully made way for him. It exasperated me that even in the street I could not be on an even footing with him.

"Why must you invariably be the first to move aside?" I kept asking myself in hysterical rage, waking up sometimes at three o'clock in the morning. "Why is it you and not he? There's no regulation about it; there's no written law. Let the making way be equal as it usually is when refined people meet: he moves half-way and you move half-way; you pass with mutual respect."

But that never happened, and I always moved aside, while he did not even notice my making way for him. And lo and behold a bright idea dawned upon me! "What," I thought, "if I meet him and don't move on one side? What if I don't move aside on purpose, even if I knock up against him? How would that be?" This audacious idea took such a hold on me that it gave me no peace. I was dreaming of it continually, horribly, and I purposely went more frequently to the Nevsky in order to picture more vividly how I should do it when I did do it. I was delighted. This intention seemed to me more and more practical and possible.

"Of course I shall not really push him," I thought, already more good-natured in my joy. "I will simply not turn aside, will run up against him, not very violently, but just shouldering each other — just as much as decency permits. I will push against him just as much as he pushes against me." At last I made up my mind completely. But my preparations took a great deal of time. To begin with, when I carried out my plan I should need to be looking rather more decent, and so I had to think of my get-up. "In case of emergency, if, for instance, there were any sort of public scandal (and the public there is of the most *recherché:* the Countess walks there; Prince D. walks there; all the literary world is there), I must be well dressed; that inspires respect and of itself puts us on an equal footing in the eyes of society."

With this object I asked for some of my salary in advance, and bought at Tchurkin's a pair of black gloves and a decent hat. Black gloves seemed to me both more dignified and *bon ton* than the lemon-coloured ones which I had contemplated at first. "The colour is too gaudy, it looks as though one were trying to be conspicuous," and I did not take the lemon-coloured ones. I had got ready long beforehand a good shirt, with white bone studs; my overcoat was the only thing that held me back. The coat in itself was a very good one, it kept me warm; but it was wadded and it had a raccoon collar which was the height of vulgarity. I had to change the collar at any sacrifice, and to have a beaver one like an officer's. For this purpose I began visiting the Gostiny Dvor and after several attempts I pitched upon a piece of cheap German beaver. Though these German beavers soon grow shabby and look wretched, yet at first they look exceedingly well, and I only needed it for one occasion. I asked the price; even so, it was too expensive. After thinking it over thoroughly I decided to sell my raccoon collar. The rest of the money — a considerable sum for me, I decided to borrow from Anton Antonitch Syetotchkin, my immediate superior, an unassuming person, though grave and judicious. He never lent money to any one, but I had, on entering the service, been specially recommended to him by an important personage who had got me my berth. I was horribly worried. To borrow from Anton Antonitch seemed to me monstrous and shameful. I did not sleep for two or three nights. Indeed, I did not sleep well at that time, I was in a fever; I had a vague sinking at my heart or else a sudden throbbing, throbbing, throbbing! Anton Antonitch was surprised at first, then he frowned, then he reflected, and did after all lend me the money, receiving from me a written authorization to take from my salary a fortnight later the sum that he had lent me.

In this way everything was at last ready. The handsome beaver replaced the mean-looking raccoon, and I began by degrees to get to work. It would never have done to act off-hand, at random; the plan had to be carried out skillfully, by degrees. But I must confess that after many efforts I began to despair: we simply could not run into each other. I made every preparation, I was quite determined — it seemed as though we should run into one another directly — and before I knew what I was doing I had stepped aside for him again and he had passed without noticing me. I even prayed as I approached him that God would grant me determination. One time I had made up my mind thoroughly, but it ended in my stumbling and falling at his feet because at the very last instant when I was six inches from him my courage failed me. He very calmly stepped over me, while I flew on one side like a ball. That night I was ill again, feverish and delirious.

And suddenly it ended most happily. The night before I had made up my mind not to carry out my fatal plan and to abandon it all, and with that object I went to the Nevsky for the last time, just to see how I would abandon it all. Suddenly, three paces from my enemy, I unexpectedly made up my mind — I closed my eyes, and we ran full tilt, shoulder to shoulder, against one another! I did not budge an inch and passed him on a perfectly equal footing! He did not even look round and pretended not to notice it; but he was only pretending, I am convinced of that. I am convinced of that to this day! Of course, I got the worst of it — he was stronger, but that was not the point. The point was that I had attained my object, I had kept up my dignity, I had not yielded a step, and had put myself publicly on an equal social footing with him. I returned home feeling that I was fully avenged for everything. I was delighted. I was triumphant and sang Italian arias. Of course, I will not describe to you what happened to me three days later; if you have read my first chapter you can guess that for yourself. The officer was afterwards transferred; I have not seen him now for fourteen years. What is the dear fellow doing now? Whom is he walking over?

II

But the period of my dissipation would end and I always felt very sick afterwards. It was followed by remorse — I tried to drive it away: I felt too sick. By degrees, however, I grew used to that too. I grew used to everything, or rather I voluntarily resigned myself to enduring it. But I had a means of escape that reconciled everything — that was to find refuge in "the good and the beautiful," in dreams, of course. I was a terrible dreamer, I would dream for three months on end, tucked away in my corner, and you may believe me that at those moments I had no resemblance to the gentleman who, in the perturbation of his chicken heart, put a collar of German beaver on his greatcoat. I suddenly became a hero. I would not have admitted my six-foot lieutenant even if he had called on me. I could not even picture him before me then. What were my dreams and how I could satisfy myself with them, it is hard to say now, but at the time I was satisfied with them. Though, indeed, even now I am to some extent satisfied with them. Dreams were particularly sweet and vivid after a spell of dissipation; they came with remorse and with tears, with curses and transports. There were moments of such positive intoxication, of such happiness, that there was not the faintest trace of irony within me, on my honour. I had faith, hope, love. I believed blindly at such times that by some miracle, by some external circumstance, all this would suddenly open out, expand; that suddenly a vista of suitable activity — beneficent, good, and, above all, *ready-made* (what sort of activity I had no idea, but the great thing was that it should be all ready for me) — would rise up before me, and I should come out into the light of day, almost riding a white horse and crowned with laurel. Anything but the foremost place I could not conceive for myself, and for that very reason I quite contentedly occupied the lowest in reality. Either to be a hero or to grovel in the mud — there was nothing between. That was my ruin, for when I was in the mud I comforted myself with the thought that at other times I was a hero, and the hero was a cloak for the mud: for an ordinary man it was shameful to defile himself, but a hero was too lofty to be utterly defiled, and so he might defile himself. It is worth noting that these attacks of "the good and the beautiful" visited me even during the period of dissipation and just at the times when I was touching the bottom. They came in separate spurts, as though reminding me of themselves, but did not banish the dissipation by their appearance. On the contrary, they seemed to add a zest to it by contrast, and were only sufficiently present to serve as an appetizing sauce. That sauce was made up of contradictions and sufferings, of agonizing inward analysis, and all these pangs and pinpricks gave a certain piquancy, even a significance to my dissipation — in fact, completely answered the purpose of an appetizing sauce. There was a certain depth of meaning in it. And I could hardly have resigned myself to the simple, vulgar, direct debauchery of a clerk and have endured all the filthiness of it. What could have allured me about it then and have drawn me at night into the street? No, I had a lofty way of getting out of it all.

And what loving-kindness, oh Lord, what loving-kindness I felt at times in those dreams of mine! in those "flights into the good and the beautiful"; though it was fantastic love, though it was never applied to anything human in reality, yet there was so much of this love that one did not feel afterwards even the impulse to apply it in reality; that would have been superfluous. Everything, however, passed satisfactorily by a lazy and fascinating transition into the sphere of art, that is, into the beautiful forms of life, lying ready, largely stolen from the poets and novelists and adapted to all sorts of needs and uses. I, for instance, was triumphant over every one; every one, of course, was in dust and ashes, and was forced spontaneously to recognize my superiority, and I forgave them all. I was a poet and a grand gentleman, I fell in love; I came in for countless millions and immediately devoted them to humanity, and at the same time I confessed before all the people my shameful deeds, which, of course, were not merely shameful, but had in them much that was "good and beautiful," something in the Manfred[8] style. Every one would kiss me and weep (what idiots they would be if they did not), while I should go barefoot and hungry preaching new ideas and fighting a victorious Austerlitz against the obscurantists. Then the band would play a march, an amnesty would be declared, the Pope would agree to retire from Rome to Brazil; then there would be a ball for the whole of Italy at the Villa Borghese on the shores of Lake Como, Lake Como being for that purpose transferred to the neighbourhood of Rome; then would come a scene in the bushes, and so on, and so on — as though you did not know all about it!

You will say that it is vulgar and contemptible to drag all this into public after all the tears and transports which I have myself confessed. But why is it contemptible? Can you imagine that I am ashamed of it all, and that it was stupider than anything in your life, gentlemen? And I can assure you that some of these fancies were by no means badly composed. . . . It did not all happen on the shores of Lake Como. And yet you are right — it really is vulgar and contemptible. And most contemptible of all it is that now I am attempting to justify myself to you. And even more contemptible than that is my making this remark now. But that's enough, or there will be no end to it: each step will be more contemptible than the last. . . .

I could never stand more than three months of dreaming at a time without feeling an irresistible desire to plunge into society. To plunge into society meant to visit my superior at the office, Anton Antonitch Syetotchkin. He was the only permanent acquaintance I have had in my life, and I wonder at the fact myself now. But I only went to see him when that phase came over me, and when my dreams had reached such a point of bliss that it became essential at once to embrace my fellows and all mankind; and for that purpose I needed at least one human being, actually existing. I had to call on Anton Antonitch, however, on Tuesday — his at-home day; so I had always to time my passionate desire to embrace humanity so that it might fall on a Tuesday.

This Anton Antonitch lived on the fourth storey in a house in Five Corners, in four low-pitched rooms, one smaller than the other, of a particularly frugal and sallow appearance. He had two daughters and their aunt, who used to pour out the tea. Of the daughters one was thirteen and another fourteen, they both had snub noses, and I was awfully shy of them because they were always whis-

8 [The guilt-ridden romantic hero in a dramatic poem (1817) by Byron. — Editors' note.]

pering and giggling together. The master of the house usually sat in his study on a leather couch in front of the table with some grey-headed gentleman, usually a colleague from our office or some other department. I never saw more than two or three visitors there, always the same. They talked about the excise duty, about business in the senate, about salaries, about promotions, about His Excellency, and the best means of pleasing him, and so on. I had the patience to sit like a fool beside these people for four hours at a stretch, listening to them without knowing what to say to them or venturing to say a word. I became stupefied, several times I felt myself perspiring, I was overcome by a sort of paralysis; but this was pleasant and good for me. On returning home I deferred for a time my desire to embrace all mankind.

I had, however, one other acquaintance of a sort, Simonov, who was an old schoolfellow. I had a number of schoolfellows indeed in Petersburg, but I did not associate with them and had even given up nodding to them in the street. I believe I had transferred into the department I was in simply to avoid their company and to cut off all connection with my hateful childhood. Curses on that school and all those terrible years of penal servitude! In short, I parted from my schoolfellows as soon as I got out into the world. There were two or three left to whom I nodded in the street. One of them was Simonov, who had been in no way distinguished at school, was of a quiet and equable disposition; but I discovered in him a certain independence of character and even honesty. I don't even suppose that he was particularly stupid. I had at one time spent some rather soulful moments with him, but these had not lasted long and had somehow been suddenly clouded over. He was evidently uncomfortable at these reminiscences, and was, I fancy, always afraid that I might take up the same tone again. I suspected that he had an aversion for me, but still I went on going to see him, not being quite certain of it.

And so on one occasion, unable to endure my solitude and knowing that as it was Thursday Anton Antonitch's door would be closed, I thought of Simonov. Climbing up to his fourth storey I was thinking that the man disliked me and tnat it was a mistake to go and see him. But as it always happened that such reflections impelled me, as though purposely, to put myself into a false position, I went in. It was almost a year since I had last seen Simonov.

III

I found two of my old schoolfellows with him. They seemed to be discussing an important matter. All of them took scarcely any notice of my entrance, which was strange, for I had not met them for years. Evidently they looked upon me as something on the level of a common fly. I had not been treated like that even at school, though they all hated me. I knew, of course, that they must despise me now for my lack of success in the service, and for my having let myself sink so low, going about badly dressed and so on — which seemed to them a sign of my incapacity and insignificance. But I had not expected such contempt. Simonov was positively surprised at my turning up. Even in the old days he had always seemed surprised at my coming. All this disconcerted me: I sat down, feeling rather miserable, and began listening to what they were saying.

They were engaged in warm and earnest conversation about a farewell dinner which they wanted to arrange for the next day to a comrade of theirs called Zverkov, an officer in the army, who was going away to a distant province. This Zverkov had been all the time at school with me too. I had begun to hate him particularly in the upper forms. In the lower forms he had simply been a pretty, playful boy whom everybody liked. I had hated him, however, even in the lower forms, just because he was a pretty and playful boy. He was always bad at his lessons and got worse and worse as he went on; however, he left with a good certificate, as he had powerful interest. During his last year at school he came in for an estate of two hundred serfs, and as almost all of us were poor he took up a swaggering tone among us. He was vulgar in the extreme, but at the same time he was a good-natured fellow, even in his swaggering. In spite of superficial, fantastic and sham notions of honour and dignity, all but very few of us positively grovelled before Zverkov, and the more so the more he swaggered. And it was not from any interested motive that they grovelled, but simply because he had been favoured by the gifts of nature. Moreover, it was, as it were, an accepted idea among us that Zverkov was a specialist in regard to tact and the social graces. This last fact particularly infuriated me. I hated the abrupt self-confident tone of his voice, his admiration of his own witticisms, which were often frightfully stupid, though he was bold in his language; I hated his handsome but stupid face (for which I would, however, have gladly exchanged my intelligent one), and the free-and-easy military manners in fashion in the "forties." I hated the way in which he used to talk of his future conquests of women (he did not venture to begin his attack upon women until he had the epaulettes of an officer, and was looking forward to them with impatience), and boasted of the duels he would constantly be fighting. I remember how I, invariably so taciturn, suddenly fastened upon Zverkov, when one day talking at a leisure moment with his schoolfellows of his future relations with the fair sex, and growing as sportive as a puppy in the sun, he all at once declared that he would not leave a single village girl on his estate unnoticed, that that was his *droit de seigneur*,[9] and that

9 [Lord's privilege. — Editors' note.]

if the peasants dared to protest he would have them all flogged and double the tax on them, the bearded rascals. Our servile rabble applauded, but I attacked him, not from compassion for the girls and their fathers, but simply because they were applauding such an insect. I got the better of him on that occasion, but though Zverkov was stupid he was lively and impudent, and so laughed it off, and in such a way that my victory was not really complete: the laugh was on his side. He got the better of me on several occasions afterwards, but without malice, jestingly, casually. I remained angrily and contemptuously silent and would not answer him. When we left school he made advances to me; I did not rebuff them, for I was flattered, but we soon parted and quite naturally. Afterwards I heard of his barrack-room success as a lieutenant, and of the fast life he was leading. Then there came other rumours — of his successes in the service. By then he had taken to cutting me in the street, and I suspected that he was afraid of compromising himself by greeting a personage as insignificant as I. I saw him once in the theatre, in the third tier of boxes. By then he was wearing shoulder-straps. He was twisting and twirling about, ingratiating himself with the daughters of an ancient general. In three years he had gone off considerably, though he was still rather handsome and adroit. One could see that by the time he was thirty he would be corpulent. So it was to this Zverkov that my schoolfellows were going to give a dinner on his departure. They had kept up with him for those three years, though privately they did not consider themselves on an equal footing with him, I am convinced of that.

Of Simonov's two visitors, one was Ferfitchkin, a Russianized German — a little fellow with the face of a monkey, a blockhead who was always deriding every one, a very bitter enemy of mine from our days in the lower forms — a vulgar, impudent, swaggering fellow, who affected a most sensitive feeling of personal honour, though, of course, he was a wretched little coward at heart. He was one of those worshippers of Zverkov who made up to the latter from interested motives, and often borrowed money from him. Simonov's other visitor, Trudolyubov, was a person in no way remarkable — a tall young fellow, in the army, with a cold face, fairly honest, though he worshipped success of every sort, and was only capable of thinking of promotion. He was some sort of distant relative of Zverkov's, and this, foolish as it seems, gave him a certain importance among us. He always thought me of no consequence whatever; his behaviour to me, though not quite courteous, was tolerable.

"Well, with seven roubles each," said Trudolyubov, "twenty-one roubles between the three of us, we ought to be able to get a good dinner. Zverkov, of course, won't pay."

"Of course not, since we are inviting him," Simonov decided.

"Can you imagine," Ferfitchkin interrupted hotly and conceitedly, like some insolent flunkey boasting of his master the general's decorations, "can you imagine that Zverkov will let us pay alone? He will accept from delicacy, but he will order half a dozen bottles of champagne."

"Do we want half a dozen for the four of us? observed Trudolyubov, taking notice only of the half-dozen.

"So the three of us, with Zverkov for the fourth, twenty-one roubles, at the Hôtel de Paris at five o'clock to-morrow," Simonov, who had been asked to make the arrangements, concluded finally.

"How twenty-one roubles?" I asked in some agitation, with a show of being offended; "if you count me it will not be twenty-one, but twenty-eight roubles."

It seemed to me that to invite myself so suddenly and unexpectedly would be positively graceful, and that they would all be conquered at once and would look at me with respect.

"Do you want to join, too?" Simonov observed, with no appearance of pleasure, seeming to avoid looking at me. He knew me through and through.

It infuriated me that he knew me so thoroughly.

"Why not? I am an old schoolfellow of his too, I believe, and I must own I feel hurt that you have left me out," I said, boiling over again.

"And where were we to find you?" Ferfitchkin put in roughly.

"You never were on good terms with Zverkov," Trudolyubov added, frowning.

But I had already clutched at the idea and would not give it up.

"It seems to me that no one has a right to form an opinion upon that," I retorted in a shaking voice, as though something tremendous had happened. "Perhaps that is just my reason for wishing it now, that I have not always been on good terms with him."

"Oh, there's no making you out . . . with these refinements," Trudolyubov jeered.

"We'll put your name down," Simonov decided, addressing me. "To-morrow at five o'clock at the Hôtel de Paris."

"What about the money?" Ferfitchkin began in an undertone, indicating me to Simonov, but he broke off, for even Simonov was embarrassed.

"That will do," said Trudolyubov, getting up. "If he wants to come so much, let him."

"But it's a private thing, between us friends," Ferfitchkin said crossly, as he too picked up his hat. "It's not an official gathering."

"We do not want at all, perhaps. . . ."

They went away. Ferfitchkin did not greet me in any way as he went out, Trudolyubov barely nodded. Simonov, with whom I was left *tête-à-tête*, was in a state of vexation and perplexity, and looked at me queerly. He did not sit down and did not ask me to.

"H'm . . . yes . . . to-morrow, then. Will you pay your subscription now? I just ask so as to know," he muttered in embarrassment.

I flushed crimson, and as I did so I remembered that I had owed Simonov fifteen roubles for ages — which I had, indeed, never forgotten, though I had not paid it.

"You will understand, Simonov, that I could have no idea when I came here . . . I am very much vexed that I have forgotten. . . ."

"All right, all right, that doesn't matter. You can pay to-morrow after the dinner. I simply wanted to know. . . . Please don't . . ."

He broke off and began pacing the room still more vexed. As he walked he began to stamp with his heels.

"Am I keeping you?" I asked, after two minutes of silence.

"Oh!" he said, starting, "that is — to be truthful — yes. I have to go and see some one . . . not far from here," he added in an apologetic voice, somewhat abashed.

"My goodness, why didn't you say so?" I cried, seizing my cap with an astonishingly free-and-easy air, which was the last thing I should have expected of myself.

"It's close by . . . not two paces away," Simonov repeated, accompanying me to the front door with a fussy air which did not suit him at all. "So five o'clock, punctually, to-morrow," he called down the stairs after me. He was very glad to get rid of me. I was in a fury.

"What possessed me, what possessed me to force myself upon them?" I wondered, grinding my teeth as I strode along the street. "For a scoundrel, a pig like that Zverkov! Of course, I had better not go; of course, I must just snap my fingers at them. I am not bound in any way. I'll send Simonov a note by to-morrow's post. . . ."

But what made me furious was that I knew for certain that I should go, that I should make a point of going; and the more tactless, the more unseemly my going would be, the more certainly I would go.

And there was a positive obstacle to my going: I had no money. All I had was nine roubles, I had to give seven of that to my servant, Apollon, for his monthly wages. That was all I paid him — he had to keep himself.

Not to pay him was impossible, considering his character. But I will talk about that fellow, about that plague of mine, another time.

However, I knew I should go and should not pay him his wages.

That night I had the most hideous dreams. No wonder; all the evening I had been oppressed by memories of my miserable days at school, and I could not shake them off. I was sent to the school by distant relations, upon whom I was dependent and of whom I have heard nothing since — they sent me there a forlorn, silent boy, already crushed by their reproaches, already troubled by doubt, and looking with savage distrust at every one. My schoolfellows met me with spiteful and merciless jibes because I was not like any of them. But I could not endure their taunts; I could not give in to them with the ignoble readiness with which they gave in to one another. I hated them from the first, and shut myself away from every one in timid, wounded and disproportionate pride. Their coarseness revolted me. They laughed cynically at my face, at my clumsy figure; and yet what stupid faces they had themselves. In our school the boys' faces seemed in a special way to degenerate and grow stupider. How many fine-looking boys came to us! In a few years they became repulsive. Even at sixteen I wondered at them morosely; even then I was struck by the pettiness of their thoughts, the stupidity of their pursuits, their games, their conversations. They had no understanding of such essential things, they took no interest in such striking, impressive subjects, that I could not help considering them inferior to myself. It was not wounded vanity that drove me to it, and for God's sake do not thrust upon me your hackneyed remarks, repeated to nausea, that "I was only a dreamer," while they even then had an understanding of life. They understood nothing, they had no idea of real life, and I swear that that was what made me most indignant with them. On the contrary, the most obvious, striking reality they accepted with fantastic stupidity and even at that time were accustomed to respect success. Everything that was just, but oppressed and looked down upon, they laughed at heartlessly and shamefully. They took rank for intelligence; even at sixteen they were already talking about a snug berth. Of course a great deal of it was due to their stupidity, to the bad examples with which they had always been surrounded in their childhood and boyhood. They were monstrously depraved. Of course a great deal of that, too, was superficial and an assumption of cynicism; of course there were glimpses of youth and freshness even in their depravity; but even that freshness was not attractive, and showed itself in a certain rakishness. I hated them horribly, though perhaps I was worse than any of them. They repaid me in the same way, and did not conceal their aversion for me. But by then I did not desire their affection: on the contrary I continually longed for their humiliation. To escape from their derision I purposely began to make all the progress I could with my studies and forced my way to the very top. This impressed them.

Moreover, they all began by degrees to grasp that I had already read books none of them could read, and understood things (not forming part of our school curriculum) of which they had not even heard. They took a savage and sarcastic view of it, but were morally impressed, especially as the teachers began to notice me on those grounds. The mockery ceased, but the hostility remained, and cold and strained relations became permanent between us. In the end I could not put up with it: with years a craving for society, for friends, developed in me. I attempted to get on friendly terms with some of my schoolfellows; but somehow or other my intimacy with them was always strained and soon ended of itself. Once, indeed, I did have a friend. But I was already a tyrant at heart; I wanted to exercise unbounded sway over him; I tried to instill into him a contempt for his surroundings; I required of him a disdainful and complete break with those surroundings. I frightened him with my passionate affection; I reduced him to tears, to hysterics. He was a simple and devoted soul; but when he devoted himself to me entirely I began to hate him immediately and repulsed him — as though all I needed him for was to win a victory over him, to subjugate him and nothing else. But I could not subjugate all of them; my friend was not at all like them either, he was, in fact, a rare exception. The first thing I did on leaving school was to give up the special job for which I had been destined so as to break all ties, to curse my past and shake the dust from off my feet. . . . And goodness knows why, after all that, I should go trudging off to Simonov's!

Early next morning I roused myself and jumped out of bed with excitement, as though it were all about to happen at once. But I believed that some radical change in my life was coming, and would inevitably come that day. Owing to its rarity, perhaps, any external event, however trivial, always made me feel as though some radical change in my life were at hand. I went to the office, however, as usual, but sneaked away home two hours earlier to get ready. The great thing, I thought, is not to be the first to arrive, or they will think I am overjoyed at coming. But there were thousands of such great points to consider, and they all agitated and overwhelmed me. I polished my boots a second time with my own hands; nothing in the world would have induced Apollon to clean them twice a day, as he considered that it was more than his duties required of him. I stole the brushes to clean them from the passage, being careful he should not detect it, for fear of his contempt. Then I minutely examined my clothes and thought that everything looked old, worn and threadbare. I had let myself get too slovenly. My uniform, perhaps, was tidy, but I could not go out to dinner in my uniform. The worst of it was that on the knee of my trousers was a big yellow stain. I had a foreboding that that stain would deprive me of nine-tenths of my personal dignity. I knew, too, that it was very poor to think so. "But this is no time for thinking: now I am in for the real thing," I thought, and my heart sank. I knew, too, perfectly well even then, that I was monstrously exaggerating the facts. But how could I help it? I could not control myself and was already shaking with fever. With despair I pictured to myself how coldly and disdainfully that "scoundrel" Zverkov would meet me; with what dull-witted, invincible contempt the blockhead Trudolyubov would look at me; with what impudent rudeness the insect Ferfitchkin would snigger at me in order to curry favour with Zverkov; how completely Simonov would take it all in, and how he would despise me for the abjectness of my vanity and lack of spirit — and, worst of all, how paltry, *unliterary*, commonplace it would all be.

Of course, the best thing would be not to go at all. But that was most impossible of all: if I feel impelled to do anything, I seem to be pitch-forked into it. I should have jeered at myself ever afterwards: "So you funked it, you funked it, you funked the *real thing!*" On the contrary, I passionately longed to show all that "rabble" that I was by no means such a spiritless creature as I seemed to myself. What is more, even in the acutest paroxysm of this cowardly fever, I dreamed of getting the upper hand, of dominating them, carrying them away, making them like me — if only for my "elevation of thought and unmistakable wit." They would abandon Zverkov, he would sit on one side, silent and ashamed, while I should crush him. Then, perhaps, we would be reconciled and drink to our everlasting friendship; but what was most bitter and most humiliating for me was that I knew even then, knew fully and for certain, that I needed nothing of all this really, that I did not really want to crush, to subdue, to attract them, and that I did not care a straw really for the result, even if I did achieve it. Oh, how I prayed for the day to pass quickly! In unutterable anguish I went to the window, opened the movable pane and looked out into the troubled darkness of the thickly falling wet snow. At last my wretched little clock hissed out five. I seized my hat and trying not to look at Apollon, who had been all day expecting his month's wages, but in his foolishness was unwilling to be the first to speak about it, I slipt between him and the door and jumping into a high-class sledge, on which I spent my last half-rouble, I drove up in grand style to the Hôtel de Paris.

IV

I had been certain the day before that I should be the first to arrive. But it was not a question of being the first to arrive. Not only were they not there, but I had difficulty in finding our room. The table was not laid even. What did it mean? After a good many questions I elicited from the waiters that the dinner had been ordered not for five, but for six o'clock. This was confirmed at the buffet too. I felt really ashamed to go on questioning them. It was only twenty-five minutes past five. If they changed the dinner hour they ought at least to have let me know — that is what the post is for, and not to have put me in an absurd position in my own eyes and . . . and even before the waiters. I sat down; the servant began laying the table; I felt even more humiliated when he was present. Towards six o'clock they brought in candles, though there were lamps burning in the room. It had not occurred to the waiter, however, to bring them in at once when I arrived. In the next room two gloomy, angry-looking persons were eating their dinners in silence at two different tables. There was a great deal of noise, even shouting, in a room further away; one could hear the laughter of a crowd of people, and nasty little shrieks in French: there were ladies at the dinner. It was sickening, in fact. I rarely passed more unpleasant moments, so much so that when they did arrive all together punctually at six I was overjoyed to see them, as though they were my deliverers, and even forgot that it was incumbent upon me to show resentment.

Zverkov walked in at the head of them; evidently he was the leading spirit. He and all of them were laughing; but, seeing me, Zverkov drew himself up a little, walked up to me deliberately with a slight, rather jaunty bend from the waist. He shook hands with me in a friendly, but not over-friendly, fashion, with a sort of circumspect courtesy like that of a general, as though in giving me his hand he were warding off something. I had imagined, on the contrary, that on coming in he would at once break into his habitual thin, shrill laugh and fall to making his insipid jokes and witticisms. I had been preparing for them ever since the previous day, but I had not expected such condescension, such high-official courtesy. So, then, he felt himself ineffably superior to me in every respect! If he only meant to insult me by that high-official tone, it would not matter, I thought — I could pay him back for it one way or another. But what if, in reality, without the least desire to be offensive, that sheep's-head had a notion in earnest that he was superior to me and could only look at me in a patronizing way? The very supposition made me gasp.

"I was surprised to hear of your desire to join us," he began, lisping and drawling, which was something new. "You and I seem to have seen nothing of one another. You fight shy of us. You shouldn't. We are not such terrible people as you think. Well, anyway, I am glad to renew our acquaintance."

And he turned carelessly to put down his hat on the window sill.

"Have you been waiting long?" Trudolyubov inquired.

"I arrived at five o'clock as you told me yesterday," I answered aloud, with an irritability that threatened an explosion.

"Didn't you let him know that we had changed the hour?" said Trudolyubov to Simonov.

"No, I didn't. I forgot," the latter replied, with no sign of regret, and without even apologizing to me he went off to order the *hors d'œuvres.*

"So you've been here a whole hour? Oh, poor fellow!" Zverkov cried ironically, for to his notions this was bound to be extremely funny. That rascal Ferfitchkin followed with his nasty little snigger like a puppy yapping. My position struck him, too, as exquisitely ludicrous and embarrassing.

"It isn't funny at all!" I cried to Ferfitchkin, more and more irritated. "It wasn't my fault, but other people's. They neglected to let me know. It was . . . it was . . . it was simply absurd."

"It's not only absurd, but something else as well," muttered Trudolyubov, naïvely taking my part. "You are not hard enough upon it. It was simply rudeness — unintentional, of course. And how could Simonov . . . h'm!"

"If a trick like that had been played on me," observed Ferfitchkin, "I should. . . ."

"But you should have ordered something for yourself," Zverkov interrupted, "or simply asked for dinner without waiting for us."

"You will allow that I might have done that without your permission," I rapped out. "If I waited, it was. . . ."

"Let us sit down, gentlemen," cried Simonov, coming in. "Everything is ready; I can answer for the champagne; it is capitally frozen. . . . You see, I did not know your address, where was I to look for you?" He suddenly turned to me, but again he seemed to avoid looking at me. Evidently he had something against me. It must have been what happened yesterday.

All sat down; I did the same. It was a round table. Trudolyubov was on my left, Simonov on my right. Zverkov was sitting opposite, Ferfitchkin next to him, between him and Trudolyubov.

"Tell me, are you . . . in a government office?" Zverkov went on attending to me. Seeing that I was embarrassed, he seriously thought that he ought to be friendly to me, and, so to speak, cheer me up.

"Does he want me to throw a bottle at his head?" I thought, in a fury. In my novel surroundings I was unnaturally ready to be irritated.

"In the N—— office," I answered jerkily, with my eyes on my plate.

"And ha-ave you a go-od berth? I say, what ma-a-de you leave your original job?"

"What ma-a-de me was that I wanted to leave my original job," I drawled more than he, hardly able to control myself. Ferfitchkin went off into a guffaw. Simonov looked at me ironically. Trudolyubov left off eating and began looking at me with curiosity.

Zverkov winced, but he tried not to notice it.

"And the remuneration?"

"What remuneration?"

"I mean, your sa-a-lary?"

"Why are you cross-examining me?" However, I told him at once what my salary was. I turned horribly red.

"It is not very handsome," Zverkov observed majestically.

"Yes, you can't afford to dine at cafés on that," Ferfitchkin added insolently.

"To my thinking it's very poor," Trudolyubov observed gravely.

"And how thin you have grown! How you have changed!" added Zverkov, with a shade of venom in his voice, scanning me and my attire with a sort of insolent compassion.

"Oh, spare his blushes," cried Ferfitchkin, sniggering.

"My dear sir, allow me to tell you I am not blushing," I broke out at last; "do you hear? I am dining here, at this café, at my own expense, not at other people's — note that, Mr. Ferfitchkin."

"Wha-at? Isn't every one here dining at his own expense? You would seem to be. . . ." Ferfitchkin flew out at me, turning as red as a lobster, and looking me in the face with fury.

"Tha-at," I answered, feeling I had gone too far, "and I imagine it would be better to talk of something more intelligent."

"You intend to show off your intelligence, I suppose?"

"Don't disturb yourself, that would be quite out of place here."

"Why are you clacking away like that, my good sir, eh? Have you gone out of your wits in your office?"

"Enough, gentlemen, enough!" Zverkov cried, authoritatively.

"How stupid it is!" muttered Simonov.

"It really is stupid. We have met here, a company of friends, for a farewell dinner to a comrade and you carry on an altercation," said Trudolyubov, rudely addressing himself to me alone. "You invited yourself to join us, so don't disturb the general harmony."

"Enough, enough!" cried Zverkov. "Give over, gentlemen, it's out of place. Better let me tell you how I nearly got married the day before yesterday. . . ."

And then followed a burlesque narrative of how this gentleman had almost been married two days before. There was not a word about the marriage, however, but the story was adorned with generals, colonels and kammer-junkers, while Zverkov almost took the lead among them. It was greeted with approving laughter; Ferfitchkin positively squealed.

No one paid any attention to me, and I sat crushed and humiliated.

"Good heavens, these are not the people for me!" I thought. "And what a fool I have made of myself before them! I let Ferfitchkin go too far, though. The brutes imagine they are doing me an honour in letting me sit down with them. They don't understand that it's an honour to them and not to me! I've grown thinner! My clothes! Oh, damn my trousers! Zverkov noticed the yellow stain on the knee as soon as he came in. . . . But what's the use! I must get up at once, this very minute, take my hat and simply go without a word . . . with contempt! And to-morrow I can send a challenge. The scoundrels! As though I cared about the seven roubles. They may think. . . . Damn it! I don't care about the seven roubles. I'll go this minute!"

Of course I remained. I drank sherry and Lafitte by the glassful in my discomfiture. Being unaccustomed to it, I was quickly affected. My annoyance increased as the wine went to my head. I longed all at once to insult them all in a most flagrant manner and then go away. To seize the moment and show what I could do, so that they would say, "He's clever, though he is absurd," and . . . and . . . in fact, damn them all!

I scanned them all insolently with my drowsy eyes. But they seemed to have forgotten me altogether. They were noisy, vociferous, cheerful. Zverkov was talking all the time. I began listening. Zverkov was talking of some exuberant lady whom he had at last led on to declaring her love (of course, he was lying like a horse), and how he had been helped in this affair by an intimate friend of his, a Prince Kolya, an officer in the Hussars, who had three thousand serfs.

"And yet this Kolya, who has three thousand serfs, has not put in an appearance here to-night to see you off," I cut in suddenly.

For a minute every one was silent. "You are drunk already." Trudolyubov deigned to notice me at last, glancing contemptuously in my direction. Zverkov, without a word, examined me as though I were an insect. I dropped my eyes. Simonov made haste to fill up the glasses with champagne.

Trudolyubov raised his glass, as did every one else but me.

"Your health and good luck on the journey!" he cried to Zverkov. "To old times, to our future, hurrah!"

They all tossed off their glasses, and crowded round Zverkov to kiss him. I did not move; my full glass stood untouched before me.

"Why, aren't you going to drink it?" roared Trudolyubov, losing patience and turning menacingly to me.

"I want to make a speech separately, on my own account . . . and then I'll drink it, Mr. Trudolyubov."

"Spiteful brute!" muttered Simonov. I drew myself up in my chair and feverishly seized my glass, prepared for something extraordinary, though I did not know myself precisely what I was going to say.

"*Silence!*" cried Ferfitchkin. "Now for a display of wit!"

Zverkov waited very gravely, knowing what was coming.

"Mr. Lieutenant Zverkov," I began, "let me tell you that I hate phrases, phrasemongers and men in corsets . . . that's the first point, and there is a second one to follow it."

There was a general stir.

"The second point is: I hate ribaldry and ribald talkers. Especially ribald talkers! The third point: I love justice, truth and honesty." I went on almost mechanically, for I was beginning to shiver with horror myself and had no idea how I came to be talking like this. "I love thought, Monsieur Zverkov; I love true comradeship, on an equal footing and not. . . . H'm. . . . I love. . . . But, however, why not? I will drink your health, too, Mr. Zverkov. Seduce the Circassian girls, shoot the enemies of the fatherland and . . . and . . . to your health, Monsieur Zverkov!"

Zverkov got up from his seat, bowed to me and said:

"I am very much obliged to you." He was frightfully offended and turned pale.

"Damn the fellow!" roared Trudolyubov, bringing his fist down on the table.

"Well, he wants a punch in the face for that," squealed Ferfitchkin.

"We ought to turn him out," muttered Simonov.

"Not a word, gentlemen, not a movement!" cried Zverkov solemnly, checking the general indignation. "I thank you all, but I can show him for myself how much value I attach to his words."

"Mr. Ferfitchkin, you will give me satisfaction to-morrow for your words just now!" I said aloud, turning with dignity to Ferfitchkin.

"A duel, you mean? Certainly," he answered. But probably I was so ridiculous as I challenged him and it was so out of keeping with my appearance that everyone, including Ferfitchkin, was prostrate with laughter.

"Yes, let him alone, of course! He is quite drunk," Trudolyubov said with disgust.

"I shall never forgive myself for letting him join us," Simonov muttered again.

"Now is the time to throw a bottle at their heads," I thought to myself. I picked up the bottle . . . and filled my glass. . . . "No, I'd better sit on to the end," I went on thinking; "you would be pleased, my friends, if I went away. Nothing will induce me to go. I'll go on sitting here and drinking to the end, on purpose, as a sign that I don't think you of the slightest consequence. I will go on sitting and drinking, because this is a public-house and I paid my entrance money. I'll sit here and drink, for I look upon you as so many pawns, as inanimate pawns. I'll sit here and drink . . . and sing if I want to, yes, sing, for I have the right to . . . to sing. . . . H'm!"

But I did not sing. I simply tried not to look at any of them. I assumed most unconcerned attitudes and waited with impatience for them to speak *first.* But alas, they did not address me! And oh, how I wished, how I wished at that moment to be reconciled to them! It struck eight, at last nine. They moved from the table to the sofa. Zverkov stretched himself on a lounge and put one foot on a round table. Wine was brought there. He did, as a fact, order three bottles on his own account. I, of course, was not invited to join them. They all sat round him on the sofa. They listened to him, almost with reverence. It was evident that they were fond of him. "What for? What for?" I wondered. From time to time they were moved to drunken enthusiasm and kissed each other. They talked of the Caucasus, of the nature of true passion, of snug berths in the service, of the income of an hussar called Podharzhevsky, whom none of them knew personally, and rejoiced in the largeness of it, of the extraordinary grace and beauty of a Princess D., whom none of them had ever seen; then it came to Shakespeare's being immortal.

I smiled contemptuously and walked up and down the other side of the room, opposite the sofa, from the table to the stove and back again. I tried my very utmost to show them that I could do without them, and yet I purposely made a noise with my boots, thumping with my heels. But it was all in vain. They paid no attention. I had the patience to walk up and down in front of them from eight o'clock till eleven, in the same place, from the table to the stove and back again. "I walk up and down to please myself and no one can prevent me." The waiter who came into the room stopped, from time to time, to look at me. I was somewhat giddy from turning round so often; at moments it seemed to me that I was in delirium. During those three hours I was three times soaked with sweat and dry again. At times, with an intense, acute pang I was stabbed to the heart by the thought that ten years, twenty years, forty years would pass, and that even in forty years I would remember with loathing and humiliation those filthiest, most ludicrous, and most awful moments of my life. No one could have gone out of his way to degrade himself more shamelessly, and I fully realized it, fully, and yet I went on pacing up and down from the table to the stove. "Oh, if you only knew what thoughts and feelings I am capable of, how cultured I am!" I thought at moments, mentally addressing the sofa on which my enemies were sitting. But my enemies behaved as though I were not in the room. Once — only once — they turned towards me, just when Zverkov was talking about Shakespeare, and I suddenly gave a contemptuous laugh. I laughed in such an affected and disgusting way that they all at once broke off their conversation, and silently and gravely for two minutes watched me walking up and down from the table to the stove, *taking no notice of them*. But nothing came of it: they said nothing, and two minutes later they ceased to notice me again. It struck eleven.

"Friends," cried Zverkov getting up from the sofa, "let us all be off now, *there!*"

"Of course, of course," the others assented. I turned sharply to Zverkov. I was so harassed, so exhausted, that I would have cut my throat to put an end to it. I was in a fever; my hair, soaked with perspiration, stuck to my forehead and temples.

"Zverkov, I beg your pardon," I said abruptly and resolutely. "Ferfitchkin, yours too, and every one's, every one's: I have insulted you all!"

"Aha! A duel is not in your line, old man," Ferfitchkin hissed venomously.

It sent a sharp pang to my heart.

"No, it's not the duel I am afraid of, Ferfitchkin! I am ready to fight you to-morrow, after we are reconciled. I insist upon it, in fact, and you cannot refuse. I want to show you that I am not afraid of a duel. You shall fire first and I shall fire into the air."

"He is comforting himself," said Simonov.

"He's simply raving," said Trudolyubov.

"But let us pass. Why are you barring our way? What do you want?" Zverkov answered disdainfully.

They were all flushed; their eyes were bright: they had been drinking heavily.

"I ask for your friendship, Zverkov; I insulted you, but. . . ."

"Insulted? *You* insulted *me?* Understand, sir, that you never, under any circumstances, could possibly insult *me.*"

"And that's enough for you. Out of the way!" concluded Trudolyubov.

"Olympia is mine, friends, that's agreed!" cried Zverkov.

"We won't dispute your right, we won't dispute your right," the others answered, laughing.

I stood as though spat upon. The party went noisily out of the room. Trudolyubov struck up some stupid song. Simonov remained behind for a moment to tip the waiters. I suddenly went up to him.

"Simonov! give me six roubles!" I said, with desperate resolution.

He looked at me in extreme amazement, with vacant eyes. He, too, was drunk.

"You don't mean you are coming with us?"

"Yes."

"I've no money," he snapped out, and with a scornful laugh he went out of the room.

I clutched at his overcoat. It was a nightmare.

"Simonov, I saw you had money. Why do you refuse me? Am I a scoundrel? Beware of refusing me: if you knew, if you knew why I am asking! My whole future, my whole plans depend upon it!"

Simonov pulled out the money and almost flung it at me.

"Take it, if you have no sense of shame!" he pronounced pitilessly, and ran to overtake them.

I was left for a moment alone. Disorder, the remains of dinner, a broken wine-glass on the floor, spilt wine, cigarette ends, fumes of drink and delirium in my brain, an agonizing misery in my heart and finally the waiter, who had seen and heard all and was looking inquisitively into my face.

"I am going there!" I cried. "Either they shall all go down on their knees to beg for my friendship, or I will give Zverkov a slap in the face!"

V

"So this is it, this is it at last — contact with real life," I muttered as I ran headlong downstairs. "This is very different from the Pope's leaving Rome and going to Brazil, very different from the ball on the shores of Lake Como!"

"You are a scoundrel," a thought flashed through my mind, "if you laugh at this now."

"No matter!" I cried, answering myself. "Now everything is lost!"

There was no trace to be seen of them, but that made no difference — I knew where they had gone.

At the steps was standing a solitary night sledge-driver in a rough peasant coat, powdered over with the still falling, wet, and as it were warm, snow. It was hot and steamy. The little shaggy piebald horse was also covered with snow and coughing, I remember that very well. I made a rush for the roughly made sledge; but as soon as I raised my foot to get into it, the recollection of how Simonov had just given me six roubles seemed to double me up and I tumbled into the sledge like a sack.

"No, I must do a great deal to make up for all that," I cried. "But I will make up for it or perish on the spot this very night. Start!"

We set off. There was a perfect whirl in my head.

"They won't go down on their knees to beg for my friendship. That is a mirage, cheap mirage, revolting, romantic and fantastical — that's another ball at Lake Como. And so I am bound to slap Zverkov's face! It is my duty to. And so it is settled; I am flying to give him a slap in the face. Hurry up!"

The driver tugged at the reins.

"As soon as I go in I'll give it him. Ought I before giving him the slap to say a few words by way of preface? No. I'll simply go in and give it him. They will all be sitting in the drawing-room, and he with Olympia on the sofa. That damned Olympia! She laughed at my looks on one occasion and refused me. I'll pull Olympia's hair, pull Zverkov's ears! No, better one ear, and pull him by it round the room. Maybe they will all begin beating me and will kick me out. That's most likely, indeed. No matter! Anyway, I shall first slap him; the initiative will be mine; and by the laws of honour that is everything: he will be branded and cannot wipe off the slap by any blows, by nothing but a duel. He will be forced to fight. And let them beat me now. Let them, the ungrateful wretches! Trudolyubov will beat me hardest, he is so strong; Ferfitchkin will be sure to catch hold sideways and tug at my hair. But no matter, no matter! That's what I am going for. The blockheads will be forced at last to see the tragedy of it all! When they drag me to the door I shall call out to them that in reality they are not worth my little finger. Get on, driver, get on!" I cried to the driver. He started and flicked his whip, I shouted so savagely.

"We shall fight at daybreak, that's a settled thing. I've done with the office. Ferfitchkin made a joke about it just now. But where can I get pistols? Nonsense! I'll get my salary in advance and buy them. And powder, and bullets? That's the second's business. And how can it all be done by daybreak? And where am I to get a second? I have no friends. Nonsense!" I cried, lashing myself up more and more. "It's of no consequence! the first person I meet in the street is bound to be my second, just as he would be bound to pull a drowning man out of water. The most eccentric things may happen. Even if I were to ask the Director himself to be my second to-morrow, he would be bound to consent, if only from a feeling of chivalry, and to keep the secret! Anton Antonitch. . . ."

The fact is, that at that very minute the disgusting absurdity of my plan and the other side of the question was clearer and more vivid to my imagination than it could be to any one on earth. But. . . .

"Get on, driver, get on, you rascal, get on!"

"Ugh, sir!" said the son of toil.

Cold shivers suddenly ran down me. Wouldn't it be better . . . to go straight home? My God, my God! Why did I invite myself to this dinner yesterday? But no, it's impossible. And my walking up and down for three hours from the table to the stove? No, they, they and no one else must pay for my walking up and down! They must wipe out this dishonour! Drive on!

And what if they give me into custody? They won't dare! They'll be afraid of the scandal. And what if Zverkov is so contemptuous that he refuses to fight a duel? He is sure to; but in that case I'll show them . . . I will turn up at the posting station when he is setting off to-morrow, I'll catch him by the leg, I'll pull off his coat when he gets into the carriage. I'll get my teeth into his hand, I'll bite him. "See what lengths you can drive a desperate man to!" He may hit me on the head and they may belabour me from behind. I will shout to the assembled multitude: "Look at this young puppy who is driving off to captivate the Circassian girls after letting me spit in his face!"

Of course, after that everything will be over! The office will have vanished off the face of the earth. I shall be arrested, I shall be tried, I shall be dismissed from the service, thrown in prison, sent to Siberia. Never mind! In fifteen years when they let me out of prison I will trudge off to him, a beggar, in rags. I shall find him in some provincial town. He will be married and happy. He will have a grown-up daughter. . . . I shall say to him: "Look, monster, at my hollow cheeks and my rags! I've lost everything — my career, my happiness, art, science, *the woman I loved*, and all through you. Here are pistols. I have come to discharge my pistol and . . . and I . . . forgive you. Then I shall fire into the air and he will hear nothing more of me. . . ."

I was actually on the point of tears, though I knew perfectly well at that moment that all this was out of Pushkin's *Silvio* and Lermontov's *Masquerade*. And all at once I felt horribly ashamed, so ashamed that I stopped the horse, got out of the sledge, and stood still in the snow in the middle of the street. The driver gazed at me, sighing and astonished.

What was I to do? I could not go on there — it was evidently stupid, and I could not leave things as they were, because that would seem as though. . . . Heavens, how could I leave things! And after such insults! "No!" I cried, throwing myself into the sledge again. "It is ordained! It is fate! Drive on, drive on!"

And in my impatience I punched the sledge-driver on the back of the neck.

"What are you up to? What are you hitting me for?" the peasant shouted, but he whipped up his nag so that it began kicking.

The wet snow was falling in big flakes; I unbuttoned myself, regardless of it. I forgot everything else, for I had finally decided on the slap, and felt with horror that it was going to happen *now, at once*, and that *no force could stop it*. The deserted street lamps gleamed sullenly in the snowy darkness like torches at a funeral. The snow drifted under my greatcoat, under my coat, under my cravat, and melted there. I did not wrap myself up — all was lost, anyway.

At last we arrived. I jumped out, almost unconscious, ran up the steps and began knocking and kicking at the door. I felt fearfully weak, particularly in my legs and my knees. The door was opened quickly as though they knew I was coming. As a fact, Simonov had warned them that perhaps another gentleman would arrive, and this was a place in which one had to give notice and to observe certain precautions. It was one of those "millinery establishments" which were abolished by the police a good time ago. By day it really was a shop; but at night, if one had an introduction, one might visit it for other purposes.

I walked rapidly through the dark shop into the familiar drawing-room, where there was only one candle burning, and stood still in amazement: there was no one there. "Where are they?" I asked somebody. But by now, of course, they had separated. Before me was standing a person with a stupid smile, the "madam" herself, who had seen me before. A minute later a door opened and another person came in.

Taking no notice of anything, I strode about the room, and, I believe, I talked to myself. I felt as though I had been saved from death and was conscious of this, joyfully, all over: I should have given that slap, I should certainly, certainly have given it! But now they were not here and . . . everything had vanished and changed! I looked round. I could not realize my condition yet. I looked mechanically at the girl who had come in: and had a glimpse of a fresh, young, rather pale face, with straight, dark eyebrows, and with grave, as it were wondering, eyes that attracted me at once; I should have hated her if she had been smiling. I began looking at her more intently and, as it were, with effort. I had not fully collected my thoughts. There was something simple and good-natured in her face, but something strangely grave. I am sure that this stood in her way here, and no one of those fools had noticed her. She could not, however, have been called a beauty, though she was tall, strong-looking, and well built. She was very simply dressed. Something loathsome stirred within me. I went straight up to her.

I chanced to look into the glass. My harassed face struck me as revolting in the extreme, pale, angry, abject, with dishevelled hair. "No matter, I am glad of it," I thought; "I am glad that I shall seem repulsive to her; I like that."

VI

. . . Somewhere behind a screen a clock began wheezing, as though oppressed by something, as though some one were strangling it. After an unnaturally prolonged wheezing there followed a shrill, nasty, and as it were unexpectedly rapid, chime — as though some one were suddenly jumping forward. It struck two. I woke up, though I had indeed not been asleep but lying half-conscious.

It was almost completely dark in the narrow, cramped, low-pitched room, cumbered up with an enormous wardrobe and piles of cardboard boxes and all sorts of frippery and litter. The candle end that had been burning on the table was going out and gave a faint flicker from time to time. In a few minutes there would be complete darkness.

I was not long in coming to myself; everything came back to my mind at once, without an effort, as though it had been in ambush to pounce upon me again. And, indeed, even while I was unconscious a point seemed continually to remain in my memory unforgotten, and round it my dreams moved drearily. But strange to say, everything that had happened to me in that day seemed to me now, on waking, to be in the far, far away past, as though I had long, long ago lived all that down.

My head was full of fumes. Something seemed to be hovering over me, rousing me, exciting me, and making me restless. Misery and spite seemed surging up in me again and seeking an outlet. Suddenly I saw beside me two wide-open eyes scrutinizing me curiously and persistently. The look in those eyes was coldly detached, sullen, as it were utterly remote; it weighed upon me.

A grim idea came into my brain and passed all over my body, as a horrible sensation, such as one feels when one goes into a damp and mouldy cellar. There was something unnatural in those two eyes, beginning to look at me only now. I recalled, too, that during those two hours I had not said a single word to this creature, and had, in fact, considered it utterly superfluous; in fact, the silence had for some reason gratified me. Now I suddenly realized vividly the hideous idea — revolting as a spider — of vice, which, without love, grossly and shamelessly begins with that in which true love finds its consummation. For a long time we gazed at each other like that, but she did not drop her eyes before mine and her expression did not change, so that at last I felt uncomfortable.

"What is your name?" I asked abruptly, to put an end to it.

"Liza," she answered almost in a whisper, but somehow far from graciously, and she turned her eyes away.

I was silent.

"What weather! The snow . . . it's disgusting!" I said, almost to myself, putting my arm under my head despondently, and gazing at the ceiling.

She made no answer. This was horrible.

"Have you always lived in Petersburg?" I asked a minute later, almost angrily, turning my head slightly towards her.

"No."

"Where do you come from?"

"From Riga," she answered reluctantly.

"Are you a German?"

"No, Russian."

"Have you been here long?"

"Where?"

"In this house?"

"A fortnight."

She spoke more and more jerkily. The candle went out; I could no longer distinguish her face.

"Have you a father and mother?"

"Yes . . . no . . . I have."

"Where are they?"

"There . . . in Riga."

"What are they?"

"Oh, nothing."

"Nothing? Why, what class are they?"

"Tradespeople."

"Have you always lived with them?"

"Yes."

"How old are you?"

"Twenty."

"Why did you leave them?"

"Oh, for no reason."

That answer meant "Let me alone; I feel sick, sad."

We were silent.

God knows why I did not go away. I felt myself more and more sick and dreary. The images of the previous day began of themselves, apart from my will, flitting through my memory in confusion. I suddenly recalled something I had seen that morning when, full of anxious thoughts, I was hurrying to the office.

"I saw them carrying a coffin out yesterday and they nearly dropped it," I suddenly said aloud, not that I desired to open the conversation, but as it were by accident.

"A coffin?"

"Yes, in the Haymarket; they were bringing it up out of a cellar."

"From a cellar?"

"Not from a cellar, but from a basement. Oh, you know . . . down below . . . from a house of ill-fame. It was filthy all round. . . . Eggshells, litter . . . a stench. It was loathsome."

Silence.

"A nasty day to be buried," I began, simply to avoid being silent.

"Nasty, in what way?"

"The snow, the wet." (I yawned.)

"It makes no difference," she said suddenly, after a brief silence.

"No, it's horrid." (I yawned again.) "The grave-diggers must have sworn at getting drenched by the snow. And there must have been water in the grave."

"Why water in the grave?" she asked, with a sort of curiosity, but speaking even more harshly and abruptly than before.

I suddenly began to feel provoked.

"Why, there must have been water at the bottom a foot deep. You can't dig a dry grave in Volkovo Cemetery."

"Why?"

"Why? Why, the place is waterlogged. It's a regular marsh. So they bury them in water. I've seen it myself . . . many times."

(I had never seen it once, indeed I had never been in Volkovo, and had only heard stories of it.)

"Do you mean to say you don't mind how you die?"

"But why should I die?" she answered, as though defending herself.

"Why, some day you will die, and you will die just the same as that dead woman. She was . . . a girl like you. She died of consumption."

"A wench would have died in a hospital. . . ." (She knows all about it already: she said "wench," not "girl.")

"She was in debt to her madam," I retorted, more and more provoked by the discussion; "and went on earning money for her up to the end, though she was in consumption. Some sledge-drivers standing by were talking about her to some soldiers and telling them so. No doubt they knew her. They were laughing. They were going to meet in a pot-house to drink to her memory."

A great deal of this was my invention. Silence followed, profound silence. She did not stir.

"And is it better to die in a hospital?"

"Isn't it just the same? Besides, why should I die?" she added irritably.

"If not now, a little later."

"Why a little later?"

"Why, indeed? Now you are young, pretty, fresh, you fetch a high price. But after another year of this life you will be very different — you will go off."

"In a year?"

"Anyway, in a year you will be worth less," I continued malignantly. "You will go from here to something lower, another house; a year later — to a third, lower and lower, and in seven years you will come to a basement in the Haymarket. That will be if you were lucky. But it would be much worse if you got some disease, consumption, say . . . and caught a chill, or something or other. It's not easy to get over an illness in your way of life. If you catch anything you may not get rid of it. And so you would die."

"Oh, well, then I shall die," she answered, quite vindictively, and she made a quick movement.

"But one is sorry."

"Sorry for whom?"

"Sorry for life."

Silence.

"Have you been engaged to be married? Eh?"

"What's that to you?"

"Oh, I am not cross-examining you. It's nothing to me. Why are you so cross? Of course you may have had your own troubles. What is it to me? It's simply that I felt sorry."

"Sorry for whom?"

"Sorry for you."

"No need," she whispered hardly audibly, and again made a faint movement.

That incensed me at once. What! I was so gentle with her, and she. . . .

"Why, do you think that you are on the right path?"

"I don't think anything."

"That's what's wrong, that you don't think. Realize it while there is still time. There still is time. You are still young, good-looking; you might love, be married, be happy. . . ."

"Not all married women are happy," she snapped out in the rude abrupt tone she had used at first.

"Not all, of course, but anyway it is much better than the life here. Infinitely better. Besides, with love one can live even without happiness. Even in sorrow life is sweet; life is sweet, however one lives. But here what is there but . . . foulness. Phew!"

I turned away with disgust; I was no longer reasoning coldly. I began to feel myself what I was saying and warmed to the subject. I was already longing to expound the cherished ideas I had brooded over in my corner. Something suddenly flared up in me. An object had appeared before me.

"Never mind my being here, I am not an example for you. I am, perhaps, worse than you are. I was drunk when I came here, though," I hastened, however, to say in self-defence. "Besides, a man is no example for a woman. It's a different thing. I may degrade and defile myself, but I am not any one's slave. I come and go, and that's an end of it. I shake it off, and I am a different man. But you are a slave from the start. Yes, a slave! You give up everything, your whole freedom. If you want to break your chains afterwards, you won't be able to: you will be more and more fast in the snares. It is an accursed bondage. I know it. I won't speak of anything else, maybe you won't understand, but tell me: no doubt you are in debt to your madam? There, you see," I added, though she made no answer, but only listened in silence, entirely absorbed, "that's a bondage for you! You will never buy your freedom. They will see to that. It's like selling your soul to the Devil. . . . And besides . . . perhaps I, too, am just as unlucky — how do you know — and wallow in the mud on purpose, out of misery? You know, men take to drink from grief; well, maybe I am here from grief. Come, tell me, what is there good here? Here you and I . . . came together . . . just now and did not say one word to one another all the time, and it was only afterwards you began staring at me like a wild creature, and I at you. Is that loving? Is that how one human being should meet another? It's hideous, that's what it is!"

"Yes!" she assented sharply and hurriedly.

I was positively astounded by the promptitude of this "Yes." So the same thought may have been straying through her mind when she was staring at me just before. So she, too, was capable of certain thoughts? "Damn it all, this was interesting, this was a point of likeness!" I thought, almost rubbing my hands. And indeed it's easy to turn a young soul like that!

It was the exercise of my power that attracted me most.

She turned her head nearer to me, and it seemed to me in the darkness that she propped herself on her arm. Perhaps she was scrutinizing me. How I regretted that I could not see her eyes. I heard her deep breathing.

"Why have you come here?" I asked her, with a note of authority already in my voice.

"Oh, I don't know."

"But how nice it would be to be living in your father's house! It's warm and free; you have a home of your own."

"But what if it's worse than this?"

"I must take the right tone," flashed through my mind. "I may not get far with sentimentality." But it was only a momentary thought. I swear she really did interest me. Besides, I was exhausted and moody. And cunning so easily goes hand in hand with feeling.

"Who denies it!" I hastened to answer. "Anything may happen. I am convinced that some one has wronged you, and that you are more sinned against than sinning. Of course, I know nothing of your story, but it's not likely a girl like you has come here of her own inclination. . . ."

"A girl like me?" she whispered, hardly audibly; but I heard it.

Damn it all, I was flattering her. That was horrid. But perhaps it was a good thing. . . . She was silent.

"See, Liza, I will tell you about myself. If I had had a home from childhood, I shouldn't be what I am now. I often think that. However bad it may be at home, anyway they are your father and mother, and not enemies, strangers. Once a year at least, they'll show their love of you. Anyway, you know you are at home. I grew up without a home; and perhaps that's why I've turned so . . . unfeeling."

I waited again. "Perhaps she doesn't understand," I thought, "and, indeed, it is absurd — it's moralizing."

"If I were a father and had a daughter, I believe I should love my daughter more than my sons, really," I began indirectly, as though talking of something else, to distract her attention. I must confess I blushed.

"Why so?" she asked.

Ah! so she was listening!

"I don't know, Liza. I knew a father who was a stern, austere man, but used to go down on his knees to his daughter, used to kiss her hands, her feet, he couldn't make enough of her, really. When she danced at parties he used to stand for five hours at a stretch, gazing at her. He was mad over her: I understand that! She would fall asleep tired at night, and he would wake to kiss her in her sleep and make the sign of the cross over her. He would go about in a dirty old coat, he was stingy to every one else, but would spend his last penny for her, giving her expensive presents, and it was his greatest delight when she was pleased with what he gave her. Fathers always love their daughters more than the mothers do. Some girls live happily at home! And I believe I should never let my daughters marry."

"What next?" she said, with a faint smile.

"I should be jealous, I really should. To think that she should kiss any one else! That she should love a stranger more than her father! It's painful to imagine it. Of course, that's all nonsense, of course every father would be reasonable at last. But I believe before I should let her marry, I should worry myself to death; I should find fault with all her suitors. But I should end by letting her marry whom she herself loved. The one whom the daughter loves always seems the worst to the father, you know. That is always so. So many family troubles come from that."

"Some are glad to sell their daughters, rather than marrying them honourably."

Ah, so that was it!

"Such a thing, Liza, happens in those accursed families in which there is neither love nor God," I retorted warmly, "and where there is no love, there is no sense either. There are such families, it's true, but I am not speaking of them. You must have seen wickedness in your own family, if you talk like that. Truly, you must have been unlucky. H'm! . . . that sort of thing mostly comes about through poverty."

"And is it any better with the gentry? Even among the poor, honest people live happily."

"H'm . . . yes. Perhaps. Another thing, Liza, man is fond of reckoning up his troubles, but does not count his joys. If he counted them up as he ought, he would see that every lot has enough happiness provided for it. And what if all goes well with the family, if the blessing of God is upon it, if the husband is a good one, loves you, cherishes you, never leaves you! There is happiness in such a family! Even sometimes there is happiness in the midst of sorrow; and indeed sorrow is everywhere. If you marry *you will find out for yourself*. But think of the first years of married life with one you love: what happiness, what happiness there sometimes is in it! And indeed it's the ordinary thing. In those early days even quarrels with one's husband end happily. Some women get up quarrels with their husbands just because they love them. Indeed, I knew a woman like that: she seemed to say that because she loved him, she would torment him and make him feel it. You know that you may torment a man on purpose through love. Women are particularly given to that, thinking to themselves 'I will love him so, I will make so much of him afterwards, that it's no sin to torment him a little now.' And all in the house rejoice in the sight of you, and you are happy and gay and peaceful and honourable. . . . Then there are some women who are jealous. If he went off anywhere — I knew one such woman, she couldn't restrain herself, but would jump up at night and run off on the sly to find out where he was, whether he was with some other woman. That's a pity.

"And the woman knows herself it's wrong, and her heart fails her and she suffers, but she loves — it's all through love. And how sweet it is to make it up after quarrels, to own herself in the wrong or to forgive him! And they are both so happy all at once — as though they had met anew, been married over again; as though their love had begun afresh. And no one, no one should know what passes between husband and wife if they love one another. And whatever quarrels there may be between them they ought not to call in their own mothers to judge between them and tell tales of one another. They are their own judges.

"Love is a holy mystery and ought to be hidden from all other eyes, whatever happens. That makes it holier and better. They respect one another more, and much is built on respect. And if once there has been love, if they have been married for love, why should love pass away? Surely one can keep it! It is rare that one cannot keep it. And if the husband is kind and straightforward, why should not love last? The first phase of married love will pass, it is true, but then there will come a love that is better still. Then there will be the union of souls, they will have everything in common, there will be no secrets between them.

"And once they have children, the most difficult times will seem to them happy, so long as there is love and courage. Even toil will be a joy, you may deny yourself bread for your children and even that will be a joy. They will love you for it afterwards; so you are laying by for your future. As the children grow up you feel that you are an example, a support for them; that even after you die your children will always keep your thoughts and feelings, because they have received them from you, they will take on your semblance and likeness. So you see this is a great duty. How can it fail to draw the father and mother nearer? People say it's a trial to have children. Who says that? It is heavenly happiness! Are you fond of little children, Liza? I am awfully fond of them. You know — a little rosy baby boy at your bosom, and what husband's heart is not touched, seeing his wife nursing his child! A plump little rosy baby, sprawling and snuggling, chubby little hands and feet, clean tiny little nails, so tiny that it makes one laugh to look at them; eyes that look as if they understand everything. And while it sucks it clutches at your bosom with its little hand, plays. When its father comes up, the child tears itself away from the bosom, flings itself back, looks at its father, laughs, as though it were fearfully funny, and falls to sucking again. Or it will bite its mother's breast when its little teeth are coming, while it looks sideways at her with its little eyes as though to say, 'Look, I am biting!' Is not all that happiness when they are the three together, husband, wife and child? One can forgive a great deal for the sake of such moments. Yes, Liza, one must first learn to live oneself before one blames others!"

"It's by pictures, pictures like that one must get at you," I thought to myself, though I did speak with real feeling, and all at once I flushed crimson. "What if she were suddenly to burst out laughing, what should I do then?" That idea drove me to fury. Towards the end of my speech I really was excited, and now my vanity was somehow wounded. The silence continued. I almost nudged her.

"Why are you. . . ." she began and stopped. But I understood: there was a quiver of something different in her voice, not abrupt, harsh and unyielding as before, but something soft and shamefaced, so shamefaced that I suddenly felt ashamed and guilty.

"What?" I asked, with tender curiosity.

"Why, you. . . ."

"What?"

"Why, you . . . speak somehow like a book," she said, and again there was a note of irony in her voice.

That remark sent a pang to my heart. It was not what I was expecting.

I did not understand that she was hiding her feelings under irony, that this is usually the last refuge of modest and chaste-souled people when the privacy of their soul is coarsely and intrusively invaded, and that their pride makes them refuse to surrender till the last moment and shrink from giving expression to their feelings before you. I ought to have guessed the truth from the timidity with which she had repeatedly approached her sarcasm, only bringing herself to utter it at last with an effort. But I did not guess, and an evil feeling took possession of me.

"Wait a bit!" I thought.

VII

"Oh, hush, Liza! How can you talk about being like a book when it makes even me, an outsider, feel sick? Though I don't look at it as an outsider, for, indeed, it touches me to the heart. . . . Is it possible, is it possible that you do not feel sick at being here yourself? Evidently habit does wonders! God knows what habit can do with any one. Can you seriously think that you will never grow old, that you will always be good-looking, and that they will keep you here for ever and ever? I say nothing of the loathsomeness of the life here. . . . Though let me tell you this about it — about your present life, I mean; here though you are young now, attractive, nice, with soul and feeling, yet you know as soon as I came to myself just now I felt at once sick at being here with you! One can only come here when one is drunk. But if you were anywhere else, living as good people live, I should perhaps be more than attracted by you, should fall in love with you, should be glad of a look from you, let alone a word; I should hang about your door, should go down on my knees to you, should look upon you as my betrothed and think it an honour to be allowed to. I should not dare to have an impure thought about you. But here, you see, I know that I have only to whistle and you have to come with me whether you like it or not. I don't consult your wishes, but you mine. The lowest labourer hires himself as a workman but he doesn't make a slave of himself altogether; besides, he knows that he will be free again presently. But when are you free? Only think what you are giving up here! What is it you are making a slave of? It is your soul, together with your body; you are selling your soul which you have no right to dispose of! You give your love to be outraged by every drunkard! Love! But that's everything, you know, it's a priceless diamond, it's a maiden's treasure, love — why, a man would be ready to give his soul, to face death to gain that love. But how much is your love worth now? You are sold, all of you, body and soul, and there is no need to strive for love when you can have everything without love. And you know there is no greater insult to a girl than that, do you understand? To be sure, I have heard that they comfort you, poor fools, they let you have lovers of your own here. But you know that's simply a farce, that's simply a sham, it's just laughing at you, and you are taken in by it!

"Why, do you suppose he really loves you, that lover of yours? I don't believe it. How can he love you when he knows you may be called away from him any minute? He would be a low fellow if he did! Will he have a grain of respect for you? What have you in common with him? He laughs at you and robs you — that is all his love amounts to! You are lucky if he does not beat you. Very likely he does beat you, too. Ask him, if you have got one, whether he will marry you. He will laugh in your face, if he doesn't spit in it or give you a blow — though maybe he is not worth a bad halfpenny himself. And for what have you ruined your life, if you come to think of it? For the coffee they give you to drink and the plentiful meals? But with what object are they feeding you up? An honest girl couldn't swallow the food, for she would know what she was being fed for. You are in debt here, and, of course, you will always be in debt, and you will go on in debt to the end, till the visitors here begin to scorn you. And that will soon happen, don't rely upon your youth — all that flies by express train here, you know. You will be kicked out. And not simply kicked out; long before that she'll begin nagging at you, scolding you, abusing you, as though you had not sacrificed your health for her, had not thrown away your youth and your soul for her benefit, but as though you had ruined her, beggared her, robbed her. And don't expect any one to take your part: the others, your companions, will attack you, too, to win her favour, for all are in slavery here, and have lost all conscience and pity here long ago. They have become utterly vile, and nothing on earth is viler, more loathsome, and more insulting than their abuse.

"And you are laying down everything here, unconditionally, youth and health and beauty and hope, and at twenty-two you will look like a woman of five-and-thirty, and you will be lucky if you are not diseased, pray to God for that! No doubt, you are thinking now that you have a gay time and no work to do! Yet there is no work harder or more dreadful in the world or ever has been. One would think that the heart alone would be worn out with tears. And you won't dare to say a word, not half a word when they drive you away from here; you will go away as though you were to blame. You will change to another house, then to a third, then somewhere else, till you come down at last to the Haymarket. There you will be beaten at every turn; that is good manners there, the visitors don't know how to be friendly without beating you. You don't believe that it is so hateful there? Go and look for yourself some time, you can see with your own eyes. Once, one New Year's Day, I saw a woman at a door. They had turned her out as a joke, to give her a taste of the frost because she had been crying so much, and they shut the door behind her. At nine o'clock in the morning she was already quite drunk, dishevelled, half-naked, covered with bruises, her face was powdered, but she had a black eye, blood was trickling from her nose and her teeth; some cabman had just given her a drubbing. She was sitting on the stone steps, a salt fish of some sort was in her hand; she was crying, wailing something about her luck and beating with the fish on the steps, and cabmen and drunken soldiers were crowding in the doorway taunting her. You don't believe that you will ever be like that? I should be sorry to believe it, too, but how do you know; maybe ten years, eight years ago that very woman with the salt fish came here fresh as a cherub, innocent, pure, knowing no evil, blushing at every word. Perhaps she was like you, proud, ready to take offence, not like the others; perhaps she looked like a queen, and knew what happiness was in store for the man who should love her and whom she should love. Do you see how it ended? And what if at that very minute when she was beating on the filthy steps with that fish, drunken and dishevelled—what if at that very minute she recalled the pure early days in her father's house, when she used to go to school and the neighbour's son watched for her on the way, declaring that he would love her as long as he lived, that he would devote his life to her, and when they vowed to love one another for ever and be married as soon as they were grown up!

"No, Liza, it would be happy for you if you were to die soon of consumption in some corner, in some cellar like that woman just now. In the hospital, do you say? You will be lucky if they take you, but what if you are still of use to the madam here? Consumption is a queer disease, it is not like fever. The patient goes on hoping till the last minute and says he is all right. He deludes himself. And that just suits your madam. Don't doubt it, that's how it is; you have sold your soul, and what is more you owe money, so you daren't say a word. But when you are dying, all will abandon you, all will turn away from you, for then there will be nothing to get from you. What's more, they will reproach you for cumbering the place, for being so long over dying. However you beg you won't get a drink of water without abuse: 'Whenever are you going off, you nasty hussy, you won't let us sleep with your moaning, you make the gentlemen sick.' That's true, I have heard such things said myself. They will thrust you dying into the filthiest corner in the cellar — in the damp and darkness; what will your thoughts be, lying there alone? When you die, strange hands will lay you out, with grumbling and impatience; no one will bless you, no one will sigh for you, they only want to get rid of you as soon as may be; they will buy a coffin, take you to the grave as they did that poor woman to-day, and celebrate your memory at the tavern. In the grave sleet, filth, wet snow — no need to put themselves out for you — 'Let her down, Vanuha; it's just like her luck — even here, she is head-foremost, the hussy. Shorten the cord, you rascal.' 'It's all right as it is.' 'All right, is it? Why, she's on her side! She was a fellow-creature, after all! But, never mind, throw the earth on her.' And they won't care to waste much time quarrelling over you. They will scatter the wet blue clay as quick as they can and go off to the tavern . . . and there your memory on earth will end; other women have children to go to their graves, fathers, husbands. While for you neither tear, nor sigh, nor remembrance; no one in the whole world will ever come to you, your name will vanish from the face of the earth — as though you had never existed, never been born at all! Nothing but filth and mud, however you knock at your coffin lid at night, when the dead arise, however you cry: 'Let me out, kind people, to live in the light of day! My life was no life at all; my life has been thrown away like a dishclout; it was drunk away in the tavern at the Haymarket; let me out, kind people, to live in the world again.' "

And I worked myself up to such a pitch that I began to have a lump in my throat myself, and . . . and all at once I stopped, sat up in dismay, and bending over apprehensively, began to listen with a beating heart. I had reason to be troubled.

I had felt for some time that I was turning her soul upside down and rending her heart, and — the more I was convinced of it, the more eagerly I desired to gain my object as quickly and as effectually as possible. It was the exercise of my skill that carried me away; yet it was not merely sport. . . .

I knew I was speaking stiffly, artificially, even bookishly, in fact, I could not speak except "like a book." But that did not trouble me: I knew, I felt that

I should be understood and that this very bookishness might be an assistance. But now, having attained my effect, I was suddenly panic-stricken. Never before had I witnessed such despair! She was lying on her face, thrusting her face into the pillow and clutching it in both hands. Her heart was being torn. Her youthful body was shuddering all over as though in convulsions. Suppressed sobs rent her bosom and suddenly burst out in weeping and wailing, then she pressed closer into the pillow: she did not want any one here, not a living soul, to know of her anguish and her tears. She bit the pillow, bit her hand till it bled (I saw that afterwards), or, thrusting her fingers into her dishevelled hair, seemed rigid with the effort of restraint, holding her breath and clenching her teeth. I began saying something, begging her to calm herself, but felt that I did not dare; and all at once, in a sort of cold shiver, almost in terror, began fumbling in the dark, trying hurriedly to get dressed to go. It was dark: though I tried my best I could not finish dressing quickly. Suddenly I felt a box of matches and a candlestick with a whole candle in it. As soon as the room was lighted up, Liza sprang up, sat up in bed, and with a contorted face, with a half-insane smile, looked at me almost senselessly. I sat down beside her and took her hands; she came to herself, made an impulsive movement towards me, would have caught hold of me, but did not dare, and slowly bowed her head before me.

"Liza, my dear, I was wrong . . . forgive me, my dear," I began, but she squeezed my hand in her fingers so tightly that I felt I was saying the wrong thing and stopped.

"This is my address, Liza, come to me."

"I will come," she answered resolutely, her head still bowed.

"But now I am going, good-bye . . . till we meet again."

I got up; she, too, stood up and suddenly flushed all over, gave a shudder, snatched up a shawl that was lying on a chair and muffled herself in it to her chin. As she did this she gave another sickly smile, blushed and looked at me strangely. I felt wretched; I was in haste to get away — to disappear.

"Wait a minute," she said suddenly, in the passage just at the doorway, stopping me with her hand on my overcoat. She put down the candle in hot haste and ran off; evidently she had thought of something or wanted to show me something. As she ran away she flushed, her eyes shone, and there was a smile on her lips — what was the meaning of it? Against my will I waited: she came back a minute later with an expression that seemed to ask forgiveness for something. In fact, it was not the same face, not the same look as the evening before: sullen, mistrustful and obstinate. Her eyes now were imploring, soft, and at the same time trustful, caressing, timid. The expression with which children look at people they are very fond of, of whom they are asking a favour. Her eyes were a light hazel, they were lovely eyes, full of life, and capable of expressing love as well as sullen hatred.

Making no explanation, as though I, as a sort of higher being, must understand everything without explanations, she held out a piece of paper to me. Her whole face was positively beaming at that instant with naïve, almost childish, triumph. I unfolded it. It was a letter to her from a medical student or some one of that sort — a very high-flown and flowery, but extremely respectful, love-letter. I don't recall the words now, but I remember well that through the high-flown phrases there was apparent a genuine feeling, which cannot be feigned. When I had finished reading it I met her glowing, questioning, and childishly impatient eyes fixed upon me. She fastened her eyes upon my face and waited impatiently for what I should say. In a few words, hurriedly, but with a sort of joy and pride, she explained to me that she had been to a dance somewhere in a private house, a family of "very nice people, *who knew nothing*, absolutely nothing, for she had only come here so lately and it had all happened . . . and she hadn't made up her mind to stay and was certainly going away as soon as she had paid her debt. . . ." and at that party there had been the student who had danced with her all the evening. He had talked to her, and it turned out that he had known her in old days at Riga when he was a child, they had played together, but a very long time ago — and he knew her parents, but *about this* he knew nothing, nothing whatever, and had no suspicion! And the day after the dance (three days ago) he had sent her that letter through the friend with whom she had gone to the party . . . and . . . "well, that was all."

She dropped her shining eyes with a sort of bashfulness as she finished.

The poor girl was keeping that student's letter as a precious treasure, and had run to fetch it, her only treasure, because she did not want me to go away without knowing that she, too, was honestly and genuinely loved; that she, too, was addressed respectfully. No doubt that letter was destined to lie in her box and lead to nothing. But none the less, I am certain that she would keep it all her life as a precious treasure, as her pride and justification, and now at such a minute she had thought of that letter and brought it with naïve pride to raise herself in my eyes that I might see, that I, too, might think well of her. I said nothing, pressed her hand and went out. I so longed to get away. . . . I walked all the way home, in spite of the fact that the melting snow was still falling in heavy flakes. I was exhausted, shattered, in bewilderment. But behind the bewilderment the truth was already gleaming. The loathsome truth.

VIII

It was some time, however, before I consented to recognize that truth. Waking up in the morning after some hours of heavy, leaden sleep, and immediately realizing all that had happened on the previous day, I was positively amazed at my last night's *sentimentality* with Liza, at all those "outcries of horror and pity." "To think of having such an attack of womanish hysteria, pah!" I concluded. And what did I thrust my address upon her for? What if she comes? Let her come, though; it doesn't matter. . . . But *obviously* that was not now the chief and the most important matter: I had to make haste and at all costs save my reputation in the eyes of Zverkov and Simonov as quickly as possible; that was the chief business. And I was so taken up that morning that I actually forgot all about Liza.

First of all I had at once to repay what I had borrowed the day before from Simonov. I resolved on a desperate measure: to borrow fifteen roubles straight off from Anton Antonitch. As luck would have it he was in the best of humours that morning, and gave it to me at once, on the first asking. I was so delighted at this that, as I signed the I O U with a swaggering air, I told him casually that the night before "I had been keeping it up with some friends at the Hôtel de Paris; we were giving a farewell party to a comrade, in fact, I might say a friend of my childhood, and you know — a desperate rake, fearfully spoilt — of course, he belongs to a good family, and has considerable means, a brilliant career; he is witty, charming, a regular Lovelace,[11] you understand; we drank an extra 'half-dozen' and. . . ." And it went off all right; all this was uttered very easily, unconstrainedly and complacently.

On reaching home I promptly wrote to Simonov.

To this hour I am lost in admiration when I recall the truly gentlemanly, good-humoured, candid tone of my letter. With tact and good breeding, and, above all, entirely without superfluous words, I blamed myself for all that had happened. I defended myself, "if I really may be allowed to defend myself," by alleging that being utterly unaccustomed to wine, I had been intoxicated with the first glass, which I said I had drunk before they arrived, while I was waiting for them at the Hôtel de Paris between five and six o'clock. I begged Simonov's pardon especially; I asked him to convey my explanations to all the others, especially to Zverkov, whom "I seemed to remember as though in a dream" I had insulted. I added that I would have called upon all of them myself, but my head ached, and besides I had not the face to. I was particularly pleased with a certain lightness, almost carelessness (strictly within the bounds of politeness, however), which was apparent in my style, and better than any possible arguments, gave them at once to understand that I took rather an independent view of "all that unpleasantness last night"; that I was by no means so utterly crushed as you, my friends, probably imagine; but on the contrary, looked upon it as a

11 [The charming but unscrupulous character in Samuel Richardson's novel, *Clarissa Harlowe* (1747–48). — Editors' note.]

gentleman serenely respecting himself should look upon it. "On a young hero's past no censure is cast!"

"There is actually an aristocratic playfulness about it!" I thought admiringly, as I read over the letter. "And it's all because I am an intellectual and cultivated man! Another man in my place would not have known how to extricate himself, but here I have got out of it and am as jolly as ever again, and all because I am a cultivated and educated man of our day." And, indeed, perhaps, everything was due to the wine yesterday. H'm! . . . no, it was not the wine. I did not drink anything at all between five and six when I was waiting for them. I had lied to Simonov; I had lied shamelessly; and indeed I wasn't ashamed now. . . . Hang it all, though, the great thing was that I was rid of it.

I put six roubles in the letter, sealed it up, and asked Apollon to take it to Simonov. When he learned that there was money in the letter, Apollon became more respectful and agreed to take it. Towards evening I went out for a walk. My head was still aching and giddy after yesterday. But as evening came on and the twilight grew denser, my impressions and, following them, my thoughts grew more and more different and confused. Something was not dead within me, in the depths of my heart and conscience it would not die, and it showed itself in acute depression. For the most part I jostled my way through the most crowded business streets, along Myeshtchansky Street, along Sadovy Street and in Yusupov Garden. I always liked particularly sauntering along these streets in the dusk, just when there were crowds of working people of all sorts going home from their daily work, with faces looking cross with anxiety. What I liked was just that cheap bustle, that bare prose. On this occasion the jostling of the streets irritated me more than ever. I could not make out what was wrong with me, I could not find the clue, something seemed rising up continually in my soul, painfully, and refusing to be appeased. I returned home completely upset; it was just as though some crime were lying on my conscience.

The thought that Liza was coming worried me continually. It seemed queer to me that of all my recollections of yesterday this tormented me, as it were, especially, as it were, quite separately. Everything else I had quite succeeded in forgetting by the evening; I dismissed it all and was still perfectly satisfied with my letter to Simonov. But on this point I was not satisfied at all. It was as though I were worried only by Liza. "What if she comes," I thought incessantly, "well, it doesn't matter, let her come! H'm! it's horrid that she should see, for instance, how I live. Yesterday I seemed such a hero to her, while now, h'm! It's horrid, though, that I have let myself go so, the room looks like a beggar's. And I brought myself to go out to dinner in such a suit! And my American leather sofa with the stuffing sticking out. And my dressing-gown, which will not cover me, such tatters, and she will see all this and she will see Apollon. That beast is certain to insult her. He will fasten upon her in order to be rude to me. And I, of course, shall be panic-stricken as usual, I shall begin bowing and scraping before her and pulling my dressing-gown round me, I shall begin smiling, telling lies. Oh, the beastliness! And it isn't the beastliness of it that matters most! There is something more important, more loathsome, viler! Yes, viler! And to put on that dishonest lying mask again!" . . .

When I reached that thought I fired up all at once.

"Why dishonest? How dishonest? I was speaking sincerely last night. I remember there was real feeling in me, too. What I wanted was to excite an honourable feeling in her. . . . Her crying was a good thing, it will have a good effect."

Yet I could not feel at ease. All that evening, even when I had come back home, even after nine o'clock, when I calculated that Liza could not possibly come, she still haunted me, and what was worse, she came back to my mind always in the same position. One moment out of all that had happened last night stood vividly before my imagination; the moment when I struck a match and saw her pale, distorted face, with its look of torture. And what a pitiful, what an unnatural, what a distorted smile she had at that moment! But I did not know then that fifteen years later I should still in my imagination see Liza, always with the pitiful, distorted, inappropriate smile which was on her face at that minute.

Next day I was ready again to look upon it all as nonsense, due to over-excited nerves, and, above all, as *exaggerated.* I was always conscious of that weak point of mine, and sometimes very much afraid of it. "I exaggerate everything, that is where I go wrong," I repeated to myself every hour. But, however, "Liza will very likely come all the same" was the refrain with which all my reflections ended. I was so uneasy that I sometimes flew into a fury: "She'll come, she is certain to come!" I cried, running about the room, "if not to-day, she will come to-morrow; she'll find me out! The damnable romanticism of these pure hearts! Oh, the vileness — oh, the silliness — oh, the stupidity of these 'wretched sentimental souls'! Why, how fail to understand? How could one fail to understand?" . . .

But at this point I stopped short, and in great confusion, indeed.

And how few, how few words, I thought, in passing, were needed; how little of the idyllic (and affectedly, bookishly, artificially idyllic too) had sufficed to turn a whole human life at once according to my will. That's virginity, to be sure! Freshness of soil!

At times a thought occurred to me, to go to her, "to tell her all," and beg her not to come to me. But this thought stirred such wrath in me that I believed I should have crushed that "damned" Liza if she had chanced to be near me at the time. I should have insulted her, have spat at her, have turned her out, have struck her!

One day passed, however, another and another; she did not come and I began to grow calmer. I felt particularly bold and cheerful after nine o'clock, I even sometimes began dreaming, and rather sweetly: I, for instance, became the salvation of Liza, simply through her coming to me and my talking to her. . . . I develop her, educate her. Finally, I notice that she loves me, loves me passionately. I pretend not to understand (I don't know, however, why I pretend, just for effect, perhaps). At last all confusion, transfigured, trembling and sobbing, she flings herself at my feet and says that I am her saviour, and that she loves me better than anything in the world. I am amazed, but. . . .

"Liza," I say, "can you imagine that I have not noticed your love? I saw it all, I divined it, but I did not dare to approach you first, because I had an influence over you and was afraid that you would force yourself, from gratitude, to respond to my love, would try to rouse in your heart a feeling which was perhaps absent, and I did not wish that . . . because it would be tyranny . . . it would be indelicate (in short, I launch off at that point into European, inexplicably lofty subtleties à la George Sand),[12] but now, now you are mine, you are my creation, you are pure, you are good, you are my noble wife.

"Into my house come bold and free,
Its rightful mistress there to be."

Then we begin living together, go abroad and so on, and so on. In fact, in the end it seemed vulgar to me myself, and I began putting out my tongue at myself.

Besides, they won't let her out, "the hussy!" I thought. They don't let them go out very readily, especially in the evening (for some reason I fancied she would come in the evening, and at seven o'clock precisely). Though she did say she was not altogether a slave there yet, and had certain rights; so, h'm! Damn it all, she will come, she is sure to come!

It was a good thing, in fact, that Apollon distracted my attention at that time by his rudeness. He drove me beyond all patience! He was the bane of my life, the curse laid upon me by Providence. We had been squabbling continually for years, and I hated him. My God, how I hated him! I believe I had never hated anyone in my life as I hated him, especially at some moments. He was an elderly, dignified man, who worked part of his time as a tailor. But for some unknown reason he despised me beyond all measure, and looked down upon me insufferably. Though, indeed, he looked down upon every one. Simply to glance at that flaxen, smoothly brushed head, at the tuft of hair he combed upon his forehead and oiled with sunflower oil, at that dignified mouth, compressed into the shape

12 [Pseudonym of Armandine Lucile Aurore Dupin (1804–76), French novelist. — Editors' note.]

of the letter V, made one feel one was confronting a man who never doubted of himself. He was a pedant, to the most extreme point, the greatest pedant I had met on earth, and with that had a vanity only befitting Alexander of Macedon. He was in love with every button on his coat, every nail on his fingers — absolutely in love with them, and he looked it! In his behaviour to me he was a perfect tyrant, he spoke very little to me, and if he chanced to glance at me he gave me a firm, majestically self-confident and invariably ironical look that drove me sometimes to fury. He did his work with the air of doing me the greatest favour. Though he did scarcely anything for me, and did not, indeed, consider himself bound to do anything. There could be no doubt that he looked upon me as the greatest fool on earth, and that he did not "get rid of me" was simply that he could get wages from me every month. He consented to do nothing for me for seven roubles a month. Many sins should be forgiven me for what I suffered from him. My hatred reached such a point that sometimes his very step almost threw me into convulsions. What I loathed particularly was his lisp. His tongue must have been a little too long or something of that sort, for he continually lisped, and seemed to be very proud of it, imagining that it greatly added to his dignity. He spoke in a slow, measured tone, with his hands behind his back and his eyes fixed on the ground. He maddened me particularly when he read aloud the Psalms to himself behind his partition. Many a battle I waged over that reading! But he was awfully fond of reading aloud in the evenings, in a slow, even, singsong voice, as though over the dead. It is interesting that that is how he has ended: he hires himself out to read the Psalms over the dead, and at the same time he kills rats and makes blacking. But at that time I could not get rid of him, it was as though he were chemically combined with my existence. Besides, nothing would have induced him to consent to leave me. I could not live in furnished lodgings: my lodging was my private solitude, my shell, my cave, in which I concealed myself from all mankind, and Apollon seemed to me, for some reason, an integral part of that flat, and for seven years I could not turn him away.

To be two or three days behind with his wages, for instance, was impossible. He would have made such a fuss, I should not have known where to hide my head. But I was so exasperated with every one during those days, that I made up my mind for some reason and with some object to *punish* Apollon and not to pay him for a fortnight the wages that were owing him. I had for a long time — for the last two years — been intending to do this, simply in order to teach him not to give himself airs with me, and to show him that if I liked I could withhold his wages. I purposed to say nothing to him about it, and was purposely silent indeed, in order to score off his pride and force him to be the first to speak of his wages. Then I would take the seven roubles out of a drawer, show him I have the money put aside on purpose, but that I won't, I won't, I simply won't pay him his wages, I won't just because that is "what I wish," because "I am master, and it is for me to decide," because he has been disrespectful, because he has been rude; but if he were to ask respectfully I might be softened and give it to him, otherwise he might wait another fortnight, another three weeks, a whole month. . . .

But angry as I was, yet he got the better of me. I could not hold out for four days. He began as he always did begin in such cases, for there had been such cases already, there had been attempts (and it may be observed I knew all this beforehand, I knew his nasty tactics by heart). He would begin by fixing upon me an exceedingly severe stare, keeping it up for several minutes at a time, particularly on meeting me or seeing me out of the house. If I held out and pretended not to notice these stares, he would, still in silence, proceed to further tortures. All at once, apropos of nothing, he would walk softly and smoothly into my room, when I was pacing up and down or reading, stand at the door, one hand behind his back and one foot behind the other, and fix upon me a stare more than severe, utterly contemptuous. If I suddenly asked him what he wanted, he would make me no answer, but continue staring at me persistently for some seconds, then, with a peculiar compression of his lips and a most significant air, deliberately turn round and deliberately go back to his room. Two hours later he would come out again and again present himself before me in the same way. It had happened that in my fury I did not even ask him what he wanted, but simply raised my head sharply and imperiously and began staring back at him. So we stared at one another for two minutes; at last he turned with deliberation and dignity and went back again for two hours.

If I were still not brought to reason by all this, but persisted in my revolt, he would suddenly begin sighing while he looked at me, long, deep sighs as though measuring by them the depths of my moral degradation, and, of course, it ended at last by his triumphing completely: I raged and shouted, but still was forced to do what he wanted.

This time the usual staring manoeuvres had scarcely begun when I lost my temper and flew at him in a fury. I was irritated beyond endurance apart from him.

"Stay," I cried, in a frenzy, as he was slowly and silently turning, with one hand behind his back, to go to his room, "stay! Come back, come back, I tell you!" and I must have bawled so unnaturally, that he turned round and even looked at me with some wonder. However, he persisted in saying nothing, and that infuriated me.

"How dare you come and look at me like that without being sent for? Answer!"

After looking at me calmly for half a minute, he began turning round again.

"Stay!" I roared, running up to him, "don't stir! There. Answer, now: what did you come in to look at?"

"If you have any order to give me it's my duty to carry it out," he answered, after another silent pause, with a slow, measured lisp, raising his eyebrows and calmly twisting his head from one side to another, all this with exasperating composure.

"That's not what I am asking you about, you torturer!" I shouted, turning crimson with anger. "I'll tell you why you came here myself: you see, I don't give you your wages, you are so proud you don't want to bow down and ask for it, and so you come to punish me with your stupid stares, to worry me and you have no sus-pic-ion how stupid it is — stupid, stupid, stupid, stupid!" . . .

He would have turned round again without a word, but I seized him.

"Listen," I shouted to him. "Here's the money, do you see, here it is" (I took it out of the table drawer); "here's the seven roubles complete, but you are not going to have it, you . . . are . . . not . . . going . . . to . . . have it until you come respectfully with bowed head to beg my pardon. Do you hear?"

"That cannot be," he answered, with the most unnatural self-confidence.

"It shall be so," I said, "I give you my word of honour, it shall be!"

"And there's nothing for me to beg your pardon for," he went on, as though he had not noticed my exclamations at all. "Why, besides, you called me a 'torturer,' for which I can summon you at the police-station at any time for insulting behaviour."

"Go, summon me," I roared, "go at once, this very minute, this very second! You are a torturer all the same! a torturer!"

But he merely looked at me, then turned, and regardless of my loud calls to him, he walked to his room with an even step and without looking round.

"If it had not been for Liza nothing of this would have happened," I decided inwardly. Then, after waiting a minute, I went myself behind his screen with a dignified and solemn air, though my heart was beating slowly and violently.

"Apollon," I said quietly and emphatically, though I was breathless, "go at once without a minute's delay and fetch the police-officer."

He had meanwhile settled himself at his table, put on his spectacles and taken up some sewing. But, hearing my order, he burst into a guffaw.

"At once, go this minute! Go on, or else you can't imagine what will happen."

"You are certainly out of your mind," he observed, without even raising his head, lisping as deliberately as ever and threading his needle. "Whoever heard of a man sending for the police against himself? And as for being frightened — you are upsetting yourself about nothing, for nothing will come of it."

"Go!" I shrieked, clutching him by the shoulder. I felt I should strike him in a minute.

But I did not notice the door from the passage softly and slowly open at that instant and a figure come in, stop short, and begin staring at us in perplexity. I glanced, nearly swooned with shame, and rushed back to my room. There, clutching at my hair with both hands, I leaned my head against the wall and stood motionless in that position.

Two minutes later I heard Apollon's deliberate footsteps. "There is some woman asking for you," he said, looking at me with peculiar severity. Then he stood aside and let in Liza. He would not go away, but stared at us sarcastically.

"Go away, go away," I commanded in desperation. At that moment my clock began whirring and wheezing and struck seven.

IX

Into my house come bold and free,
Its rightful mistress there to be.

I stood before her crushed, crestfallen, revoltingly confused, and I believe I smiled as I did my utmost to wrap myself in the skirts of my ragged wadded dressing-gown — exactly as I had imagined the scene not long before in a fit of depression. After standing over us for a couple of minutes Apollon went away, but that did not make me more at ease. What made it worse was that she, too, was overwhelmed with confusion, more so, in fact, than I should have expected. At the sight of me, of course.

"Sit down," I said mechanically, moving a chair up to the table, and I sat down on the sofa. She obediently sat down at once and gazed at me open-eyed, evidently expecting something from me at once. This naïveté of expectation drove me to fury, but I restrained myself.

She ought to have tried not to notice, as though everything had been as usual, while instead of that, she . . . and I dimly felt that I should make her pay dearly for *all this.*

"You have found me in a strange position, Liza," I began, stammering and knowing that this was the wrong way to begin. "No, no, don't imagine anything," I cried, seeing that she had suddenly flushed. "I am not ashamed of my poverty. . . . On the contrary I look with pride on my poverty. I am poor but honourable. . . . One can be poor and honourable," I muttered. "However . . . would you like tea?" . . .

"No," she was beginning.

"Wait a minute."

I leapt up and ran to Apollon. I had to get out of the room somehow.

"Apollon," I whispered in feverish haste, flinging down before him the seven roubles which had remained all the time in my clenched fist, "here are your wages, you see I give them to you; but for that you must come to my rescue: bring me tea and a dozen rusks from the restaurant. If you won't go, you'll make me a miserable man! You don't know what this woman is. . . . This is — everything! You may be imagining something. . . . But you don't know what that woman is!" . . .

Apollon, who had already sat down to his work and put on his spectacles again, at first glanced askance at the money without speaking or putting down his needle; then, without paying the slightest attention to me or making any answer he went on busying himself with his needle, which he had not yet threaded. I waited before him for three minutes with my arms crossed *à la Napoléon.* My temples were moist with sweat. I was pale, I felt it. But, thank God, he must have been moved to pity, looking at me. Having threaded his needle, he deliberately got up from his seat, deliberately moved back his chair, deliberately took off his spectacles, deliberately counted the money, and finally asking me over his shoulder: "Shall I get a whole portion?" deliberately walked out of the room. As I was going back to Liza, the thought occurred to me on the way: shouldn't I run away just as I was in my dressing-gown, no matter where, and then let happen what would?

I sat down again. She looked at me uneasily. For some minutes we were silent.

"I will kill him," I shouted suddenly, striking the table with my fist so that the ink spurted out of the inkstand.

"What are you saying!" she cried, starting.

"I will kill him! kill him!" I shrieked, suddenly striking the table in absolute frenzy, and at the same time fully understanding how stupid it was to be in such a frenzy. "You don't know, Liza, what that torturer is to me. He is my torturer. . . . He has gone now to fetch some rusks; he. . . ."

And suddenly I burst into tears. It was an hysterical attack. How ashamed I felt in the midst of my sobs; but still I could not restrain them.

She was frightened.

"What is the matter? What is wrong?" she cried, fussing about me.

"Water, give me water, over there!" I muttered in a faint voice, though I was inwardly conscious that I could have got on very well without water and without muttering in a faint voice. But I was what is called *putting it on,* to save appearances, though the attack was a genuine one.

She gave me water, looking at me in bewilderment. At that moment Apollon brought in the tea. It suddenly seemed to me that this commonplace, prosaic tea was horribly undignified and paltry after all that had happened, and I blushed crimson. Liza looked at Apollon with positive alarm. He went out without a glance at either of us.

"Liza, do you despise me?" I asked, looking at her fixedly, trembling with impatience to know what she was thinking.

She was confused, and did not know what to answer.

"Drink your tea," I said to her angrily. I was angry with myself, but, of course, it was she who would have to pay for it. A horrible spite against her suddenly surged up in my heart; I believe I could have killed her. To revenge myself on her I swore inwardly not to say a word to her all the time. "She is the cause of it all," I thought.

Our silence lasted for five minutes. The tea stood on the table; we did not touch it. I had got to the point of purposely refraining from beginning in order to embarrass her further; it was awkward for her to begin alone. Several times she glanced at me with mournful perplexity. I was obstinately silent. I was, of course, myself the chief sufferer, because I was fully conscious of the disgusting meanness of my spiteful stupidity, and yet at the same time I could not restrain myself.

"I want to . . . get away . . . from there altogether," she began, to break the silence in some way, but, poor girl, that was just what she ought not to have spoken about at such a stupid moment to a man so stupid as I was. My heart positively ached with pity for her tactless and unnecessary straightforwardness. But something hideous at once stifled all compassion in me; it even provoked me to greater venom. I did not care what happened. Another five minutes passed.

"Perhaps I am in your way," she began timidly, hardly audibly, and was getting up.

But as soon as I saw this first impulse of wounded dignity I positively trembled with spite, and at once burst out.

"Why have you come to me, tell me that, please?" I began, gasping for breath and regardless of logical connection in my words. I longed to have it all out at once, at one burst; I did not even trouble how to begin. "Why have you come? Answer, answer," I cried, hardly knowing what I was doing. "I'll tell you, my good girl, why you have come. You've come because I talked sentimental stuff to you then. So now you are soft as butter and longing for fine sentiments again. So you may as well know that I was laughing at you then. And I am laughing at you now. Why are you shuddering? Yes, I was laughing at you! I had been insulted just before, at dinner, by the fellows who came that evening before me. I came to you, meaning to thrash one of them, an officer; but I didn't succeed, I didn't find him; I had to avenge the insult on some one to get back my own again; you turned up, I vented my spleen on you and laughed at you. I had been humiliated, so I wanted to humiliate; I had been treated like a rag, so I wanted to show my power. . . . That's what it was, and you imagined I had come there on purpose to save you. Yes? You imagined that? You imagined that?"

I knew that she would perhaps be muddled and not take it all in exactly, but I knew, too, that she would grasp the gist of it, very well indeed. And so, indeed, she did. She turned white as a handkerchief, tried to say something, and her lips worked painfully; but she sank on a chair as though she had been felled by an axe. And all the time afterwards she listened to me with her lips parted and her eyes wide-open, shuddering with awful terror. The cynicism, the cynicism of my words overwhelmed her.

"Save you!" I went on, jumping up from my chair and running up and down the room before her. "Save you from what? But perhaps I am worse than you myself. Why didn't you throw it in my teeth when I was giving you that sermon: 'But what did you come here yourself for? Was it to read us a sermon?' Power, power was what I wanted then, sport was what I wanted, I wanted to wring out your tears, your humiliation, your hysteria — that was what I wanted then! Of course, I couldn't keep it up then, because I am a wretched creature, I was frightened, and, the devil knows why, gave you my address in my folly. Afterwards, before I got home, I was cursing and swearing at you because of that address, I hated you already because of the lies I had told you. Because I only like playing with words, only dreaming, but, do you know, what I really want is that you should all go to hell. That is what I want. I want peace; yes, I'd sell the whole world for a farthing, straight off, so long as I was left in peace. Is the world to go to pot, or am I to go without my tea? I say that the world may go to pot for me so long as I always get my tea. Did you know that, or not? Well, anyway, I know that I am a blackguard, a scoundrel, an egoist, a sluggard. Here I have been shuddering for the last three days at the thought of your coming. And do you know what has worried me particularly for these three days? That I posed as such a hero to you, and now you would see me in a wretched torn dressing-gown, beggarly, loathsome. I told you just now that I was not ashamed of my poverty; so you may as well know that I am ashamed of it; I am more ashamed of it than of anything, more afraid of it than of being found out if I were a thief, because I am as vain as though I had been skinned and the very air blowing on me hurt. Surely by now you must realize that I shall never forgive you for having found me in this wretched dressing-gown, just as I was flying at Apollon like a spiteful cur. The saviour, the former hero, was flying like a mangy, unkempt sheep-dog at his lackey, and the lackey was jeering at him! And I shall never forgive you for the tears I could not help shedding before you just now, like some silly woman put to shame! And for what I am confessing to you now,

I shall never forgive *you* either! Yes — you must answer for it all because you turned up like this, because I am a blackguard, because I am the nastiest, stupidest, absurdest and most envious of all the worms on earth, who are not a bit better than I am, but, the devil knows why, are never put to confusion; while I shall always be insulted by every louse, that is my doom! And what is it to me that you don't understand a word of this! And what do I care, what do I care about you, and whether you go to ruin there or not? Do you understand? How I shall hate you now after saying this, for having been here and listening. Why, it's not once in a lifetime a man speaks out like this, and then it is in hysterics! . . . What more do you want? Why do you still stand confronting me, after all this? Why are you worrying me? Why don't you go?"

But at this point a strange thing happened: I was so accustomed to think and imagine everything from books, and to picture everything in the world to myself just as I had made it up in my dreams beforehand, that I could not all at once take in this strange circumstance. What happened was this: Liza, insulted and crushed by me, understood a great deal more than I imagined. She understood from all this what a woman understands first of all, if she feels genuine love, that is, that I was myself unhappy.

The frightened and wounded expression on her face was followed first by a look of sorrowful perplexity. When I began calling myself a scoundrel and a blackguard and my tears flowed (the tirade was accompanied throughout by tears) her whole face worked convulsively. She was on the point of getting up and stopping me; when I finished she took no notice of my shouting: "Why are you here, why don't you go away?" but realized only that it must have been very bitter to me to say all this. Besides, she was so crushed, poor girl; she considered herself infinitely beneath me; how could she feel anger or resentment? She suddenly leapt up from her chair with an irresistible impulse and held out her hands, yearning towards me, though still timid and not daring to stir. . . . At this point there was a revulsion in my heart, too. Then she suddenly rushed to me, threw her arms round me and burst into tears. I, too, could not restrain myself, and sobbed as I never had before.

"They won't let me . . . I can't be good!" I managed to articulate; then I went to the sofa, fell on it face downwards, and sobbed on it for a quarter of an hour in genuine hysterics. She came close to me, put her arms round me and stayed motionless in that position. But the trouble was that the hysterics could not go on for ever, and (I am writing the loathsome truth) lying face downwards on the sofa with my face thrust into my nasty leather pillow, I began by degrees to be aware of a far-away, involuntary but irresistible feeling that it would be awkward now for me to raise my head and look Liza straight in the face. Why was I ashamed? I don't know, but I was ashamed. The thought, too, came into my overwrought brain that our parts now were completely changed, that she was now the heroine, while I was just such a crushed and humiliated creature as she had been before me that night — four days before. . . . And all this came into my mind during the minutes I was lying on my face on the sofa.

My God! surely I was not envious of her then.

I don't know, to this day I cannot decide, and at the time, of course, I was still less able to understand what I was feeling than now. I cannot get on without domineering and tyrannizing over some one, but . . . there is no explaining anything by reasoning and so it is useless to reason.

I conquered myself, however, and raised my head; I had to do so sooner or later . . . and I am convinced to this day that it was just because I was ashamed to look at her that another feeling was suddenly kindled and flamed up in my heart . . . a feeling of mastery and possession. My eyes gleamed with passion, and I gripped her hands tightly. How I hated her and how I was drawn to her at that minute! The one feeling intensified the other. It was almost like an act of vengeance. At first there was a look of amazement, even of terror, on her face, but only for one instant. She warmly and rapturously embraced me.

X

A quarter of an hour later I was rushing up and down the room in frenzied impatience, from minute to minute I went up to the screen and peeped through the crack at Liza. She was sitting on the ground with her head leaning against the bed, and must have been crying. But she did not go away, and that irritated me. This time she understood it all. I had insulted her finally, but . . . there's no need to describe it. She realized that my outburst of passion had been simply revenge, a fresh humiliation, and that to my earlier, almost causeless hatred was added now a *personal hatred,* born of envy. . . . Though I do not maintain positively that she understood all this distinctly; but she certainly did fully understand that I was a despicable man, and what was worse, incapable of loving her.

I know I shall be told that this is incredible — but it is incredible to be as spiteful and stupid as I was; it may be added that it was strange I should not love her, or at any rate, appreciate her love. Why is it strange? In the first place, by then I was incapable of love, for, I repeat, with me loving meant tyrannizing and showing my moral superiority. I have never in my life been able to imagine any other sort of love, and have nowadays come to the point of sometimes thinking that love really consists in the right — freely given by the beloved object — to tyrannize over her.

Even in my underground dreams I did not imagine love except as a struggle. I began it always with hatred and ended it with moral subjugation, and afterwards I never knew what to do with the subjugated object. And what is there to wonder at in that, since I had succeeded in so corrupting myself, since I was so out of touch with "real life," as to have actually thought of reproaching her, and putting her to shame for having come to me to hear "fine sentiments"; and did not even guess that she had come not to hear fine sentiments, but to love me, because to a woman all reformation — all salvation from any sort of ruin, and all moral renewal — is included in love and can only show itself in that form.

I did not hate her so much, however, when I was running about the room and peeping through the crack in the screen. I was only insufferably oppressed by her being here. I wanted her to disappear. I wanted "peace," to be left alone in my underground world. Real life oppressed me with its novelty so much that I could hardly breathe.

But several minutes passed and she still remained without stirring, as though she were unconscious. I had the shamelessness to tap softly at the screen as though to remind her. . . . She started, sprang up, and flew to seek her kerchief, her hat, her coat, as though making her escape from me. . . . Two minutes later she came from behind the screen and looked with heavy eyes at me. I gave a spiteful grin, which was forced, however, to *keep up appearances,* and I turned away from her eyes.

"Good-bye," she said, going towards the door.

I ran up to her, seized her hand, opened it, thrust something in it and closed it again. Then I turned at once and dashed away in haste to the other corner of the room to avoid seeing, anyway. . . .

I did mean a moment since to tell a lie — to write that I did this accidentally, not knowing what I was doing through foolishness, through losing my head. But I don't want to lie, and so I will say straight out that I opened her hand and put the money in it . . . from spite. It came into my head to do this while I was running up and down the room and she was sitting behind the screen. But this I can say for certain: though I did that cruel thing purposely, it was not an impulse from the heart, but came from my evil brain. This cruelty was so affected, so purposely made up, so completely a product of the brain, of books, that I could not even keep it up a minute — first I dashed away to avoid seeing her, and then in shame and despair rushed after Liza. I opened the door in the passage and began listening.

"Liza! Liza!" I cried on the stairs, but in a low voice, not boldly.

There was no answer, but I fancied I heard her footsteps, lower down on the stairs.

"Liza!" I cried, more loudly.

No answer. But at that minute I heard the stiff outer glass door open heavily with a creak and slam violently, the sound echoed up the stairs.

She had gone. I went back to my room in hesitation. I felt horribly oppressed.

I stood still at the table beside the chair on which she had sat and looked aimlessly before me. A minute passed, suddenly I started; straight before me on the table I saw. . . . In short, I saw a crumpled blue five-rouble note, the one I had thrust into her hand a minute before. It was the same note; it could be no other, there was no other in the flat. So she had managed to fling it from her hand on the table at the moment when I had dashed into the further corner.

Well! I might have expected that she would do that. Might I have expected it? No, I was such an egoist, I was so lacking in respect for my fellow-creatures that I could not even imagine she would do so. I could not endure it. A minute later I flew like a madman to dress, flinging on what I could at random and ran headlong after her. She could not have got two hundred paces away when I ran out into the street.

It was a still night and the snow was coming down in masses and falling almost perpendicularly, covering the pavement and the empty street as though with a pillow. There was no one in the street, no sound was to be heard. The street lamps gave a disconsolate and useless glimmer. I ran two hundred paces to the cross-roads and stopped short.

Where had she gone? And why was I running after her?

Why? To fall down before her, to sob with remorse, to kiss her feet, to entreat her forgiveness! I longed for that, my whole breast was being rent to pieces, and never, never shall I recall that minute with indifference. But — what for? I thought. Should I not begin to hate her, perhaps, even to-morrow, just because I had kissed her feet to-day? Should I give her happiness? Had I not recognized that day, for the hundredth time, what I was worth? Should I not torture her?

I stood in the snow, gazing into the troubled darkness and pondered this.

"And will it not be better?" I mused fantastically, afterwards at home, stifling the living pang of my heart with fantastic dreams. "Will it not be better that she should keep the resentment of the insult for ever? Resentment — why, it is purification; it is a most stinging and painful consciousness! To-morrow I should have defiled her soul and have exhausted her heart, while now the feeling of insult will never die in her heart, and however loathsome the filth awaiting her — the feeling of insult will elevate and purify her . . . by hatred . . . h'm! . . . perhaps too, by forgiveness. . . . Will all that make things easier for her, though? . . ."

And, indeed, I will ask on my own account here an idle question: which is better — cheap happiness or exalted sufferings? Well, which is better?

So I dreamed as I sat at home that evening, almost dead with the pain in my soul. Never had I endured such suffering and remorse, yet could there have been the faintest doubt when I ran out from my lodging that I should turn back halfway? I never met Liza again and I have heard nothing of her. I will add, too, that

I remained for a long time afterwards pleased with the phrase about the benefit from resentment and hatred, in spite of the fact that I almost fell ill from misery.

Even now, so many years later, all this is somehow a very evil memory. I have many evil memories now, but . . . hadn't I better end my "Notes" here? I believe I made a mistake in beginning to write them, anyway I have felt ashamed all the time I've been writing this story; so it's hardly literature so much as a corrective punishment. Why, to tell long stories, showing how I have spoiled my life through morally rotting in my corner, through lack of fitting environment, through divorce from real life, and rankling spite in my underground world, would certainly not be interesting; a novel needs a hero, and all the traits for an anti-hero are *expressly* gathered together here, and what matters most, it all produces an unpleasant impression, for we are all divorced from life, we are all cripples, every one of us, more or less. We are so divorced from it that we feel at once a sort of loathing for real life, and so cannot bear to be reminded of it. Why, we have come almost to looking upon real life as an effort, almost as hard work, and we are all privately agreed that it is better in books. And why do we fuss and fume sometimes? Why are we perverse and ask for something else? We don't know what ourselves. It would be the worse for us if our petulant prayers were answered. Come, try, give any one of us, for instance, a little more independence, untie our hands, widen the spheres of our activity, relax the control and we . . . yes, I assure you . . . we should be begging to be under control again at once. I know that you will very likely be angry with me for that, and will begin shouting and stamping. Speak for yourself, you will say, and for your miseries in your underground holes, and don't dare to say all of us — excuse me, gentlemen, I am not justifying myself with that "all of us." As for what concerns me in particular I have only in my life carried to an extreme what you have not dared to carry halfway, and what's more, you have taken your cowardice for good sense, and have found comfort in deceiving yourselves. So that perhaps, after all, there is more life in me than in you. Look into it more carefully! Why, we don't even know what living means now, what it is, and what it is called! Leave us alone without books and we shall be lost and in confusion at once. We shall not know what to join on to, what to cling to, what to love and what to hate, what to respect and what to despise. We are oppressed at being men — men with a real individual body and blood, we are ashamed of it, we think it a disgrace and try to contrive to be some sort of impossible generalized man. We are still-born, and for generations past have been begotten, not by living fathers, and that suits us better and better. We are developing a taste for it. Soon we shall contrive to be born somehow from an idea. But enough; I don't want to write more from "Underground."

[The notes of this paradoxalist do not end here, however. He could not refrain from going on with them, but it seems to us that we may stop here.]

AFTERWORD

When one sets out to read a book that has achieved the status of a classic one may reasonably expect to be able to experience much of the book without first boning up on the background, either of the author's life or his times. And surely every reader responds immediately to *Notes from Underground,* partly because the alienated narrator seems so curiously modern, partly because the topics of freedom and security are so much our concern. And yet, although it is evident that this book, like all classics, is our contemporary, it is also evident that any book, no matter how universal its appeal, is written at a particular time, and some familiarity with the times may deepen our understanding and enjoyment. And when the book can with some justice be called a philosophical novel or a novel of ideas, familiarity with these ideas is highly desirable. All this by way of prefacing a few broad remarks on the climate of opinion in which Dostoevsky wrote.

The slow process of the secularization of Western Europe and England began at least as early as the beginnings of the Renaissance, but Russia did not really share in this secularization until several centuries later, when in the eighteenth century Peter the Great looked to the West for ideas that would strengthen his despotism. He built a new palace (designed by a Frenchman and modeled on Versailles), imported cannon and French military engineers for his army, and created the Russian navy, but Russia's social structure remained unaltered. The high culture of the aristocracy (e.g., literature, ballet, painting) underwent a fairly steady transformation, but the masses remained ignorant serfs. Thus when totalitarian Russia in the middle of the nineteenth century was forced into genuine contact with the philosophic and economic ideas that had slowly evolved and become organic in the West, the shock in Russia was enormous. Russia was still an agrarian society ruled by a despot who had the support of a church which exerted a spiritual authority immensely greater than the churches of, say, England or France. One index of the time-lag between Russia and Western Europe is the fact that even up to the beginning of the last decade of the nineteenth century almost all the important Russian writers were members of the aristocracy, whereas in Western Europe they were members of the bourgeoisie, a class that was not yet of importance in Russia. (Dostoevsky's father, a physician who owned serfs, was an impoverished nobleman.) There were, of course, merchants, bureaucrats, and members of intellectual professions in Russia, but there was not really a unified bourgeoisie, and so the chief characters in Russian fiction of the nineteenth century, unlike those in English and French fiction, are usually aristocrats or civil servants.

When the Western glorification of reason and science was belatedly encountered in nineteenth-century Russia, it was passionately embraced by the radical Westernizers, who extolled European achievements and argued that Russia should share in them, and it was passionately denounced by the conservative Slavophils, who extolled the old values of humility and brotherly love and who argued that Peter the Great's interest in the West was an unfortunate interruption in Russian tradition. For the Slavophils, Russian culture was essentially religious, and the people had delegated to the Czar the temporal power needed to maintain this culture. Among the Westernizers was Nicolai Chernyshevsky, whose Utopian novel, *What Is to Be Done?* (1863), written while he was imprisoned as an enemy of the state, propounded a doctrine that he called "rational egoism": happiness is achieved when everyone pursues his own rational desires. Chernyshevsky was a follower of the English Utilitarian philosopher John Stuart Mill (the fact that Chernyshevsky was exiled for twenty-one years in Siberia, while Mill was esteemed in England says a good deal about the differences between their countries). Chernyshevsky subscribed to the assumptions that (1) man is innately good; (2) reason and self-interest alone are the sanctions of morality; (3) enlightened man, guided by reason, seeks his self-interest; (4) reason and self-interest, displacing authoritarianism, especially the authoritarianism of the church, will usher in an ideal society. Dostoevsky's *Notes from Underground* is a potent reply, and one of the great anticipations of the twentieth century's perception that when the Age of Reason displaced religious values and offered a creed of rational self-interest, it claimed for its values a finality that they did not have. Later, when the limitations of these values became evident, confidence gave way to an anguished sense of meaninglessness.

Dostoevsky's underground man several times refers to the Crystal Palace, the building that housed the Great Exhibition (a trade fair) of 1851 in England, and we can take as an example of Western confidence in reason and science Prince Albert's speech celebrating the Exhibition:

> We are living at a period of most wonderful transition which tends rapidly to accomplish that great end, to which, indeed, all history points — *the realisation of the unity of mankind.* . . . On the other hand, the *great principle of the division of labor,* which may be called the moving power of civilisation, is being extended to all branches of science, indus-

> try and art. . . . The products of all quarters of the globe are placed at our disposal, and we have only to choose which is the best and the cheapest for our purposes, and the powers of production are intrusted to the stimulus of *competition and capital.*
>
> So man is approaching a more complete fulfilment of that great and sacred mission which he has to perform in this world. His reason being created after the image of God, he has to use it to discover the laws by which the Almighty governs His creation, and, by making these laws his standard of action, to conquer nature to his use, himself a divine instrument.

The bourgeois deification of man is evident here, in its overall complacency, in its praise of technology (England of course was the leader of the Industrial Revolution), and in its pride in using reason as a tool to exploit nature. Later generations learned to view technology as a source of enormous danger, division of labor as a source of man's alienation from his work, and unregulated competition or free enterprise as cruel and dehumanizing. In the middle of the nineteenth century, however, sentiments such as Albert's could be met only with general applause, except in such a place as Russia where old social and theological values belatedly survived. That Prince Albert's speech, so evidently bourgeois, was in accord with Western Europe's most modern thinking, can be seen by comparing it with a strikingly similar passage from *The Communist Manifesto* (1848), by Marx and Engels. They wrote:

> National differences and antagonisms are daily vanishing more and more, owing to freedom of commerce and uniformity in modes of production. . . . In proportion as antagonism between classes vanishes, the hostility of one nation to another will come to an end. . . . We shall have an association in which the free development of each is the free development of all.

It was against such neat and confident middle-class ideas that Dostoevsky wrote *Notes from Underground,* the confession of a man who does not wish to be encased in a crystal palace and who, in fact, prefers to throw stones. The bland confidence that reason and science can discover the laws of nature and that we will be pleased by this discovery is countered by a hatred of a thoroughly predictable world, a world still sought by those engaged in "human engineering."

> You say, science itself will teach man . . . that he never has really had any caprice or will of his own, and that he himself is something of the

> nature of a piano-key or the stop of an organ, and that there are, besides, things called the laws of nature; so that everything he does is not done by his willing it, but is done of itself, by the laws of nature. Consequently we have only to discover these laws of nature, and man will no longer have to answer for his actions and life will become exceedingly easy for him. All human actions will then, of course, be tabulated according to these laws, mathematically, like tables of logarithms up to 108,000, and entered in an index. . . .

And a curious consequence of this predictable, comfortable, rational world, the underground man points out, may be a desire for *dis*comfort, even for intense pain, a longing for something that lets us feel that we are human beings rather than keys on a piano. As a very simple example of our discontent with predictable perfection and our preference for the unexpected and imperfect, consider our response to those excellent frozen baked-goods we can buy at supermarkets. Our first experience with, say, an apple pie, is that it is delicious, and so is our second. But after a while we become bored with the sameness, and we prefer a homemade apple pie that one time may be a bit sweet, another time a bit tart, another time a bit overdone. The variations themselves afford pleasure; confronted with a succession of perfect pies, we will chose imperfection over the monotony of predictably persistent perfection.

Traditionally philosophers have argued that man has freedom of will if he can modify his conduct in the direction of an ideal; the ideal was often said to be self-interest, and reason was the guide toward this goal. The underground man argues that freedom to do anything at all, i.e., the mere exertion of will — even against one's self-interest — may be more satisfying than the achievement of self-interest through reason. There is much that is persuasive here; certainly in Part I the underground man's remorseless analysis of the problem and of his own character and motive arouses our deep interest and strikes responsive chords in us. Not reason, but a will to freedom, we recognize, is what often moves us. (The term "underground" has the appropriate revolutionary implication.) But we cannot help sensing, too, especially in Part II, that his furious insistence on freedom reveals what Matthew Arnold, Dostoevsky's English contemporary, called "bondage to the passing moment." The underground man is often persuasive, and certainly he is entertaining, in his analysis of the simple dreams of the Utopian rationalists, but his concept of freedom involves not only a rejection of external determinism (e.g., a planned society) but also a rejection of what can be called consistency of character. Most of us believe that we can most fully be ourselves if we have some settled character, and so, for example, we try to develop certain habits, say, the habit of honesty. If we find a wallet we return it, and we do not say that our action was not free, even though no other course of conduct might have been entertained. In short, the underground man's drive for freedom, though appealing deeply to our hatred of a society in which everything might be predicted, substitutes a terrifying world in which every trivial action is agonized over and which finally deprives the individual of any full experience of life. The underground man admits this: not only is he not a hero, he is less than a man; he often sees himself as some sort of animal "in a corner," a mouse, a fly, a worm:

> A novel needs a hero, and all the traits for an antihero are *expressly* gathered together here, and what matters most, it all produces an unpleasant impression, for we are all divorced from life, we are all cripples. ... We are so divorced from it that we feel at once a sort of loathing for real life, and so cannot bear to be reminded of it.

The underground man's misery is apparent in every line; if we are sympathetic to his regret that twice two equals four, we nevertheless are also aware that he cannot achieve any identity of his own:

> I did not know how to become anything: neither spiteful nor kind, neither a rascal nor an honest man, neither a hero nor an insect. ... I could not even become an insect.

The bourgeois novelists of the nineteenth century had dethroned the traditional hero and replaced him with more or less respectable bourgeois figures; Dostoevsky goes further, annihilating bourgeois values and giving us a protagonist whose values leave him unable to achieve an identity.

Notes from Underground, it seems fair to say (without implying that this is a fault), satirizes rationalistic reformers but offers no solution. Elsewhere in his writings Dostoevsky does offer a solution, faith in Christ, but in *Notes* the closest we come to such a vision is the pity and love offered by the prostitute Liza. The underground man's self-hatred could, of course, be a step toward a perception of God, but this is not the story that Dostoevsky gives us — though in a letter to his brother Dostoevsky says that the censors deleted a passage on "the necessity of belief in Christ." Had this novel, which uses the form of journal or a confession, moved toward an awareness of Christ, it would have more evidently been in the tradition of St. Augustine's *Confessions* (ca. 400), the Western world's first fully developed autobiography, recording Augustine's conversion from misery to joy, describing not only "confession of sin ... which showeth the wound to the physician" but also "confession of praise ... which giveth thanks for health." But as the text of *Notes* stands, the closest that the underground man comes to a religious solution is to raise a question:

> Why am I made with such desires? Can I have been constructed simply in order to come to the conclusion that all my construction is a cheat? Can this be my whole purpose? I do not believe it.

We are far, too, from another book called *Confessions,* Jean-Jacques Rousseau's, written in the mid-eighteenth century, which argued that the unaided individual is fundamentally good and that he can be trusted to judge between good and evil. But we can say that Dostoevsky's anti-hero, in his refusal to deceive himself with assumptions about his honesty or his rationality, and in his refusal to console himself with conventional, shallow ideas, displays a sort of heroism. We can say, too, that this novel of ideas is always a novel, never a treatise: we continually sense the urgency of the argument and yet we never feel that the narrative is a thin fable (as in, say, Voltaire's *Candide*), merely the vehicle for abstract ideas. In *Notes* the ideas are inseparable from the speaker, and we are at least as much concerned with the character and career of this bruised and vengeful man struggling for self-esteem in a brutal world as we are concerned with the abstracted ideas. We again and again find in the novel — as we do not find in philosophic treatises — an image of life.

LEO N. TOLSTOY

Count Leo Nikolayevich Tolstoy (1828–1910), son of a wealthy Russian nobleman, was orphaned at an early age, at which time he inherited vast estates in Central Russia. He was brought up by an aunt and attended Kazan University, but he left before receiving a degree. In 1851, at twenty-three, he joined the army and for the next five years led the dissolute life of an army officer in the Caucasus during the Crimean War. After the war he returned to his ancestral estate, where he eventually married. Some time around 1876 he underwent a spiritual conversion: he emancipated his serfs, traveled in Europe to study methods of education, and began a progressive school to educate the children of peasants. He became a vegetarian and a teetotaler, learned Greek in order to study early translations of the New Testament, finally renounced the Russian Orthodox Church, condemned the State, renounced his property, and lived the life of a peasant. Throughout Russia, Europe, and even in America, he was looked upon as a religious prophet. *My Confession,* Tolstoy's dramatic, autobiographical description of his spiritual conversion, was published in 1882. At eighty-two he abandoned his wife and, accompanied by one of his young daughters, began a last pilgrimage to preach his beliefs. He died in an obscure railroad station on the way. Tolstoy's major novels were written over a thirty-year period: *War and Peace* (1865–72), *Anna Karenina* (1875–76), *The Death of Ivan Ilych* (1884), *The Kreutzer Sonata* (1890), and *Resurrection* (1899). His treatise on esthetics, *What Is Art?,* was published in 1896.

THE DEATH OF IVAN ILYCH

Translated by Louise and Aylmer Maude

I

During an interval in the Melvinski trial in the large building of the Law Courts, the members and public prosecutor met in Ivan Egorovich Shebek's private room, where the conversation turned on the celebrated Krasovski case. Fëdor Vasilievich warmly maintained that it was not subject to their jurisdiction, Ivan Egorovich maintained the contrary, while Peter Ivanovich, not having entered into the discussion at the start, took no part in it but looked through the *Gazette* which had just been handed in.

"Gentlemen," he said, "Ivan Ilych has died!"

"You don't say so!"

"Here, read it yourself," replied Peter Ivanovich, handing Fëdor Vasilievich the paper still damp from the press. Surrounded by a black border were the words: "Praskovya Fëdorovna Goloviná, with profound sorrow, informs relatives and friends of the demise of her beloved husband Ivan Ilych Golovin, Member of the Court of Justice, which occurred on February the 4th of this year 1882. The funeral will take place on Friday at one o'clock in the afternoon."

Ivan Ilych had been a colleague of the gentlemen present and was liked by them all. He had been ill for some weeks with an illness said to be incurable. His post had been kept open for him, but there had been conjectures that in case of his death Alexeev might receive his appointment, and that either Vinnikov or Shtabel would succeed Alexeev. So on receiving the news of Ivan Ilych's death the first thought of each of the gentlemen in that private room was of the changes and promotions it might occasion among themselves or their acquaintances.

"I shall be sure to get Shtabel's place or Vinnikov's," thought Fëdor Vasilievich. "I was promised that long ago, and the promotion means an extra eight hundred rubles a year for me besides the allowance."

"Now I must apply for my brother-in-law's transfer from Kaluga," thought Peter Ivanovich. "My wife will be very glad, and then she won't be able to say that I never do anything for her relations."

"I thought he would never leave his bed again," said Peter Ivanovich aloud. "It's very sad."

"But what really was the matter with him?"

"The doctors couldn't say — at least they could, but each of them said something different. When last I saw him I thought he was getting better."

"And I haven't been to see him since the holidays. I always meant to go."

"Had he any property?"

"I think his wife had a little — but something quite trifling."

"We shall have to go to see her, but they live so terribly far away."

"Far away from you, you mean. Everything's far away from your place."

"You see, he never can forgive my living on the other side of the river," said Peter Ivanovich, smiling at Shebek. Then, still talking of the distances between different parts of the city, they returned to the Court.

Besides considerations as to the possible transfers and promotions likely to result from Ivan Ilych's death, the mere fact of the death of a near acquaintance aroused, as usual, in all who heard of it the complacent feeling that, "it is he who is dead and not I."

Each one thought or felt, "Well, he's dead but I'm alive!" But the more intimate of Ivan Ilych's acquaintances, his so-called friends, could not help thinking also that they would now have to fulfil the very tiresome demands of propriety by attending the funeral service and paying a visit of condolence to the widow.

Fëdor Vasilievich and Peter Ivanovich had been his nearest acquaintances. Peter Ivanovich had studied law with Ivan Ilych and had considered himself to be under obligations to him.

Having told his wife at dinner-time of Ivan Ilych's death and of his conjecture that it might be possible to get her brother transferred to their circuit, Peter Ivanovich sacrificed his usual nap, put on his evening clothes, and drove to Ivan Ilych's house.

At the entrance stood a carriage and two cabs. Leaning against the wall in the hall downstairs near the cloak-stand was a coffin-lid covered with cloth of gold, ornamented with gold cord and tassels, that had been polished up with metal powder. Two ladies in black were taking off their fur cloaks. Peter Ivanovich recognized one of them as Ivan Ilych's sister, but the other was a stranger to him. His colleague Schwartz was just coming downstairs, but on seeing Peter Ivanovich enter he stopped and winked at him, as if to say: "Ivan Ilych has made a mess of things — not like you and me."

Schwartz's face with his Piccadilly whiskers[1] and his slim figure in evening dress had as usual an air of elegant solemnity which contrasted with the play-

1 [Side-whiskers. — Editors' note.]

fulness of his character and had a special piquancy here, or so it seemed to Peter Ivanovich.

Peter Ivanovich allowed the ladies to precede him and slowly followed them upstairs. Schwartz did not come down but remained where he was, and Peter Ivanovich understood that he wanted to arrange where they should play bridge that evening. The ladies went upstairs to the widow's room, and Schwartz with seriously compressed lips but a playful look in his eyes, indicated by a twist of his eyebrows the room to the right where the body lay.

Peter Ivanovich, like everyone else on such occasions, entered feeling uncertain what he would have to do. All he knew was that at such times it is always safe to cross oneself. But he was not quite sure whether one should make obeisances while doing so. He therefore adopted a middle course. On entering the room he began crossing himself and made a slight movement resembling a bow. At the same time, as far as the motion of his head and arm allowed, he surveyed the room. Two young men — apparently nephews, one of whom was a high-school pupil — were leaving the room, crossing themselves as they did so. An old woman was standing motionless, and a lady with strangely arched eyebrows was saying something to her in a whisper. A vigorous, resolute Church Reader, in a frock-coat, was reading something in a loud voice with an expression that precluded any contradiction. The butler's assistant, Gerasim, stepping lightly in front of Peter Ivanovich, was strewing something on the floor. Noticing this, Peter Ivanovich was immediately aware of a faint odour of a decomposing body.

The last time he had called on Ivan Ilych, Peter Ivanovich had seen Gerasim in the study. Ivan Ilych had been particularly fond of him and he was performing the duty of a sick nurse.

Peter Ivanovich continued to make the sign of the cross, slightly inclining his head in an intermediate direction between the coffin, the Reader, and the icons on the table in a corner of the room. Afterwards, when it seemed to him that this movement of his arm in crossing himself had gone on too long, he stopped and began to look at the corpse.

The dead man lay, as dead men always lie, in a specially heavy way, his rigid limbs sunk in the soft cushions of the coffin, with the head forever bowed on the pillow. His yellow waxen brow with bald patches over his sunken temples was thrust up in the way peculiar to the dead, the protruding nose seeming to press on the upper lip. He was much changed and had grow even thinner since Peter Ivanovich had last seen him, but, as is always the case with the dead, his face was handsomer and above all more dignified than when he was alive. The expression on the face said that what was necessary had been accomplished, and accomplished rightly. Besides this there was in that expression a reproach and a warning to the living. This warning seemed to Peter Ivanovich out of place, or at least not applicable to him. He felt a certain discomfort and so he hurriedly crossed himself once more and turned and went out of the door — too hurriedly and too regardless of propriety, as he himself was aware.

Schwartz was waiting for him in the adjoining room with legs spread wide apart and both hands toying with his top-hat behind his back. The mere sight of that playful, well-groomed, and elegant figure refreshed Peter Ivanovich. He felt that Schwartz was above all these happenings and would not surrender to any depressing influences. His very look said that this incident of a church service for Ivan Ilych could not be a sufficient reason for infringing the order of the session — in other words, that it would certainly not prevent his unwrapping a new pack of cards and shuffling them that evening while a footman placed four fresh candles on the table: in fact, that there was no reason for supposing that this incident would hinder their spending the evening agreeably. Indeed he said this in a whisper as Peter Ivanovich passed him, proposing that they should meet for a game at Fëdor Vasilievich's. But apparently Peter Ivanovich was not destined to play bridge that evening. Praskovya Fëdorovna (a short, fat woman who despite all efforts to the contrary had continued to broaden steadily from her shoulders downwards and who had the same extraordinarily arched eyebrows as the lady who had been standing by the coffin), dressed all in black, her head covered with lace, came out of her own room with some other ladies, conducted them to the room where the dead body lay, and said: "The service will begin immediately. Please go in."

Schwartz, making an indefinite bow, stood still, evidently neither accepting nor declining this invitation. Praskovya Fëdorovna, recognizing Peter Ivanovich, sighed, went close up to him, took his hand, and said: "I know you were a true friend of Ivan Ilych . . ." and looked at him awaiting some suitable response. And Peter Ivanovich knew that, just as it had been the right thing to cross himself in that room, so what he had to do here was to press her hand, sigh, and say, "Believe me. . . ." So he did all this and as he did it felt that the desired result had been achieved: that both he and she were touched.

"Come with me. I want to speak to you before it begins," said the widow. "Give me your arm."

Peter Ivanovich gave her his arm and they went to the inner rooms, passing Schwartz, who winked at Peter Ivanovich compassionately.

"That does for our bridge! Don't object if we find another player. Perhaps you can cut in when you do escape," said his playful look.

Peter Ivanovich sighed still more deeply and despondently, and Praskovya Fëdorovna pressed his arm gratefully. When they reached the drawing-room, upholstered in pink cretonne and lighted by a dim lamp, they sat down at the table — she on a sofa and Peter Ivanovich on a low pouffe, the springs of which yielded spasmodically under his weight. Praskovya Fëdorovna had been on the point of warning him to take another seat, but felt that such a warning was out of keeping with her present condition and so changed her mind. As he sat down on the pouffe Peter Ivanovich recalled how Ivan Ilych had arranged this room and had consulted him regarding this pink cretonne with green leaves. The whole room was full of furniture and knick-knacks, and on her way to the sofa the lace of the widow's black shawl caught on the carved edge of the table. Peter Ivanovich rose to detach it, and the springs of the pouffe, relieved of his weight, rose also and gave him a push. The widow began detaching her shawl herself, and Peter Ivanovich again sat down, suppressing the rebellious springs of the pouffe under him. But the widow had not quite freed herself and Peter Ivanovich got up again, and again the pouffe rebelled and even creaked. When this was all over she took out a clean cambric handkerchief and began to weep. The episode with the shawl and the struggle with the pouffe had cooled Peter Ivanovich's emotions and he sat there with a sullen look on his face. This awkward situation was interrupted by Sokolov, Ivan Ilych's butler, who came to report that the plot in the cemetery that Praskovya Fëdorovna had chosen would cost two hundred rubles. She stopped weeping and, looking at Peter Ivanovich with the air of a victim, remarked in French that it was very hard for her. Peter Ivanovich made a silent gesture signifying his full conviction that it must indeed be so.

"Please smoke," she said in a magnanimous yet crushed voice, and turned to discuss with Sokolov the price of the plot for the grave.

Peter Ivanovich while lighting his cigarette heard her inquiring very circumstantially into the prices of different plots in the cemetery and finally decide which she would take. When that was done she gave instructions about engaging the choir. Sokolov then left the room.

"I look after everything myself," she told Peter Ivanovich, shifting the albums that lay on the table; and noticing that the table was endangered by his cigarette-ash, she immediately passed him an ashtray, saying as she did so: "I consider it an affectation to say that my grief prevents my attending to practical affairs. On the contrary, if anything can — I won't say console me, but — distract me, it is seeing to everything concerning him." She again took out her handkerchief as if preparing to cry, but suddenly, as if mastering her feeling, she shook herself and began to speak calmly. "But there is something I want to talk to you about."

Peter Ivanovich bowed, keeping control of the springs of the pouffe, which immediately began quivering under him.

"He suffered terribly the last few days."

"Did he?" said Peter Ivanovich.

"Oh, terribly! He screamed unceasingly, not for minutes but for hours. For the last three days he screamed incessantly. It was unendurable. I cannot understand how I bore it; you could hear him three rooms off. Oh, what I have suffered!"

"Is it possible that he was conscious all that time?" asked Peter Ivanovich.

"Yes," she whispered. "To the last moment. He took leave of us a quarter of an hour before he died, and asked us to take Volodya away."

The thought of the sufferings of this man he had known so intimately, first as a merry little boy, then as a school-mate, and later as a grown-up colleague, suddenly struck Peter Ivanovich with horror, despite an unpleasant consciousness of his own and this woman's dissimulation. He again saw that brow, and that nose pressing down on the lip, and felt afraid for himself.

"Three days of frightful suffering and then death! Why, that might suddenly, at any time, happen to me," he thought, and for a moment felt terrified. But — he did not himself know how — the customary reflection at once occurred to him that this had happened to Ivan Ilych and not to him, and that it should not and could not happen to him, and that to think that it could would be yielding to depression which he ought not to do, as Schwartz's expression plainly showed. After which reflection Peter Ivanovich felt reassured, and began to ask with interest about the details of Ivan Ilych's death, as though death was an accident natural to Ivan Ilych but certainly not to himself.

After many details of the really dreadful physical sufferings Ivan Ilych had endured (which details he learnt only from the effect those sufferings had produced on Praskovya Fëdorovna's nerves) the widow apparently found it necessary to get to business.

"Oh, Peter Ivanovich, how hard it is! How terribly, terribly hard!" and she again began to weep.

Peter Ivanovich sighed and waited for her to finish blowing her nose. When she had done so he said, "Believe me . . ." and she again began talking and brought out what was evidently her chief concern with him — namely, to question him as to how she could obtain a grant of money from the government on the occasion of her husband's death. She made it appear that she was asking Peter Ivanovich's advice about her pension, but he soon saw that she already knew about that to the minutest detail, more even than he did himself. She knew how much could be got out of the government in consequence of her husband's death, but wanted to find out whether she could not possibly extract something more. Peter Ivanovich tried to think of some means of doing so, but after reflecting for a while and, out of propriety, condemning the government for its niggardliness, he said he thought that nothing more could be got. Then she sighed and evidently began to devise means of getting rid of her visitor. Noticing this, he put out his cigarette, rose, pressed her hand, and went out into the anteroom.

In the dining-room where the clock stood that Ivan Ilych had liked so much and had bought at an antique shop, Peter Ivanovich met a priest and a few acquaintances who had come to attend the service, and he recognized Ivan Ilych's daughter, a handsome young woman. She was in black and her slim figure appeared slimmer than ever. She had a gloomy, determined, almost angry expression, and bowed to Peter Ivanovich as though he were in some way to blame. Behind her, with the same offended look, stood a wealthy young man, an examining magistrate, whom Peter Ivanovich also knew and who was her fiancé, as he had heard. He bowed mournfully to them and was about to pass into the death-chamber, when from under the stairs appeared the figure of Ivan Ilych's schoolboy son, who was extremely like his father. He seemed a little Ivan Ilych, such as Peter Ivanovich remembered when they studied law together. His tear-stained eyes had in them the look that is seen in the eyes of boys of thirteen or fourteen who are not pure-minded. When he saw Peter Ivanovich he scowled morosely and shamefacedly. Peter Ivanovich nodded to him and entered the death-chamber. The service began: candles, groans, incense, tears, and sobs. Peter Ivanovich stood looking gloomily down at his feet. He did not look once at the dead man, did not yield to any depressing influence, and was one of the first to leave the room. There was no one in the anteroom, but Gerasim darted out of the dead man's room, rummaged with his strong hands among the fur coats to find Peter Ivanovich's, and helped him on with it.

"Well, friend Gerasim," said Peter Ivanovich, so as to say something. "It's a sad affair, isn't it?"

"It's God's will. We shall all come to it some day," said Gerasim, displaying his teeth — the even, white teeth of a healthy peasant — and, like a man in the thick of urgent work, he briskly opened the front door, called the coachman, helped Peter Ivanovich into the sledge, and sprang back to the porch as if in readiness for what he had to do next.

Peter Ivanovich found the fresh air particularly pleasant after the smell of incense, the dead body, and carbolic acid.

"Where to, sir?" asked the coachman.

"It's not too late even now. . . . I'll call round on Fëdor Vasilievich."

He accordingly drove there and found them just finishing the first rubber, so that it was quite convenient for him to cut in.

II

Ivan Ilych's life had been most simple and most ordinary and therefore most terrible.

He had been a member of the Court of Justice, and died at the age of forty-five. His father had been an official who after serving in various ministries and departments in Petersburg had made the sort of career which brings men to positions from which by reason of their long service they cannot be dismissed, though they are obviously unfit to hold any responsible position, and for whom therefore posts are specially created, which though fictitious carry salaries of from six to ten thousand rubles that are not fictitious, and in receipt of which they live on to a great age.

Such was the Privy Councillor and superfluous member of various superfluous institutions, Ilya Epimovich Golovin.

He had three sons, of whom Ivan Ilych was the second. The eldest son was following in his father's footsteps only in another department, and was already approaching that stage in the service at which a similar sinecure would be reached. The third son was a failure. He had ruined his prospects in a number of positions and was now serving in the railway department. His father and brothers, and still more their wives, not merely disliked meeting him, but avoided remembering his existence unless compelled to do so. His sister had married Baron Greff, a Petersburg official of her father's type. Ivan Ilych was *le phénix de la famille*[2] as people said. He was neither as cold and formal as his elder brother nor as wild as the younger, but was a happy mean between them — an intelligent, polished, lively, and agreeable man. He had studied with his younger brother at the School of Law, but the latter had failed to complete the course and was expelled when he was in the fifth class. Ivan Ilych finished the course well. Even when he was at the School of Law he was just what he remained for the rest of his life: a capable, cheerful, good-natured, and sociable man, though strict in the fulfilment of what he considered to be his duty: and he considered his duty to be what was so considered by those in authority. Neither as a boy nor as a man was he a toady, but from early youth was by nature attracted to people of high station as a fly is drawn to the light, assimilating their ways and views of life and establishing friendly relations with them. All the enthusiasms of childhood and youth passed without leaving much trace on him; he succumbed to sensuality, to vanity, and latterly among the highest classes to liberalism, but always within limits which his instinct unfailingly indicated to him as correct.

At school he had done things which had formerly seemed to him very horrid and made him feel disgusted with himself when he did them; but when later on he saw that such actions were done by people of good position and that they did not regard them as wrong, he was able not exactly to regard them as right, but to forget about them entirely or not be at all troubled at remembering them.

2 [The unique (and perfect) member of the family. — Editors' note.]

Having graduated from the School of Law and qualified for the tenth rank of the civil service, and having received money from his father for his equipment, Ivan Ilych ordered himself clothes at Scharmer's, the fashionable tailor, hung a medallion inscribed *respice finem*[3] on his watch-chain, took leave of his professor and the prince who was patron of the school, had a farewell dinner with his comrades at Donon's first-class restaurant, and with his new and fashionable portmanteau, linen, clothes, shaving and other toilet appliances, and a travelling rug all purchased at the best shops, he set off for one of the provinces where, through his father's influence, he had been attached to the Governor as an official for special service.

In the province Ivan Ilych soon arranged as easy and agreeable a position for himself as he had had at the School of Law. He performed his official tasks, made his career, and at the same time amused himself pleasantly and decorously. Occasionally he paid official visits to country districts, where he behaved with dignity both to his superiors and inferiors, and performed the duties entrusted to him, which related chiefly to the sectarians,[4] with an exactness and incorruptible honesty of which he could not but feel proud.

In official matters, despite his youth and taste for frivolous gaiety, he was exceedingly reserved, punctilious, and even severe; but in society he was often amusing and witty, and always good-natured, correct in his manner, and *bon enfant*,[5] as the Governor and his wife — with whom he was like one of the family — used to say of him.

In the province he had an affair with a lady who made advances to the elegant young lawyer, and there was also a milliner; and there were carousals with aides-de-camp who visited the district, and after-supper visits to a certain outlying street of doubtful reputation; and there was too some obsequiousness to his chief and even to his chief's wife, but all this was done with such a tone of good breeding that no hard names could be applied to it. It all came under the heading of the French saying: *"Il faut que jeunesse se passe."*[6] It was all done with clean hands, in clean linen, with French phrases, and above all among people of the best society and consequently with the approval of people of rank.

So Ivan Ilych served for five years and then came a change in his official life. The new and reformed judicial institutions were introduced, and new men were needed. Ivan Ilych became such a new man. He was offered the post of examining magistrate, and he accepted it though the post was in another province and obliged him to give up the connexions he had formed and to make new ones. His friends met to give him a send-off; they had a group-photograph

3 [Think about your end. — Editors' note.]
4 [Christian sects that had broken with the Russian Orthodox Church. — Editors' note.]
5 [I.e., well-behaved toward his elders. — Editors' note.]
6 [Youth must have its fling. — Editors' note.]

taken and presented him with a silver cigarette-case, and he set off to his new post.

As examining magistrate Ivan Ilych was just as *comme il faut*[7] and decorous a man, inspiring general respect and capable of separating his official duties from his private life, as he had been when acting as an official on special service. His duties now as examining magistrate were far more interesting and attractive than before. In his former position it had been pleasant to wear an undress uniform made by Scharmer, and to pass through the crowd of petitioners and officials who were timorously awaiting an audience with the Governor, and who envied him as with free and easy gait he went straight into his chief's private room to have a cup of tea and a cigarette with him. But not many people had been directly dependent on him — only police officials and the sectarians when he went on special missions — and he liked to treat them politely, almost as comrades, as if he were letting them feel that he who had the power to crush them was treating them in this simple, friendly way. There were then but few such people. But now, as an examining magistrate, Ivan Ilych felt that everyone without exception, even the most important and self-satisfied, was in his power, and that he need only write a few words on a sheet of paper with a certain heading, and this or that important, self-satisfied person would be brought before him in the role of an accused person or a witness, and if he did not choose to allow him to sit down, would have to stand before him and answer his questions. Ivan Ilych never abused his power; he tried on the contrary to soften its expression, but the consciousness of it and of the possibility of softening its effect, supplied the chief interest and attraction of his office. In his work itself, especially in his examinations, he very soon acquired a method of eliminating all considerations irrelevant to the legal aspect of the case, and reducing even the most complicated case to a form in which it would be presented on paper only in its externals, completely excluding his personal opinion of the matter, while above all observing every prescribed formality. The work was new and Ivan Ilych was one of the first men to apply the new Code of 1864.[8]

On taking up the post of examining magistrate in a new town, he made new acquaintances and connexions, placed himself on a new footing, and assumed a somewhat different tone. He took up an attitude of rather dignified aloofness towards the provincial authorities, but picked out the best circle of legal gentlemen and wealthy gentry living in the town and assumed a tone of slight dissatisfaction with the government, of moderate liberalism, and of enlightened citizenship. At the same time, without at all altering the elegance of his toilet, he ceased shaving his chin and allowed his beard to grow as it pleased.

7 [Proper. — Editors' note.]
8 [The emancipation of the serfs in 1861 was followed by a thorough all-round reform of judicial proceedings. — Translators' note.]

Ivan Ilych setted down very pleasantly in this new town. The society there, which inclined towards opposition to the Governor, was friendly, his salary was larger, and he began to play *vint,*[9] which he found added not a little to the pleasure of life, for he had a capacity for cards, played good-humouredly, and calculated rapidly and astutely, so that he usually won.

After living there for two years he met his future wife, Praskovya Fëdorovna Mikhel, who was the most attractive, clever, and brilliant girl of the set in which he moved, and among other amusements and relaxations from his labours as examining magistrate, Ivan Ilych established light and playful relations with her.

While he had been an official on special service he had been accustomed to dance, but now as an examining magistrate it was exceptional for him to do so. If he danced now, he did it as if to show that though he served under the reformed order of things, and had reached the fifth official rank, yet when it came to dancing he could do it better than most people. So at the end of an evening he sometimes danced with Praskovya Fëdorovna, and it was chiefly during these dances that he captivated her. She fell in love with him. Ivan Ilych had at first no definite intention of marrying, but when the girl fell in love with him he said to himself: "Really, why shouldn't I marry?"

Praskovya Fëdorovna came of a good family, was not bad-looking, and had some little property. Ivan Ilych might have aspired to a more brilliant match, but even this was good. He had his salary, and she, he hoped, would have an equal income. She was well connected, and was a sweet, pretty, and thoroughly correct young woman. To say that Ivan Ilych married because he fell in love with Praskovya Fëdorovna and found that she sympathized with his views of life would be as incorrect as to say that he married because his social circle approved of the match. He was swayed by both these considerations: the marriage gave him personal satisfaction, and at the same time it was considered the right thing by the most highly placed of his associates.

So Ivan Ilych got married.

The preparations for marriage and the beginning of married life, with its conjugal caresses, the new furniture, new crockery, and new linen, were very pleasant until his wife became pregnant — so that Ivan Ilych had begun to think that marriage would not impair the easy, agreeable, gay, and always decorous character of his life, approved of by society and regarded by himself as natural, but would even improve it. But from the first months of his wife's pregnancy, something new, unpleasant, depressing, and unseemly, and from which there was no way of escape, unexpectedly showed itself.

His wife, without any reason — *de gaieté de cœur*[10] as Ivan Ilych expressed

9 [A form of bridge. — Translators' note.]
10 [Out of wantonness. — Editors' note.]

it to himself — began to disturb the pleasure and propriety of their life. She began to be jealous without any cause, expected him to devote his whole attention to her, found fault with everything, and made coarse and ill-mannered scenes.

At first Ivan Ilych hoped to escape from the unpleasantness of this state of affairs by the same easy and decorous relation to life that had served him heretofore: he tried to ignore his wife's disagreeable moods, continued to live in his usual easy and pleasant way, invited friends to his house for a game of cards, and also tried going out to his club or spending his evenings with friends. But one day his wife began upbraiding him so vigorously, using such coarse words, and continued to abuse him every time he did not fulfil her demands, so resolutely and with such evident determination not to give way till he submitted — that is, till he stayed at home and was bored just as she was — that he became alarmed. He now realized that matrimony — at any rate with Praskovya Fëdorovna — was not always conducive to the pleasures and amenities of life, but on the contrary often infringed both comfort and propriety, and that he must therefore entrench himself against such infringement. And Ivan Ilych began to seek for means of doing so. His official duties were the one thing that imposed upon Praskovya Fëdorovna, and by means of his official work and the duties attached to it he began struggling with his wife to secure his own independence.

With the birth of their child, the attempts to feed it and the various failures in doing so, and with the real and imaginary illnesses of mother and child, in which Ivan Ilych's sympathy was demanded but about which he understood nothing, the need of securing for himself an existence outside his family life became still more imperative.

As his wife grew more irritable and exacting and Ivan Ilych transferred the centre of gravity of his life more and more to his official work, so did he grow to like his work better and become more ambitious than before.

Very soon, within a year of his wedding, Ivan Ilych had realized that marriage, though it may add some comforts to life, is in fact a very intricate and difficult affair towards which in order to perform one's duty, that is, to lead a decorous life approved of by society, one must adopt a definite attitude just as towards one's official duties.

And Ivan Ilych evolved such an attitude towards married life. He only required of it those conveniences — dinner at home, housewife, and bed — which it could give him, and above all that propriety of external forms required by public opinion. For the rest he looked for light-hearted pleasure and propriety, and was very thankful when he found them, but if he met with antagonism and querulousness he at once retired into his separate fenced-off world of official duties, where he found satisfaction.

Ivan Ilych was esteemed a good official, and after three years was made

Assistant Public Prosecutor. His new duties, their importance, the possibility of indicting and imprisoning anyone he chose, the publicity his speeches received, and the success he had in all these things, made his work still more attractive.

More children came. His wife became more and more querulous and ill-tempered, but the attitude Ivan Ilych had adopted towards his home life rendered him almost impervious to her grumbling.

After seven years' service in that town he was transferred to another province as Public Prosecutor. They moved, but were short of money and his wife did not like the place they moved to. Though the salary was higher the cost of living was greater, besides which two of their children died and family life became still more unpleasant for him.

Praskovya Fëdorovna blamed her husband for every inconvenience they encountered in their new home. Most of the conversations between husband and wife, especially as to the children's education, led to topics which recalled former disputes, and those disputes were apt to flare up again at any moment. There remained only those rare periods of amorousness which still came to them at times but did not last long. These were islets at which they anchored for a while and then again set out upon that ocean of veiled hostility which showed itself in their aloofness from one another. This aloofness might have grieved Ivan Ilych had he considered that it ought not to exist, but he now regarded the position as normal, and even made it the goal at which he aimed in family life. His aim was to free himself more and more from those unpleasantnesses and to give them a semblance of harmlessness and propriety. He attained this by spending less and less time with his family, and when obliged to be at home he tried to safeguard his position by the presence of outsiders. The chief thing however was that he had his official duties. The whole interest of his life now centred in the official world and that interest absorbed him. The consciousness of his power, being able to ruin anybody he wished to ruin, the importance, even the external dignity of his entry into court, or meetings with his subordinates, his success with superiors and inferiors, and above all his masterly handling of cases, of which he was conscious — all this gave him pleasure and filled his life, together with chats with his colleagues, dinners, and bridge. So that on the whole Ivan Ilych's life continued to flow as he considered it should do — pleasantly and properly.

So things continued for another seven years. His eldest daughter was already sixteen, another child had died, and only one son was left, a schoolboy and a subject of dissension. Ivan Ilych wanted to put him in the School of Law, but to spite him Praskovya Fëdorovna entered him at the High School. The daughter had been educated at home and had turned out well: the boy did not learn badly either.

III

So Ivan Ilych lived for seventeen years after his marriage. He was already a Public Prosecutor of long standing, and had declined several proposed transfers while awaiting a more desirable post, when an unanticipated and unpleasant occurrence quite upset the peaceful course of his life. He was expecting to be offered the post of presiding judge in a University town, but Happe somehow came to the front and obtained the appointment instead. Ivan Ilych became irritable, reproached Happe, and quarrelled both with him and with his immediate superiors — who became colder to him and again passed him over when other appointments were made.

This was in 1880, the hardest year of Ivan Ilych's life. It was then that it became evident on the one hand that his salary was insufficient for them to live on, and on the other that he had been forgotten, and not only this, but that what was for him the greatest and most cruel injustice appeared to others a quite ordinary occurrence. Even his father did not consider it his duty to help him. Ivan Ilych felt himself abandoned by everyone, and that they regarded his position with a salary of 3,500 rubles as quite normal and even fortunate. He alone knew that with the consciousness of the injustices done him, with his wife's incessant nagging, and with the debts he had contracted by living beyond his means, his position was far from normal.

In order to save money that summer he obtained leave of absence and went with his wife to live in the country at her brother's place.

In the country, without his work, he experienced *ennui* for the first time in his life, and not only *ennui* but intolerable depression, and he decided that it was impossible to go on living like that, and that it was necessary to take energetic measures.

Having passed a sleepless night pacing up and down the veranda, he decided to go to Petersburg and bestir himself, in order to punish those who had failed to appreciate him and to get transferred to another ministry.

Next day, despite many protests from his wife and her brother, he started for Petersburg with the sole object of obtaining a post with a salary of five thousand rubles a year. He was no longer bent on any particular department, or tendency, or kind of activity. All he now wanted was an appointment to another post with a salary of five thousand rubles, either in the administration, in the banks, with the railways, in one of the Empress Marya's Institutions,[11] or even in the customs — but it had to carry with it a salary of five thousand rubles and be in a ministry other than that in which they had failed to appreciate him.

11 [Orphanage-schools for girls. — Editors' note.]

And this quest of Ivan Ilych's was crowned with remarkable and unexpected success. At Kursk an acquaintance of his, F. I. Ilyin, got into the first-class carriage, sat down beside Ivan Ilych, and told him of a telegram just received by the Governor of Kursk announcing that a change was about to take place in the ministry: Peter Ivanovich was to be superseded by Ivan Semënovich.

The proposed change, apart from its significance for Russia, had a special significance for Ivan Ilych, because by bringing forward a new man, Peter Petrovich, and consequently his friend Zachar Ivanovich, it was highly favourable for Ivan Ilych, since Zachar Ivanovich was a friend and colleague of his.

In Moscow this news was confirmed, and on reaching Petersburg Ivan Ilych found Zachar Ivanovich and received a definite promise of an appointment in his former department of Justice.

A week later he telegraphed to his wife: "Zachar in Miller's place. I shall receive appointment on presentation of report."

Thanks to this change of personnel, Ivan Ilych had unexpectedly obtained an appointment in his former ministry which placed him two stages above his former colleagues besides giving him five thousand rubles salary and three thousand five hundred rubles for expenses connected with his removal. All his ill humour towards his former enemies and the whole department vanished, and Ivan Ilych was completely happy.

He returned to the country more cheerful and contented than he had been for a long time. Praskovya Fëdorovna also cheered up and a truce was arranged between them. Ivan Ilych told of how he had been fêted by everybody in Petersburg, how all those who had been his enemies were put to shame and now fawned on him, how envious they were of his appointment, and how much everybody in Petersburg had liked him.

Praskovya Fëdorovna listened to all this and appeared to believe it. She did not contradict anything, but only made plans for their life in the town to which they were going. Ivan Ilych saw with delight that these plans were his plans, that he and his wife agreed, and that, after a stumble, his life was regaining its due and natural character of pleasant lightheartedness and decorum.

Ivan Ilych had come back for a short time only, for he had to take up his new duties on the 10th of September. Moreover, he needed time to settle into the new place, to move all his belongings from the province, and to buy and order many additional things: in a word, to make such arrangements as he had resolved on, which were almost exactly what Praskovya Fëdorovna too had decided on.

Now that everything had happened so fortunately, and that he and his wife were at one in their aims and moreover saw so little of one another, they got on together better than they had done since the first years of marriage. Ivan Ilych had thought of taking his family away with him at once, but the insistence of his wife's brother and her sister-in-law, who had suddenly become particularly amiable and friendly to him and his family, induced him to depart alone.

So he departed, and the cheerful state of mind induced by his success and by the harmony between his wife and himself, the one intensifying the other, did not leave him. He found a delightful house, just the thing both he and his wife had dreamt of. Spacious, lofty reception rooms in the old style, a convenient and dignified study, rooms for his wife and daughter, a study for his son — it might have been specially built for them. Ivan Ilych himself superintended the arrangements, chose the wallpapers, supplemented the furniture (preferably with antiques which he considered particularly *comme il faut*), and supervised the upholstering. Everything progressed and progressed and approached the ideal he had set himself: even when things were only half completed they exceeded his expectations. He saw what a refined and elegant character, free from vulgarity, it would all have when it was ready. On falling asleep he pictured to himself how the reception-room would look. Looking at the yet unfinished drawing-room he could see the fireplace, the screen, the what-not, the little chairs dotted here and there, the dishes and plates on the walls, and the bronzes, as they would be when everything was in place. He was pleased by the thought of how his wife and daughter, who shared his taste in this matter, would be impressed by it. They were certainly not expecting as much. He had been particularly successful in finding, and buying cheaply, antiques which gave a particularly aristocratic character to the whole place. But in his letters he intentionally understated everything in order to be able to surprise them. All this so absorbed him that his new duties — though he liked his official work — interested him less than he had expected. Sometimes he even had moments of absentmindedness during the Court Sessions, and would consider whether he should have straight or curved cornices for his curtains. He was so interested in it all that he often did things himself, rearranging the furniture, or rehanging the curtains. Once when mounting a stepladder to show the upholsterer, who did not understand, how he wanted the hangings draped, he made a false step and slipped, but being a strong and agile man he clung on and only knocked his side against the knob of the window frame. The bruised place was painful but the pain soon passed, and he felt particularly bright and well just then. He wrote: "I feel fifteen years younger." He thought he would have everything ready by September, but it dragged on till mid-October. But the result was charming not only in his eyes but to everyone who saw it.

In reality it was just what is usually seen in the houses of people of moderate means who want to appear rich, and therefore succeed only in resembling others like themselves: there were damasks, dark wood, plants, rugs, and dull and polished bronzes — all the things people of a certain class have in order to resemble other people of that class. His house was so like the others that it would never have been noticed, but to him it all seemed to be quite exceptional. He was very happy when he met his family at the station and brought them to the newly furnished house all lit up, where a footman in a white tie opened the door into the hall decorated with plants, and when they went on into the drawing-room and the study uttering exclamations of delight. He conducted them everywhere, drank in their praises eagerly, and beamed with pleasure. At tea that evening, when Praskovya Fëdorovna among other things asked him about his fall, he laughed and showed them how he had gone flying and had frightened the upholsterer.

"It's a good thing I'm a bit of an athlete. Another man might have been killed, but I merely knocked myself, just here; it hurts when it's touched, but it's passing off already — it's only a bruise."

So they began living in their new home — in which, as always happens, when they got thoroughly settled in they found they were just one room short — and with the increased income, which as always was just a little (some five hundred rubles) too little, but it was all very nice.

Things went particularly well at first, before everything was finally arranged and while something had still to be done: this thing bought, that thing ordered, another thing moved, and something else adjusted. Though there were some disputes between husband and wife, they were both so well satisfied and had so much to do that it all passed off without any serious quarrels. When nothing was left to arrange it became rather dull and something seemed to be lacking, but they were then making acquaintances, forming habits, and life was growing fuller.

Ivan Ilych spent his mornings at the law courts and came home to dinner, and at first he was generally in a good humour, though he occasionally became irritable just on account of his house. (Every spot on the tablecloth or the upholstery, and every broken window-blind string, irritated him. He had devoted so much trouble to arranging it all that every disturbance of it distressed him.) But on the whole his life ran its course as he believed life should do: easily, pleasantly, and decorously.

He got up at nine, drank his coffee, read the paper, and then put on his undress uniform and went to the law courts. There the harness in which he worked had already been stretched to fit him and he donned it without a hitch: petitioners, inquiries at the chancery, the chancery itself, and the sittings public and administrative. In all this the thing was to exclude everything fresh and vital, which always disturbs the regular course of official business, and to admit only official relations with people, and then only on official grounds. A man would come, for instance, wanting some information. Ivan Ilych, as one in whose sphere the matter did not lie, would have nothing to do with him: but if the man had some business with him in his official capacity, something that could be expressed on officially stamped paper, he would do everything, positively everything he could within the limits of such relations, and in doing so would maintain the semblance of friendly human relations, that is, would observe the courtesies of life. As soon as the official relations ended, so did everything else. Ivan Ilych possessed this capacity to separate his real life from the official side of affairs and not mix the two, in the highest degree, and by long practice and natural aptitude had brought it to such a pitch that sometimes, in the manner of a virtuoso, he would even allow himself to let the human and official relations mingle. He let himself do this just because he felt that he could at any time he chose resume the strictly official attitude again and drop the human relation. And he did it all easily, pleasantly, correctly, and even artistically. In the intervals between the sessions he smoked, drank tea, chatted a little about politics, a little about general topics, a little about cards, but most of all about official appointments. Tired, but with the feelings of a virtuoso — one of the first violins who has played his part in an orchestra with precision — he would return home to find that his wife and daughter had been out paying calls, or had a visitor, and that his son had been to school, had done his homework with his tutor, and was duly learning what is taught at High Schools. Everything was as it should be. After dinner, if they had no visitors, Ivan Ilych sometimes read a book that was being much discussed at the time, and in the evening settled down to work, that is, read official papers, compared the depositions of witnesses, and noted paragraphs of the Code applying to them. This was neither dull nor amusing. It was dull when he might have been playing bridge, but if no bridge was available it was at any rate better than doing nothing or sitting with his wife. Ivan Ilych's chief pleasure was giving little dinners to which he invited men and women of good social position, and just as his drawing-room resembled all other drawing-rooms so did his enjoyable little parties resemble all other such parties.

Once they even gave a dance. Ivan Ilych enjoyed it and everything went off well, except that it led to a violent quarrel with his wife about the cakes and sweets. Praskovya Fëdorovna had made her own plans, but Ivan Ilych insisted on getting everything from an expensive confectioner and ordered too many cakes, and the quarrel occurred because some of those cakes were left over and the confectioner's bill came to forty-five rubles. It was a great and disagreeable quarrel. Praskovya Fëdorovna called him "a fool and an imbecile," and he clutched at his head and made angry allusions to divorce.

But the dance itself had been enjoyable. The best people were there, and Ivan Ilych had danced with Princess Trufonova, a sister of the distinguished founder of the Society "Bear my Burden."

The pleasures connected with his work were pleasures of ambition; his social pleasures were those of vanity; but Ivan Ilych's greatest pleasure was playing bridge. He acknowledged that whatever disagreeable incident happened in his life, the pleasure that beamed like a ray of light above everything else was to sit down to bridge with good players, not noisy partners, and of course to four-handed bridge (with five players it was annoying to have to stand out, though one pretended not to mind), to play a clever and serious game (when the cards allowed it), and then to have supper and drink a glass of wine. After a game of bridge, especially if he had won a little (to win a large sum was unpleasant), Ivan Ilych went to bed in specially good humour.

So they lived. They formed a circle of acquaintances among the best people and were visited by people of importance and by young folk. In their views as to their acquaintances, husband, wife, and daughter were entirely agreed, and tacitly and unanimously kept at arm's length and shook off the various shabby friends and relations who, with much show of affection, gushed into the drawing-room with its Japanese plates on the walls. Soon these shabby friends ceased to obtrude themselves and only the best people remained in the Golovins' set.

Young men made up to Lisa, and Petrishchev, an examining magistrate and Dmitri Ivanovich Petrishchev's son and sole heir, began to be so attentive to her that Ivan Ilych had already spoken to Praskovya Fëdorovna about it, and considered whether they should not arrange a party for them, or get up some private theatricals.

So they lived, and all went well, without change, and life flowed pleasantly.

IV

They were all in good health. It could not be called ill health if Ivan Ilych sometimes said that he had a queer taste in his mouth and felt some discomfort in his left side.

But this discomfort increased and, though not exactly painful, grew into a sense of pressure in his side accompanied by ill humour. And his irritability became worse and worse and began to mar the agreeable, easy, and correct life that had established itself in the Golovin family. Quarrels between husband and wife became more and more frequent, and soon the ease and amenity disappeared and even the decorum was barely maintained. Scenes again became frequent, and very few of those islets remained on which husband and wife could meet without an explosion. Praskovya Fëdorovna now had good reason to say that her husband's temper was trying. With characteristic exaggeration she said he had always had a dreadful temper, and that it had needed all her good nature to put up with it for twenty years. It was true that now the quarrels were started by him. His bursts of temper always came just before dinner, often just as he began to eat his soup. Sometimes he noticed that a plate or dish was chipped, or the food was not right, or his son put his elbow on the table, or his daughter's hair was not done as he liked it, and for all this he blamed Praskovya Fëdorovna. At first she retorted and said disagreeable things to him, but once or twice he fell into such a rage at the beginning of dinner that she realized it was due to some physical derangement brought on by taking food, and so she restrained herself and did not answer, but only hurried to get the dinner over. She regarded this self-restraint as highly praiseworthy. Having come to the conclusion that her husband had a dreadful temper and made her life miserable, she began to feel sorry for herself, and the more she pitied herself the more she hated her husband. She began to wish he would die; yet she did not want him to die because then his salary would cease. And this irritated her against him still more. She considered herself dreadfully unhappy just because not even his death could save her, and though she concealed her exasperation, that hidden exasperation of hers increased his irritation also.

After one scene in which Ivan Ilych had been particularly unfair and after which he had said in explanation that he certainly was irritable but that it was due to his not being well, she said that if he was ill it should be attended to, and insisted on his going to see a celebrated doctor.

He went. Everything took place as he had expected and as it always does. There was the usual waiting and the important air assumed by the doctor, with which he was so familiar (resembling that which he himself assumed in court), and the sounding and listening, and the questions which called for answers that were foregone conclusions and were evidently unnecessary, and the look of importance which implied that "if only you put yourself in our hands we will arrange everything — we know indubitably how it has to be done, always in the same way for everybody alike." It was all just as it was in the law courts. The doctor put on just the same air towards him as he himself put on towards an accused person.

The doctor said that so-and-so indicated that there was so-and-so inside the patient, but if the investigation of so-and-so did not confirm this, then he must assume that and that. If he assumed that and that, then . . . and so on. To Ivan Ilych only one question was important: was his case serious or not? But the doctor ignored that inappropriate question. From his point of view it was not the one under consideration, the real question was to decide between a floating kidney, chronic catarrh, or appendicitis. It was not a question of Ivan Ilych's life or death, but one between a floating kidney and appendicitis. And that question the doctor solved brilliantly, as it seemed to Ivan Ilych, in favour of the appendix, with the reservation that should an examination of the urine give fresh indications the matter would be reconsidered. All this was just what Ivan Ilych had himself brilliantly accomplished a thousand times in dealing with men on trial. The doctor summed up just as brilliantly, looking over his spectacles triumphantly and even gaily at the accused. From the doctor's summing up Ivan Ilych concluded that things were bad, but that for the doctor, and perhaps for everybody else, it was a matter of indifference, though for him it was bad. And this conclusion struck him painfully, arousing in him a great feeling of pity for himself and of bitterness towards the doctor's indifference to a matter of such importance.

He said nothing of this, but rose, placed the doctor's fee on the table, and remarked with a sigh: "We sick people probably often put inappropriate questions. But tell me, in general, is this complaint dangerous, or not? . . ."

The doctor looked at him sternly over his spectacles with one eye, as if to say: "Prisoner, if you will not keep to the questions put to you, I shall be obliged to have you removed from the court."

"I have already told you what I consider necessary and proper. The analysis may show something more." And the doctor bowed.

Ivan Ilych went out slowly, seated himself disconsolately in his sledge, and drove home. All the way home he was going over what the doctor had said, trying to translate those complicated, obscure, scientific phrases into plain language and find in them an answer to the question: "Is my condition bad? Is it very bad? Or is there as yet nothing much wrong?" And it seemed to him that the meaning of what the doctor had said was that it was very bad. Everything in the streets seemed depressing. The cabmen, the houses, the passers-by, and the shops, were dismal. His ache, this dull gnawing ache that never ceased for a moment, seemed to have acquired a new and more serious significance from the doctor's dubious remarks. Ivan Ilych now watched it with a new and oppressive feeling.

He reached home and began to tell his wife about it. She listened, but in the middle of his account his daughter came in with her hat on, ready to go out with her mother. She sat down reluctantly to listen to this tedious story, but could not stand it long, and her mother too did not hear him to the end.

"Well, I am very glad," she said. "Mind now to take your medicine regularly. Give me the prescription and I'll send Gerasim to the chemist's." And she went to get ready to go out.

While she was in the room Ivan Ilych had hardly taken time to breathe, but he sighed deeply when she left it.

"Well," he thought, "perhaps it isn't so bad after all."

He began taking his medicine and following the doctor's directions, which had been altered after the examination of the urine. But then it happened that there was a contradiction between the indications drawn from the examination of the urine and the symptoms that showed themselves. It turned out that what was happening differed from what the doctor had told him, and that he had either forgotten, or blundered, or hidden something from him. He could not, however, be blamed for that, and Ivan Ilych still obeyed his orders implicitly and at first derived some comfort from doing so.

From the time of his visit to the doctor, Ivan Ilych's chief occupation was the exact fulfilment of the doctor's instructions regarding hygiene and the taking of medicine, and the observation of his pain and his excretions. His chief interests came to be people's ailments and people's health. When sickness, deaths, or recoveries were mentioned in his presence, especially when the illness resembled his own, he listened with agitation which he tried to hide, asked questions, and applied what he heard to his own case.

The pain did not grow less, but Ivan Ilych made efforts to force himself to think that he was better. And he could do this so long as nothing agitated him. But as soon as he had any unpleasantness with his wife, any lack of success in his official work, or held bad cards at bridge, he was at once acutely sensible of his disease. He had formerly borne such mischances, hoping soon to adjust what was wrong, to master it and attain success, or make a grand slam. But now every mischance upset him and plunged him into despair. He would say to himself: "There now, just as I was beginning to get better and the medicine had begun to take effect, comes this accursed misfortune, or unpleasantness. . . ." And he was furious with the mishap, or with the people who were causing the unpleasantness and killing him, for he felt that this fury was killing him but could not restrain it. One would have thought that it should have been clear to him that this exasperation with circumstances and people aggravated his illness, and that he ought therefore to ignore unpleasant occurrences. But he drew the very opposite conclusion: he said that he needed peace, and he watched for everything that might disturb it and became irritable at the slightest infringement of it. His condition was rendered worse by the fact that he read medical books and consulted doctors. The progress of his disease was so gradual that he could deceive himself when comparing one day with another — the difference was so slight. But when he consulted the doctors it seemed to him that he was getting worse, and even very rapidly. Yet despite this he was continually consulting them.

That month he went to see another celebrity, who told him almost the same as the first had done but put his questions rather differently, and the interview with this celebrity only increased Ivan Ilych's doubts and fears. A friend of a friend of his, a very good doctor, diagnosed his illness again quite differently from the others, and though he predicted recovery, his questions and suppositions bewildered Ivan Ilych still more and increased his doubts. A homœopathist diagnosed the disease in yet another way, and prescribed medicine which Ivan Ilych took secretly for a week. But after a week, not feeling any improvement and having lost confidence both in the former doctor's treatment and in this one's, he became still more despondent. One day a lady acquaintaince mentioned a cure effected by a wonder-working icon. Ivan Ilych caught himself listening attentively and beginning to believe that it had occurred. This incident alarmed him. "Has my mind really weakened to such an extent?" he asked himself. "Nonsense! It's all rubbish. I mustn't give way to nervous fears but having chosen a doctor must keep strictly to his treatment. That is what I will do. Now it's all settled. I won't think about it, but will follow the treatment seriously till summer, and then we shall see. From now there must be no more of this wavering!" This was easy to say but impossible to carry out. The pain in his side oppressed him and seemed to grow worse and more incessant, while the taste in his mouth grew stranger and stranger. It seemed to him that his breath had a disgusting smell, and he was conscious of a loss of appetite and strength. There was no deceiving himself: something terrible, new, and more important than anything before in his life, was taking place within him of which he alone was aware. Those about him did not understand or would not understand it, but thought everything in the world was going on as usual. That tormented Ivan Ilych more than anything. He saw that his household, especially his wife and daughter who were in a perfect whirl of visiting, did not understand anything of it and were annoyed that he was so depressed and so exacting, as if he were to blame for it. Though they tried to disguise it he saw that he was an obstacle in their path, and that his wife had adopted a definite line in regard to his illness and kept to it regardless of anything he said or did. Her attitude was this: "You know," she would say to her friends, "Ivan Ilych can't do as other people do, and keep to the treatment prescribed for him. One day he'll take his drops and keep strictly to his diet and go to bed in good time, but the next day unless I watch him he'll suddenly forget his medicine, eat sturgeon — which is forbidden — and sit up playing cards till one o'clock in the morning."

"Oh, come, when was that?" Ivan Ilych would ask in vexation. "Only once at Peter Ivanovich's."

"And yesterday with Shebek."

"Well, even if I hadn't stayed up, this pain would have kept me awake."

"Be that as it may you'll never get well like that, but will always make us wretched."

Praskovya Fëdorovna's attitude to Ivan Ilych's illness, as she expressed it both to others and to him, was that it was his own fault and was another of the annoyances he caused her. Ivan Ilych felt that this opinion escaped her involuntarily — but that did not make it easier for him.

At the law courts too, Ivan Ilych noticed, or thought he noticed, a strange attitude towards himself. It sometimes seemed to him that people were watching him inquisitively as a man whose place might soon be vacant. Then again, his friends would suddenly begin to chaff him in a friendly way about his low spirits, as if the awful, horrible, and unheard-of thing that was going on within him, incessantly gnawing at him and irresistibly drawing him away, was a very agreeable subject for jests. Schwartz in particular irritated him by his jocularity, vivacity, and *savoir-faire,* which reminded him of what he himself had been ten years ago.

Friends came to make up a set and they sat down to cards. They dealt, bending the new cards to soften them, and he sorted the diamonds in his hand and found he had seven. His partner said "No trumps" and supported him with two diamonds. What more could be wished for? It ought to be jolly and lively. They would make a grand slam. But suddenly Ivan Ilych was conscious of that gnawing pain, that taste in his mouth, and it seemed ridiculous that in such circumstances he should be pleased to make a grand slam.

He looked at his partner Mikhail Mikhaylovich, who rapped the table with his strong hand and instead of snatching up the tricks pushed the cards courteously and indulgently towards Ivan Ilych that he might have the pleasure of gathering them up without the trouble of stretching out his hand for them. "Does he think I am too weak to stretch out my arm?" thought Ivan Ilych, and forgetting what he was doing he over-trumped his partner, missing the grand slam by three tricks. And what was most awful of all was that he saw how upset Mikhail Mikhaylovich was about it but did not himself care. And it was dreadful to realize why he did not care.

They all saw that he was suffering, and said: "We can stop if you are tired. Take a rest." Lie down? No, he was not at all tired, and he finished the rubber. All were gloomy and silent. Ivan Ilych felt that he had diffused this gloom over them and could not dispel it. They had supper and went away, and Ivan Ilych was left alone with the consciousness that his life was poisoned and was poisoning the lives of others, and that this poison did not weaken but penetrated more and more deeply into his whole being.

With this consciousness, and with physical pain besides the terror, he must go to bed, often to lie awake the greater part of the night. Next morning he had to get up again, dress, go to the law courts, speak, and write; or if he did not go out, spend at home those twenty-four hours a day each of which was a torture. And he had to live thus all alone on the brink of an abyss, with no one who understood or pitied him.

V

So one month passed and then another. Just before the New Year his brother-in-law came to town and stayed at their house. Ivan Ilych was at the law courts and Praskovya Fëdorovna had gone shopping. When Ivan Ilych came home and entered his study he found his brother-in-law there — a healthy, florid man — unpacking his portmanteau himself. He raised his head on hearing Ivan Ilych's footsteps and looked up at him for a moment without a word. That stare told Ivan Ilych everything. His brother-in-law opened his mouth to utter an exclamation of surprise but checked himself, and that action confirmed it all.

"I have changed, eh?"

"Yes, there is a change."

And after that, try as he would to get his brother-in-law to return to the subjects of his looks, the latter would say nothing about it. Praskovya Fëdorovna came home and her brother went out to her. Ivan Ilych locked the door and began to examine himself in the glass, first full face, then in profile. He took up a portrait of himself taken with his wife, and compared it with what he saw in the glass. The change in him was immense. Then he bared his arms to the elbow, looked at them, drew the sleeves down again, sat down on an ottoman, and grew blacker than night.

"No, no, this won't do!" he said to himself, and jumped up, went to the table, took up some law papers, and began to read them, but could not continue. He unlocked the door and went into the reception-room. The door leading to the drawing-room was shut. He approached it on tiptoe and listened.

"No, you are exaggerating!" Praskovya Fëdorovna was saying.

"Exaggerating! Don't you see it? Why, he's a dead man! Look at his eyes — there's no light in them. But what is it that is wrong with him?"

"No one knows. Nikolaevich said something, but I don't know what. And Leshchetitsky[12] said quite the contrary. . . ."

Ivan Ilych walked away, went to his own room, lay down, and began musing: "The kidney, a floating kidney." He recalled all the doctors had told him of how it detached itself and swayed about. And by an effort of imagination he tried to catch that kidney and arrest it and support it. So little was needed

12 [Nikolaevich, Leshchetitsky, two doctors, the latter a celebrated specialist. — Translators' note.]

for this, it seemed to him. "No, I'll go to see Peter Ivanovich again."[13] He rang, ordered the carriage, and got ready to go.

"Where are you going, Jean?" asked his wife, with a specially sad and exceptionally kind look.

This exceptionally kind look irritated him. He looked morosely at her.

"I must go to see Peter Ivanovich."

He went to see Peter Ivanovich, and together they went to see his friend, the doctor. He was in, and Ivan Ilych had a long talk with him.

Reviewing the anatomical and physiological details of what in the doctor's opinion was going on inside him, he understood it all.

There was something, a small thing, in the vermiform appendix. It might all come right. Only stimulate the energy of one organ and check the activity of another, then absorption would take place and everything would come right. He got home rather late for dinner, ate his dinner, and conversed cheerfully, but could not for a long time bring himself to go back to work in his room. At last, however, he went to his study and did what was necessary, but the consciousness that he had put something aside — an important, intimate matter which he would revert to when his work was done — never left him. When he had finished his work he remembered that this intimate matter was the thought of his vermiform appendix. But he did not give himself up to it, and went to the drawing-room for tea. There were callers there, including the examining magistrate who was a desirable match for his daughter, and they were conversing, playing the piano, and singing. Ivan Ilych, as Praskovya Fëdorovna remarked, spent that evening more cheerfully than usual, but he never for a moment forgot that he had postponed the important matter of the appendix. At eleven o'clock he said good-night and went to his bedroom. Since his illness he had slept alone in a small room next to his study. He undressed and took up a novel by Zola, but instead of reading it he fell into thought, and in his imagination that desired improvement in the vermiform appendix occurred. There was the absorption and evacuation and the re-establishment of normal activity. "Yes, that's it!" he said to himself. "One need only assist nature, that's all." He remembered his medicine, rose, took it, and lay down on his back watching for the beneficent action of the medicine and for it to lessen the pain. "I need only take it regularly and avoid all injurious influences. I am already feeling better, much better." He began touching his side: it was not painful to the touch. "There, I really don't feel it. It's much better already." He put out the light and turned on his side. . . . "The appendix is getting better, absorption is occurring." Suddenly he felt the old, familiar, dull, gnawing pain, stubborn and serious. There was the same familiar

13 [That was the friend whose friend was a doctor. — Translators' note.]

loathsome taste in his mouth. His heart sank and he felt dazed. "My God! My God!" he muttered. "Again, again! and it will never cease." And suddenly the matter presented itself in a quite different aspect. "Vermiform appendix! Kidney!" he said to himself. "It's not a question of appendix or kidney, but of life and . . . death. Yes, life was there and now it is going, going and I cannot stop it. Yes. Why deceive myself? Isn't it obvious to everyone but me that I'm dying, and that it's only a question of weeks, days . . . it may happen this moment. There was light and now there is darkness. I was here and now I'm going there! Where?" A chill came over him, his breathing ceased, and he felt only the throbbing of his heart.

"When I am not, what will there be? There will be nothing. Then where shall I be when I am no more? Can this be dying? No, I don't want to!" He jumped up and tried to light the candle, felt for it with trembling hands, dropped candle and candlestick on the floor, and fell back on his pillow.

"What's the use? It makes no difference," he said to himself, staring with wide-open eyes into the darkness. "Death. Yes, death. And none of them know or wish to know it, and they have no pity for me. Now they are playing." (He heard through the door the distant sound of a song and its accompaniment.) "It's all the same to them, but they will die too! Fools! I first, and they later, but it will be the same for them. And now they are merry . . . the beasts!"

Anger choked him and he was agonizingly, unbearably miserable. "It is impossible that all men have been doomed to suffer this awful horror!" He raised himself.

"Something must be wrong. I must calm myself — must think it all over from the beginning." And he again began thinking. "Yes, the beginning of my illness: I knocked my side, but I was still quite well that day and the next. It hurt a little, then rather more. I saw the doctors, then followed despondency and anguish, more doctors, and I drew nearer to the abyss. My strength grew less and I kept coming nearer and nearer, and now I have wasted away and there is no light in my eyes. I think of the appendix — but this is death! I think of mending the appendix, and all the while here is death! Can it really be death?" Again terror seized him and he gasped for breath. He leant down and began feeling for the matches, pressing with his elbow on the stand beside the bed. It was in his way and hurt him, he grew furious with it, pressed on it still harder, and upset it. Breathless and in despair he fell on his back, expecting death to come immediately.

Meanwhile the visitors were leaving. Praskovya Fëdorovna was seeing them off. She heard something fall and came in.

"What has happened?"

"Nothing. I knocked it over accidentally."

She went out and returned with a candle. He lay there panting heavily, like a man who has run a thousand yards, and stared upwards at her with a fixed look.

"What is it, Jean?"

"No . . . o . . . thing. I upset it." ("Why speak of it? She won't understand," he thought.)

And in truth she did not understand. She picked up the stand, lit his candle, and hurried away to see another visitor off. When she came back he still lay on his back, looking upwards.

"What is it? Do you feel worse?"

"Yes."

She shook her head and sat down.

"Do you know, Jean, I think we must ask Leshchetitsky to come and see you here."

This meant calling in the famous specialist, regardless of expense. He smiled malignantly and said "No." She remained a little longer and then went up to him and kissed his forehead.

While she was kissing him he hated her from the bottom of his soul and with difficulty refrained from pushing her away.

"Good-night. Please God you'll sleep."

"Yes."

VI

Ivan Ilych saw that he was dying, and he was in continual despair.

In the depth of his heart he knew he was dying, but not only was he not accustomed to the thought, he simply did not and could not grasp it.

The syllogism he had learnt from Kiezewetter's Logic: "Caius is a man, men are mortal, therefore Caius is mortal," had always seemed to him correct as applied to Caius, but certainly not as applied to himself. That Caius — man in the abstract — was mortal, was perfectly correct, but he was not Caius, not an abstract man, but a creature quite, quite separate from all others. He had been little Vanya, with a mamma and a papa, with Mitya and Volodya, with the toys, a coachman and a nurse, afterwards with Katenka and with all the joys, griefs, and delights of childhood, boyhood, and youth. What did Caius know of the smell of that striped leather ball Vanya had been so fond of? Had Caius kissed his mother's hand like that, and did the silk of her dress rustle so for Caius? Had he rioted like that at school when the pastry was bad? Had Caius been in love like that? Could Caius preside at a session as he did? "Caius really was mortal, and it was right for him to die; but for me, little Vanya, Ivan Ilych, with all my thoughts and emotions, it's altogether a different matter. It cannot be that I ought to die. That would be too terrible."

Such was his feeling.

"If I had to die like Caius I should have known it was so. An inner voice would have told me so, but there was nothing of the sort in me and I and all my friends felt that our case was quite different from that of Caius. And now here it is!" he said to himself. "It can't be. It's impossible! But here it is. How is this? How is one to understand it?"

He could not understand it, and tried to drive this false, incorrect, morbid thought away and to replace it by other proper and healthy thoughts. But that thought, and not the thought only but the reality itself, seemed to come and confront him.

And to replace that thought he called up a succession of others, hoping to find in them some support. He tried to get back into the former current of thoughts that had once screened the thought of death from him. But strange to say, all that had formerly shut off, hidden, and destroyed his consciousness of death, no longer had that effect. Ivan Ilych now spent most of his time in attempting to re-establish that old current. He would say to himself: "I will take up my duties again — after all I used to live by them." And banishing all doubts he would go to the law courts, enter into conversation with his colleagues, and sit carelessly as was his wont, scanning the crowd with a thoughtful look and leaning both his emaciated arms on the arms of his oak chair; bending over as usual to a colleague and drawing his papers nearer he would interchange whispers with him, and then suddenly raising his eyes and sitting erect would pronounce certain words and open the proceedings. But suddenly in the midst of those proceedings the pain in his side, regardless of the stage the proceedings had reached, would begin its own gnawing work. Ivan Ilych would turn his attention to it and try to drive the thought of it away, but without success. *It* would come and stand before him and look at him, and he would be petrified and the light would die out of his eyes, and he would again begin asking himself whether *It* alone was true. And his colleagues and subordinates would see with surprise and distress that he, the brilliant and subtle judge, was becoming confused and making mistakes. He would shake himself, try to pull himself together, manage somehow to bring the sitting to a close, and return home with the sorrowful consciousness that his judicial labours could not as formerly hide from him what he wanted them to hide, and could not deliver him from *It*. And what was worst of all was that *It* drew his attention to itself not in order to make him take some action but only that he should look at *It*, look it straight in the face: look at it and, without doing anything, suffer inexpressibly.

And to save himself from this condition Ivan Ilych looked for consolations — new screens — and new screens were found and for a while seemed to save him, but then they immediately fell to pieces or rather became transparent, as if *It* penetrated them and nothing could veil *It*.

In these latter days he would go into the drawing-room he had arranged — that drawing-room where he had fallen and for the sake of which (how bitterly ridiculous it seemed) he had sacrificed his life — for he knew that his illness originated with that knock. He would enter and see that something had scratched the polished table. He would look for the cause of this and find that it was the bronze ornamentation of an album, that had got bent. He would take up the expensive album which he had lovingly arranged, and feel vexed with his daughter and her friends for their untidiness — for the album was torn here and there and some of the photographs turned upside down. He would put it carefully in order and bend the ornamentation back into position. Then it would occur to him to place all those things in another corner of the room, near the plants. He could call the footman, but his daughter or wife would come to help him. They would not agree, and his wife would contradict him, and he would dispute and grow angry. But that was all right, for then he did not think about *It*. *It* was invisible.

But then, when he was moving something himself, his wife would say: "Let the servants do it. You will hurt yourself again." And suddenly *It* would flash through the screen and he would see it. It was just a flash, and he hoped it would disappear, but he would involuntarily pay attention to his side. "It sits there as before, gnawing just the same!" And he could no longer forget *It*, but could distinctly see it looking at him from behind the flowers. "What is it all for?"

"It really is so! I lost my life over that curtain as I might have done when storming a fort. Is that possible? How terrible and how stupid. It can't be true! It can't, but it is."

He would go to his study, lie down, and again be alone with *It:* face to face with *It*. And nothing could be done with *It* except to look at it and shudder.

VII

How it happened it is impossible to say because it came about step by step, unnoticed, but in the third month of Ivan Ilych's illness, his wife, his daughter, his son, his acquaintances, the doctors, the servants, and above all he himself, were aware that the whole interest he had for other people was whether he would soon vacate his place, and at last release the living from the discomfort caused by his presence and be himself released from his sufferings.

He slept less and less. He was given opium and hypodermic injections of morphine, but this did not relieve him. The dull depression he experienced in a somnolent condition at first gave him a little relief, but only as something new, afterwards it became as distressing as the pain itself or even more so.

Special foods were prepared for him by the doctors' orders, but all those foods became increasingly distasteful and disgusting to him.

For his excretions also special arrangements had to be made, and this was a torment to him every time — a torment from the uncleanliness, the unseemliness, and the smell, and from knowing that another person had to take part in it.

But just through this most unpleasant matter, Ivan Ilych obtained comfort. Gerasim, the butler's young assistant, always came in to carry the things out. Gerasim was a clean, fresh peasant lad, grown stout on town food and always cheerful and bright. At first the sight of him, in his clean Russian peasant costume, engaged on that disgusting task embarrassed Ivan Ilych.

Once when he got up from the commode too weak to draw up his trousers, he dropped into a soft armchair and looked with horror at his bare, enfeebled thighs with the muscles so sharply marked on them.

Gerasim with a firm light tread, his heavy boots emitting a pleasant smell of tar and fresh winter air, came in wearing a clean Hessian apron, the sleeves of his print shirt tucked up over his strong, bare young arms; and refraining from looking at his sick master out of consideration for his feelings, and restraining the joy of life that beamed from his face, he went up to the commode.

"Gerasim!" said Ivan Ilych in a weak voice.

Gerasim started, evidently afraid he might have committed some blunder, and with a rapid movement turned his fresh, kind, simple young face which just showed the first downy signs of a beard.

"Yes, sir?"

"That must be very unpleasant for you. You must forgive me. I am helpless."

"Oh, why, sir," and Gerasim's eyes beamed and he showed his glistening white teeth, "what's a little trouble? It's a case of illness with you, sir."

And his deft strong hands did their accustomed task, and he went out of the room stepping lightly. Five minutes later he as lightly returned.

Ivan Ilych was still sitting in the same position in the armchair.

"Gerasim," he said when the latter had replaced the freshly-washed utensil. "Please come here and help me." Gerasim went up to him. "Lift me up. It is hard for me to get up, and I have sent Dmitri away."

Gerasim went up to him, grasped his master with his strong arms deftly but gently, in the same way that he stepped — lifted him, supported him with one hand, and with the other drew up his trousers and would have set him down again, but Ivan Ilych asked to be led to the sofa. Gerasim, without an effort and without apparent pressure, led him, almost lifting him, to the sofa and placed him on it.

"Thank you. How easily and well you do it all!"

Gerasim smiled again and turned to leave the room. But Ivan Ilych felt his presence such a comfort that he did not want to let him go.

"One thing more, please move up that chair. No, the other one — under my feet. It is easier for me when my feet are raised."

Gerasim brought the chair, set it down gently in place, and raised Ivan Ilych's legs on to it. It seemed to Ivan Ilych that he felt better while Gerasim was holding up his legs.

"It's better when my legs are higher," he said. "Place that cushion under them."

Gerasim did so. He again lifted the legs and placed them, and again Ivan Ilych felt better while Gerasim held his legs. When he set them down Ivan Ilych fancied he felt worse.

"Gerasim," he said. "Are you busy now?"

"Not at all, sir," said Gerasim, who had learnt from the townsfolk how to speak to gentlefolk.

"What have you still to do?"

"What have I to do? I've done everything except chopping the logs for tomorrow."

"Then hold my legs up a bit higher, can you?"

"Of course I can. Why not?" And Gerasim raised his master's legs higher and Ivan Ilych thought that in that position he did not feel any pain at all.

"And how about the logs?"

"Don't trouble about that, sir. There's plenty of time."

Ivan Ilych told Gerasim to sit down and hold his legs, and began to talk to him. And strange to say it seemed to him that he felt better while Gerasim held his legs up.

After that Ivan Ilych would sometimes call Gerasim and get him to hold his legs on his shoulders, and he liked talking to him. Gerasim did it all easily, willingly, simply, and with a good nature that touched Ivan Ilych. Health, strength, and vitality in other people were offensive to him, but Gerasim's strength and vitality did not mortify but soothed him.

What tormented Ivan Ilych most was the deception, the lie, which for some reason they all accepted, that he was not dying but was simply ill, and that he only need keep quiet and undergo a treatment and then something very good would result. He however knew that do what they would nothing would come of it, only still more agonizing suffering and death. This deception tortured him — their not wishing to admit what they all knew and what he knew, but wanting to lie to him concerning his terrible condition, and wishing and forcing him to participate in that lie. Those lies — lies enacted over him on the eve of his death and destined to degrade this awful, solemn act to the level of their visitings, their curtains, their sturgeon for dinner — were a terrible agony for Ivan Ilych. And strangely enough, many times when they were going through their antics over him he had been within a hairbreadth of calling out to them: "Stop lying! You know and I know that I am dying. Then at least stop lying about it!" But he had never had the spirit to do it. The awful, terrible act of his dying was, he could see, reduced by those about him to the level of a casual, unpleasant, and almost indecorous incident (as if someone entered a drawing-room diffusing an unpleasant odour) and this was done by that very decorum which he had served all his life long. He saw that no one felt for him, because no one even wished to grasp his position. Only Gerasim recognized it and pitied him. And so Ivan Ilych felt at ease only with him. He felt comforted when Gerasim supported his legs (sometimes all night long) and refused to go to bed, saying: "Don't you worry, Ivan Ilych. I'll get sleep enough later on," or when he suddenly became familiar and exclaimed: "If you weren't sick it would be another matter, but as it is, why should I grudge a little trouble?" Gerasim alone did not lie; everything showed that he alone understood the facts of the case and did not consider it necessary to disguise them, but simply felt sorry for his emaciated and enfeebled master. Once when Ivan Ilych was sending him away he even said straight out: "We shall all of us die, so why should I grudge a little trouble?" — expressing the fact that he did not think his work burdensome, because he was doing it for a dying man and hoped someone would do the same for him when his time came.

Apart from this lying, or because of it, what most tormented Ivan Ilych was that no one pitied him as he wished to be pitied. At certain moments after prolonged suffering he wished most of all (though he would have been ashamed to confess it) for someone to pity him as a sick child is pitied. He longed to be petted and comforted. He knew he was an important functionary, that he had a beard turning grey, and that therefore what he longed for was impossible, but still he longed for it. And in Gerasim's attitude towards him there was something akin to what he wished for, and so that attitude comforted him. Ivan Ilych wanted to weep, wanted to be petted and cried over, and then his colleague Shebek would come, and instead of weeping and being petted, Ivan Ilych would assume a serious, severe, and profound air, and by force of habit would express his opinion on a decision of the Court of Cassation and would stubbornly insist on that view. This falsity around him and within him did more than anything else to poison his last days.

VIII

It was morning. He knew it was morning because Gerasim had gone, and Peter the footman had come and put out the candles, drawn back one of the curtains, and begun quietly to tidy up. Whether it was morning or evening, Friday or Sunday, made no difference, it was all just the same: the gnawing, unmitigated, agonizing pain, never ceasing for an instant, the consciousness of life inexorably waning but not yet extinguished, the approach of that ever dreaded and hateful

Death which was the only reality, and always the same falsity. What were days, weeks, hours, in such a case?

"Will you have some tea, sir?"

"He wants things to be regular, and wishes the gentlefolk to drink tea in the morning," thought Ivan Ilych, and only said "No."

"Wouldn't you like to move onto the sofa, sir?"

"He wants to tidy up the room, and I'm in the way. I am uncleanliness and disorder," he thought, and said only:

"No, leave me alone."

The man went on bustling about. Ivan Ilych stretched out his hand. Peter came up, ready to help.

"What is it, sir?"

"My watch."

Peter took the watch which was close at hand and gave it to his master.

"Half-past eight. Are they up?"

"No, sir, except Vladimir Ivanovich" (the son) "who has gone to school. Praskovya Fëdorovna ordered me to wake her if you asked for her. Shall I do so?"

"No, there's no need to." "Perhaps I'd better have some tea," he thought, and added aloud: "Yes, bring me some tea."

Peter went to the door, but Ivan Ilych dreaded being left alone. "How can I keep him here? Oh yes, my medicine." "Peter, give me my medicine." "Why not? Perhaps it may still do me some good." He took a spoonful and swallowed it. "No, it won't help. It's all tomfoolery, all deception," he decided as soon as he became aware of the familiar, sickly, hopeless taste. "No, I can't believe in it any longer. But the pain, why this pain? If it would only cease just for a moment!" And he moaned. Peter turned towards him. "It's all right. Go and fetch me some tea."

Peter went out. Left alone Ivan Ilych groaned not so much with pain, terrible though that was, as from mental anguish. Always and forever the same, always these endless days and nights. If only it would come quicker! If only *what* would come quicker? Death, darkness? . . . No, no! Anything rather than death!

When Peter returned with the tea on a tray, Ivan Ilych stared at him for a time in perplexity, not realizing who and what he was. Peter was disconcerted by that look and his embarrassment brought Ivan Ilych to himself.

"Oh, tea! All right, put it down. Only help me to wash and put on a clean shirt."

And Ivan Ilych began to wash. With pauses for rest, he washed his hands and then his face, cleaned his teeth, brushed his hair, and looked in the glass.

He was terrified by what he saw, especially by the limp way in which his hair clung to his pallid forehead.

While his shirt was being changed he knew that he would be still more frightened at the sight of his body, so he avoided looking at it. Finally he was ready. He drew on a dressing-gown, wrapped himself in a plaid, and sat down in the armchair to take his tea. For a moment he felt refreshed, but soon as he began to drink the tea he was again aware of the same taste, and the pain also returned. He finished it with an effort, and then lay down stretching out his legs, and dismissed Peter.

Always the same. Now a spark of hope flashes up, then a sea of despair rages, and always pain; always pain, always despair, and always the same. When alone he had a dreadful and distressing desire to call someone, but he knew beforehand that with others present it would be still worse. "Another dose of morphine — to lose consciousness. I will tell him, the doctor, that he must think of something else. It's impossible, impossible, to go on like this."

An hour and another pass like that. But now there is a ring at the door bell. Perhaps it's the doctor? It is. He comes in fresh, hearty, plump, and cheerful, with that look on his face that seems to say: "There now, you're in a panic about something, but we'll arrange it all for you directly!" The doctor knows this expression is out of place here, but he has put it on once for all and can't take it off — like a man who has put on a frock-coat in the morning to pay a round of calls.

The doctor rubs his hands vigorously and reassuringly.

"Brr! How cold it is! There's such a sharp frost; just let me warm myself!" he says, as if it were only a matter of waiting till he was warm, and then he would put everything right.

"Well now, how are you?"

Ivan Ilych feels that the doctor would like to say: "Well, how are our affairs?" but that even he feels that this would not do, and says instead: "What sort of a night have you had?"

Ivan Ilych looks at him as much as to say: "Are you really never ashamed of lying?" But the doctor does not wish to understand this question, and Ivan Ilych says: "Just as terrible as ever. The pain never leaves me and never subsides. If only something. . . ."

"Yes, you sick people are always like that. . . . There, now I think I am warm enough. Even Praskovya Fëdorovna, who is so particular, could find no fault with my temperature. Well, now I can say good-morning," and the doctor presses his patient's hand.

Then, dropping his former playfulness, he begins with a most serious face to examine the patient, feeling his pulse and taking his temperature, and then begins the sounding and auscultation.

Ivan Ilych knows quite well and definitely that all this is nonsense and pure deception, but when the doctor, getting down on his knee, leans over him, putting his ear first higher then lower, and performs various gymnastic movements over him with a significant expression on his face, Ivan Ilych submits to it all as he used to submit to the speeches of the lawyers, though he knew very well that they were all lying and why they were lying.

The doctor, kneeling on the sofa, is still sounding him when Praskovya Fëdorovna's silk dress rustles at the door and she is heard scolding Peter for not having let her know of the doctor's arrival.

She comes in, kisses her husband, and at once proceeds to prove that she has been up a long time already, and only owing to a misunderstanding failed to be there when the doctor arrived.

Ivan Ilych looks at her, scans her all over, sets against her the whiteness and plumpness and cleanness of her hands and neck, the gloss of her hair, and the sparkle of her vivacious eyes. He hates her with his whole soul. And the thrill of hatred he feels for her makes him suffer from her touch.

Her attitude towards him and his disease is still the same. Just as the doctor had adopted a certain relation to his patient which he could not abandon, so had she formed one towards him — that he was not doing something he ought to do and was himself to blame, and that she reproached him lovingly for this — and she could not now change that attitude.

"You see he doesn't listen to me and doesn't take his medicine at the proper time. And above all he lies in a position that is no doubt bad for him — with his legs up."

She described how he made Gerasim hold his legs up.

The doctor smiled with a contemptuous affability that said: "What's to be done? These sick people do have foolish fancies of that kind, but we must forgive them."

When the examination was over the doctor looked at his watch, and then Praskovya Fëdorovna announced to Ivan Ilych that it was of course as he pleased, but she had sent today for a celebrated specialist who would examine him and have a consultation with Michael Danilovich (their regular doctor).

"Please don't raise any objections. I am doing this for my own sake," she said ironically, letting it be felt that she was doing it all for his sake and only said this to leave him no right to refuse. He remained silent, knitting his brows. He felt that he was so surrounded and involved in a mesh of falsity that it was hard to unravel anything.

Everything she did for him was entirely for her own sake, and she told him she was doing for herself what she actually was doing for herself, as if that was so incredible that he must understand the opposite.

At half-past eleven the celebrated specialist arrived. Again the sounding began and the significant conversations in his presence and in another room, about the kidneys and the appendix, and the questions and answers, with such an air of importance that again, instead of the real question of life and death which now alone confronted him, the question arose of the kidney and appendix which were not behaving as they ought to and would now be attacked by Michael Danilovich and the specialist and forced to amend their ways.

The celebrated specialist took leave of him with a serious though not hopeless look, and in reply to the timid question Ivan Ilych, with eyes glistening with fear and hope, put to him as to whether there was a chance of recovery, said that he could not vouch for it but there was a possibility. The look of hope with which Ivan Ilych watched the doctor out was so pathetic that Praskovya Fëdorovna, seeing it, even wept as she left the room to hand the doctor his fee.

The gleam of hope kindled by the doctor's encouragement did not last long. The same room, the same pictures, curtains, wallpaper, medicine bottles, were all there, and the same aching suffering body, and Ivan Ilych began to moan. They gave him a subcutaneous injection and he sank into oblivion.

It was twilight when he came to. They brought him his dinner and he swallowed some beef tea with difficulty, and then everything was the same again and night was coming on.

After dinner, at seven o'clock, Praskovya Fëdorovna came into the room in evening dress, her full bosom pushed up by her corset, and with traces of powder on her face. She had reminded him in the morning that they were going to the theatre. Sarah Bernhardt was visiting the town and they had a box, which he had insisted on their taking. Now he had forgotten about it and her toilet offended him, but he concealed his vexation when he remembered that he had himself insisted on their securing a box and going because it would be an instructive and aesthetic pleasure for the children.

Praskovya Fëdorovna came in, self-satisfied but yet with a rather guilty air. She sat down and asked how he was, but, as he saw, only for the sake of asking and not in order to learn about it, knowing that there was nothing to learn — and then went on to what she really wanted to say: that she would not on any account have gone but that the box had been taken and Helen and their daughter were going, as well as Petrishchev (the examining magistrate, their daughter's fiancé), and that it was out of the question to let them go alone; but that she would have much preferred to sit with him for a while; and he must be sure to follow the doctor's orders while she was away.

"Oh, and Fëdor Petrovich" (the fiancé) "would like to come in. May he? And Lisa?"

"All right."

Their daughter came in in full evening dress, her fresh young flesh exposed (making a show of that very flesh which in his own case caused so much suffering), strong, healthy, evidently in love, and impatient with illness, suffering, and death, because they interfered with her happiness.

Fëdor Petrovich came in too, in evening dress, his hair curled *à la Capoul*,[14] a tight stiff collar round his long sinewy neck, an enormous white shirt-front, and narrow black trousers tightly stretched over his strong thighs. He had one white glove tightly drawn on, and was holding his opera hat in his hand.

Following him the schoolboy crept in unnoticed, in a new uniform, poor little fellow, and wearing gloves. Terribly dark shadows showed under his eyes, the meaning of which Ivan Ilych knew well.

His son had always seemed pathetic to him, and now it was dreadful to see the boy's frightened look of pity. It seemed to Ivan Ilych that Vasya was the only one besides Gerasim who understood and pitied him.

They all sat down and again asked how he was. A silence followed. Lisa asked her mother about the opera-glasses, and there was an altercation between mother and daughter as to who had taken them and where they had been put. This occasioned some unpleasantness.

Fëdor Petrovich inquired of Ivan Ilych whether he had ever seen Sarah Bernhardt. Ivan Ilych did not at first catch the question, but then replied: "No, have you seen her before?"

"Yes, in *Adrienne Lecouvreur*."[15]

Praskovya Fëdorovna mentioned some rôles in which Sarah Bernhardt was particularly good. Her daughter disagreed. Conversation sprang up as to the elegance and realism of her acting — the sort of conversation that is always repeated and is always the same.

In the midst of the conversation Fëdor Petrovich glanced at Ivan Ilych and became silent. The others also looked at him and grew silent. Ivan Ilych was staring with glittering eyes straight before him, evidently indignant with them. This had to be rectified, but it was impossible to do so. The silence had to be broken, but for a time no one dared to break it and they all became afraid that the conventional deception would suddenly become obvious and the truth become plain to all. Lisa was the first to pluck up courage and break that silence, but by trying to hide what everybody was feeling, she betrayed it.

"Well, if we are going it's time to start," she said, looking at her watch, a present from her father, and with a faint and significant smile at Fëdor Petrovich relating to something known only to them. She got up with a rustle of her dress.

They all rose, said good-night, and went away.

14 [I.e., in the elaborate style of the French singer Victor Capoul. — Editors' note.]
15 [A French tragedy by Scribe and Legouvé. — Editors' note.]

When they had gone it seemed to Ivan Ilych that he felt better; the falsity had gone with them. But the pain remained — that same pain and that same fear that made everything monotonously alike, nothing harder and nothing easier. Everything was worse.

Again minute followed minute and hour followed hour. Everything remained the same and there was no cessation. And the inevitable end of it all became more and more terrible.

"Yes, send Gerasim here," he replied to a question Peter asked.

IX

His wife returned late at night. She came in on tiptoe, but he heard her, opened his eyes, and made haste to close them again. She wished to send Gerasim away and to sit with him herself, but he opened his eyes and said: "No, go away."

"Are you in great pain?"

"Always the same."

"Take some opium."

He agreed and took some. She went away.

Till about three in the morning he was in a state of stupefied misery. It seemed to him that he and his pain were being thrust into a narrow, deep black sack, but though they were pushed further and further in they could not be pushed to the bottom. And this, terrible enough in itself, was accompanied by suffering. He was frightened yet wanted to fall through the sack, he struggled but yet cooperated. And suddenly he broke through, fell, and regained consciousness. Gerasim was sitting at the foot of the bed dozing quietly and patiently, while he himself lay with his emaciated stockinged legs resting on Gerasim's shoulders; the same shaded candle was there and the same unceasing pain.

"Go away, Gerasim," he whispered.

"It's all right, sir. I'll stay a while."

"No. Go away."

He removed his legs from Gerasim's shoulders, turned sideways onto his arm, and felt sorry for himself. He only waited till Gerasim had gone into the next room and then restrained himself no longer but wept like a child. He wept on account of his helplessness, his terrible loneliness, the cruelty of man, the cruelty of God, and the absence of God.

"Why hast Thou done all this? Why hast Thou brought me here? Why, why dost Thou torment me so terribly?"

He did not expect an answer and yet wept because there was no answer and could be none. The pain again grew more acute, but he did not stir and did not call. He said to himself: "Go on! Strike me! But what is it for? What have I done to Thee? What is it for?"

Then he grew quiet and not only ceased weeping but even held his breath and became all attention. It was as though he were listening not to an audible voice but to the voice of his soul, to the current of thoughts arising within him.

"What is it you want?" was the first clear conception capable of expression in words, that he heard.

"What do you want? What do you want?" he repeated to himself.

"What do I want? To live and not to suffer," he answered.

And again he listened with such concentrated attention that even his pain did not distract him.

"To live? How?" asked his inner voice.

"Why, to live as I used to — well and pleasantly."

"As you lived before, well and pleasantly?" the voice repeated.

And in imagination he began to recall the best moments of his pleasant life. But strange to say none of those best moments of his pleasant life now seemed at all what they had then seemed — none of them except the first recollections of childhood. There, in childhood, there had been something really pleasant with which it would be possible to live if it could return. But the child who had experienced that happiness existed no longer, it was like a reminiscence of somebody else.

As soon as the period began which had produced the present Ivan Ilych, all that had then seemed joys now melted before his sight and turned into something trivial and often nasty.

And the further he departed from childhood and the nearer he came to the present the more worthless and doubtful were the joys. This began with the School of Law. A little that was really good was still found there — there was lightheartedness, friendship, and hope. But in the upper classes there had already been fewer of such good moments. Then during the first years of his official career, when he was in the service of the Governor, some pleasant moments again occurred; they were the memories of love for a woman. Then all became confused and there was still less of what was good; later on again there was still less that was good, and the further he went the less there was. His marriage, a mere accident, then the disenchantment that followed it, his wife's bad breath and the sensuality and hypocrisy: then that deadly official life and those preoccupations about money, a year of it, and two, and ten, and twenty, and always the same thing. And the longer it lasted the more deadly it became. "It is as if I had been going downhill while I imagined I was going up. And that is really what it was. I was going up in public opinion, but to the same extent life was ebbing away from me. And now it is all done and there is only death."

"Then what does it mean? Why? It can't be that life is so senseless and horrible. But if it really has been so horrible and senseless, why must I die and die in agony? There is something wrong!"

"Maybe I did not live as I ought to have done," it suddenly occurred to him. "But how could that be, when I did everything properly?" he replied, and immediately dismissed from his mind this, the sole solution of all the riddles of life and death, as something quite impossible.

"Then what do you want now? To live? Live how? Live as you lived in the law courts when the usher proclaimed 'The judge is coming!' The judge is coming, the judge!" he repeated to himself. "Here he is, the judge. But I am not guilty!" he exclaimed angrily. "What is it for?" And he ceased crying, but turning his face to the wall continued to ponder on the same question: Why, and for what purpose, is there all this horror? But however much he pondered he found no answer. And whenever the thought occurred to him, as it often did, that it all resulted from his not having lived as he ought to have done, he at once recalled the correctness of his whole life and dismissed so strange an idea.

X

Another fortnight passed. Ivan Ilych now no longer left his sofa. He would not lie in bed but lay on the sofa, facing the wall nearly all the time. He suffered ever the same unceasing agonies and in his loneliness pondered always on the same insoluble question: "What is this? Can it be that it is Death?" And the inner voice answered: "Yes, it is Death."

"Why these sufferings?" And the voice answered, "For no reason — they just are so." Beyond and besides this there was nothing.

From the very beginning of his illness, ever since he had first been to see the doctor, Ivan Ilych's life had been divided between two contrary and alternating moods: now it was despair and the expectation of this uncomprehended and terrible death, and now hope and an intently interested observation of the functioning of his organs. Now before his eyes there was only a kidney or an intestine that temporarily evaded its duty, and now only that incomprehensible and dreadful death from which it was impossible to escape.

These two states of mind had alternated from the very beginning of his illness, but the further it progressed the more doubtful and fantastic became the conception of the kidney, and the more real the sense of impending death.

He had but to call to mind what he had been three months before and what he was now, to call to mind with what regularity he had been going downhill, for every possibility of hope to be shattered.

Latterly during that loneliness in which he found himself as he lay facing the back of the sofa, a loneliness in the midst of a populous town and surrounded by numerous acquaintances and relations but that yet could not have been more complete anywhere — either at the bottom of the sea or under the earth — during that terrible loneliness Ivan Ilych had lived only in memories of the past. Pictures of his past rose before him one after another. They always began with what was nearest in time and then went back to what was most remote — to his childhood — and rested there. If he thought of the stewed prunes that had been offered him that day, his mind went back to the raw shrivelled French plums of his childhood, their peculiar flavour and the flow of saliva when he sucked their stones, and along with the memory of that taste came a whole series of memories of those days: his nurse, his brother, and their toys. "No, I mustn't think of that. . . . It is too painful," Ivan Ilych said to himself, and brought himself back to the present — to the button on the back of the sofa and the creases in its morocco. "Morocco is expensive, but it does not wear well: there had been a quarrel about it. It was a different kind of quarrel and a different kind of morocco that time when we tore father's portfolio and were punished, and mamma brought us some tarts. . . ." And again his thoughts dwelt on his childhood, and again it was painful and he tried to banish them and fix his mind on something else.

Then again together with that chain of memories another series passed through his mind — of how his illness had progressed and grown worse. There also the further back he looked the more life there had been. There had been more of what was good in life and more of life itself. The two merged together. "Just as the pain went on getting worse and worse, so my life grew worse and worse," he thought. "There is one bright spot there at the back, at the beginning of life, and afterwards all becomes blacker and blacker and proceeds more and more rapidly — in inverse ratio to the square of the distance from death," thought Ivan Ilych. And the example of a stone falling downwards with increasing velocity entered his mind. Life, a series of increasing sufferings, flies further and further towards its end — the most terrible suffering. "I am flying. . . ." He shuddered, shifted himself, and tried to resist, but was already aware that resistance was impossible, and again, with eyes weary of gazing but unable to cease seeing what was before them, he stared at the back of the sofa and waited — awaiting that dreadful fall and shock and destruction.

"Resistance is impossible!" he said to himself. "If I could only understand what it is all for! But that too is impossible. An explanation would be possible if it could be said that I have not lived as I ought to. But it is impossible to say that," and he remembered all the legality, correctitude, and propriety of his life. "That at any rate can certainly not be admitted," he thought, and his lips smiled ironically as if someone could see that smile and be taken in by it. "There is no explanation! Agony, death. . . . What for?"

XI

Another two weeks went by in this way and during that fortnight an event occurred that Ivan Ilych and his wife had desired. Petrishchev formally proposed. It happened in the evening. The next day Praskovya Fëdorovna came into her husband's room considering how best to inform him of it, but that very night there had been a fresh change for the worse in his condition. She found him still lying on the sofa but in a different position. He lay on his back, groaning and staring fixedly straight in front of him.

She began to remind him of his medicines, but he turned his eyes towards her with such a look that she did not finish what she was saying; so great an animosity, to her in particular, did that look express.

"For Christ's sake let me die in peace!" he said.

She would have gone away, but just then their daughter came in and went up to say good morning. He looked at her as he had done at his wife, and in reply to her inquiry about his health said dryly that he would soon free them all of himself. They were both silent and after sitting with him for a while went away.

"Is it our fault?" Lisa said to her mother. "It's as if we were to blame! I am sorry for papa, but why should we be tortured?"

The doctor came at his usual time. Ivan Ilych answered "Yes" and "No," never taking his angry eyes from him, and at last said: "You know you can do nothing for me, so leave me alone."

"We can ease your sufferings."

"You can't even do that. Let me be."

The doctor went into the drawing-room and told Praskovya Fëdorovna that the case was very serious and that the only resource left was opium to allay her husband's sufferings, which must be terrible.

It was true, as the doctor said, that Ivan Ilych's physical sufferings were terrible, but worse than the physical sufferings were his mental sufferings, which were his chief torture.

His mental sufferings were duc to the fact that that night, as he looked at Gerasim's sleepy, good-natured face with its prominent cheekbones, the question suddenly occurred to him: "What if my whole life has really been wrong?"

It occurred to him that what had appeared perfectly impossible before, namely that he had not spent his life as he should have done, might after all be true. It occurred to him that his scarcely perceptible attempts to struggle against what was considered good by the most highly placed people, those scarcely noticeable impulses which he had immediately suppressed, might have been the real thing, and all the rest false. And his professional duties and the whole arrangement of his life and of his family, and all his social and official interests, might all have been false. He tried to defend all those things to himself and suddenly felt the weakness of what he was defending. There was nothing to defend.

"But if that is so," he said to himself, "and I am leaving this life with the consciousness that I have lost all that was given me and it is impossible to rectify it — what then?"

He lay on his back and began to pass his life in review in quite a new way. In the morning when he saw first his footman, then his wife, then his daughter, and then the doctor, their every word and movement confirmed to him the awful truth that had been revealed to him during the night. In them he saw himself — all that for which he had lived — and saw clearly that it was not real at all, but a terrible and huge deception which had hidden both life and death. This consciousness intensified his physical suffering tenfold. He groaned and tossed about, and pulled at his clothing which choked and stifled him. And he hated them on that account.

He was given a large dose of opium and became unconscious, but at noon his sufferings began again. He drove everybody away and tossed from side to side.

His wife came to him and said:

"Jean, my dear, do this for me. It can't do any harm and often helps. Healthy people often do it."

He opened his eyes wide.

"What? Take communion? Why? It's unnecessary! However. . . ."

She began to cry.

"Yes, do, my dear. I'll send for our priest. He is such a nice man."

"All right. Very well," he muttered.

When the priest came and heard his confession, Ivan Ilych was softened and seemed to feel a relief from his doubts and consequently from his sufferings, and for a moment there came a ray of hope. He again began to think of the vermiform appendix and the possibility of correcting it. He received the sacrament with tears in his eyes.

When they laid him down again afterwards he felt a moment's ease, and the hope that he might live awoke in him again. He began to think of the operation that had been suggested to him. "To live! I want to live!" he said to himself.

His wife came in to congratulate him after his communion, and when uttering the usual conventional words she added:

"You feel better, don't you?"

Without looking at her he said "Yes."

Her dress, her figure, the expression of her face, the tone of her voice, all revealed the same thing. "This is wrong, it is not as it should be. All you have lived for and still live for is falsehood and deception, hiding life and death from you." And as soon as he admitted that thought, his hatred and his agonizing physical suffering again sprang up, and with that suffering a consciousness of the unavoidable, approaching end. And to this was added a new sensation of grinding shooting pain and a feeling of suffocation.

The expression of his face when he uttered that "yes" was dreadful. Having uttered it, he looked her straight in the eyes, turned on his face with a rapidity extraordinary in his weak state and shouted:

"Go away! Go away and leave me alone!"

XII

From that moment the screaming began that continued for three days, and was so terrible that one could not hear it through two closed doors without horror. At the moment he answered his wife he realized that he was lost, that there was no return, that the end had come, the very end, and his doubts were still unsolved and remained doubts.

"Oh! Oh! Oh!" he cried in various intonations. He had begun by screaming "I won't!" and continued screaming on the letter *O*.

For three whole days, during which time did not exist for him, he struggled in that black sack into which he was being thrust by an invisible, resistless force. He struggled as a man condemned to death struggles in the hands of the executioner, knowing that he cannot save himself. And every moment he felt that despite all his efforts he was drawing nearer and nearer to what terrified him. He felt that his agony was due to his being thrust into that black hole and still more to his not being able to get right into it. He was hindered from getting into it by his conviction that his life had been a good one. That very justification of his life held him fast and prevented his moving forward, and it caused him most torment of all.

Suddenly some force struck him in the chest and side, making it still harder to breathe, and he fell through the hole and there at the bottom was a light. What had happened to him was like the sensation one sometimes experiences in a railway carriage when one thinks one is going backwards while one is really going forwards and suddenly becomes aware of the real direction.

"Yes, it was all not the right thing," he said to himself, "but that's no matter. It can be done. But what *is* the right thing?" he asked himself, and suddenly grew quiet.

This occurred at the end of the third day, two hours before his death. Just then his schoolboy son had crept softly in and gone up to the bedside. The dying man was still screaming desperately and waving his arms. His hand fell on the boy's head, and the boy caught it, pressed it to his lips, and began to cry.

At that very moment Ivan Ilych fell through and caught sight of the light, and it was revealed to him that though his life had not been what it should have been, this could still be rectified. He asked himself, "What *is* the right thing?" and grew still, listening. Then he felt that someone was kissing his hand. He opened his eyes, looked at his son, and felt sorry for him. His wife came up to him and he glanced at her. She was gazing at him open-mouthed, with undried tears on her nose and cheek and a despairing look on her face. He felt sorry for her too.

"Yes, I am making them wretched," he thought. "They are sorry, but it will be better for them when I die." He wished to say this but had not the strength to utter it. "Besides, why speak? I must act," he thought. With a look at his wife he indicated his son and said: "Take him away . . . sorry for him . . . sorry for you too. . . ." He tried to add, "Forgive me," but said "forgo" and waved his hand, knowing that He whose understanding mattered would understand.

And suddenly it grew clear to him that what had been oppressing him and would not leave him was all dropping away at once from two sides, from ten sides, and from all sides. He was sorry for them, he must act so as not to hurt them: release them and free himself from these sufferings. "How good and how simple!" he thought. "And the pain?" he asked himself. "What has become of it? Where are you, pain?"

He turned his attention to it.

"Yes, here it is. Well, what of it? Let the pain be."

"And death . . . where is it?"

He sought his former accustomed fear of death and did not find it. "Where is it? What death?" There was no fear because there was no death.

In place of death there was light.

"So that's what it is!" he suddenly exclaimed aloud. "What joy!"

To him all this happened in a single instant, and the meaning of that instant did not change. For those present his agony continued for another two hours. Something rattled in his throat, his emaciated body twitched, then the gasping and rattle became less and less frequent.

"It is finished!" said someone near him.

He heard these words and repeated them in his soul.

"Death is finished," he said to himself. "It is no more!"

He drew in a breath, stopped in the midst of a sigh, stretched out, and died.

AFTERWORD

No author need apologize for writing about death, a topic of such enormous interest that it is rivaled only by sex. But if we think for a moment about *The Death of Ivan Ilych*, we realize that it is largely about the *life* of Ivan Ilych, or, more precisely, about his deathbed realization that he has scarcely lived. Despite the recurrent references to Ivan Ilych's illness, the story reveals not a morbid interest in illness and dying but a heartening interest in living.

The first sentence of the second part of the story makes this clear: "Ivan Ilych's life had been most simple and most ordinary and therefore most terrible." In the remainder of the story Tolstoy (clearly the narrator is Tolstoy, or someone so close to him that we need scarcely speak delicately of "the narrator") goes on to demonstrate the terribleness of this ordinariness. Superficially Ivan Ilych's life would seem to be unusual and successful: he climbs fairly high up the social ladder, achieves a substantial salary, has a wife, children, and an ample home, and he has some power which he savors even if he does not abuse it. But the point, of course, is that after he falls ill and nears death, he becomes aware — as Tolstoy has kept the reader aware — that Ivan Ilych's interests are so narrow, and even his vices so trivial, that however he may be envied he can scarcely be said to have lived. He learns this through sickness, which forces intense awareness of oneself, as anyone realizes who has had even so trivial a sickness as a running nose. And one of the facts about us, which we are scarcely aware of until we become sick, is that someday we will die.

Tolstoy makes it clear that, in a way, Ivan Ilych knew this: in a logic text he had learned that "Caius is a man, men are mortal, therefore Caius is mortal," but, Tolstoy says, these words "had always seemed to him correct as applied to Caius, but certainly not as applied to himself." And here we can digress for a moment on one of the differences between literature and philosophy. Literature, it has long been recognized, has a concreteness or immediacy that at least in some considerable degree forces the reader to sense or experience the reality that is being presented: to some degree we believe in and understand the experiences of the characters in good literature (at least in realistic prose fiction such as this story). *Why* do we identify with such figures? Probably for at least two reasons: (1) We are given a fairly convincing detailed picture of their surroundings, and (2) we are given revelations of character or psychological insights whose truth we recognize from our own experiences. Each of these two points may be discussed a bit.

Most novels, long or short, carefully build up a picture of the characters' surroundings. Thus, *The Death of Ivan Ilych* begins with a reference to an apparently public event ("the Melvinski trial") and to a public building ("the Law Courts"), specifies the name of a particular person, and moves through other people's names to the name of a newspaper. We know, of course, that we are reading fiction, but it is fiction that insists on facts, rather than fiction that begins "Once upon a time in a far-off country there lived a woodsman who had three sons." But it is not merely the specification of names of buildings, people, and newspapers that gives us a sense of a believable world. Tolstoy continually gives us a sense of the solidity of things. For example, describing the players beginning a card game Tolstoy mentions that "they dealt, bending the new cards to soften them." We need not look here for symbolism, we need not fancy that the cards, like Ivan Ilych, are being forced into a new shape; we can be content simply with our sense of the reality of this (fictional) card game. It is through such details, which pervade the story, that the writer gains our confidence. Illustrations need not be multiplied, but we might look briefly at one other scene before proceeding to the second point, the author's psychological astuteness. In the first section of the story there is a highly comic scene when Peter Ivanovich sits "on a low pouffe, the springs of which yielded spasmodically under his weight." There again, most literally, is the sense of the weight of things. When Peter must get up to assist the widow in detaching a shawl which catches on the carved edge of a table (again, convincing even if apparently irrelevant detail) "the springs of the pouffe, relieved of his weight, rose also and gave him a push." It probably is not fanciful to see here, in the pouffe's mechanical behavior, satiric commentary on the mechanical (conventional, unspontaneous) behavior of Peter and the widow, but it would be wrong to neglect the fact that Tolstoy also sees the pouffe as a pouffe, a thing with a density of its own, and it is through a world of believable things that his characters move.

Now for the second point, the revelation of convincing characters. Possibly the presentation of convincing *things* is a sort of sleight of hand whereby an author wins our confidence in his perceptions. After all, it does not follow that because a writer is perceptive enough to notice that card players bend new cards and that pouffes have springs, he is a shrewd perceiver of human nature. But in page after page Tolstoy does indeed give us shrewd perceptions of human nature. He catches the irritability and the hypersensitivity of a sick man, for example, in the scene when his partner "pushed the cards courteously and indulgently towards Ivan Ilych that he might have the pleasure of gathering them up without the trouble of stretching out his hand for them" and Ivan Ilych's mental response is "Does he think I am too weak to stretch out my arm?"

As we begin to read the story, perceiving the mutual insincerity which passes between Peter Ivanovich and the widow he is supposed to be consoling, and perceiving Ivan Ilych's shallowness, we may feel superior to the characters, but it soon becomes evident that although these people are not very amiable, we can scarcely look down on them. Too much is revealed about them that we recognize in ourselves. We have been pushed by pouffes, we have experienced "the complacent feeling that, 'it is he who is dead and not I,' " we have said to widows what we believe we are supposed to say, and — most telling — we know from experience the truth of Tolstoy's assertion that after Peter pressed the widow's hand because it was "the right thing," "both he and she were touched." That hurts, this perception that we are moved by our own calculating gestures.

Most of all, of course, we are concerned with Ivan Ilych, not with his widow or his acquaintances, and here again, we are compelled to recognize that we cannot take a superior attitude. We simply find him too recognizable, too human, too much ourself, to take refuge in thoughts of our superiority. Interestingly, he is *not* given much external characterization: he has a name, he is somewhat bald, he has a prominent nose and a graying beard, but he is not described in such detail as to become a "character" and therefore someone apart from us. The story, after all, is the story of Everyman: near the end of one's life one finds that death terrifies, and that one has not loved and therefore in any significant sense one has scarcely lived. Ivan Ilych very late and very painfully comes to an awareness of these things; his body racks him first into an awareness of physical existence and then into an awareness of spirit whereby he is at last able to recognize his lifetime of failure and to experience — terribly late — a compassion that banishes the fear of death. In a very crude sense, then, the story has a happy ending: a man in his last couple of hours experiences a pity for others that is perhaps indistinguishable from love and dies without fear; but Tolstoy does not let us off that easily with a comforting message. We continue to remember the agony of Ivan Ilych's dying months, and the waste of his life.

JOSEPH CONRAD

Joseph Conrad (1857–1924), born Josef Teodor Nalecz Korzeniowski in Poland, traveled to Marseilles in 1874 and from there, at the age of seventeen, went to sea on French merchant ships. In 1878, when he was twenty-one, he joined an English ship and in the following years learned English while sailing in the English merchant service. In 1886 he became a British citizen and won his master's (i.e., captain's) certificate. In 1890 he served as the master of a river steamer on the Congo River, undergoing many of the experiences set forth in *Heart of Darkness.* Apparently as early as 1889 he had already begun a novel, *Almayer's Folly,* and when it was published in 1895 he decided to change his profession from seaman to writer. *Heart of Darkness* was written from December 1898 to February 1899, published serially in a magazine in three parts in 1899, and very slightly revised for publication as a book in 1902. Some of his best-known works are *The Nigger of the "Narcissus,"* 1897; *Lord Jim,* 1900; *Nostromo,* 1904; *The Secret Sharer,* 1912.

HEART OF DARKNESS

I

The *Nellie*, a cruising yawl, swung to her anchor without a flutter of the sails, and was at rest. The flood had made, the wind was nearly calm, and being bound down the river, the only thing for it was to come to and wait for the turn of the tide.

The sea-reach of the Thames stretched before us like the beginning of an interminable waterway. In the offing the sea and the sky were welded together without a joint, and in the luminous space the tanned sails of the barges drifting up with the tide seemed to stand still in red clusters of canvas sharply peaked, with gleams of varnished sprits. A haze rested on the low shores that ran out to sea in vanishing flatness. The air was dark above Gravesend, and farther back still seemed condensed into a mournful gloom, brooding motionless over the biggest, and the greatest, town on earth.

The Director of Companies was our captain and our host. We four affectionately watched his back as he stood in the bows looking to seaward. On the whole river there was nothing that looked half so nautical. He resembled a pilot, which to a seaman is trustworthiness personified. It was difficult to realize his work was not out there in the luminous estuary, but behind him, within the brooding gloom.

Between us there was, as I have already said somewhere, the bond of the sea. Besides holding our hearts together through long periods of separation, it had the effect of making us tolerant of each other's yarns — and even convictions. The Lawyer — the best of old fellows — had, because of his many years and many virtues, the only cushion on deck, and was lying on the only rug. The Accountant had brought out already a box of dominoes, and was toying architecturally with the bones. Marlow sat cross-legged right aft, leaning against the mizzenmast. He had sunken cheeks, a yellow complexion, a straight back, an ascetic aspect, and, with his arms dropped, the palms of hands outwards, resembled an idol. The director, satisfied the anchor had good hold, made his way aft and sat down amongst us. We exchanged a few words lazily. Afterwards there was silence on board the yacht. For some reason or other we did not begin that game of dominoes. We felt meditative, and fit for nothing but placid staring. The day was ending in a serenity of still and exquisite brilliance. The water shone pacifically; the sky, without a speck, was a benign immensity of unstained light; the very mist on the Essex marsh was like a gauzy and radiant fabric, hung from the wooded rises inland, and draping the low shores in diaphanous folds. Only the gloom to the west, brooding over the upper reaches, became more sombre every minute, as if angered by the approach of the sun.

And at last, in its curved and imperceptible fall, the sun sank low, and from glowing white changed to a dull red without rays and without heat, as if about to go out suddenly, stricken to death by the touch of that gloom brooding over a crowd of men.

Forthwith a change came over the waters, and the serenity became less brilliant but more profound. The old river in its broad reach rested unruffled at the decline of day, after ages of good service done to the race that peopled its banks, spread out in the tranquil dignity of a waterway leading to the uttermost ends of the earth. We looked at the venerable stream not in the vivid flush of a short day that comes and departs for ever, but in the august light of abiding memories. And indeed nothing is easier for a man who has, as the phrase goes, "followed the sea" with reverence and affection, than to evoke the great spirit of the past upon the lower reaches of the Thames. The tidal current runs to and fro in its unceasing service, crowded with memories of men and ships it had borne to the rest of home or to the battles of the sea. It had known and served all the men of whom the nation is proud, from Sir Francis Drake to Sir John Franklin, knights all, titled and untitled — the great knights-errant of the sea. It had borne all the ships whose names are like jewels flashing in the night of time, from the *Golden Hind* returning with her round flanks full of treasure, to be visited by the Queen's Highness and thus pass out of the gigantic tale, to the *Erebus* and *Terror*, bound on other conquests — and that never returned. It had known the ships and the men. They had sailed from Deptford, from Greenwich, from Erith — the adventurers and the settlers; kings' ships and the ships of men on 'Change; captains, admirals, the dark "interlopers" of the Eastern trade, and the commissioned "generals" of East India fleets. Hunters for gold or pursuers of fame, they all had gone out on that stream, bearing the sword, and often the torch, messengers of the might within the land, bearers of a spark from the sacred fire. What greatness had not floated on the ebb of that river into the mystery of an unknown earth! . . . The dreams of men, the seed of commonwealths, the germs of empires.

The sun set; the dusk fell on the stream, and lights began to appear along the shore. The Chapman lighthouse, a three-legged thing erect on a mud-flat, shone strongly. Lights of ships moved in the fairway — a great stir of lights going up and going down. And farther west on the upper reaches the place of the monstrous town was still marked ominously on the sky, a brooding gloom in sunshine, a lurid glare under the stars.

"And this also," said Marlow suddenly, "has been one of the dark places of the earth."

He was the only man of us who still "followed the sea." The worst that could be said of him was that he did not represent his class. He was a seaman, but he was a wanderer, too, while most seamen lead, if one may so express it, a sedentary life. Their minds are of the stay-at-home order, and their home is always with them — the ship; and so is their country — the sea. One ship is very much like another, and the sea is always the same. In the immutability of their surroundings the foreign shores, the foreign faces, the changing immensity of life, glide past, veiled not by a sense of mystery but by a slightly disdainful ignorance; for there is nothing mysterious to a seaman unless it be the sea itself, which is the mistress of his existence and as inscrutable as Destiny. For the rest, after his hours of work, a casual stroll or a casual spree on shore suffices to unfold for him the secret of a whole continent, and generally he finds the secret not worth knowing. The yarns of seamen have a direct simplicity, the whole meaning of which lies within the shell of a cracked nut. But Marlow was not typical (if his propensity to spin yarns be excepted), and to him the meaning of an episode was not inside like a kernel but outside, enveloping the tale which brought it out only as a glow brings out a haze, in the likeness of one of these misty halos that sometimes are made visible by the spectral illumination of moonshine.

His remark did not seem at all surprising. It was just like Marlow. It was accepted in silence. No one took the trouble to grunt even; and presently he said, very slow —

"I was thinking of very old times, when the Romans first came here, nineteen hundred years ago — the other day. . . . Light came out of this river since — you say Knights? Yes; but it is like a running blaze on a plain, like a flash of lightning in the clouds. We live in the flicker — may it last as long as the old earth keeps rolling! But darkness was here yesterday. Imagine the feelings of a commander of a fine — what d'ye call 'em? — trireme in the Mediterranean, ordered suddenly to the north; run overland across the Gauls in a hurry; put in charge of one of these craft the legionaries — a wonderful lot of handy men they must have been, too — used to build, apparently by the hundred, in a month or two, if we may believe what we read. Imagine him here — the very end of the world, a sea the colour of lead, a sky the colour of smoke, a kind of ship about as rigid as a concertina — and going up this river with stores, or orders, or what you like. Sand-banks, marshes, forests, savages, — precious little to eat fit for a civilized man, nothing but Thames water to drink. No Falernian wine here, no going ashore. Here and there a military camp lost in a wilderness, like a needle in a bundle of hay — cold, fog, tempests, disease, exile, and death — death skulking in the air, in the water, in the bush. They must have been dying like flies here. Oh, yes — he did it. Did it very well, too, no doubt, and without thinking much about it either, except afterwards to brag of what he had gone through in his time, perhaps. They were men enough to face the darkness. And perhaps he was cheered by keeping his eye on a chance of promotion to the fleet at Ravenna by and by, if he had good friends in Rome and survived the awful climate. Or think of a decent young citizen in a toga — perhaps too much dice, you know — coming out here in the train of some prefect, or tax-gatherer, or trader even, to mend his fortunes. Land in a swamp, march through the woods, and in some inland post feel the savagery, the utter savagery, had closed round him — all that mysterious life of the wilderness that stirs in the forest, in the jungles, in the hearts of wild men. There's no initiation either into such mysteries. He has to live in the midst of the incomprehensible, which is also detestable. And it has a fascination, too, that goes to work upon him. The fascination of the abomination — you know, imagine the growing regrets, the longing to escape, the powerless disgust, the surrender, the hate."

He paused.

"Mind," he began again, lifting one arm from the elbow, the palm of the hand outwards, so that, with his legs folded before him, he had the pose of a Buddha preaching in European clothes and without a lotus-flower — "Mind, none of us would feel exactly like this. What saves us is efficiency — the devotion to efficiency. But these chaps were not much account, really. They were no colonists; their administration was merely a squeeze, and nothing more, I suspect. They were conquerors, and for that you want only brute force — nothing to boast of, when you have it, since your strength is just an accident arising from the weakness of others. They grabbed what they could get for the sake of what was to be got. It was just robbery with violence, aggravated murder on a great scale, and men going at it blind — as is very proper for those who tackle a darkness. The conquest of the earth, which mostly means the taking it away from those who have a different complexion or slightly flatter noses than ourselves, is not a pretty thing when you look into it too much. What redeems it is the idea only. An idea at the back of it; not a sentimental pretence but an idea; and an unselfish belief in the idea — something you can set up, and bow down before, and offer a sacrifice to. . . ."

He broke off. Flames glided in the river, small green flames, red flames, white flames, pursuing, overtaking, joining, crossing each other — then separating slowly or hastily. The traffic of the great city went on in the deepening night upon the sleepless river. We looked on, waiting patiently — there was nothing else to do till the end of the flood; but it was only after a long silence, when he said, in a hesitating voice, "I suppose you fellows remember I did once turn fresh-water sailor for a bit," that we knew we were fated, before the ebb began to run, to hear about one of Marlow's inconclusive experiences.

"I don't want to bother you much with what happened to me personally," he began, showing in this remark the weakness of many tellers of tales who seem so often unaware of what their audience would best like to hear; "yet to understand the effect of it on me you ought to know how I got out there, what I saw, how I went up that river to the place where I first met the poor chap. It was the farthest point of navigation and the culminating point of my experience. It seemed somehow to throw a kind of light on everything about me — and into my thoughts. It was sombre enough, too — and pitiful — not extraordinary in any way — not very clear either. No, not very clear. And yet it seemed to throw a kind of light.

"I had then, as you remember, just returned to London after a lot of Indian Ocean, Pacific, China Seas — a regular dose of the East — six years or so, and I was loafing about, hindering you fellows in your work and invading your homes, just as though I had got a heavenly mission to civilize you. It was very fine for a time, but after a bit I did get tired of resting. Then I began to look for a ship — I should thing the hardest work on earth. But the ships wouldn't even look at me. And I got tired of that game, too.

"Now when I was a little chap I had a passion for maps. I would look for hours at South America, or Africa, or Australia, and lose myself in all the glories of exploration. At that time there were many blank spaces on the earth, and when I saw one that looked particularly inviting on a map (but they all look that) I would put my finger on it and say, 'When I grow up I will go there.' The North Pole was one of these places, I remember. Well, I haven't been there yet, and shall not try now. The glamour's off. Other places were scattered about the Equator, and in every sort of latitude all over the two hemispheres. I have been in some of them, and . . . well, we won't talk about that. But there was one yet — the biggest, the most blank, so to speak — that I had a hankering after.

"True, by this time it was not a blank space any more. It had got filled since my boyhood with rivers and lakes and names. It had ceased to be a blank space of delightful mystery — a white patch for a boy to dream gloriously over. It had become a place of darkness. But there was in it one river especially, a mighty big river, that you could see on the map, resembling an immense snake uncoiled, with its head in the sea, its body at rest curving afar over a vast country, and its tail lost in the depths of the land. And as I looked at the map of it in a shop-window, it fascinated me as a snake would a bird — a silly little bird. Then I remembered there was a big concern, a Company for trade on that river. Dash it all! I thought to myself, they can't trade without using some kind of craft on that lot of fresh water — steamboats! Why shouldn't I try to get charge of one? I went on along Fleet Street, but could not shake off the idea. The snake had charmed me.

"You understand it was a Continental concern, that Trading society; but I have a lot of relations living on the Continent, because it's cheap and not so nasty as it looks, they say.

"I am sorry to own I began to worry them. This was already a fresh departure for me. I was not used to get things that way, you know. I always went my own road and on my own legs where I had a mind to go. I wouldn't have believed it of myself; but, then — you see — I felt somehow I must get there by hook or by crook. So I worried them. The men said 'My dear fellow,' and did nothing. Then — would you believe it? — I tried the women. I, Charlie Marlow, set the women to work — to get a job. Heavens! Well, you see, the notion drove me. I had an aunt, a dear enthusiastic soul. She wrote: 'It will be delightful. I am ready to do anything, anything for you. It is a glorious idea. I know the wife of a very high personage in the Administration, and also a man who has lots of influence with,' etc., etc. She was determined to make no end of fuss to get me appointed skipper of a river steamboat, if such was my fancy.

"I got my appointment — of course; and I got it very quick. It appears the Company had received news that one of their captains had been killed in a scuffle with the natives. This was my chance, and it made me the more anxious to go. It was only months and months afterwards, when I made the attempt to recover what was left of the body, that I heard the original quarrel arose from a misunderstanding about some hens. Yes, two black hens. Fresleven — that was the fellow's name, a Dane — thought himself wronged somehow in the bargain, so he went ashore and started to hammer the chief of the village with a stick. Oh, it didn't surprise me in the least to hear this, and at the same time to be told that Fresleven was the gentlest, quietest creature that ever walked on two legs. No doubt he was; but he had been a couple of years already out there engaged in the noble cause, you know, and he probably felt the need at last of asserting his self-respect in some way. Therefore he whacked the old nigger mercilessly, while a big crowd of his people watched him, thunderstruck, till some man — I was told the chief's son — in desperation at hearing the old chap yell, made a tentative jab with a spear at the white man — and of course it went quite easy between the shoulder blades. Then the whole population cleared into the forest, expecting all kinds of calamities to happen, while, on the other hand, the steamer Fresleven commanded left also in a bad panic, in charge of the engineer, I believe.

Afterwards nobody seemed to trouble much about Fresleven's remains, till I got out and stepped into his shoes. I couldn't let it rest, though; but when an opportunity offered at last to meet my predecessor, the grass growing through his ribs was tall enough to hide his bones. They were all there. The supernatural being had not been touched after he fell. And the village was deserted, the huts gaped black, rotting, all askew within the fallen enclosures. A calamity had come to it, sure enough. The people had vanished. Mad terror had scattered them, men, women, and children, through the bush, and they had never returned. What became of the hens I don't know either. I should think the cause of progress got them, anyhow. However, through this glorious affair I got my appointment, before I had fairly begun to hope for it.

"I flew around like mad to get ready, and before forty-eight hours I was crossing the Channel to show myself to my employers, and sign the contract. In a very few hours I arrived in a city that always makes me think of a whited sepulchre. Prejudice no doubt. I had no difficulty in finding the Company's offices. It was the biggest thing in the town, and everybody I met was full of it. They were going to run an over-sea empire, and make no end of coin by trade.

"A narrow and deserted street in deep shadow, high houses, innumerable windows with venetian blinds, a dead silence, grass sprouting between the stones, imposing carriage archways right and left, immense double doors standing ponderously ajar. I slipped through one of these cracks, went up a swept and ungarnished staircase, as arid as a desert, and opened the first door I came to. Two women, one fat and the other slim, sat on strawbottomed chairs, knitting black wool. The slim one got up and walked straight at me — still knitting with downcast eyes — and only just as I began to think of getting out of her way, as you would for a somnambulist, stood still, and looked up. Her dress was as plain as an umbrella-cover, and she turned round without a word and preceded me into a waiting-room. I gave my name, and looked about. Deal table in the middle, plain chairs all round the walls, on one end a large shining map, marked with all the colours of a rainbow. There was a vast amount of red — good to see at any time, because one knows that some real work is done in there, a deuce of a lot of blue, a little green, smears of orange, and, on the East Coast, a purple patch, to show where the jolly pioneers of progress drink the jolly lager-beer. However, I wasn't going into any of these. I was going into the yellow. Dead in the centre. And the river was there — fascinating — deadly — like a snake. Ough! A door opened, a white-haired secretarial head, but wearing a compassionate expression, appeared, and a skinny forefinger beckoned me into the sanctuary. Its light was dim, and a heavy writing-desk squatted in the middle. From behind that structure came out an impression of pale plumpness in a frock-coat. The great man himself. He was five feet six, I should judge, and had his grip on the handle-end of ever so many millions. He shook hands, I fancy, murmured vaguely, was satisfied with my French. *Bon voyage.*

"In about forty-five seconds I found myself again in the waiting-room with the compassionate secretary, who, full of desolation and sympathy, made me sign some document. I believe I undertook amongst other things not to disclose any trade secrets. Well, I am not going to.

"I began to feel slightly uneasy. You know I am not used to such ceremonies, and there was something ominous in the atmosphere. It was just as though I had been let into some conspiracy — I don't know — something not quite right; and I was glad to get out. In the outer room the two women knitted black wool feverishly. People were arriving, and the younger one was walking back and forth introducing them. The old one sat on her chair. Her flat cloth slippers were propped up on a footwarmer, and a cat reposed on her lap. She wore a starched white affair on her head, had a wart on one cheek, and silver-rimmed spectacles hung on the tip of her nose. She glanced at me above the glasses. The swift and indifferent placidity of that look troubled me. Two youths with foolish and cheery countenances were being piloted over, and she threw at them the same quick glance of unconcerned wisdom. She seemed to know all about them and me, too. An eerie feeling came over me. She seemed uncanny and fateful. Often far away there I thought of these two, guarding the door of Darkness, knitting black wool as for a warm pall, one introducing, introducing continuously to the unknown, the other scrutinizing the cheery and foolish faces with unconcerned old eyes. *Ave!* Old knitter of black wool. *Morituri te salutant.*[1] Not many of those she looked at ever saw her again — not half, by a long way.

"There was yet a visit to the doctor. 'A simple formality,' assured me the secretary, with an air of taking an immense part in all my sorrows. Accordingly a young chap wearing his hat over the left eyebrow, some clerk I suppose — there must have been clerks in the business, though the house was as still as a house in a city of the dead — came from somewhere up-stairs, and led me forth. He was shabby and careless, with inkstains on the sleeves of his jacket, and his cravat was large and billowy, under a chin shaped like the toe of an old boot. It was a little too early for the doctor, so I proposed a drink, and thereupon he developed a vein of joviality. As we sat over our vermouths he glorified the Company's business, and by and by I expressed casually my surprise at him not going out there. He became very cool and collected all at once. 'I am not such a fool as I look, quoth Plato to his disciples,' he said sententiously, emptied his glass with great resolution, and we rose.

"The old doctor felt my pulse, evidently thinking of something else the

1 [Hail. . . . Those who are about to die salute you. — Editors' note.]

while. 'Good, good for there,' he mumbled, and then with a certain eagerness asked me whether I would let him measure my head. Rather surprised, I said Yes, when he produced a thing like calipers and got the dimensions back and front and every way, taking notes carefully. He was an unshaven little man in a threadbare coat like a gaberdine, with his feet in slippers, and I thought him a harmless fool. 'I always ask leave, in the interests of science, to measure the crania of those going out there,' he said. 'And when they come back, too?' I asked. 'Oh, I never see them,' he remarked; 'and, moreover, the changes take place inside, you know.' He smiled, as if at some quiet joke. 'So you are going out there. Famous. Interesting, too.' He gave me a searching glance, and made another note. 'Ever any madness in your family?' he asked, in a matter-of-fact tone. I felt very annoyed. 'Is that question in the interests of science, too?' 'It would be,' he said, without taking notice of my irritation, 'interesting for science to watch the mental changes of individuals, on the spot, but. . . .' 'Are you an alienist?'[2] I interrupted. 'Every doctor should be — a little,' answered that original, imperturbably. 'I have a little theory which you messieurs who go out there must help me to prove. This is my share in the advantages my country shall reap from the possession of such a magnificent dependency. The mere wealth I leave to others. Pardon my questions, but you are the first Englishman coming under my observation. . . .' I hastened to assure him I was not in the least typical. 'If I were,' said I, 'I wouldn't be talking like this with you.' 'What you say is rather profound, and probably erroneous,' he said, with a laugh. 'Avoid irritation more than exposure to the sun. Adieu. How do you English say, eh? Good-bye. Ah! Good-bye. Adieu. In the tropics one must before everything keep calm.' . . . He lifted a warning forefinger. . . . *'Du calme, du calme. Adieu.'*

"One thing more remained to do — say good-bye to my excellent aunt. I found her triumphant. I had a cup of tea — the last decent cup of tea for many days — and in a room that most soothingly looked just as you would expect a lady's drawing-room to look, we had a long quiet chat by the fireside. In the course of these confidences it became quite plain to me I had been represented to the wife of the high dignitary, and goodness knows to how many more people besides, as an exceptional and gifted creature — a piece of good fortune for the Company — a man you don't get hold of every day. Good heavens! and I was going to take charge of a two-penny-half-penny river-steamboat with a penny whistle attached! It appeared, however, I was also one of the Workers, with a capital — you know. Something like an emissary of light, something like a lower sort of apostle. There had been a lot of such rot let loose in print and talk just about that time, and the excellent woman, living right in the rush of all that

2 [Psychiatrist. — Editors' note.]

humbug, got carried off her feet. She talked about 'weaning those ignorant millions from their horrid ways,' till, upon my word, she made me quite uncomfortable. I ventured to hint that the Company was run for profit.

" 'You forget, dear Charlie, that the labourer is worthy of his hire,' she said, brightly. It's queer how out of touch with truth women are. They live in a world of their own, and there has never been anything like it, and never can be. It is too beautiful altogether, and if they were to set it up it would go to pieces before the first sunset. Some confounded fact we men have been living contentedly with ever since the day of creation would start up and knock the whole thing over.

"After this I got embraced, told to wear flannel, be sure to write often, and so on — and I left. In the street — I don't know why — a queer feeling came to me that I was an impostor. Odd thing that I, who used to clear out for any part of the world at twenty-four hours' notice, with less thought than most men give to the crossing of a street, had a moment — I won't say of hesitation, but of startled pause, before this commonplace affair. The best way I can explain it to you is by saying that, for a second or two, I felt as though, instead of going to the centre of a continent, I were about to set off for the centre of the earth.

"I left in a French steamer, and she called in every blamed port they have out there, for, as far as I could see, the sole purpose of landing soldiers and custom-house officers. I watched the coast. Watching a coast as it slips by the ship is like thinking about an enigma. There it is before you — smiling, frowning, inviting, grand, mean, insipid, or savage, and always mute with an air of whispering, 'Come and find out.' This one was almost featureless, as if still in the making, with an aspect of monotonous grimness. The edge of a colossal jungle, so dark-green as to be almost black, fringed with white surf, ran straight, like a ruled line, far, far away along a blue sea whose glitter was blurred by a creeping mist. The sun was fierce, the land seemed to glisten and drip with steam. Here with a flag flying above them perhaps. Settlements some centuries old, and still no bigger than pinheads on the untouched expanse of their background. We pounded along, stopped, landed soldiers; went on, landed custom-house clerks to levy toll in what looked like a God-forsaken wilderness, with a tin shed and a flag-pole lost in it; landed more soldiers — to take care of the custom-house clerks, presumably. Some, I heard, got drowned in the surf; but whether they did or not, nobody seemed particularly to care. They were just flung out there, and on we went. Every day the coast looked the same, as though we had not moved; but we passed various places — trading places — with names like Gran' Bassam, Little Popo; names that seemed to belong to some sordid farce acted in front of a sinister back-cloth. The idleness of a passenger, my isolation amongst all these men with whom I had no point of contact, the oily and languid sea, the uniform sombreness of the coast, seemed to keep me away from the truth of things, within the toil of a mournful and senseless delusion. The voice of the surf heard now and then was a positive pleasure, like the speech of a brother. It was something natural, that had its reason, that had a meaning. Now and then a boat from the shore gave one a momentary contact with reality. It was paddled by black fellows. You could see from afar the white of their eyeballs glistening. They shouted, sang; their bodies streamed with perspiration; they had faces like grotesque masks — these chaps; but they had bone, muscle, a wild vitality, an intense energy of movement, that was as natural and true as the surf along their coast. They wanted no excuse for being there. They were a great comfort to look at. For a time I would feel I belonged still to a world of straightforward facts; but the feeling would not last long. Something would turn up to scare it away. Once, I remember, we came upon a man-of-war anchored off the coast. There wasn't even a shed there, and she was shelling the bush. It appears the French had one of their wars going on thereabouts. Her ensign dropped limp like a rag; the muzzles of the long six-inch guns stuck out all over the low hull; the greasy, slimy swell swung her up lazily and let her down, swaying her thin masts. In the empty immensity of earth, sky, and water, there she was, incomprehensible, firing into a continent. Pop, would go one of the six-inch guns; a small flame would dart and vanish, a little white smoke would disappear, a tiny projectile would give a feeble screech — and nothing happened. Nothing could happen. There was a touch of insanity in the proceeding, a sense of lugubrious drollery in the sight; and it was not dissipated by somebody on board assuring me earnestly there was a camp of natives — he called them enemies! — hidden out of sight somewhere.

"We gave her her letters (I heard the men in that lonely ship were dying of fever at the rate of three a day) and went on. We called at some more places with farcical names, where the merry dance of death and trade goes on in a still and earthy atmosphere as of an overheated catacomb; all along the formless coast bordered by dangerous surf, as if Nature herself had tried to ward off intruders; in and out of rivers, streams of death in life, whose banks were rotting into mud, whose waters, thickened into slime, invaded the contorted mangroves, that seemed to writhe at us in the extremity of an impotent despair. Nowhere did we stop long enough to get a particularized impression, but the general sense of vague and oppressive wonder grew upon me. It was like a weary pilgrimage amongst hints for nightmares.

"It was upward of thirty days before I saw the mouth of the big river. We anchored off the seat of the government. But my work would not begin till some two hundred miles farther on. So as soon as I could I made a start for a place thirty miles higher up.

"I had my passage on a little sea-going steamer. Her captain was a Swede, and knowing me for a seaman, invited me on the bridge. He was a young man, lean, fair, and morose, with lanky hair and a shuffling gait. As we left the miserable little wharf, he tossed his head contemptuously at the shore. 'Been living there?' he asked. I said, 'Yes.' 'Fine lot these government chaps — are they not?' he went on, speaking English with great precision and considerable bitterness. 'It is funny what some people will do for a few francs a month. I wonder what becomes of that kind when it goes upcountry?' I said to him I expected to see that soon. 'So-o-o!' he exclaimed. He shuffled athwart, keeping one eye ahead vigilantly. 'Don't be too sure,' he continued. 'The other day I took up a man who hanged himself on the road. He was a Swede, too.' 'Hanged himself! Why, in God's name?' I cried. He kept on looking out watchfully. 'Who knows? The sun too much for him, or the country perhaps.'

"At last we opened a reach. A rocky cliff appeared, mounds of turned-up earth by the shore, houses on a hill, others with iron roofs, amongst a waste of excavations, or hanging to the declivity. A continuous noise of the rapids above hovered over this scene of inhabited devastation. A lot of people, mostly black and naked, moved about like ants. A jetty projected into the river. A blinding sunlight drowned all this at times in a sudden recrudescence of glare. 'There's your Company's station,' said the Swede, pointing to three wooden barrack-like structures on the rocky slope. 'I will send your things up. Four boxes did you say? So. Farewell.'

"I came upon a boiler wallowing in the grass, then found a path leading up the hill. It turned aside for the boulders, and also for an undersized railway-truck lying there on its back with its wheels in the air. One was off. The thing looked as dead as the carcass of some animal. I came upon more pieces of decaying machinery, a stack of rusty nails. To the left a clump of trees made a shady spot, where dark things seemed to stir feebly. I blinked, the path was steep. A horn tooted to the right, and I saw the black people run. A heavy and dull detonation shook the ground, a puff of smoke came out of the cliff, and that was all. No change appeared on the face of the rock. They were building a railway. The cliff was not in the way or anything; but this objectless blasting was all the work going on.

"A slight clinking behind me made me turn my head. Six black men advanced in a file, toiling up the path. They walked erect and slow, balancing small baskets full of earth on their heads, and the clink kept time with their footsteps. Black rags were wound round their loins, and the short ends behind waggled to and fro like tails. I could see every rib, the joints of their limbs were like knots in a rope; each had an iron collar on his neck, and all were connected together with a chain whose bights swung between them, rhythmically clinking. Another report from the cliff made me think suddenly of that ship of war I had seen firing into a continent. It was the same kind of ominous voice; but these men could by no stretch of imagination be called enemies. They were called criminals, and the outraged law, like the bursting shells, had come to them, an insoluble mystery from the sea. All their meagre breasts panted together, the violently dilated nostrils quivered, the eyes stared stonily uphill. They passed me within six inches, without a glance, with that complete, deathlike indifference of unhappy savages. Behind this raw matter one of the reclaimed, the product of the new forces at work, strolled despondently, carrying a rifle by its middle. He had a uniform jacket with one button off, and seeing a white man on the path, hoisted his weapon to his shoulder with alacrity. This was simple prudence, white men being so much alike at a distance that he could not tell who I might be. He was speedily reassured, and with a large, white, rascally grin, and a glance at his charge, seemed to take me into partnership in his exalted trust. After all, I also was a part of the great cause of these high and just proceedings.

"Instead of going up, I turned and descended to the left. My idea was to let that chain-gang get out of sight before I climbed the hill. You know I am not particularly tender; I've had to strike and to fend off. I've had to resist and to attack sometimes — that's only one way of resisting — without counting the exact cost, according to the demands of such sort of life as I had blundered into. I've seen the devil of violence, and the devil of greed, and the devil of hot desire; but, by all the stars! these were strong, lusty, red-eyed devils, that swayed and drove men — men, I tell you. But as I stood on this hillside, I foresaw that in the blinding sunshine of that land I would become acquainted with a flabby, pretending, weak-eyed devil of a rapacious and pitiless folly. How insidious he could be, too, I was only to find out several months later and a thousand miles farther. For a moment I stood appalled, as though by a warning. Finally I descended the hill, obliquely, towards the trees I had seen.

"I avoided a vast artificial hole somebody had been digging on the slope, the purpose of which I found it impossible to divine. It wasn't a quarry or a sandpit, anyhow. It was just a hole. It might have been connected with the philanthropic desire of giving the criminals something to do. I don't know. Then I nearly fell into a very narrow ravine, almost no more than a scar in the hillside. I discovered that a lot of imported drainage-pipes for the settlement had been tumbled in there. There wasn't one that was not broken. It was a wanton smash-up. At last I got under the trees. My purpose was to stroll into the shade for a moment; but no sooner within than it seemed to me I had stepped into the gloomy circle of some Inferno. The rapids were near, and an uninterrupted, uniform, headlong, rushing noise filled the mournful stillness of the grove, where not a breath stirred, not a leaf moved, with a mysterious sound — as though the tearing pace of the launched earth had suddenly become audible.

"Black shapes crouched, lay, sat between the trees leaning against the trunks, clinging to the earth, half coming out, half effaced within the dim light, in all the attitudes of pain, abandonment, and despair. Another mine on the cliff went off, followed by a slight shudder of the soil under my feet. The work was going on. The work! And this was the place where some of the helpers had withdrawn to die.

"They were dying slowly — it was very clear. They were not enemies, they were not criminals, they were nothing earthly now — nothing but black shadows of disease and starvation, lying confusedly in the greenish gloom. Brought from all the recesses of the coast in all the legality of time contracts, lost in uncongenial surroundings, fed on unfamiliar food, they sickened, became inefficient, and were then allowed to crawl away and rest. These moribund shapes were free as air — and nearly as thin. I began to distinguish the gleam of the eyes under the trees. Then, glancing down, I saw a face near my hand. The black bones reclined at full length with one shoulder against the tree, and slowly the eyelids rose and the sunken eyes looked up at me, enormous and vacant, a kind of blind, white flicker in the depths of the orbs, which died out slowly. The man seemed young — almost a boy — but you know with them it's hard to tell. I found nothing else to do but to offer him one of my good Swede's ship's biscuits I had in my pocket. The fingers closed slowly on it and held — there was no other movement and no other glance. He had tied a bit of white worsted round his neck — Why? Where did he get it? Was it a badge — an ornament — a charm — a propitiatory act? Was there any idea at all connected with it? It looked startling round his black neck, this bit of white thread from beyond the seas.

"Near the same tree two more bundles of acute angles sat with their legs drawn up. One, with his chin propped on his knees, stared at nothing, in an intolerable and appalling manner: his brother phantom rested its forehead, as if overcome with a great weariness; and all about others were scattered in every pose of contorted collapse, as in some picture of a massacre or a pestilence. While I stood horror-struck, one of these creatures rose to his hands and knees, and went off on all-fours towards the river to drink. He lapped out of his hand, then sat up in the sunlight, crossing his shins in front of him, and after a time let his woolly head fall on his breastbone.

"I didn't want any more loitering in the shade, and I made haste towards the station. When near the buildings I met a white man, in such an unexpected elegance of getup that in the first moment I took him for a sort of vision. I saw a high starched collar, white cuffs, a light alpaca jacket, snowy trousers, a clean necktie, and varnished boots. No hat. Hair parted, brushed, oiled, under a green-lined parasol held in a big white hand. He was amazing, and had a penholder behind his ear.

"I shook hands with this miracle, and I learned he was the Company's chief accountant, and that all the bookkeeping was done at this station. He had come out for a moment, he said, 'to get a breath of fresh air.' The expression sounded wonderfully odd, with its suggestion of sedentary desk-life. I wouldn't have mentioned the fellow to you at all, only it was from his lips that I first heard the name of the man who is so indissolubly connected with the memories of that time. Moreover, I respected the fellow. Yes; I respected his collars, his vast cuffs, his brushed hair. His appearance was certainly that of a hairdresser's dummy; but in the great demoralization of the land he kept up his appearance. That's backbone. His starched collars and got-up shirt-fronts were achievements of character. He had been out nearly three years; and, later, I could not help asking him how he managed to sport such linen. He had just the faintest blush, and said modestly, 'I've been teaching one of the native women about the station. It was difficult. She had a distaste for the work.' Thus this man had verily accomplished something. And he was devoted to his books, which were in apple-pie order.

"Everything else in the station was in a muddle — heads, things, buildings. Strings of dusty niggers with splay feet arrived and departed; a stream of manufactured goods, rubbishy cottons, beads, and brass-wire set into the depths of darkness, and in return came a precious trickle of ivory.

"I had to wait in the station for ten days — an eternity. I lived in a hut in the yard, but to be out of the chaos I would sometimes get into the accountant's office. It was built of horizontal planks, and so badly put together that, as he bent over his high desk, he was barred from neck to heels with narrow strips of sunlight. There was no need to open the big shutter to see. It was hot there, too; big flies buzzed fiendishly, and did not sting, but stabbed. I sat generally on the floor, while, of faultless appearance (and even slightly scented), perching on a high stool, he wrote, he wrote. Sometimes he stood up for exercise. When a truckle-bed with a sick man (some invalid agent from upcountry) was put in there, he exhibited a gentle annoyance. 'The groans of this sick person,' he said, 'distract my attention. And without that it is extremely difficult to guard against clerical errors in this climate.'

"One day he remarked, without lifting his head, 'In the interior you will no doubt meet Mr. Kurtz.' On my asking who Mr. Kurtz was, he said he was a first-class agent; and seeing my disappointment at this information, he added slowly, laying down his pen, 'He is a very remarkable person.' Further questions elicited from him that Mr. Kurtz was at present in charge of a trading-post, a very important one, in the true ivory-country, at 'the very bottom of there. Sends in as much ivory as all the others put together. . . .' He began to write again. The sick man was too ill to groan. The flies buzzed in a great peace.

"Suddenly there was a growing murmur of voices and a great tramping of feet. A caravan had come in. A violent babble of uncouth sounds burst out on the other side of the planks. All the carriers were speaking together, and in the midst of the uproar the lamentable voice of the chief agent was heard 'giving it up' tearfully for the twentieth time that day. . . . He rose slowly. 'What a frightful row,' he said. He crossed the room gently to look at the sick man, and returning, said to me, 'He does not hear.' 'What! Dead?' I asked, startled. 'No, not yet,' he answered, with great composure. Then, alluding with a toss of the head to the tumult in the station-yard, 'When one has got to make correct entries, one comes to hate those savages — hate them to the death.' He remained thoughtful for a moment. 'When you see Mr. Kurtz,' he went on, 'tell him from me that everything here' — he glanced at the deck — 'is very satisfactory. I don't like to write to him — with those messengers of ours you never know who may get hold of your letter — at that Central Station.' He stared at me for a moment with his mild, bulging eyes. 'Oh, he will go far, very far,' he began again. 'He will be a somebody in the Administration before long. They, above — the Council in Europe, you know — mean him to be.'

"He turned to his work. The noise outside had ceased, and presently in going out I stopped at the door. In the steady buzz of flies the homeward-bound agent was lying flushed and insensible; the other, bent over his books, was making correct entries of perfectly correct transactions; and fifty feet below the doorstep I could see the still treetops of the grove of death.

"Next day I left that station at last, with a caravan of sixty men, for a two-hundred-mile tramp.

"No use telling you much about that. Paths, paths, everywhere; a stamped-in network of paths spreading over the empty land, through the long grass, through burnt grass, through thickets, down and up chilly ravines, up and down stony hills ablaze with heat; and a solitude, a solitude, nobody, not a hut. The population had cleared out a long time ago. Well, if a lot of mysterious niggers armed with all kinds of fearful weapons suddenly took to travelling on the road between Deal and Gravesend, catching the yokels right and left to carry heavy loads for them, I fancy every farm and cottage thereabouts would get empty very soon. Only here the dwellings were gone, too. Still I passed through several abandoned villages. There's something pathetically childish in the ruins of grass walls. Day after day, with the stamp and shuffle of sixty pair of bare feet behind me, each pair under a 60-lb. load. Camp, cook, sleep, strike camp, march. Now and then a carrier dead in harness, at rest in the long grass near the path, with an empty water-gourd and his long staff lying by his side. A great silence around and above. Perhaps on some quiet night the tremor of faroff drums, sinking, swelling, a tremor vast, faint; a sound weird, appealing, suggestive, and wild — and perhaps with as profound a meaning as the sound of bells in a Christian country. Once a white man in an unbuttoned uniform, camping on the path with an armed escort of lank Zanzibaris, very hospitable and festive — not to say drunk. Was looking after the upkeep of the road, he declared. Can't say I saw any road or any upkeep, unless the body of a middle-aged negro, with a bullet-hole in the forehead, upon which I absolutely stumbled three miles farther on, may be considered as a permanent improvement. I had a white companion, too, not a bad chap, but rather too fleshy and with the exasperating habit of fainting on the hot hillsides, miles away from the least bid of shade and water. Annoying, you know, to hold your own coat like a parasol over a man's head while he is coming to. I couldn't help asking him once what he meant by coming there at all. 'To make money, of course. What do you think?' he said, scornfully. Then he got fever, and had to be carried in a hammock slung under a pole. As he weighed sixteen stone[3] I had no end of rows with the carriers. They jibbed, ran away, sneaked off with their loads in the night — quite a mutiny. So, one evening, I made a speech in English with gestures, not one of which was lost to the sixty pairs of eyes before me, and the next morning I started the hammock off in front all right. An hour afterwards I came upon the whole concern wrecked in a bush — man, hammock, groans, blankets, horrors. The heavy pole had skinned his poor nose. He was very anxious for me to kill somebody, but there wasn't the shadow of a carrier near. I remembered the old doctor — 'It would be interesting for science to watch the mental changes of individuals, on the spot.' I felt I was becoming scientifically interesting. However, all that is to no purpose. On the fifteenth day I came in sight of the big river again, and hobbled into the Central Station. It was on a back water surrounded by scrub and forest, with a pretty border of smelly mud on one side, and on the three others enclosed by a crazy fence of rushes. A neglected gap was all the gate it had, and the first glance at the place was enough to let you see the flabby devil was running that show. White men with long staves in their hands appeared languidly from amongst the buildings, strolling up to take a look at me, and then retired out of sight somewhere. One of them, a stout, excitable chap with black moustaches, informed me with great volubility and many digressions, as soon as I told him who I was, that my steamer was at the bottom of the river. I was thunderstruck. What, how, why? Oh, it was 'all right.' The 'manager himself' was there. All quite correct. 'Everybody had behaved splendidly! splendidly!' — 'you must,' he said in agitation, 'go and see the general manager at once. He is waiting!'

"I did not see the real significance of that wreck at once. I fancy I see it now, but I am not sure — not at all. Certainly the affair was too stupid — when I think of it — to be altogether natural. Still. . . . But at the moment it presented itself simply as a confounded nuisance. The steamer was sunk. They had started

3 [Two hundred and twenty-four pounds. — Editors' note.]

two days before in a sudden hurry up the river with the manager on board, in charge of some volunteer skipper, and before they had been out three hours they tore the bottom out of her on stones, and she sank near the south bank. I asked myself what I was to do there, now my boat was lost. As a matter of fact, I had plenty to do in fishing my command out of the river. I had to set about it the very next day. That, and the repairs when I brought the pieces to the station, took some months.

"My first interview with the manager was curious. He did not ask me to sit down after my twenty-mile walk that morning. He was commonplace in complexion, in feature, in manners, and in voice. He was of middle size and of ordinary build. His eyes, of the usual blue, were perhaps remarkably cold, and he certainly could make his glance fall on one as trenchant and heavy as an axe. But even at these times the rest of his person seemed to disclaim the intention. Otherwise there was only an indefinable, faint expression of his lips, something stealthy — a smile — not a smile — I remember it, but I can't explain. It was unconscious, this smile was, though just after he had said something it got intensified for an instant. It came at the end of his speeches like a seal applied on the words to make the meaning of the commonest phrase appear absolutely inscrutable. He was a common trader, from his youth up employed in these parts — nothing more. He was obeyed, yet he inspired neither love nor fear, nor even respect. He inspired uneasiness. That was it! Uneasiness. Not a definite mistrust — just uneasiness — nothing more. You have no idea how effective such a . . . a . . . faculty can be. He had no genius for organizing, for initiative, or for order even. That was evident in such things as the deplorable state of the station. He had no learning, and no intelligence. His position had come to him — why? Perhaps because he was never ill. . . . He had served three terms of three years out there. . . . Because triumphant health in the general rout of constitutions is a kind of power in itself. When he went home on leave he rioted on a large scale — pompously. Jack ashore — with a difference — in externals only. This one could gather from his casual talk. He originated nothing, he could keep the routine going — that's all. But he was great. He was great by this little thing that it was impossible to tell what could control such a man. He never gave that secret away. Perhaps there was nothing within him. Such a suspicion made one pause — for out there there were no external checks. Once when various tropical diseases had laid low almost every 'agent' in the station, he was heard to say, 'Men who come out here should have no entrails.' He sealed the utterance with that smile of his, as though it had been a door opening into a darkness he had in his keeping. You fancied you had seen things — but the seal was on. When annoyed at meal-times by the constant quarrels of the white men about precedence, he ordered an immense round table to be made, for which a special house had to be built. This was the station's mess-room. Where he sat was the first place — the rest were nowhere. One felt this to be his unalterable conviction. He was neither civil nor uncivil. He was quiet. He allowed his 'boy' — an overfed young negro from the coast — to treat the white men, under his very eyes, with provoking insolence.

"He began to speak as soon as he saw me. I had been very long on the road. He could not wait. Had to start without me. The up-river stations had to be relieved. There had been so many delays already that he did not know who was dead and who was alive, and how they got on — and so on, and so on. He paid no attention to my explanations, and, playing with a stick of sealing-wax, repeated several times that the situation was 'very grave, very grave.' There were rumours that a very important station was in jeopardy, and its chief, Mr. Kurtz, was ill. Hoped it was not true. Mr. Kurtz was . . . I felt weary and irritable. Hang Kurtz, I thought. I interrupted him by saying I had heard of Mr. Kurtz on the coast. 'Ah! So they talk of him down there,' he murmured to himself. Then he began again, assuring me Mr. Kurtz was the best agent he had, an exceptional man, of the greatest importance to the Company; therefore I could understand his anxiety. He was, he said, 'very, very uneasy.' Certainly he fidgeted on his chair a good deal, exclaimed, 'Ah, Mr. Kurtz!' broke the stick of sealing-wax and seemed dumfounded by the accident. Next thing he wanted to know 'how long it would take to' . . . I interrupted him again. Being hungry, you know, and kept on my feet too, I was getting savage. 'How can I tell?' I said. 'I haven't even seen the wreck yet — some months, no doubt.' All this talk seemed to me so futile. 'Some months,' he said. 'Well, let us say three months before we can make a start. Yes. That ought to do the affair.' I flung out of his hut (he lived all alone in a clay hut with a sort of verandah) muttering to myself my opinion of him. He was a chattering idiot. Afterwards I took it back when it was borne in upon me startlingly with what extreme nicety he had estimated the time requisite for the 'affair.'

"I went to work the next day, turning, so to speak, my back on that station. In that way only it seemed to me I could keep my hold on the redeeming facts of life. Still, one must look about sometimes; and then I saw this station, these men strolling aimlessly about in the sunshine of the yard. I asked myself sometimes what it all meant. They wandered here and there with their absurd long staves in their hands, like a lot of faithless pilgrims bewitched inside a rotten fence. The word 'ivory' rang in the air, was whispered, was sighed. You would think they were praying to it. A taint of imbecile rapacity blew through it all, like a whiff from some corpse. By Jove! I've never seen anything so unreal in my life. And outside, the silent wilderness surrounding this cleared speck on the earth struck me as something great and invincible, like evil or truth, waiting patiently for the passing away of this fantastic invasion.

"Oh, these months! Well, never mind. Various things happened. One evening a grass shed full of calico, cotton prints, beads, and I don't know what else, burst into a blaze so suddenly that you would have thought the earth had opened to let an avenging fire consume all that trash. I was smoking my pipe quietly by my dismantled steamer, and saw them all cutting capers in the light, with their arms lifted high, when the stout man with moustaches came tearing down to the river, a tin pail in his hand, assured me that everybody was 'behaving splendidly, splendidly,' dipped about a quart of water and tore back again. I noticed there was a hole in the bottom of his pail.

"I strolled up. There was no hurry. You see the thing had gone off like a box of matches. It had been hopeless from the very first. The flame had leaped high, driven everybody back, lighted up everything — and collapsed. The shed was already a heap of embers glowing fiercely. A nigger was being beaten near by. They said he had caused the fire in some way; be that as it may, he was screeching most horribly. I saw him, later, for several days, sitting in a bit of shade looking very sick and trying to recover himself: afterwards he arose and went out — and the wilderness without a sound took him into its bosom again. As I approached the glow from the dark I found myself at the back of two men, talking. I heard the name of Kurtz pronounced, then the words, 'take advantage of this unfortunate accident.' One of the men was the manager. I wished him a good evening. 'Did you ever see anything like it — eh? it is incredible,' he said, and walked off. The other man remained. He was a first-class agent, young, gentlemanly, a bit reserved, with a forked little beard and a hooked nose. He was stand-offish with the other agents, and they on their side said he was the manager's spy upon them. As to me, I had hardly ever spoken to him before. We got into talk, and by and by we strolled away from the hissing ruins. Then he asked me to his room, which was in the main building of the station. He struck a match, and I perceived that this young aristocrat had not only a silver-mounted dressing-case but also a whole candle all to himself. Just at that time the manager was the only man supposed to have any right to candles. Native mats covered the clay walls; a collection of spears, assegais,[4] shields, knives was hung up in trophies. The business intrusted to this fellow was the making of bricks — so I had been informed; but there wasn't a fragment of a brick anywhere in the station, and he had been there more than a year — waiting. It seems he could not make bricks without something, I don't know what — straw maybe. Anyway, it could not be found there and as it was not likely to be sent from Europe, it did not appear clear to me what he was waiting for. An act of special creation perhaps. However, they were all waiting — all the sixteen or twenty pilgrims of

4 [Thin spears. — Editors' note.]

them — for something; and upon my word it did not seem an uncongenial occupation, from the way they took it, though the only thing that ever came to them was disease — as far as I could see. They beguiled the time by backbiting and intriguing against each other in a foolish kind of way. There was an air of plotting about that station, but nothing came of it, of course. It was as unreal as everything else — as the philanthropic pretence of the whole concern, as their talk, as their government, as their show of work. The only real feeling was a desire to get appointed to a trading-post where ivory was to be had, so that they could earn percentages. They intrigued and slandered and hated each other only on that account — but as to effectually lifting a little finger — oh, no. By heavens! there is something after all in the world allowing one man to steal a horse while another must not look at a halter. Steal a horse straight out. Very well. He has done it. Perhaps he can ride. But there is a way of looking at a halter that would provoke the most charitable of saints into a kick.

"I had no idea why he wanted to be sociable, but as we chatted in there it suddenly occurred to me the fellow was trying to get at something — in fact, pumping me. He alluded constantly to Europe, to the people I was supposed to know there — putting leading questions as to my acquaintances in the sepulchral city, and so on. His little eyes glittered like mica discs — with curiosity — though he tried to keep up a bit of superciliousness. At first I was astonished, but very soon I became awfully curious to see what he would find out from me. I couldn't possibly imagine what I had in me to make it worth his while. It was very pretty to see how he baffled himself, for in truth my body was full only of chills, and my head had nothing in it but that wretched steamboat business. It was evident he took me for a perfectly shameless prevaricator. At last he got angry, and, to conceal a movement of furious annoyance, he yawned. I rose. Then I noticed a small sketch in oils, on a panel, representing a woman, draped and blindfolded, carrying a lighted torch. The background was sombre — almost black. The movement of the woman was stately, and the effect of the torchlight on the face was sinister.

"It arrested me, and he stood by civilly, holding an empty half-pint champagne bottle (medical comforts) with the candle stuck in it. To my question he said Mr. Kurtz had painted this — in this very station more than a year ago — while waiting for means to go to his trading-post. 'Tell me, pray,' said I, 'who is this Mr. Kurtz?'

" 'The chief of the Inner Station,' he answered in a short tone, looking away. 'Much obliged,' I said, laughing. 'And you are the brickmaker of the Central Station. Every one knows that.' He was silent for a while. 'He is a prodigy,' he said at last. 'He is an emissary of pity and science and progress, and devil knows what else. We want,' he began to declaim suddenly, 'for the guidance of the cause intrusted to us by Europe, so to speak, higher intelligence, wide sympathies, a singleness of purpose.' 'Who says that?' I asked. 'Lots of them,' he replied. 'Some even write that; and so *he* comes here, a special being, as you ought to know.' 'Why ought I to know?' I interrupted, really surprised. He paid no attention. 'Yes. Today he is chief of the best station, next year he will be assistant-manager, two years more and . . . but I daresay you know what he will be in two years' time. You are of the new gang — the gang of virtue. The same people who sent him specially also recommended you. Oh, don't say no. I've my own eyes to trust.' Light dawned upon me. My dear aunt's influential acquaintances were producing an unexpected effect upon that young man. I nearly burst into a laugh. 'Do you read the Company's confidential correspondence?' I asked. He hadn't a word to say. It was great fun. 'When Mr. Kurtz,' I continued, severely, 'is General Manager, you won't have the opportunity.'

"He blew the candle out suddenly, and we went outside. The moon had risen. Black figures strolled about listlessly, pouring water on the glow, whence proceeded a sound of hissing; steam ascended in the moonlight, the beaten nigger groaned somewhere. 'What a row the brute makes!' said the indefatigable man with the moustaches, appearing near us. 'Serve him right. Transgression — punishment — bang! Pitiless, pitiless. That's the only way. This will prevent all conflagrations for the future. I was just telling the manager. . . .' He noticed my companion, and became crestfallen all at once. 'Not in bed yet,' he said, with a kind of servile heartiness; 'it's so natural. Ha! Danger — agitation.' He vanished. I went on to the riverside, and the other followed me. I heard a scathing murmur at my ear, 'Heap of muffs — go to.' The pilgrims could be seen in knots gesticulating, discussing. Several had still their staves in their hands. I verily believe they took these sticks to bed with them. Beyond the fence the forest stood up spectrally in the moonlight, and through the dim stir, through the faint sounds of that lamentable courtyard, the silence of the land went home to one's very heart — its mystery, its greatness, the amazing reality of its concealed life. The hurt nigger moaned feebly somewhere near by, and then fetched a deep sigh that made me mend my pace away from there. I felt a hand introducing itself under my arm. 'My dear sir,' said the fellow, 'I don't want to be misunderstood, and especially by you, who will see Mr. Kurtz long before I can have that pleasure. I wouldn't like him to get a false idea of my disposition. . . .'

"I let him run on, this papier-maché Mephistopheles, and it seemed to me that if I tried I could poke my forefinger through him, and would find nothing inside but a little loose dirt, maybe. He, don't you see, had been planning to be assistant-manager by and by under the present man, and I could see that the coming of that Kurtz had upset them both not a little. He talked precipitately, and I did not try to stop him. I had my shoulders against the wreck of my steamer, hauled up on the slope like a carcass of some big river animal. The smell of mud, of primeval mud, by Jove! was in my nostrils, the high stillness of primeval forest was before my eyes; there were shiny patches on the black creek. The moon had spread over everything a thin layer of silver — over the rank grass, over the mud, upon the wall of matted vegetation standing higher than the wall of a temple, over the great river I could see through a sombre gap glittering, glittering, as it flowed broadly by without a murmur. All this was great, expectant, mute, while the man jabbered about himself. I wondered whether the stillness on the face of the immensity looking at us two were meant as an appeal or as a menace. What were we who had strayed in here? Could we handle that dumb thing, or would it handle us? I felt how big, how confoundedly big, was that thing that couldn't talk, and perhaps was deaf as well. What was in there? I could see a little ivory coming out from there, and I had heard Mr. Kurtz was in there. I had heard enough about it, too — God knows! Yet somehow it didn't bring any image with it — no more than if I had been told an angel or a fiend was in there. I believed it in the same way one of you might believe there are inhabitants in the planet Mars. I knew once a Scotch sailmaker who was certain, dead sure, there were people in Mars. If you asked him for some idea how they looked and behaved, he would get shy and mutter something about 'walking on all-fours.' If you as much as smiled, he would — though a man of sixty — offer to fight you. I would not have gone so far as to fight for Kurtz, but I went for him near enough to a lie. You know I hate, detest, and can't bear a lie, not because I am straighter than the rest of us, but simply because it appalls me. There is a taint of death, a flavour of mortality in lies — which is exactly what I hate and detest in the world — what I want to forget. It makes me miserable and sick, like biting something rotten would do. Temperament, I suppose. Well, I went near enough to it by letting the young fool there believe anything he liked to imagine as to my influence in Europe. I became in an instant as much of a pretence as the rest of the bewitched pilgrims. This simply because I had a notion it somehow would be of help to that Kurtz whom at the time I did not see — you understand. He was just a word for me. I did not see the man in the name any more than you do. Do you see him? Do you see the story? Do you see anything? It seems to me I am trying to tell you a dream — making a vain attempt, because no relation of a dream can convey the dream-sensation, that commingling of absurdity, surprise, and bewilderment in a tremor of struggling revolt, that notion of being captured by the incredible which is of the very essence of dreams. . . ."

He was silent for a while.

". . . No, it is imposible; it is impossible to convey the life-sensation of any given epoch of one's existence — that which makes its truth, its meaning — its subtle and penetrating essence. It is impossible. We live, as we dream — alone. . . ."

He paused again as if reflecting, then added:

"Of course in this you fellows see more than I could then. You see me, whom you know. . . ."

It had become so pitch dark that we listeners could hardly see one another. For a long time already he, sitting apart, had been no more to us than a voice. There was not a word from anybody. The others might have been asleep, but I was awake. I listened, I listened on the watch for the sentence, for the word, that would give me the clue to the faint uneasiness inspired by this narrative that seemed to shape itself without human lips in the heavy night-air of the river.

". . . Yes — I let him run on," Marlow began again, "and think what he pleased about the powers that were behind me. I did! And there was nothing behind me! There was nothing but that wretched, old, mangled steamboat I was leaning against, while he talked fluently about 'the necessity for every man to get on.' 'And when one comes out here, you conceive, it is not to gaze at the moon.' Mr. Kurtz was a 'universal genius,' but even a genius would find it easier to work with 'adequate tools — intelligent men.' He did not make bricks — why, there was a physical impossibility in the way — as I was well aware; and if he did secretarial work for the manager, it was because 'no sensible man rejects wantonly the confidence of his superiors.' Did I see it? I saw it. What more did I want? What I really wanted was rivets, by heaven! Rivets. To get on with the work — to stop the hole. Rivets I wanted. There were cases of them down at the coast — cases — piled up — burst — split! You kicked a loose rivet at every second step in that station-yard on the hillside. Rivets had rolled into the grove of death. You could fill your pockets with rivets for the trouble of stooping down — and there wasn't one rivet to be found where it was wanted. We had plates that would do, but nothing to fasten them with. And every week the messenger, a lone negro, letter-bag on shoulder and staff in hand, left our station for the coast. And several times a week a coast caravan came in with trade goods — ghastly glazed calico that made you shudder only to look at it, glass beads value about a penny a quart, confounded spotted cotton handkerchiefs. And no rivets. Three carriers could have brought all that was wanted to set that steamboat afloat.

"He was becoming confidential now, but I fancy my unresponsive attitude must have exasperated him at last, for he judged it necessary to inform me he feared neither God nor devil, let alone any mere man. I said I could see that very well, but what I wanted was a certain quantity of rivets — and rivets were what really Mr. Kurtz wanted, if he had only known it. Now letters went to the coast every week. . . . 'My dear sir,' he cried, 'I write from dictation.' I demanded rivets. There was a way — for an intelligent man. He changed his manner; became very cold, and suddenly began to talk about a hippopotamus; wondered whether sleeping on board the steamer (I stuck to my salvage night and day) I wasn't disturbed.

There was an old hippo that had the bad habit of getting out on the bank and roaming at night over the station grounds. The pilgrims used to turn out in a body and empty every rifle they could lay hands on at him. Some even had sat up o' nights for him. All this energy was wasted, though. 'That animal has a charmed life,' he said; 'but you can say this only of brutes in this country. No man — you apprehend me? — no man here bears a charmed life.' He stood there for a moment in the moonlight with his delicate hooked nose set a little askew, and his mica eyes glittering without a wink, then, with a curt Good-night, he strode off. I could see he was disturbed and considerably puzzled, which made me feel more hopeful than I had been for days. It was a great comfort to turn from that chap to my influential friend, the battered, twisted, ruined, tin-pot steamboat. I clambered on board. She rang under my feet like an empty Huntley & Palmer biscuit-tin kicked along a gutter; she was nothing so solid in make, and rather less pretty in shape, but I had expended enough hard work on her to make me love her. No influential friend would have served me better. She had given me a chance to come out a bit — to find out what I could do. No, I don't like work. I had rather laze about and think of all the fine things that can be done. I don't like work — no man does — but I like what is in the work — the chance to find yourself. Your own reality — for yourself, not for others — what no other man can ever know. They can only see the mere show, and never can tell what it really means.

"I was not surprised to see somebody sitting aft, on the deck, with his legs dangling over the mud. You see I rather chummed with the few mechanics there were in that station, whom the other pilgrims naturally despised — on account of their imperfect manners, I suppose. This was the foreman — a boiler-maker by trade — a good worker. He was a lank, bony, yellow-faced man, with big intense eyes. His aspect was worried, and his head was as bald as the palm of my hand; but his hair in falling seemed to have stuck to his chin, and had prospered in the new locality, for his beard hung down to his waist. He was a widower with six young children (he had left them in charge of a sister of his to come out there), and the passion of his life was pigeon-flying. He was an enthusiast and a connoisseur. He would rave about pigeons. After work hours he used sometimes to come over from his hut for a talk about his children and his pigeons; at work, when he had to crawl in the mud under the bottom of the steamboat, he would tie up that beard of his in a kind of white serviette he brought for the purpose. It had loops to go over his ears. In the evening he could be seen squatted on the bank rinsing that wrapper in the creek with great care, then spreading it solemnly on a bush to dry.

"I slapped him on the back and shouted, 'We shall have rivets!' He scrambled to his feet exclaiming, 'No! Rivets!' as though he couldn't believe his ears. Then in a low voice, 'You . . . eh?' I don't know why we behaved like lunatics. I put my finger to the side of my nose and nodded mysteriously. 'Good for you!' he cried, snapped his fingers above his head, lifting one foot. I tried a jig. We capered on the iron deck. A frightful clatter came out of that hulk, and the virgin forest on the other bank of the creek sent it back in a thundering roll upon the sleeping station. It must have made some of the pilgrims sit up in their hovels. A dark figure obscured the lighted doorway of the manager's hut, vanished, then, a second or so after, the doorway itself vanished, too. We stopped, and the silence driven away by the stamping of our feet flowed back again from the recesses of the land. The great wall of vegetation, an exuberant and entangled mass of trunks, branches, leaves, boughs, festoons, motionless in the moonlight, was like a rioting invasion of soundless life, a rolling wave of plants, piled up, crested, ready to topple over the creek, to sweep every little man of us out of his little existence. And it moved not. A deadened burst of mighty splashes and snorts reached us from afar, as though an ichthyosaurus had been taking a bath of glitter in the great river. 'After all,' said the boiler-maker in a reasonable tone, 'why shouldn't we get the rivets?' Why not, indeed! I did not know of any reason why we shouldn't. 'They'll come in three weeks,' I said, confidently.

"But they didn't. Instead of rivets there came an invasion, an infliction, a visitation. It came in sections during the next three weeks, each section headed by a donkey carrying a white man in new clothes and tan shoes, bowing from that elevation right and left to the impressed pilgrims. A quarrelsome band of footsore sulky niggers trod on the heels of the donkey; a lot of tents, campstools, tin boxes, white cases, brown bales would be shot down in the court-yard, and the air of mystery would deepen a little over the muddle of the station. Five such instalments came, with their absurd air of disorderly flight with the loot of innumerable outfit shops and provision stores, that, one would think, they were lugging, after a raid, into the wilderness for equitable division. It was an inextricable mess of things decent in themselves but that human folly made look like the spoils of thieving.

"This devoted band called itself the Eldorado Exploring Expedition, and I believe they were sworn to secrecy. Their talk, however, was the talk of sordid buccaneers: it was reckless without hardihood, greedy without audacity, and cruel without courage; there was not an atom of foresight or of serious intention in the whole batch of them, and they did not seem aware these things are wanted for the work of the world. To tear treasure out of the bowels of the land was their desire, with no more moral purpose at the back of it than there is in burglars breaking into a safe. Who paid the expenses of the noble enterprise I don't know; but the uncle of our manager was leader of that lot.

"In exterior he resembled a butcher in a poor neighbourhood, and his eyes had a look of sleepy cunning. He carried his fat paunch with ostentation on his short legs, and during the time his gang infested the station spoke to no one but his nephew. You could see these two roaming about all day long with their heads close together in an everlasting confab.

"I had given up worrying myself about the rivets. One's capacity for that kind of folly is more limited than you would suppose. I said Hang! — and let things slide. I had plenty of time for meditation, and now and then I would give some thought to Kurtz. I wasn't very interested in him. No. Still, I was curious to see whether this man, who had come out equipped with moral ideas of some sort, would climb to the top after all and how he would set about his work when there."

II

"One evening as I was lying flat on the deck of my steamboat, I heard voices approaching — and there were the nephew and the uncle strolling along the bank. I laid my head on my arm again, and had nearly lost myself in a doze, when somebody said in my ear, as it were: 'I am as harmless as a little child, but I don't like to be dictated to. Am I the manager — or am I not? I was ordered to send him there. It's incredible.' . . . I became aware that the two were standing on the shore alongside the forepart of the steamboat, just below my head. I did not move; it did not occur to me to move: I was sleepy. 'It *is* unpleasant,' grunted the uncle. 'He has asked the Administration to be sent there,' said the other, 'with the idea of showing what he could do; and I was instructed accordingly. Look at the influence that man must have. Is it not frightful?' They both agreed it was frightful, then made several bizarre remarks: 'Make rain and fine weather — one man — the Council — by the nose' — bits of absurd sentences that got the better of my drowsiness, so that I had pretty near the whole of my wits about me when the uncle said, 'The climate may do away with this difficulty for you. Is he alone there? 'Yes,' answered the manager; 'he sent his assistant down the river with a note to me in these terms: "Clear this poor devil out of the country, and don't bother sending more of that sort. I had rather be alone than have the kind of men you can dispose of with me." It was more than a year ago. Can you imagine such impudence!' 'Anything since then?' asked the other hoarsely. 'Ivory,' jerked the nephew; 'lots of it — prime sort — lots — most annoying, from him.' 'And with that?' questioned the heavy rumble. 'Invoice,' was the reply fired out, so to speak. Then silence. They had been talking about Kurtz.

"I was broad awake by this time, but, lying perfectly at ease, remained still, having no inducement to change my position. 'How did that ivory come all this way?' growled the elder man, who seemed very vexed. The other explained that it had come with a fleet of canoes in charge of an English half-caste clerk Kurtz had with him; that Kurtz had apparently intended to return himself, the station being by that time bare of goods and stores, but after coming three hundred miles, had suddenly decided to go back, which he started to do alone in a small dugout with four paddlers, leaving the half-caste to continue down the river with the ivory. The two fellows there seemed astounded at anybody attempting such a thing. They were at a loss for an adequate motive. As to me, I seemed to see Kurtz for the first time. It was a distinct glimpse: the dugout, four paddling savages, and the lone white man turning his back suddenly on the headquarters, on relief, on thoughts of home — perhaps; setting his face towards the depths of the wilderness, towards his empty and desolate station. I did not know the motive. Perhaps he was just simply a fine fellow who stuck to his work for its own sake. His name, you understand, had not been pronounced once. He was 'that man.' The half-caste, who, as far as I could see, had conducted a difficult trip with great prudence and pluck, was invariably alluded to as 'that scoundrel.' The 'scoundrel' had reported that the 'man' had been very ill — had recovered imperfectly. . . . The two below me moved away then a few paces, and strolled back and forth at some little distance. I heard: 'Military post — doctor — two hundred miles — quite alone now — unavoidable delays — nine months — no news — strange rumours.' They approached again, just as the manager was saying, 'No one, as far as I know, unless a species of wandering trader — a pestilential fellow, snapping ivory from the natives.' Who was it they were talking about now? I gathered in snatches that this was some man supposed to be in Kurtz's district, and of whom the manager did not approve. 'We will not be free from unfair competition till one of these fellows is hanged for an example,' he said. 'Certainly,' grunted the other; 'get him hanged! Why not? Anything — anything can be done in this country. That's what I say; nobody here, you understand, *here,* can endanger your position. And why? You stand the climate — you outlast them all. The danger is in Europe; but there before I left I took care to ——' They moved off and whispered, then their voices rose again. 'The extraordinary series of delays is not my fault. I did my best.' The fat man sighed. 'Very sad.' 'And the pestiferous absurdity of his talk,' continued the other; 'he bothered me enough when he was here. "Each station should be like a beacon on the road towards better things, a centre for trade of course, but also for humanizing, improving, instructing." Conceive you — that ass! And he wants to be manager! No, it's ——' Here he got choked by excessive indignation, and I lifted my head the least bit. I was surprised to see how near they were — right under me. I could have spat upon their hats. They were looking on the ground, absorbed in thought. The manager was switching his leg with a slender twig: his sagacious relative lifted his head. 'You have been well since you came out this time?' he asked. The other gave a start. 'Who? I? Oh! Like a charm — like a charm. But the rest — oh, my goodness! All sick. They die so quick, too, that I haven't the time to send them out of the country — it's incredible!' 'H'm. Just so,' grunted the uncle. 'Ah! my boy, trust to this — I say, trust to this.' I saw him extend his short flipper of an arm for a gesture that took in the forest, the creek, the mud, the river — seemed to beckon with a dishonouring flourish before the sunlit face of the land a treacherous appeal to the lurking death, to the hidden evil, to the profound darkness of its heart. It was so startling that I leaped to my feet and looked back at the edge of the forest, as though I had expected an answer of some sort to that black display of confidence. You know the foolish notions that come to one sometimes. The high stillness confronted these two figures with its ominous patience, waiting for the passing away of a fantastic invasion.

"They swore aloud together — out of sheer fright, I believe — then pretending not to know anything of my existence, turned back to the station. The sun was low; and leaning forward side by side, they seemed to be tugging painfully uphill their two ridiculous shadows of unequal length, that trailed behind them slowly over the tall grass without bending a single blade.

"In a few days the Eldorado Expedition went into the patient wilderness, that closed upon it as the sea closes over a diver. Long afterwards the news came that all the donkeys were dead. I know nothing as to the fate of the less valuable animals. They, no doubt, like the rest of us, found what they deserved. I did not inquire. I was then rather excited at the prospect of meeting Kurtz very soon. When I say very soon I mean it comparatively. It was just two months from the day we left the creek when we came to the bank below Kurtz's station.

"Going up that river was like travelling back to the earliest beginnings of the world, when vegetation rioted on the earth and the big trees were kings. An empty stream, a great silence, an impenetrable forest. The air was warm, thick, heavy, sluggish. There was no joy in the brilliance of sunshine. The long stretches of the waterway ran on, deserted, into the gloom of over-shadowed distances. On silvery sand-banks hippos and alligators sunned themselves side by side. The broadening waters flowed through a mob of wooded islands; you lost your way on that river as you would in a desert, and butted all day long against shoals, trying to find the channel, till you thought yourself bewitched and cut off for ever from everything you had known once — somewhere — far away — in another existence perhaps. There were moments when one's past came back to one, as it will sometimes when you have not a moment to spare to yourself; but it came in the shape of an unrestful and noisy dream, remembered with wonder amongst the overwhelming realities of this strange world of plants, and water, and silence. And this stillness of life did not in the least resemble a peace. It was the stillness of an implacable force brooding over an inscrutable intention. It looked at you with a vengeful aspect. I got used to it afterwards;

I did not see it any more; I had no time. I had to keep guessing at the channel; I had to discern, mostly by inspiration, the signs of hidden banks; I watched for sunken stones; I was learning to clap my teeth smartly before my heart flew out, when I shaved by a fluke some infernal sly old snag that would have ripped the life out of the tin-pot steamboat and drowned all the pilgrims; I had to keep a lookout for the signs of dead wood we could cut up in the night for next day's steaming. When you have to attend to things of that sort, to the mere incidents of the surface, the reality — the reality, I tell you — fades. The inner truth is hidden — luckily, luckily. But I felt it all the same; I felt often its mysterious stillness watching me at my monkey tricks, just as it watches you fellows performing on your respective tight-ropes for — what is it? half-a-crown a tumble ——"

"Try to be civil, Marlow," growled a voice, and I knew there was at least one listener awake besides myself.

"I beg your pardon. I forgot the heartache which makes up the rest of the price. And indeed what does the price matter, if the trick be well done? You do your tricks very well. And I didn't do badly either, since I managed not to sink that steamboat on my first trip. It's a wonder to me yet. Imagine a blindfolded man set to drive a van over a bad road. I sweated and shivered over that business considerably, I can tell you. After all, for a seaman, to scrape the bottom of the thing that's supposed to float all the time under his care is the unpardonable sin. No one may know of it, but you never forget the thump — eh? A blow on the very heart. You remember it, you dream of it, you wake up at night and think of it — years after — and go hot and cold all over. I don't pretend to say that steamboat floated all the time. More than once she had to wade for a bit, with twenty cannibals splashing around and pushing. We had enlisted some of these chaps on the way for a crew. Fine fellows — cannibals — in their place. They were men one could work with, and I am grateful to them. And, after all, they did not eat each other before my face: they had brought along a provision of hippo-meat which went rotten, and made the mystery of the wilderness stink in my nostrils. Phoo! I can sniff it now. I had the manager on board and three or four pilgrims with their staves — all complete. Sometimes we came upon a station close by the bank, clinging to the skirts of the unknown, and the white men rushing out of a tumble-down hovel, with great gestures of joy and surprise and welcome, seemed very strange — had the appearance of being held there captive by a spell. The word ivory would ring in the air for a while — and on we went again into the silence, along empty reaches, round the still bends, between the high walls of our winding way, reverberating in hollow claps the ponderous beat of the sternwheel. Trees, trees, millions of trees, massive, immense, running up high; and at their foot, hugging the bank against the stream, crept the little begrimed steamboat, like a sluggish beetle crawling on the floor of a lofty portico. It made you feel very small, very lost, and yet it was not altogether depressing, that feeling. After all, if you were small, the grimy beetle crawled on — which was just what you wanted it to do. Where the pilgrims imagined it crawled to I don't know. To some place where they expected to get something. I bet! For me it crawled towards Kurtz — exclusively; but when the steam-pipes started leaking we crawled very slow. The reaches opened before us and closed behind, as if the forest had stepped leisurely across the water to bar the way for our return. We penetrated deeper and deeper into the heart of darkness. It was very quiet there. At night sometimes the roll of drums behind the curtain of trees would run up the river and remain sustained faintly, as if hovering in the air high over our heads, till the first break of day. Whether it meant war, peace, or prayer we could not tell. The dawns were heralded by the descent of a chill stillness; the woodcutters slept, their fires burned low; the snapping of a twig would make you start. We were wanderers on a prehistoric earth, on an earth that wore the aspect of an unknown planet. We could have fancied ourselves the first of men taking possession of an accursed inheritance, to be subdued at the cost of profound anguish and of excessive toil. But suddenly, as we struggled round a bend, there would be a glimpse of rush walls, of peaked grass-roofs, a burst of yells, a whirl of black limbs, a mass of hands clapping, of feet stamping, of bodies swaying, of eyes rolling, under the droop of heavy and motionless foliage. The steamer toiled along slowly on the edge of a black and incomprehensible frenzy. The prehistoric man was cursing us, praying to us, welcoming us — who could tell? We were cut off from the comprehension of our surroundings; we glided past like phantoms, wondering and secretly appalled, as sane men would be before an enthusiastic outbreak in a madhouse. We could not understand because we were too far and could not remember because we were travelling in the night of first ages, of those ages that are gone, leaving hardly a sign — and no memories.

"The earth seemed unearthly. We are accustomed to look upon the shackled form of a conquered monster, but there — there you could look at a thing monstrous and free. It was unearthly, and the men were —— No, they were not inhuman. Well, you know, that was the worst of it — this suspicion of their not being inhuman. It would come slowly to one. They howled and leaped, and spun, and made horrid faces; but what thrilled you was just the thought of their humanity — like yours — the thought of your remote kinship with this wild and passionate uproar. Ugly. Yes, it was ugly enough; but if you were man enough you would admit to yourself that there was in you just the faintest trace of a response to the terrible frankness of that noise, a dim suspicion of there being a meaning in it which you — you so remote from the night of first ages — could comprehend. And why not? The mind of man is capable of anything — because everything is in it, all the past as well as all the future. What was there after all? Joy, fear, sorrow, devotion, valour, rage — who can tell? — but truth — truth stripped of its cloak of time. Let the fool gape and shudder — the man knows, and can look on without a wink. But he must at least be as much of a man as these on the shore. He must meet that truth with his own true stuff — with his own inborn strength. Principles won't do. Acquisitions, clothes, pretty rags — rags that would fly off at the first good shake. No; you want a deliberate belief. An appeal to me in this fiendish row — is there? Very well; I hear; I admit, but I have a voice, too, and for good or evil mine is the speech that cannot be silenced. Of course, a fool, what with sheer fright and fine sentiments, is always safe. Who's that grunting? You wonder I didn't go ashore for a howl and a dance? Well, no — I didn't. Fine sentiments, you say? Fine sentiments, be hanged! I had no time. I had to mess about with white-lead and strips of woolen blanket helping to put bandages on those leaky steampipes — I tell you. I had to watch the steering, and circumvent those snags, and get the tin-pot along by hook or by crook. There was surface-truth enough in these things to save a wiser man. And between whiles I had to look after the savage who was fireman. He was an improved specimen; he could fire up a vertical boiler. He was there below me, and, upon my word, to look at him was as edifying as seeing a dog in a parody of breeches and a feather hat, walking on his hind-legs. A few months of training had done for that really fine chap. He squinted at the steam-gauge and at the water-gauge with an evident effort of intrepidity — and he had filed teeth, too, the poor devil, and the wool of his pate shaved into queer patterns, and three ornamental scars on each of his cheeks. He ought to have been clapping his hands and stamping his feet on the bank, instead of which he was hard at work, a thrall to strange witchcraft, full of improving knowledge. He was useful because he had been instructed; and what he knew was this — that should the water in that transparent thing disappear, the evil spirit inside the boiler would get angry through the greatness of his thirst, and take a terrible vengeance. So he sweated and fired up and watched the glass fearfully (with an impromptu charm, made of rags, tied to his arm, and a piece of polished bone, as big as a watch, stuck flatways through his lower lip), while the wooded banks slipped past us slowly, the short noise was left behind, the interminable miles of silence — and we crept on, towards Kurtz. But the snags were thick, the water was treacherous and shallow, the boiler seemed indeed to have a sulky devil in it, and thus neither that fireman nor I had any time to peer into our creepy thoughts.

"Some fifty miles below the Inner Station we came upon a hut of reeds, an inclined and melancholy pole, with the unrecognizable tatters of what had been a flag of some sort flying from it, and a neatly stacked woodpile. This was unexpected. We came to the bank, and on the stack of firewood found a flat piece of board with some faded pencil-writing on it. When deciphered it said: 'Wood for you. Hurry up. Approach cautiously.' There was a signature, but it was illegible — not Kurtz — a much longer word. 'Hurry up.' Where? Up the river? 'Approach cautiously.' We had not done so. But the warning could not have been meant for the place where it could be only found after approach. Something was wrong above. But what — and how much? That was the question. We commented adversely upon the imbecility of that telegraphic style. The bush around said nothing, and would not let us look very far, either. A torn curtain of red twill hung in the doorway of the hut, and flapped sadly in our faces. The dwelling was dismantled; but we could see a white man had lived there not very long ago. There remained a rude table — a plank on two posts; a heap of rubbish reposed in a dark corner, and by the door I picked up a book. It had lost its covers, and the pages had been thumbed into a state of extremely dirty softness; but the back had been lovingly stitched afresh with white cotton thread, which looked clean yet. It was an extraordinary find. Its title was, *An Inquiry into some Points of Seamanship*, by a man Towser, Towson — some such name — Master in his Majesty's Navy. The matter looked dreary reading enough, with illustrative diagrams and repulsive tables of figures, and the copy was sixty years old. I handled this amazing antiquity with the greatest possible tenderness, lest it should dissolve in my hands. Within, Towson or Towser was inquiring earnestly into the breaking strain of ships' chains and tackle, and other such matters. Not a very enthralling book; but at the first glance you could see there a singleness of intention, an honest concern for the right way of going to work, which made these humble pages, thought out so many years ago, luminous with another than a professional light. The simple old sailor, with his talk of chains and purchases, made me forget the jungle and the pilgrims in a delicious sensation of having come upon something unmistakably real. Such a book being there was wonderful enough but still more astounding were the notes pencilled in the margin, and plainly referring to the text. I couldn't believe my eyes! They were in cipher! Yes, it looked like cipher. Fancy a man lugging with him a book of that description into this nowhere and studying it — and making notes — in cipher at that! It was an extravagant mystery.

"I had been dimly aware for some time of a worrying noise, and when I lifted my eyes I saw the woodpile was gone, and the manager, aided by all the pilgrims, was shouting at me from the riverside. I slipped the book into my pocket. I assure you to leave off reading was like tearing myself away from the shelter of an old and solid friendship.

"I started the lame engine ahead. 'It must be this miserable trader — this intruder,' exclaimed the manager, looking back malevolently at the place we had left. 'He must be English,' I said. 'It will not save him from getting into trouble if he is not careful,' muttered the manager darkly. I observed with assumed innocence that no man was safe from trouble in this world.

"The current was more rapid now, the steamer seemed at her last gasp, the stern-wheel flopped languidly, and I caught myself listening on tiptoe for the next beat of the float,[5] for in sober truth I expected the wretched thing to give up every moment. It was like watching the last flickers of a life. But still we crawled. Sometimes I would pick out a tree a little way ahead to measure our progress towards Kurtz by, but I lost it invariably before we got abreast. To keep the eyes so long on one thing was too much for human patience. The manager displayed a beautiful resignation. I fretted and fumed and took to arguing with myself whether or no I would talk openly with Kurtz; but before I could come to any conclusion it occurred to me that my speech or my silence, indeed any action of mine, would be a mere futility. What did it matter what any one knew or ignored? What did it matter who was manager? One gets sometimes such a flash of insight. The essentials of this affair lay deep under the surface, beyond my reach, and beyond my power of meddling.

"Towards the evening of the second day we judged ourselves about eight miles from Kurtz's station. I wanted to push on; but the manager looked grave, and told me the navigation up there was so dangerous that it would be advisable, the sun being very low already, to wait where we were till next morning. Moreover, he pointed out that if the warning to approach cautiously were to be followed, we must approach in daylight — not at dusk or in the dark. This was sensible enough. Eight miles meant nearly three hours' steaming for us, and I could also see suspicious ripples at the upper end of the reach. Nevertheless, I was annoyed beyond expression at the delay, and most unreasonably, too, since one night more could not matter much after so many months. As we had plenty of wood, and caution was the word, I brought up in the middle of the stream. The reach was narrow, straight, with high sides like a railway cutting. The dusk came gliding into it long before the sun had set. The current ran smooth and swift, but a dumb immobility sat on the banks. The living trees, lashed together by the creepers and every living bush of the undergrowth, might have been changed into stone, even to the slenderest twig, to the lightest leaf. It was not sleep — it seemed unnatural, like a state of trance. Not the faintest sound of any kind could be heard. You looked on amazed, and began to suspect yourself of being deaf — then the night came suddenly, and struck you blind as well. About three in the morning some large fish leaped, and the loud splash made me jump as though a gun had been fired. When the sun rose there was a white fog, very warm and clammy, and more blinding than the night. It did not shift or drive; it was just there, standing all round you like something solid. At eight or nine,

5 [Blade on the paddle-wheel. — Editors' note.]

perhaps, it lifted as a shutter lifts. We had a glimpse of the towering multitude of trees, of the immense matted jungle, with the blazing little ball of the sun hanging over it — all perfectly still — and then the white shutter came down again, smoothly, as if sliding in greased grooves. I ordered the chain, which we had begun to heave in, to be paid out again. Before it stopped running with a muffled rattle, a cry, a very loud cry, as of infinite desolation, soared slowly in the opaque air. It ceased. A complaining clamour, modulated in savage discords, filled our ears. The sheer unexpectedness of it made my hair stir under my cap. I don't know how it struck the others: to me it seemed as though the mist itself had screamed, so suddenly, and apparently from all sides at once, did this tumultuous and mournful uproar arise. It culminated in a hurried outbreak of almost intolerably excessive shrieking, which stopped short, leaving us stiffened in a variety of silly attitudes, and obstinately listening to the nearly as appalling and excessive silence. 'Good God! What is the meaning ——' stammered at my elbow one of the pilgrims — a little fat man, with sandy hair and red whiskers, who wore sidespring boots, and pink pyjamas tucked into his socks. Two others remained open-mouthed a whole minute, then dashed into the little cabin, to rush out incontinently and stand darting scared glances, with Winchesters at 'ready' in their hands. What we could see was just the steamer we were on, her outlines blurred as though she had been on the point of dissolving, and a misty strip of water, perhaps two feet broad, around her — and that was all. The rest of the world was nowhere, as far as our eyes and ears were concerned. Just nowhere. Gone, disappeared; swept off without leaving a whisper or a shadow behind.

"I went forward, and ordered the chain to be hauled in short, so as to be ready to trip the anchor and move the steamboat at once if necessary. 'Will they attack?' whispered an awed voice. 'We will be all butchered in this fog,' murmured another. The faces twitched with the strain, the hands trembled slightly, the eyes forgot to wink. It was very curious to see the contrast of expressions of the white men and of the black fellows of our crew, who were as much strangers to that part of the river as we, though their homes were only eight hundred miles away. The whites, of course greatly discomposed, had besides a curious look of being painfully shocked by such an outrageous row. The others had an alert, naturally interested expression; but their faces were essentially quiet, even those of the one or two who grinned as they hauled at the chain. Several exchanged short, grunting phrases, which seemed to settle the matter to their satisfaction. Their headman, a young, broad-chested black, severely draped in dark-blue fringed cloths, with fierce nostrils and his hair all done up artfully in oily ringlets, stood near me. 'Aha!' I said, just for good fellowship's sake. 'Catch 'im,' he snapped, with a bloodshot widening of his eyes and a flash of sharp teeth — 'catch 'im. Give 'im to us.' 'To you, eh?' I asked; 'what would you do with them?' 'Eat 'im!' he said curtly, and, leaning his elbow on the rail, looked out into the fog in a dignified and profoundly pensive attitude. I would no doubt have been properly horrified, had it not occurred to me that he and his chaps must be very hungry: that they must have been growing increasingly hungry for at least this month past. They had been engaged for six months (I don't think a single one of them had any clear idea of time, as we at the end of countless ages have. They still belonged to the beginnings of time — had no inherited experience to teach them as it were), and of course, as long as there was a piece of paper written over in accordance with some farcical law or other made down the river, it didn't enter anybody's head to trouble how they would live. Certainly they had brought with them some rotten hippo-meat, which couldn't have lasted very long, anyway, even if the pilgrims hadn't, in the midst of a shocking hullabaloo, thrown a considerable quantity of it overboard. It looked like a high-handed proceeding; but it was really a case of legitimate self-defence. You can't breathe dead hippo waking, sleeping, and eating, and at the same time keep your precarious grip on existence. Besides that, they had given them every week three pieces of brass wire, each about nine inches long; and the theory was they were to buy their provisions with that currency in riverside villages. You can see how *that* worked. There were either no villages, or the people were hostile, or the director, who like the rest of us fed out of tins, with an occasional old he-goat thrown in, didn't want to stop the steamer for some more or less recondite reason. So, unless they swallowed the wire itself, or made loops of it to snare the fishes with, I don't see what good their extravagant salary could be to them. I must say it was paid with a regularity worthy of a large and honourable trading company. For the rest, the only thing to eat — though it didn't look eatable in the least — I saw in their possession was a few lumps of some stuff like half-cooked dough, of a dirty lavender colour, they kept wrapped in leaves, and now and then swallowed a piece of, but so small that it seemed done more for the looks of the thing than for any serious purpose of sustenance. Why in the name of all the gnawing devils of hunger they didn't go for us — they were thirty to five — and have a good tuck-in for once, amazes me now when I think of it. They were big powerful men, with not much capacity to weigh the consequences, with courage, with strength, even yet, though their skins were no longer glossy and their muscles no longer hard. And I saw that something restraining, one of those human secrets that baffle probability, had come into play there. I looked at them with a swift quickening of interest — not because it occurred to me I might be eaten by them before very long, though I own to you that just then I perceived — in a new light, as it were — how unwholesome the pilgrims looked, and I hoped, yes, I positively hoped, that my aspect was not so — what shall I say? — so — unappetizing: a touch of fantastic vanity which fitted well with the dream-sensation that pervaded all my days at that time. Perhaps I had a little fever, too. One can't live with one's finger everlastingly on one's pulse. I had often 'a little fever,' or a little touch of other things — the playful paw-strokes of the wilderness, the preliminary trifling before the more serious onslaught which came in due course. Yes; I looked at them as you would on any human being, with a curiosity of their impulses, motives, capacities, weaknesses, when brought to the test of an inexorable physical necessity. Restraint! What possible restraint? Was it superstition, disgust, patience, fear — or some kind of primitive honour? No fear can stand up to hunger, no patience can wear it out, disgust simply does not exist where hunger is; and as to superstition, beliefs, and what you may call principles, they are less than chaff in a breeze. Don't you know the devilry of lingering starvation, its exasperating torment, its black thoughts, its sombre and brooding ferocity? Well, I do. It takes a man all his inborn strength to fight hunger properly. It's really easier to face bereavement, dishonour, and the perdition of one's soul — than this kind of prolonged hunger. Sad, but true. And these chaps, too, had no earthly reason for any kind of scruple. Restraint! I would just as soon have expected restraint from a hyena prowling amongst the corpses of a battlefield. But there was the fact facing me — the fact dazzling, to be seen, like the foam on the depths of the sea, like a ripple on an unfathomable enigma, a mystery greater — when I thought of it — than the curious, inexplicable note of desperate grief in this savage clamour that had swept by us on the river-bank, behind the blind whiteness of the fog.

"Two pilgrims were quarrelling in hurried whispers as to which bank. 'Left.' 'No, no; how can you? Right, right, of course.' 'It is very serious,' said the manager's voice behind me; 'I would be desolated if anything should happen to Mr. Kurtz before we came up.' I looked at him, and had not the slightest doubt he was sincere. He was just the kind of man who would wish to preserve appearances. That was his restraint. But when he muttered something about going on at once, I did not even take the trouble to answer him. I knew, and he knew, that it was impossible. Were we to let go our hold of the bottom, we would be absolutely in the air — in space. We wouldn't be able to tell where we were going to — whether up or down stream, or across — till we fetched against one bank or the other — and then we wouldn't know at first which it was. Of course I made no move. I had no mind for a smash-up. You couldn't imagine a more deadly place for a shipwreck. Whether drowned at once or not, we were sure to perish speedily in one way or another. 'I authorize you to take all the risks,' he said, after a short silence. 'I refuse to take any,' I said shortly; which was just the answer he expected, though its tone might have surprised him. 'Well, I must defer to your judgment. You are captain,' he said with marked civility. I turned my shoulder to him in sign of my appreciation, and looked into the fog. How long would it last? It was the most hopeless lookout. The approach to this Kurtz grubbing for ivory in the wretched bush was beset by as many dangers as though he had been an enchanted princess sleeping in a fabulous castle. 'Will they attack, do you think?" asked the manager, in a confidential tone.

"I did not think they would attack, for several obvious reasons. The thick fog was one. If they left the bank in their canoes they would get lost in it, as we would be if we attempted to move. Still, I had also judged the jungle of both banks quite impenetrable — and yet eyes were in it, eyes that had seen us. The riverside bushes were certainly very thick; but the undergrowth behind was evidently penetrable. However, during the short lift I had seen no canoes anywhere in the reach — certainly not abreast of the steamer. But what made the idea of attack inconceivable to me was the nature of the noise — of the cries we had heard. They had not the fierce character boding immediate hostile intention. Unexpected, wild, and violent as they had been, they had given me an irresistible impression of sorrow. The glimpse of the steamboat had for some reason filled those savages with unrestrained grief. The danger, if any, I expounded, was from our proximity to a great human passion let loose. Even extreme grief may ultimately vent itself in violence — but more generally takes the form of apathy. . . .

"You should have seen the pilgrims stare! They had no heart to grin, or even to revile me: But I believe they thought me gone mad — with fright, maybe. I delivered a regular lecture. My dear boys, it was no good bothering. Keep a lookout? Well, you may guess I watched the fog for the signs of lifting as a cat watches a mouse; but for anything else our eyes were of no more use to us than if we had been buried miles deep in a heap of cotton-wool. It felt like it, too — choking, warm, stifling. Besides, all I said, though it sounded extravagant, was absolutely true to fact. What we afterwards alluded to as an attack was really an attempt at repulse. The action was very far from being aggressive — it was not even defensive, in the usual sense: it was undertaken under the stress of desperation, and in its essence was purely protective.

"It developed itself, I should say, two hours after the fog lifted, and its commencement was at a spot, roughly speaking, about a mile and a half below Kurtz's station. We had just floundered and flopped round a bend, when I saw an islet, a mere grassy hummock of bright green, in the middle of the stream. It was the only thing of the kind; but as we opened the reach more, I perceived it was the head of a long sand-bank, or rather of a chain of shallow patches stretching down the middle of the river. They were discoloured, just awash, and the whole lot was seen just under the water, exactly as a man's backbone is seen running down the middle of his back under the skin. Now, as far as I did see, I could go to the right or to the left of this. I didn't know either channel, of course. The banks looked pretty well alike, the depth appeared the same; but as I had been informed the station was on the west side, I naturally headed for the western passage.

"No sooner had we fairly entered it than I became aware it was much narrower than I had supposed. To the left of us there was the long uninterrupted shoal, and to the right a high, steep bank heavily overgrown with bushes. Above the bush the trees stood in serried ranks. The twigs overhung the current thickly, and from distance to distance a large limb of some tree projected rigidly over the stream. It was then well on in the afternoon, the face of the forest was gloomy, and a broad strip of shadow had already fallen on the water. In this shadow we steamed up — very slowly, as you may imagine. I sheered her well inshore — the water being deepest near the bank, as the sounding-pole informed me.

"One of my hungry and forbearing friends was sounding in the bows just below me. This steamboat was exactly like a decked scow. On the deck, there were two little teakwood houses, with doors and windows. The boiler was in the fore-end, and the machinery right astern. Over the whole there was a light roof, supported on stanchions. The funnel projected through that roof, and in front of the funnel a small cabin built of light planks served for a pilot-house. It contained a couch, two campstools, a loaded Martini-Henry[6] leaning in one corner, a tiny table, and the steering-wheel. It had a wide door in front and a broad shutter at each side. All these were always thrown open, of course. I spent my days perched up there on the extreme fore-end of that roof, before the door. At night I slept, or tried to, on the couch. An athletic black belonging to some coast tribe and educated by my poor predecessor, was the helmsman. He sported a pair of brass earrings, wore a blue cloth wrapper from the waist to the ankles, and thought all the world of himself. He was the most unstable kind of fool I had ever seen. He steered with no end of a swagger while you were by; but if he lost sight of you, he became instantly the prey of an abject funk, and would let that cripple of a steamboat get the upper hand of him in a minute.

"I was looking down at the sounding-pole, and feeling much annoyed to see at each try a little more of it stick out of that river, when I saw my poleman give up the business suddenly, and stretch himself flat on the deck, without even taking the trouble to haul his pole in. He kept hold on it though, and it trailed in the water. At the same time the fireman, whom I could also see below me, sat down abruptly before his furnace and ducked his head. I was amazed. Then I had to look at the river mighty quick, because there was a snag in the fairway. Sticks, little sticks, were flying about — thick: they were whizzing before my nose, dropping below me, striking behind me against my pilot-house. All this time the river, the shore, the woods, were very quiet — perfectly quiet. I could only hear

6 [Rifle. — Editors' note.]

the heavy splashing thump of the stern-wheel and the patter of these things. We cleared the snag clumsily. Arrows, by Jove! We were being shot at! I stepped in quickly to close the shutter on the landside. That fool-helmsman, his hands on the spokes, was lifting his knees high, stamping his feet, champing his mouth, like a reined-in horse. Confound him! And we were staggering within ten feet of the bank. I had to lean right out to swing the heavy shuttter, and I saw a face amongst the leaves on the level with my own, looking at me very fierce and steady; and then suddenly, as though a veil had been removed from my eyes, I made out, deep in the tangled gloom, naked breasts, arms, legs, glaring eyes — the bush was swarming with human limbs in movement, glistening, of bronze colour. The twigs shook, swayed, and rustled, the arrows flew out of them, and then the shutter came to. 'Steer her straight,' I said to the helmsman. He held his head rigid, face forward; but his eyes rolled, he kept on lifting and setting down his feet gently, his mouth foamed a little. 'Keep quiet!' I said in a fury. I might just as well have ordered a tree not to sway in the wind. I darted out. Below me there was a great scuffle of feet on the iron deck; confused exclamations; a voice screamed, 'Can you turn back?' I caught sight of a V-shaped ripple on the water ahead. What? Another snag! A fusillade burst out under my feet. The pilgrims had opened with their Winchesters, and were simply squirting lead into that bush. A deuce of a lot of smoke came up and drove slowly forward. I swore at it. Now I couldn't see the ripple or the snag either. I stood in the doorway, peering, and the arrows came in swarms. They might have been poisoned, but they looked as though they wouldn't kill a cat. The bush began to howl. Our wood-cutters raised a warlike whoop; the report of a rifle just at my back deafened me. I glanced over my shoulder, and the pilot-house was yet full of noise and smoke when I made a dash at the wheel. The fool-nigger had dropped everything, to throw the shutter open and let off that Martini-Henry. He stood before the wide opening, glaring, and I yelled at him to come back, while I straightened the sudden twist out of that steamboat. There was no room to turn even if I had wanted to, the snag was somewhere very near ahead in that confounded smoke, there was no time to lose, so I just crowded her into the bank — right into the bank, where I knew the water was deep.

"We tore slowly along the overhanging bushes in a whirl of broken twigs and flying leaves. The fusillade below stopped short, as I had foreseen it would when the squirts got empty. I threw my head back to a glinting whizz that traversed the pilot-house, in at one shutter-hole and out at the other. Looking past that mad helmsman, who was shaking the empty rifle and yelling at the shore, I saw vague forms of men running bent double, leaping, gliding, distinct, incomplete, evanescent. Something big appeared in the air before the shutter, the rifle went overboard, and the man stepped back swiftly, looked at me over his shoulder in an extraordinary, profound, familiar manner, and fell upon my feet. The side of his head hit the wheel twice, and the end of what appeared a long cane clattered round and knocked over a little campstool. It looked as though after wrenching that thing from somebody ashore he had lost his balance in the effort. The thin smoke had blown away, we were clear of the snag, and looking ahead I could see that in another hundred yards or so I would be free to sheer off, away from the bank; but my feet felt so very warm and wet that I had to look down. The man had rolled on his back and stared straight up at me; both his hands clutched that cane. It was the shaft of a spear that, either thrown or lunged through the opening, had caught him in the side just below the ribs; the blade had gone in out of sight, after making a frightful gash; my shoes were full; a pool of blood lay very still, gleaming dark-red under the wheel; his eyes shone with an amazing lustre. The fusillade burst out again. He looked at me anxiously, gripping the spear like something precious, with an air of being afraid I would try to take it away from him. I had to make an effort to free my eyes from his gaze and attend to the steering. With one hand I felt above my head for the line of the steam whistle, and jerked out screech after screech hurriedly. The tumult of angry and warlike yells was checked instantly, and then from the depths of the woods went out such a tremulous and prolonged wail of mournful fear and utter despair as may be imagined to follow the flight of the last hope from the earth. There was a great commotion in the bush; the shower of arrows stopped, a few dropping shots rang out sharply — then silence, in which the languid beat of the stern-wheel came plainly to my ears. I put the helm hard a-starboard at the moment when the pilgrim in pink pyjamas, very hot and agitated, appeared in the doorway. 'The manager sends me ——' he began in an official tone, and stopped short. 'Good God!' he said, glaring at the wounded man.

"We two whites stood over him, and his lustrous and inquiring glance enveloped us both. I declare it looked as though he would presently put to us some question in an understandable language; but he died without uttering a sound, without moving a limb, without twitching a muscle. Only in the very last moment, as though in response to some sign we could not see, to some whisper we could not hear, he frowned heavily, and that frown gave to his black death-mask an inconceivably sombre, brooding, and menacing expression. The lustre of inquiring glance faded swiftly into vacant glassiness. 'Can you steer?' I asked the agent eagerly. He looked very dubious; but I made a grab at his arm, and he understood at once I meant him to steer whether or no. To tell you the truth, I was morbidly anxious to change my shoes and socks. 'He is dead,' murmured the fellow, immensely impressed. 'No doubt about it,' said I, tugging like mad at the shoe-laces. 'And by the way, I suppose Mr. Kurtz is dead as well by this time.'

"For the moment that was the dominant thought. There was a sense of extreme disappointment, as though I had found out I had been striving after something altogether without a substance. I couldn't have been more disgusted if I had travelled all this way for the sole purpose of talking with Mr. Kurtz. Talking with . . . I flung one shoe overboard, and became aware that that was exactly what I had been looking forward to — a talk with Kurtz. I made the strange discovery that I had never imagined him as doing, you know, but as discoursing. I didn't say to myself, 'Now I will never see him,' or 'Now I will never shake him by the hand,' but, 'Now I will never hear him.' The man presented himself as a voice. Not of course that I did not connect him with some sort of action. Hadn't I been told in all the tones of jealousy and admiration that he had collected, bartered, swindled, or stolen more ivory than all the other agents together? That was not the point. The point was in his being a gifted creature, and that of all his gifts the one that stood out preëminently, that carried with it a sense of real presence, was his ability to talk, his words — the gift of expression, the bewildering, the illuminating, the most exalted and the most contemptible, the pulsating stream of light, or the deceitful flow from the heart of an impenetrable darkness.

"The other shoe went flying unto the devil-god of that river. I thought, 'By Jove! it's all over. We are too late; he has vanished — the gift has vanished, by means of some spear, arrow, or club. I will never hear that chap speak after all' — and my sorrow had a startling extravagance of emotion, even such as I had noticed in the howling sorrow of these savages in the bush. I couldn't have felt more of lonely desolation somehow, had I been robbed of a belief or had missed my destiny in life. . . . Why do you sigh in this beastly way, somebody? Absurd? Well, absurd. Good Lord! mustn't a man ever —— Here, give me some tobacco." . . .

There was a pause of profound stillness, then a match flared, and Marlow's lean face appeared, worn, hollow, with downward folds and dropped eyelids, with an aspect of concentrated attention; and as he took vigorous draws at his pipe, it seemed to retreat and advance out of the night in the regular flicker of tiny flame. The match went out.

"Absurd!" he cried. "This is the worst of trying to tell. . . . Here you all are, each moored with two good addresses, like a hulk with two anchors, a butcher round one corner, a policeman round another, excellent appetites, and temperature normal — you hear — normal from year's end to year's end. And you say, Absurd! Absurd be — exploded! Absurd! My dear boys, what can you expect from a man who out of sheer nervousness had just flung overboard a pair of new shoes! Now I think of it, it is amazing I did not shed tears. I am, upon the whole, proud of my fortitude. I was cut to the quick at the idea of having lost the inestimable privilege of listening to the gifted Kurtz. Of course I was wrong. The privilege was waiting for me. Oh, yes, I heard more than enough. And I was right, too. A voice. He was very little more than a voice. And I heard — him — it — this voice — other voices — all of them were so little more than voices — and the memory of that time itself lingers around me, impalpable, like a dying vibration of one immense jabber, silly, atrocious, sordid, savage, or simply mean, without any kind of sense. Voices, voices — even the girl herself — now —— "

He was silent for a long time.

"I laid the ghost of his gifts at last with a lie," he began, suddenly. "Girl! What? Did I mention a girl? Oh, she is out of it — completely. They — the women I mean — are out of it — should be out of it. We must help them to stay in that beautiful world of their own, lest ours gets worse. Oh, she had to be out of it. You should have heard the disinterred body of Mr. Kurtz saying, 'My Intended.' You would have perceived directly then how completely she was out of it. And the lofty frontal bone of Mr. Kurtz! They say the hair goes on growing sometimes, but this — ah — specimen, was impressively bald. The wilderness had patted him on the head, and, behold, it was like a ball — an ivory ball; it had caressed him, and — lo! — he had withered; it had taken him, loved him, embraced him, got into his veins, consumed his flesh, and sealed his soul to its own by the inconceivable ceremonies of some devilish initiation. He was its spoiled and pampered favourite. Ivory? I should think so. Heaps of it, stacks of it. The old mud shanty was bursting with it. You would think there was not a single tusk left either above or below the ground in the whole country. 'Mostly fossil,' the manager had remarked, disparagingly. It was no more fossil than I am; but they call it fossil when it is dug up. It appears these niggers do bury the tusks sometimes — but evidently they couldn't bury this parcel deep enough to save the gifted Mr. Kurtz from his fate. We filled the steamboat with it, and had to pile a lot on the deck. Thus he could see and enjoy as long as he could see, because the appreciation of this favour had remained with him to the last. You should have heard him say, 'My ivory.' Oh, yes, I heard him. 'My Intended, my ivory, my station, my river, my —— ' everything belonged to him. It made me hold my breath in expectation of hearing the wilderness burst into a prodigious peal of laughter that would shake the fixed stars in their places. Everything belonged to him — but that was a trifle. The thing was to know what he belonged to, how many powers of darkness claimed him for their own. That was the reflection that made you creepy all over. It was impossible — it was not good for one either — trying to imagine. He had taken a high seat amongst the devils of the land — I mean literally. You can't understand. How could you? — with solid pavement under your feet, surrounded by kind neighbours ready to cheer you or to fall on you, stepping delicately between the butcher and the policeman, in the holy terror of scandal and gallows and lunatic asylums — how can you imagine what particular region of the first ages a man's untrammelled feet may take him into by the way of solitude — utter solitude without a policeman — by the way of silence — utter silence, where no warning voice of a kind neighbour can be heard whispering of public opinion? These little things make all the great difference. When they are gone you must fall back upon your own innate strength, upon your own capacity for faithfulness. Of course you may be too much of a fool to go wrong — too dull even to know you are being assaulted by the powers of darkness. I take it, no fool ever made a bargain for his soul with the devil; the fool is too much of a fool, or the devil too much of a devil — I don't know which. Or you may be such a thunderingly exalted creature as to be altogether deaf and blind to anything but heavenly sights and sounds. Then the earth for you is only a standing place — and whether to be like this is your loss or your gain I won't pretend to say. But most of us are neither one nor the other. The earth for us is a place to live in, where we must put up with sights, with sounds, with smells, too, by Jove! — breathe dead hippo, so to speak, and not be contaminated. And there, don't you see? Your strength comes in, the faith in your ability for the digging of unostentatious holes to bury the stuff in — your power of devotion, not to yourself, but to an obscure, back-breaking business. And that's difficult enough. Mind, I am not trying to excuse or even explain — I am trying to account to myself for — for — Mr. Kurtz — for the shade of Mr. Kurtz. This initiated wraith from the back of Nowhere honoured me with its amazing confidence before it vanished altogether. This was because it could speak English to me. The original Kurtz had been educated partly in England, and — as he was good enough to say himself — his sympathies were in the right place. His mother was half-English, his father was half-French. All Europe contributed to the making of Kurtz; and by and by I learned that, most appropriately, the International Society for the Suppression of Savage Customs had intrusted him with the making of a report, for its future guidance. And he had written it, too. I've seen it. I've read it. It was eloquent, vibrating with eloquence, but too high-strung, I think. Seventeen pages of close writing he had found time for! But this must have been before his — let us say — nerves, went wrong, and caused him to preside at certain midnight dances ending with unspeakable rites, which — as far as I reluctantly gathered from what I heard at various times — were offered up to him — do you understand? — to Mr. Kurtz himself. But it was a beautiful piece of writing. The opening paragraph, however, in the light of later information, strikes me now as ominous. He began with the argument that we whites, from the point of development we had arrived at, 'must necessarily appear to them [savages] in the nature of supernatural beings — we approach them with the might as of a deity,' and so on, and so on. 'By the simple exercise of our will we can exert a power for good practically unbounded,' etc., etc. From that point he soared and took me with him. The peroration was magnificent, though difficult to remember, you know. It gave me the notion of an exotic Immensity ruled by an august Benevolence. It made me tingle with enthusiasm. This was the unbounded power of eloquence — of words — of burning noble words. There were no practical hints to interrupt the magic current of phrases, unless a kind of note at the foot of the last page, scrawled evidently much later, in an unsteady hand, may be regarded as the exposition of a method. It was very simple, and at the end of that moving appeal to every altruistic sentiment it blazed at you, luminous and terrifying, like a flash of lightning in a serene sky: 'Exterminate all the brutes!' The curious part was that he had apparently forgotten all about that valuable postscriptum, because, later on, when he in a sense came to himself, he repeatedly entreated me to take good care of 'my pamphlet' (he called it), as it was sure to have in the future a good influence upon his career. I had full information about all these things, and, besides, as it turned out, I was to have the care of his memory. I've done enough for it to give me the indisputable right to lay it, if I choose, for an everlasting rest in the dust-bin of progress, amongst all the sweepings and, figuratively speaking, all the dead cats of civilization. But then, you see, I can't choose. He won't be forgotten. Whatever he was, he was not common. He had the power to charm or frighten rudimentary souls into an aggravated witch-dance in his honour; he could also fill the small souls of the pilgrims with bitter misgivings: he had one devoted friend at least, and he had conquered one soul in the world that was neither rudimentary nor tainted with self-seeking. No; I can't forget him, though I am not prepared to affirm the fellow was exactly worth the life we lost in getting to him. I missed my late helmsman awfully — I missed him even while his body was still lying in the pilot-house. Perhaps you will think it passing strange this regret for a savage who was no more account than a grain of sand in a black Sahara. Well, don't you see, he had done something, he had steered; for months I had him at my back — a help — an instrument. It was a kind of partnership. He steered for me — I had to look after him, I worried about his deficiencies, and thus a subtle bond had been created, of which I only became aware when it was suddenly broken. And the intimate profundity of that look he gave me when he received his hurt remains to this day in my memory — like a claim of distant kinship affirmed in a supreme moment.

"Poor fool! If he had only left that shutter alone. He had no restraint, no restraint — just like Kurtz — a tree swayed by the wind. As soon as I had put on a dry pair of slippers, I dragged him out, after first jerking the spear out of his side, which operation I confess I performed with my eyes shut tight. His heels leaped together over the little doorstep; his shoulders were pressed to my breast; I hugged him from behind desperately. Oh! he was heavy, heavy; heavier than any man on earth, I should imagine. Then without more ado I tipped him overboard. The current snatched him as though he had been a wisp of grass, and I saw the body roll over twice before I lost sight of it for ever. All the pilgrims and the manager were then congregated on the awning-deck about the pilot-house, chattering at each other like a flock of excited magpies, and there was a scandalized murmur at my heartless promptitude. What they wanted to keep that body hanging about for I can't guess. Embalm it, maybe. But I had also heard another, and a very ominous, murmur on the deck below. My friends the woodcutters were likewise scandalized, and with a better show of reason — though I admit that the reason itself was quite inadmissible. Oh, quite! I had made up my mind that if my late helmsman was to be eaten, the fishes alone should have him. He had been a very second-rate helmsman while alive, but now he was dead he might have become a first-class temptation, and possibly cause some startling trouble. Besides, I was anxious to take the wheel, the man in pink pyjamas showing himself a hopeless duffer at the business.

"This I did directly the simple funeral was over. We were going half-speed, keeping right in the middle of the stream, and I listened to the talk about me. They had given up Kurtz, they had given up the station; Kurtz was dead, and the station had been burnt — and so on — and so on. The red-haired pilgrim was beside himself with the thought that at least this poor Kurtz had been properly avenged. 'Say! We must have made a glorious slaughter of them in the bush. Eh? What do you think? Say?' He positively danced, the bloodthirsty little gingery beggar. And he had nearly fainted when he saw the wounded man! I could not help saying, 'You made a glorious lot of smoke, anyhow.' I had seen, from the way the tops of the bushes rustled and flew, that almost all the shots had gone too high. You can't hit anything unless you take aim and fire from the shoulder; but these chaps fired from the hip with their eyes shut. The retreat, I maintained — and I was right — was caused by the screeching of the steam whistle. Upon this they forgot Kurtz, and began to howl at me with indignant protests.

"The manager stood by the wheel murmuring confidentially about the necessity of getting well away down the river before dark at all events, when I saw in the distance a clearing on the riverside and the outlines of some sort of building. 'What's this?' I asked. He clapped his hands in wonder. 'The station!' he cried. I edged in at once, still going half-speed.

"Through my glasses I saw the slope of a hill interspersed with rare trees and perfectly free from undergrowth. A long decaying building on the summit was half buried in the high grass; the large holes in the peaked roof gaped black from afar; the jungle and the woods made a background. There was no enclosure or fence of any kind; but there had been one apparently, for near the house half-a-dozen slim posts remained in a row, roughly trimmed, and with their upper ends ornamented with round carved balls. The rails, or whatever there had been between, had disappeared. Of course the forest surrounded all that. The river-bank was clear, and on the waterside I saw a white man under a hat like a cartwheel beckoning persistently with his whole arm. Examining the edge of the forest above and below, I was almost certain I could see movements — human forms gliding here and there. I steamed past prudently, then stopped the engines and let her drift down. The man on the shore began to shout, urging us to land. 'We have been attacked,' screamed the manager. 'I know — I know. It's all right,' yelled back the other, as cheerful as you please. 'Come along. It's all right. I am glad.'

"His aspect reminded me of something I had seen — something funny I had seen somewhere. As I manœuvred to get alongside, I was asking myself, 'What does this fellow look like?' Suddenly I got it. He looked like a harlequin. His clothes had been made of some stuff that was brown holland probably, but it was covered with patches all over, with bright patches, blue, red, and yellow — patches on the back, patches on the front, patches on elbows, on knees; coloured binding around his jacket, scarlet edging at the bottom of his trousers; and the sunshine made him look extremely gay and wonderfully neat withal, because you could see how beautifully all this patching had been done. A beardless, boyish face, very fair, no features to speak of, nose peeling, little blue eyes, smiles and frowns chasing each other over that open countenance like sunshine and shadow on a wind-swept plain. 'Look out, captain!' he cried; 'there's a snag lodged in here last night.' What! Another snag? I confess I swore shamefully. I had nearly holed my cripple, to finish off that charming trip. The harlequin on the bank turned his little pug-nose up to me. 'You English?' he asked, all smiles. 'Are you?' I shouted from the wheel. The smiles vanished, and he shook his head as if sorry for my disappointment. Then he brightened up. 'Never mind!' he cried encouragingly. 'Are we in time?' I asked. 'He is up there,' he replied, with a toss of the head up the hill, and becoming gloomy all of a sudden. His face was like the autumn sky, overcast one moment and bright the next.

"When the manager, escorted by the pilgrims, all of them armed to the teeth, had gone to the house this chap came on board. 'I say, I don't like this. These natives are in the bush,' I said. He assured me earnestly it was all right. 'They are simple people,' he added; 'well, I am glad you came. It took me all my time to keep them off.' 'But you said it was all right,' I cried. 'Oh, they meant no harm,' he said; and as I stared he corrected himself, 'Not exactly.' Then vivaciously, 'My faith, your pilot-house wants a clean-up!' In the next breath he advised me to keep enough steam on the boiler to blow the whistle in case of any trouble. 'One good screech will do more for you than all your rifles. They are simple people,' he repeated. He rattled away at such a rate he quite overwhelmed me. He seemed to be trying to make up for lots of silence, and actually hinted, laughing, that such was the case. 'Don't you talk with Mr. Kurtz?' I said. 'You don't talk with that man — you listen to him,' he exclaimed with severe exaltation. 'But now —— ' He waved his arm, and in the twinkling of an eye was in the uttermost depths of despondency. In a moment he came up again with a jump, possessed himself of both my hands, shook them continuously, while he gabbled: 'Brother sailor . . . honour . . . pleasure . . . delight . . . introduce myself . . . Russian . . . son of an arch-priest. . . . Government of Tambov. . . . What? Tobacco! English tobacco; the excellent English tobacco! Now, that's brotherly. Smoke? Where's a sailor that does not smoke?"

"The pipe soothed him, and gradually I made out he had run away from school, had gone to sea in a Russian ship; ran away again; served some time in English ships; was now reconciled with the arch-priest. He made a point of that. 'But when one is young one must see things, gather experience, ideas; enlarge the mind.' 'Here!' I interrupted. 'You can never tell! Here I met Mr. Kurtz,' he said, youthfully solemn and reproachful. I held my tongue after that. It appears he had persuaded a Dutch trading-house on the coast to fit him out with stores and goods, and had started for the interior with a light heart and no more idea of what would happen to him than a baby. He had been wandering about that river for nearly two years alone, cut off from everybody and everything. 'I am not so young as I look. I am twenty-five,' he said. 'At first old Van Shuyten would tell me to go to the devil,' he narrated with keen enjoyment; 'but I stuck to him, and talked and talked, till at last he got afraid I would talk the hind-leg off his favourite dog, so he gave me some cheap things and a few guns, and told me he hoped he would never see my face again. Good old Dutchman, Van Shuyten. I've sent him one small lot of ivory a year ago, so that he can't call me a little thief when I get back. I hope he got it. And for the rest I don't care. I had some wood stacked for you. That was my old house. Did you see?'

"I gave him Towson's book. He made as though he would kiss me, but restrained himself. 'The only book I had left, and I thought I had lost it,' he said, looking at it ecstatically. 'So many accidents happen to a man going about alone, you know. Canoes get upset sometimes — and sometimes you've got to clear out so quick when the people get angry.' He thumbed the pages. 'You made notes in Russian?' I asked. He nodded. 'I thought they were written in cipher,' I said. He laughed, then became serious. 'I had lots of trouble to keep these people off,' he said. 'Did they want to kill you?' I asked. 'Oh, no!' he cried, and checked himself. 'Why did they attack us?' I pursued. He hesitated, then said shamefacedly, 'They don't want him to go.' 'Don't they?' I said curiously. He nodded a nod full of mystery and wisdom. 'I tell you,' he cried, 'this man has enlarged my mind.' He opened his arms wide, staring at me with his little blue eyes that were perfectly round."

III

"I looked at him, lost in astonishment. There he was before me, in motley, as though he had absconded from a troupe of mimes, enthusiastic, fabulous. His very existence was improbable, inexplicable, and altogether bewildering. He was an insoluble problem. It was inconceivable how he had existed, how he had succeeded in getting so far, how he had managed to remain — why he did not instantly disappear. 'I went a little farther,' he said, 'then still a little farther — till I had gone so far that I don't know how I'll ever get back. Never mind. Plenty time. I can manage. You take Kurtz away quick — quick — I tell you.' The glamour of youth enveloped his parti-coloured rags, his destitution, his loneliness, the essential desolation of his futile wanderings. For months — for years — his life hadn't been worth a day's purchase; and there he was gallantly, thoughtlessly alive, to all appearance indestructible solely by the virtue of his few years and of his unreflecting audacity. I was seduced into something like admiration — like envy. Glamour urged him on, glamour kept him unscathed. He surely wanted nothing from the wilderness but space to breathe in and to push on through. His need was to exist, and to move onwards at the greatest possible risk, and with a maximum of privation. If the absolutely pure, uncalculating, unpractical spirit of adventure had ever ruled a human being, it ruled this bepatched youth. I almost envied him the possession of this modest and clear flame. It seemed to have consumed all thought of self so completely, that even while he was talking to you, you forgot that it was he — the man before your eyes — who had gone through these things. I did not envy him his devotion to Kurtz, though. He had not meditated over it. It came to him, and he accepted it with a sort of eager fatalism. I must say that to me it appeared about the most dangerous thing in every way he had come upon so far.

"They had come together unavoidably, like two ships becalmed near each other, and lay rubbing sides at last. I suppose Kurtz wanted an audience, because on a certain occasion, when encamped in the forest, they had talked all night, or more probably Kurtz had talked. 'We talked of everything,' he said, quite transported at the recollection. 'I forgot there was such a thing as sleep. The night did not seem to last an hour. Everything! Everything! . . . Of love, too.' 'Ah, he talked to you of love!' I said, much amused. 'It isn't what you think,' he cried, almost passionately. 'It was in general. He made me see things — things.'

"He threw his arms up. We were on deck at the time, and the headman of my wood-cutters, lounging near by, turned upon him his heavy and glittering eyes. I looked around, and I don't know why, but I assure you that never, never before, did this land, this river, this jungle, the very arch of this blazing sky, appear to me so hopeless and so dark, so impenetrable to human thought, so pitiless to human weakness. 'And, ever since, you have been with him, of course?' I said.

'On the contrary. It appears their intercourse had been very much broken by various causes. He had, as he informed me proudly, managed to nurse Kurtz through two illnesses (he alluded to it as you would to some risky feat), but as a rule Kurtz wandered alone, far in the depths of the forest. 'Very often coming to this station, I had to wait days and days before he would turn up,' he said. 'Ah, it was worth waiting for! — sometimes.' 'What was he doing? exploring or what?' I asked. 'Oh, yes, of course'; he had discovered lots of villages, a lake, too — he did not know exactly in what direction; it was dangerous to inquire too much — but mostly his expeditions had been for ivory. 'But he had no goods to trade with by that time,' I objected. 'There's a good lot of cartridges left even yet,' he answered, looking away. 'To speak plainly, he raided the country,' I said. He nodded. 'Not alone, surely!' He muttered something about the villages round that lake. 'Kurtz got the tribe to follow him, did he?' I suggested. He fidgeted a little. 'They adored him,' he said. The tone of these words was so extraordinary that I looked at him searchingly. It was curious to see his mingled eagerness and reluctance to speak of Kurtz. The man filled his life, occupied his thoughts, swayed his emotions. 'What can you expect?' he burst out; 'he came to them with thunder and lightning, you know — and they had never seen anything like it — and very terrible. He could be very terrible. You can't judge Mr. Kurtz as you would an ordinary man. No, no, no! Now — just to give you an idea — I don't mind telling you, he wanted to shoot me, too, one day — but I don't judge him.' 'Shoot you!' I cried. 'What for?' 'Well, I had a small lot of ivory the chief of that village near my house gave me. You see I used to shoot game for them. Well, he wanted it, and wouldn't hear reason. He declared he would shoot me unless I gave him the ivory and then cleared out of the country, because he could do so, and had a fancy for it, and there was nothing on earth to prevent him killing whom he jolly well pleased. And it was true, too. I gave him the ivory. What did I care! But I didn't clear out. No, no. I couldn't leave him. I had to be careful, of course, till we got friendly again for a time. He had his second illness then. Afterwards I had to keep out of the way; but I didn't mind. He was living for the most part in those villages on the lake. When he came down to the river, sometimes he would take to me, and sometimes it was better for me to be careful. This man suffered too much. He hated all this, and somehow he couldn't get away. When I had a chance I begged him to try and leave while there was time; I offered to go back with him. And he would say yes, and then he would remain; go off on another ivory hunt; disappear for weeks; forget himself amongst these people — forget himself — you know.' 'Why! he's mad,' I said. He protested indignantly. Mr. Kurtz couldn't be mad.

If I had heard him talk, only two days ago, I wouldn't dare hint at such a thing. . . . I had taken up my binoculars while we talked, and was looking at the shore, sweeping the limit of the forest at each side and at the back of the house. The consciousness of there being people in that bush, so silent, so quiet — as silent and quiet as the ruined house on the hill — made me uneasy. There was no sign on the face of nature of this amazing tale that was not so much told as suggested to me in desolate exclamations, completed by shrugs, in interrupted phrases, in hints ending in deep sighs. The woods were unmoved, like a mask — heavy, like the closed door of a prison — they looked with their air of hidden knowledge, of patient expectation, of unapproachable silence. The Russian was explaining to me that it was only lately that Mr. Kurtz had come down to the river, bringing along with him all the fighting men of that lake tribe. He had been absent for several months — getting himself adored, I suppose — and had come down unexpectedly, with the intention to all appearance of making a raid either across the river or down stream. Evidently the appetite for more ivory had got the better of the — what shall I say? — less material aspirations. However he had got much worse suddenly. 'I heard he was lying helpless, and so I came up — took my chance,' said the Russian. 'Oh, he is bad, very bad.' I directed my glass to the house. There were no signs of life, but there was the ruined roof, the long mud wall peeping above the grass, with three little square window-holes, no two of the same size; all this brought within reach of my hand, as it were. And then I made a brusque movement, and one of the remaining posts of that vanished fence leaped up in the field of my glass. You remember I told you I had been struck at the distance by certain attempts at ornamentation, rather remarkable in the ruinous aspect of the place. Now I had suddenly a nearer view, and its first result was to make me throw my head back as if before a blow. Then I went carefully from post to post with my glass, and I saw my mistake. These round knobs were not ornamental but symbolic; they were expressive and puzzling, striking and disturbing — food for thought and also for vultures if there had been any looking down from the sky; but at all events for such ants as were industrious enough to ascend the pole. They would have been even more impressive, those heads on the stakes, if their faces had not been turned to the house. Only one, the first I had made out, was facing my way. I was not so shocked as you may think. The start back I had given was really nothing but a movement of surprise. I had expected to see a knob of wood there, you know. I returned deliberately to the first I had seen — and there it was, black, dried, sunken, with closed eyelids — a head that seemed to sleep at the top of that pole, and, with the shrunken dry lips showing a narrow white line of the teeth, was smiling, too, smiling continuously at some endless and jocose dream of that eternal slumber.

"I am not disclosing any trade secrets. In fact, the manager said afterwards that Mr. Kurtz's methods had ruined the district. I have no opinion on that point, but I want you clearly to understand that there was nothing exactly profitable in these heads being there. They only showed that Mr. Kurtz lacked restraint in the gratification of his various lusts, that there was something wanting in him — some small matter which, when the pressing need arose, could not be found under his magnificent eloquence. Whether he knew of this deficiency himself I can't say. I think the knowledge came to him at last — only at the very last. But the wilderness had found him out early, and had taken on him a terrible vengeance for the fantastic invasion. I think it had whispered to him things about himself which he did not know, things of which he had no conception till he took counsel with this great solitude — and the whisper had proved irresistibly fascinating. It echoed loudly within him because he was hollow at the core. . . . I put down the glass, and the head that had appeared near enough to be spoken to seemed at once to have leaped away from me into inaccessible distance.

"The admirer of Mr. Kurtz was a bit crestfallen. In a hurried, indistinct voice he began to assure me he had not dared to take these — say, symbols — down. He was not afraid of the natives; they would not stir till Mr. Kurtz gave the word. His ascendancy was extraordinary. The camps of these people surrounded the place, and the chiefs came every day to see him. They would crawl. . . . 'I don't want to know anything of the ceremonies used when approaching Mr. Kurtz,' I shouted. Curious, this feeling that came over me that such details would be more intolerable than those heads drying on the stakes under Mr. Kurtz's windows. After all, that was only a savage sight, while I seemed at one bound to have been transported into some lightless region of subtle horrors, where pure, uncomplicated savagery was a positive relief, being something that had a right to exist — obviously — in the sunshine. The young man looked at me with surprise. I suppose it did not occur to him that Mr. Kurtz was no idol of mine. He forgot I hadn't heard any of these splendid monologues on, what was it? on love, justice, conduct of life — or what not. If it had come to crawling before Mr. Kurtz, he crawled as much as the veriest savage of them all. I had no idea of the conditions, he said: these heads were the heads of rebels. I shocked him excessively by laughing. Rebels! What would be the next definition I was to hear? There had been enemies, criminals, workers — and these were rebels. Those rebellious heads looked very subdued to me on their sticks. 'You don't know how such a life tries a man like Kurtz,' cried Kurtz's last disciple. 'Well, and you?' I said. 'I! I! I am a simple man. I have no great thoughts. I want nothing from anybody. How can you compare me to . . . ?' His feelings were too much for speech, and suddenly he broke down. 'I don't understand,' he groaned.

'I've been doing my best to keep him alive, and that's enough. I had no hand in all this. I have no abilities. There hasn't been a drop of medicine or a mouthful of invalid food for months here. He was shamefully abandoned. A man like this, with such ideas. Shamefully! Shamefully! I — I — haven't slept for the last ten nights. . . .'

"His voice lost itself in the calm of the evening. The long shadows of the forest had slipped downhill while we talked, had gone far beyond the ruined hovel, beyond the symbolic row of stakes. All this was in the gloom, while we down there were yet in the sunshine, and the stretch of the river abreast of the clearing glittered in a still and dazzling splendour, with a murky and overshadowed bend above and below. Not a living soul was seen on the shore. The bushes did not rustle.

"Suddenly round the corner of the house a group of men appeared, as though they had come up from the ground. They waded waist-deep in the grass, in a compact body, bearing an improvised stretcher in their midst. Instantly, in the emptiness of the landscape, a cry arose whose shrillness pierced the still air like a sharp arrow flying straight to the very heart of the land; and, as if by enchantment, streams of human beings — of naked human beings — with spears in their hands, with bows, with shields, with wild glances and savage movements, were poured into the clearing by the dark-faced and pensive forest. The bushes shook, the grass swayed for a time, and then everything stood still in attentive immobility.

" 'Now, if he does not say the right thing to them we are all done for,' said the Russian at my elbow. The knot of men with the stretcher had stopped, too, halfway to the steamer, as if petrified. I saw the man on the stretcher sit up, lank and with an uplifted arm, above the shoulders of the bearers. 'Let us hope that the man who can talk so well of love in general will find some particular reason to spare us this time,' I said. I resented bitterly the absurd danger of our situation, as if to be at the mercy of that atrocious phantom had been a dishonouring necessity. I could not hear a sound, but through my glasses I saw the thin arm extended commandingly, the lower jaw moving, the eyes of that apparition shining darkly far in its bony head that nodded with grotesque jerks. Kurtz — Kurtz — that means short in German — don't it? Well, the name was as true as everything else in his life — and death. He looked at least seven feet long. His covering had fallen off, and his body emerged from it pitiful and appalling as from a winding-sheet. I could see the cage of his ribs all astir, the bones of his arm waving. It was as though an animated image of death carved out of old ivory had been shaking its hand with menaces at a motionless crowd of men made of dark and glittering bronze. I saw him open his mouth wide — it gave him a weirdly voracious aspect, as though he had wanted to swallow all the air, all the earth, all the men before him. A deep voice reached me faintly. He must have been shouting. He fell back suddenly. The stretcher shook as the bearers staggered forward again, and almost at the same time I noticed that the crowd of savages was vanishing without any perceptible movement of retreat, as if the forest that had ejected these beings so suddenly had drawn them in again as the breath is drawn in a long aspiration.

"Some of the pilgrims behind the stretcher carried his arms — two shotguns, a heavy rifle, and a light revolver-carbine — the thunderbolts of that pitiful Jupiter. The manager bent over him murmuring as he walked beside his head. They laid him down in one of the little cabins — just a room for a bed place and a campstool or two, you know. We had brought his belated correspondence, and a lot of torn envelopes and open letters littered his bed. His hand roamed feebly amongst these papers. I was struck by the fire of his eyes and the composed languor of his expression. It was not so much the exhaustion of disease. He did not seem in pain. This shadow looked satiated and calm, as though for the moment it had had its fill of all the emotions.

"He rustled one of the letters, and looking straight in my face said, 'I am glad.' Somebody had been writing to him about me. These special recommendations were turning up again. The volume of tone he emitted without effort, almost without the trouble of moving his lips, amazed me. A voice! a voice! It was grave, profound, vibrating, while the man did not seem capable of a whisper. However, he had enough strength in him — factitious no doubt — to very nearly make an end of us, as you shall hear directly.

"The manager appeared silently in the doorway; I stepped out at once and he drew the curtain after me. The Russian, eyed curiously by the pilgrims, was staring at the shore. I followed the direction of his glance.

"Dark human shapes could be made out in the distance, flitting indistinctly against the gloomy border of the forest, and near the river two bronze figures, leaning on tall spears, stood in the sunlight under fantastic head-dresses of spotted skins, warlike and still in statuesque repose. And from right to left along the lighted shore moved a wild and gorgeous apparition of a woman.

"She walked with measured steps, draped in striped and fringed cloths, treading the earth proudly, with a slight jingle and flash of barbarous ornaments. She carried her head high; her hair was done in the shape of a helmet; she had brass leggings to the knee, brass wire gauntlets to the elbow, a crimson spot on her tawny cheek, innumerable necklaces of glass beads on her neck; bizarre things, charms, gifts of witch-men, that hung about her, glittered and trembled at every step. She must have had the value of several elephant tusks upon her. She was savage and superb, wild-eyed and magnificent; there was something ominous and stately in her deliberate progress. And in the hush that had fallen suddenly upon the whole sorrowful land, the immense wilderness, the colossal body of the fecund and mysterious life seemed to look at her, pensive, as though it had been looking at the image of its own tenebrous and passionate soul.

"She came abreast of the steamer, stood still, and faced us. Her long shadow fell to the water's edge. Her face had a tragic and fierce aspect of wild sorrow and of dumb pain mingled with the fear of some struggling, half-shaped resolve. She stood looking at us without a stir, and like the wilderness itself, with an air of brooding over an inscrutable purpose. A whole minute passed, and then she made a step forward. There was a low jingle, a glint of yellow metal, a sway of fringed draperies, and she stopped as if her heart had failed her. The young fellow by my side growled. The pilgrims murmured at my back. She looked at us all as if her life had depended upon the unswerving steadiness of her glance. Suddenly she opened her bared arms and threw them up rigid above her head, as though in an uncontrollable desire to touch the sky, and at the same time the swift shadows darted out on the earth, swept around on the river, gathering the steamer into a shadowy embrace. A formidable silence hung over the scene.

"She turned away slowly, walked on, following the bank, and passed into the bushes to the left. Once only her eyes gleamed back at us in the dusk of the thickets before she disappeared.

" 'If she had offered to come aboard I really think I would have tried to shoot her,' said the man of patches, nervously. 'I have been risking my life every day for the last fortnight to keep her out of the house. She got in one day and kicked up a row about those miserable rags I picked up in the storeroom to mend my clothes with. I wasn't decent. At least it must have been that, for she talked like a fury to Kurtz for an hour, pointing at me now and then. I don't understand the dialect of this tribe. Luckily for me, I fancy Kurtz felt too ill that day to care, or there would have been mischief. I don't understand. . . . No — it's too much for me. Ah, well, it's all over now.'

"At this moment I heard Kurtz's deep voice behind the curtain: 'Save me! — save the ivory, you mean. Don't tell me. Save *me!* Why, I've had to save you. You are interrupting my plans now. Sick! Sick! Not so sick as you would like to believe. Never mind. I'll carry my ideas out yet — I will return. I'll show you what can be done. You with your little peddling notions — you are interfering with me. I will return. I. . . .'

"The manager came out. He did me the honour to take me under the arm and lead me aside. 'He is very low, very low,' he said. He considered it necessary to sigh, but neglected to be consistently sorrowful. 'We have done all we could for him — haven't we? But there is no disguising the fact, Mr. Kurtz has done more harm than good to the Company. He did not see the time was not ripe for vigorous action. Cautiously, cautiously — that's my principle. We must be cautious yet. The district is closed to us for a time. Deplorable! Upon the whole, the trade will suffer. I don't deny there is a remarkable quantity of ivory — mostly fossil. We must save it, at all events — but look how precarious the position is — and why? Because the method is unsound.' 'Do you,' said I, looking at the shore, 'call it "unsound method"?' 'Without doubt,' he exclaimed hotly. 'Don't you?' . . . 'No method at all,' I murmured after a while. 'Exactly,' he exulted. 'I anticipated this. Shows a complete want of judgment. It is my duty to point it out in the proper quarter.' 'Oh,' said I, 'that fellow — what's his name? — the brickmaker, will make a readable report for you.' He appeared confounded for a moment. It seemed to me I had never breathed an atmosphere so vile, and I turned mentally to Kurtz for relief — positively for relief. 'Nevertheless I think Mr. Kurtz is a remarkable man,' I said with emphasis. He started, dropped on me a cold heavy glance, said very quietly, 'he *was,*' and turned his back on me. My hour of favour was over; I found myself lumped along with Kurtz as a partisan of methods for which the time was not ripe: I was unsound! Ah! but it was something to have at least a choice of nightmares.

"I had turned to the wilderness really, not to Mr. Kurtz, who, I was ready to admit, was as good as buried. And for a moment it seemed to me as if I also were buried in a vast grave full of unspeakable secrets. I felt an intolerable weight oppressing my breast, the smell of the damp earth, the unseen presence of victorious corruption, the darkness of an impenetrable night. . . . The Russian tapped me on the shoulder. I heard him mumbling and stammering something about 'brother seaman — couldn't conceal — knowledge of matters that would affect Mr. Kurtz's reputation.' I waited. For him evidently Mr. Kurtz was not in his grave; I suspect that for him Mr. Kurtz was one of the immortals. 'Well!' said I at last, 'speak out. As it happens, I am Mr. Kurtz's friend — in a way.'

"He stated with a good deal of formality that had we not been 'of the same profession,' he would have kept the matter to himself without regard to consequences. 'He suspected there was an active ill-will towards him on the part of these white men that ——' 'You are right,' I said, remembering a certain conversation I had overheard. 'The manager thinks you ought to be hanged.' He showed a concern at this intelligence which amused me at first. 'I had better get out of the way quietly,' he said earnestly. 'I can do no more for Kurtz now, and they would soon find some excuse. What's to stop them? There's a military post three hundred miles from here.' 'Well, upon my word,' said I, 'perhaps you had better go if you have any friends amongst the savages near by.' 'Plenty,' he said. 'They are simple people — and I want nothing, you know.' He stood biting his lip, then: 'I don't want any harm to happen to these whites here, but of course I was thinking of Mr. Kurtz's reputation — but you are a brother seaman and ——' 'All right,' said I, after a time. 'Mr. Kurtz's reputation is safe with me.' I did not know how truly I spoke.

"He informed me, lowering his voice, that it was Kurtz who had ordered the attack to be made on the steamer. 'He hated sometimes the idea of being taken away — and then again. . . . But I don't understand these matters. I am a simple man. He thought it would scare you away — that you would give it up, thinking him dead. I could not stop him. Oh, I had an awful time of it this last month.' 'Very well,' I said. 'He is all right now.' 'Ye-e-es,' he muttered, not very convinced apparently. 'Thanks,' said I; 'I shall keep my eyes open.' 'But quiet — eh?' he urged anxiously. 'It would be awful for his reputation if anybody here ——' I promised a complete discretion with great gravity. 'I have a canoe and three black fellows waiting not very far. I am off. Could you give me a few Martini-Henry cartridges?' I could, and did, with proper secrecy. He helped himself, with a wink at me, to a handful of my tobacco. 'Between sailors — you know — good English tobacco.' At the door of the pilot-house he turned round — 'I say, haven't you a pair of shoes you could spare?' He raised one leg. 'Look.' The soles were tied with knotted strings sandalwise under his bare feet. I rooted out an old pair, at which he looked with admiration before tucking it under his left arm. One of his pockets (bright red) was bulging with cartridges, from the other (dark blue) peeped 'Towson's Inquiry,' etc., etc. He seemed to think himself excellently well equipped for a renewed encounter with the wilderness. 'Ah! I'll never, never meet such a man again. You ought to have heard him recite poetry — his own, too, it was, he told me. Poetry!' He rolled his eyes at the recollection of these delights. 'Oh, he enlarged my mind!' 'Good-bye,' said I. He shook hands and vanished in the night. Sometimes I ask myself whether I had ever really seen him — whether it was possible to meet such a phenomenon! . . .

"When I woke up shortly after midnight his warning came to my mind with its hint of danger that seemed, in the starred darkness, real enough to make me get up for the purpose of having a look round. On the hill a big fire burned, illuminating fitfully a crooked corner of the station-house. One of the agents with a picket of a few of our blacks, armed for the purpose, was keeping guard over the ivory; but deep within the forest, red gleams that wavered, that seemed to sink and rise from the ground amongst confused columnar shapes of intense blackness, showed the exact position of the camp where Mr. Kurtz's adorers were keeping their uneasy vigil. The monotonous beating of a big drum filled the air with muffled shocks and a lingering vibration. A steady droning sound of many men chanting each to himself some weird incantation came out from the black, flat wall of the woods as the humming of bees comes out of a hive, and had a strange narcotic effect upon my half-awake senses. I believe I dozed off leaning over the rail, till an abrupt burst of yells, an overwhelming outbreak of a pent-up and mysterious frenzy, woke me up in a bewildered wonder. It was cut short all at once, and the low droning went on with an effect of audible and soothing silence. I glanced casually into the little cabin. A light was burning within, but Mr. Kurtz was not there.

"I think I would have raised an outcry if I had believed my eyes. But I didn't believe them at first — the thing seemed so impossible. The fact is I was completely unnerved by a sheer blank fright, pure abstract terror, unconnected with any distinct shape of physical danger. What made this emotion so overpowering was — how shall I define it? — the moral shock I received, as if something altogether monstrous, intolerable to thought and odious to the soul, had been thrust upon me unexpectedly. This lasted of course the merest fraction of a second, and then the usual sense of commonplace, deadly danger, the possibility of a sudden onslaught and massacre, or something of the kind, which I saw impending, was positively welcome and composing. It pacified me, in fact, so much that I did not raise an alarm.

"There was an agent buttoned up inside an ulster and sleeping on a chair on deck within three feet of me. The yells had not awakened him; he snored very slightly; I left him to his slumbers and leaped ashore. I did not betray Mr. Kurtz — it was ordered I should never betray him — it was written I should be loyal to the nightmare of my choice. I was anxious to deal with this shadow by myself alone — and to this day I don't know why I was so jealous of sharing with any one the peculiar blackness of that experience.

"As soon as I got on the bank I saw a trail — a broad trail through the grass. I remember the exultation with which I said to myself, 'He can't walk — he is crawling on all-fours — I've got him.' The grass was wet with dew. I strode rapidly with clenched fists. I fancy I had some vague notion of falling upon him and giving him a drubbing. I don't know. I had some imbecile thoughts. The knitting old woman with the cat obtruded herself upon my memory as a most improper person to be sitting at the other end of such an affair. I saw a row of pilgrims squirting lead in the air out of Winchesters held to the hip. I thought I would never get back to the steamer, and imagined myself living alone and unarmed in the woods to an advanced age. Such silly things — you know. And I remember I confounded the beat of the drum with the beating of my heart, and was pleased at its calm regularity.

"I kept to the track though — then stopped to listen. The night was very clear; a dark blue space, sparkling with dew and starlight, in which black things stood very still. I thought I could see a kind of motion ahead of me. I was strangely cocksure of everything that night. I actually left the track and ran in a wide semicircle (I verily believe chuckling to myself) so as to get in front of that stir, of that motion I had seen — if indeed I had seen anything. I was circumventing Kurtz as though it had been a boyish game.

"I came upon him, and, if he had not heard me coming, I would have fallen over him, too, but he got up in time. He rose, unsteady, long, pale, indistinct, like a vapour exhaled by the earth, and swayed slightly, misty and silent before me; while at my back the fires loomed between the trees, and the murmur of many voices issued from the forest. I had cut him off cleverly; but when actually confronting him I seemed to come to my senses, I saw the danger in its right proportion. It was by no means over yet. Suppose he began to shout? Though he could hardly stand, there was still plenty of vigour in his voice. 'Go away — hide yourself,' he said, in that profound tone. It was very awful. I glanced back. We were within thirty yards from the nearest fire. A black figure stood up, strode on long black legs, waving long black arms, across the glow. It had horns — antelope horns, I think — on its head. Some sorcerer, some witch-man, no doubt: it looked fiendlike enough. 'Do you know what you are doing?' I whispered. 'Perfectly,' he answered, raising his voice for that single word: it sounded to me far off and yet loud, like a hail through a speaking-trumpet. 'If he makes a row we are lost,' I thought to myself. This clearly was not a case for fisticuffs, even apart from the very natural aversion I had to beat that Shadow — this wandering and tormented thing. 'You will be lost,' I said — 'utterly lost.' One gets sometimes such a flash of inspiration, you know. I did say the right thing, though indeed he could not have been more irretrievably lost than he was at this very moment, when the foundations of our intimacy were being laid — to endure — to endure — even to the end — even beyond.

" 'I had immense plans,' he muttered irresolutely. 'Yes,' said I; 'but if you try to shout I'll smash your head with ——' There was not a stick or a stone near. 'I will throttle you for good,' I corrected myself. 'I was on the threshold of great things,' he pleaded, in a voice of longing, with a wistfulness of tone that made my blood run cold. 'And now for this stupid scoundrel ——' 'Your success in Europe is assured in any case,' I affirmed steadily. I did not want to have the throttling of him, you understand — and indeed it would have been very little use for any practical purpose. I tried to break the spell — the heavy, mute spell of the wilderness — that seemed to draw him to its pitiless breast by the awakening of forgotten and brutal instincts, by the memory of gratified and monstrous passions. This alone, I was convinced, had driven him out to the edge of the forest, to the bush, towards the gleam of fires, the throb of drums, the drone of weird incantations; this alone had beguiled his unlawful soul beyond the bounds of permitted aspirations. And, don't you see, the terror of the position was not in being knocked on the head — though I had a very lively sense of that danger, too — but in this, that I had to deal with a being to whom I could not appeal in the name of anything high or low. I had, even like the niggers, to invoke him — himself — his own exalted and incredible degradation. There was nothing either above or below him, and I knew it. He had kicked himself loose of the earth. Confound the man! he had kicked the very earth to pieces. He was alone, and I before him did not know whether I stood on the ground or floated in the air. I've been telling you what we said — repeating the phrases we pronounced — but what's the good? They were common everyday words — the familiar, vague sounds exchanged on every waking day of life. But what of that? They had behind them, to my mind, the terrific suggestiveness of words heard in dreams, of phrases spoken in nightmares. Soul! If anybody ever struggled with a soul, I am the man. And I wasn't arguing with a lunatic either. Believe me or not, his intelligence was perfectly clear — concentrated, it is true, upon himself with horrible intensity, yet clear; and therein was my only chance — barring, of course, the killing him there and then, which wasn't so good, on account of unavoidable noise. But his soul was mad. Being alone in the wilderness, it had looked within itself, and, by heavens! I tell you, it had gone mad. I had — for my sins, I suppose — to go through the ordeal of looking into it myself. No eloquence could have been so withering to one's belief in mankind as his final burst of sincerity. He struggled with himself, too. I saw it — I heard it. I saw the inconceivable mystery of a soul that knew no restraint, no faith, and no fear, yet struggling blindly with itself. I kept my head pretty well; but when I had him at last stretched on the couch, I wiped my forehead, while my legs shook under me as though I had carried half a ton on my back down that hill. And yet I had only supported him, his bony arm clasped round my neck — and he was not much heavier than a child.

"When next day we left at noon, the crowd, of whose presence behind the curtain of trees I had been acutely conscious all the time, flowed out of the woods again, filled the clearing, covered the slope with a mass of naked, breathing, quivering, bronze bodies. I steamed up a bit, then swung down stream, and two thousand eyes followed the evolutions of the splashing, thumping, fierce river-demon beating the water with its terrible tail and breathing black smoke into the air. In front of the first rank, along the river, three men, plastered with bright red earth from head to foot, strutted to and fro restlessly. When we came abreast again, they faced the river, stamped their feet, nodded their horned heads, swayed their scarlet bodies; they shook towards the fierce river-demon a bunch of black feathers, a mangy skin with a pendent tail — something that looked like a dried gourd; they shouted periodically together strings of amazing words that resembled no sounds of human language; and the deep murmurs of the crowd, interrupted suddenly, were like the responses of some satanic litany.

"We had carried Kurtz into the pilot-house: there was more air there.

Lying on the couch, he stared through the open shutter. There was an eddy in the mass of human bodies, and the woman with helmeted head and tawny cheeks rushed out to the very brink of the stream. She put out her hands, shouted something, and all that wild mob took up the shout in a roaring chorus of articulated, rapid, breathless utterance.

" 'Do you understand this?' I asked.

"He kept on looking out past me with fiery, longing eyes, with a mingled expression of wistfulness and hate. He made no answer, but I saw a smile, a smile of indefinable meaning, appear on his colourless lips that a moment after twitched convulsively. 'Do I not?' he said slowly, gasping, as if the words had been torn out of him by a supernatural power.

"I pulled the string of the whistle, and I did this because I saw the pilgrims on deck getting out their rifles with an air of anticipating a jolly lark. At the sudden screech there was a movement of abject terror through that wedged mass of bodies. 'Don't! don't you frighten them away,' cried some one on deck disconsolately. I pulled the string time after time. They broke and ran, they leaped, they crouched, they swerved, they dodged the flying terror of the sound. The three red chaps had fallen flat, face down on the shore, as though they had been shot dead. Only the barbarous and superb woman did not so much as flinch, and stretched tragically her bare arms after us over the sombre and glittering river.

"And then that imbecile crowd down on the deck started their little fun, and I could see nothing more for smoke.

"The brown current ran swiftly out of the heart of darkness, bearing us down towards the sea with twice the speed of our upward progress; and Kurtz's life was running swiftly, too, ebbing, ebbing out of his heart into the sea of inexorable time. The manager was very placid, he had no vital anxieties now, he took us both in with a comprehensive and satisfied glance: the 'affair' had come off as well as could be wished. I saw the time approaching when I would be left alone of the party of 'unsound method.' The pilgrims looked upon me with disfavour. I was, so to speak, numbered with the dead. It is strange how I accepted this unforeseen partnership, this choice of nightmares forced upon me in the tenebrous land invaded by these mean and greedy phantoms.

"Kurtz discoursed. A voice! a voice! It rang deep to the very last. It survived his strength to hide in the magnificent folds of eloquence the barren darkness of his heart. Oh, he struggled! he struggled! The wastes of his weary brain were haunted by shadowy images now — images of wealth and fame revolving obsequiously round his unextinguishable gift of noble and lofty expression. My Intended, my station, my career, my ideas — these were the subjects for the occasional utterances of elevated sentiments. The shade of the original Kurtz frequented the bedside of the hollow sham, whose fate it was to be buried presently in the mould of primeval earth. But both the diabolic love and the unearthly hate of the mysteries it had penetrated fought for the possession of that soul satiated with primitive emotions, avid of lying fame, of sham distinction, of all the appearances of success and power.

"Sometimes he was contemptibly childish. He desired to have kings meet him at railway-stations on his return from some ghastly Nowhere, where he intended to accomplish great things. 'You show them you have in you something that is really profitable, and then there will be no limits to the recognition of your ability,' he would say. 'Of course you must take care of the motives — right motives — always.' The long reaches that were like one and the same reach, monotonous bends that were exactly alike, slipped past the steamer with their multitude of secular[7] trees looking patiently after this grimy fragment of another world, the forerunner of change, of conquest, of trade, of massacres, of blessings. I looked ahead — piloting. 'Close the shutter,' said Kurtz suddenly one day; 'I can't bear to look at this.' I did so. There was a silence. 'Oh, but I will wring your heart yet!' he cried at the invisible wilderness.

"We broke down — as I had expected — and had to lie up for repairs at the head of an island. This delay was the first thing that shook Kurtz's confidence. One morning he gave me a packet of papers and a photograph — the lot tied together with a shoe-string. 'Keep this for me,' he said. 'This noxious fool' (meaning the manager) 'is capable of prying into my boxes when I am not looking.' In the afternoon I saw him. He was lying on his back with closed eyes, and I withdrew quietly, but I heard him mutter, 'Live rightly, die, die . . .' I listened. There was nothing more. Was he rehearsing some speech in his sleep, or was it a fragment of a phrase from some newspaper article? He had been writing for the papers and meant to do so again, 'for the furthering of my ideas. It's a duty.'

"His was an impenetrable darkness. I looked at him as you peer down at a man who is lying at the bottom of a precipice where the sun never shines. But I had not much time to give him, because I was helping the engine-driver to take to pieces the leaky cylinders, to straighten a bent connecting-rod, and in other such matters. I lived in an infernal mess of rust, filings, nuts, bolts, spanners, hammers, ratchet-drills — things I abominate, because I don't get on with them. I tended the little forge we fortunately had aboard; I toiled wearily in a wretched scrap-heap — unless I had the shakes too bad to stand.

"One evening coming in with a candle I was startled to hear him say a little tremulously, 'I am lying here in the dark waiting for death.' The light was within a foot of his eyes. I forced myself to murmur, 'Oh, nonsense!' and stood over him as if transfixed.

7 [Ancient. — Editors' note.]

"Anything approaching the change that came over his features I have never seen before, and hope never to see again. Oh, I wasn't touched. I was fascinated. It was as though a veil had been rent. I saw on that ivory face the expression of sombre pride, of ruthless power, of craven terror — of an intense and hopeless despair. Did he live his life again in every detail of desire, temptation, and surrender during that supreme moment of complete knowledge? He cried in a whisper at some image, at some vision — he cried out twice, a cry that was no more than a breath:

" 'The horror! The horror!'

"I blew the candle out and left the cabin. The pilgrims were dining in the mess-room, and I took my place opposite the manager, who lifted his eyes to give me a questioning glance, which I successfully ignored. He leaned back, serene, with that peculiar smile of his sealing the unexpressed depths of his meanness. A continuous shower of small flies streamed upon the lamp, upon the cloth, upon our hands and faces. Suddenly the manager's boy put his insolent black head in the doorway, and said in a tone of scathing contempt:

" 'Mistah Kurtz — he dead.'

"All the pilgrims rushed out to see. I remained, and went on with my dinner. I believe I was considered brutally callous. However, I did not eat much. There was a lamp in there — light, don't you know — and outside it was so beastly, beastly dark. I went no more near the remarkable man who had pronounced a judgment upon the adventures of his soul on this earth. The voice was gone. What else had been there? But I am of course aware that next day the pilgrims buried something in a muddy hole.

"And then they very nearly buried me.

"However, as you see, I did not go to join Kurtz there and then. I did not. I remained to dream the nightmare out to the end, and to show my loyalty to Kurtz once more. Destiny. My destiny! Droll thing life is — that mysterious arrangement of merciless logic for a futile purpose. The most you can hope from it is some knowledge of yourself — that comes too late — a crop of unextinguishable regrets. I have wrestled with death. It is the most unexciting contest you can imagine. It takes place in an impalpable greyness, with nothing underfoot, with nothing around, without spectators, without clamour, without glory, without the great desire of victory, without the great fear of defeat, in a sickly atmosphere of tepid scepticism, without much belief in your own right, and still less in that of your adversary. If such is the form of ultimate wisdom, then life is a greater riddle than some of us think it to be. I was within a hair's breadth of the last opportunity for pronouncement, and I found with humiliation that probably I would have nothing to say. This is the reason why I affirm that Kurtz was a remarkable man. He had something to say. He said it. Since I had peeped over the edge myself, I understand better the meaning of his stare, that could not see the flame of the candle, but was wide enough to embrace the whole universe, piercing enough to penetrate all the hearts that beat in the darkness. He had summed up — he had judged. 'The horror!' He was a remarkable man. After all, this was the expression of some sort of belief; it had candour, it had conviction, it had a vibrating note of revolt in its whisper, it had the appalling face of a glimpsed truth — the strange commingling of desire and hate. And it is not my own extremity I remember best — a vision of greyness without form filled with physical pain, and a careless contempt for the evanescence of all things — even of this pain itself. No! It is his extremity that I seem to have lived through. True, he had made that last stride, he had stepped over the edge, while I had been permitted to draw back my hesitating foot. And perhaps in this is the whole difference; perhaps all the wisdom, and all truth, and all sincerity, are just compressed into that inappreciable moment of time in which we step over the threshold of the invisible. Perhaps! I like to think my summing-up would not have been a word of careless contempt. Better his cry — much better. It was an affirmation, a moral victory paid for by innumerable defeats, by abominable terrors, by abominable satisfactions. But it was a victory! That is why I have remained loyal to Kurtz to the last and even beyond, when a long time after I heard once more, not his own voice, but the echo of his magnificent eloquence thrown to me from a soul as translucently pure as a cliff of crystal.

"No, they did not bury me, though there is a period of time which I remember mistily, with a shuddering wonder, like a passage through some inconceivable world that had no hope in it and no desire. I found myself back in the sepulchral city resenting the sight of people hurrying through the streets to filch a little money from each other, to devour their infamous cookery, to gulp their unwholesome beer, to dream their insignificant and silly dreams. They trespassed upon my thoughts. They were intruders whose knowledge of life was to me an irritating pretence, because I felt so sure they could not possibly know the things I knew. Their bearing, which was simply the bearing of commonplace individuals going about their business in the assurance of perfect safety, was offensive to me like the outrageous flauntings of folly in the face of a danger it is unable to comprehend. I had no particular desire to enlighten them, but I had some difficulty in restraining myself from laughing in their faces so full of stupid importance. I daresay I was not very well at that time. I tottered about the streets — there were various affairs to settle — grinning bitterly at perfectly respectable persons. I admit my behaviour was inexcusable, but then my temperature was seldom normal in these days. My dear aunt's endeavours to 'nurse up my strength' seemed altogether beside the mark. It was not my strength that wanted nursing, it was my imagination that wanted soothing. I kept the bundle of papers given me by Kurtz, not knowing exactly what to do with it. His mother had died lately, watched over, as I was told, by his Intended. A clean-shaved man, with an official manner and wearing gold-rimmed spectacles, called on me one day and made inquiries, at first circuitous, afterwards suavely pressing, about what he was pleased to denominate certain 'documents.' I was not surprised, because I had had two rows with the manager on the subject out there. I had refused to give up the smallest scrap out of that package, and I took the same attitude with the spectacled man. He became darkly menacing at last, and with much heat argued that the Company had the right to every bit of information about its 'territories.' And said he, 'Mr. Kurtz's knowledge of unexplored regions must have been necessarily extensive and peculiar — owing to his great abilities and to the deplorable circumstances in which he had been placed: therefore ——' I assured him Mr. Kurtz's knowledge, however extensive, did not bear upon the problems of commerce or administration. He invoked then the name of science. 'It would be an incalculable loss if,' etc., etc. I offered him the report on the 'Suppression of Savage Customs,' with the postscriptum torn off. He took it up eagerly, but ended by sniffing at it with an air of contempt. 'This is not what we had a right to expect,' he remarked. 'Expect nothing else,' I said. 'There are only private letters.' He withdrew upon some threat of legal proceedings, and I saw him no more; but another fellow, calling himself Kurtz's cousin, appeared two days later, and was anxious to hear all the details about his dear relative's last moments. Incidentally he gave me to understand that Kurtz had been essentially a great musician. 'There was the making of an immense success,' said the man, who was an organist, I believe, with lank grey hair flowing over a greasy coat-collar. I had no reason to doubt his statement; and to this day I am unable to say what was Kurtz's profession, whether he ever had any — which was the greatest of his talents. I had taken him for a painter who wrote for the papers, or else for a journalist who could paint — but even the cousin (who took snuff during the interview) could not tell me what he had been — exactly. He was a universal genius — on that point I agreed with the old chap, who thereupon blew his note noisily into a large cotton handkerchief and withdrew in senile agitation, bearing off some family letters and memoranda without importance. Ultimately a journalist anxious to know something of the fate of his 'dear colleague' turned up. This visitor informed me Kurtz's proper sphere ought to have been politics 'on the popular side.' He had furry straight eyebrows, bristly hair cropped short, an eyeglass on a broad ribbon, and, becoming expansive, confessed his opinion that Kurtz really couldn't write a bit — 'but heavens! how that man could talk. He electrified large meetings. He had faith — don't you see? — he had the faith. He could get himself to believe anything — anything. He would have been a splendid leader of an extreme party.' 'What party?' I asked. 'Any party,' answered the other. 'He was an — an — extremist.' Did I not think so? I assented. Did I know, he asked, with a sudden flash of curiosity, 'what it was that had induced him to go out there?' 'Yes,' said I, and forthwith handed him the famous Report for publication, if he thought fit. He glanced through it hurriedly, mumbling all the time, judged 'it would do,' and took himself off with this plunder.

"Thus I was left at last with a slim packet of letters and the girl's portrait. She struck me as beautiful — I mean she had a beautiful expression. I know that the sunlight can be made to lie, too, yet one felt that no manipulation of light and pose could have conveyed the delicate shade of truthfulness upon those features. She seemed ready to listen without mental reservation, without suspicion, without a thought for herself. I concluded I would go and give her back her portrait and those letters myself. Curiosity? Yes; and also some other feeling perhaps. All that had been Kurtz's had passed out of my hands: his soul, his body, his station, his plans, his ivory, his career. There remained only his memory and his Intended — and I wanted to give that up, too, to the past, in a way — to surrender personally all that remained of him with me to that oblivion which is the last word of our common fate. I don't defend myself. I had no clear perception of what it was I really wanted. Perhaps it was an impulse of unconscious loyalty, or the fulfilment of one of those ironic necessities that lurk in the facts of human existence. I don't know. I can't tell. But I went.

"I thought his memory was like the other memories of the dead that accumulate in every man's life — a vague impress on the brain of shadows that had fallen on it in their swift and final passage; but before the high and ponderous door, between the tall houses of a street as still and decorous as a well-kept alley in a cemetery, I had a vision of him on the stretcher, opening his mouth voraciously, as if to devour all the earth with all its mankind. He lived then before me; he lived as much as he had ever lived — a shadow insatiable of splendid appearances, of frightful realities; a shadow darker than the shadow of the night, and draped nobly in the folds of a gorgeous eloquence. The vision seemed to enter the house with me — the stretcher, the phantom-bearers, the wild crowd of obedient worshippers, the gloom of the forests, the glitter of the reach between the murky bends, the beat of the drum, regular and muffled like the beating of a heart — the heart of a conquering darkness. It was a moment of triumph for the wilderness, an invading and vengeful rush which, it seemed to me, I would have to keep back alone for the salvation of another soul. And the memory of what I had heard him say afar there, with the horned shapes stirring at my back, in the glow of fires, within the patient woods, those broken phrases came back to me, were heard again in their ominous and terrifying simplicity. I remembered his abject pleading, his abject threats, the colossal scale of his vile desires, the meanness, the torment, the tempestuous anguish of his soul. And later on I seemed to see his collected languid manner, when he said one day, 'This lot of ivory now is really mine. The Company did not pay for it. I collected it myself at a very great personal risk. I am afraid they will try to claim it as theirs though. H'm. It is a difficult case. What do you think I ought to do — resist? Eh? I want no more than justice.' . . . He wanted no more than justice — no more than justice. I rang the bell before a mahogany door on the first floor, and while I waited he seemed to stare at me out of the glassy panel — stare with that wide and immense stare embracing, condemning, loathing all the universe. I seemed to hear the whispered cry, 'The horror! The horror!'

"The dusk was falling. I had to wait in a lofty drawing-room with three long windows from floor to ceiling that were like three luminous and bedraped columns. The bent gilt legs and backs of the furniture shone in indistinct curves. The tall marble fireplace had a cold and monumental whiteness. A grand piano stood massively in a corner; with dark gleams on the flat surfaces like a sombre and polished sarcophagus. A high door opened — closed. I rose.

"She came forward, all in black, with a pale head, floating towards me in the dusk. She was in mourning. It was more than a year since his death, more than a year since the news came; she seemed as though she would remember and mourn forever. She took both my hands in hers and murmured, 'I had heard you were coming.' I noticed she was not very young — I mean not girlish. She had a mature capacity for fidelity, for belief, for suffering. The room seemed to have grown darker, as if all the sad light of the cloudy evening had taken refuge on her forehead. This fair hair, this pale visage, this pure brow, seemed surrounded by an ashy halo from which the dark eyes looked out at me. Their glance was guileless, profound, confident, and trustful. She carried her sorrowful head as though she were proud of that sorrow, as though she would say, 'I — I alone know how to mourn for him as he deserves.' But while we were still shaking hands, such a look of awful desolation came upon her face that I perceived she was one of those creatures that are not the playthings of Time. For her he had died only yesterday. And, by Jove! the impression was so powerful that for me, too, he seemed to have died only yesterday — nay, this very minute. I saw her and him in the same instant of time — his death and her sorrow — I saw her sorrow in the very moment of his death. Do you understand? I saw them together — I heard them together. She had said, with a deep catch of the breath, 'I have survived' while my strained ears seemed to hear distinctly, mingled with her tone of despairing regret, the summing up whisper of his eternal condemnation. I asked myself what I was doing there, with a sensation of panic in my heart as though I had blundered into a place of cruel and absurd mysteries not fit for a human being to behold. She motioned me to a chair. We sat down. I laid the packet gently on the little table, and she put her hand over it. . . . 'You knew him well,' she murmured, after a moment of mourning silence.

" 'Intimacy grows quickly out there,' I said. 'I knew him as well as it is possible for one man to know another.'

" 'And you admired him,' she said. 'It was impossible to know him and not to admire him. Was it?'

" 'He was a remarkable man,' I said, unsteadily. Then before the appealing fixity of her gaze, that seemed to watch for more words on my lips, I went on, 'It was impossible not to ——'

" 'Love him,' she finished eagerly, silencing me into an appalled dumbness. 'How true! how true! But when you think that no one knew him so well as I! I had all his noble confidence. I knew him best.'

" 'You knew him best,' I repeated. And perhaps she did. But with every word spoken the room was growing darker, and only her forehead, smooth and white, remained illumined by the unextinguishable light of belief and love.

" 'You were his friend,' she went on. 'His friend,' she repeated, a little louder. 'You must have been, if he had given you this, and sent you to me. I feel I can speak to you — and oh! I must speak. I want you — you who have heard his last words — to know I have been worthy of him. . . . It is not pride. . . . Yes! I am proud to know I understood him better than any one on earth — he told me so himself. And since his mother died I have had no one — no one — to — to ——'

"I listened. The darkness deepened. I was not even sure whether he had given me the right bundle. I rather suspect he wanted me to take care of another batch of his papers which, after his death, I saw the manager examining under the lamp. And the girl talked, easing her pain in the certitude of my sympathy; she talked as thirsty men drink. I had heard that her engagement with Kurtz had been disapproved by her people. He wasn't rich enough or something. And indeed I don't know whether he had not been a pauper all his life. He had given me some reason to infer that it was his impatience of comparative poverty that drove him out there.

" '. . . Who was not his friend who had heard him speak once?' she was saying. 'He drew men towards him by what was best in them.' She looked at me with intensity. 'It is the gift of the great,' she went on, and the sound of her low voice seemed to have the accompaniment of all the other sounds, full of mystery, desolation, and sorrow, I had ever heard — the ripple of the river, the soughing of the trees swayed by the wind, the murmurs of the crowds, the faint ring of incomprehensible words cried from afar, the whisper of a voice speaking from beyond the threshold of an eternal darkness. 'But you have heard him! You know!' she cried.

" 'Yes, I know,' I said with something like despair in my heart, but bowing my head before the faith that was in her, before that great and saving illusion that shone with an unearthly glow in the darkness, in the triumphant darkness from which I could not have defended her — from which I could not even defend myself.

" 'What a loss to me — to us!' — she corrected herself with beautiful generosity; then added in a murmur, 'To the world.' By the last gleams of twilight I could see the glitter of her eyes, full of tears — of tears that would not fall.

" 'I have been very happy — very fortunate — very proud,' she went on. 'Too fortunate. Too happy for a little while. And now I am unhappy for — for life.'

"She stood up; her fair hair seemed to catch all the remaining light in a glimmer of gold. I rose, too.

" 'And of all this,' she went on mournfully, 'of all his promise, and of all his greatness, of his generous mind, of his noble heart, nothing remains — nothing but a memory. You and I ——'

" 'We shall always remember him,' I said hastily.

" 'No!' she cried. 'It is impossible that all this should be lost — that such a life should be sacrificed to leave nothing — but sorrow. You know what vast plans he had. I knew of them, too — I could not perhaps understand — but others knew of them. Something must remain. His words, at least, have not died.'

" 'His words will remain,' I said.

" 'And his example,' she whispered to herself. 'Men looked up to him — his goodness shone in every act. His example ——'

" 'True,' I said; 'his example, too. Yes, his example. I forgot that.'

" 'But I do not. I cannot — I cannot believe — not yet. I cannot believe that I shall never see him again, that nobody will see him again, never, never, never.'

"She put out her arms as if after a retreating figure, stretching them back and with clasped pale hands across the fading and narrow sheen of the window. Never see him! I saw him clearly enough then. I shall see this eloquent phantom as long as I live, and I shall see her, too, a tragic and familiar Shade, resembling in this gesture another one, tragic also, and bedecked with powerless charms, stretching bare brown arms over the glitter of the infernal stream, the stream of darkness. She said suddenly very low, 'He died as he lived.'

" 'His end,' said I, with dull anger stirring in me, 'was in every way worthy of his life.'

" 'And I was not with him,' she murmured. My anger subsided before a feeling of infinite pity.

" 'Everything that could be done ——' I mumbled.

" 'Ah, but I believed in him more than any one on earth — more than his own mother, more than — himself. He needed me! Me! I would have treasured every sigh, every word, every sign, every glance.'

"I felt like a chill grip on my chest. 'Don't,' I said, in a muffled voice.

" 'Forgive me. I — I have mourned so long in silence — in silence. . . . You were with him — to the last? I think of his loneliness. Nobody near to understand him as I would have understood. Perhaps no one to hear. . . .'

" 'To the very end,' I said, shakily. 'I heard his very last words. . . .' I stopped in a fright.

" 'Repeat them,' she murmured in a heart-broken tone. 'I want — I want — something — something — to — to live with.'

"I was on the point of crying at her, 'Don't you hear them?' The dusk was repeating them in a persistent whisper all around us, in a whisper that seemed to swell menacingly like the first whisper of a rising wind. 'The horror! The horror!'

" 'His last word — to live with,' she insisted. 'Don't you understand I loved him — I loved him — I loved him!'

"I pulled myself together and spoke slowly.

" 'The last word he pronounced was — your name.'

"I heard a light sigh and then my heart stood still, stopped dead short by an exulting and terrible cry, by the cry of inconceivable triumph and of unspeakable pain. 'I knew it — I was sure!' . . . She knew. She was sure. I heard her weeping; she had hidden her face in her hands. It seemed to me that the house would collapse before I could escape, that the heavens would fall upon my head. But nothing happened. The heavens do not fall for such a trifle. Would they have fallen, I wonder, if I had rendered Kurtz that justice which was his due? Hadn't he said he wanted only justice? But I couldn't. I could not tell her. It would have been too dark — too dark altogether. . . ."

Marlow ceased, and sat apart, indistinct and silent, in the pose of a meditating Buddha. Nobody moved for a time. "We have lost the first of the ebb," said the Director suddenly. I raised my head. The offing was barred by a black bank of clouds, and the tranquil waterway leading to the uttermost ends of the earth flowed sombre under an overcast sky — seemed to lead into the heart of an immense darkness.

AFTERWORD

Midway in *Heart of Darkness* Marlow uses an astounding image to describe his arduous quest: "The approach to this Kurtz grubbing for ivory in the wretched bush was beset by as many dangers as though he had been an enchanted princess sleeping in a fabulous castle." What is immediately astounding is the comparison of Kurtz — at this stage a grubber and later described as one who engaged in "devilish" practices — to an enchanted princess, with implications of innocence and tranquility. Perhaps we are astounded, too, for a moment, by the introduction of the idea of a fairy-tale world, for we have been reading an account of a search in a place that, although geographically remote and sometimes associated with romance, is described here in realistic and sordid detail. Much of the book is devoted to what Conrad later called "the vilest scramble for loot that ever disfigured the history of human conscience and geographical exploration." Many passages in *Heart of Darkness* ring with similar indignation; for the moment, one example will have to serve for all:

> This devoted band called itself the Eldorado Exploring Expedition, and I believe they were sworn to secrecy. Their talk, however, was the talk of sordid buccaneers: it was reckless without hardihood, greedy without audacity, and cruel without courage; there was not an atom of foresight or of serious intention in the whole batch of them, and they did not seem aware that these things are wanted for the work of the world. To tear treasure out of the bowels of the land was their desire, with no more moral purpose at the back of it than there is in burglars breaking into a safe.

And yet, while reading *Heart of Darkness*, one is continually aware that one is also reading about matters other than the rapacious colonization of Africa. If we were reading the story in its first appearance in book form, *Youth . . . and Two Other Stories* (1902), the epigraph from Grimm's Fairy Tales that Conrad prefixed to this book might have alerted us that the story is not merely history with some names changed, but art, with symbolic and moral implications: "But the dwarf answered: No; something human is dearer to me than the wealth of all the world." Throughout *Heart of Darkness* Conrad gives us both the realist's detail (the smell of rotting hippo, etc.) and the fabulist's halo of implications. Thus, the arduous journey takes Marlow past rusted useless vehicles, dying men, stupid men, all described in convincing detail, and it is at the same time a kind of mysterious descent to the underworld in a quest for knowledge, a "travelling back to the earliest beginnings of the world." Marlow himself suggests the literal and symbolic implications in the journey: it "was the farthest point of navigation and the culminating point of my experience." Occasionally the symbolism is highly explicit (Kurtz's "mother was half-English, his father was half-French. All Europe contributed to the making of Kurtz"), and shortly after revising the story for publication in book form, he confided to his publisher that he had committed "the fault of having made Kurtz too symbolic or rather symbolic at all." Not every reader will agree.

Despite his uneasy confession, for Conrad there was usually no incompatibility between the demands of realism and the symbolic quality of literature if symbolism is taken in the sense of the Victorian sage Thomas Carlyle: in a symbol, Carlyle said, "the Infinite is made to blend itself with the Finite, to stand visible, and as it were, attainable there." Here is Conrad on literary inventions, fictions, as the presentation of the real and through it the attainment of what is otherwise invisible:

> Fiction is history, human history, or it is nothing. But it is also more than that; it stands on firmer ground, being based on the reality of forms and the observation of social phenomena, whereas history is based on documents, and the reading of print and handwriting — on second-hand impression.

Another, and only slightly different, way of putting it is to say that fiction is not the rendering of an invisible world but is the fairest treatment, the fullest revelation, of the visible world:

> Art itself may be defined as a single-minded attempt to render the highest kind of justice to the visible universe, by bringing to light the truth, manifold and one, underlying its every aspect. It is an attempt to find in its forms, in its colours, in its light, in its shadows, in the aspects of matter and in the facts of life, what of each is fundamental, what is enduring and essential — their one illuminating and convincing quality — the very truth of their existence.

And yet one more quotation from Conrad on art, again calling attention to art as a revelation of implications:

> My task which I am trying to achieve is, by the power of the written word, to make you hear, to make you feel — it is, before all, to make you *see*.

Some of the implications of the word "task" in this quotation and the expression "single-minded attempt" in the previous quotation will be touched on in a moment, but first it may be appropriate to say that *Heart of Darkness*, then, is not only the detailed story of a man's adventure in the Congo, and an indictment of Europe's assault on Africa, but it is also a revelation of certain facts (as Conrad saw them) of human nature. Briefly, Conrad's central character Marlow learns to understand himself through Kurtz (and we learn to understand ourselves through Marlow's story); in the voyage into Africa and the simultaneous voyage into the deepest recesses of the self he learns of man's enormous capacity for wickedness. Kurtz, too, learned about himself, for the last words of this degraded man were a moral judgment: "The horror! The horror!"

Shortly after the Congo voyage, when Conrad was recuperating from the diseases he had encountered there, he received an earnest letter from a relative adjuring him "to avoid all meditations which lead to pessimistic conclusions." Conrad could scarcely stop meditating, but *Heart of Darkness* shows us that his vision of man is not one of unmitigated pessimism. We can put aside the somewhat puzzling material near the end of the story, where the woman, Kurtz's "Intended," is preserved in her innocence by Marlow's lie. (Are we convinced that Marlow is being loyal to Kurtz because Kurtz had finally won "a moral victory"? Or is Conrad weaseling on his earlier commitment to the truth? Or is the Intended unworthy of knowing the truth? Or does this "pure brow" indeed deserve to be exempted from needless suffering?) In many passages in *Heart of Darkness* Marlow emphasizes duty, an unselfish belief in service, and — another way of putting it — "restraint," no matter how severe the pressures. Putting aside fools who are too dull to know that they are being "assaulted by the powers of darkness," and "exalted creatures" who are "deaf and blind to anything but heavenly sights," "the earth for us is a place to live in, where we must put up with sights, with sounds, with smells, too, by Jove! — breathe dead hippo, so to speak, and not be contaminated. And there, don't you see? Your strength comes in, the faith in your ability for the digging of unostentatious holes to bury the stuff in — your power of devotion, not to yourself, to an obscure, back-breaking business." True, some of Conrad's pictures of people devoted to "obscure, back-breaking business" include ironic elements. For example, the accountant's books commendably "were in apple-pie order," but it is hard to admire him unequivocally when he complains that "the groans of this sick person distract my attention." Yet it is clear that Conrad has genuine reverence for Towson's *Inquiry into Some Points of Seamanship,* whose pages, concerned with "the breaking strain of ships' chains and tackle, and other such matters," displayed "a singleness of intention, an honest concern for the right way of going to work, which made these humble pages . . . luminous with another than a professional light."

We can connect "the right way of going to *work*" with the passages quoted earlier about the writer's "single-minded attempt" and his "task." There is something very Victorian about Conrad's — and Marlow's — emphasis on salvation through work. (That we admire the achievements of Conrad and of many of his immediate predecessors in the novel is, of course, telling evidence that Victorianism is not contemptible.) By the latter part of the nineteenth century the Puritan emphasis on the divinely ordained necessity of unselfish work had (for many people) lost its theological force, but dedication to unselfish work remained a code of behavior, often the only code for those who could no longer believe in God. Early in *Heart of Darkness* it is work — the sheer business of salvaging the ship and of protecting it from attack — that keeps Marlow sane and alive. This attention to surface reality does not lead to the deepest wisdom, but it keeps him going, and going decently in a world where most of the white people have yielded to slovenliness — not only of behavior but of morals, as we see most easily in the Eldorado Exploring Expedition. Against this omnipresent flaccid evil — and later against the vigorous evil of Kurtz — Conrad juxtaposes fidelity to an ideal. He is fully aware that most colonizing is "merely a squeeze," "robbery with violence, aggravated murder on a great scale"; but at moments "what redeems it is the idea only. An idea at the back of it; not a sentimental pretence but an idea; and an unselfish belief in the idea — something you can set up, and bow down before, and offer a sacrifice to. . . ."

That Conrad himself held in reverence the "idea" of service through writing cannot be doubted. He gave to the task of creating fictions the same sort of patient dedication that Towson gave to his *Inquiry into Some Points of Seamanship*, and the same sort of patient dedication that earlier earned him his master's certificate in the British merchant service. The writer, he said, "descends within himself," into a "lonely region of stress and strife" which, apparently, is not very remote from a voyage into the heart of darkness. Although thoughtless people may believe that a writer is a trifler, Conrad spoke from experience when he said that writing was "hard labor for life," but it was labor made meaningful by an idea.

FRANZ KAFKA

Franz Kafka (1883–1924), the son of a wealthy Jewish merchant, was born in Prague (then the capital of Bohemia, part of the Austrian Empire), where he attended the German school and eventually the German university, receiving a doctorate of jurisprudence in 1906. From 1908 he held a position in the Workers Accident Insurance, a semigovernmental institution, which allowed him time to write, an activity that his authoritarian father opposed. (All of his stories, he said, were attempts to escape from his father.) Kafka longed for integration into society through marriage, but a deep distrust of himself kept him unmarried, although he was engaged three times. Never of robust health, by 1917 his sickness was diagnosed as tuberculosis, and for the next seven years he traveled from one sanatorium to another. He continued to write fables, short stories, and novels, though most of the works he is best known for were not published until after his death when his friend Max Brod disregarded Kafka's request to destroy all the work that Kafka himself had not. Among his most important works are two short novels, *In the Penal Colony* (1914) and *The Metamorphosis* (1915, but translated into English only in 1937), and three longer novels, *The Trial* (1925), *The Castle* (1926), and *Amerika* (1927).

THE METAMORPHOSIS

Translated by Edwin Muir

I

As Gregor Samsa awoke one morning from uneasy dreams he found himself transformed in his bed into a gigantic insect. He was lying on his hard, as it were armor-plated, back and when he lifted his head a little he could see his dome-like brown belly divided into stiff arched segments on top of which the bed quilt could hardly keep in position and was about to slide off completely. His numerous legs, which were pitifully thin compared to the rest of his bulk, waved helplessly before his eyes.

What has happened to me? he thought. It was no dream. His room, a regular human bedroom, only rather too small, lay quiet between the four familiar walls. Above the table on which a collection of cloth samples was unpacked and spread out — Samsa was a commercial traveler[1] — hung the picture which he had recently cut out of an illustrated magazine and put into a pretty gilt frame. It showed a lady, with a fur cap on and a fur stole, sitting upright and holding out to the spectator a huge fur muff into which the whole of her forearm had vanished!

Gregor's eyes turned next to the window, and the overcast sky — one could hear rain drops beating on the window gutter — made him quite melancholy. What about sleeping a little longer and forgetting all this nonsense, he thought, but it could not be done, for he was accustomed to sleep on his right side and in his present condition he could not turn himself over. However violently he forced himself towards his right side he always rolled on to his back again. He tried it at least a hundred times, shutting his eyes to keep from seeing his struggling legs, and only desisted when he began to feel in his side a faint dull ache he had never experienced before.

Oh God, he thought, what an exhausting job I've picked on! Traveling

1 [Traveling salesman. — Editors' note.]

about day in, day out. It's much more irritating work than doing the actual business in the office, and on top of that there's the trouble of constant traveling, of worrying about train connections, the bed and irregular meals, casual acquaintances that are always new and never become intimate friends. The devil take it all! He felt a slight itching up on his belly; slowly pushed himself on his back nearer to the top of the bed so that he could lift his head more easily; identified the itching place which was surrounded by many small white spots the nature of which he could not understand and made to touch it with a leg, but drew the leg back immediately, for the contact made a cold shiver run through him.

He slid down again into his former position. This getting up early, he thought, makes one quite stupid. A man needs his sleep. Other commercials live like harem women. For instance, when I come back to the hotel of a morning to write up the orders I've got, these others are only sitting down to breakfast. Let me just try that with my chief; I'd be sacked on the spot. Anyhow, that might be quite a good thing for me, who can tell? If I didn't have to hold my hand because of my parents I'd have given notice long ago, I'd have gone to the chief and told him exactly what I think of him. That would knock him endways from his desk! It's a queer way of doing, too, this sitting on high at a desk and talking down to employees, especially when they have to come quite near because the chief is hard of hearing. Well, there's still hope; once I've saved enough money to pay back my parents' debts to him — that should take another five or six years — I'll do it without fail. I'll cut myself completely loose then. For the moment, though, I'd better get up, since my train goes at five.

He looked at the alarm clock ticking on the chest. Heavenly Father! he thought. It was half-past six o'clock and the hands were quietly moving on, it was even past the half-hour, it was getting on toward a quarter to seven. Had the alarm clock not gone off? From the bed one could see that it had been properly set for four o'clock; of course it must have gone off. Yes, but was it possible to sleep quietly through that ear-splitting noise? Well, he had not slept quietly, yet apparently all the more soundly for that. But what was he to do now? The next train went at seven o'clock; to catch that he would need to hurry like mad and his samples weren't even packed up, and he himself wasn't feeling particularly fresh and active. And even if he did catch the train he wouldn't avoid a row with the chief, since the firm's porter would have been waiting for the five o'clock train and would have long since reported his failure to turn up. The porter was a creature of the chief's, spineless and stupid. Well, supposing he were to say he was sick? But that would be most unpleasant and would look suspicious, since during his five years' employment he had not been ill once. The chief himself would be sure to come with the sick-insurance doctor, would reproach his parents with their son's laziness and would cut all excuses short by referring to the insurance doctor, who of course regarded all mankind as perfectly healthy malingerers. And would he be so far wrong on this occasion? Gregor really felt quite well, apart from a drowsiness that was utterly superfluous after such a long sleep, and he was even unusually hungry.

As all this was running through his mind at top speed without his being able to decide to leave his bed — the alarm clock had just struck a quarter to seven — there came a cautious tap at the door behind the head of his bed. "Gregor," said a voice — it was his mother's — "it's a quarter to seven. Hadn't you a train to catch?" That gentle voice! Gregor had a shock as he heard his own voice answering hers, unmistakably his own voice, it was true, but with a persistent horrible twittering squeak behind it like an undertone, that left the words in their clear shape only for the first moment and then rose up reverberating round them to destroy their sense, so that one could not be sure one had heard them rightly. Gregor wanted to answer at length and explain everything, but in the circumstances he confined himself to saying: "Yes, yes, thank you, Mother, I'm getting up now." The wooden door between them must have kept the change in his voice from being noticeable outside, for his mother contented herself with this statement and shuffled away. Yet this brief exchange of words had made the other members of the family aware that Gregor was still in the house, as they had not expected, and at one of the side doors his father was already knocking, gently, yet with his fist. "Gregor, Gregor," he called, "what's the matter with you?" And after a little while he called again in a deeper voice: "Gregor! Gregor!" At the other side door his sister was saying in a low, plaintive tone: "Gregor? Aren't you well? Are you needing anything?" He answered them both at once: "I'm just ready," and did his best to make his voice sound as normal as possible by enunciating the words very clearly and leaving long pauses between them. So his father went back to his breakfast, but his sister whispered: "Gregor, open the door, do." However, he was not thinking of opening the door, and felt thankful for the prudent habit he had acquired in traveling of locking all doors during the night, even at home.

His immediate intention was to get up quietly without being disturbed, to put on his clothes and above all eat his breakfast, and only then to consider what else was to be done, since in bed, he was well aware, his meditations would come to no sensible conclusion. He remembered that often enough in bed he had felt small aches and pains, probably caused by awkward postures, which had proved purely imaginary once he got up, and he looked forward eagerly to seeing this morning's delusions gradually fall away. That the change in his voice was nothing but the precursor of a severe chill, a standing ailment of commercial travelers, he had not the least possible doubt.

To get rid of the quilt was quite easy; he had only to inflate himself a little and it fell off by itself. But the next move was difficult, especially because he was so uncommonly broad. He would have needed arms and hands to hoist himself up; instead he had only the numerous little legs which never stopped waving in all directions and which he could not control in the least. When he tried to bend one of them it was the first to stretch itself straight; and did he succeed at last in making it do what he wanted, all the other legs meanwhile waved the more wildly in a high degree of unpleasant agitation. "But what's the use of lying idle in bed," said Gregor to himself.

He thought that he might get out of bed with the lower part of his body first, but this lower part, which he had not yet seen and of which he could form no clear conception, proved too difficult to move; it shifted so slowly; and when finally, almost wild with annoyance, he gathered his forces together and thrust out recklessly, he had miscalculated the direction and bumped heavily against the lower end of the bed, and the stinging pain he felt informed him that precisely this lower part of his body was at the moment probably the most sensitive.

So he tried to get the top part of himself out first, and cautiously moved his head towards the edge of the bed. That proved easy enough, and despite its breadth and mass bulk of his body at last slowly followed the movement of his head. Still, when he finally got his head free over the edge of the bed he felt too scared to go on advancing, for after all if he let himself fall in this way it would take a miracle to keep his head from being injured. And at all costs he must not lose consciousness now, precisely now; he would rather stay in bed.

But when after a repetition of the same efforts he lay in his former position again, sighing, and watched his little legs struggling against each other more wildly than ever, if that were possible, and saw no way of bringing any order into this arbitrary confusion, he told himself again that it was impossible to stay in bed and that the most sensible course was to risk everything for the smallest hope of getting away from it. At the same time he did not forget meanwhile to remind himself that cool reflection, the coolest possible, was much better than desperate resolves. In such moments he focused his eyes as sharply as possible on the window, but, unfortunately, the prospect of the morning fog, which muffled even the other side of the narrow street, brought him little encouragement and comfort. "Seven o'clock already," he said to himself when the alarm clock chimed again, "seven o'clock already and still such a thick fog." And for a little while he lay quiet, breathing lightly, as if perhaps expecting such complete repose to restore all things to their real and normal condition.

But then he said to himself: "Before it strikes a quarter past seven I must be quite out of this bed, without fail. Anyhow, by that time someone will have come from the office to ask for me, since it opens before seven." And he set himself to rocking his whole body at once in a regular rhythm, with the idea of swinging it out of the bed. If he tipped himself out in that way he could keep his head from injury by lifting it at an acute angle when he fell. His back seemed to be hard and was not likely to suffer from a fall on the carpet. His biggest worry was the loud crash he would not be able to help making, which would probably cause anxiety, if not terror, behind all the doors. Still, he must take the risk.

When he was already half out of the bed — the new method was more a game than an effort, for he needed only to hitch himself across by rocking to and fro — it struck him how simple it would be if he could get help. Two strong people — he thought of his father and the servant girl — would be amply sufficient; they would only have to thrust their arms under his convex back, lever him out of the bed, bend down with their burden and then be patient enough to let him turn himself right over on to the floor, where it was to be hoped his legs would then find their proper function. Well, ignoring the fact that the doors were all locked, ought he really to call for help? In spite of his misery he could not suppress a smile at the very idea of it.

He had got so far that he could barely keep his equilibrium when he rocked himself strongly, and he would have to nerve himself very soon for the final decision since in five minutes' time it would be a quarter past seven — when the front door bell rang. "That's someone from the office," he said to himself, and grew almost rigid, while his little legs only jigged about all the faster. For a moment everything stayed quiet. "They're not going to open the door," said Gregor to himself, catching at some kind of irrational hope. But then of course the servant girl went as usual to the door with her heavy tread and opened it. Gregor needed only to hear the first good morning of the visitor to know immediately who it was — the chief clerk himself. What a fate, to be condemned to work for a firm where the smallest omission at once gave rise to the gravest suspicion! Were all employees in a body nothing but scoundrels, was there not among them one single loyal devoted man who, had he wasted only an hour or so of the firm's time in a morning, was so tormented by conscience as to be driven out of his mind and actually incapable of leaving his bed? Wouldn't it really have been sufficient to send an apprentice to inquire — if any inquiry were necessary at all — did the chief clerk himself have to come and thus indicate to the entire family, an innocent family, that this suspicious circumstance could be investigated by no one less versed in affairs than himself? And more through the agitation caused by these reflections than through any act of will Gregor swung himself out of bed with all his strength. There was a loud thump, but it was not really a crash. His fall was broken to some extent by the carpet, his back, too, was less stiff than he thought, and so there was merely a dull thud, not so very startling. Only he had not lifted his head carefully enough and had hit it; he turned it and rubbed it on the carpet in pain and irritation.

"That was something falling down in there," said the chief clerk in the next room to the left. Gregor tried to suppose to himself that something like what had happened to him today might some day happen to the chief clerk; one really could not deny that it was possible. But as if in brusque reply to this supposition the chief clerk took a couple of firm steps in the next-door room and his patent leather boots creaked. From the right-hand room his sister was whispering to inform him of the situation: "Gregor, the chief clerk's here." "I know," muttered Gregor to himself; but he didn't dare to make his voice loud enough for his sister to hear it.

"Gregor," said his father now from the left-hand room, "the chief clerk has come and wants to know why you didn't catch the early train. We don't know what to say to him. Besides, he wants to talk to you in person. So open the door, please. He will be good enough to excuse the untidiness of your room." "Good morning, Mr. Samsa," the chief clerk was calling amiably meanwhile. "He's not well," said his mother to the visitor, while his father was still speaking through the door, "he's not well, sir, believe me. What else would make him miss a train! The boy thinks about nothing but his work. It makes me almost cross the way he never goes out in the evenings; he's been here the last eight days and has stayed at home every single evening. He just sits there quietly at the table reading a newspaper or looking through railway timetables. The only amusement he gets is doing fretwork. For instance, he spent two or three evenings cutting out a little picture frame; you would be surprised to see how pretty it is; it's hanging in his room; you'll see it in a minute when Gregor opens the door. I must say I'm glad you've come, sir; we should never have got him to unlock the door by ourselves; he's so obstinate; and I'm sure he's unwell, though he wouldn't have it to be so this morning." "I'm just coming," said Gregor slowly and carefully, not moving an inch for fear of losing one word of the conversation. "I can't think of any other explanation, madam," said the chief clerk, "I hope it's nothing serious. Although on the other hand I must say that we men of business — fortunately or unfortunately — very often simply have to ignore any slight indisposition, since business must be attended to." "Well, can the chief clerk come in now?" asked Gregor's father impatiently, again knocking on the door. "No," said Gregor. In the left-hand room a painful silence followed this refusal, in the right-hand room his sister began to sob.

Why didn't his sister join the others? She was probably newly out of bed and hadn't even begun to put on her clothes yet. Well, why was she crying? Because he wouldn't get up and let the chief clerk in, because he was in danger of losing his job, and because the chief would begin dunning his parents again for the old debts? Surely these were things one didn't need to worry about for the present. Gregor was still at home and not in the least thinking of deserting the family. At the moment, true, he was lying on the carpet and no one who knew the condition he was in could seriously expect him to admit the chief clerk. But for such a small discourtesy, which could plausibly be explained away somehow later on, Gregor could hardly be dismissed on the spot. And it seemed to Gregor that it would be much more sensible to leave him in peace for the present than to trouble him with tears and entreaties. Still, of course, their uncertainty bewildered them all and excused their behavior.

"Mr. Samsa," the chief clerk called now in a louder voice, "what's the matter with you? Here you are, barricading yourself in your room, giving only 'yes' and 'no' for answers, causing your parents a lot of unnecessary trouble and neglecting — I mention this only in passing — neglecting your business duties in an incredible fashion. I am speaking here in the name of your parents and of your chief, and I beg you quite seriously to give me an immediate and precise explanation. You amaze me, you amaze me. I thought you were a quiet, dependable person, and now all at once you seem bent on making a disgraceful exhibition of yourself. The chief did hint to me early this morning a possible explanation for your disappearance — with reference to the cash payments that were entrusted to you recently — but I almost pledged my solemn word of honor that this could not be so. But now that I see how incredibly obstinate you are, I no longer have the slightest desire to take your part at all. And your position in the firm is not so unassailable. I came with the intention of telling you all this in private, but since you are wasting my time so needlessly I don't see why your parents shouldn't hear it too. For some time past your work has been most unsatisfactory; this is not the season of the year for a business boom, of course, we admit that, but a season of the year for doing no business at all, that does not exist, Mr. Samsa, must not exist."

"But, sir," cried Gregor, beside himself and in his agitation forgetting everything else, "I'm just going to open the door this very minute. A slight illness, an attack of giddiness, has kept me from getting up. I'm still lying in bed. But I feel all right again. I'm getting out of bed now. Just give me a moment or two longer! I'm not quite so well as I thought. But I'm all right, really. How a thing like that can suddenly strike one down! Only last night I was quite well, my parents can tell you, or rather I did have a slight presentiment. I must have showed some sign of it. Why didn't I report it at the office! But one always thinks that an indisposition can be got over without staying in the house. Oh sir, do spare my parents! All that you're reproaching me with now has no foundation; no one has ever said a word to me about it. Perhaps you haven't looked at the last orders I sent in. Anyhow, I can still catch the eight o'clock train, I'm much the better for my few hours' rest. Don't let me detain you here, sir; I'll be attending to business very soon, and do be good enough to tell the chief so and to make my excuses to him!"

And while all this was tumbling out pell-mell and Gregor hardly knew what he was saying, he had reached the chest quite easily, perhaps because of the practice he had had in bed, and was now trying to lever himself upright by means of it. He meant actually to open the door, actually to show himself and speak to the chief clerk; he was eager to find out what the others, after all their insistence, would say at the sight of him. If they were horrified then the responsibility was no longer his and he could stay quiet. But if they took it calmly, then he had no reason either to be upset, and could really get to the station for the eight o'clock train if he hurried. At first he slipped down a few times from the polished surface of the chest, but at length with a last heave he stood upright; he paid no more attention to the pains in the lower part of his body, however they smarted. Then he let himself fall against the back of a near-by chair, and clung with his little legs to the edges of it. That brought him into control of himself again and he stopped speaking, for now he could listen to what the chief clerk was saying.

"Did you understand a word of it?" the chief clerk was asking; "surely he can't be trying to make fools of us?" "Oh dear," cried his mother, in tears, "perhaps he's terribly ill and we're tormenting him. Grete! Grete!" she called out then. "Yes Mother?" called his sister from the other side. They were calling to each other across Gregor's room. "You must go this minute for the doctor. Gregor is ill. Go for the doctor, quick. Did you hear how he was speaking?" "That was no human voice," said the chief clerk in a voice noticeably low beside the shrillness of the mother's. "Anna! Anna!" his father was calling through the hall to the kitchen, clapping his hands, "get a locksmith at once!" And the two girls were already running through the hall with a swish of skirts — how could his sister have got dressed so quickly? — and were tearing the front door open. There was no sound of its closing again; they had evidently left it open, as one docs in houses where some great misfortune has happened.

But Gregor was now much calmer. The words he uttered were no longer understandable, apparently, although they seemed clear enough to him, even clearer than before, perhaps because his ear had grown accustomed to the sound of them. Yet at any rate people now believed that something was wrong with him, and were ready to help him. The positive certainty with which these first measures had been taken comforted him. He felt himself drawn once more into the human circle and hoped for great and remarkable results from both the doctor and the locksmith, without really distinguishing precisely between them. To make his voice as clear as possible for the decisive conversation that was now imminent he coughed a little, as quietly as he could, of course, since this noise too might not sound like a human cough for all he was able to judge. In the next room meanwhile there was complete silence. Perhaps his parents were sitting at the table with the chief clerk, whispering, perhaps they were all leaning against the door and listening.

Slowly Gregor pushed the chair towards the door, then let go of it, caught hold of the door for support — the soles at the end of his little legs were somewhat sticky — and rested against it for a moment after his efforts. Then he set himself to turning the key in the lock with his mouth. It seemed, unhappily, that he hadn't really any teeth — what could he grip the key with? — but on the other hand his jaws were certainly very strong; with their help he did manage to set the key in motion, heedless of the fact that he was undoubtedly damaging them somewhere, since a brown fluid issued from his mouth, flowed over the key and dripped on the floor. "Just listen to that," said the chief clerk next door; "he's turning the key." That was a great encouragement to Gregor; but they should all have shouted encouragement to him, his father and mother too: "Go on, Gregor," they should have called out, "keep going, hold on to that key!" And in the belief that they were all following his efforts intently, he clenched his jaws recklessly on the key with all the force at his command. As the turning of the key progressed he circled round the lock, holding on now only with his mouth, pushing on the key, as required, or pulling it down again with all the weight of his body. The louder click of the finally yielding lock literally quickened Gregor. With a deep breath of relief he said to himself: "So I didn't need the locksmith," and laid his head on the handle to open the door wide.

Since he had to pull the door towards him, he was still invisible when it was really wide open. He had to edge himself slowly round the near half of the double door, and to do it very carefully if he was not to fall plump upon his back just on the threshold. He was still carrying out this difficult manoeuvre, with no time to observe anything else, when he heard the chief clerk utter a loud "Oh!" — it sounded like a gust of wind — and now he could see the man, standing as he was nearest to the door, clapping one hand before his open mouth and slowly backing away as if driven by some invisible steady pressure. His mother — in spite of the chief clerk's being there her hair was still undone and sticking up in all directions — first clasped her hands and looked at his father, then took two steps towards Gregor and fell on the floor among her outspread skirts, her face quite hidden on her breast. His father knotted his fist with a fierce expression on his face as if he meant to knock Gregor back into his room, then looked uncertainly round the living room, covered his eyes with his hands and wept till his great chest heaved.

Gregor did not go now into the living room, but leaned against the inside of the firmly shut wing of the door, so that only half his body was visible and his head above it bending sideways to look at the others. The light had meanwhile strengthened; on the other side of the street one could see clearly a section of the endlessly long, dark gray building opposite — it was a hospital — abruptly punctuated by its row of regular windows; the rain was still falling, but only in large singly discernible and literally singly splashing drops. The breakfast dishes were set out on the table lavishly, for breakfast was the most important meal of the day to Gregor's father, who lingered it out for hours over various newspapers. Right opposite Gregor on the wall hung a photograph of himself on military service, as a lieutenant, hand on sword, a carefree smile on his face, inviting one to respect his uniform and military bearing. The door leading to the hall was open, and one could see that the front door stood open too, showing the landing beyond and the beginning of the stairs going down.

"Well," said Gregor, knowing perfectly that he was the only one who had retained any composure, "I'll put my clothes on at once, pack up my samples and start off. Will you only let me go? You see, sir, I'm not obstinate, and I'm willing to work; traveling is a hard life, but I couldn't live without it. Where are you going, sir? To the office? Yes? Will you give a true account of all this? One can be temporarily incapacitated, but that's just the moment for remembering former services and bearing in mind that later on, when the incapacity has been got over, one will certainly work with all the more industry and concentration. I'm loyally bound to serve the chief, you know that very well. Besides, I have to provide for my parents and my sister. I'm in great difficulties, but I'll get out of them again. Don't make things any worse for me than they are. Stand up for me in the firm. Travelers are not popular there, I know. People think they earn sacks of money and just have a good time. A prejudice there's no particular reason for revising. But you, sir, have a more comprehensive view of affairs than the rest of the staff, yes, let me tell you in confidence, a more comprehensive view than the chief himself, who, being the owner, lets his judgment easily be swayed against one of his employees. And you know very well that the traveler, who is never seen in the office almost the whole year round, can so easily fall a victim to gossip and ill luck and unfounded complaints, which he mostly knows nothing about, except when he comes back exhausted from his rounds, and only then suffers in person from their evil consequences, which he can no longer trace back to the original causes. Sir, sir, don't go away without a word to me to show that you think me in the right at least to some extent!"

But at Gregor's very first words the chief clerk had already backed away and only stared at him with parted lips over one twitching shoulder. And while Gregor was speaking he did not stand still one moment but stole away towards the door, without taking his eyes off Gregor, yet only an inch at a time, as if obeying some secret injunction to leave the room. He was already at the hall, and the suddenness with which he took his last step out of the living room would have made one believe he had burned the sole of his foot. Once in the hall he stretched his right arm before him towards the staircase, as if some supernatural power were waiting there to deliver him.

Gregor perceived that the chief clerk must on no account be allowed to go away in this frame of mind if his position in the firm were not to be endangered to the utmost. His parents did not understand this so well; they had convinced themselves in the course of years that Gregor was settled for life in this firm, and besides they were so occupied with their immediate troubles that all foresight had forsaken them. Yet Gregor had this foresight. The chief clerk must be detained, soothed, persuaded and finally won over; the whole future of Gregor and his family depended on it! If only his sister had been there! She was intelligent; she had begun to cry while Gregor was still lying quietly on his back. And no doubt the chief clerk, so partial to ladies, would have been guided by her; she would have shut the door of the flat and in the hall talked him out of his horror. But she was not there, and Gregor would have to handle the situation himself. And without remembering that he was still unaware what powers of movement he possessed, without even remembering that his words in all possibility, indeed in all likelihood, would again be unintelligible, he let go the wing of the door, pushed himself through the opening, started to walk towards the chief clerk, who was already ridiculously clinging with both hands to the railing on the landing; but immediately, as he was feeling for a support, he fell down with a little cry upon all his numerous legs. Hardly was he down when he experienced for the first time this morning a sense of physical comfort; his legs had firm ground under them; they were completely obedient, as he noted with joy; they even strove to carry him forward in whatever direction he chose; and he was inclined to believe that a final relief from all his sufferings was at hand. But in the same moment as he found himself on the floor, rocking with suppressed eagerness to move, not far from his mother, indeed just in front of her, she, who had seemed so completely crushed, sprang all at once to her feet, her arms and fingers outspread, cried: "Help, for God's sake, help!" bent her head down as if to see Gregor better, yet on the contrary kept backing senselessly away; had quite forgotten that the laden table stood behind her; sat upon it hastily, as if in absence of mind, when she bumped into it; and seemed altogether unaware that the big coffee pot beside her was upset and pouring coffee in a flood over the carpet.

"Mother, Mother," said Gregor in a low voice, and looked up at her. The chief clerk, for the moment, had quite slipped from his mind; instead, he could not resist snapping his jaws together at the sight of the streaming coffee. That made his mother scream again, she fled from the table and fell into the arms of his father, who hastened to catch her. But Gregor had now no time to spare for his parents; the chief clerk was already on the stairs; with his chin on the banisters he was taking one last backward look. Gregor made a spring, to be as sure as possible of overtaking him; the chief clerk must have divined his intention, for he leaped down several steps and vanished; he was still yelling "Ugh!" and it echoed through the whole staircase.

Unfortunately, the flight of the chief clerk seemed completely to upset Gregor's father, who had remained relatively calm until now, for instead of running after the man himself, or at least not hindering Gregor in his pursuit, he seized in his right hand the walking stick which the chief clerk had left behind on a chair, together with a hat and greatcoat, snatched in his left hand a large newspaper from the table and began stamping his feet and flourishing the stick and the newspaper to drive Gregor back into his room. No entreaty of Gregor's availed, indeed no entreaty was even understood, however humbly he bent his head his father only stamped on the floor the more loudly. Behind his father his mother had torn open a window, despite the cold weather, and was leaning far out of it with her face in her hands. A strong draught set in from the street to the staircase, the window curtains blew in, the newspapers on the table fluttered, stray pages whisked over the floor. Pitilessly Gregor's father drove him back, hissing and crying "Shoo!" like a savage. But Gregor was quite unpracticed in walking backwards, it really was a slow business. If he only had a chance to turn round he could get back to his room at once, but he was afraid of exasperating his father by the slowness of such a rotation and at any moment the stick in his father's hand might hit him a fatal blow on the back or on the head. In the end, however, nothing else was left for him to do since to his horror he observed that in moving backwards he could not even control the direction he took; and so, keeping an anxious eye on his father all the time over his shoulder, he began to turn round as quickly as he could, which was in reality very slowly. Perhaps his father noted his good intentions, for he did not interfere except every now and then to help him in the manoeuvre from a distance with the point of the stick. If only he would have stopped making that unbearable hissing noise! It made Gregor quite lose his head. He had turned almost completely round when the hissing noise so distracted him that he even turned a little the wrong way again. But when at last his head was fortunately right in front of the doorway, it appeared that his body was too broad simply to get through the opening. His father, of course, in his present mood was far from thinking of such a thing as opening the other half of the door, to let Gregor have enough space. He had merely the fixed idea of driving Gregor back into his room as quickly as possible. He would never have suffered Gregor to make the circumstantial preparations for standing up on end and perhaps slipping his way through the door. Maybe he was now making more noise than ever to urge Gregor forward, as if no obstacle impeded him; to Gregor, anyhow, the noise in his rear sounded no longer like the voice of one single father; this was really no joke, and Gregor thrust himself — come what might — into the doorway. One side of his body rose up, he was tilted at an angle in the doorway, his flank was quite bruised, horrid blotches stained the white door, soon he was stuck fast and, left to himself, could not have moved at all, his legs on one side fluttered trembling in the air, those on the other were crushed painfully to the floor — when from behind his father gave him a strong push which was literally a deliverance and he flew far into the room, bleeding freely. The door was slammed behind him with the stick, and then at last there was silence.

II

Not until it was twilight did Gregor awake out of a deep sleep, more like a swoon than a sleep. He would certainly have waked up of his own accord not much later, for he felt himself sufficiently rested and well-slept, but it seemed to him as if a fleeting step and a cautious shutting of the door leading into the hall had aroused him. The electric lights in the street cast a pale sheen here and there on the ceiling and the upper surfaces of the furniture, but down below, where he lay, it was dark. Slowly, awkwardly trying out his feelers, which he now first learned to appreciate, he pushed his way to the door to see what had been happening there. His left side felt like one single long, unpleasantly tense scar, and he had actually to limp on his two rows of legs. One little leg, moreover, had been severely damaged in the course of that morning's events — it was almost a miracle that only one had been damaged — and trailed uselessly behind him.

He had reached the door before he discovered what had really drawn him to it: the smell of food. For there stood a basin filled with fresh milk in which floated little sops of white bread. He could almost have laughed with joy, since he was now still hungrier than in the morning, and he dipped his head almost over the eyes straight into the milk. But soon in disappointment he withdrew it again; not only did he find it difficult to feed because of his tender left side — and he could only feed with the palpitating collaboration of his whole body — he did not like the milk either, although milk had been his favorite drink and that was certainly why his sister had set it there for him, indeed it was almost with repulsion that he turned away from the basin and crawled back to the middle of the room.

He could see through the crack of the door that the gas was turned on in the living room, but while usually at this time his father made a habit of reading the afternoon newspaper in a loud voice to his mother and occasionally to his sister as well, not a sound was now to be heard. Well, perhaps his father had recently given up this habit of reading aloud, which his sister had mentioned so often in conversation and in her letters. But there was the same silence all around, although the flat was certainly not empty of occupants. "What a quiet life our family has been leading," said Gregor to himself, and as he sat there motionless staring into the darkness he felt great pride in the fact that he had been able to provide such a life for his parents and sister in such a fine flat. But what if all the quiet, the comfort, the contentment were now to end in horror? To keep himself from being lost in such thoughts Gregor took refuge in movement and crawled up and down the room.

Once during the long evening one of the side doors was opened a little and quickly shut again, later the other side door too; someone had apparently wanted to come in and then thought better of it. Gregor now stationed himself immediately before the living-room door, determined to persuade any hesitating visitor to come in or at least to discover who it might be; but the door was not opened again and he waited in vain. In the early morning, when the doors were locked, they had all wanted to come in, now that he had opened one door and the other had apparently been opened during the day, no one came in and even the keys were on the other side of the doors.

It was late at night before the gas went out in the living room, and Gregor could easily tell that his parents and his sister had all stayed awake until then, for he could clearly hear the three of them stealing away on tiptoe. No one was likely to visit him, not until the morning, that was certain; so he had plenty of time to meditate at his leisure on how he was to arrange his life afresh. But the lofty, empty room in which he had to lie flat on the floor filled him with an apprehension he could not account for, since it had been his very own room for the past five years — and with a half-unconscious action, not without a slight feeling of shame, he scuttled under the sofa, where he felt comfortable at once, although his back was a little cramped and he could not lift his head up, and his only regret was that his body was too broad to get the whole of it under the sofa.

He stayed there all night, spending the time partly in a light slumber, from which his hunger kept waking him up with a start, and partly in worrying and sketching vague hopes, which all led to the same conclusion, that he must lie low for the present and, by exercising patience and the utmost consideration, help the family to bear the inconvenience he was bound to cause them in his present condition.

Very early in the morning, it was still almost night, Gregor had the chance to test the strength of his new resolutions, for his sister, nearly fully dressed, opened the door from the hall and peered in. She did not see him at once, yet when she caught sight of him under the sofa — well, he had to be somewhere, he couldn't have flown away, could he? — she was so startled that without being able to help it she slammed the door shut again. But as if regretting her behavior she opened the door again immediately and came in on tiptoe, as if she were visiting an invalid or even a stranger. Gregor had pushed his head forward to the very edge of the sofa and watched her. Would she notice that he had left the milk standing, and not for lack of hunger, and would she bring in some other kind of food more to his taste? If she did not do it of her own accord, he would rather starve than draw her attention to the fact, although he felt a wild impulse to dart out from under the sofa, throw himself at her feet and beg her for something to eat. But his sister at once noticed, with surprise, that the basin was still full, except for a little milk that had been spilt all around it, she lifted it immediately, not with her bare hands, true, but with a cloth and carried it away. Gregor was wildly curious to know what she would bring instead, and made various speculations about it. Yet what she actually did next, in the goodness of her heart, he could never have guessed at. To find out what he liked she brought him a whole selection of food, all set out on an old newspaper. There were old, half-decayed vegetables, bones from last night's supper covered with a white sauce that had thickened; some raisins and almonds; a piece of cheese that Gregor would have called uneatable two days ago; a dry roll of bread, a buttered roll, and a roll both buttered and salted. Besides all that, she set down again the same basin, into which she had poured some water, and which was apparently to be reserved for his exclusive use. And with fine tact, knowing that Gregor would not eat in her presence, she withdrew quickly and even turned the key, to let him understand that he could take his ease as much as he liked. Gregor's legs all whizzed towards the food. His wounds must have healed completely, moreover, for he felt no disability, which amazed him and made him reflect how more than a month ago he had cut one finger a little with a knife and had still suffered pain from the wound only the day before yesterday. Am I less sensitive now? he thought, and sucked greedily at the cheese, which above all the other edibles attracted him at once and strongly. One after another and with tears of satisfaction in his eyes he quickly devoured the cheese, the vegetables and the sauce; the fresh food, on the other hand, had no charms for him, he could not even stand the smell of it and actually dragged away to some little distance the things he could eat. He had long finished his meal and was only lying lazily on the same spot when his sister turned the key slowly as a sign for him to retreat. That roused him at once, although he was nearly asleep, and he hurried under the sofa again. But it took considerable self-control for him to stay under the sofa, even for the short time his sister was in the room, since the large meal had swollen his body somewhat and he was so cramped he could hardly breathe. Slight attacks of breathlessness afflicted him and his eyes were starting a little out of his head as he watched his unsuspecting sister sweeping together with a broom not only the remains of what he had eaten but even the things he had not touched, as if these were now of no use to anyone, and hastily shoveling it all into a bucket, which she covered with a wooden lid and carried away. Hardly had she turned her back when Gregor came from under the sofa and stretched and puffed himself out.

In this manner Gregor was fed, once in the early morning while his parents and the servant girl were still asleep, and a second time after they had all had their midday dinner, for then his parents took a short nap and the servant girl could be sent out on some errand or other by his sister. Not that they would have wanted him to starve, of course, but perhaps they could not have borne to know more about his feeding than from hearsay, perhaps too his sister wanted to spare them such little anxieties wherever possible, since they had quite enough to bear as it was.

Under what pretext the doctor and the locksmith had been got rid of on that first morning Gregor could not discover, for since what he said was not understood by the others it never struck any of them, not even his sister, that he could understand what they said, and so whenever his sister came into his room he had to content himself with hearing her utter only a sigh now and then and an occasional appeal to the saints. Later on, when she had got a little used to the situation — of course she could never get completely used to it — she sometimes threw out a remark which was kindly meant or could be so interpreted. "Well, he liked his dinner today," she would say when Gregor had made a good clearance of his food; and when he had not eaten, which gradually happened more and more often, she would say almost sadly: "Everything's been left standing again."

But although Gregor could get no news directly, he overheard a lot from the neighboring rooms, and as soon as voices were audible, he would run to the door of the room concerned and press his whole body against it. In the first few days especially there was no conversation that did not refer to him somehow, even if only indirectly. For two whole days there were family consultations at every mealtime about what should be done; but also between meals the same subject was discussed, for there were always at least two members of the family at home, since no one wanted to be alone in the flat and to leave it quite empty was unthinkable. And on the very first of these days the household cook — it was not quite clear what and how much she knew of the situation — went down on her knees to his mother and begged leave to go, and when she departed, a quarter of an hour later, gave thanks for her dismissal with tears in her eyes as if for the greatest benefit that could have been conferred on her, and without any prompting swore a solemn oath that she would never say a single word to anyone about what had happened.

Now Gregor's sister had to cook too, helping her mother; true, the cooking did not amount to much, for they ate scarcely anything. Gregor was always hearing one of the family vainly urging another to eat and getting no answer but: "Thanks, I've had all I want," or something similar. Perhaps they drank nothing either. Time and again his sister kept asking his father if he wouldn't like some beer and offered kindly to go and fetch it herself, and when he made no answer suggested that she could ask the concierge to fetch it, so that he need feel no sense of obligation, but then a round "No" came from his father and no more was said about it.

In the course of that very first day Gregor's father explained the family's financial position and prospects to both his mother and his sister. Now and then he rose from the table to get some voucher or memorandum out of the small safe he had rescued from the collapse of his business five years earlier. One could hear him opening the complicated lock and rustling papers out and shutting it again. This statement made by his father was the first cheerful information Gregor had heard since his imprisonment. He had been of the opinion that nothing at all was left over from his father's business, at least his father had never said anything to the contrary, and of course he had not asked him directly. At that time Gregor's sole desire was to do his utmost to help the family to forget as soon as possible the catastrophe which had overwhelmed the business and thrown them all into a state of complete despair. And so he had set to work with unusual ardor and almost overnight had become a commercial traveler instead of a little clerk, with of course much greater chances of earning money, and his success was immediately translated into good round coin which he could lay on the table for his amazed and happy family. These had been fine times, and they had never recurred, at least not with the same sense of glory, although later on Gregor had earned so much money that he was able to meet the expenses of the whole household and did so. They had simply got used to it, both the family and Gregor; the money was gratefully accepted and gladly given, but there was no special uprush of warm feeling. With his sister alone had he remained intimate, and it was a secret plan of his that she, who loved music, unlike himself, and could play movingly on the violin, should be sent next year to study at the Conservatorium, despite the great expense that would entail, which must be made up in some other way. During his brief visits home the Conservatorium was often mentioned in the talks he had with his sister, but always merely as a beautiful dream which could never come true, and his parents discouraged even these innocent references to it; yet Gregor had made up his mind firmly about it and meant to announce the fact with due solemnity on Christmas Day.

Such were the thoughts, completely futile in his present condition, that went through his head as he stood clinging upright to the door and listening. Sometimes out of sheer weariness he had to give up listening and let his head fall negligently against the door, but he always had to pull himself together again at once, for even the slight sound his head made was audible next door and brought all conversation to a stop. "What can he be doing now?" his father would say after a while, obviously turning towards the door, and only then would the interrupted conversation gradually be set going again.

Gregor was now informed as amply as he could wish — for his father tended to repeat himself in his explanations, partly because it was a long time since he had handled such matters and partly because his mother could not always grasp things at once — that a certain amount of investments, a very small amount it was true, had survived the wreck of their fortunes and had even increased a little because the dividends had not been touched meanwhile. And besides that, the money Gregor brought home every month — he had kept only a few dollars for himself — had never been quite used up and now amounted to a small capital sum. Behind the door Gregor nodded his head eagerly, rejoiced at this evidence of unexpected thrift and foresight. True, he could really have paid off some more of his father's debts to the chief with his extra money, and so brought much nearer the day on which he could quit his job, but doubtless it was better the way his father had arranged it.

Yet this capital was by no means sufficient to let the family live on the interest of it; for one year, perhaps, or at the most two, they could live on the principal, that was all. It was simply a sum that ought not to be touched and should be kept for a rainy day; money for living expenses woud have to be earned. Now his father was still hale enough but an old man, and he had done no work for the past five years and could not be expected to do much; during these five years, the first years of leisure in his laborious though unsuccessful life, he had grown rather fat and become sluggish. And Gregor's old mother, how was she to earn a living with her asthma, which troubled her even when she walked through the flat and kept her lying on a sofa every other day panting for breath beside an open window? And was his sister to earn her bread, she who was still a child of seventeen and whose life hitherto had been so pleasant, consisting as it did in dressing herself nicely, sleeping long, helping in the housekeeping, going out to a few modest entertainments and above all playing the violin? At first whenever the need for earning money was mentioned Gregor let go his hold on the door and threw himself down on the cool leather sofa beside it, he felt so hot with shame and grief.

Often he just lay there the long nights through without sleeping at all, scrabbling for hours on the leather. Or he nerved himself to the great effort of pushing an armchair to the window, then crawled up over the window sill and, braced against the chair, leaned against the window panes, obviously in some recollection of the sense of freedom that looking out of a window always used to give him. For in reality day by day things that were even a little way off were growing dimmer to his sight; the hospital across the street, which he used to execrate for being all too often before his eyes, was now quite beyond his range of vision, and if he had not known that he lived in Charlotte Street, a quiet street but still a city street, he might have believed that his window gave on a desert waste where gray sky and gray land blended indistinguishably into each other. His quick-witted sister only needed to observe twice that the armchair stood by the window; after that whenever she had tidied the room she always pushed the chair back to the same place at the window and even left the inner casements open.

If he could have spoken to her and thanked her for all she had to do for him, he could have borne her ministrations better; as it was, they oppressed him. She certainly tried to make as light as possible of whatever was disagreeable in her task, and as time went on she succeeded, of course, more and more, but time brought more enlightenment to Gregor too. The very way she came in distressed him. Hardly was she in the room when she rushed to the window, without even taking time to shut the door, careful as she was usually to shield the sight of Gregor's room from the others, and as if she were almost suffocating tore the casements open with hasty fingers, standing then in the open draught for a while even in the bitterest cold and drawing deep breaths. This noisy scurry of hers upset Gregor twice a day; he would crouch trembling under the sofa all the time, knowing quite well that she would certainly have spared him such a disturbance had she found it at all possible to stay in his presence without opening the window.

On one occasion, about a month after Gregor's metamorphosis, when there was surely no reason for her to be still startled at his appearance, she came a little earlier than usual and found him gazing out of the window, quite motionless, and thus well placed to look like a bogey. Gregor would not have been surprised had she not come in at all, for she could not immediately open the window while he was there, but not only did she retreat, she jumped back as if in alarm and banged the door shut; a stranger might well have thought that he had been lying in wait for her there meaning to bite her. Of course he hid himself under the sofa at once, but he had to wait until midday before she came again, and she seemed more ill at ease than usual. This made him realize how repulsive the sight of him still was to her, and that it was bound to go on being repulsive, and what an effort it must cost her not to run away even from the sight of the small portion of his body that stuck out from under the sofa. In order to spare her that, therefore, one day he carried a sheet on his back to the sofa — it cost him four hours' labor — and arranged in there in such a way as to hide him completely, so that even if she were to bend down she could not see him. Had she considered the sheet unnecessary, she would certainly have stripped it off the sofa again, for it was clear enough that this curtaining and confining of himself was not likely to conduce Gregor's comfort, but she left it where it was, and Gregor even fancied that he caught a thankful glance from her eye when he lifted the sheet carefully a very little with his head to see how she was taking the new arrangement.

For the first fortnight his parents could not bring themselves to the point of entering his room, and he often heard them expressing their appreciation of his sister's activities, whereas formerly they had frequently scolded her for being as they thought a somewhat useless daughter. But now, both of them often waited outside the door, his father and his mother, while his sister tidied his room, and as soon as she came out she had to tell them exactly how things were in the room, what Gregor had eaten, how he had conducted himself this time and whether there was not perhaps some slight improvement in his condition. His mother, moreover, began relatively soon to want to visit him, but his father and sister dissuaded her at first with arguments which Gregor listened to very attentively and altogether approved. Later, however, she had to be held back by main force, and when she cried out: "Do let me in to Gregor, he is my unfortunate son! Can't you understand that I must go to him?" Gregor thought that it might be well to have her come in, not every day, of course, but perhaps once a week; she understood things, after all, much better than his sister, who was only a child despite the efforts she was making and had perhaps taken on so difficult a task merely out of childish thoughtlessness.

Gregor's desire to see his mother was soon fulfilled. During the daytime he did not want to show himself at the window, out of consideration for his parents, but he could not crawl very far around the few square yards of floor space he had, nor could he bear lying quietly at rest all during the night, while he was fast losing any interest he had ever taken in food, so that for mere recreation he had formed the habit of crawling crisscross over the walls and ceiling. He especially enjoyed hanging suspended from the ceiling; it was much better than lying on the floor; one could breathe more freely; one's body swung and rocked lightly; and in the almost blissful absorption induced by this suspension it could happen to his own surprise that he let go and fell plump on the floor. Yet he now had his body much better under control than formerly, and even such a big fall did him no harm. His sister at once remarked the new distraction Gregor had found for himself — he left traces behind him of the sticky stuff on his soles wherever he crawled — and she got the idea in her head of giving him as wide a field as possible to crawl in and of removing the pieces of furniture that hindered him, above all the chest of drawers and the writing desk. But that was more than she could manage all by herself; she did not dare ask her father to help her; and as for the servant girl, a young creature of sixteen who had had the courage to stay on after the cook's departure, she could not be asked to help, for she had begged as an especial favor that she might keep the kitchen door locked and open it only on a definite summons; so there was nothing left but to apply to her mother at an hour when her father was out. And the old lady did come, with exclamations of joyful eagerness, which, however, died away at the door of Gregor's room. Gregor's sister, of course, went in first, to see that everything was in order before letting his mother enter. In great haste Gregor pulled the sheet lower and rucked it more in folds so that it really looked as if it had been thrown accidentally over the sofa. And this time he did not peer out from under it; he renounced the pleasure of seeing his mother on this occasion and was only glad that she had come at all. "Come in, he's out of sight," said his sister, obviously leading her mother in by the hand. Gregor could now hear the two women struggling to shift the heavy old chest from its place, and his sister claiming the greater part of the labor for herself, without listening to the admonitions of her mother who feared she might overstrain herself. It took a long time. After at least a quarter of an hour's tugging his mother objected that the chest had better be left where it was, for in the first place it was too heavy and could never be got out before his father came home, and standing in the middle of the room like that it would only hamper Gregor's movements, while in the second place it was not at all certain that removing the furniture would be doing a service to Gregor. She was inclined to think to the contrary; the sight of the naked walls made her own heart heavy, and why shouldn't Gregor have the same feeling, considering that he had been used to his furniture for so long and might feel forlorn without it. "And doesn't it look," she concluded in a low voice — in fact she had been almost whispering all the time as if to avoid letting Gregor, whose exact whereabouts she did not know, hear even the tones of her voice, for she was convinced that he could not understand her words — "doesn't it look as if we were showing him, by taking away his furniture, that we have given up hope of his ever getting better and are just leaving him coldly to himself? I think it would be best to keep his room exactly as it has always been, so that when he comes back to us he will find everything unchanged and be able all the more easily to forget what has happened in between."

On hearing these words from his mother Gregor realized that the lack of all direct human speech for the past two months together with the monotony of family life must have confused his mind, otherwise he could not account for the fact that he had quite earnestly looked forward to having his room emptied of furnishing. Did he really want his warm room, so comfortably fitted with old family furniture, to be turned into a naked den in which he would certainly be able to crawl unhampered in all directions but at the price of shedding simultaneously all recollection of his human background? He had indeed been so near the brink of forgetfulness that only the voice of his mother, which he had not heard for so long, had drawn him back from it. Nothing should be taken out of his room; everything must stay as it was; he could not dispense with the good influence of the furniture on his state of mind; and even if the furniture did hamper him in his senseless crawling round and round, that was no drawback but a great advantage.

Unfortunately his sister was of the contrary opinion; she had grown accustomed, and not without reason, to consider herself an expert in Gregor's affairs as against her parents, and so her mother's advice was now enough to make her determined on the removal not only of the chest and the writing desk, which had been her first intention, but of all the furniture except the indispensable sofa. This determination was not, of course, merely the outcome of childish recalcitrance and of the self-confidence she had recently developed so unexpectedly and at such cost; she had in fact perceived that Gregor needed a lot of space to crawl about in, while on the other hand he never used the furniture at all, so far as could be seen. Another factor might have been also the enthusiastic temperament of an adolescent girl, which seeks to indulge itself on every opportunity and which now tempted Grete to exaggerate the horror of her brother's circumstances in order that she might do all the more for him. In a room where Gregor lorded it all alone over empty walls no one save herself was likely ever to set foot.

And so she was not to be moved from her resolve by her mother who seemed moreover to be ill at ease in Gregor's room and therefore unsure of herself, was soon reduced to silence and helped her daughter as best she could to push the chest outside. Now, Gregor could do without the chest, if need be, but the writing desk he must retain. As soon as the two women had got the chest out of his room, groaning as they pushed it, Gregor stuck his head out from under the sofa to see how he might intervene as kindly and cautiously as possible. But as bad luck would have it, his mother was the first to return, leaving Grete clasping the chest in the room next door where she was trying to shift it all by herself, without of course moving it from the spot. His mother however was not accustomed to the sight of him, it might sicken her and so in alarm Gregor backed quickly to the other end of the sofa, yet could not prevent the sheet from swaying a little in front. That was enough to put her on the alert. She paused, stood still for a moment and then went back to Grete.

Although Gregor kept reassuring himself that nothing out of the way was happening, but only a few bits of furniture were being changed round, he soon had to admit that all this trotting to and fro of the two women, their little ejaculations and the scraping of furniture along the floor affected him like a vast disturbance coming from all sides at once, and however much he tucked in his head and legs and cowered to the very floor he was bound to confess that he would not be able to stand it for long. They were clearing his room out; taking away everything he loved; the chest in which he kept his fret saw and other tools was already dragged off; they were now loosening the writing desk which had almost sunk into the floor, the desk at which he had done all his homework when he was at the commercial academy, at the grammar school before that, and, yes, even at the primary school — he had no more time to waste in weighing the good intentions of the two women, whose existence he had by now almost forgotten, for they were so exhausted that they were laboring in silence and nothing could be heard but the heavy scuffling of their feet.

And so he rushed out — the women were just leaning against the writing desk in the next room to give themselves a breather — and four times changed his direction, since he really did not know what to rescue first, then on the wall opposite, which was already otherwise cleared, he was struck by the picture of the lady muffled in so much fur and quickly crawled up to it and pressed himself to the glass, which was a good surface to hold on to and comforted his hot belly. This picture at least, which was entirely hidden beneath him, was going to be removed by nobody. He turned his head towards the door of the living room so as to observe the women when they came back.

They had not allowed themselves much of a rest and were already coming; Grete had twined her arm round her mother and was almost supporting her. "Well, what shall we take now?" said Grete, looking round. Her eyes met Gregor's from the wall. She kept her composure, presumably because of her mother, bent her head down to her mother, to keep her from looking up, and said, although in a fluttering, unpremeditated voice: "Come, hadn't we better go back to the living room for a moment?" Her intentions were clear enough to Gregor, she wanted to bestow her mother in safety and then chase him down from the wall. Well, just let her try it! He clung to his picture and would not give it up. He would rather fly in Grete's face.

But Grete's words had succeeded in disquieting her mother, who took a step to one side, caught sight of the huge brown mass on the flowered wallpaper, and before she was really conscious that what she saw was Gregor screamed in a loud, hoarse voice: "Oh God, oh God!" fell with outspread arms over the sofa as if giving up and did not move. "Gregor!" cried his sister, shaking her fist and glaring at him. This was the first time she had directly addressed him since his metamorphosis. She ran into the next room for some aromatic essence with which to rouse her mother from her fainting fit. Gregor wanted to help too — there was still time to rescue the picture — but he was stuck fast to the glass and had to tear himself loose; he then ran after his sister into the next room as if he could advise her, as he used to do; but then had to stand helplessly behind her; she meanwhile searched among various small bottles and when she turned round started in alarm at the sight of him; one bottle fell on the floor and broke; a splinter of glass cut Gregor's face and some kind of corrosive medicine splashed him; without pausing a moment longer Grete gathered up all the bottles she could carry and ran to her mother with them; she banged the door shut with her foot. Gregor was now cut off from his mother, who was perhaps nearly dying because of him; he dared not open the door for fear of frightening away his sister, who had to stay with her mother; there was nothing he could do but wait; and harassed by self-reproach and worry he began now to crawl to and fro, over everything, walls, furniture and ceiling, and finally in his despair, when the whole room seemed to be reeling round him, fell down on to the middle of the big table.

A little while elapsed, Gregor was still lying there feebly and all around was quiet, perhaps that was a good omen. Then the doorbell rang. The servant girl was of course locked in her kitchen, and Grete would have to open the door. It was his father. "What's been happening?" were his first words; Grete's face must have told him everything. Grete answered in a muffled voice, apparently hiding her head on his breast: "Mother has been fainting, but she's better now. Gregor's broken loose." "Just what I expected," said his father, "just what I've been telling you, but you women would never listen." It was clear to Gregor that his father had taken the worst interpretation of Grete's all too brief statement and was assuming that Gregor had been guilty of some violent act. Therefore Gregor must now try to propitiate his father, since he had neither time nor means for an explanation. And so he fled to the door of his own room and crouched against it, to let his father see as soon as he came in from the hall that his son had the good intention of getting back into his room immediately and that it was not necessary to drive him there, but that if only the door were opened he would disappear at once.

Yet his father was not in the mood to perceive such fine distinctions. "Ah!" he cried as soon as he appeared, in a tone which sounded at once angry and exultant. Gregor drew his head back from the door and lifted it to look at his father. Truly, this was not the father he had imagined to himself; admittedly he had been too absorbed of late in his new recreation of crawling over the ceiling to take the same interest as before in what was happening elsewhere in the flat, and he ought really to be prepared for some changes. And yet, and yet, could that be his father? The man who used to lie wearily sunk in bed whenever Gregor set out on a business journey; who welcomed him back of an evening lying in a long chair in a dressing gown; who could not really rise to his feet but only lifted his arms in greeting, and on the rare occasions when he did go out with his family, on one or two Sundays a year and on high holidays, walked between Gregor and his mother, who were slow walkers anyhow, even more slowly than they did, muffled in his old greatcoat, shuffling laboriously forward with the help of his crook-handled stick which he set down most cautiously at every step and, whenever he wanted to say anything, nearly always came to a full stop and gathered his escort around him? Now he was standing there in fine shape; dressed in a smart blue uniform with gold buttons, such as bank messengers wear; his strong double chin bulged over the stiff high collar of his jacket; from under his bushy eyebrows his black eyes darted fresh and penetrating glances; his onetime tangled white hair had been combed flat on either side of a shining and carefully exact parting. He pitched his cap, which bore a gold monogram, probably the badge of some bank, in a wide sweep across the whole room on to a sofa and with the tail-ends of his jacket thrown back, his hands in his trouser pockets, advanced with a grim visage towards Gregor. Likely enough he did not himself know what he meant to do; at any rate he lifted his feet uncommonly high, and Gregor was dumbfounded at the enormous size of his shoe soles. But Gregor could not risk standing up to him, aware as he had been from the very first day of his new life that his father believed only the severest measures suitable for dealing with him. And so he ran before his father, stopping when he stopped and scuttling forward again when his father made any kind of move. In this way they circled the room several times without anything decisive happening, indeed the whole operation did not even look like a pursuit because it was carried out so slowly. And so Gregor did not leave the floor, for he feared that his father might take as a piece of peculiar wickedness any excursion of his over the walls or the ceiling. All the same, he could not stay this course much longer, for while his father took one step he had to carry out a whole series of movements. He was already beginning to feel breathless, just as in his former life his lungs had not been very dependable. As he was staggering along, trying to concentrate his energy on running, hardly keeping his eyes open; in his dazed state never even thinking of any other escape than simply going forward; and having almost forgotten that the walls were free to him, which in this room were well provided with finely carved pieces of furniture full of knobs and crevices — suddenly something lightly flung landed close behind him and rolled before him. It was an apple; a second apple followed immediately; Gregor came to a stop in alarm; there was no point in running on, for his father was determined to bombard him. He had filled his pockets with fruit from the dish on the sideboard and was now shying apple after apple, without taking particularly good aim for the moment. The small red apples rolled about the floor as if magnetized and cannoned into each other. An apple thrown without much force grazed Gregor's back and glanced off harmlessly. But another following immediately landed right on his back and sank in; Gregor wanted to drag himself forward, as if this startling, incredible pain could be left behind him; but he felt as if nailed to the spot and flattened himself out in a complete derangement of all his senses. With his last conscious look he saw the door of his room being torn open and his mother rushing out ahead of his screaming sister, in her underbodice, for her daughter had loosened her clothing to let her breathe more freely and recover from her swoon, he saw his mother rushing towards his father, leaving one after another behind her on the floor her loosened petticoats, stumbling over her petticoats straight to his father and embracing him, in complete union with him — but here Gregor's sight began to fail — with her hands clasped round his father's neck as she begged for her son's life.

III

The serious injury done to Gregor, which disabled him for more than a month — the apple went on sticking in his body as a visible reminder, since no one ventured to remove it — seemed to have made even his father recollect that Gregor was a member of the family, despite his present unfortunate and repulsive shape, and ought not to be treated as an enemy, that, on the contrary, family duty required the suppression of disgust and the exercise of patience, nothing but patience.

And although his injury had impaired, probably for ever, his power of movement, and for the time being it took him long, long minutes to creep across his room like an old invalid — there was no question now of crawling up the wall — yet in his own opinion he was sufficiently compensated for this worsening of his condition by the fact that towards evening the living-room door, which he used to watch intently for an hour or two beforehand, was always thrown open, so that lying in the darkness of his room, invisible to the family, he could see them all at the lamp-lit table and listen to their talk, by general consent as it were, very different from his earlier eavesdropping.

True, their intercourse lacked the lively character of former times, which he had always called to mind with a certain wistfulness in the small hotel bedrooms where he had been wont to throw himself down, tired out, on damp bedding. They were now mostly very silent. Soon after supper his father would fall asleep in his armchair; his mother and sister would admonish each other to be silent; his mother, bending low over the lamp, stitched at fine sewing for an underwear firm; his sister, who had taken a job as a salesgirl, was learning shorthand and French in the evenings on the chance of bettering herself. Sometimes his father woke up, and as if quite unaware that he had been sleeping said to his mother: "What a lot of sewing you're doing today!" and at once fell asleep again, while the two women exchanged a tired smile.

With a kind of mulishness his father persisted in keeping his uniform on even in the house; his dressing gown hung uselessly on its peg and he slept fully dressed where he sat, as if he were ready for service at any moment and even here only at the beck and call of his superior. As a result, his uniform, which was not brand-new to start with, began to look dirty, despite all the loving care of the mother and sister to keep it clean, and Gregor often spent whole evenings gazing at the many greasy spots on the garment, gleaming with gold buttons always in a high state of polish, in which the old man sat sleeping in extreme discomfort and yet quite peacefully.

As soon as the clock struck ten his mother tried to rouse his father with gentle words and to persuade him after that to get into bed, for sitting there he could not have a proper sleep and that was what he needed most, since he had to go to duty at six. But with the mulishness that had obsessed him since he became a bank messenger he always insisted on staying longer at the table, although he regularly fell asleep again and in the end only with the greatest trouble could be got out of his armchair and into his bed. However insistently Gregor's mother and sister kept urging him with gentle reminders, he would go on slowly shaking his head for a quarter of an hour, keeping his eyes shut, and refuse to get to his feet. The mother plucked at his sleeve, whispering endearments in his ear, the sister left her lessons to come to her mother's help, but Gregor's father was not to be caught. He would only sink down deeper in his chair. Not until the two women hoisted him up by the armpits did he open his eyes and look at them both, one after the other, usually with the remark: "This is a life. This is the peace and quiet of my old age." And leaning on the two of them he would heave himself up, with difficulty, as if he were a great burden to himself, suffer them to lead him as far as the door and then wave them off and go on alone, while the mother abandoned her needlework and the sister her pen in order to run after him and help him farther.

Who could find time, in this overworked and tired-out family, to bother about Gregor more than was absolutely needful? The household was reduced more and more; the servant girl was turned off; a gigantic bony charwoman with white hair flying round her head came in morning and evening to do the rough work; everything else was done by Gregor's mother, as well as great piles of sewing. Even various family ornaments, which his mother and sister used to wear with pride at parties and celebrations, had to be sold, as Gregor discovered of an evening from hearing them all discuss the prices obtained. But what they lamented most was the fact that they could not leave the flat which was much too big for their present circumstances, because they could not think of any way to shift Gregor. Yet Gregor saw well enough that consideration for him was not the main difficulty preventing the removal, for they could have easily shifted him in some suitable box with a few air holes in it; what really kept them from moving into another flat was rather their own complete hopelessness and the belief that they had been singled out for a misfortune such as had never happened to any of their relations or acquaintances. They fulfilled to the uttermost all that the world demands of poor people, the father fetched breakfast for the small clerks in the bank, the mother devoted her energy to making underwear for strangers, the sister trotted to and fro behind the counter at the behest of customers, but more than this they had not the strength to do. And the wound in Gregor's back began to nag at him afresh when his mother and sister, after getting his father into bed, came back again, left their work lying, drew close to each other and sat cheek by cheek; when his mother, pointing towards his room, said: "Shut that door now, Grete," and he was left again in darkness, while next door the women mingled their tears or perhaps sat dry-eyed staring at the table.

Gregor hardly slept at all by night or by day. He was often haunted by the idea that next time the door opened he would take the family's affairs in hand again just as he used to do; once more, after this long interval, there appeared in his thoughts the figures of the chief and the chief clerk, the commercial travelers and the apprentices, the porter who was so dull-witted, two or three friends in other firms, a chambermaid in one of the rural hotels, a sweet and fleeting memory, a cashier in a milliner's shop, whom he had wooed earnestly but too slowly — they all appeared, together with strangers or people he had quite forgotten, but instead of helping him and his family they were one and all unapproachable and he was glad when they vanished. At other times he would not be in the mood to bother about his family, he was only filled with rage at the way they were neglecting him, and although he had no clear idea of what he might care to eat he would make plans for getting into the larder to take the food that was after all his due, even if he were not hungry. His sister no longer took thought to bring him what might especially please him, but in the morning and at noon before she went to business hurriedly pushed into his room with her foot any food that was available, and in the evening cleared it out again with one sweep of the broom, heedless of whether it had been merely tasted, or — as most frequently happened — left untouched. The cleaning of his room, which she now did always in the evenings, could not have been more hastily done. Streaks of dirt stretched along the walls, here and there lay balls of dust and filth. At first Gregor used to station himself in some particularly filthy corner when his sister arrived, in order to reproach her with it, so to speak. But he could have sat there for weeks without getting her to make any improvements; she could see the dirt as well as he did, but she had simply made up her mind to leave it alone. And yet, with a touchiness that was new to her, which seemed anyhow to have infected the whole family, she jealously guarded her claim to be the sole caretaker of Gregor's room. His mother once subjected his room to a thorough cleaning, which was achieved only by means of several buckets of water — all this dampness of course upset Gregor too and he lay widespread, sulky and motionless on the sofa — but she was well punished for it. Hardly had his sister noticed the changed aspect of his room that evening than she rushed in high dudgeon into the living room and, despite the imploringly raised hands of her mother, burst into a storm of weeping, while her parents — her father had of course been startled out of his chair — looked on at first in helpless amazement; then they too began to go into action; the father reproached the mother on his right for not having left the cleaning of Gregor's room to his sister; shrieked at the sister on his left that never again was she to be allowed to clean Gregor's room; while the mother tried to pull the father into his bedroom, since he was beyond himself with agitation; the sister, shaken with sobs, then beat upon the table with her small fists; and Gregor hissed loudly with rage because not one of them thought of shutting the door to spare him such a spectacle and so much noise.

Still, even if the sister, exhausted by her daily work, had grown tired of looking after Gregor as she did formerly, there was no need for his mother's intervention or for Gregor's being neglected at all. The charwoman was there. This old widow, whose strong bony frame had enabled her to survive the worst a long life could offer, by no means recoiled from Gregor. Without being in the least curious she had once by chance opened the door of his room and at the sight of Gregor, who, taken by surprise, began to rush to and fro although no one was chasing him, merely stood there with her arms folded. From that time she never failed to open his door a little for a moment, morning and evening, to have a look at him. At first she even used to call him to her, with words which apparently she took to be friendly, such as: "Come along, then, you old dung beetle!" or "Look at the old dung beetle, then!" To such allocutions Gregor made no answer, but stayed motionless where he was, as if the door had never been opened. Instead of being allowed to disturb him so senselessly whenever the whim took her, she should rather have been ordered to clean out his room daily, that charwoman! Once, early in the morning — heavy rain was lashing on the windowpanes, perhaps a sign that spring was on the way — Gregor was so exasperated when she began addressing him again that he ran at her, as if to attack her, although slowly and feebly enough. But the charwoman instead of showing fright merely lifted high a chair that happened to be beside the door, and as she stood there with her mouth wide open it was clear that she meant to shut it only when she brought the chair down on Gregor's back. "So you're not coming any nearer?" she asked, as Gregor turned away again, and quietly put the chair back into the corner.

Gregor was now eating hardly anything. Only when he happened to pass the food laid out for him did he take a bit of something in his mouth as a pastime, kept it there for an hour at a time and usually spat it out again. At first he thought it was chagrin over the state of his room that prevented him from eating, yet he soon got used to the various changes in his room. It had become a habit in the family to push into his room things there was no room for elsewhere, and there were plenty of these now, since one of the rooms had been let to three lodgers. These serious gentlemen — all three of them with full beards, as Gregor once observed through a crack in the door — had a passion for order, not only in their own room but, since they were now members of the household, in all its arrangements, especially in the kitchen. Superfluous, not to say dirty, objects they could not bear. Besides, they had brought with them most of the furnishings they needed. For this reason many things could be dispensed with that it was no use trying to sell but that should not be thrown away either. All of them found their way into Gregor's room. The ash can likewise and the kitchen garbage can. Anything that was not needed for the moment was simply flung into Gregor's room by the charwoman, who did everything in a hurry; fortunately Gregor usually saw only the object, whatever it was, and the hand that held it. Perhaps she intended to take the things away again as time and opportunity offered, or to collect them until she could throw them all out in a heap, but in fact they just lay wherever she happened to throw them, except when Gregor pushed his way through the junk heap and shifted it somewhat, at first out of necessity, because he had not room enough to crawl, but later with increasing enjoyment, although after such excursions, being sad and weary to death, he would lie motionless for hours. And since the lodgers often ate their supper at home in the common living room, the living-room door stayed shut many an evening, yet Gregor reconciled himself quite easily to the shutting of the door, for often enough on evenings when it was opened he had disregarded it entirely and lain in the darkest corner of his room, quite unnoticed by the family. But on one occasion the charwoman left the door open a little and it stayed ajar even when the lodgers came in for supper and the lamp was lit. They set themselves at the top end of the table where formerly Gregor and his father and mother had eaten their meals, unfolded their napkins and took knife and fork in hand. At once his mother appeared in the other doorway with a dish of meat and close behind her his sister with a dish of potatoes piled high. The food steamed with a thick vapor. The lodgers bent over the food set before them as if to scrutinize it before eating, in fact the man in the middle, who seemed to pass for an authority with the other two, cut a piece of meat as it lay on the dish, obviously to discover if it were tender or should be sent back to the kitchen. He showed satisfaction, and Gregor's mother and sister, who had been watching anxiously, breathed freely and began to smile.

The family itself took its meals in the kitchen. None the less, Gregor's father came into the living room before going into the kitchen and with one prolonged bow, cap in hand, made a round of the table. The lodgers all stood up and murmured something in their beards. When they were alone again they ate their food in almost complete silence. It seemed remarkable to Gregor that among the various noises coming from the table he could always distinguish the sound of their masticating teeth, as if this were a sign to Gregor that one needed teeth in order to eat, and that with toothless jaws even of the finest make one could do nothing. "I'm hungry enough," said Gregor sadly to himself, "but not for that kind of food. How these lodgers are stuffing themselves, and here am I dying of starvation!"

On that very evening — during the whole of his time there Gregor could not remember ever having heard the violin — the sound of violin-playing came from the kitchen. The lodgers had already finished their supper, the one in the middle had brought out a newspaper and given the other two a page apiece, and now they were leaning back at ease reading and smoking. When the violin began to play they pricked up their ears, got to their feet, and went on tiptoe to the hall door where they stood huddled together. Their movements must have been heard in the kitchen, for Gregor's father called out: "Is the violin-playing disturbing you, gentlemen? It can be stopped at once." "On the contrary," said the middle lodger, "could not Fräulein Samsa come and play in this room, beside us, where it is much more convenient and comfortable?" "Oh certainly," cried Gregor's father, as if he were the violin-player. The lodgers came back into the living room and waited. Presently Gregor's father arrived with the music stand, his mother carrying the music and his sister with the violin. His sister quietly made everything ready to start playing; his parents, who had never let rooms before and so had an exaggerated idea of the courtesy due to lodgers, did not venture to sit down on their own chairs; his father leaned against the door, the right hand thrust between two buttons of his livery coat, which was formally buttoned up; but his mother was offered a chair by one of the lodgers and, since she left the chair just where he had happened to put it, sat down in a corner to one side.

Gregor's sister began to play; the father and mother, from either side, intently watched the movements of her hands. Gregor, attracted by the playing, ventured to move forward a little until his head was actually inside the living room. He felt hardly any surprise at his growing lack of consideration for the others; there had been a time when he prided himself on being considerate. And yet just on this occasion he had more reason than ever to hide himself, since owing to the amount of dust which lay thick in his room and rose into the air at the slightest movement, he too was covered with dust; fluff and hair and remnants of food trailed with him, caught on his back and along his sides; his indifference to everything was much too great for him to turn on his back and scrape himself clean on the carpet, as once he had done several times a day. And in spite of his condition, no shame deterred him from advancing a little over the spotless floor of the living room.

To be sure, no one was aware of him. The family was entirely absorbed in the violin-playing; the lodgers, however, who first of all had stationed themselves, hands in pockets, much too close behind the music stand so that they could all have read the music, which must have bothered his sister, had soon retreated to the window, half-whispering with downbent heads, and stayed there while his father turned an anxious eye on them. Indeed, they were making it more than obvious that they had been disappointed in their expectation of hearing good or enjoyable violin-playing, that they had had more than enough of the performance and only out of courtesy suffered a continued disturbance of their peace. From the way they all kept blowing the smoke of their cigars high in the air through nose and mouth one could divine their irritation. And yet Gregor's sister was playing so beautifully. Her face leaned sideways, intently and sadly her eyes followed the notes of music. Gregor crawled a little farther forward and lowered his head to the ground so that it might be possible for his eyes to meet hers. Was he an animal, that music had such an effect upon him? He felt as if the way were opening before him to the unknown nourishment he craved. He was determined to push forward till he reached his sister, to pull at her skirt and so let her know that she was to come into his room with her violin, for no one here appreciated her playing as he would appreciate it. He would never let her out of his room, at least, not so long as he lived; his frightful appearance would become, for the first time, useful to him; he would watch all the doors of his room at once and spit at intruders; but his sister should need no constraint, she should stay with him of her own free will; she should sit beside him on the sofa, bend down her ear to him and hear him confide that he had had the firm intention of sending her to the Conservatorium, and that, but for his mishap, last Christmas — surely Christmas was long past? — he would have announced it to everybody without allowing a single objection. After this confession his sister would be so touched that she would burst into tears, and Gregor would then raise himself to her shoulder and kiss her on the neck, which, now that she went to business, she kept free of any ribbon or collar.

"Mr. Samsa!" cried the middle lodger, to Gregor's father, and pointed, without wasting any more words, at Gregor, now working himself slowly forwards. The violin fell silent, the middle lodger first smiled to his friends with a shake of the head and then looked at Gregor again. Instead of driving Gregor out, his father seemed to think it more needful to begin by soothing down the lodgers, although they were not at all agitated and apparently found Gregor more entertaining than the violin-playing. He hurried towards them and, spreading out his arms, tried to urge them back into their own room and at the same time to block their view of Gregor. They now began to be really a little angry, one could not tell whether because of the old man's behavior or because it had just dawned on them that all unwittingly they had such a neighbor as Gregor next door. They demanded explanations of his father, they waved their arms like him, tugged uneasily at their beards, and only with reluctance backed towards their room. Meanwhile Gregor's sister, who stood there as if lost when her playing was so abruptly broken off, came to life again, pulled herself together all at once after standing for a while holding violin and bow in nervelessly hanging hands and staring at her music, pushed her violin into the lap of her mother, who was still sitting in her chair fighting asthmatically for breath, and ran into the lodgers' room to which they were now being shepherded by her father rather more quickly than before. One could see the pillows and blankets on the beds flying under her accustomed fingers and being laid in order. Before the lodgers had actually reached their room she had finished making the beds and slipped out.

The old man seemed once more to be so possessed by his mulish self-assertiveness that he was forgetting all the respect he should show to his lodgers. He kept driving them on and driving them on until in the very door of the bedroom the middle lodger stamped his foot loudly on the floor and so brought him to a halt. "I beg to announce," said the lodger, lifting one hand and looking also at Gregor's mother and sister, "that because of the disgusting conditions prevailing in this household and family" — here he spat on the floor with emphatic brevity — "I give you notice on the spot. Naturally I won't pay you a penny for the days I have lived here, on the contrary I shall consider bringing an action for damages against you, based on claims — believe me — that will be easily susceptible of proof." He ceased and stared straight in front of him, as if he expected something. In fact his two friends at once rushed into the breach with these words: "And we too give notice on the spot." On that he seized the door-handle and shut the door with a slam.

Gregor's father, groping with his hands, staggered forward and fell into his chair; it looked as if he were stretching himself there for his ordinary evening nap, but the marked jerkings of his head, which was as if uncontrollable, showed that he was far from asleep. Gregor had simply stayed quietly all the time on the spot where the lodgers had espied him. Disappointment at the failure of his plan, perhaps also the weakness arising from extreme hunger, made it impossible for him to move. He feared, with a fair degree of certainty, that at any moment the general tension would discharge itself in a combined attack upon him, and he lay waiting. He did not react even to the noise made by the violin as it fell off his mother's lap from under her trembling fingers and gave out a resonant note.

"My dear parents," said his sister, slapping her hand on the table by way of introduction, "things can't go on like this. Perhaps you don't realize that, but I do. I won't utter my brother's name in the presence of this creature, and so all I say is: we must try to get rid of it. We've tried to look after it and to put up with it as far as is humanly possible, and I don't think anyone could reproach us in the slightest."

"She is more than right," said Gregor's father to himself. His mother, who was still choking for lack of breath, began to cough hollowly into her hand with a wild look in her eyes.

His sister rushed over to her and held her forehead. His father's thoughts seemed to have lost their vagueness at Grete's words, he sat more upright, fingering his service cap that lay among the plates still lying on the table from the lodgers' supper, and from time to time looked at the still form of Gregor.

"We must try to get rid of it," his sister now said explicitly to her father, since her mother was coughing too much to hear a word, "it will be the death of both of you, I can see that coming. When one has to work as hard as we do, all of us, one can't stand this continual torment at home on top of it. At least I can't stand it any longer." And she burst into such a passion of sobbing that her tears dropped on her mother's face, where she wiped them off mechanically.

"My dear," said the old man sympathetically, and with evident understanding, "but what can we do?"

Gregor's sister merely shrugged her shoulders to indicate the feeling of helplessness that had now overmastered her during her weeping fit, in contrast to her former confidence.

"If he could understand us," said her father, half questioningly; Grete, still sobbing, vehemently waved a hand to show how unthinkable that was.

"If he could understand us," repeated the old man, shutting his eyes to consider his daughter's conviction that understanding was impossible, "then perhaps we might come to some agreement with him. But as it is —"

"He must go," cried Gregor's sister, "that's the only solution, Father. You must just try to get rid of the idea that this is Gregor. The fact that we've believed it for so long is the root of all our trouble. But how can it be Gregor? If this were

Gregor, he would have realized long ago that human beings can't live with such a creature, and he'd have gone away on his own accord. Then we wouldn't have any brother, but we'd be able to go on living and keep his memory in honor. As it is, this creature persecutes us, drives away our lodgers, obviously wants the whole apartment to himself and would have us all sleep in the gutter. Just look, Father," she shrieked all at once, "he's at it again!" And in an access of panic that was quite incomprehensible to Gregor she even quitted her mother, literally thrusting the chair from her as if she would rather sacrifice her mother than stay so near to Gregor, and rushed behind her father, who also rose up, being simply upset by her agitation, and half-spread his arms out as if to protect her.

Yet Gregor had not the slightest intention of frightening anyone, far less his sister. He had only begun to turn round in order to crawl back to his room, but it was certainly a startling operation to watch, since because of his disabled condition he could not execute the difficult turning movements except by lifting his head and then bracing it against the floor over and over again. He paused and looked round. His good intentions seemed to have been recognized; the alarm had only been momentary. Now they were all watching him in melancholy silence. His mother lay in her chair, her legs stiffly outstretched and pressed together, her eyes almost closing for sheer weariness; his father and his sister were sitting beside each other, his sister's arm around the old man's neck.

Perhaps I can go on turning round now, thought Gregor, and began his labors again. He could not stop himself from panting with the effort, and had to pause now and then to take breath. Nor did anyone harass him, he was left entirely to himself. When he had completed the turn-round he began at once to crawl straight back. He was amazed at the distance separating him from his room and could not understand how in his weak state he had managed to accomplish the same journey so recently, almost without remarking it. Intent on crawling as fast as possible, he barely noticed that not a single word, not an ejaculation from his family, interfered with his progress. Only when he was already in the doorway did he turn his head round, not completely, for his neck muscles were getting stiff, but enough to see that nothing had changed behind him except that his sister had risen to her feet. His last glance fell on his mother, who was not quite overcome by sleep.

Hardly was he well inside his room when the door was hastily pushed shut, bolted and locked. The sudden noise in his rear startled him so much that his little legs gave beneath him. It was his sister who had shown such haste. She had been standing ready waiting and had made a light spring forward, Gregor had not even heard her coming, and she cried "At last!" to her parents as she turned the key in the lock.

"And what now?" said Gregor to himself, looking round in the darkness.

Soon he made the discovery that he was now unable to stir a limb. This did not surprise him, rather it seemed unnatural that he should ever actually have been able to move on these feeble little legs. Otherwise he felt relatively comfortable. True, his whole body was aching, but it seemed that the pain was gradually growing less and would finally pass away. The rotting apple in his back and the inflamed area around it, all covered with soft dust, already hardly troubled him. He thought of his family with tenderness and love. The decision that he must disappear was one that he held to even more strongly than his sister, if that were possible. In this state of vacant and peaceful meditation he remained until the tower clock struck three in the morning. The first broadening of light in the world outside the window entered his consciousness once more. Then his head sank to the floor of its own accord and from his nostrils came the last faint flicker of his breath.

When the charwoman arrived early in the morning — what between her strength and her impatience she slammed all the doors so loudly, never mind how often she had been begged not to do so, that no one in the whole apartment could enjoy any quiet sleep after her arrival — she noticed nothing unusual as she took her customary peep into Gregor's room. She thought he was lying motionless on purpose, pretending to be in the sulks; she credited him with every kind of intelligence. Since she happened to have the long-handled broom in her hand she tried to tickle him up with it from the doorway. When that too produced no reaction she felt provoked and poked at him a little harder, and only when she had pushed him along the floor without meeting any resistance was her attention aroused. It did not take her long to establish the truth of the matter, and her eyes widened, she let out a whistle, yet did not waste much time over it but tore open the door of the Samsas' bedroom and yelled into the darkness at the top of her voice: "Just look at this, it's dead; it's lying here dead and done for!"

Mr. and Mrs. Samsa started up in their double bed and before they realized the nature of the charwoman's announcement had some difficulty in overcoming the shock of it. But then they got out of bed quickly, one on either side, Mr. Samsa throwing a blanket over his shoulders, Mrs. Samsa in nothing but her nightgown; in this array they entered Gregor's room. Meanwhile the door of the living room opened, too, where Grete had been sleeping since the advent of the lodgers; she was completely dressed as if she had not been to bed, which seemed to be confirmed also by the paleness of her face. "Dead?" said Mrs. Samsa, looking questioningly at the charwoman, although she could have investigated for herself, and the fact was obvious enough without investigation. "I should say so," said the charwoman, proving her words by pushing Gregor's corpse a long way to one side with her broomstick. Mrs. Samsa made a movement as if to stop her, but checked it. "Well," said Mr. Samsa, "now thanks be to God." He crossed himself, and the three women followed his example. Grete, whose eyes never left the corpse, said: "Just see how thin he was. It's such a long time since he's eaten anything. The food came out again just as it went in." Indeed, Gregor's body was completely flat and dry, as could only now be seen when it was no longer supported by the legs and nothing prevented one from looking closely at it.

"Come in beside us, Grete, for a little while," said Mrs. Samsa with a tremulous smile, and Grete, not without looking back at the corpse, followed her parents into their bedroom. The charwoman shut the door and opened the window wide. Although it was so early in the morning a certain softness was perceptible in the fresh air. After all, it was already the end of March.

The three lodgers emerged from their room and were surprised to see no breakfast; they had been forgotten. "Where's our breakfast?" said the middle lodger peevishly to the charwoman. But she put her finger to her lips and hastily, without a word, indicated by gestures that they should go into Gregor's room. They did so and stood, their hands in the pockets of their somewhat shabby coats, around Gregor's corpse in the room where it was now fully light.

At that the door of the Samsas' bedroom opened and Mr. Samsa appeared in his uniform, his wife on one arm, his daughter on the other. They all looked a little as if they had been crying; from time to time Grete hid her face on her father's arm.

"Leave my house at once!" said Mr. Samsa, and pointed to the door without disengaging himself from the women. "What do you mean by that?" said the middle lodger, taken somewhat aback, with a feeble smile. The two others put their hands behind them and kept rubbing them together, as if in gleeful expectation of a fine set-to in which they were bound to come off the winners. "I mean just what I say," answered Mr. Samsa, and advanced in a straight line with his two companions towards the lodger. He stood his ground at first quietly, looking at the floor as if his thoughts were taking a new pattern in his head. "Then let us go, by all means," he said, and looked up at Mr. Samsa as if in a sudden access of humility he were expecting some renewed sanction for this decision. Mr. Samsa merely nodded briefly once or twice with meaning eyes. Upon that the lodger really did go with long strides into the hall, his two friends had been listening and had quite stopped rubbing their hands for some moments and now went scuttling after him as if afraid that Mr. Samsa might get into the hall before them and cut them off from their leader. In the hall they all three took their hats from the rack, their sticks from the umbrella stand, bowed in silence and quitted the apartment. With a suspiciousness which proved quite unfounded Mr. Samsa and the two women followed them out to the landing; leaning over the banister they watched the three figures slowly but surely going down the long stairs, vanishing from sight at a certain turn of the staircase on every floor and coming into view again after a moment or so; the more they dwindled, the more the Samsa family's interest in them dwindled, and when a butcher's boy met them and passed them on the stairs coming up proudly with a tray on his head, Mr. Samsa and the two women soon left the landing and as if a burden had been lifted from them went back into their apartment.

They decided to spend this day in resting and going for a stroll; they had not only deserved such a respite from work, but absolutely needed it. And so they sat down at the table and wrote three notes of excuse, Mr. Samsa to his board of management, Mrs. Samsa to her employer and Grete to the head of her firm. While they were writing, the charwoman came in to say that she was going now, since her morning's work was finished. At first they only nodded without looking up, but as she kept hovering there they eyed her irritably. "Well?" said Mr. Samsa. The charwoman stood grinning in the doorway as if she had good news to impart to the family but meant not to say a word unless properly questioned. The small ostrich feather standing upright on her hat, which had annoyed Mr. Samsa ever since she was engaged, was waving gaily in all directions. "Well, what is it then?" asked Mrs. Samsa, who obtained more respect from the charwoman than the others. "Oh," said the charwoman, giggling so amiably that she could not at once continue, "just this, you don't need to bother about how to get rid of the thing next door. It's been seen to already." Mrs. Samsa and Grete bent over their letters again, as if preoccupied; Mr. Samsa, who perceived that she was eager to begin describing it all in detail, stopped her with a decisive hand. But since she was not allowed to tell her story, she remembered the great hurry she was in, being obviously deeply huffed: "Bye, everybody," she said, whirling off violently, and departed with a frightful slamming of doors.

"She'll be given notice tonight," said Mr. Samsa, but neither from his wife nor his daughter did he get any answer, for the charwoman seemed to have shattered again the composure they had barely achieved. They rose, went to the window and stayed there, clasping each other tight. Mr. Samsa turned in his chair to look at them and quietly observed them for a little. Then he called out: "Come along, now, do. Let bygones be bygones. And you might have some consideration for me." The two of them complied at once, hastened to him, caressed him and quickly finished their letters.

Then they all three left the apartment together, which was more than they had done for months, and went by tram into the open country outside the town. The tram, in which they were the only passengers, was filled with warm sunshine. Leaning comfortably back in their seats they canvassed their prospects for the future, and it appeared on closer inspection that these were not at all bad, for the jobs they had got, which so far they had never really discussed with each other, were all three admirable and likely to lead to better things later on. The greatest immediate improvement in their condition would of course arise from moving to another house; they wanted to take a smaller and cheaper but also better situated and more easily run apartment than the one they had, which Gregor had selected. While they were thus conversing, it struck both Mr. and Mrs. Samsa, almost at the same moment, as they became aware of their daughter's increasing vivacity, that in spite of all the sorrow of recent times, which had made her cheeks pale, she had bloomed into a pretty girl with a good figure. They grew quieter and half unconsciously exchanged glances of complete agreement, having come to the conclusion that it would soon be time to find a good husband for her. And it was like a confirmation of their new dreams and excellent intentions that at the end of their journey their daughter sprang to her feet first and stretched her young body.

AFTERWORD

If we call something Shakespearian, the something is likely to be a passage of poetry; if we call something Shavian, the something is likely to be a play. But if we call something Kafkaesque, the something is not likely to be literature, but an experience — a maddening encounter with bureaucracy, or a supremely banal moment of horror.

Horror fiction used to deal with misshapen people and strange instruments of torture, but Kafka probably more than any other literary figure changed all that, and gave us a literature of commonplace horror: encounters with bewildering officials, dreamlike efforts of ordinary people to clear up petty things, incomprehensible interruptions in our routines, a sense of isolation from one's fellows and even from oneself. These experiences are set forth in a matter-of-fact style that serves, by its passionless recording of precise details, to relate them convincingly to the reader's daily life. *The Metamorphosis* is somewhat unusual in its fantastic premise, but even this story about a man who has turned into an insect is told with no sense of wonder. Here is the first paragraph:

> As Gregor Samsa awoke one morning from uneasy dreams he found himself transformed in his bed into a gigantic insect. He was lying on his hard, as it were armor-plated, back and when he lifted his head a little he could see his dome-like brown belly divided into stiff arched

> segments on top of which the bed quilt could hardly keep in position and was about to slide off completely. His numerous legs, which were pitifully thin compared to the rest of his bulk, waved helplessly before his eyes.

The reader is not allowed to believe that he is entering a world of hallucination; he is firmly told, "It was no dream"; the literal is insisted on.

If we remember any of the metamorphoses in earlier literature — say in Ovid's *Metamorphoses,* or the change from fallen angel to snake in Milton's *Paradise Lost* — we see how far from mystery we have come, and how deeply immersed in the commonplace we now are. Of course, in the world of fairy tales there was always mystery mixed with daily life (grandmother might be gobbled up by a wolf who would then don her clothes), but in the fairy-tale world a metamorphosed character, the handsome prince whom an enchantress had turned into a frog, would always finally resume his rightful, ordinary appearance, and the world would again make sense. In Kafka this redemption never occurs.

In fact, in Kafka's *Metamorphosis* nothing very much occurs, or so it seems if we are used to novels that show the development of a character by taking him through a series of crucial situations. The most startling thing that happens in the story is Gregor's transformation into an insect, and we are told in the first sentence that this has already taken place. The process of transformation is never described, as it *is* described over and over again in Ovid's *Metamorphoses,* a book of Latin poems recounting how various mortals are changed into stones, plants, animals, and insects. (Why is the spider so skillful a weaver? Because the spider was once a mortal, Arachne, who, proud of her weaving, challenged the Goddess Athena to a contest and was changed into a spider for her presumption.) Ovid's poems share with Aesop's *Fables* the implication that men sometimes act like beasts, but Ovid dwells on the picturesque description of the change, whereas Aesop emphasizes a narrative that reveals beastly qualities. Kafka, in a sense, begins where they both leave off: a man is a particularly low sort of an animal, and the pathos of this condition itself — especially the inability to communicate that accompanies it — is described with a minimum of narrative.

Something like Kafka's initial perception is not, of course, unprecedented. Hamlet, surrounded by foulness and filled with self-loathing, asks, "What should such fellows as I do crawling between earth and heaven?" and Dostoevsky's narrator in *Notes from Underground* says he often wished to become an insect; but Hamlet was using a metaphor, and Dostoevsky's underground man could not succeed in becoming an insect. Kafka's imaginative triumph was to give us a man who *is* an insect, not a man *like* an insect or a man who failed to become an insect.

The sense of exile is Kafka's recurrent theme, and no writer on Kafka fails to point out this deep sense of isolation; he was a Jew in a Gentile world, a German speaker in Prague, a victim of tuberculosis, neurotically estranged from his domineering father, and a literary man in a bourgeois society. An entry in his diary, where he imagines himself as some sort of impotent winged creature, is of special interest to readers of *The Metamorphosis,* and it may help to reveal the sense of isolation that he felt his literary gift had imposed on him:

> What will be my fate as a writer is very simple. My talent for portraying my dreamlike inner life has thrust all other matters into the background; my life has dwindled dreadfully, nor will it cease to dwindle. . . . I waver, continually fly to the summit of the mountain, but then fall back in a moment.

His *Letter to His Father,* a lucid account of the sense of inferiority that his authoritarian father instilled in him, also has some images that connect interestingly with *The Metamorphosis:* Kafka's friends are, in his father's words, "vermin" and "fleas," and Kafka imagines his father replying to the *Letter* by calling Kafka a kind of "vermin" that "sucks blood in order to sustain its own life." But what is especially important for us, since we are interested in Kafka's novel rather than in his life, is a passage in which he describes a moment of intense humiliation and then — astoundingly — adds, "I was frantic with desperation and at such moments all my bad experiences in all spheres fitted magnificently together." "Magnificently" is the astounding word: the chaos and traumas sometimes cohered and he was able to make them into something magnificent.

Exactly what this magnificent thing in front of us, *The Metamorphosis,* is, can be much debated, but debate tends to reduce it to simple formulas such as man's unconscious feelings of guilt, the Jew in a Gentile society, the writer in a bourgeois society, or the writer's inability to communicate his vision. Probably something of all of these interpretations, and a good many more, is in the novel; but, surely, as we read it, we respond, rather than interpret, and we respond at least partly because the emotions described in the story are recognizably our own. The first five or six pages, for instance, carefully record normal responses on awakening: "What about sleeping a little longer," "What an exhausting job I've picked," "A man needs his sleep," "Well, supposing he were to say he was sick." There are, of course, in addition to the astounding premise of a man who changes into a bug, strange dreamlike passages, such as those concerning the three lodgers, and Gregor's father's insistence on wearing his uniform even when off duty. But on the whole the story holds us not by its fantasy but by its realism, its patient recounting of familiar states of mind and its patient description of the insect.

These states of mind, doubtless occasionally felt in all ages, seem especially modern, and it is highly appropriate that Kafka chose for his hero, or anti-hero, a traveling salesman, for the salesman's profession necessarily imposes rootlessness and discontinuity upon him. One is tempted to say that Kafka depicts alienation — the individual's sense that he is separated from his "real self" and forced to adopt a role that does not involve the "real self." But Gregor, at the start, is only intermittently aware that the life he leads is alien to his true self: he grumbles, of course, but he also takes pleasure in being the support of his family, and he is almost wholly devoted to his work. We are told that he does not go out of the house during the evenings but spends his time reading newspapers and railway timetables, and the only suggestions of a life other than his life of drudgery are his interest in fretwork and the pinup girl on the wall. Spineless, he is not so much a man who feels he is forced into the role of a bug, as he is a bug itself, which is why the story begins, rather than ends, with Gregor's metamorphosis. (But we cannot easily feel superior to Gregor; we somehow recognize that Kafka's image of human feelings within an insect's body is a brilliant representation of our dual nature.) The remainder, and bulk, of the story, recounts society's rejection of this drudge, and his perception that he is utterly unloved, a perception that causes him to cease to hang on to life. (This is Gregor's most notable perception, but in the story there are a few other passages indicating, curiously, that as a bug Gregor occasionally is more perceptive than he had been earlier. The description of his response to his sister's music is especially suggestive.) His family feels an enormous relief when this bug dies, and Kafka takes some pains to let the reader share in this relief, for the story — even while it ends with the parents plotting to marry off the daughter to some suitable husband — concludes with references to "the open country" (it began inside a bedroom, on a rainy and overcast day), "vivacity," and the daughter rising and stretching. It is almost as though the metamorphosis at the beginning is balanced by another — this one of the entire family. In his *Diaries* Kafka refers cryptically to the "unreadable ending" of *The Metamorphosis,* but he did not suggest an alternative; he was too honest to suggest that Gregor's death — so unlike Ivan Ilych's in other ways — could be anything other than a relief to Gregor and to all who knew him or heard his story.

JEAN TOOMER

Jean Toomer (1894–1967) was born in Washington, D.C., though both his father's and his mother's families were originally from Georgia. His maternal grandfather, after the Civil War, was acting governor of Louisiana. Toomer attended both the University of Wisconsin and the City College of New York but left both without degrees, since neither gave him what he wanted. He worked at various odd jobs in Chicago and New York, and in 1918 he began publishing poems and sketches in magazines. In 1922, feeling the need to nourish his sense of black identity, he went to Sparta, Georgia, where he was the principal of a school, and where he must have gathered much of the material for *Cane,* which was published the following year. *Cane* achieved some critical acclaim but it was a financial failure, selling only about five hundred copies in the first year. Toomer's interest in mysticism, noticeable in *Cane,* was strengthened when he came under the influence of the Russian mystic Gurdjieff, and in 1926 he spent the summer at the Gurdjieff Institute in Fontainebleau, France. In 1932 he married a writer who died while giving birth to their only child. His second marriage, in 1934, was to a daughter of a member of the New York Stock Exchange. Though he continued to write, no further book was accepted for publication. After living in artists' colonies in Carmel, California, and Taos, New Mexico, he eventually became a member of the Society of Friends and wrote articles for its paper, *Friends Intelligencer.* He died on March 30, 1967, near Philadelphia.

CANE

KARINTHA

Her skin is like dusk on the eastern horizon,
O cant you see it, O cant you see it,
Her skin is like dusk on the eastern horizon
. . . When the sun goes down.

Men had always wanted her, this Karintha, even as a child, Karintha carrying beauty, perfect as dusk when the sun goes down. Old men rode her hobby-horse upon their knees. Young men danced with her at frolics when they should have been dancing with their grownup girls. God grant us youth, secretly prayed the old men. The young fellows counted the time to pass before she would be old enough to mate with them. This interest of the male, who wishes to ripen a growing thing too soon, could mean no good to her.

Karintha, at twelve, was a wild flash that told the other folks just what it was to live. At sunset, when there was no wind, and the pine-smoke from over by the sawmill hugged the earth, and you couldn't see more than a few feet in front, her sudden darting past you was a bit of vivid color, like a black bird that flashes in light. With the other children one could hear, some distance off, their feet flopping in the two-inch dust. Karintha's running was a whir. It had the sound of the red dust that sometimes makes a spiral in the road. At dusk, during the hush just after the sawmill had closed down, and before any of the women had started their supper-getting-ready songs, her voice, high-pitched, shrill, would put one's ears to itching. But no one ever thought to make her stop because of it. She stoned the cows, and beat her dog, and fought the other children. . . Even the preacher, who caught her at mischief, told himself that she was as innocently lovely as a November cotton flower. Already, rumors were out about her. Homes in Georgia are most often built on the two-room plan. In one, you cook and eat, in the other you sleep, and there love goes on. Karintha had seen or heard, perhaps she had felt her parents loving. One could but imitate one's parents, for to follow them was the way of God. She played "home" with a small boy who was not afraid to do her bidding. That started the whole thing. Old men could no longer ride her hobby-horse upon their knees. But young men counted faster.

Her skin is like dusk,
O cant you see it,
Her skin is like dusk,
When the sun goes down.

Karintha is a woman. She who carries beauty, perfect as dusk when the sun goes down. She has been married many times. Old men remind her that a few years back they rode her hobby-horse upon their knees. Karintha smiles, and indulges them when she is in the mood for it. She has contempt for them. Karintha is a woman. Young men run stills to make her money. Young men go to the big cities and run on the road. Young men go away to college. They all want to bring her money. These are the young men who thought that all they had to do was to count time. But Karintha is a woman, and she has had a child. A child fell out of her womb onto a bed of pine-needles in the forest. Pine-needles are smooth and sweet. They are elastic to the feet of rabbits... A sawmill was nearby. Its pyramidal sawdust pile smouldered. It is a year before one completely burns. Meanwhile, the smoke curls up and hangs in odd wraiths about the trees, curls up, and spreads itself out over the valley... Weeks after Karintha returned home the smoke was so heavy you tasted it in water. Some one made a song:

Smoke is on the hills. Rise up.
Smoke is on the hills, O rise
And take my soul to Jesus.

Karintha is a woman. Men do not know that the soul of her was a growing thing ripened too soon. They will bring their money; they will die not having found it out... Karintha at twenty, carrying beauty, perfect as dusk when the sun goes down. Karintha...

Her skin is like dusk on the eastern horizon,
O cant you see it. O cant you see it,
Her skin is like dusk on the eastern horizon
... When the sun goes down.

Goes down...

REAPERS

Black reapers with the sound of steel on stones
Are sharpening scythes. I see them place the hones
In their hip-pockets as a thing that's done,
And start their silent swinging, one by one.
Black horses drive a mower through the weeds,
And there, a field rat, startled, squealing bleeds,
His belly close to ground. I see the blade,
Blood-stained, continue cutting weeds and shade.

NOVEMBER COTTON FLOWER

Boll-weevil's coming, and the winter's cold,
Made cotton-stalks look rusty, seasons old,
And cotton, scarce as any southern snow,
Was vanishing; the branch, so pinched and slow,
Failed in its function as the autumn rake;
Drouth fighting soil had caused the soil to take
All water from the streams; dead birds were found
In wells a hundred feet below the ground —
Such was the season when the flower bloomed.
Old folks were startled, and it soon assumed
Significance. Superstition saw
Something it had never seen before:
Brown eyes that loved without a trace of fear,
Beauty so sudden for that time of year.

BECKY

Becky was the white woman who had two Negro sons. She's dead; they've gone away. The pines whisper to Jesus. The Bible flaps its leaves with an aimless rustle on her mound.

Becky had one Negro son. Who gave it to her? Damn buck nigger, said the white folks' mouths. She wouldnt tell. Common, God-forsaken, insane white shameless wench, said the white folks' mouths. Her eyes were sunken, her neck stringy, her breasts fallen, till then. Taking their words, they filled her, like a bubble rising — then she broke. Mouth setting in a twist that held her eyes, harsh, vacant, staring. . . Who gave it to her? Low-down nigger with no self-respect, said the black folks' mouths. She wouldnt tell. Poor Catholic poor-white crazy woman, said the black folks' mouths. White folks and black folks built her cabin, fed her and her growing baby, prayed secretly to God who'd put His cross upon her and cast her out.

When the first was born, the white folks said they'd have no more to do with her. And black folks, they too joined hands to cast her out. . . The pines whispered to Jesus. . . The railroad boss said not to say he said it, but she could live, if she wanted to, on the narrow strip of land between the railroad and the road. John Stone, who owned the lumber and the bricks, would have shot the man who told he gave the stuff to Lonnie Deacon, who stole out there at night and built the cabin. A single room held down to earth. . . O fly away to Jesus . . . by a leaning chimney. . .

Six trains each day rumbled past and shook the ground under her cabin. Fords, and horse- and mule-drawn buggies went back and forth along the road. No one ever saw her. Trainmen, and passengers who'd heard about her, threw out papers and food. Threw out little crumpled slips of paper scribbled with prayers, as they passed her eye-shaped piece of sandy ground. Ground islandized between the road and railroad track. Pushed up where a blue-sheen God with listless eyes could look at it. Folks from the town took turns, unknown, of course, to each other, in bringing corn and meat and sweet potatoes. Even sometimes snuff. . . O thank y Jesus. . . Old David Georgia, grinding cane and boiling syrup, never went her way without some sugar sap. No one ever saw her. The boy grew up and ran around. When he was five years old as folks reckoned it, Hugh Jourdon saw him carrying a baby. "Becky has another son," was what the whole town knew. But nothing was said, for the part of man that says things to the likes of that had told itself that if there was a Becky, that Becky now was dead.

The two boys grew. Sullen and cunning. . . O pines, whisper to Jesus; tell Him to come and press sweet Jesus-lips against their lips and eyes. . . It seemed as though with those two big fellows there, there could be no room for Becky. The part that prayed wondered if perhaps she'd really died, and they had buried her. No one dared ask. They'd beat and cut a man who meant nothing at all in mentioning that they lived along the road. White or colored? No one knew, and least of all themselves. They drifted around from job to job. We, who had cast out their mother because of them, could we take them in? They answered black and white folks by shooting up two men and leaving town. "Godam the white folks; godam the niggers," they shouted as they left town. Becky? Smoke curled up from her chimney; she must be there. Trains passing shook the ground. The ground shook the leaning chimney. Nobody noticed it. A creepy feeling came over all who saw that thin wraith of smoke and felt the trembling of the ground. Folks began to take her food again. They quit it soon because they had a fear. Becky if dead might be a hant, and if alive — it took some nerve even to mention it. . . O pines, whisper to Jesus. . .

It was Sunday. Our congregation had been visiting at Pulverton, and were coming home. There was no wind. The autumn sun, the bell from Ebenezer Church, listless and heavy. Even the pines were stale, sticky, like the smell of food that makes you sick. Before we turned the bend of the road that would show us the Becky cabin, the horses stopped stock-still, pushed back their ears, and nervously whinnied. We urged, then whipped them on. Quarter of a mile away thin smoke curled up from the leaning chimney. . . O pines, whisper to Jesus. . . Goose-flesh came on my skin though there still was neither chill nor wind. Eyes left their sockets for the cabin. Ears burned and throbbed. Uncanny eclipse! fear closed my mind. We were just about to pass. . . Pines shout to Jesus! . . the ground trembled as a ghost train rumbled by. The chimney fell into the cabin. Its thud was like a hollow report, ages having passed since it went off. Barlo and I were pulled out of our seats. Dragged to the door that had swung open. Through the dust we saw the bricks in a mound upon the floor. Becky, if she was there, lay under them. I thought I heard a groan. Barlo, mumbling something, threw his Bible on the pile. (No one has ever touched it.) Somehow we got away. My buggy was still on the road. The last thing that I remember was whipping old Dan like fury; I remember nothing after that — that is, until I reached town and folks crowded round to get the true word of it.

> Becky was the white woman who had two Negro sons. She's dead; they've gone away. The pines whisper to Jesus. The Bible flaps its leaves with an aimless rustle on her mound.

FACE

Hair —
silver-gray,
like streams of stars,

Brows —
recurved canoes
quivered by the ripples blown by pain,
Her eyes —
mist of tears
condensing on the flesh below
And her channeled muscles
are cluster grapes of sorrow
purple in the evening sun
nearly ripe for worms.

COTTON SONG

Come, brother, come. Lets lift it;
Come now, hewit! roll away!
Shackles fall upon the Judgment Day
But lets not wait for it.

God's body's got a soul,
Bodies like to roll the soul,
Cant blame God if we dont roll,
Come, brother, roll, roll!

Cotton bales are the fleecy way
Weary sinner's bare feet trod,
Softly, softly to the throne of God,
"We aint agwine t wait until th Judgment Day!

Nassur; nassur,
Hump.
Eoho, eoho, roll away!
We aint agwine t wait until th Judgment Day!"

God's body's got a soul,
Bodies like to roll the soul,
Cant blame God if we dont roll,
Come, brother, roll, roll!

CARMA

Wind is in the cane. Come along.
Cane leaves swaying, rusty with talk,
Scratching choruses above the guinea's squawk,
Wind is in the cane. Come along.

Carma, in overalls, and strong as any man, stands behind the old brown mule, driving the wagon home. It bumps, and groans, and shakes as it crosses the railroad track. She, riding it easy. I leave the men around the stove to follow her with my eyes down the red dust road. Nigger woman driving a Georgia chariot down an old dust road. Dixie Pike is what they call it. Maybe she feels my gaze, perhaps she expects it. Anyway, she turns. The sun, which has been slanting over her shoulder, shoots primitive rockets into her mangrove-gloomed, yellow flower face. Hi! Yip! God has left the Moses-people for the nigger. "Gedap." Using reins to slap the mule, she disappears in a cloudy rumble at some indefinite point along the road.

(The sun is hammered to a band of gold. Pine-needles, like mazda, are brilliantly aglow. No rain has come to take the rustle from the falling sweet-gum leaves. Over in the forest, across the swamp, a sawmill blows its closing whistle. Smoke curls up. Marvelous web spun by the spider sawdust pile. Curls up and spreads itself pine-high above the branch, a single silver band along the eastern valley. A black boy . . . you are the most sleepiest man I ever seed, Sleeping Beauty . . . cradled on a gray mule, guided by the hollow sound of cowbells, heads for them through a rusty cotton field. From down the railroad track, the chugchug of a gas engine announces that the repair gang is coming home. A girl in the yard of a whitewashed shack not much larger than the stack of worn ties piled before it, sings. Her voice is loud. Echoes, like rain, sweep the valley. Dusk takes the polish from the rails. Lights twinkle in scattered houses. From far away, a sad strong song. Pungent and composite, the smell of farmyards is the fragrance of the woman. She does not sing; her body is a song. She is in the forest, dancing. Torches flare . . . juju men, greegree, witch-doctors . . . torches go out. . . The Dixie Pike has grown from a goat path in Africa.

Night.

Foxie, the bitch, slicks back her ears and barks at the rising moon.)

Wind is in the corn. Come along.
Corn leaves swaying, rusty with talk,
Scratching choruses above the guinea's squawk,
Wind is in the corn. Come along.

Carma's tale is the crudest melodrama. Her husband's in the gang. And its her fault he got there. Working with a contractor, he was away most of the time. She had others. No one blames her for that. He returned one day and hung around the town where he picked up week-old boasts and rumors. . . Bane accused her. She denied. He couldnt see that she was becoming hysterical. He would have liked to take his fists and beat her. Who was strong as a man. Stronger. Words, like corkscrews, wormed to her strength. It fizzled out. Grabbing a gun, she rushed from the house and plunged across the road into a canebrake. . . There, in quarter heaven shone the crescent moon. . . Bane was afraid to follow till he heard the gun go off. Then he wasted half an hour gathering the neighbor men. They met in the road where lamp-light showed tracks dissolving in the loose earth about the cane. The search began. Moths flickered the lamps. They put them out. Really, because she still might be live enough to shoot. Time and space have no meaning in a canefield. No more than the interminable stalks. . . Some one stumbled over her. A cry went up. From the road, one would have thought that they were cornering a rabbit or a skunk. . . It is difficult carrying dead weight through cane. They placed her on the sofa. A curious, nosey somebody looked for the wound. This fussing with her clothes aroused her. Her eyes were weak and pitiable for so strong a woman. Slowly, then like a flash, Bane came to know that the shot she fired, with averted head, was aimed to whistle like a dying hornet through the cane. Twice deceived, and one deception proved the other. His head went off. Slashed one of the men who'd helped, the man who'd stumbled over her. Now he's in the gang. Who was her husband. Should she not take others, this Carma, strong as a man, whose tale as I have told it is the crudest melodrama?

Wind is in the cane. Come along.
Cane leaves swaying, rusty with talk,
Scratching choruses above the guinea's squawk,
Wind is in the cane. Come along.

SONG OF THE SON

Pour O pour that parting soul in song,
O pour it in the sawdust glow of night,
Into the velvet pine-smoke air to-night,
And let the valley carry it along.
And let the valley carry it along.

O land and soil, red soil and sweet-gum tree,
So scant of grass, so profligate of pines,
Now just before an epoch's sun declines
Thy son, in time, I have returned to thee,
Thy son, I have in time returned to thee.

In time, for though the sun is setting on
A song-lit race of slaves, it has not set;
Though late, O soil, it is not too late yet
To catch thy plaintive soul, leaving, soon gone,
Leaving, to catch thy plaintive soul soon gone.

O Negro slaves, dark purple ripened plums,
Squeezed, and bursting in the pine-wood air,
Passing, before they stripped the old tree bare
One plum was saved for me, one seed becomes

An everlasting song, a singing tree,
Caroling softly souls of slavery,
What they were, and what they are to me,
Caroling softly souls of slavery.

GEORGIA DUSK

The sky, lazily disdaining to pursue
  The setting sun, too indolent to hold
  A lengthened tournament for flashing gold,
Passively darkens for night's barbecue,

A feast of moon and men and barking hounds,
  An orgy for some genius of the South
  With blood-hot eyes and cane-lipped scented mouth,
Surprised in making folk-songs from soul sounds.

The sawmill blows its whistle, buzz-saws stop,
  And silence breaks the bud of knoll and hill,
  Soft settling pollen where plowed lands fulfill
Their early promise of a bumper crop.

Smoke from the pyramidal sawdust pile
   Curls up, blue ghosts of trees, tarrying low
   Where only chips and stumps are left to show
The solid proof of former domicile.

Meanwhile, the men, with vestiges of pomp,
   Race memories of king and caravan,
   High-priests, an ostrich, and a juju-man,
Go singing through the footpaths of the swamp.

Their voices rise . . . the pine trees are guitars,
   Strumming, pine-needles fall like sheets of rain . . .
   Their voices rise . . . the chorus of the cane
Is caroling a vesper to the stars. . .

O singers, resinous and soft your songs
   Above the sacred whisper of the pines,
   Give virgin lips to cornfield concubines,
Bring dreams of Christ to dusky cane-lipped throngs.

FERN

Face flowed into her eyes. Flowed in soft cream foam and plaintive ripples, in such a way that wherever your glance may momentarily have rested, it immediately thereafter wavered in the direction of her eyes. The soft suggestion of down slightly darkened, like the shadow of a bird's wing might, the creamy brown color of her upper lip. Why, after noticing it, you sought her eyes, I cannot tell you. Her nose was aquiline, Semitic. If you have heard a Jewish cantor sing, if he has touched you and made your own sorrow seem trivial when compared with his, you will know my feeling when I follow the curves of her profile, like mobile rivers, to their common delta. They were strange eyes. In this, that they sought nothing — that is, nothing that was obvious and tangible and that one could see, and they gave the impression that nothing was to be denied. When a woman seeks, you will have observed, her eyes deny. Fern's eyes desired nothing that you could give her; there was no reason why they should withhold. Men saw her eyes and fooled themselves. Fern's eyes said to them that she was easy. When she was young, a few men took her, but got no joy from it. And then, once done, they felt bound to her (quite unlike their hit and run with other girls), felt as though it would take them a lifetime to fulfill an obligation which they could find no name for. They became attached to her, and hungered after finding the barest trace of what she might desire. As she grew up, new men who came to town felt as almost everyone did who ever saw her: that they would not be denied. Men were everlastingly bringing her their bodies. Something inside of her got tired of them, I guess, for I am certain that for the life of her she could not tell why or how she began to turn them off. A man in fever is no trifling thing to send away. They began to leave her, baffled and ashamed, yet vowing to themselves that some day they would do some fine thing for her: send her candy every week and not let her know whom it came from, watch out for her wedding-day and give her a magnificent something with no name on it, buy a house and deed it to her, rescue her from some unworthy fellow who had tricked her into marrying him. As you know, men are apt to idolize or fear that which they cannot understand, especially if it be a woman. She did not deny them, yet the fact was that they were denied. A sort of superstition crept into their consciousness of her being somehow above them. Being above them meant that she was not to be approached by anyone. She became a virgin. Now a virgin in a small southern town is by no means the usual thing, if you will believe me. That the sexes were made to mate is the practice of the South. Particularly, black folks were made to mate. And it is black folks whom I have been talking about thus far. What white men thought of Fern I can arrive at only by analogy. They let her alone.

Anyone, of course, could see her, could see her eyes. If you walked up the Dixie Pike most any time of day, you'd be most like to see her resting listless-like on the railing of her porch, back propped against a post, head tilted a little forward because there was a nail in the porch post just where her head came which for some reason or other she never took the trouble to pull out. Her eyes, if it were sunset, rested idly where the sun, molten and glorious, was pouring down between the fringe of pines. Or maybe they gazed at the gray cabin on the knoll from which an evening folk-song was coming. Perhaps they followed a cow that had been turned loose to roam and feed on cotton-stalks and corn leaves. Like as not they'd settle on some vague spot above the horizon, though hardly a trace of wistfulness would come to them. If it were dusk, then they'd wait for the search-light of the evening train which you could see miles up the track before it flared across the Dixie Pike, close to her home. Wherever they looked, you'd follow them and then waver back. Like her face, the whole countryside seemed to flow into her eyes. Flowed into them with the soft listless cadence of Georgia's South. A young Negro, once, was looking at her, spellbound, from the road. A white man passing in a buggy had to flick him with his whip if he was to get by without running him over. I first saw her on her porch. I was passing with a fellow whose crusty numbness (I was from the North and suspected of being prejudiced and stuck-up) was melting as he found me warm. I asked him who she was. "That's Fern," was all that I could get from him. Some folks already thought that I was given to nosing around; I let it go at that, so far as questions were concerned. But at first sight of her I felt as if I heard a Jewish cantor sing. As if his singing rose above the unheard chorus of a folk-song. And I felt bound to her. I too had my dreams: something I would do for her. I have knocked about from town to town too much not to know the futility of mere change of place. Besides, picture if you can, this cream-colored solitary girl sitting at a tenement window looking down on the indifferent throngs of Harlem. Better that she listen to folk-songs at dusk in Georgia, you would say, and so would I. Or, suppose she came up North and married. Even a doctor or a lawyer, say, one who would be sure to get along — that is, make money. You and I know, who have had experience in such things, that love is not a thing like prejudice which can be bettered by changes of town. Could men in Washington, Chicago, or New York, more than the men of Georgia, bring her something left vacant by the bestowal of their bodies? You and I who know men in these cities will have to say, they could not. See her out and out a prostitute along State Street in Chicago. See her move into a southern town where white men are more aggressive. See her become a white man's concubine. . . Something I must do for her. There was myself. What could I do for her? Talk, of course. Push back the fringe of pines upon new horizons. To what purpose? and what for? Her? Myself? Men in her case seem to lose their selfishness. I lost mine before I touched her. I ask you, friend (it makes no difference if you sit in the Pullman or the Jim Crow as the train crosses her road), what thoughts would come to you — that is, after you'd finished with the thoughts that leap into men's minds at the sight of a pretty woman who will not deny them; what thoughts would come to you, had you seen her in a quick flash, keen and intuitively, as she sat there on her porch when your train thundered by? Would you have got off at the next station and come back for her to take her where? Would you have completely forgotten her as soon as you reached Macon, Atlanta, Augusta, Pasadena, Madison, Chicago, Boston, or New Orleans? Would you tell your wife or sweetheart about a girl you saw? Your thoughts can help me, and I would like to know. Something I would do for her. . .

One evening I walked up the Pike on purpose, and stopped to say hello. Some of her family were about, but they moved away to make room for me. Damn if I knew how to begin. Would you? Mr. and Miss So-and-So, people, the weather, the crops, the new preacher, the frolic, the church benefit, rabbit and possum hunting, the new soft drink they had at old Pap's store, the schedule of the trains, what kind of town Macon was, Negro's migration north, boll-weevils, syrup, the Bible — to all these things she gave a yassur or nassur, without further comment. I began to wonder if perhaps my own emotional sensibility had played one of its tricks on me. "Lets take a walk," I at last ventured. The suggestion, coming after so long an isolation, was novel enough, I guess, to surprise. But it wasnt that. Something told me that men before me had said just that as a prelude to the offering of their bodies. I tried to tell her with my eyes. I think she understood. The thing from her that made my throat catch, vanished. Its passing left her visible in a way I'd thought, but never seen. We walked down the Pike with people on all the porches gaping at us. "Doesnt it make you mad?" She meant the row of petty gossiping people. She meant the world. Through a canebrake that was ripe for cutting, the branch was reached. Under a sweet-gum tree, and where reddish leaves had dammed the creek a little, we sat down. Dusk, suggesting the almost imperceptible procession of giant trees, settled with a purple haze about the cane. I felt strange, as I always do in Georgia, particularly at dusk. I felt that things unseen to men were tangibly immediate. It would not have surprised me had I had vision. People have them in Georgia more often than you would suppose. A black woman once saw the mother of Christ and drew her in charcoal on the courthouse wall. . . When one is on the soil of one's ancestors, most anything can come to one. . . From force of habit, I suppose, I held Fern in my arms — that is, without at first noticing it. Then my mind came back to her. Her eyes, unusually weird and open, held me. Held God. He flowed in as I've seen the countryside flow in. Seen men. I must have done something — what, I dont know, in the confusion of my emotion. She sprang up. Rushed some distance from me. Fell to her knees, and began swaying, swaying. Her body was tortured with something it could not let out. Like boiling sap it flooded arms and fingers till she shook them as if they burned her. It found her throat, and spattered inarticulately in plaintive, convulsive sounds, mingled with calls to Christ Jesus. And then she sang, brokenly. A Jewish cantor singing with a broken voice. A child's voice, uncertain, or an old man's. Dusk hid her; I could hear only her song. It seemed to me as though she were pounding her head in anguish upon the ground. I rushed to her. She fainted in my arms.

There was talk about her fainting with me in the canefield. And I got one or two ugly looks from town men who'd set themselves up to protect her. In fact, there was talk of making me leave town. But they never did. They kept a watch-out for me, though. Shortly after, I came back North. From the train window I saw her as I crossed her road. Saw her on her porch, head tilted a little forward where the nail was, eyes vaguely focused on the sunset. Saw her face flow into them, the countryside and something that I call God, flowing into them... Nothing ever really happened. Nothing ever came to Fern, not even I. Something I would do for her. Some fine unnamed thing... And, friend, you? She is still living, I have reason to know. Her name, against the chance that you might happen down that way, is Fernie May Rosen.

NULLO

A spray of pine-needles,
Dipped in western horizon gold,
Fell onto a path.
Dry moulds of cow-hoofs.
In the forest.
Rabbits knew not of their falling,
Nor did the forest catch aflame.

EVENING SONG

Full moon rising on the waters of my heart,
Lakes and moon and fires,
Cloine tires,
Holding her lips apart.

Promises of slumber leaving shore to charm the moon,
Miracle made vesper-keeps,
Cloine sleeps,
And I'll be sleeping soon.

Cloine, curled like the sleepy waters where the moon-waves start,
Radiant, resplendently she gleams,
Cloine dreams,
Lips pressed against my heart.

ESTHER

I

Nine.

Esther's hair falls in soft curls about her high-cheek-boned chalk-white face. Esther's hair would be beautiful if there were more gloss to it. And if her face were not prematurely serious, one could call it pretty. Her cheeks are too flat and dead for a girl of nine. Esther looks like a little white child, starched, frilled, as she walks slowly from her home towards her father's grocery store. She is about to turn in Broad from Maple Street. White and black men loafing on the corner hold no interest for her. Then a strange thing happens. A clean-muscled, magnificent, black-skinned Negro, whom she had heard her father mention as King Barlo, suddenly drops to his knees on a spot called the Spittoon. White men, unaware of him, continue squirting tobacco juice in his direction. The saffron fluid splashes on his face. His smooth black face begins to glisten and to shine. Soon, people notice him, and gather round. His eyes are rapturous upon the heavens. Lips and nostrils quiver. Barlo is in a religious trance. Town folks know it. They are not startled. They are not afraid. They gather round. Some beg boxes from the grocery stores. From old McGregor's notion shop. A coffin-case is pressed into use. Folks line the curb-stones. Business men close shop. And Banker Warply parks his car close by. Silently, all await the prophet's voice. The sheriff, a great florid fellow whose leggings never meet around his bulging calves, swears in three deputies. "Wall, y cant never tell what a nigger like King Barlo might be up t." Soda bottles, five fingers full of shine, are passed to those who want them. A couple of stray dogs start a fight. Old Goodlow's cow comes flopping up the street. Barlo, still as an Indian fakir, has not moved. The town bell strikes six. The sun slips in behind a heavy mass of horizon cloud. The crowd is hushed and expectant. Barlo's under jaw relaxes, and his lips begin to move.

"Jesus has been awhisperin strange words deep down, O way down deep, deep in my ears."

Hums of awe and of excitement.

"He called me to His side an said, 'Git down on your knees beside me, son, Ise gwine t whisper in your ears.' "

An old sister cries, "Ah, Lord."

" 'Ise agwine t whisper in your ears,' he said, and I replied, 'Thy will be done on earth as it is in heaven.' "

"Ah, Lord. Amen. Amen."

"An Lord Jesus whispered strange good words deep down, O way down deep, deep in my ears. An He said, 'Tell em till you feel your throat on fire.' I saw a vision. I saw a man arise, an he was big an black an powerful —"

Some one yells, "Preach it, preacher, preach it!"

"— but his head was caught up in th clouds. An while he was agazin at th heavens, heart filled up with th Lord, some little white-ant biddies came an tied his feet to chains. They led him t th coast, they led him t th sea, they led him across th ocean an they didnt set him free. The old coast didnt miss him, and th new coast wasnt free, he left the old-coast brothers, t give birth t you an me. O Lord, great God Almighty, t give birth t you an me."

Barlo pauses. Old gray mothers are in tears. Fragments of melodies are being hummed. White folks are touched and curiously awed. Off to themselves, white and black preachers confer as to how best to rid themselves of the vagrant, usurping fellow. Barlo looks as though he is struggling to continue. People are hushed. One can hear weevils work. Dusk is falling rapidly, and the customary store lights fail to throw their feeble glow across the gray dust and flagging of the Georgia town. Barlo rises to his full height. He is immense. To the people he assumes the outlines of his visioned African. In a mighty voice he bellows:

"Brothers an sisters, turn your faces t th sweet face of the Lord, an fill your hearts with glory. Open your eyes an see th dawnin of th mornin light. Open your ears —"

Years afterwards Esther was told that at that very moment a great, heavy, rumbling voice actually was heard. That hosts of angels and of demons paraded up and down the streets all night. That King Barlo rode out of town astride a pitch-black bull that had a glowing gold ring in its nose. And that old Limp Underwood, who hated niggers, woke up next morning to find that he held a black man in his arms. This much is certain: an inspired Negress, of wide reputation for being sanctified, drew a portrait of a black madonna on the court-house wall. And King Barlo left town. He left his image indelibly upon the mind of Esther. He became the starting point of the only living patterns that her mind was to know.

II

Sixteen.

Esther begins to dream. The low evening sun sets the windows of McGregor's notion shop aflame. Esther makes believe that they really are aflame. The town fire department rushes madly down the road. It ruthlessly shoves black and white idlers to one side. It whoops. It clangs. It rescues from the second-story window a dimpled infant which she claims for her own. How had she come by it? She thinks of it immaculately. It is a sin to think of it immaculately. She must dream no more. She must repent her sin. Another dream comes. There is no fire department. There are no heroic men. The fire starts. The loafers on the corner form a circle, chew their tobacco faster, and squirt juice just as fast as they can chew. Gallons on top of gallons they squirt upon the flames. The air reeks with the stench of scorched tobacco juice. Women, fat chunky Negro women, lean scrawny white women, pull their skirts up above their heads and display the most ludicrous underclothes. The women scoot in all directions from the danger zone. She alone is left to take the baby in her arms. But what a baby! Black, singed, woolly, tobacco-juice baby — ugly as sin. Once held to her breast, miraculous thing: its breath is sweet and its lips can nibble. She loves it frantically. Her joy in it changes the town folks' jeers to harmless jealousy, and she is left alone.

Twenty-two.

Esther's schooling is over. She works behind the counter of her father's grocery store. "To keep the money in the family," so he said. She is learning to make distinctions between the business and the social worlds. "Good business comes from remembering that the white folks dont divide the niggers, Esther. Be just as black as any man who has a silver dollar." Esther listlessly forgets that she is near white, and that her father is the richest colored man in town. Black folk who drift in to buy lard and snuff and flour of her, call her a sweet-natured, accommodating girl. She learns their names. She forgets them. She thinks about men. "I dont appeal to them. I wonder why." She recalls an affair she had with a little fair boy while still in school. It had ended in her shame when he as much as told her that for sweetness he preferred a lollipop. She remembers the salesman from the North who wanted to take her to the movies that first night he was in town. She refused, of course. And he never came back, having found out who she was. She thinks of Barlo. Barlo's image gives her a slightly stale thrill. She spices it by telling herself his glories. Black. Magnetically so. Best cotton picker in the county, in the state, in the whole world for that matter. Best man with his fists, best man with dice, with a razor. Promoter of church benefits. Of colored fairs. Vagrant preacher. Lover of all the women for miles and miles around. Esther decides that she loves him. And with a vague sense of life slipping by, she resolves that she will tell him so, whatever people say, the next time he comes to town. After the making of this resolution which becomes a sort of wedding cake for her to tuck beneath her pillow and go to sleep upon, she sees nothing of Barlo for five years. Her hair thins. It looks like the dull silk on puny corn ears. Her face pales until it is the color of the gray dust that dances with dead cotton leaves.

III

Esther is twenty-seven.

Esther sells lard and snuff and flour to vague black faces that drift in her store to ask for them. Her eyes hardly see the people to whom she gives change. Her body is lean and beaten. She rests listlessly against the counter, too weary to sit down. From the street some one shouts, "King Barlo has come back to town." He passes her window, driving a large new car. Cut-out open. He veers to the curb, and steps out. Barlo has made money on cotton during the war. He is as rich as anyone. Esther suddenly is animate. She goes to her door. She sees him at a distance, the center of a group of credulous men. She hears the deep-bass rumble of his talk. The sun swings low. McGregor's windows are aflame again. Pale flame. A sharply dressed white girl passes by. For a moment Esther wishes that she might be like her. Not white; she has no need for being that. But sharp, sporty, with get-up about her. Barlo is connected with that wish. She mustnt wish. Wishes only make you restless. Emptiness is a thing that grows by being moved. "I'll not think. Not wish. I just set my mind against it." Then the thought comes to her that those purposeless, easy-going men will possess him, if she doesnt. Purpose is not dead in her, now that she comes to think of it. That loose women will have their arms around him at Nat Bowle's place to-night. As if her veins are full of fired sun-bleached southern shanties, a swift heat sweeps them. Dead dreams, and a forgotten resolution are carried upward by the flames. Pale flames. "They shant have him. Oh, they shall not. Not if it kills me they shant have him." Jerky, aflutter, she closes the store and starts home. Folks lazing on store windowsills wonder what on earth can be the matter with Jim Crane's gal, as she passes them. "Come to remember, she always was a little off, a little crazy, I reckon." Esther seeks her own room, and locks the door. Her mind is a pink mesh-bag filled with baby toes.

Using the noise of the town clock striking twelve to cover the creaks of her departure, Esther slips into the quiet road. The town, her parents, most everyone is sound asleep. This fact is a stable thing that comforts her. After sundown a chill wind came up from the west. It is still blowing, but to her it is a steady, settled thing like the cold. She wants her mind to be like that.

Solid, contained, and blank as a sheet of darkened ice. She will not permit herself to notice the peculiar phosphorescent glitter of the sweet-gum leaves. Their movement would excite her. Exciting too, the recession of the dull familiar homes she knows so well. She doesnt know them at all. She closes her eyes, and holds them tightly. Wont do. Her being aware that they are closed recalls her purpose. She does not want to think of it. She opens them. She turns now into the deserted business street. The corrugated iron canopies and mule- and horse-gnawed hitching posts bring her a strange composure. Ghosts of the commonplaces of her daily life take stride with her and become her companions. And the echoes of her heels upon the flagging are rhythmically monotonous and soothing. Crossing the street at the corner of McGregor's notion shop, she thinks that the windows are a dull flame. Only a fancy. She walks faster. Then runs. A turn into a side street brings her abruptly to Nat Bowle's place. The house is squat and dark. It is always dark. Barlo is within. Quietly she opens the outside door and steps in. She passes through a small room. Pauses before a flight of stairs down which people's voices, muffled, come. The air is heavy with fresh tobacco smoke. It makes her sick. She wants to turn back. She goes up the steps. As if she were mounting to some great height, her head spins. She is violently dizzy. Blackness rushes to her eyes. And then she finds that she is in a large room. Barlo is before her.

"Well, I'm sholy damned — skuse me, but what, what brought you here, lil milk-white gal?"

"You." Her voice sounds like a frightened child's that calls homeward from some point miles away.

"Me?"

"Yes, you Barlo."

"This aint th place fer y. This aint th place fer y."

"I know. I know. But I've come for you."

"For me for what?"

She manages to look deep and straight into his eyes. He is slow at understanding. Guffaws and giggles break out from all around the room. A coarse woman's voice remarks, "So thats how the dictie[1] niggers does it." Laughs. "Mus give em credit fo their gall."

Esther doesnt hear. Barlo does. His faculties are jogged. She sees a smile, ugly and repulsive to her, working upward through thick licker fumes. Barlo seems hideous. The thought comes suddenly, that conception with a drunken man must be a mighty sin. She draws away, frozen. Like a somnambulist she wheels around and walks stiffly to the stairs. Down them. Jeers and hoots

1 [Affected, high-toned. — Editors' note.]

pelter bluntly upon her back. She steps out. There is no air, no street, and the town has completely disappeared.

CONVERSION

African Guardian of Souls,
Drunk with rum,
Feasting on a strange cassava,
Yielding to new words and a weak palabra
Of a white-faced sardonic god —
Grins, cries
Amen,
Shouts hosanna.

PORTRAIT IN GEORGIA

Hair — braided chestnut,
    coiled like a lyncher's rope,
Eyes — fagots,
Lips — old scars, or the first red blisters,
Breath — the last sweet scent of cane,
And her slim body, white as the ash
    of black flesh after flame.

BLOOD-BURNING MOON

I

Up from the skeleton stone walls, up from the rotting floor boards and the solid hand-hewn beams of oak of the pre-war cotton factory, dusk came. Up from the dusk the full moon came. Glowing like a fired pine-knot, it illumined the great door and soft showered the Negro shanties aligned along the single street of factory town. The full moon in the great door was an omen. Negro women improvised songs against its spell.

Louisa sang as she came over the crest of the hill from the white folks' kitchen. Her skin was the color of oak leaves on young trees in fall. Her breasts, firm and up-pointed like ripe acorns. And her singing had the low murmur of winds in fig trees. Bob Stone, younger son of the people she worked for, loved her. By the way the world reckons things, he had won her. By measure of that warm glow which came into her mind at thought of him, he had won her. Tom Burwell, whom the whole town called Big Boy, also loved her. But working in the fields all day, and far away from her, gave him no chance to show it. Though often enough of evenings he had tried to. Somehow, he never got along. Strong as he was with hands upon the ax or plow, he found it difficult to hold her. Or so he thought. But the fact was that he held her to factory town more firmly than he thought for. His black balanced, and pulled against, the white of Stone, when she thought of them. And her mind was vaguely upon them as she came over the crest of the hill, coming from the white folks' kitchen. As she sang softly at the evil face of the full moon.

A strange stir was in her. Indolently, she tried to fix upon Bob or Tom as the cause of it. To meet Bob in the canebrake, as she was going to do an hour or so later, was nothing new. And Tom's proposal which she felt on its way to her could be indefinitely put off. Separately, there was no unusual significance to either one. But for some reason, they jumbled when her eyes gazed vacantly at the rising moon. And from the jumble came the stir that was strangely within her. Her lips trembled. The slow rhythm of her song grew agitant and restless. Rusty black and tan spotted hounds, lying in the dark corners of porches or prowling around back yards, put their noses in the air and caught its tremor. They began plaintively to yelp and howl. Chickens woke up and cackled. Intermittently, all over the countryside dogs barked and roosters crowed as if heralding a weird dawn or some ungodly awakening. The women sang lustily. Their songs were cotton-wads to stop their ears. Louisa came down into factory town and sank wearily upon the step before her home. The moon was rising towards a thick cloud-bank which soon would hide it.

> Red nigger moon. Sinner!
> Blood-burning moon. Sinner!
> Come out that fact'ry door.

II

Up from the deep dusk of a cleared spot on the edge of the forest a mellow glow arose and spread fan-wise into the low-hanging heavens. And all around the air was heavy with the scent of boiling cane. A large pile of cane-stalks lay like ribboned shadows upon the ground. A mule, harnessed to a pole, trudged lazily round and round the pivot of the grinder. Beneath a swaying oil lamp, a Negro alternately whipped out at the mule, and fed cane-stalks to the grinder. A fat boy waddled pails of fresh ground juice between the grinder and the boiling stove. Steam came from the copper boiling pan. The scent of cane came from the copper pan and drenched the forest and the hill that sloped to factory town, beneath its fragrance. It drenched the men in circle seated around the stove. Some of them chewed at the white pulp of stalks, but there was no need for them to, if all they wanted was to taste the cane. One tasted it in factory town. And from factory town one could see the soft haze thrown by the glowing stove upon the low-hanging heavens.

Old David Georgia stirred the thickening syrup with a long ladle, and ever so often drew it off. Old David Georgia tended his stove and told tales about the white folks, about moonshining and cotton picking, and about sweet nigger gals, to the men who sat there about his stove to listen to him. Tom Burwell chewed cane-stalk and laughed with the others till someone mentioned Louisa. Till someone said something about Louisa and Bob Stone, about the silk stockings she must have gotten from him. Blood ran up Tom's neck hotter than the glow that flooded from the stove. He sprang up. Glared at the men and said, "She's my gal." Will Manning laughed. Tom strode over to him. Yanked him up and knocked him to the ground. Several of Manning's friends got up to fight for him. Tom whipped out a long knife and would have cut them to shreds if they hadnt ducked into the woods. Tom had had enough. He nodded to Old David Georgia and swung down the path to factory town. Just then, the dogs started barking and the roosters began to crow. Tom felt funny. Away from the fight, away from the stove, chill got to him. He shivered. He shuddered when he saw the full moon rising towards the cloud-bank. He who didnt give a godam for the fears of old women. He forced his mind to fasten on Louisa. Bob Stone. Better not be. He turned into the street and saw Louisa sitting before her home. He went towards her, ambling, touched the brim of a marvelously shaped, spotted, felt hat, said he wanted to say something to her, and then found that he didnt know what he had to say, or if he did, that he couldnt say it. He shoved his big fists in his overalls, grinned, and started to move off.

"Youall want me, Tom?"

"Thats what us wants, sho, Louisa."

"Well, here I am —"

"An here I is, but that aint ahelpin none, all th same."

"You wanted to say something? . ."

"I did that, sho. But words is like th spots on dice: no matter how y fumbles em, there's times when they jes wont come. I dunno why. Seems like th love I feels fo yo done stole m tongue. I got it now. Whee! Louisa, honey, I oughtnt tell y, I feel I oughtnt cause yo is young an goes t church an I has had other gals, but Louisa I sho do love y. Lil gal, Ise watched y from them first days when youall sat right here befo yo door befo th well an sang sometimes in a way that like t broke m heart. Ise carried y with me into th fields, day after day, an after that, an I sho can plow when yo is there, an I can pick cotton. Yassur! Come near beatin Barlo yesterday. I sho did. Yassur! An next year if ole Stone'll trust me, I'll have a farm. My own. My bales will buy yo what y gets from white folks now. Silk stockings an purple dresses — course I dont believe what some folks been whisperin as t how y gets them things now. White folks always did do for niggers what they likes. An they jes cant help alikin yo, Louisa. Bob Stone likes y. Course he does. But not th way folks is awhisperin. Does he, hon?"

"I dont know what you mean, Tom."

"Course y dont. Ise already cut two niggers. Had t hon, t tell em so. Niggers always tryin t make somethin out a nothin. An then besides, white folks aint up t them tricks so much nowadays. Godam better not be. Leastawise not with yo. Cause I wouldnt stand f it. Nassur."

"What would you do, Tom?"

"Cut him jes like I cut a nigger."

"No, Tom —"

"I said I would an there aint no mo to it. But that aint th talk f now. Sing, honey Louisa, an while I'm listenin t y I'll be makin love."

Tom took her hand in his. Against the tough thickness of his own, hers felt soft and small. His huge body slipped down to the step beside her. The full moon sank upward into the deep purple of the cloud-bank. An old woman brought a lighted lamp and hung it on the common well whose bulky shadow squatted in the middle of the road, opposite Tom and Louisa. The old woman lifted the well-lid, took hold the chain, and began drawing up the heavy bucket. As she did so, she sang. Figures shifted, restless-like, between lamp and window in the front rooms of the shanties. Shadows of the figures fought each other on the gray dust of the road. Figures raised the windows and joined the old woman in song. Louisa and Tom, the whole street, singing:

Red nigger moon. Sinner!
Blood-burning moon. Sinner!
Come out that fact'ry door.

III

Bob Stone sauntered from his veranda out into the gloom of fir trees and magnolias. The clear white of his skin paled, and the flush of his cheeks turned purple. As if to balance this outer change, his mind became consciously a white man's. He passed the house with its huge open hearth which, in the days of slavery, was the plantation cookery. He saw Louisa bent over that hearth. He went in as a master should and took her. Direct, honest, bold. None of this sneaking that he had to go through now. The contrast was repulsive to him. His family had lost ground. Hell no, his family still owned the niggers, practically. Damned if they did, or he wouldnt have to duck around so. What would they think if they knew? His mother? His sister? He shouldnt mention them, shouldnt think of them in this connection. There in the dusk he blushed at doing so. Fellows about town were all right, but how about his friends up North? He could see them incredible, repulsed. They didnt know. The thought first made him laugh. Then, with their eyes still upon him, he began to feel embarrassed. He felt the need of explaining things to them. Explain hell. They wouldnt understand, and moreover, who ever heard of a Southerner getting on his knees to any Yankee, or anyone. No sir. He was going to see Louisa to-night, and love her. She was lovely — in her way. Nigger way. What way was that? Damned if he knew. Must know. He'd known her long enough to know. Was there something about niggers that you couldnt know? Listening to them at church didnt tell you anything. Looking at them didnt tell you anything. Talking to them didnt tell you anything — unless it was gossip, unless they wanted to talk. Of course, about farming, and licker, and craps — but those werent nigger. Nigger was something more. How much more? Something to be afraid of, more? Hell no. Who ever heard of being afraid of a nigger? Tom Burwell. Cartwell had told him that Tom went with Louisa after she reached home. No sir. No nigger had ever been with his girl. He'd like to see one try. Some position for him to be in. Him, Bob Stone, of the old Stone family, in a scrap with a nigger over a nigger girl. In the good old days. . . Ha! Those were the days. His family had lost ground. Not so much, though. Enough for him to have to cut through old Lemon's canefield by way of the woods, that he might meet her. She was worth it. Beautiful nigger gal. Why nigger? Why not, just gal? No, it was because she was nigger that he went to her. Sweet. . . The scent of boiling cane came to him. Then he saw the rich glow of the stove. He heard the voices of the men circled around it. He was about to skirt the clearing when he heard his own name mentioned. He stopped. Quivering. Leaning against a tree, he listened.

"Bad nigger. Yassur, he sho is one bad nigger when he gets started."

"Tom Burwell's been on th gang three times fo cuttin men."

"What y think he's agwine t do t Bob Stone?"

"Dunno yet. He aint found out. When he does — Baby!"

"Aint no tellin."

"Young Stone aint no quitter an I ken tell y that. Blood of th old uns in his veins."

"Thats right. He'll scrap, sho."

"Be gettin too hot f niggers round this away."

"Shut up, nigger. Y dont know what y talkin bout."

Bob Stone's ears burned as though he had been holding them over the stove. Sizzling heat welled up within him. His feet felt as if they rested on red-hot coals. They stung him to quick movement. He circled the fringe of the glowing. Not a twig cracked beneath his feet. He reached the path that led to factory town. Plunged furiously down it. Halfway along, a blindness within him veered him aside. He crashed into the bordering canebrake. Cane leaves cut his face and lips. He tasted blood. He threw himself down and dug his fingers in the ground. The earth was cool. Cane-roots took the fever from his hands. After a long while, or so it seemed to him, the thought came to him that it must be time to see Louisa. He got to his feet and walked calmly to their meeting place. No Louisa. Tom Burwell had her. Veins in his forehead bulged and distended. Saliva moistened the dried blood on his lips. He bit down on his lips. He tasted blood. Not his own blood; Tom Burwell's blood. Bob drove through the cane and out again upon the road. A hound swung down the path before him towards factory town. Bob couldnt see it. The dog loped aside to let him pass. Bob's blind rushing made him stumble over it. He fell with a thud that dazed him. The hound yelped. Answering yelps came from all over the countryside. Chickens cackled. Roosters crowed, heralding the bloodshot eyes of southern awakening. Singers in the town were silenced. They shut their windows down. Palpitant between the rooster crows, a chill hush settled upon the huddled forms of Tom and Louisa. A figure rushed from the shadow and stood before them. Tom popped to his feet.

"Whats y want?"

"I'm Bob Stone."

"Yassur — an I'm Tom Burwell. Whats y want?"

Bob lunged at him. Tom side-stepped, caught him by the shoulder, and flung him to the ground. Straddled him.

"Let me up."

"Yassur — but watch yo doins, Bob Stone."

A few dark figures, drawn by the sound of scuffle, stood about them. Bob sprang to his feet.

"Fight like a man, Tom Burwell, an I'll lick y."

Again he lunged. Tom side-stepped and flung him to the ground. Straddled him.

"Get off me, you godam nigger you."

"Yo sho has started somethin now. Get up."

Tom yanked him up and began hammering at him. Each blow sounded as if it smashed into a precious, irreplaceable soft something. Beneath them, Bob staggered back. He reached in his pocket and whipped out a knife.

"Thats my game, sho."

Blue flash, a steel blade slashed across Bob Stone's throat. He had a sweetish sick feeling. Blood began to flow. Then he felt a sharp twitch of pain. He let his knife drop. He slapped one hand against his neck. He pressed the other on top of his head as if to hold it down. He groaned. He turned, and staggered towards the crest of the hill in the direction of white town. Negroes who had seen the fight slunk into their homes and blew the lamps out. Louisa, dazed, hysterical, refused to go indoors. She slipped, crumbled, her body loosely propped against the woodwork of the well. Tom Burwell leaned against it. He seemed rooted there.

Bob reached Broad Street. White men rushed up to him. He collapsed in their arms.

"Tom Burwell. . ."

White men like ants upon a forage rushed about. Except for the taut hum of their moving, all was silent. Shotguns, revolvers, rope, kerosene, torches. Two high-powered cars with glaring search-lights. They came together. The taut hum rose to a low roar. Then nothing could be heard but the flop of their feet in the thick dust of the road. The moving body of their silence preceded them over the crest of the hill into factory town. It flattened the Negroes beneath it. It rolled to the wall of the factory, where it stopped. Tom knew that they were coming. He couldnt move. And then he saw the search-lights of the two cars glaring down on him. A quick shock went through him. he stiffened. He started to run. A yell went up from the mob. Tom wheeled about and faced them. They poured down on him. They swarmed. A large man with dead-white face and flabby cheeks came to him and almost jabbed a gun-barrel through his guts.

"Hands behind y, nigger."

Tom's wrists were bound. The big man shoved him to the well. Burn him over it, and when the woodwork caved in, his body would drop to the bottom. Two deaths for a godam nigger. Louisa was driven back. The mob pushed in. Its pressure, its momentum was too great. Drag him to the factory. Wood and stakes already there. Tom moved in the direction indicated. But they had to drag him. They reached the great door. Too many to get in there. The mob divided and flowed around the walls to either side. The big man shoved him through the door. The mob pressed in from the sides. Taut humming. No words. A stake was sunk into the ground. Rotting floor boards piled around it. Kerosene poured on the rotting floor boards. Tom bound to the stake. His breast was bare.

Nails scratches let little lines of blood trickle down and mat into the hair. His face, his eyes were set and stony. Except for irregular breathing, one would have thought him already dead. Torches were flung onto the pile. A great flare muffled in black smoke shot upward. The mob yelled. The mob was silent. Now Tom could be seen within the flames. Only his head, erect, lean, like a blackened stone. Stench of burning flesh soaked the air. Tom's eyes popped. His head settled downward. The mob yelled. Its yell echoed against the skeleton stone walls and sounded like a hundred yells. Like a hundred mobs yelling. Its yell thudded against the thick front wall and fell back. Ghost of a yell slipped through the flames and out the great door of the factory. It fluttered like a dying thing down the single street of factory town. Louisa, upon the step before her home, did not hear it, but her eyes opened slowly. They saw the full moon glowing in the great door. The full moon, an evil thing, an omen, soft showering the homes of folks she knew. Where were they, these people? She'd sing, and perhaps they'd come out and join her. Perhaps Tom Burwell would come. At any rate, the full moon in the great door was an omen which she must sing to:

> Red nigger moon. Sinner!
> Blood-burning moon. Sinner!
> Come out that fact'ry door.

SEVENTH STREET

Money burns the pocket, pocket hurts,
Bootleggers in silken shirts,
Ballooned, zooming Cadillacs,
Whizzing, whizzing down the street-car tracks.

Seventh Street is a bastard of Prohibition and the War. A crude-boned, soft-skinned wedge of nigger life breathing its loafer air, jazz songs and love, thrusting unconscious rhythms, black reddish blood into the white and white-washed wood of Washington. Stale soggy wood of Washington. Wedges rust in soggy wood. . . Split it! In two! Again! Shred it! . . the sun. Wedges are brilliant in the sun; ribbons of wet wood dry and blow away. Black reddish blood. Pouring for crude-boned soft-skinned life, who set you flowing? Blood suckers of the War would spin in a frenzy of dizziness if they drank your blood. Prohibition would put a stop to it. Who set you flowing? White and whitewash disappear in blood. Who set you flowing? Flowing down the smooth asphalt of Seventh Street, in shanties, brick office buildings, theaters, drug stores, restaurants, and cabarets? Eddying on the corners? Swirling like a blood-red smoke up where the buzzards fly in heaven? God would not dare to suck black red blood. A Nigger God! He would duck his head in shame and call for the Judgment Day. Who set you flowing?

Money burns the pocket, pocket hurts,
Bootleggers in silken shirts,
Ballooned, zooming Cadillacs,
Whizzing, whizzing down the street-car tracks.

RHOBERT

Rhobert wears a house, like a monstrous diver's helmet, on his head. His legs are banty-bowed and shaky because as a child he had rickets. He is way down. Rods of the house like antennæ of a dead thing, stuffed, prop up in the air. He is way down. He is sinking. His house is a dead thing that weights him down. He is sinking as a diver would sink in mud should the water be drawn off. Life is a murky, wiggling, microscopic water that compresses him. Compresses his helmet and would crush it the minute that he pulled his head out. He has to keep it in. Life is water that is being drawn off.

Brother, life is water that is being drawn off.
Brother, life is water that is being drawn off.

The dead house is stuffed. The stuffing is alive. It is sinful to draw one's head out of live stuffing in a dead house. The propped-up antennæ would cave in and the stuffing be strewn . . . shredded life-pulp . . . in the water. It is sinful to have one's own head crushed. Rhobert is an upright man whose legs are banty-bowed and shaky because as a child he had rickets. The earth is round. Heaven is a sphere that surrounds it. Sink where you will. God is a Red Cross man with a dredge and a respiration-pump who's waiting for you at the opposite periphery. God built the house. He blew His breath into its stuffing. It is good to die obeying Him who can do these things.

A futile something like the dead house wraps the live stuffing of the question: how long before the water will be drawn off? Rhobert does not care. Like most men who wear monstrous helmets, the pressure it exerts is enough to convince him of its practical infinity. And he cares not two straws as to whether or not he will ever see his wife and children again. Many a time he's seen them drown in his dreams and has kicked about joyously in the mud for days after. One thing about him goes straight to the heart. He has an Adam's-apple which strains sometimes as if he were painfully gulping great globules of air . . . air floating shredded life-pulp. It is a sad thing to see a banty-bowed, shaky, ricket-legged man straining the raw insides of his throat against smooth air. Holding furtive thoughts about the glory of pulp-heads strewn in water. . . He is way down. Down. Mud, coming to his banty knees, almost hides them. Soon people will be looking at him and calling him a strong man. No doubt he is for one who has had rickets. Lets give it to him. Lets call him great when the water shall have been all drawn off. Lets build a monument and set it in the ooze where he goes down. A monument of hewn oak, carved in nigger-heads. Lets open our throats, brother, and sing "Deep River" when he goes down.

Brother, Rhobert is sinking.
Lets open our throats, brother,
Lets sing Deep River when he goes down.

AVEY

For a long while she was nothing more to me than one of those skirted beings whom boys at a certain age disdain to play with. Just how I came to love her, timidly, and with secret blushes, I do not know. But that I did was brought home to me one night, the first night that Ned wore his long pants. Us fellers were seated on the curb before an apartment house where she had gone in. The young trees had not outgrown their boxes then. V Street was lined with them. When our legs grew cramped and stiff from the cold of the stone, we'd stand around a box and whittle it. I like to think now that there was a hidden purpose in the way we hacked them with our knives. I like to feel that something deep in me responded to the trees, the young trees that whinnied like colts impatient to be let free. . . On the particular night I have in mind, we were waiting for the top-floor light to go out. We wanted to see Avey leave the flat. This night she stayed longer than usual and gave us a chance to complete the plans of how we were going to stone and beat that feller on the top floor out of town. Ned especially had it in for him. He was about to throw a brick up at the window when at last the room went dark. Some minutes passed. Then Avey, as unconcerned as if she had been paying an old-maid aunt a visit, came out. I don't remember what she had on, and all that sort of thing. But I do know that I turned hot as bare pavements in the summertime at Ned's boast: "Hell, bet I could get her too if you little niggers weren't always spying and crabbing everything." I didnt say a word to him. It wasnt my way then. I just stood there like the others, and something like a fuse burned up inside of me. She never noticed us, but swung along lazy and easy as anything. We sauntered to the corner and watched her till her door banged to. Ned repeated what he'd said. I didnt seem to care. Sitting around old Mush-Head's bread box, the discussion began. "Hang if I can see how she gets away with it," Doc started. Ned knew, of course. There was nothing he didnt know when it came to women. He dilated on the emotional needs of girls. Said they werent much different from men in that respect. And concluded with the solemn avowal: "It does em good." None of us liked Ned much. We all talked dirt; but it was the way he said it. And then too, a couple of the fellers had sisters and had caught Ned playing with them. But there was no disputing the superiority of his smutty wisdom. Bubs Sanborn, whose mother was friendly with Avey's, had overheard the old ladies talking. "Avey's mother's ont her," he said. We thought that only natural and began to guess at what would happen. Some one said she'd marry that feller on the top floor. Ned called that a lie because Avey was going to marry nobody but him. We had our doubts about that, but we did agree that she'd soon leave school and marry some one. The gang broke up, and I went home, picturing myself as married.

Nothing I did seemed able to change Avey's indifference to me. I played basket-ball, and when I'd make a long clean shot she'd clap with the others, louder than they, I thought. I'd meet her on the street, and there'd be no difference in the way she said hello. She never took the trouble to call me by my name. On the days for drill, I'd let my voice down a tone and call for a complicated maneuver when I saw her coming. She'd smile appreciation, but it was an impersonal smile, never for me. It was on a summer excursion down to Riverview that she first seemed to take me into account. The day had been spent riding merry-go-rounds, scenic-railways, and shoot-the-chutes. We had been in swimming and we had danced. I was a crack swimmer then. She didnt know how. I held her up and showed her how to kick her legs and draw her arms. Of course she didnt learn in one day, but she thanked me for bothering with her. I was also somewhat of a dancer. And I had already noticed that love can start on a dance floor. We danced. But though I held her tightly in my arms, she was way away. That college feller who lived on the top floor was somewhere making money for the next year. I imagined that she was thinking, wishing for him. Ned was along. He treated her until his money gave out. She went with another feller. Ned got sore. One by one the boys' money gave out. She left them. And they got sore. Every one of them but me got sore. This is the reason, I guess, why I had her to myself on the top deck of the *Jane Mosely* that night as we puffed up the Potomac, coming home. The moon was brilliant. The air was sweet like clover. And every now and then, a salt tang, a stale drift of sea-weed. It was not my mind's fault if it went romancing. I should have taken her in my arms the minute we were stowed in that old lifeboat. I dallied, dreaming. She took me in hers. And I could feel by the touch of it that it wasnt a man-to-woman love. It made me restless. I felt chagrined. I didnt know what it was, but I did know that I couldnt handle it. She ran her fingers through my hair and kissed my forehead. I itched to break through her tenderness to passion. I wanted her to take me in her arms as I knew she had that college feller. I wanted her to love me passionately as she did him. I gave her one burning kiss. Then she laid me in her lap as if I were a child. Helpless. I got sore when she started to hum a lullaby. She wouldnt let me go. I talked. I knew damned well that I could beat her at that. Her eyes were soft and misty, the curves of her lips were wistful, and her smile seemed indulgent of the irrelevance of my remarks. I gave up at last and let her love me, silently, in her own way. The moon was brilliant. The air was sweet like clover, and every now and then, a salt tang, a stale drift of sea-weed. . .

The next time I came close to her was the following summer at Harpers Ferry. We were sitting on a flat projecting rock they give the name of Lover's Leap. Some one is supposed to have jumped off it. The river is about six hundred feet beneath. A railroad track runs up the valley and curves out of sight where part of the mountain rock had to be blasted away to make room for it. The engines of this valley have a whistle, the echoes of which sound like iterated gasps and sobs. I always think of them as crude music from the soul of Avey.

We sat there holding hands. Our palms were soft and warm against each other. Our fingers were not tight. She would not let them be. She would not let me twist them. I wanted to talk. To explain what I meant to her. Avey was as silent as those great trees whose tops we looked down upon. She has always been like that. At least, to me. I had the notion that if I really wanted to, I could do with her just what I pleased. Like one can strip a tree. I did kiss her. I even let my hands cup her breasts. When I was through, she'd seek my hand and hold it till my pulse cooled down. Evening after evening we sat there. I tried to get her to talk about that college feller. She never would. There was no set time to go home. None of my family had come down. And as for hers, she didnt give a hang about them. The general gossips could hardly say more than they had. The boarding-house porch was always deserted when we returned. No one saw us enter, so the time was set conveniently for scandal. This worried me a little, for I thought it might keep Avey from getting an appointment in the schools. She didnt care. She had finished normal school. They could give her a job if they wanted to. As time went on, her indifference to things began to pique me; I was ambitious. I left the Ferry earlier than she did. I was going off to college. The more I thought of it, the more I resented, yes, hell, thats what it was, her downright laziness. Sloppy indolence. There was no excuse for a healthy girl taking life so easy. Hell! she was no better than a cow. I was certain that she was a cow when I felt an udder in a Wisconsin stockjudging class. Among those energetic Swedes, or whatever they are, I decided to forget her. For two years I thought I did. When I'd come home for the summer she'd be away. And before she returned, I'd be gone. We never wrote; she was too damned lazy for that. But what a bluff I put up about forgetting her. The girls up that way, at least the ones I knew, havent got the stuff: they dont know how to love. Giving themselves completely was tame beside just the holding of Avey's hand. One day I received a note from her. The writing, I decided, was slovenly. She wrote on a torn bit of note-book paper. The envelope had a faint perfume that I remembered. A single line told me she had lost her school and was going away. I comforted myself with the reflection that shame held no pain for one so indolent as she. Nevertheless, I left Wisconsin that year for good. Washington had seemingly forgotten her. I hunted Ned. Between curses, I caught his opinion of her. She was no better than a whore. I saw her mother on the street. The same old pinch-beck, jerky-gaited creature that I'd always known.

Perhaps five years passed. The business of hunting a job or something or other had bruised my vanity so that I could recognize it. I felt old. Avery and my real relation to her, I thought I came to know. I wanted to see her. I had been told that she was in New York. As I had no money, I hiked and bummed my way there. I got work in a ship-yard and walked the streets at night, hoping to meet her. Failing in this, I saved enough to pay my fare back home. One evening in early June, just at the time when dusk is most lovely on the eastern horizon, I saw Avey, indolent as ever, leaning on the arm of a man, strolling under the recently lit arc-lights of U Street. She had almost passed before she recognized me. She showed no surprise. The puff over her eyes had grown heavier. The eyes themselves were still sleepy-large, and beautiful. I had almost concluded — indifferent. "You look older," was what she said. I wanted to convince her that I was, so I asked her to walk with me. The man whom she was with, and whom she never took the trouble to introduce, at a nod from her, hailed a taxi, and drove away. That gave me a notion of what she had been used to. Her dress was of some fine, costly stuff. I suggested the park, and then added that the grass might stain her skirt. Let it get stained, she said, for where it came from there are others.

I have a spot in Soldier's Home to which I always go when I want the simple beauty of another's soul. Robins spring about the lawn all day. They leave their footprints in the grass. I imagine that the grass at night smells sweet and fresh because of them. The ground is high. Washington lies below. Its light spreads like a blush against the darkened sky. Against the soft dusk sky of Washington. And when the wind is from the South, soil of my homeland falls like a fertile shower upon the lean streets of the city. Upon my hill in Soldier's Home. I know the policeman who watches the place of nights. When I go there alone, I talk to him. I tell him I come there to find the truth that people bury in their hearts. I tell him that I do not come there with a girl to do the thing he's paid to watch out for. I look deep in his eyes when I say these things, and he believes me. He comes over to see who it is on the grass. I say hello to him. He greets me in the same way and goes off searching for other black splotches upon the lawn. Avey and I went there. A band in one of the buildings a fair distance off was playing a march. I wished they would stop. Their playing was like a tin spoon in one's mouth. I wanted the Howard Glee Club to sing "Deep River," from the road. To sing "Deep River, Deep River," from the road. . . Other than the first comments, Avey had been silent. I started to hum a folk-tune. She slipped her hand in mine. Pillowed her head as best she could upon my arm. Kissed the hand that she was holding and listened, or so I thought, to what I had to say. I traced my development from the early days up to the present time, the phase in which I could understand her. I described her own nature and temperament. Told how they needed a larger life for their expression. How incapable Washington was of understanding that need. How it could not meet it. I pointed out that in lieu of proper channels, her emotions had overflowed into paths that dissipated them. I talked, beautifully I thought, about an art that would be born, an art that would open the way for women the likes of her. I asked her to hope, and build up an inner life against the coming of that day. I recited some of my own things to her. I sang, with a strange quiver in my voice, a promise-song. And then I began to wonder why her hand had not once returned a single pressure. My old-time feeling about her laziness came back. I spoke sharply. My policeman friend passed by. I said hello to him. As he went away, I began to visualize certain possibilities. An immediate and urgent passion swept over me. Then I looked at Avey. Her heavy eyes were closed. Her breathing was as faint and regular as a child's in slumber. My passion died. I was afraid to move lest I disturb her. Hours and hours, I guess it was, she lay there. My body grew numb. I shivered. I coughed. I wanted to get up and whittle at the boxes of young trees. I withdrew my hand. I raised her head to waken her. She did not stir. I got up and walked around. I found my policeman friend and talked to him. We both came up, and bent over her. He said it would be all right for her to stay there just so long as she got away before the workmen came at dawn. A blanket was borrowed from a neighbor house. I sat beside her through the night. I saw the dawn steal over Washington. The Capitol dome looked like a gray ghost ship drifting in from sea. Avey's face was pale, and her eyes were heavy. She did not have the gray crimson-splashed beauty of the dawn. I hated to wake her. Orphan-woman...

BEEHIVE

Within this black hive to-night
There swarm a million bees;
Bees passing in and out the moon,
Bees escaping out the moon,
Bees returning through the moon,
Silver bees intently buzzing,
Silver honey dripping from the swarm of bees
Earth is a waxen cell of the world comb,
And I, a drone,
Lying on my back,
Lipping honey,
Getting drunk with silver honey,
Wish that I might fly out past the moon
And curl forever in some far-off farmyard flower.

STORM ENDING

Thunder blossoms gorgeously above our heads,
Great, hollow, bell-like flowers,
Rumbling in the wind,
Stretching clappers to strike our ears . . .
Full-lipped flowers
Bitten by the sun
Bleeding rain
Dripping rain like golden honey —
And the sweet earth flying from the thunder.

THEATER

Life of nigger alleys, of pool rooms and restaurants and near-beer saloons soaks into the walls of Howard Theater and sets them throbbing jazz songs. Black-skinned, they dance and shout above the tick and trill of white-walled buildings. At night, they open doors to people who come in to stamp their feet and shout. At night, road-shows volley songs into the mass-heart of black people. Songs soak the walls and seep out to the nigger life of alleys and near-beer saloons, of the Poodle Dog and Black Bear cabarets. Afternoons, the house is dark, and the walls are sleeping singers until rehearsal begins. Or until John comes within them. Then they start throbbing to a subtle syncopation. And the space-dark air grows softly luminous.

John is the manager's brother. He is seated at the center of the theater, just before rehearsal. Light streaks down upon him from a window high above. One half his face is orange in it. One half his face is in shadow. The soft glow of the house rushes to, and compacts about, the shaft of light. John's mind coincides with the shaft of light. Thoughts rush to, and compact about it. Life of the house and of the slowly awakening stage swirls to the body of John, and thrills it. John's body is separate from the thoughts that pack his mind.

Stage-lights, soft, as if they shine through clear pink fingers. Beneath them, hid by the shadow of a set, Dorris. Other chorus girls drift in. John feels them in the mass. And as if his own body were the mass-heart of a black audience listening to them singing, he wants to stamp his feet and shout. His mind, contained above desires of his body, singles the girls out, and tries to trace origins and plot destinies.

A pianist slips into the pit and improvises jazz. The walls awake. Arms of the girls, and their limbs, which . . . jazz, jazz . . . by lifting up their tight street skirts they set free, jab the air and clog the floor in rhythm to the music. (Lift your skirts, Baby, and talk t papa!) Crude, individualized, and yet . . . monotonous. . .

John: Soon the director will herd you, my full-lipped, distant beauties, and tame you, and blunt your sharp thrusts in loosely suggestive movements, appropriate to Broadway. (O dance!) Soon the audience will paint your dusk faces white, and call you beautiful. (O dance!) Soon I. . . (O dance!) I'd like. . .

Girls laugh and shout. Sing discordant snatches of other jazz songs. Whirl with loose passion into the arms of passing show-men.

John: Too thick. Too easy. Too monotonous. Her whom I'd love I'd leave before she knew that I was with her. Her? Which? (O dance!) I'd like to. . .

Girls dance and sing. Men clap. The walls sing and press inward. They press the men and girls, they press John towards a center of physical ecstasy. Go to it, Baby! Fan yourself, and feed your papa! Put . . . nobody lied . . . and take . . . when they said I cried over you. No lie! The glitter and color of stacked scenes, the gilt and brass and crimson of the house, converge towards a center of physical ecstasy. John's feet and torso and his blood press in. He wills thought to rid his mind of passion.

"All right, girls. Alaska. Miss Reynolds, please."

The director wants to get the rehearsal through with.

The girls line up. John sees the front row: dancing ponies. The rest are in shadow. The leading lady fits loosely in the front. Lack-life, monotonous. "One, two, three —" Music starts. The song is somewhere where it will not strain the leading lady's throat. The dance is somewhere where it will not strain the girls. Above the staleness, one dancer throws herself into it. Dorris. John sees her. Her hair, crisp-curled, is bobbed. Bushy, black hair bobbing about her lemon-colored face. Her lips are curiously full, and very red. Her limbs in silk purple stockings are lovely. John feels them. Desires her. Holds off.

John: Stage-door johnny; chorus-girl. No, that would be all right. Dictie, educated, stuckup; show-girl. Yep. Her suspicion would be stronger than her passion. It wouldnt work. Keep her loveliness. Let her go.

Dorris sees John and knows that he is looking at her. Her own glowing is too rich a thing to let her feel the slimness of his diluted passion.

"Who's that?" she asks her dancing partner.

"Th manager's brother. Dictie. Nothin doin, hon."

Dorris tosses her head and dances for him until she feels she has him. Then, withdrawing disdainfully, she flirts with the director.

Dorris: Nothin doin? How come? Aint I as good as him? Couldnt I have got an education if I'd wanted one? Dont I know respectable folks, lots of em, in Philadelphia and New York and Chicago? Aint I had men as good as him? Better. Doctors an lawyers. Whats a manager's brother, anyhow?

Two steps back, and two steps front.

"Say, Mame, where do you get that stuff?"

"Whatshmean, Dorris?"

"If you two girls cant listen to what I'm telling you, I know where I can get some who can. Now listen."

Mame: Go to hell, you black bastard.

Dorris: Whats eatin at him, anyway?

"Now follow me in this, you girls. Its three counts to the right, three counts to the left, and then you shimmy —"

John: — and then you shimmy. I'll bet she can. Some good cabaret, with rooms upstairs. And what in hell do you think you'd get from it? Youre going wrong. Here's right: get her to herself — (Christ, but how she'd bore you after the first five minutes) — not if you get her right she wouldnt. Touch her, I mean. To herself — in some room perhaps. Some cheap, dingy bedroom. Hell no. Cant be done. But the point is, brother John, it can be done. Get her to herself somewhere, anywhere. Go down in yourself — and she'd be calling you all sorts of asses while you were in the process of going down. Hold em, bud. Cant be done. Let her go. (Dance and I'll love you!) And keep her loveliness.

"All right now, Chicken Chaser. Dorris and girls. Where's Dorris? I told you to stay on the stage, didnt I? Well? Now thats enough. All right. All right there, Professor? All right. One, two, three —"

Dorris swings to the front. The line of girls, four deep, blurs within the shadow of suspended scenes. Dorris wants to dance. The director feels that and steps to one side. He smiles, and picks her for a leading lady, one of these days. Odd ends of stage-men emerge from the wings, and stare and clap. A crap game in the alley suddenly ends. Black faces crowd the rear stage doors. The girls, catching joy from Dorris, whip up within the footlights' glow. They forget set steps; they find their own. The director forgets to bawl them out. Dorris dances.

John: Her head bobs to Broadway. Dance from yourself. Dance! O just a little more.

Dorris' eyes burn across the space of seats to him.

Dorris: I bet he can love. Hell, he cant love. He's too skinny. His lips are too skinny. He wouldnt love me anyway, only for that. But I'd get a pair of silk stockings out of it. Red silk. I got purple. Cut it, kid. You cant win him to respect you that away. He wouldnt anyway. Maybe he would. Maybe he'd love. I've heard em say that men who look like him (what does he look like?) will marry if they love. O will you love me? And give me kids, and a home, and everything? (I'd like to make your nest, and honest, hon, I wouldnt run out on you.) You will if I make you. Just watch me.

Dorris dances. She forgets her tricks. She dances.

Glorious songs are the muscles of her limbs.

And her singing is of canebrake loves and mangrove feastings.

The walls press in, singing. Flesh of a throbbing body, they press close to John and Dorris. They close them in. John's heart beats tensely against her dancing body. Walls press his mind within his heart. And then, the shaft of light goes out the window high above him. John's mind sweeps up to follow it. Mind pulls him upward into dream. Dorris dances. . . John dreams:

> Dorris is dressed in a loose black gown splashed with lemon ribbons. Her feet taper long and slim from trim ankles. She waits for him just inside the stage door. John, collar and tie colorful and flaring, walks towards the stage door. There are no trees in the alley. But his feet feel as though they step on autumn leaves whose rustle has been pressed out of them by the passing of a million satin slippers. The air is sweet with roasting chestnuts, sweet with bonfires of old leaves. John's melancholy is a deep thing that seals all senses but his eyes, and makes him whole.
>
> Dorris knows that he is coming. Just at the right moment she steps from the door, as if there were no door. Her face is tinted like the autumn alley. Of old flowers, or of a southern canefield, her perfume. "Glorious Dorris." So his eyes speak. And their sadness is too deep for sweet untruth. She barely touches his arm. They glide off with footfalls softened on the leaves, the old leaves powdered by a million satin slippers.
>
> They are in a room. John knows nothing of it. Only, that the flesh and blood of Dorris are its walls. Singing walls. Lights, soft, as if they shine through clear pink fingers. Soft lights, and warm.
>
> John reaches for a manuscript of his, and reads. Dorris, who has no eyes, has eyes to understand him. He comes to a dancing scene. The scene is Dorris. She dances. Dorris dances. Glorious Dorris. Dorris whirls, whirls, dances. . .

Dorris dances.

The pianist crashes a bumper chord. The whole stage claps. Dorris, flushed, looks quick at John. His whole face is in shadow. She seeks for her dance in it. She finds it a dead thing in the shadow which is his dream. She rushes from the stage. Falls down the steps into her dressing-room. Pulls her hair. Her eyes, over a floor of tears, stare at the whitewashed ceiling. (Smell of dry paste, and paint, and soiled clothing.) Her pal comes in. Dorris flings herself into the old safe arms, and cries bitterly.

"I told you nothin doin," is what Mame says to comfort her.

HER LIPS ARE COPPER WIRE

whisper of yellow globes
gleaming on lamp-posts that sway
like bootleg licker drinkers in the fog

and let your breath be moist against me
like bright beads on yellow globes

telephone the power-house
that the main wires are insulate

(her words play softly up and down
dewy corridors of billboards)

then with your tongue remove the tape
and press your lips to mine
till they are incandescent

CALLING JESUS

Her soul is like a little thrust-tailed dog that follows her, whimpering. She is large enough, I know, to find a warm spot for it. But each night when she comes home and closes the big outside storm door, the little dog is left in the vestibule, filled with chills till morning. Some one . . . eoho Jesus . . . soft as a cotton boll brushed against the milk-pod cheek of Christ, will steal in and cover it that it need not shiver, and carry it to her where she sleeps upon clean hay cut in her dreams.

When you meet her in the daytime on the streets, the little dog keeps coming. Nothing happens at first, and then, when she has forgotten the streets and alleys, and the large house where she goes to bed of nights, a soft thing like fur begins to rub your limbs, and you hear a low, scared voice, lonely, calling, and you know that a cool something nozzles moisture in your palms. Sensitive things like nostrils, quiver. Her breath comes sweet as honeysuckle whose pistils bear the life of coming song. And her eyes carry to where builders find no need for vestibules, for swinging on iron hinges, storm doors.

Her soul is like a little thrust-tailed dog, that follows her, whimpering. I've seen it tagging on behind her, up streets where chestnut trees flowered, where dusty asphalt had been freshly sprinkled with clean water. Up alleys where niggers sat on low door-steps before tumbled shanties and sang and loved. At night, when she comes home, the little dog is left in the vestibule, nosing the crack beneath the big storm door, filled with chills till morning. Some one . . . eoho Jesus . . . soft as the bare feet of Christ moving across bales of southern cotton, will steal in and cover it that it need not shiver, and carry it to her where she sleeps: cradled in dream-fluted cane.

BOX SEAT

I

Houses are shy girls whose eyes shine reticently upon the dusk body of the street. Upon the gleaming limbs and asphalt torso of a dreaming nigger. Shake your curled wool-blossoms, nigger. Open your liver lips to the lean, white spring. Stir the root-life of a withered people. Call them from their houses, and teach them to dream.

Dark swaying forms of Negroes are street songs that woo virginal houses.

Dan Moore walks southward on Thirteenth Street. The low limbs of budding chestnut trees recede above his head. Chestnut buds and blossoms are wool he walks upon. The eyes of houses faintly touch him as he passes them. Soft girl-eyes, they set him singing. Girl-eyes within him widen upward to promised faces. Floating away, they dally wistfully over the dusk body of the street. Come on, Dan Moore, come on. Dan sings. His voice is a little hoarse. It cracks. He strains to produce tones in keeping with the houses' loveliness. Cant be done. He whistles. His notes are shrill. They hurt him. Negroes open gates, and go indoors, perfectly. Dan thinks of the house he's going to. Of the girl. Lips, flesh-notes of a forgotten song, plead with him. . .

Dan turns into a side-street, opens an iron gate, bangs it to. Mounts the steps, and searches for the bell. Funny, he cant find it. He fumbles around. The thought comes to him that some one passing by might see him, and not understand. Might think that he is trying to sneak, to break in.

Dan: Break in. Get an ax and smash in. Smash in their faces. I'll show em. Break into an engine-house, steal a thousand horse-power fire truck. Smash in with the truck. I'll show em. Grab an ax and brain em. Cut em up. Jack the Ripper. Baboon from the zoo. And then the cops come. "No, I aint a baboon. I aint Jack the Ripper. I'm a poor man out of work. Take your hands off me, you bull-necked bears. Look into my eyes. I am Dan Moore. I was born in a canefield. The hands of Jesus touched me. I am come to a sick world to heal it. Only the other day, a dope fiend brushed against me — Dont laugh, you mighty, juicy, meat-hook men. Give me your fingers and I will peel them as if they were ripe bananas."

Some one might think he is trying to break in. He'd better knock. His knuckles are raw bone against the thick glass door. He waits. No one comes. Perhaps they havent heard him. He raps again. This time, harder. He waits. No one comes. Some one is surely in. He fancies that he sees their shadows on the glass. Shadows of gorillas. Perhaps they saw him coming and dont want to let him in. He knocks. The tension of his arms makes the glass rattle. Hurried steps come towards him. The door opens.

"Please, you might break the glass — the bell — oh, Mr. Moore! I thought it must be some stranger. How do you do? Come in, wont you? Muriel? Yes. I'll call her. Take your things off, wont you? And have a seat in the parlor. Muriel will be right down. Muriel! Oh Muriel! Mr. Moore to see you. She'll be right down. You'll pardon me, wont you? So glad to see you."

Her eyes are weak. They are bluish and watery from reading newspapers. The blue is steel. It gimlets Dan while her mouth flaps amiably to him.

Dan: Nothing for you to see, old mussel-head. Dare I show you? If I did, delirium would furnish you headlines for a month. Now look here. Thats enough. Go long, woman. Say some nasty thing and I'll kill you. Huh. Better damned sight not. Ta-ta, Mrs. Pribby.

Mrs. Pribby retreats to the rear of the house. She takes up a newspaper. There is a sharp click as she fits into her chair and draws it to the table. The click is metallic like the sound of a bolt being shot into place. Dan's eyes sting. Sinking into a soft couch, he closes them. The house contracts about him. It is a sharp-edged, massed, metallic house. Bolted. About Mrs. Pribby. Bolted to the endless rows of metal houses. Mrs. Pribby's house. The rows of houses belong to other Mrs. Pribbys. No wonder he couldn't sing to them.

Dan: What's Muriel doing here? God, what a place for her. Whats she doing? Putting her stockings on? In the bathroom. Come out of there, Dan

Moore. People must have their privacy. Peeping-toms. I'll never peep. I'll listen. I like to listen.

Dan goes to the wall and places his ear against it. A passing street car and something vibrant from the earth sends a rumble to him. That rumble comes from the earth's deep core. It is the mutter of powerful underground races. Dan has a picture of all the people rushing to put their ears against walls, to listen to it. The next world-savior is coming up that way. Coming up. A continent sinks down. The new-world Christ will need consummate skill to walk upon the waters where huge bubbles burst... Thuds of Muriel coming down. Dan turns to the piano and glances through a stack of jazz music sheets. "Ji-ji-bo, JI-JI-BO!"..

"Hello, Dan, stranger, what brought you here?"

Muriel comes in, shakes hands, and then clicks into a high-armed seat under the orange glow of a floor-lamp. Her face is fleshy. It would tend to coarseness but for the fresh fragrant something which is the life of it. Her hair like an Indian's. But more curly and bushed and vagrant. Her nostrils flare. The flushed ginger of her cheeks is touched orange by the shower of color from the lamp.

"Well, you havent told me, you havent answered my question, stranger. What brought you here?"

Dan feels the pressure of the house, of the rear room, of the rows of houses, shift to Muriel. He is light. He loves her. He is doubly heavy.

"Dont know, Muriel — wanted to see you — wanted to talk to you — to see you and tell you that I know what you've been through — what pain the last few months must have been —"

"Lets dont mention that."

"But why not, Muriel? I —"

"Please."

"But Muriel, life is full of things like that. One grows strong and beautiful in facing them. What else is life?"

"I dont know, Dan. And I dont believe I care. Whats the use? Lets talk about something else. I hear there's a good show at the Lincoln this week."

"Yes, so Harry was telling me. Going?"

"To-night."

Dan starts to rise.

"I didnt know. I dont want to keep you."

"Its all right. You dont have to go till Bernice comes. And she wont be here till eight. I'm all dressed. I'll let you know."

"Thanks."

Silence. The rustle of a newspaper being turned comes from the rear room.

Muriel: Shame about Dan. Something awfully good and fine about him. But he don't fit in. In where? Me? Dan, I could love you if I tried. I dont have to try. I do. O Dan, dont you know I do? Timid lover, brave talker that you are. Whats the good of all you know if you dont know that? I wont let myself. I? Mrs. Pribby who reads newspapers all night wont. What has she got to do with me? She *is* me, somehow. No she's not. Yes she is. She is the town, and the town wont let me love you, Dan. Dont you know? You could make it let me if you would. Why wont you? Youre selfish. I'm not strong enough to buck it. Youre too selfish to buck it, for me. I wish you'd go. You irritate me. Dan, please go.

"What are you doing now, Dan?"

"Same old thing, Muriel. Nothing, as the world would have it. Living, as I look at things. Living as much as I can without —"

"But you cant live without money, Dan. Why dont you get a good job and settle down?"

Dan: Same old line. Shoot it at me, sister. Hell of a note, this loving business. For ten minutes of it youve got to stand the torture of an intolerable heaviness and a hundred platitudes. Well, damit, shoot on.

"To what? my dear. Rustling newspapers?"

"You mustnt say that, Dan. It isnt right. Mrs. Pribby has been awfully good to me."

"Dare say she has. Whats that got to do with it?"

"Oh, Dan, youre so unconsiderate and selfish. All you think of is yourself."

"I think of you."

"Too much — I mean, you ought to work more and think less. Thats the best way to get along."

"Mussel-heads get along, Muriel. There is more to you than that —"

"Sometimes I think there is, Dan. But I dont know. I've tried. I've tried to do something with myself. Something real and beautiful, I mean. But whats the good of trying? I've tried to make people, every one I come in contact with, happy —"

Dan looks at her, directly. Her animalism, still unconquered by zoo-restrictions and keeper-taboos, stirs him. Passion tilts upward, bringing with it the elements of an old desire. Muriel's lips become the flesh-notes of a futile, plaintive longing. Dan's impulse to direct her is its fresh life.

"Happy, Muriel? No, not happy. Your aim is wrong. There is no such thing as happiness. Life blends joy and pain, beauty and ugliness, in such a way that no one may isolate them. No one should want to. Perfect joy, or perfect pain, with no contrasting element to define them, would mean a monotony of consciousness, would mean death. Not happy, Muriel. Say that you have tried to make them create. Say that you have used your own capacity for life to cradle them. To start them upward-flowing. Or if you cant say that you have, then say that you will. My talking to you will make you aware of your power to do so. Say that you will love, that you will give yourself in love —"

"To you, Dan?"

Dan's consciousness crudely swerves into his passions. They flare up in his eyes. They set up quivers in his abdomen. He is suddenly over-tense and nervous.

"Muriel —"

The newspaper rustles in the rear room.

"Muriel —"

Dan rises. His arms stretch towards her. His fingers and his palms, pink in the lamplight, are glowing irons. Muriel's chair is close and stiff about her. The house, the rows of houses locked about her chair. Dan's fingers and arms are fire to melt and bars to wrench and force and pry. Her arms hang loose. Her hands are hot and moist. Dan takes them. He slips to his knees before her.

"Dan, you mustnt."

"Muriel —"

"Dan, really you mustnt. No, Dan. No."

"Oh, come, Muriel. Must I —"

"Shhh. Dan, please get up. Please. Mrs. Pribby is right in the next room. She'll hear you. She may come in. Dont, Dan. She'll see you —"

"Well then, lets go out."

"I cant. Let go, Dan. Oh, wont you please let go."

Muriel tries to pull her hands away. Dan tightens his grip. He feels the strength of his fingers. His muscles are tight and strong. He stands up. Thrusts out his chest. Muriel shrinks from him. Dan becomes aware of his crude absurdity. His lips curl. His passion chills. He has an obstinate desire to possess her.

"Muriel, I love you. I want you, whatever the world of Pribby says. Damn your Pribby. Who is she to dictate my love? I've stood enough of her. Enough of you. Come here."

Muriel's mouth works in and out. Her eyes flash and waggle. She wrenches her hands loose and forces them against his breast to keep him off. Dan grabs her wrists. Wedges in between her arms. Her face is close to him. It is hot and blue and moist. Ugly.

"Come here now."

"Dont, Dan. Oh, dont. What are you killing?"

"Whats weak in both of us and a whole litter of Pribbys. For once in your life youre going to face whats real, by God —"

A sharp rap on the newspaper in the rear room cuts between them. The rap is like cool thick glass between them. Dan is hot on one side. Muriel, hot on the other. They straighten. Gaze fearfully at one another. Neither moves. A clock in the rear room, in the rear room, the rear room, strikes eight. Eight slow, cool sounds. Bernice. Muriel fastens on her image. She smooths her dress. She adjusts her skirt. She becomes prim and cool. Rising, she skirts Dan as if to keep the glass between them. Dan, gyrating nervously above the easy swing of his limbs, follows her to the parlor door. Muriel retreats before him till she reaches the landing of the steps that lead upstairs. She smiles at him. Dan sees his face in the hall mirror. He runs his fingers through his hair. Reaches for his hat and coat and puts them on. He moves towards Muriel. Muriel steps backward up one step. Dan's jaw shoots out. Muriel jerks her arm in warning of Mrs. Pribby. She gasps and turns and starts to run. Noise of a chair scraping as Mrs. Pribby rises from it, ratchets down the hall. Dan stops. He makes a wry face, wheels round, goes out, and slams the door.

II

People come in slowly . . . mutter, laughs, flutter, whishadwash, "I've changed my workclothes —" . . . and fill vacant seats of Lincoln Theater. Muriel, leading Bernice who is a cross between a washerwoman and a blue-blood lady, a washer-blue, a washer-lady, wanders down the right aisle to the lower front box. Muriel has on an orange dress. Its color would clash with the crimson box-draperies, its color would contradict the sweet rose smile her face is bathed in, should she take her coat off. She'll keep it on. Pale purple shadows rest on the planes of her cheeks. Deep purple comes from her thick-shocked hair. Orange of the dress goes well with these. Muriel presses her coat down from around her shoulders. Teachers are not supposed to have bobbed hair. She'll keep her hat on. She takes the first chair, and indicates that Bernice is to take the one directly behind her. Seated thus, her eyes are level with, and near to, the face of an imaginary man upon the stage. To speak to Berny she must turn. When she does, the audience is square upon her.

People come in slowly . . . "— for my Sunday-go-to-meeting dress. O glory God! O shout Amen!" . . . and fill vacant seats of Lincoln Theater. Each one is a bolt that shoots into a slot, and is locked there. Suppose the Lord should ask, where was Moses when the light went out? Suppose Gabriel should blow his trumpet! The seats are slots. The seats are bolted houses. The mass grows denser. Its weight at first is impalpable upon the box. Then Muriel begins to feel it. She props her arm against the brass box-rail, to ward it off. Silly. These people are friends of hers: a parent of a child she teaches, an old school friend. She smiles at them. They return her courtesy, and she is free to chat with Berny. Berny's tongue, started, runs on, and on. O washer-blue! O washer-lady!

Muriel: Never see Dan again. He makes me feel queer. Starts things he doesnt finish. Upsets me. I am not upset. I am perfectly calm. I am going to enjoy the show. Good show. I've had some show! This damn tame thing. O Dan. Wont see Dan again. Not alone. Have Mrs. Pribby come in. She *was* in. Keep Dan out. If I love him, can I keep him out? Well then, I dont love him. Now he's out. Who is that coming in? Blind as a bat. Ding-bat. Looks like Dan. He mustnt see me. Silly. He cant reach me. He wont dare come in here. He'd put his head down like a goring bull and charge me. He'd trample them. He'd gore. He'd rape! Berny! He won't dare come in here.

"Berny, who was that who just came in? I havent my glasses."

"A friend of yours, a *good* friend so I hear. Mr. Daniel Moore, Lord."

"Oh. He's no friend of mine."

"No? I hear he is."

"Well, he isnt."

Dan is ushered down the aisle. He has to squeeze past the knees of seated people to reach his own seat. He treads on a man's corns. The man grumbles, and shoves him off. He shrivels close beside a portly Negress whose huge rolls of flesh meet about the bones of seat-arms. A soil-soaked fragrance comes from her. Through the cement floor her strong roots sink down. They spread under the asphalt streets. Dreaming, the streets roll over on their bellies, and suck their glossy health from them. Her strong roots sink down and spread under the river and disappear in blood-lines that waver south. Her roots shoot down. Dan's hands follow them. Roots throb. Dan's heart beats violently. He places his palms upon the earth to cool them. Earth throbs. Dan's heart beats violently. He sees all the people in the house rush to the walls to listen to the rumble. A new-world Christ is coming up. Dan comes up. He is startled. The eyes of the woman dont belong to her. They look at him unpleasantly. From either aisle, bolted masses press in. He doesnt fit. The mass grows agitant. For an instant, Dan's and Muriel's eyes meet. His weight there slides the weight on her. She braces an arm against the brass rail, and turns her head away.

Muriel: Damn fool; dear Dan, what did you want to follow me here for? Oh cant you ever do anything right? Must you always pain me, and make me hate you? I do hate you. I wish some one would come in with a horse-whip and lash you out. I wish some one would drag you up a back alley and brain you with the whip-butt.

Muriel glances at her wrist-watch.

"Quarter of nine. Berny, what time have you?"

"Eight-forty. Time to begin. Oh, look Muriel, that woman with the plume; doesnt she look good! They say she's going with, oh, whats his name. You know. Too much powder. I can see it from here. Here's the orchestra now. O fine! Jim Clem at the piano!"

The men fill the pit. Instruments run the scale and tune. The saxophone moans and throws a fit. Jim Clem, poised over the piano, is ready to begin. His head nods forward. Opening crash. The house snaps dark. The curtain recedes upward from the blush of the footlights. Jazz overture is over. The first act is on.

Dan: Old stuff. Muriel — bored. Must be. But she'll smile and she'll clap. Do what youre bid, you she-slave. Look at her. Sweet, tame woman in a brass box seat. Clap, smile, fawn, clap. Do what youre bid. Drag me in with you. Dirty me. Prop me in your brass box seat. I'm there, am I not? because of you. He-slave. Slave of a woman who is a slave. I'm a damned sight worse than you are. I sing your praises, Beauty! I exalt thee, O Muriel! A slave, thou art greater than all Freedom because I love thee.

Dan fidgets, and disturbs his neighbors. His neighbors glare at him. He glares back without seeing them. The man whose corns have been trod upon speaks to him.

"Keep quiet, cant you, mister. Other people have paid their money besides yourself to see the show."

The man's face is a blur about two sullen liquid things that are his eyes. The eyes dissolve in the surrounding vagueness. Dan suddenly feels that the man is an enemy whom he has long been looking for.

Dan bristles. Glares furiously at the man.

"All right. All right then. Look at the show. I'm not stopping you."

"Shhh," from some one in the rear.

Dan turns around.

"Its that man there who started everything. I didnt say a thing to him until he tried to start something. What have I got to do with whether he has paid his money or not? Thats the manager's business. Do I look like the manager?"

"Shhhh. Youre right. Shhhh."

"Dont tell me to shhh. Tell him. That man there. He started everything. If what he wanted was to start a fight, why didnt he say so?"

The man leans forward.

"Better be quiet, sonny. I aint said a thing about fight, yet."

"Its a good thing you havent."

"Shhhh."

Dan grips himself. Another act is on. Dwarfs, dressed like prize-fighters, foreheads bulging like boxing gloves, are led upon the stage. They are going to fight for the heavy-weight championship. Gruesome. Dan glances at Muriel. He imagines that she shudders. His mind curves back into himself, and picks up tail-ends of experiences. His eyes are open, mechanically. The dwarfs pound and bruise and bleed each other, on his eyeballs.

Dan: Ah, but she was some baby! And not vulgar either. Funny how some women can do those things. Muriel dancing like that! Hell. She rolled and wabbled. Her buttocks rocked. She pulled up her dress and showed her pink drawers. Baby! And then she caught my eyes. Dont know what my eyes had in them. Yes I do. God, dont I though! Sometimes I think, Dan Moore, that your eyes could burn clean . . . burn clean . . . BURN CLEAN! . .

The gong rings. The dwarfs set to. They spar grotesquely, playfully, until one lands a stiff blow. This makes the other sore. He commences slugging. A real scrap is on. Time! The dwarfs go to their corners and are sponged and fanned off. Gloves bulge from their wrists. Their wrists are necks for the tight-faced gloves. The fellow to the right lets his eyes roam over the audience. He sights Muriel. He grins.

Dan: Those silly women arguing feminism. Here's what I should have said to them. "It should be clear to you women, that the proposition must be stated thus:

> Me, horizontally above her.
> Action: perfect strokes downward oblique.
> Hence, man dominates because of limitation.
> Or, so it shall be until women learn their stuff.

So framed, the proposition is a mental-filler, Dentist, I want gold teeth. It should become cherished of the technical intellect. I hereby offer it to posterity as one of the important machine-age designs. P.S. It should be noted, that because it *is* an achievement of this age, its growth and hence its causes, up to the point of maturity, antedate machinery. Ery . . ."

The gong rings. No fooling this time. The dwarfs set to. They clinch. The referee parts them. One swings a cruel upper-cut and knocks the other down. A huge head hits the floor. Pop! The house roars. The fighter, groggy, scrambles up. The referee whispers to the contenders not to fight so hard. They ignore him. They charge. Their heads jab like boxing-gloves. They kick and spit and bite. They pound each other furiously. Muriel pounds. The house pounds. Cut lips. Bloody noses. The referee asks for the gong. Time! The house roars. The dwarfs bow, are made to bow. The house wants more. The dwarfs are led from the stage.

Dan: Strange I never really noticed him before. Been sitting there for years. Born a slave. Slavery not so long ago. He'll die in his chair. Swing low, sweet chariot. Jesus will come and roll him down the river Jordan. Oh, come along, Moses, you'll get lost; stretch out your rod and come across. LET MY PEOPLE GO! Old man. Knows everyone who passes the corners. Saw the first horse-cars. The first Oldsmobile. And he was born in slavery. I did see his eyes. Never miss eyes. But they were bloodshot and watery. It hurt to look at them. It hurts to look in most people's eyes. He saw Grant and Lincoln. He saw Walt — old man, did you see Walt Whitman? Did you see Walt Whitman! Strange force that drew me to him. And I went up to see. The woman thought I saw crazy. I told him to look into the heavens. He did, and smiled. I asked him if he knew what that rumbling is that comes up from the ground. Christ, what a stroke that was. And the jabbering idiots crowding around. And the crossing-cop leaving his job to come over and wheel him away . . .

The house applauds. The house wants more. The dwarfs are led back. But no encore. Must give the house something. The attendant comes out and announces that Mr. Barry, the champion, will sing one of his own songs, "for your approval." Mr. Barry grins at Muriel as he wabbles from the wing. He holds a fresh white rose, and a small mirror. He wipes blood from his nose. He signals Jim Clem. The orchestra starts. A sentimental love song, Mr. Barry sings, first to one girl, and then another in the audience. He holds the mirror in such a way that it flashes in the face of each one he sings to. The light swings around.

Dan: I am going to reach up and grab the girders of this building and pull them down. The crash will be a signal. Hid by the smoke and dust Dan Moore will arise. In his right hand will be a dynamo. In his left, a god's face that will flash white light from ebony. I'll grab a girder and swing it like a walking-stick. Lightning will flash. I'll grab its black knob and swing it like a crippled cane. Lightning . . . Some one's flashing . . . some one's flashing . . . Who in hell is flashing that mirror? Take it off me, godam you.

Dan's eyes are half blinded. He moves his head. The light follows. He hears the audience laugh. He hears the orchestra. A man with a high-pitched, sentimental voice is singing. Dan sees the dwarf. Along the mirror flash the song comes. Dan ducks his head. The audience roars. The light swings around to Muriel. Dan looks. Muriel is too close. Mr. Barry covers his mirror. He sings to her. She shrinks away. Nausea. She clutches the brass box-rail. She moves to face away. The audience is square upon her. Its eyes smile. Its hands itch to clap. Muriel turns to the dwarf and forces a smile at him. With a showy blare of orchestration, the song comes to its close. Mr. Barry bows. He offers Muriel the rose, first having kissed it. Blood of his battered lips is a vivid stain upon its petals. Mr. Barry offers Muriel the rose. The house applauds. Muriel flinches back. The dwarf steps forward, diffident; threatening. Hate pops from his eyes and crackles like a brittle heat about the box. The thick hide of his face is drawn in tortured wrinkles. Above his eyes, the bulging, tight-skinned brow. Dan looks at it. It grows calm and massive. It grows profound. It is a thing of wisdom and tenderness, of suffering and beauty. Dan looks down. The eyes are calm and luminous. Words come from them . . . Arms of the audience reach out, grab Muriel, and hold her there. Claps are steel fingers that manacle her wrists and move them forward to acceptance. Berny leans forward and whispers:

"Its all right. Go on — take it."

Words form in the eyes of the dwarf:

> Do not shrink. Do not be afraid of me.
> *Jesus*
> See how my eyes look at you.
> *the Son of God*
> I too was made in His image.
> *was once —*
> I give you the rose.

Muriel, tight in her revulsion, sees black, and daintily reaches for the offering. As her hand touches it, Dan springs up in his seat and shouts:

"JESUS WAS ONCE A LEPER!"

•

• •

Dan steps down.

He is as cool as a green stem that has just shed its flower.

Rows of gaping faces strain towards him. They are distant, beneath him, impalpable. Squeezing out, Dan again treads upon the corn-foot man. The man shoves him.

"Watch where youre going, mister. Crazy or no, you aint going to walk over me. Watch where youre going there."

Dan turns, and serenely tweaks the fellow's nose. The man jumps up. Dan is jammed against a seat-back. A slight swift anger flicks him. His fist hooks the other's jaw.

"Now you have started something. Aint no man living can hit me and get away with it. Come on on the outside."

The house, tumultuously stirring, grabs its wraps and follows the men.

The man leads Dan up a black alley. The alley-air is thick and moist with smells of garbage and wet trash. In the morning, singing niggers will drive by and ring their gongs. . . Heavy with the scent of rancid flowers and with the scent of fight. The crowd, pressing forward, is a hollow roar. Eyes of houses, soft girl-eyes, glow reticently upon the hubbub and blink out. The man stops. Takes off his hat and coat. Dan, having forgotten him, keeps going on.

PRAYER

My body is opaque to the soul.
Driven of the spirit, long have I sought to temper it unto the spirit's longing,
But my mind, too, is opaque to the soul.
A closed lid is my soul's flesh-eye.
O Spirits of whom my soul is but a little finger,
Direct it to the lid of its flesh-eye.
I am weak with much giving.
I am weak with the desire to give more.
(How strong a thing is the little finger!)
So weak that I have confused the body with the soul,
And the body with its little finger.
(How frail is the little finger.)
My voice could not carry to you did you dwell in stars,
O Spirits of whom my soul is but a little finger . . .

HARVEST SONG

I am a reaper whose muscles set at sundown. All my oats are cradled.
But I am too chilled, and too fatigued to bind them. And I hunger.

I crack a grain between my teeth. I do not taste it.
I have been in the fields all day. My throat is dry. I hunger.

My eyes are caked with dust of oatfields at harvesttime.
I am a blind man who stares across the hills, seeking stack'd fields of other harvesters.

It would be good to see them . . . crook'd, split, and iron-ring'd handles of the scythes. It would be good to see them, dust-caked and blind. I hunger.

(Dusk is a strange fear'd sheath their blades are dull'd in.)
My throat is dry. And should I call, a cracked grain like the oats . . . eoho —

I fear to call. What should they hear me, and offer me their grain, oats, or wheat, or corn? I have been in the fields all day. I fear I could not taste it. I fear knowledge of my hunger.

My ears are caked with dust of oatfields at harvesttime.
I am a deaf man who strains to hear the calls of other harvesters whose throats are also dry.

It would be good to hear their songs . . . reapers of the sweet-stalk'd cane, cutters of the corn . . . even though their throats cracked and the strangeness of their voices deafened me.

I hunger. My throat is dry. Now that the sun has set and I am chilled, I fear to call. (Eoho, my brothers!)

I am a reaper. (Eoho!) All my oats are cradled. But I am too fatigued to bind them. And I hunger. I crack a grain. It has no taste to it. My throat is dry. . .

O my brothers, I beat my palms, still soft, against the stubble of my harvesting. (You beat your soft palms, too.) My pain is sweet. Sweeter than the oats or wheat or corn. It will not bring me knowledge of my hunger.

BONA AND PAUL

I

On the school gymnasium floor, young men and women are drilling. They are going to be teachers, and go out into the world . . . thud, thud . . . and give precision to the movements of sick people who all their lives have been drilling. One man is out of step. In step. The teacher glares at him. A girl in bloomers, seated on a mat in the corner because she has told the director that she is sick, sees that the footfalls of the men are rhythmical and syncopated. The dance of his blue-trousered limbs thrills her.

Bona: He is a candle that dances in a grove swung with pale balloons.

Columns of the drillers thud towards her. He is in the front row. He is in no row at all. Bona can look close at him. His red-brown face —

Bona: He is a harvest moon. He is an autumn leaf. He is a nigger. Bona! But dont all the dorm girls say so? And dont you, when you are sane, say so? Thats why I love — Oh, nonsense. You have never loved a man who didnt first love you. Besides —

Columns thud away from her. Come to a halt in line formation. Rigid. The period bell rings, and the teacher dismisses them.

A group collects around Paul. They are choosing sides for basket-ball. Girls against boys. Paul has his. He is limbering up beneath the basket. Bona runs to the girl captain and asks to be chosen. The girls fuss. The director comes to quiet them. He hears what Bona wants.

"But, Miss Hale, you were excused —"

"So I was, Mr. Boynton, but —"

"— you can play basket-ball, but you are too sick to drill."

"If you wish to put it that way."

She swings away from him to the girl captain.

"Helen, I want to play, and you must let me. This is the first time I've asked and I dont see why —"

"Thats just it, Bona. We have our team."

"Well, team or no team, I want to play and thats all there is to it."

She snatches the ball from Helen's hands, and charges down the floor.

Helen shrugs. One of the weaker girls says that she'll drop out. Helen accepts this. The team is formed. The whistle blows. The game starts. Bona, in center, is jumping against Paul. He plays with her. Out-jumps her, makes a quick pass, gets a quick return, and shoots a goal from the middle of the floor. Bona burns crimson. She fights, and tries to guard him. One of her team-mates advises her not to play so hard. Paul shoots his second goal.

Bona begins to feel a little dizzy and all in. She drives on. Almost hugs Paul to guard him. Near the basket, he attempts to shoot, and Bona lunges into his body and tries to beat his arms. His elbow, going up, gives her a sharp crack on the jaw. She whirls. He catches her. Her body stiffens. Then becomes strangely vibrant, and bursts to a swift life within her anger. He is about to give way before her hatred when a new passion flares at him and makes his stomach fall. Bona squeezes him. He suddenly feels stifled, and wonders why in hell the ring of silly gaping faces that's caked about him doesnt make way and give him air. He has a swift illusion that it is himself who has been struck. He looks at Bona. Whir. Whir. They seem to be human distortions spinning tensely in a fog. Spinning . . . dizzy . . . spinning. . . Bona jerks herself free, flushes a startling crimson, breaks through the bewildered teams, and rushes from the hall.

II

Paul is in his room of two windows.

Outside, the South-Side L track cuts them in two.

Bona is one window. One window, Paul.

Hurtling Loop-jammed L trains throw them in swift shadow.

Paul goes to his. Gray slanting roofs of houses are tinted lavender in the setting sun. Paul follows the sun, over the stock-yards where a fresh stench is just arising, across wheat lands that are still waving above their stubble, into the sun. Paul follows the sun to a pine-matted hillock in Georgia. He sees the slanting roofs of gray unpainted cabins tinted lavender. A Negress chants a lullaby beneath the mate-eyes of a southern planter. Her breasts are ample for the suckling of a song. She weans it, and sends it, curiously weaving, among lush melodies of cane and corn. Paul follows the sun into himself in Chicago.

He is at Bona's window.

With his own glow he looks through a dark pane.

Paul's room-mate comes in.

"Say, Paul, I've got a date for you. Come on. Shake a leg, will you?"

His blonde hair is combed slick. His vest is snug about him.

He is like the electric light which he snaps on.

"Whatdoysay, Paul? Get a wiggle on. Come on. We havent got much time by the time we eat and dress and everything."

His bustling concentrates on the brushing of his hair.

Art: What in hell's getting into Paul of late, anyway? Christ, but he's getting moony. Its his blood. Dark blood: moony. Doesnt get anywhere unless you boost it. You've got to keep it going—

"Say, Paul!"

—or it'll go to sleep on you. Dark blood; nigger? Thats what those jealous she-hens say. Not Bona though, or she . . . from the South . . . wouldnt want me to fix a date for him and her. Hell of a thing, that Paul's dark: you've got to always be answering questions.

"Say, Paul, for Christ's sake leave that window, cant you?"

"Whats it, Art?"

"Hell, I've told you about fifty times. Got a date for you. Come on."

"With who?"

Art: He didnt use to ask; now he does. Getting up in the air. Getting funny.

"Heres your hat. Want a smoke? Paul! Here. I've got a match. Now come on and I'll tell you all about it on the way to supper."

Paul: He's going to Life this time. No doubt of that. Quit your kidding. Some day, dear Art, I'm going to kick the living slats out of you, and you wont know what I've done it for. And your slats will bring forth Life . . . beautiful woman. . .

Pure Food Restaurant.

"Bring me some soup with a lot of crackers, understand? And then a roastbeef dinner. Same for you, eh, Paul? Now as I was saying, you've got a swell chance with her. And she's game. Best proof: she dont give a damn what the dorm girls say about you and her in the gym, or about the funny looks that Boynton gives her, or about what they say about, well, hell, you know, Paul. And say, Paul, she's a sweetheart. Tall, not puffy and pretty, more serious and deep — the kind you like these days. And they say she's got a car. And say, she's on fire. But you know all about that. She got Helen to fix it up with me. The four of us — remember the last party? Crimson Gardens! Boy!"

Paul's eyes take on a light that Art can settle in.

III

Art has on his patent-leather pumps and fancy vest. A loose fall coat is swung across his arm. His face has been massaged, and over a close shave, powdered. It is a healthy pink the blue of evening tints a purple pallor. Art is happy and confident in the good looks that his mirror gave him. Bubbling over with a joy he must spend now if the night is to contain it all. His bubbles, too, are curiously tinted purple as Paul watches them. Paul, contrary to what he had thought he would be like, is cool like the dusk, and like the dusk, detached. His dark face is a floating shade in evening's shadow. He sees Art, curiously. Art is a purple fluid, carbon-charged, that effervesces besides him. He loves Art. But is it not queer, this pale purple facsimile of a red-blooded Norwegian friend of his? Perhaps for some reason, white skins are not supposed to live at night. Surely, enough nights would transform them fantastically, or kill them. And their red passion? Night paled that too, and made it moony. Moony. Thats what Art thought of him. Bona didnt, even in the daytime. Bona, would she be pale? Impossible. Not that red glow. But the conviction did not set his emotion flowing.

"Come right in, wont you? The young ladies will be right down. Oh, Mr. Carlstrom, do play something for us while you are waiting. We just love to listen to your music. You play so well."

Houses, and dorm sitting-rooms are places where white faces seclude themselves at night. There is a reason. . .

Art sat on the piano and simply tore it down. Jazz. The picture of Our Poets hung perilously.

Paul: I've got to get the kid to play that stuff for me in the daytime. Might be different. More himself. More nigger. Different? There is. Curious, though.

The girls come in. Art stops playing, and almost immediately takes up a petty quarrel, where he had last left it, with Helen.

Bona, black-hair curled staccato, sharply contrasting with Helen's puffy yellow, holds Paul's hand. She squeezes it. Her own emotion supplements the return pressure. And then, for no tangible reason, her spirits drop. Without them, she is nervous, and slightly afraid. She resents this. Paul's eyes are critical. She resents Paul. She flares at him. She flares to poise and security.

"Shall we be on our way?"

"Yes, Bona, certainly."

The Boulevard is sleek in asphalt, and, with arc-lights and limousines, aglow. Dry leaves scamper behind the whir of cars. The scent of exploded gasoline that mingles with them is faintly sweet. Mellow stone mansions overshadow clapboard homes which now resemble Negro shanties in some southern alley. Bona and Paul, and Art and Helen, move along an island-like, far-stretching strip of leaf-soft ground. Above them, worlds of shadow-planes and solids, silently moving. As if on one of these, Paul looks down on Bona. No doubt of it: her face is pale. She is talking. Her words have no feel to them. One sees them. They are pink petals that fall upon velvet cloth. Bona is soft, and pale, and beautiful.

"Paul, tell me something about yourself — or would you rather wait?"

"I'll tell you anything you'd like to know."

"Not what I want to know, Paul; what you want to tell me."

"You have the beauty of a gem fathoms under sea."

"I feel that, but I dont want to be. I want to be near you. Perhaps I will be if I tell you something. Paul, I love you."

The sea casts up its jewel into his hands, and burns them furiously. To tuck her arm under his and hold her hand will ease the burn.

"What can I say to you, brave dear woman — I cant talk love. Love is a dry grain in my mouth unless it is wet with kisses."

"You would dare? right here on the Boulevard? before Arthur and Helen?"

"Before myself? I dare."

"Here then."

Bona, in the slim shadow of a tree trunk, pulls Paul to her. Suddenly she stiffens. Stops.

"But you have not said you love me."

"I cant — yet — Bona."

"Ach, you never will. Youre cold. Cold."

Bona: Colored; cold. Wrong somewhere.

She hurries and catches up with Art and Helen.

IV

Crimson Gardens. Hurrah! So one feels. People . . . University of Chicago students, members of the stock exchange, a large Negro in crimson uniform who guards the door . . . had watched them enter. Had leaned towards each other over ash-smeared tablecloths and highballs and whispered: What is he, a Spaniard, an Indian, an Italian, a Mexican, a Hindu, or a Japanese? Art had at first fidgeted under their stares . . . what are *you* looking at, you godam pack of owl-eyed hyenas? . . but soon settled into his fuss with Helen, and forgot them. A strange thing happened to Paul. Suddenly he knew that he was apart from the people around him. Apart from the pain which they had unconsciously caused. Suddenly he knew that people saw, not attractiveness in his dark skin, but difference. Their stares, giving him to himself, filled something long empty within him, and were like green blades sprouting in his consciousness. There was fullness, and strength and peace about it all. He saw himself, cloudy, but real. He saw the faces of the people at the tables round him. White lights, or as now, the pink lights of the Crimson Gardens gave a glow and immediacy to white faces. The pleasure of it, equal to that of love or dream, of seeing this. Art and Bona and Helen? He'd look. They were wonderfully flushed and beautiful. Not for himself; because they were. Distantly. Who were they, anyway? God, if he knew them. He'd come in with them. Of that he was sure. Come where? Into life? Yes. No. Into the Crimson Gardens. A part of life. A carbon bubble. Would it look purple if he went out into the night and looked at it? His sudden starting to rise almost upset the table.

"What in hell — pardon — whats the matter, Paul?"

"I forgot my cigarettes —"

"Youre smoking one."

"So I am. Pardon me."

The waiter straightens them out. Takes their order.

Art: What in hell's eating Paul? Moony aint the word for it. From bad to worse. And those godam people staring so. Paul's a queer fish. Doesnt seem to mind. . . He's my pal, let me tell you, you horn-rimmed owl-eyed hyena at that table, and a lot better than you whoever you are. . . Queer about him. I could stick up for him if he'd only come out, one way or the other, and tell a feller. Besides, a room-mate has a right to know. Thinks I wont understand. Said so. He's got a swell head when it comes to brains, all right. God, he's a good straight feller, though. Only, moony. Nut. Nuttish. Nuttery. Nutmeg. . . "What'd you say, Helen?"

"I was talking to Bona, thank you."

"Well, its nothing to get spiffy about."

"What? Oh, of course not. Please lets dont start some silly argument all over again."

"Well."

"Well."

"Now thats enough. Say, waiter, whats the matter with our order? Make it snappy, will you?"

Crimson Gardens. Hurrah! So one feels. The drinks come. Four highballs. Art passes cigarettes. A girl dressed like a bare-back rider in flaming pink, makes her way through tables to the dance floor. All lights are dimmed till they seem a lush afterglow of crimson. Spotlights the girl. She sings. "Liza, Little Liza Jane."

Paul is rosy before his window.

He moves, slightly, towards Bona.

With his own glow, he seeks to penetrate a dark pane.

Paul: From the South. What does that mean, precisely, except that you'll love or hate a nigger? Thats a lot. What does it mean except that in Chicago you'll have the courage to neither love or hate. A priori. But it would seem that you have. Queer words, arent these, for a man who wears blue pants on a gym floor in the daytime. Well, never matter. You matter. I'd like to know you whom I look at. Know, not love. Not that knowing is a greater pleasure; but that I have just found the joy of it. You came just a month too late. Even this afternoon I dreamed. To-night, along the Boulevard, you found me cold. Paul Johnson, cold! Thats a good one, eh, Art, you fine old stupid fellow, you! But I feel good! The color and the music and the song. . . A Negress chants a lullaby beneath the mate-eyes of a southern planter. O song! . . And those flushed faces. Eager brilliant eyes. Hard to imagine them as unawakened. Your own. Oh, they're awake all right. "And you know it too, dont you Bona?"

"What, Paul?"

"The truth of what I was thinking."

"I'd like to know I know — something of you."

"You will — before the evening's over. I promise it."

Crimson Gardens. Hurrah! So one feels. The bare-back rider balances agilely on the applause which is the tail of her song. Orchestral instruments warm up for jazz. The flute is a cat that ripples its fur against the deep-purring saxophone. The drum throws sticks. The cat jumps on the piano keyboard. Hi diddle, hi diddle, the cat and the fiddle. Crimson Gardens . . . hurrah! . . jumps over the moon. Crimson Gardens! Helen . . . O Eliza . . . rabbit-eyes sparkling, plays up to, and tries to placate what she considers to be Paul's contempt. She always does that . . . Little Liza Jane. . . Once home, she burns with the thought of what she's done. She says all manner of snidy things about him, and swears that she'll never go out again when he is along. She tries to get Art to break with him, saying, that if Paul, whom the whole dormitory calls a nigger, is more to him than she is, well, she's through. She does not break with Art. She goes out as often as she can with Art and Paul. She explains this to herself by a piece of information which a friend of hers had given her: men like him (Paul) can fascinate. One is not responsible for fascination. Not one girl had really loved Paul; he fascinated them. Bona didnt; only thought she did. Time would tell. And of course, *she* didnt. Liza. . . She plays up to, and tries to placate, Paul.

"Paul is so deep these days, and I'm so glad he's found some one to interest him."

"I dont believe I do."

The thought escapes from Bona just a moment before her anger at having said it.

Bona: You little puffy cat, I do. I do!

Dont I, Paul? her eyes ask.

Her answer is a crash of jazz from the palm-hidden orchestra. Crimson Gardens is a body whose blood flows to a clot upon the dance floor. Art and Helen clot. Soon, Bona and Paul. Paul finds her a little stiff, and his mind, wandering to Helen (silly little kid who wants every highball spoon her hands touch, for a souvenir), supple, perfect little dancer, wishes for the next dance when he and Art will exchange.

Bona knows that she must win him to herself.

"Since when have men like you grown cold?"

"The first philosopher."

"I thought you were a poet — or a gym director."

"Hence, your failure to make love."

Bona's eyes flare. Water. Grow red about the rims. She would like to tear away from him and dash across the clotted floor.

"What do you mean?"

"Mental concepts rule you. If they were flush with mine — good. I dont believe they are."

"How do you know, Mr. Philosopher?"

"Mostly a priori."

"You talk well for a gym director."

"And you —"

"I hate you. Ou!"

She presses away. Paul, conscious of the convention in it, pulls her to him. Her body close. Her head still strains away. He nearly crushes her. She tries to pinch him. Then sees people staring, and lets her arms fall. Their eyes meet. Both, contemptuous. The dance takes blood from their minds and packs it, tingling, in the torsos of their swaying bodies. Passionate blood leaps back into their eyes. They are a dizzy blood clot on a gyrating floor. They know that the pink-faced people have no part in what they feel. Their instinct leads them away from Art and Helen, and towards the big uniformed black man who opens and closes the gilded exit door. The cloak-room girl is tolerant of their impatience over such trivial things as wraps. And slightly superior. As the black man swings the door for them, his eyes are knowing. Too many couples have passed out, flushed and fidgety, for him not to know. The chill air is a shock to Paul. A strange thing happens. He sees the Gardens purple, as if he were way off. And a spot is in the purple. The spot comes furiously towards him. Face of the black man. It leers. It smiles sweetly like a child's. Paul leaves Bona and darts back so quickly that he doesnt give the door-man a chance to open. He swings in. Stops. Before the huge bulk of the Negro.

"Youre wrong."

"Yassur."

"Brother, youre wrong.

"I came back to tell you, to shake your hand, and tell you that you are wrong. That something beautiful is going to happen. That the Gardens are purple like a bed of roses would be at dusk. That I came into the Gardens, into life in the Gardens with one whom I did not know. That I danced with her, and did not know her. That I felt passion, contempt and passion for her whom I did not know. That I thought of her. That my thoughts were matches thrown into a dark window. And all the while the Gardens were purple like a bed of roses would be at dusk. I came back to tell you, brother, that white faces are petals of roses. That dark faces are petals of dusk. That I am going out and gather petals. That I am going out and know her whom I brought here with me to these Gardens which are purple like a bed of roses would be at dusk."

Paul and the black man shook hands.

When he reached the spot where they had been standing, Bona was gone.

TO WALDO FRANK.

KABNIS

I

Ralph Kabnis, propped in his bed, tries to read. To read himself to sleep. An oil lamp on a chair near his elbow burns unsteadily. The cabin room is spaced fantastically about it. Whitewashed hearth and chimney, black with sooty saw-teeth. Ceiling, patterned by the fringed globe of the lamp. The walls, unpainted, are seasoned a rosin yellow. And cracks between the boards are black. These cracks are the lips the night winds use for whispering. Night winds in Georgia are vagrant poets, whispering. Kabnis, against his will, lets his book slip down, and listens to them. The warm whiteness of his bed, the lamp-light, do not protect him from the weird chill of their song:

White-man's land.
Niggers, sing.
Burn, bear black children
Till poor rivers bring
Rest, and sweet glory
In Camp Ground.

Kabnis' thin hair is streaked on the pillow. His hand strokes the slim silk of his mustache. His thumb, pressed under his chin, seems to be trying to give squareness and projection to it. Brown eyes stare from a lemon face. Moisture gathers beneath his arm-pits. He slides down beneath the cover, seeking release.

Kabnis: Near me. Now. Whoever you are, my warm glowing sweetheart, do not think that the face that rests beside you is the real Kabnis. Ralph Kabnis is a dream. And dreams are faces with large eyes and weak chins and broad brows that get smashed by the fists of square faces. The body of the world is bull-necked. A dream is a soft face that fits uncertainly upon it. . . God, if I could develop that in words. Give what I know a bull-neck and a heaving body, all would go well with me, wouldnt it, sweetheart? If I could feel that I came to the South to face it. If I, the dream (not what is weak and afraid in me) could become the face of the South. How my lips would sing for it, my songs being the lips of its soul. Soul. Soul hell. There aint no such thing. What in hell was that?

A rat had run across the thin boards of the ceiling. Kabnis thrusts his head out from the covers. Through the cracks, a powdery faded red dust sprays down on him. Dust of slave-fields, dried, scattered. . . No use to read. Christ, if he only could drink himself to sleep. Something as sure as fate was going to happen. He couldnt stand this thing much longer. A hen, perched on a shelf in the adjoining room begins to tread. Her nails scrape the soft wood. Her feathers ruffle.

"Get out of that, you egg-laying bitch."

Kabnis hurls a slipper against the wall. The hen flies from her perch and cackles as if a skunk were after her.

"Now cut out that racket or I'll wring your neck for you."

Answering cackles arise in the chicken yard.

"Why in Christ's hell cant you leave me alone? Damn it, I wish your cackle would choke you. Choke every mother's son of them in this God-forsaken hole. Go away. By God I'll wring your neck for you if you dont. Hell of a mess I've got in: even the poultry is hostile. Go way. Go way. By God, I'll . . ."

Kabnis jumps from his bed. His eyes are wild. He makes for the door. Bursts through it. The hen, driving blindly at the windowpane, screams. Then flies and flops around trying to elude him. Kabnis catches her.

"Got you now, you she-bitch."

With his fingers about her neck, he thrusts open the outside door and steps out into the serene loveliness of Georgian autumn moonlight. Some distance off, down in the valley, a band of pine-smoke, silvered gauze, drifts steadily. The half-moon is a white child that sleeps upon the tree-tops of the forest. White winds croon its sleep-song:

> rock a-by baby . . .
> Black mother sways, holding a white child on her bosom.
> when the bough bends . . .
> Her breath hums through pine-cones.
> cradle will fall . . .
> Teat moon-children at your breasts,
> down will come baby . . .
> Black mother.

Kabnis whirls the chicken by its neck, and throws the head away. Picks up the hopping body, warm, sticky, and hides it in a clump of bushes. He wipes blood from his hands onto the coarse scant grass.

Kabnis: Thats done. Old Chromo in the big house there will wonder whats become of her pet hen. Well, it'll teach her a lesson: not to make a hen-coop of my quarters. Quarters. Hell of a fine quarters, I've got. Five years ago; look at me now. Earth's child. The earth my mother. God is a profligate red-nosed man about town. Bastardy; me. A bastard son has got a right to curse his maker. God. . .

Kabnis is about to shake his fists heavenward. He looks up, and the night's beauty strikes him dumb. He falls to his knees. Sharp stones cut through his thin pajamas. The shock sends a shiver over him. He quivers. Tears mist his eyes. He writhes.

"God Almighty, dear God, dear Jesus, do not torture me with beauty. Take it away. Give me an ugly world. Ha, ugly. Stinking like unwashed niggers. Dear Jesus, do not chain me to myself and set these hills and valleys, heaving with folk-songs, so close to me that I cannot reach them. There is a radiant beauty in the night that touches and . . . tortures me. Ugh. Hell. Get up, you damn fool. Look around. Whats beautiful there? Hog pens and chicken yards. Dirty red mud. Stinking outhouse. Whats beauty anyway but ugliness if it hurts you? God, he doesnt exist, but nevertheless He is ugly. Hence, what comes from Him is ugly. Lynchers and business men, and that cockroach Hanby, especially. How come that he gets to be principal of a school? Of the school I'm driven to teach in? God's handiwork, doubtless. God and Hanby, they belong together. Two godam moral-spouters. Oh, no, I wont let that emotion come up in me. Stay down. Stay down, I tell you. O Jesus, Thou art beautiful. . .Come, Ralph, pull yourself together. Curses and adoration dont come from what is sane. This loneliness, dumbness, awful, intangible oppression is enough to drive a man insane. Miles from nowhere. A speck on a Georgia hillside. Jesus, can you imagine it — an atom of dust in agony on a hillside? Thats a spectacle for you. Come, Ralph, old man, pull yourself together."

Kabnis has stiffened. He is conscious now of the night wind, and of how it chills him. He rises. He totters as a man would who for the first time uses artificial limbs. As a completely artificial man would. The large frame house, squatting on brick pillars, where the principal of the school, his wife, and the boarding girls sleep, seems a curious shadow of his mind. He tries, but cannot convince himself of its reality. His gaze drifts down into the vale, across the swamp, up over the solid dusk bank of pines, and rests, bewildered-like, on the court-house tower. It is dull silver in the moonlight. White child that sleeps upon the top of pines. Kabnis' mind clears. He sees himself yanked beneath that tower. He sees white minds, with indolent assumption, juggle justice and a nigger. . . Somewhere, far off in the straight line of his sight, is Augusta. Christ, how cut off from everything he is. And hours, hours north, why not say a lifetime north? Washington sleeps. Its still, peaceful streets, how desirable they are. Its people whom he had always halfway despised. New York? Impossible. It was a fiction. He had dreamed it. An impotent nostalgia grips him. It becomes intolerable. He forces himself to narrow to a cabin silhouetted on a knoll about a mile away. Peace. Negroes within it are content. They farm. They sing. They love. They sleep. Kabnis wonders if perhaps they can feel him. If perhaps he gives them bad dreams. Things are so immediate in Georgia.

Thinking that now he can go to sleep, he re-enters his room. He builds a fire in the open hearth. The room dances to the tongues of flames, and sings to the crackling and spurting of the logs. Wind comes up between the floor boards, through the black cracks of the walls.

Kabnis: Cant sleep. Light a cigarette. If that old bastard comes over here and smells smoke, I'm done for. Hell of a note, cant even smoke. The stillness of it: where they burn and hang men, you cant smoke. Cant take a swig of licker. What do they think this is, anyway, some sort of temperance school? How did I ever land in such a hole? Ugh. One might just as well be in his grave. Still as a grave. Jesus, how still everything is. Does the world know how still it is? People make noise. They are afraid of silence. Of what lives, and God, of what dies in silence. There must be many dead things moving in silence. They come here to touch me. I swear I feel their fingers. . . Come, Ralph, pull yourself together. What in hell was that? Only the rustle of leaves, I guess. You know, Ralph, old man, it wouldnt surprise me at all to see a ghost. People dont think there are such things. They rationalize their fear, and call their cowardice science. Fine bunch, they are. Damit, that was a noise. And not the wind either. A chicken maybe. Hell, chickens dont wander around this time of night. What in hell is it?

A scraping sound, like a piece of wood dragging over the ground, is coming near.

"Ha, ha. The ghosts down this way havent got any chains to rattle, so they drag trees along with them. Thats a good one. But no joke, something is outside this house, as sure as hell. Whatever it is, it can get a good look at me and I cant see it. Jesus Christ!"

Kabnis pours water on the flames and blows his lamp out. He picks up a poker and stealthily approaches the outside door. Swings it open, and lurches into the night. A calf, carrying a yoke of wood, bolts away from him and scampers down the road.

"Well, I'm damned. This godam place is sure getting the best of me. Come, Ralph, old man, pull yourself together. Nights cant last forever. Thank God for that. Its Sunday already. First time in my life I've ever wanted Sunday to come. Hell of a day. And down here there's no such thing as ducking church. Well, I'll see Halsey and Layman, and get a good square meal. Thats something. And Halsey's a damn good feller. Cant talk to him, though. Who in Christ's world can I talk to? A hen. God. Myself. . . I'm going bats, no doubt of that. Come now, Ralph, go in and make yourself go to sleep. Come now . . . in the door . . . thats right. Put the poker down. There. All right. Slip under the sheets. Close your eyes. Think nothing . . . a long time . . . nothing, nothing. Dont even think nothing. Blank. Not even blank. Count. No, mustnt count. Nothing . . . blank . . . nothing . . . blank . . . space without stars in it. No, nothing . . . nothing . . .

Kabnis sleeps. The winds, like soft-voiced vagrant poets sing:

White-man's land.
Niggers, sing.
Burn, bear black children
Till poor rivers bring
Rest, and sweet glory
In Camp Ground.

II

The parlor of Fred Halsey's home. There is a seediness about it. It seems as though the fittings have given a frugal service to at least seven generations of middle-class shop-owners. An open grate burns cheerily in contrast to the gray cold changed autumn weather. An old-fashioned mantelpiece supports a family clock (not running), a figure or two in imitation bronze, and two small group pictures. Directly above it, in a heavy oak frame, the portrait of a bearded man. Black hair, thick and curly, intensifies the pallor of the high forehead. The eyes are daring. The nose, sharp and regular. The poise suggests a tendency to adventure checked by the necessities of absolute command. The portrait is that of an English gentleman who has retained much of his culture, in that money has enabled him to escape being drawn through a land-grubbing pioneer life. His nature and features, modified by marriage and circumstances, have been transmitted to his great-grandson, Fred. To the left of this picture, spaced on the wall, is a smaller portrait of the great grandmother. That here there is a Negro strain, no one would doubt. But it is difficult to say in precisely what feature it lies. On close inspection, her mouth is seen to be wistfully twisted. The expression of her face seems to shift before one's gaze — now ugly, repulsive; now sad, and somehow beautiful in its pain. A tin woodbox rests on the floor below. To the right of the great-grandfather's portrait hangs a family group: the father, mother, two brothers, and one sister of Fred. It includes himself some thirty years ago when his face was an olive white, and his hair luxuriant and dark and wavy. The father is a rich brown. The mother, practically white. Of the children, the girl, quite young, is like Fred; the two brothers, darker. The walls of the room are plastered and painted green. An old upright piano is tucked into the corner near the window. The window looks out on a forlorn, box-like, whitewashed frame church. Negroes are gathering, on foot, driving questionable gray and brown mules, and in an occasional Ford, for afternoon service. Beyond, Georgia hills roll off into the distance, their dreary aspect heightened by the gray spots of unpainted one- and two-room shanties. Clumps of pine trees here and there are the dark points the whole landscape is approaching. The church bell tolls. Above its squat tower, a great spiral of buzzards reaches far into the heavens. An ironic comment upon the path that leads into the Christian land. . . Three rocking chairs are grouped around the grate. Sunday papers scattered on the floor indicate a recent usage. Halsey, a well-built, stocky fellow, hair cropped close, enters the room. His Sunday clothes smell of wood and glue, for it is his habit to potter around his wagon-shop even on the Lord's day. He is followed by Professor Layman, tall, heavy, loose-jointed Georgia Negro, by turns teacher and preacher, who has traveled in almost every nook and corner of the state and hence knows more than would be good for anyone other than a silent man. Kabnis, trying to force through a gathering heaviness, trails in behind them. They slip into chairs before the fire.

Layman: Sholy fine, Mr. Halsey, sholy fine. This town's right good at feedin folks, better'n most towns in th state, even for preachers, but I ken say this beats um all. Yassur. Now aint that right, Professor Kabnis?

Kabnis: Yes sir, this beats them all, all right — best I've had, and thats a fact, though my comparison doesnt carry far, y'know.

Layman: Hows that, Professor?

Kabnis: Well, this is my first time out —

Layman: For a fact. Aint seed you round so much. Whats th trouble? Dont like our folks down this away?

Halsey: Aint that, Layman. He aint like most northern niggers that way. Aint a thing stuck up about him. He likes us, you an me, maybe all — its that red mud over yonder — gets stuck in it an cant get out. (Laughs.) An then he loves th fire so, warm as its been. Coldest Yankee I've ever seen. But I'm goin t get him out now in a jiffy, eh, Kabnis?

Kabnis: Sure, I should say so, sure. Dont think its because I dont like folks down this way. Just the opposite, in fact. Theres more hospitality and everything. Its diff— that is, theres lots of northern exaggeration about the South. Its not half the terror they picture it. Things are not half bad, as one could easily figure out for himself without ever crossing the Mason and Dixie line: all these people wouldnt stay down here, especially the rich, the ones that could easily leave, if conditions were so mighty bad. And then too, sometime back, my family were southerners y'know. From Georgia, in fact —

Layman: Nothin t feel proud about, Professor. Neither your folks nor mine.

Halsey (in a mock religious tone): Amen t that, brother Layman. Amen (turning to Kabnis, half playful, yet somehow dead in earnest). An Mr. Kabnis, kindly remember youre in th land of cotton — hell of a land. Th white folks get th boll; th niggers get th stalk. An dont you dare touch th boll, or even look at it. They'll swing y sho. (Laughs.)

Kabnis: But they wouldnt touch a gentleman — fellows, men like us three here —

Layman: Nigger's a nigger down this away, Professor. An only two dividins:

good an bad. An even they aint permanent categories. They sometimes mixes um up when it comes t lynchin. I've seen um do it.

Halsey: Dont let th fear int y, though, Kabnis. This county's a good un. Aint been a stringin up I can remember. (Laughs.)

Layman: This is a good town an a good county. But theres some that makes up fer it.

Kabnis: Things are better now though since that stir about those peonage cases, arent they?

Layman: Ever hear tell of a single shot killin moren one rabbit, Professor?

Kabnis: No, of course not, that is, but then —

Halsey: Now I know you werent born yesterday, sprung up so rapid like you aint heard of th brick thrown in th hornets' nest. (Laughs.)

Kabnis: Hardly, hardly, I know —

Halsey: Course y do. (To Layman) See, northern niggers aint as dumb as they make out t be.

Kabnis (overlooking the remark): Just stirs them up to sting.

Halsey: T perfection. An put just like a professor should put it.

Kabnis: Thats what actually did happen?

Layman: Well, if it aint sos only because th stingers already movin jes as fast as they ken go. An been goin ever since I ken remember, an then some mo. Though I dont usually make mention of it.

Halsey: Damn sight better not. Say, Layman, you come from where theyre always swarmin, dont y?

Layman: Yassur. I do that, sho. Dont want t mention it, but its a fact. I've seed th time when there werent no use t even stretch out flat upon th ground. Seen um shoot an cut a man t pieces who had died th night befo. Yassur. An they didnt stop when they found out he was dead — jes went on ahackin at him anyway.

Kabnis: What did you do? What did you say to them, Professor?

Layman: Thems th things you neither does a thing or talks about if y want t stay around this away, Professor.

Halsey: Listen t what he's tellin y, Kabnis. May come in handy some day.

Kabnis: Cant something be done? But of course not. This preacher-ridden race. Pray and shout. Theyre in the preacher's hands. Thats what it is. And the preacher's hands are in the white man's pockets.

Halsey: Present company always excepted.

Kabnis: The Professor knows I wasnt referring to him.

Layman: Preacher's a preacher anywheres you turn. No use exceptin.

Kabnis: Well, of course, if you look at it that way. I didnt mean — But cant something be done?

Layman: Sho. Yassur. An done first rate an well. Jes like Sam Raymon done it.

Kabnis: Hows that? What did he do?

Layman: Th white folks (reckon I oughtnt tell it) had jes knocked two others like you kill a cow — brained um with an ax, when they caught Sam Raymon by a stream. They was about t do fer him when he up an says, "White folks, I gotter die, I knows that. But wont y let me die in my own way?" Some was fer gettin after him, but th boss held um back an says, "Jes so longs th nigger dies —" An Sam fell down ont his knees an prayed, "O Lord, Ise comin to y," an he up an jumps int th stream.

Singing from the church becomes audible. Above it, rising and falling in a plaintive moan, a woman's voice swells to shouting. Kabnis hears it. His face gives way to an expression of mingled fear, contempt, and pity. Layman takes no notice of it. Halsey grins at Kabnis. He feels like having a little sport with him.

Halsey: Lets go t church, eh, Kabnis?

Kabnis (seeking control): All right — no sir, not by a damn sight. Once a days enough for me. Christ, but that stuff gets to me. Meaning no reflection on you, Professor.

Halsey: Course not. Say, Kabnis, noticed y this morning. What'd y get up for an go out?

Kabnis: Couldnt stand the shouting, and thats a fact. We dont have that sort of thing up North. We do, but, that is, some one should see to it that they are stopped or put out when they get so bad the preacher has to stop his sermon for them.

Halsey: Is that th way youall sit on sisters up North?

Kabnis: In the church I used to go to no one ever shouted —

Halsey: Lungs weak?

Kabnis: Hardly, that is —

Halsey: Yankees are right up t th minute in tellin folk how t turn a trick. They always were good at talkin.

Kabnis: Well, anyway, they should be stopped.

Layman: Thats right. Thats true. An its th worst ones in th community that comes int th church t shout. I've sort a made a study of it. You take a man what drinks, th biggest licker-head around will come int th church an yell th loudest. An th sister whats done wrong, an is always doin wrong, will sit down in th Amen corner an swing her arms an shout her head off. Seems as if they cant control themselves out in th world; they cant control themselves in church. Now dont that sound logical, Professor?

Halsey: Reckon its as good as any. But I heard that queer cuss over yonder

—y know him, dont y, Kabnis? Well, y ought t. He had a run-in with your boss th other day—same as you'll have if you dont walk th chalk-line. An th quicker th better. I hate that Hanby. Ornery bastard. I'll mash his mouth in one of these days. Well, as I was sayin, that feller, Lewis's name, I heard him sayin somethin about a stream whats dammed has got t cut loose somewheres. An that sounds good. I know th feelin myself. He strikes me as knowin a bucketful bout most things, that feller does. Seems like he doesnt want t talk, an does, sometimes, like Layman here. Damn queer feller, him.

Layman: Cant make heads or tails of him, an I've seen lots o queer possums in my day. Everybody's wonderin about him. White folks too. He'll have t leave here soon, thats sho. Always askin questions. An I aint seed his lips move once. Pokin round an notin somethin. Noted what I said th other day, an that werent fer notin down.

Kabnis: What was that?

Layman: Oh, a lynchin that took place bout a year ago. Th worst I know of round these parts.

Halsey: Bill Burnam?

Layman: Na. Mame Lamkins.

Halsey grunts, but says nothing.

The preacher's voice rolls from the church in an insistent chanting monotone. At regular intervals it rises to a crescendo note. The sister begins to shout. Her voice, high-pitched and hysterical, is almost perfectly attuned to the nervous key of Kabnis. Halsey notices his distress, and is amused by it. Layman's face is expressionless. Kabnis wants to hear the story of Mame Lamkins. He does not want to hear it. It can be no worse than the shouting.

Kabnis (his chair rocking faster): What about Mame Lamkins?

Halsey: Tell him, Layman.

The preacher momentarily stops. The choir, together with the entire congregation, sings an old spiritual. The music seems to quiet the shouter. Her heavy breathing has the sound of evening winds that blow through pinecones. Layman's voice is uniformly low and soothing. A canebrake, murmuring the tale to its neighbor-road would be more passionate.

Layman: White folks know that niggers talk, an they dont mind jes so long as nothing comes of it, so here goes. She was in th family-way, Mame Lamkins was. They killed her in th street, an some white man seein th risin in her stomach as she lay there soppy in her blood like any cow, took an ripped her belly open, an th kid fell out. It was living; but a nigger baby aint supposed t live. So he jabbed his knife in it an stuck it t a tree. An then they all went away.

Kabnis: Christ no! What had she done?

Layman: Tried t hide her husband when they was after him.

A shriek pierces the room. The bronze pieces on the mantel hum. The sister cries frantically: "Jesus, Jesus, I've found Jesus. O Lord, glory t God, one mo sinner is acomin home." At the height of this, a stone, wrapped round with paper, crashes through the window. Kabnis springs to his feet, terror-stricken. Layman is worried. Halsey picks up the stone. Takes off the wrapper, smooths it out, and reads: "You northern nigger, its time fer y t leave. Git along now." Kabnis knows that the command is meant for him. Fear squeezes him. Caves him in. As a violent external pressure would. Fear flows inside him. It fills him up. He bloats. He saves himself from bursting by dashing wildly from the room. Halsey and Layman stare stupidly at each other. The stone, the crumpled paper are things, huge things that weight them. Their thoughts are vaguely concerned with the texture of the stone, with the color of the paper. Then they remember the words, and begin to shift them about in sentences. Layman even construes them grammatically. Suddenly the sense of them comes back to Halsey. He grips Layman by the arm and they both follow after Kabnis.

A false dusk has come early. The countryside is ashen, chill. Cabins and roads and canebrakes whisper. The church choir, dipping into a long silence, sings:

My Lord, what a mourning,
My Lord, what a mourning,
My Lord, what a mourning,
When the stars begin to fall.

Softly luminous over the hills and valleys, the faint spray of a scattered star...

III

A splotchy figure drives forward along the cane- and corn-stalk hemmed-in road. A scarecrow replica of Kabnis, awkwardly animate. Fantastically plastered with red Georgia mud. It skirts the big house whose windows shine like mellow lanterns in the dusk. Its shoulder jogs against a sweet-gum tree. The figure caroms off against the cabin door, and lunges in. It slams the door as if to prevent some one entering after it.

"God Almighty, theyre here. After me. On me. All along the road I saw their eyes flaring from the cane. Hounds. Shouts. What in God's name did I run here for? A mud-hole trap. I stumbled on a rope. O God, a rope. Their clammy hands were like the love of death playing up and down my spine. Trying to trip my legs. To trip my spine. Up and down my spine. My spine. . . My legs. . . Why in hell didn't they catch me?"

Kabnis wheels around, half defiant, half numbed with a more immediate fear.

"Wanted to trap me here. Get out o there. I see you."

He grabs a broom from beside the chimney and violently pokes it under the bed. The broom strikes a tin wash-tub. The noise bewilders. He recovers.

"Not there. In the closet."

He throws the broom aside and grips the poker. Starts towards the closet door, towards somewhere in the perfect blackness behind the chimney.

"I'll brain you."

He stops short. The barks of hounds, evidently in pursuit, reach him. A voicc, liquid in distance, yells, "Hi! Hi!"

"O God, theyre after me. Holy Father, Mother of Christ — hell, this aint no time for prayer —"

Voices, just outside the door:

"Reckon he's here."

"Dont see no light though."

The door is flung open.

Kabnis: Get back or I'll kill you.

He braces himself, brandishing the poker.

Halsey (coming in): Aint as bad as all that. Put that thing down.

Layman: Its only us, Professor. Nobody else after y.

Kabnis: Halsey. Layman. Close that door. Dont light that light. For godsake get away from there.

Halsey: Nobody's after y, Kabnis, I'm tellin y. Put that thing down an get yourself together.

Kabnis: I tell you they are. I saw them. I heard the hounds.

Halsey: These aint th days of hounds an Uncle Tom's Cabin, feller. White folks aint in fer all them theatrics these days. Theys more direct than that. If what they wanted was t get y, theyd have just marched right in an took y where y sat. Somebodys down by th branch chasin rabbits an atrccin possums.

A shot is heard.

Halsey: Got him, I reckon. Saw Tom goin out with his gun. Tom's pretty lucky most times.

He goes to the bureau and lights the lamp. The circular fringe is patterned on the ceiling. The moving shadows of the men are huge against the bare wall boards. Halsey walks up to Kabnis, takes the poker from his grip, and without more ado pushes him into a chair before the dark hearth.

Halsey: Youre a mess. Here, Layman. Get some trash an start a fire.

Layman fumbles around, finds some newspapers and old bags, puts them in the hearth, arranges the wood, and kindles the fire. Halsey sets a black iron kettle where it soon will be boiling. Then takes from his hip-pocket a bottle of corn licker which he passes to Kabnis.

Halsey: Here. This'll straighten y out a bit.

Kabnis nervously draws the cork and gulps the licker down.

Kabnis: Ha. Good stuff. Thanks. Thank y, Halsey.

Halsey: Good stuff! Youre damn right. Hanby there dont think so. Wonder he doesnt come over t find out whos burnin his oil. Miserly bastard, him. Th boys what made this stuff — are y listenin t me, Kabnis? th boys what made this stuff have got th art down like I heard you say youd like t be with words. Eh? Have some, Layman?

Layman: Dont think I care for none, thank y jes th same, Mr. Halsey.

Halsey: Care hell. Course y care. Everybody cares around these parts. Preachers an school teachers an everybody. Here. Here, take it. Dont try that line on me.

Layman limbers up a little, but he cannot quite forget that he is on school ground.

Layman: Thats right. Thats true, sho. Shinin is th only business what pays in these hard times.

He takes a nip, and passes the bottle to Kabnis. Kabnis is in the middle of a long swig when a rap sounds on the door. He almost spills the bottle, but manages to pass it to Halsey just as the door swings open and Hanby enters. He is a well-dressed, smooth, rich, black-skinned Negro who thinks there is no one quite so suave and polished as himself. To members of his own race, he affects the manners of a wealthy white planter. Or, when he is up North, he lets it be known that his ideas are those of the best New England tradition. To white men he bows, without ever completely humbling himself. Tradesmen in the town tolerate him because he spends his money with them. He delivers his words with a full consciousness of his moral superiority.

Hanby: Hum. Erer, Professor Kabnis, to come straight to the point: the progress of the Negro race is jeopardized whenever the personal habits and examples set by its guides and mentors fall below the acknowledged and hard-won standard of its average member. This institution, of which I am the humble president, was founded, and has been maintained at a cost of great labor and untold sacrifice. Its purpose is to teach our youth to live better, cleaner, more noble lives. To prove to the world that the Negro race can be just like any other race. It hopes to attain this aim partly by the salutary examples set by its instructors. I cannot hinder the progress of a race simply to indulge a single member. I have thought the matter out beforehand, I can assure you. Therefore, if I find your resignation on my desk by to-morrow morning, Mr. Kabnis, I shall not feel obliged to call in the sheriff. Otherwise. . ."

Kabnis: A fellow can take a drink in his own room if he wants to, in the privacy of his own room.

Hanby: His room, but not the institution's room, Mr. Kabnis.

Kabnis: This is my room while I'm in it.

Hanby: Mr. Clayborn (the sheriff) can inform you as to that.

Kabnis: Oh, well, what do I care — glad to get out of this mud-hole.

Hanby: I should think so from your looks.

Kabnis: You neednt get sarcastic about it.

Hanby: No, that is true. And I neednt wait for your resignation either, Mr. Kabnis.

Kabnis: Oh, you'll get that all right. Dont worry.

Hanby: And I should like to have the room thoroughly aired and cleaned and ready for your successor by to-morrow noon, Professor.

Kabnis (trying to rise): You can have your godam room right away. I dont want it.

Hanby: But I wont have your cursing.

Halsey pushes Kabnis back into his chair.

Halsey: Sit down, Kabnis, till I wash y.

Hanby (to Halsey): I would rather not have drinking men on the premises, Mr. Halsey. You will oblige me —

Halsey: I'll oblige you by stayin right on this spot, this spot, get me? till I get damned ready t leave.

He approaches Hanby. Hanby retreats, but manages to hold his dignity.

Halsey: Let me get you told right now, Mr. Samuel Hanby. Now listen t me. I aint no slick an span slave youve hired, an dont y think it for a minute. Youve bullied enough about this town. An besides, wheres that bill youve been owin me? Listen t me. If I dont get it paid in by tmorrer noon, Mr. Hanby (he mockingly assumes Hanby's tone and manner), I shall feel obliged t call th sheriff. An that sheriff'll be myself who'll catch y in th road an pull y out your buggy an rightly attend t y. You heard me. Now leave him alone. I'm takin him home with me. I got it fixed. Before you came in. He's goin t work with me. Shapin shafts and buildin wagons'll make a man of him what nobody, y get me? what nobody can take advantage of. Thats all. . .

Halsey burrs off into vague and incoherent comment.

Pause. Disagreeable.

Layman's eyes are glazed on the spurting fire.

Kabnis wants to rise and put both Halsey and Hanby in their places. He vaguely knows that he must do this, else the power of direction will completely slip from him to those outside. The conviction is just strong enough to torture him. To bring a feverish, quick-passing flare into his eyes. To mutter words soggy in hot saliva. To jerk his arms upward in futile protest. Halsey, noticing his gestures, thinks it is water that he desires. He brings a glass to him. Kabnis slings it to the floor. Heat of the conviction dies. His arms crumple. His upper lip, his mustache, quiver. Rap! rap, on the door. The sounds slap Kabnis. They bring a hectic color to his cheeks. Like huge cold finger tips they touch his skin and goose-flesh it. Hanby strikes a commanding pose. He moves towards Layman. Layman's face is innocently immobile.

Halsey: Whos there?

Voice: Lewis.

Halsey: Come in, Lewis. Come on in.

Lewis enters. He is the queer fellow who has been referred to. A tall wiry copper-colored man, thirty perhaps. His mouth and eyes suggest purpose guided by an adequate intelligence. He is what a stronger Kabnis might have been, and in an odd faint way resembles him. As he steps towards the others, he seems to be issuing sharply from a vivid dream. Lewis shakes hands with Halsey. Nods perfunctorily to Hanby, who has stiffened to meet him. Smiles rapidly at Layman, and settles with real interest on Kabnis.

Lewis: Kabnis passed me on the road. Had a piece of business of my own, and couldnt get here any sooner. Thought I might be able to help in some way or other.

Halsey: A good baths bout all he needs now. An somethin t put his mind t rest.

Lewis: I think I can give him that. That note was meant for me. Some Negroes have grown uncomfortable at my being here —

Kabnis: You mean, Mr. Lewis, some colored folks threw it? Christ Amighty!

Halsey: Thats what he means. An just as I told y. White folks more direct than that.

Kabnis: What are they after you for?

Lewis: Its a long story, Kabnis. Too long for now. And it might involve present company. (He laughs pleasantly and gestures vaguely in the direction of Hanby.) Tell you about it later on perhaps.

Kabnis: Youre not going?

Lewis: Not till my month's up.

Halsey: Hows that?

Lewis: I'm on a sort of contract with myself. (Is about to leave.) Well, glad its nothing serious —

Halsey: Come round t th shop sometime why dont y, Lewis? I've asked y enough. I'd like t have a talk with y. I aint as dumb as I look. Kabnis an me'll be in most any time. Not much work these days. Wish t hell there was. This burg get to me when there aint. (In answer to Lewis' question.) He's goin t work with me. Ya. Night air this side th branch aint good fer him. (Looks at Hanby. Laughs.)

Lewis: I see. . .

His eyes turn to Kabnis. In the instant of their shifting, a vision of the life they are to meet. Kabnis, a promise of a soil-soaked beauty; uprooted, thinning out. Suspended a few feet above the soil whose touch would resurrect him. Arm's length removed from him whose will to help. . . There is a swift intuitive interchange of consciousness. Kabnis has a sudden need to rush into the arms of this man. His eyes call, "Brother." And then a savage, cynical twistabout within him mocks his impulse and strengthens him to repulse Lewis. His lips curl cruelly. His eyes laugh. They are glittering needles, stitching. With a throbbing ache they draw Lewis to. Lewis brusquely wheels on Hanby.

Lewis: I'd like to see you, sir, a moment, if you dont mind.

Hanby's tight collar and vest effectively preserve him.

Hanby: Yes, erer, Mr. Lewis. Right away.

Lewis: See you later, Halsey.

Halsey: So long — thanks — sho hope so, Lewis.

As he opens the door and Hanby passes out, a woman, miles down the valley, begins to sing. Her song is a spark that travels swiftly to the near-by cabins. Like purple tallow flames, songs jet up. They spread a ruddy haze over the heavens. The haze swings low. Now the whole countryside is a soft chorus. Lord. O Lord. . . Lewis closes the door behind him. A flame jets out. . .

The kettle is boiling. Halsey notices it. He pulls the wash-tub from beneath the bed. He arranges for the bath before the fire.

Halsey: Told y them theatrics didnt fit a white man. Th niggers, just like I told y. An after him. Aint surprisin though. He aint bowed t none of them. Nassur. T nairy a one of them nairy an inch nairy a time. An only mixed when he was good an ready —

Kabnis: That song, Halsey, do you hear it?

Halsey: Thats a man. Hear me, Kabnis? A man —

Kabnis: Jesus, do you hear it?

Halsey: Hear it? Hear what? Course I hear it. Listen t what I'm tellin y. A man, get me? They'll get him yet if he dont watch out.

Kabnis is jolted into his fear.

Kabnis: Get him? What do you mean? How? Not lynch him?

Halsey: Na. Take a shotgun an shoot his eyes clear out. Well, anyway, it wasnt fer you, just like I told y. You'll stay over at th house an work with me, eh, boy? Good t get away from his nobs, eh? Damn big stiff though, him. An youre not th first an I can tell y. (Laughs.)

He bustles and fusses about Kabnis as if he were a child. Kabnis submits, wearily. He has no will to resist him.

Layman (his voice is like a deep hollow echo): Thats right. Thats true, sho. Everybody's been expectin that th bust up was comin. Surprised um all y held on as long as y did. Teachin in th South aint th thing fer y. Nassur. You ought t be way back up North where sometimes I wish I was. But I've hung on down this away so long —

Halsey: An there'll never be no leavin time fer y.

IV

A month has passed.

Halsey's workshop. It is an old building just off the main street of Sempter. The walls to within a few feet of the ground are of an age-worn cement mixture. On the outside they are considerably crumbled and peppered with what looks like musket-shot. Inside, the plaster has fallen away in great chunks, leaving the laths, grayed and cobwebbed, exposed. A sort of loft above the shop proper serves as a break-water for the rain and sunshine which otherwise would have free entry to the main floor. The shop is filled with old wheels and parts of wheels, broken shafts, and wooden litter. A double door, midway the street wall. To the left of this, a work-bench that holds a vise and a variety of wood-work tools. A window with as many panes broken as whole, throws light on the bench. Opposite, in the rear wall, a second window looks out upon the back yard. In the left wall, a rickety smoke-blackened chimney, and hearth with fire blazing. Smooth-worn chairs grouped about the hearth suggest the village meeting-place. Several large wooden blocks, chipped and cut and sawed on their upper surfaces are in the middle of the floor. They are the supports used in almost any sort of wagon-work. Their idleness means that Halsey has no worth-while job on foot. To the right of the central door is a junk heap, and directly behind this, stairs that lead down into the cellar. The cellar is known as "The Hole." Besides being the home of a very old man, it is used by Halsey on those occasions when he spices up the life of the small town.

Halsey, wonderfully himself in his work overalls, stands in the doorway and gazes up the street, expectantly. Then his eyes grow listless. He slouches against the smooth-rubbed frame. He lights a cigarette. Shifts his position. Braces an arm against the door. Kabnis passes the window and stoops to get in under Halsey's arm. He is awkward and ludicrous, like a schoolboy in his big brother's new overalls. He skirts the large blocks on the floor, and drops into a chair before the fire. Halsey saunters towards him.

Kabnis: Time f lunch.

Halsey: Ya.

He stands by the hearth, rocking backward and forward. He stretches his hands out to the fire. He washes them in the warm glow of the flames. They never get cold, but he warms them.

Kabnis: Saw Lewis up th street. Said he'd be down.

Halsey's eyes brighten. He looks at Kabnis. Turns away. Says nothing. Kabnis fidgets. Twists his thin blue cloth-covered limbs. Pulls closer to the fire till the heat stings his shins. Pushes back. Pokes the burned logs. Puts on several fresh ones. Fidgets. The town bell strikes twelve.

Kabnis: Fix it up f tnight?

Halsey: Leave it t me.

Kabnis: Get Lewis in?

Halsey: Tryin t.

The air is heavy with the smell of pine and resin. Green logs spurt and sizzle. Sap trickles from an old pine-knot into the flames. Layman enters. He carries a lunch-pail. Kabnis, for the moment, thinks that he is a day laborer.

Layman: Evenin, gen'lemun.

Both: Whats say, Layman.

Layman squares a chair to the fire and droops into it. Several town fellows, silent unfathomable men for the most part, saunter in. Overalls. Thick tan shoes. Felt hats marvelously shaped and twisted. One asks Halsey for a cigarette. He gets it. The blacksmith, a tremendous black man, comes in from the forge. Not even a nod from him. He picks up an axle and goes out. Lewis enters. The town men look curiously at him. Suspicion and an open liking contest for possession of their faces. They are uncomfortable. One by one they drift into the street.

Layman: Heard y was leavin, Mr. Lewis.

Kabnis: Months up, eh? Hell of a month I've got.

Halsey: Sorry y goin, Lewis. Just getting acquainted like.

Lewis: Sorry myself, Halsey, in a way —

Layman: Gettin t like our town, Mr. Lewis?

Lewis: I'm afraid its on a different basis, Professor.

Halsey: An I've yet t hear about that basis. Been waitin long enough, God knows. Seems t me like youd take pity on a feller if nothin more.

Kabnis: Somethin that old black cockroach over yonder doesnt like, whatever it is.

Layman: Thats right. Thats right, sho.

Halsey: A feller dropped in here tother day an said he knew what you was about. Said you had queer opinions. Well, I could have told him you was a queer one, myself. But not th way he was driftin. Didnt mean anything by it, but just let drop he thought you was a little wrong up here — crazy, y'know. (Laughs.)

Kabnis: Y mean old Blodson? Hell, he's bats himself.

Lewis: I remember him. We had a talk. But what he found queer, I think, was not my opinions, but my lack of them. In half an hour he had settled everything: boll weevils, God, the World War. Weevils and wars are the pests that God sends against the sinful. People are too weak to correct themselves: the Redeemer is coming back. Get ready, ye sinners, for the advent of Our Lord. Interesting, eh, Kabnis? but not exactly what we want.

Halsey: Y could have come t me. I've sho been after y enough. Most every time I've seen y.

Kabnis (sarcastically): Hows it y never came t us professors?

Lewis: I did — to one.

Kabnis: Y mean t say y got somethin from that celluloid-collar-eraser-cleaned old codger over in th mud hole?

Halsey: Rough on th old boy, aint he? (Laughs.)

Lewis: Something, yes. Layman here could have given me quite a deal, but the incentive to his keeping quiet is so much greater than anything I could have offered him to open up, that I crossed him off my mind. And you —

Kabnis: What about me?

Halsey: Tell him, Lewis, for godsake tell him. I've told him. But its somethin else he wants so bad I've heard him downstairs mumblin with th old man.

Lewis: The old man?

Kabnis: What about me? Come on now, you know so much.

Halsey: Tell him, Lewis. Tell it t him.

Lewis: Life has already told him more than he is capable of knowing. It has given him in excess of what he can receive. I have been offered. Stuff in his stomach curdled, and he vomited me.

Kabnis' face twitches. His body writhes.

Kabnis: You know a lot, you do. How about Halsey?

Lewis: Yes. . . Halsey? Fits here. Belongs here. An artist in your way, arent you, Halsey?

Halsey: Reckon I am, Lewis. Give me th work and fair pay an I aint askin nothin better. Went over-seas an saw France; an I come back. Been up North; an I come back. Went t school; but there aint no books whats got th feel t them of them there tools. Nassur. An I'm atellin y.

A shriveled, bony white man passes the window and enters the shop. He carries a broken hatchet-handle and the severed head. He speaks with a flat, drawn voice to Halsey, who comes forward to meet him.

Mr. Ramsay: Can y fix this fer me, Halsey?

Halsey (looking it over): Reckon so, Mr. Ramsay. Here, Kabnis. A little practice fer y.

Halsey directs Kabnis, showing him how to place the handle in the vise, and cut it down. The knife hangs. Kabnis thinks that it must be dull. He jerks it hard. The tool goes deep and shaves too much off. Mr. Ramsay smiles brokenly at him.

Mr. Ramsay (to Halsey): Still breakin in the new hand, eh, Halsey? Seems like a likely enough faller once he gets th hang of it.

He gives a tight laugh at his own good humor. Kabnis burns red. The back of his neck stings him beneath his collar. He feels stifled. Through Ramsay, the whole white South weighs down upon him. The pressure is terrific. He sweats under the arms. Chill beads run down his body. His brows concentrate upon the handle as though his own life was staked upon the perfect shaving of it. He begins to out and out botch the job. Halsey smiles.

Halsey: He'll make a good un some of these days, Mr. Ramsay.

Mr. Ramsay: Y ought t know. Yer daddy was a good un before y. Runs in th family, seems like t me.

Halsey: Thats right, Mr. Ramsay.

Kabnis is hopeless. Halsey takes the handle from him. With a few deft strokes he shaves it. Fits it. Gives it to Ramsay.

Mr. Ramsay: How much on this?

Halsey: No charge, Mr. Ramsay.

Mr. Ramsay (going out): All right, Halsey. Come down an take it out in trade. Shoe-strings or something.

Halsey: Yassur, Mr. Ramsay.

Halsey rejoins Lewis and Layman. Kabnis, hangdog-fashion, follows him.

Halsey: They like y if y work fer them.

Layman: Thats right, Mr. Halsey. Thats right, sho.

The group is about to resume its talk when Hanby enters. He is all energy, bustle, and business. He goes direct to Kabnis.

Hanby: An axle is out in the buggy which I would like to have shaped into a crow-bar. You will see that it is fixed for me.

Without waiting for an answer, and knowing that Kabnis will follow, he passes out. Kabnis, scowling, silent, trudges after him.

Hanby (from the outside): Have that ready for me by three o'clock, young man. I shall call for it.

Kabnis (under his breath as he comes in): Th hell you say, you old black swamp-gut.

He slings the axle on the floor.

Halsey: Wheeee!

Layman, lunch finished long ago, rises, heavily. He shakes hands with Lewis.

Layman: Might not see y again befo y leave, Mr. Lewis. I enjoys t hear y talk. Y might have been a preacher. Maybe a bishop some day. Sho do hope t see y back this away again sometime, Mr. Lewis.

Lewis: Thanks, Professor. Hope I'll see you.

Layman waves a long arm loosely to the others, and leaves. Kabnis goes to the door. His eyes, sullen, gaze up the street.

Kabnis: Carrie K.'s comin with th lunch. Bout time.

She passes the window. Her red girl's-cap, catching the sun, flashes vividly. With a stiff, awkward little movement she crosses the doorsill and gives Kabnis one of the two baskets which she is carrying. There is a slight stoop to her shoulders. The curves of her body blend with this to a soft rounded charm. Her gestures are stiffly variant. Black bangs curl over the forehead of her oval-olive face. Her expression is dazed, but on provocation it can melt into a wistful smile. Adolescent. She is easily the sister of Fred Halsey.

Carrie K.: Mother says excuse her, brother Fred an Ralph, fer bein late.

Kabnis: Everythings all right an O.K., Carrie Kate. O.K. an all right.

The two men settle on their lunch. Carrie, with hardly a glance in the direction of the hearth, as is her habit, is about to take the second basket down to the old man, when Lewis rises. In doing so he draws her unwitting attention. Their meeting is a swift sun-burst. Lewis impulsively moves towards her. His mind flashes images of her life in the southern town. He sees the nascent woman, her flesh already stiffening to cartilage, drying to bone. Her spirit-bloom, even now touched sullen, bitter. Her rich beauty fading. . . He wants to — He stretches forth his hands to hers. He takes them. They feel like warm cheeks against his palms. The sun-burst from her eyes floods up and haloes him. Christ-eyes, his eyes look to her. Fearlessly she loves into them. And then something happens. Her face blanches. Awkwardly she draws away. The sin-bogies of respectable southern colored folks clamor at her: "Look out! Be a *good* girl. A *good* girl. Look out!" She gropes for her basket that has fallen to the floor. Finds it, and marches with a rigid gravity to her task of feeding the old man. Like the glowing white ash of burned paper, Lewis' eyelids, wavering, settle down. He stirs in the direction of the rear window. From the back yard, mules tethered to odd trees and posts blink dumbly at him. They too seem burdened with an impotent pain. Kabnis and Halsey are still busy with their lunch. They havent noticed him. After a while he turns to them.

Lewis: Your sister, Halsey, whats to become of her? What are you going to do for her?

Halsey: Who? What? What am I goin t do? . .

Lewis: What I mean is, what does she do down there?

Halsey: Oh. Feeds th old man. Had lunch, Lewis?

Lewis: Thanks, yes. You have never felt her, have you, Halsey? Well, no, I guess not. I dont suppose you can. Nor can she. . . Old man? Halsey, some one lives down there? I've never heard of him. Tell me —

Kabnis takes time from his meal to answer with some emphasis:

Kabnis: Theres lots of things you aint heard of.

Lewis: Dare say. I'd like to see him.

Kabnis: You'll get all th chance you want tnight.

Halsey: Fixin a little somethin up fer tnight, Lewis. Th three of us an some girls. Come round bout ten-thirty.

Lewis: Glad to. But what under the sun does he do down there?

Halsey: Ask Kabnis. He blows off t him every chance he gets.

Kabnis gives a grunting laugh. His mouth twists. Carrie returns from the cellar. Avoiding Lewis, she speaks to her brother.

Carrie K.: Brother Fred, father hasnt eaten now goin on th second week, but mumbles an talks funny, or tries t talk when I put his hands ont th food. He frightens me, an I dunno what t do. An oh, I came near fergettin, brother, but Mr. Marmon — he was eatin lunch when I saw him — told me t tell y that th lumber wagon busted down an he wanted y t fix it fer him. Said he reckoned he could get it t y after he ate.

Halsey chucks a half-eaten sandwich in the fire. Gets up. Arranges his blocks. Goes to the door and looks anxiously up the street. The wind whirls a small spiral in the gray dust road.

Halsey: Why didnt y tell me sooner, little sister?

Carrie K.: I fergot t, an just remembered it now, brother.

Her soft rolled words are fresh pain to Lewis. He wants to take her North with him. What for? He wonders what Kabnis could do for her. What she could do for him. Mother him. Carrie gathers the lunch things, silently, and in her pinched manner, curtsies, and departs. Kabnis lights his after-lunch cigarette. Lewis, who has sensed a change, becomes aware that he is not included in it. He starts to ask again about the old man. Decides not to. Rises to go.

Lewis: Think I'll run along, Halsey.

Halsey: Sure. Glad t see y any time.

Kabnis: Dont forget tnight.

Lewis: Dont worry. I wont. So long.

Kabnis: So long. We'll be expectin y.

Lewis passes Halsey at the door. Halsey's cheeks form a vacant smile. His eyes are wide awake, watching for the wagon to turn from Broad Street into his road.

Halsey: So long.

His words reach Lewis halfway to the corner.

V

Night, soft belly of a pregnant Negress, throbs evenly against the torso of the South. Night throbs a womb-song to the South. Cane- and cotton-fields, pine forests, cypress swamps, sawmills, and factories are fecund at her touch. Night's womb-song sets them singing. Night winds are the breathing of the unborn child whose calm throbbing in the belly of a Negress sets them somnolently singing. Hear their song.

White-man's land.
Niggers, sing.
Burn, bear black children
Till poor rivers bring
Rest, and sweet glory
In Camp Ground.

Sempter's streets are vacant and still. White paint on the wealthier houses has the chill blue glitter of distant stars. Negro cabins are a purple blur. Broad Street is deserted. Winds stir beneath the corrugated iron canopies and dangle odd bits of rope tied to horse- and mule-gnawed hitching-posts. One store window has a light in it. Chesterfield cigarette and Chero-Cola cardboard advertisements are stacked in it. From a side door two men come out. Pause, for a last word and then say good night. Soon they melt in shadows thicker than they. Way off down the street four figures sway beneath iron awnings which form a sort of corridor that imperfectly echoes and jumbles what they say. A fifth form joins them. They turn into the road that leads to Halsey's workshop. The old building is phosphorescent above deep shade. The figures pass through the double door. Night winds whisper in the eaves. Sing weirdly in the ceiling cracks. Stir curls of shavings on the floor. Halsey lights a candle. A good-sized lumber wagon, wheels off, rests upon the blocks. Kabnis makes a face at it. An unearthly hush is upon the place. No one seems to want to talk. To move, lest the scraping of their feet . . .

Halsey: Come on down this way, folks.

He leads the way. Stella follows. And close after her, Cora, Lewis, and Kabnis. They descend into the Hole. It seems huge, limitless in the candle light. The walls are of stone, wonderfully fitted. They have no openings save a small iron-barred window toward the top of each. They are dry and warm. The ground slopes away to the rear of the building and thus leaves the south wall exposed to the sun. The blacksmith's shop is plumb against the right wall. The floor is clay. Shavings have at odd times been matted into it. In the right-hand corner, under the stairs, two good-sized pine mattresses, resting on cardboard, are on either side of a wooden table. On this are several half-burned candles and an oil lamp. Behind the table, an irregular piece of mirror hangs on the wall. A loose something that looks to be a gaudy ball costume dangles from a near-by hook. To the front, a second table holds a lamp and several whiskey glasses. Six rickety chairs are near this table. Two old wagon wheels rest on the floor. To the left, sitting in a high-backed chair which stands upon a low platform, the old man. He is like a bust in black walnut. Gray-bearded. Gray-haired. Prophetic. Immobile. Lewis' eyes are sunk in him. The others, unconcerned, are about to pass on to the front table when Lewis grips Halsey and so turns him that the candle flame shines obliquely on the old man's features.

Lewis: And he rules over —

Kabnis: Th smoke an fire of th forge.

Lewis: Black Vulcan? I wouldnt say so. That forehead. Great woolly beard. Those eyes. A mute John the Baptist of a new religion — or a tongue-tied shadow of an old.

Kabnis: His tongue is tied all right, an I can vouch f that.

Lewis: Has he never talked to you?

Halsey: Kabnis wont give him a chance.

He laughs. The girls laugh. Kabnis winces.

Lewis: What do you call him?

Halsey: Father.

Lewis: Good. Father what?

Kabnis: Father of hell.

Halsey: Father's th only name we have fer him. Come on. Lets sit down an get t th pleasure of the evenin.

Lewis: Father John it is from now on. . .

Slave boy whom some Christian mistress taught to read the Bible. Black man who saw Jesus in the ricefields, and began preaching to his people. Moses- and Christ-words used for songs. Dead blind father of a muted folk who feel their way upward to a life that crushes or absorbs them. (Speak, Father!) Suppose your eyes could see, old man. (The years hold hands. O Sing!) Suppose your lips . . .

Halsey, does he never talk?

Halsey: Na. But sometimes. Only seldom. Mumbles. Sis says he talks —

Kabnis: I've heard him talk.

Halsey: First I've ever heard of it. You dont give him a chance. Sis says she's made out several words, mostly one — an like as not cause it was "sin."

Kabnis: All those old fogies stutter about sin.

Cora laughs in a loose sort of way. She is a tall, thin, mulatto woman. Her eyes are deepset behind a pointed nose. Her hair is coarse and bushy. Seeing that Stella also is restless, she takes her arm and the two women move towards the table. They slip into chairs. Halsey follows and lights the lamp. He lays out a pack of cards. Stella sorts them as if telling fortunes. She is a beautifully proportioned, large-eyed, brown-skin girl. Except for the twisted line of her mouth when she smiles or laughs, there is about her no suggestion of the life she's been through. Kabnis, with great mock-solemnity, goes to the corner, takes down the robe, and dons it. He is a curious spectacle, acting a part, yet very real. He joins the others at the table. They are used to him. Lewis is surprised. He laughs. Kabnis shrinks and then glares at him with a furtive hatred. Halsey, bringing out a bottle of corn licker, pours drinks.

Halsey: Come on, Lewis. Come on, you fellers. Heres lookin at y.

Then, as if suddenly recalling something, he jerks away from the table and starts towards the steps.

Kabnis: Where y goin, Halsey?

Halsey: Where? Where y think? That oak beam in th wagon —

Kabnis: Come ere. Come ere. Sit down. What in hell's wrong with you fellers? You with your wagon. Lewis with his Father John. This aint th time fer foolin with wagons. Daytime's bad enough f that. Ere, sit down. Ere, Lewis, you too sit down. Have a drink. Thats right. Drink corn licker, love th girls, an listen t th old man mumblin sin.

There seems to be no good-time spirit to the party. Something in the air is too tense and deep for that. Lewis, seated now so that his eyes rest upon the old man, merges with his source and lets the pain and beauty of the South meet him there. White faces, pain-pollen, settle downward through a cane-sweet mist and touch the ovaries of yellow flowers. Cotton-bolls bloom, droop. Black roots twist in a parched red soil beneath a blazing sky. Magnolias, fragrant, a trifle futile, lovely, far off. . . His eyelids close. A force begins to heave and rise. . . Stella is serious, reminiscent.

Stella: Usall is brought up t hate sin worse than death —

Kabnis: An then before you have y eyes half open, youre made t love it if y want t live.

Stella: Us never —

Kabnis: Oh, I know your story: that old prim bastard over yonder, an then old Calvert's office —

Stella: It wasnt them —

Kabnis: I know. They put y out of church, an then I guess th preacher came around an asked f some. But thats your body. Now me —

Halsey (passing him the bottle): All right, kid, we believe y. Here, take another. Wheres Clover, Stel?

Stella: You know how Jim is when he's just out th swamp. Done up in shine an wouldn't let her come. Said he'd bust her head open if she went out.

Kabnis: Dont see why he doesnt stay over with Laura, where he belongs.

Stella: Ask him, an I reckon he'll tell y. More than you want.

Halsey: Th nigger hates th sight of a black woman worse than death. Sorry t mix y up this way, Lewis. But y see how tis.

Lewis' skin is tight and glowing over the fine bones of his face. His lips tremble. His nostrils quiver. The others notice this and smile knowingly at each other. Drinks and smokes are passed around. They pay no neverminds to him. A real party is being worked up. Then Lewis opens his eyes and looks at them. Their smiles disperse in hot-cold tremors. Kabnis chokes his laugh. It sputters, gurgles. His eyes flicker and turn away. He tries to pass the thing off by taking a long drink which he makes considerable fuss over. He is drawn back to Lewis. Seeing Lewis' gaze still upon him, he scowls.

Kabnis: Whatsha lookin at me for? Y want t know who I am? Well, I'm Ralph Kabnis — lot of good its goin t do y. Well? Whatsha keep lookin for? I'm Ralph Kabnis. Aint that enough f y? Want th whole family history? Its none of your godam business, anyway. Keep off me. Do y hear? Keep off me. Look at Cora. Aint she pretty enough t look at? Look at Halsey, or Stella. Clover ought t be here an you could look at her. An love her. Thats what you need. I know —

Lewis: Ralph Kabnis gets satisfied that way?

Kabnis: Satisfied? Say, quit your kiddin. Here, look at that old man there. See him? He's satisfied. Do I look like him? When I'm dead I dont expect t be satisfied. Is that enough f y, with your godam nosin, or do you want more? Well, y wont get it, understand?

Lewis: The old man as symbol, flesh, and spirit of the past, what do you think he would say if he could see you? You look at him, Kabnis.

Kabnis: Just like any done-up preacher is what he looks t me. Jam some false teeth in his mouth and crank him, an youd have God Almighty spit in torrents all around th floor. Oh, hell, an he reminds me of that black cockroach over yonder. An besides, he aint my past. My ancestors were southern blue-bloods —

Lewis: And black.

Kabnis: Aint much difference between blue an black.

Lewis: Enough to draw a denial from you. Cant hold them, can you? Master; slave. Soil; and the overarching heavens. Dusk; dawn. They fight and bastardize you. The sun tint of your cheeks, flame of the great season's multicolored leaves, tarnished, burned. Split, shredded: easily burned. No use . . .

His gaze shifts to Stella. Stella's face draws back, her breasts come towards him.

Stella: I aint got nothin f y, mister. Taint no use t look at me.

Halsey: Youre a queer feller, Lewis, I swear y are. Told y so, didnt I, girls? Just take him easy though, an he'll be ridin just th same as any Georgia mule, eh, Lewis? (Laughs.)

Stella: I'm goin t tell y somethin, mister. It aint t you, t th Mister Lewis what noses about. Its t somethin different, I dunno what. That old man there — maybe its him — is like m father used t look. He used t sing. An when he could sing no mo, they'd allus come f him an carry him t church an there he'd sit, befo th pulpit, aswayin an aleadin every song. A white man took m mother an it broke th old man's heart. He died; an then I didnt care what become of me, an I dont now. I dont care now. Dont get it in y head I'm some sentimental Susie askin for yo sop. Nassur. But theres somethin t yo th others aint got. Boars an kids an fools — thats all I've known. Boars when their fever's up. When their fever's up they come t me. Halsey asks me over when he's off th job. Kabnis — it ud be a sin t play with him. He takes it out in talk.

Halsey knows that he has trifled with her. At odd things he has been inwardly penitent before her tasking him. But now he wants to hurt her. He turns to Lewis.

Halsey: Lewis, I got a little licker in me, an thats true. True's what I said. True. But th stuff just seems t wake me up an make my mind a man of me. Listen. You know a lot, queer as hell as y are, an I want t ask y some questions. Theyre too high fer them, Stella an Cora an Kabnis, so we'll just excuse em. A chat between ourselves. (Turns to the others.) You-all cant listen in on this. Twont interest y. So just leave th table t this gen'lemun an myself. Go long now.

Kabnis gets up, pompous in his robe, grotesquely so, and makes as if to go through a grand march with Stella. She shoves him off, roughly, and in a mood swings her body to the steps. Kabnis grabs Cora and parades around, passing the old man, to whom he bows in mock-curtsy. He sweeps by the table, snatches the licker bottle, and then he and Cora sprawl on the mattresses. She meets his weak approaches after the manner she thinks Stella would use.

Halsey contemptuously watches them until he is sure that they are settled.

Halsey: This aint th sort o thing f me, Lewis, when I got work upstairs. Nassur. You an me has got things t do. Wastin time on common low-down women — say, Lewis, look at her now — Stella — aint she a picture? Common wench — na she aint, Lewis. You know she aint. I'm only tryin t fool y. I used t love that girl. Yassur. An sometimes when th moon is thick an I hear dogs up th valley barkin an some old woman fetches out her song, an th winds seem like th Lord made them fer t fetch an carry th smell o pine an cane, an there aint no big job on foot, I sometimes get t thinkin that I still do. But I want t talk t y, Lewis, queer as y are. Y know, Lewis, I went t school once. Ya. In Augusta. But it wasnt a regular school. Na. It was a pussy Sunday-school masqueradin under a regular name. Some goody-goody teachers from th North had come down t teach th niggers. If you was nearly white, they liked y. If you was black, they didnt. But it wasnt that — I was all right, y see. I couldnt stand em messin an pawin over m business like I was a child. So I cussed em out an left. Kabnis there ought t have cussed out th old duck over yonder an left. He'd a been a better man tday. But as I was sayin, I couldnt stand their ways. So I left an came here an worked with my father. An been here ever since. He died. I set in f myself. An its always been; give me a good job an sure pay an I aint far from being satisfied, so far as satisfaction goes. Prejudice is everywheres about this country. An a nigger aint in much standin anywheres. But when it comes t pottin round an doin nothing, with nothin bigger'n an ax-handle t hold a feller down, like it was a while back befo I got this job — that beam ought t be — but tmorrow mornin early's time enough f that. As I was sayin, I gets t thinkin. Play dumb naturally t white folks. I gets t thinkin. I used to subscribe t th *Literary Digest* an that helped along a bit. But there werent nothing I could sink m teeth int. Theres lots I want t ask y, Lewis. Been askin y t come around. Couldnt get y. Cant get in much tnight. (He glances at the others. His mind fastens on Kabnis.) Say, tell me this, whats on your mind t say on that feller there? Kabnis' name. One queer bird ought t know another, seems like t me.

Licker has released conflicts in Kabnis and set them flowing. He pricks his ears, intuitively feels that the talk is about him, leaves Cora, and approaches the table. His eyes are watery, heavy with passion. He stoops. He is a ridiculous pathetic figure in his showy robe.

Kabnis: Talkin bout me. I know. I'm th topic of conversation everywhere theres talk about this town. Girls an fellers. White folks as well. An if its me youre talkin bout, guess I got a right t listen in. Whats sayin? Whats sayin bout his royal guts, the Duke? Whats sayin, eh?

Halsey (to Lewis): We'll take it up another time.

Kabnis: No nother time bout it. Now. I'm here now an talkin's just begun. I was born an bred in a family of orators, thats what I was.

Halsey: Preachers.

Kabnis: Na. Preachers hell. I didnt say wind-busters. Y misapprehended me. Y understand what that means, dont y? All right then, y misapprehended me. I didnt say preachers. I said orators. ORATORS. Born one an I'll die one. You understand me, Lewis. (He turns to Halsey and begins shaking his finger in his face.) An as f you, youre all right f choppin things from blocks of wood. I was good at that th day I ducked th cradle. An since then, I've been shapin words after a design that branded here. Know whats here? M soul. Ever heard o that? Th hell y have. Been shapin words t fit m soul. Never told y that before, did I?

Thought I couldnt talk. I'll tell y. I've been shapin words; ah, but sometimes theyre beautiful an golden an have a taste that makes them fine t roll over with y tongue. Your tongue aint fit f nothin but t roll an lick hog-meat.

Stella and Cora come up to the table.

Halsey: Give him a shove there, will y, Stel?

Stella jams Kabnis in a chair. Kabnis springs up.

Kabnis: Cant keep a good man down. Those words I was tellin y about, they wont fit int th mold thats branded on m soul. Rhyme, y see? Poet, too. Bad rhyme. Bad poet. Somethin else youve learned tnight. Lewis dont know it all, an I'm atellin y. Ugh. Th form thats burned int my soul is some twisted awful thing that crept in from a dream, a godam nightmare, an wont stay still unless I feed it. An it lives on words. Not beautiful words. God Almighty no. Misshapen, split-gut, tortured, twisted words. Layman was feedin it back there that day you thought I ran out fearin things. White folks feed it cause their looks are words. Niggers, black niggers feed it cause theyre evil an their looks are words. Yallar niggers feed it. This whole damn bloated purple country feeds it cause its goin down t hell in a holy avalanche of words. I want t feed th soul — I know what that is; th preachers dont — but I've got t feed it. I wish t God some lynchin white man ud stick his knife through it an pin it to a tree. An pin it to a tree. You hear me? Thats a wish f y, you little snot-nosed pups who've been makin fun of me, an fakin that I'm weak. Me, Ralph Kabnis weak. Ha.

Halsey: Thats right, old man. There, there. Here, so much exertion merits a fittin reward. Help him t be seated, Cora.

Halsey gives him a swig of shine. Cora glides up, seats him, and then plumps herself down on his lap, squeezing his head into her breasts. Kabnis mutters. Tries to break loose. Curses. Cora almost stifles him. He goes limp and gives up. Cora toys with him. Ruffles his hair. Braids it. Parts it in the middle. Stella smiles contemptuously. And then a sudden anger sweeps her. She would like to lash Cora from the place. She'd like to take Kabnis to some distant pine grove and nurse and mother him. Her eyes flash. A quick tensioning throws her breasts and neck into a poised strain. She starts towards them. Halsey grabs her arm and pulls her to him. She struggles. Halsey pins her arms and kisses her. She settles, spurting like a pine-knot afire.

Lewis finds himself completely cut out. The glowing within him subsides. It is followed by a dead chill. Kabnis, Carrie, Stella, Halsey, Cora, the old man, the cellar, and the work-shop, the southern town descend upon him. Their pain is too intense. He cannot stand it. He bolts from the table. Leaps up the stairs. Plunges through the work-shop and out into the night.

VI

The cellar swims in a pale phosphorescence. The table, the chairs, the figure of the old man are amœba-like shadows which move about and float in it. In the corner under the steps, close to the floor, a solid blackness. A sound comes from it. A forcible yawn. Part of the blackness detaches itself so that it may be seen against the grayness of the wall. It moves forward and then seems to be clothing itself in odd dangling bits of shadow. The voice of Halsey, vibrant and deepened, calls.

Halsey: Kabnis. Cora. Stella.

He gets no response. He wants to get them up, to get on the job. He is intolerant of their sleepiness.

Halsey: Kabnis! Stella! Cora!

Gutturals, jerky and impeded, tell that he is shaking them.

Halsey: Come now, up with you.

Kabnis (sleepily and still more or less intoxicated): Whats th big idea? What in hell —

Halsey: Work. But never you mind about that. Up with you.

Cora: Oooooo! Look here, mister, I aint used t bein thrown int th street befo day.

Stella: Any bunk whats worked is worth in wages moren this. But come on. Taint no use t arger.

Kabnis: I'll arger. Its preposterous —

The girls interrupt him with none too pleasant laughs.

Kabnis: Thats what I said. Know what it means, dont y? All right, then. I said its preposterous t root an artist out o bed at this ungodly hour, when there aint no use t it. You can start your damned old work. Nobody's stoppin y. But what we got t get up for? Fraid somebody'll see th girls leavin? Some sport, you are. I hand it t y.

Halsey: Up you get, all th same.

Kabnis: Oh, th hell you say.

Halsey: Well, son, seeing that I'm th kindhearted father, I'll give y chance t open your eyes. But up y get when I come down.

He mounts the steps to the work-shop and starts a fire in the hearth. In the yard he finds some chunks of coal which he brings in and throws on the fire. He puts a kettle on to boil. The wagon draws him. He lifts an oak-beam, fingers it, and becomes abstracted. Then comes to himself and places the beam upon the work-bench. He looks over some newly cut wooden spokes. He goes to the fire and pokes it. The coals are red-hot. With a pair of long prongs he picks them up and places them in a thick iron bucket. This he carries downstairs. Outside, darkness has given way to the impalpable grayness of dawn. This early morning light, seeping through the four barred cellar windows, is the color of the stony walls. It seems to be an emanation from them. Halsey's coals throw out a rich warm glow. He sets them on the floor, a safe distance from the beds.

Halsey: No foolin now. Come. Up with you.

Other than a soft rustling, there is no sound as the girls slip into their clothes. Kabnis still lies in bed.

Stella (to Halsey): Reckon y could spare us a light?

Halsey strikes a match, lights a cigarette, and then bends over and touches flame to the two candles on the table between the beds. Kabnis asks for a cigarette. Halsey hands him his and takes a fresh one for himself. The girls, before the mirror, are doing up their hair. It is bushy hair that has gone through some straightening process. Character, however, has not all been ironed out. As they kneel there, heavy-eyed and dusky, and throwing grotesque moving shadows on the wall, they are two princesses in Africa going through the early-morning ablutions of their pagan prayers. Finished, they come forward to stretch their hands and warm them over the glowing coals. Red dusk of a Georgia sunset, their heavy, coal-lit faces. . . Kabnis suddenly recalls something.

Kabnis: Th old man talked last night.

Stella: An so did you.

Halsey: In your dreams.

Kabnis: I tell y, he did. I know what I'm talkin about. I'll tell y what he said. Wait now, lemme see.

Halsey: Look out, brother, th old man'll be getting int you by way o dreams. Come, Stel, ready? Cora? Coffee an eggs f both of you.

Halsey goes upstairs.

Stella: Gettin generous, aint he?

She blows the candles out. Says nothing to Kabnis. Then she and Cora follow after Halsey. Kabnis, left to himself, tries to rise. He has slept in his robe. His robe trips him. Finally, he manages to stand up. He starts across the floor. Halfway to the old man, he falls and lies quite still. Perhaps an hour passes. Light of a new sun is about to filter through the windows. Kabnis slowly rises to support upon his elbows. He looks hard, and internally gathers himself together. The side face of Father John is in the direct line of his eyes. He scowls at him. No one is around. Words gush from Kabnis.

Kabnis: You sit there like a black hound spiked to an ivory pedestal. An all night long I heard you murmurin that devilish word. They thought I didnt hear y, but I did. Mumblin, feedin that ornery thing thats livin on my insides. Father John. Father of Satan, more likely. What does it mean t you? Youre dead already. Death. What does it mean t you? To you who died way back there in th 'sixties. What are y throwin it in my throat for? Whats it goin t get y? A good smashin in th mouth, thats what. My fist'll sink int y black mush face clear t y guts — if y got any. Dont believe y have. Never seen signs of none. Death. Death. Sin an Death. All night long y mumbled death. (He forgets the old man as his mind begins to play with the word and its associations.) Death . . . these clammy floors . . . just like th place they used t stow away th wornout, no-count niggers in th days of slavery . . . that was long ago; not so long ago . . . no windows (he rises higher on his elbows to verify this assertion. He looks around, and, seeing no one but the old man, calls.) Halsey! Halsey! Gone an left me. Just like a nigger. I thought he was a nigger all th time. Now I know it. Ditch y when it comes right down t it. Damn him anyway. Godam him. (He looks and re-sees the old man.) Eh, you? T hell with you too. What do I care whether you can see or hear? You know what hell is cause youve been there. Its a feelin an its ragin in my soul in a way that'll pop out of me an run you through, an scorch y, an burn an rip your soul. Your soul. Ha. Nigger soul. A gin soul that gets drunk on a preacher's words. An screams. An shouts. God Almighty, how I hate that shoutin. Where's th beauty in that? Gives a buzzard a windpipe an I'll bet a dollar t a dime th buzzard ud beat y to it. Aint surprisin th white folks hate y so. When you had eyes, did you ever see th beauty of th world? Tell me that. Th hell y did. Now dont tell me. I know y didnt. You couldnt have. Oh, I'm drunk an just as good as dead, but no eyes that have seen beauty ever lose their sight. You aint got no sight. If you had, drunk as I am, I hope Christ will kill me if I couldnt see it. Your eyes are dull and watery, like fish eyes. Fish eyes are dead eyes. Youre an old man, a dead fish man, an black at that. Theyve put y here t die, damn fool y are not t know it. Do y know how many feet youre under ground? I'll tell y. Twenty. An do y think you'll ever see th light of day again, even if you wasnt blind? Do y think youre out of slavery? Huh? Youre where they used t throw th worked-out, no-count slaves. On a damp clammy floor of a dark scum-hole. An they called that an infirmary. Th sons-a . . . . Why I can already see you toppled off that stool an stretched out on th floor beside me — not beside me, damn you, by yourself, with th flies buzzin an lickin God knows what they'd find on a dirty, black, foul-breathed mouth like yours . . .

Some one is coming down the stairs. Carrie, bringing food for the old man. She is lovely in her fresh energy of the morning, in the calm untested confidence and nascent maternity which rise from the purpose of her present mission. She walks to within a few paces of Kabnis.

Carrie K.: Brother says come up now, brother Ralph.

Kabnis: Brother doesnt know what he's talkin bout.

Carrie K.: Yes he does, Ralph. He needs you on th wagon.

Kabnis: He wants me on th wagon, eh? Does he think some wooden thing can lift me up? Ask him that.

Carrie K.: He told me t help y.

Kabnis: An how would you help me, child, dear sweet little sister?

She moves forward as if to aid him.

Carrie K.: I'm not a child, as I've more than once told you, brother Ralph, an as I'll show you now.

Kabnis: Wait, Carrie. No, thats right. Youre not a child. But twont do t lift me bodily. You dont understand. But its th soul of me that needs th risin.

Carrie K: Youre a bad brother an just wont listen t me when I'm tellin y t go t church.

Kabnis doesnt hear her. He breaks down and talks to himself.

Kabnis: Great God Almighty, a soul like mine cant pin itself onto a wagon wheel an satisfy itself in spinnin round. Iron prongs an hickory sticks, an God knows what all . . . all right for Halsey . . . use him. Me? I get my life down in this scum-hole. Th old man an me —

Carrie K.: Has he been talkin?

Kabnis: Huh? Who? Him? No. Dont need to. I talk. An when I really talk, it pays th best of them t listen. Th old man is a good listener. He's deaf; but he's a good listener. An I can talk t him. Tell him anything.

Carrier K.: He's deaf an blind, but I reckon he hears, an sees too, from th things I've heard.

Kabnis: No. Cant. Cant I tell you. How's he do it?

Carrie K.: Dunno, except I've heard that th souls of old folks have a way of seein things.

Kabnis: An I've heard them call that superstition.

The old man begins to shake his head slowly. Carrie and Kabnis watch him, anxiously. He mumbles. With a grave motion his head nods up and down. And then, on one of the downswings —

Father John (remarkably clear and with great conviction): Sin.

He repeats this word several times, always on the downward nodding. Surprised, indignant, Kabnis forgets that Carrie is with him.

Kabnis: Sin! Shut up. What do you know about sin, you old black bastard. Shut up, an stop that swayin an noddin your head.

Father John: Sin.

Kabnis tries to get up.

Kabnis: Didnt I tell y t shut up?

Carrie steps forward to help him. Kabnis is violently shocked at her touch. He springs back.

Kabnis: Carrie! What . . . how . . . Baby, you shouldnt be down here. Ralph says things. Doesnt mean to. But Carrie, he doesnt know what he's talkin about.

Couldnt know. It was only a preacher's sin they knew in those old days, an that wasnt sin at all. Mind me, th only sin is whats done against th soul. Th whole world is a conspiracy t sin, especially in America, an against me. I'm th victim of their sin. I'm what sin is. Does he look like me? Have you ever heard him say th things youve heard me say? He couldnt if he had th Holy Ghost t help him. Dont look shocked, little sweetheart, you hurt me.

Father John: Sin.

Kabnis: Aw, shut up, old man.

Carrie K.: Leave him be. He wants t say somethin. (She turns to the old man.) What is it, Father?

Kabnis: Whatsha talkin t that old deaf man for? Come away from him.

Carrie K.: What is it, Father?

The old man's lips begin to work. Words are formed incoherently. Finally, he manages to articulate —

Father John: Th sin whats fixed . . . (Hesitates.)

Carrie K. (restraining a comment from Kabnis): Go on, Father.

Father John: . . . upon th white folks —

Kabnis: Suppose youre talkin about that bastard race thats roamin round th country. It looks like sin, if thats what y mean. Give us somethin new an up t date.

Father John: — f tellin Jesus — lies. O th sin th white folks 'mitted when they made th Bible lie.

Boom. Boom. BOOM! Thuds on the floor above. The old man sinks back into his stony silence. Carrie is wet-eyed. Kabnis, contemptuous.

Kabnis: So thats your sin. All these years t tell us that th white folks made th Bible lie. Well, I'll be damned. Lewis ought t have been here. You old black fakir —

Carrie K.: Brother Ralph, is that your best Amen?

She turns him to her and takes his hot cheeks in her firm cool hands. Her palms draw the fever out. With its passing, Kabnis crumples. He sinks to his knees before her, ashamed, exhausted. His eyes squeeze tight. Carrie presses his face tenderly against her. The suffocation of her fresh starched dress feels good to him. Carrie is about to lift her hands in prayer, when Halsey, at the head of the stairs, calls down.

Halsey: Well, well. Whats up? Aint you ever comin? Come on. Whats up down there? Take you all mornin t sleep off a pint? Youre weakenin, man, youre weakenin. Th axle an th beam's all ready waitin f y. Come on.

Kabnis rises and is going doggedly towards the steps. Carrie notices his robe. She catches up to him, points to it, and helps him take it off. He hangs it, with an exaggerated ceremony, on its nail in the corner. He looks down on the tousled beds. His lips curl bitterly. Turning, he stumbles over the bucket of dead coals. He savagely jerks it from the floor. And then, seeing Carrie's eyes upon him, he swings the pail carelessly and with eyes downcast and swollen, trudges upstairs to the work-shop. Carrie's gaze follows him till he is gone. Then she goes to the old man and slips to her knees before him. Her lips murmur, "Jesus, come."

Light streaks through the iron-barred cellar window. Within its soft circle, the figures of Carrie and Father John.

Outside, the sun arises from its cradle in the tree-tops of the forest. Shadows of pines are dreams the sun shakes from its eyes. The sun arises. Gold-glowing child, it steps into the sky and sends a birth-song slanting down gray dust streets and sleepy windows of the southern town.

AFTERWORD

Throughout the twentieth century, literary critics have been announcing that the novel is dead, meaning (roughly) that the interesting possibilities of the realistic depiction of bourgeois characters living through some action — usually moving from innocence to experience — have been exhausted. The motif has been effectively treated innumerable times, and a new motif and a new form long seemed needed. James Joyce's *Ulysses,* published in 1922, and Marcel Proust's *Remembrance of Things Past,* seven volumes published from 1913 to 1927, are of course the towering monuments produced by the desire for a new kind of novel. In America, especially in New York's Greenwich Village in the 1920's, writers experimented with new techniques, seeking to develop new forms of prose fiction. Jean Toomer's *Cane* (1923) is one of the most interesting of these American experiments.

First, *Cane* does not follow its characters for the length of the book. Several names recur a few times from one story to another, but the central figures of one story do not appear in the others. In this collection of sketches and poems we get something like Sherwood Anderson's *Winesburg, Ohio* (1919) crossed with Edgar Lee Masters's *Spoon River Anthology* (1915), with an infusion of Gertrude Stein's *Three Lives* (1909). *Three Lives* is especially interesting in connection with *Cane,* not only because the three lives are told in separate stories but for two additional reasons: first, because Miss Stein described her book (and one might so describe *Cane*) as being about "how men do not love, how men do love, how women and men do and do not love and so on"; second, because one of the three lives, *Melanctha,* is that of a black woman. (The Harlem Renaissance was already affirming blackness when Toomer began writing, but he must also have found in Miss Stein's book a fresh and impressive literary treatment of a black.)

Even before we read far enough in *Cane* to learn that the characters we meet in one sketch will not reappear in the next, the language strikes us as unusual for prose fiction:

> Men had always wanted her, this Karintha, even as a child, Karintha carrying beauty, perfect as dusk when the sun goes down. Old men rode her hobby-horse upon their knees. Young men danced with her at frolics when they should have been dancing with their grownup girls. . . Old men could no longer ride her hobby-horse upon their knees. But young men counted faster. . . Old men remind her that a few years back they rode her hobby-horse upon their knees.

Possibly here also Toomer shows some influence of Gertrude Stein, whose interest in the unconscious or the supposedly primitive mind revealing its thoughts unfiltered by reason led her to use a style characterized by repetition ("A rose is a rose is a rose"), but, more important, Toomer is drawing upon the black traditions of oral literature, notably the folk song, where lines are repeated, sometimes with highly significant variations that advance the narrative. Toomer's prose, often repetitive and often rhythmic, thus has affinities with poetry and is far removed from the inconspicuous prose style that realistic novelists had used. His style allows him to include poems with no sense of a break in the texture.

All these things are obvious to anyone who reads a few pages of *Cane;* no less obvious, and no less a departure from the traditional novel, is what can be called the mythologizing tendency that in *Cane* replaces the usual apparently dispassionate scrutiny of ordinary people working out their lives. Toomer, formally educated in Washington, Wisconsin, and New York, had moved in both the white and the black worlds, but he had come to feel a need for roots, which might also be expressed as a need for a mythology. In 1922 he wrote:

> Within the last two or three years . . . my growing need for artistic expression has pulled me deeper and deeper into the Negro group. And as my powers of receptivity increased, I found myself loving it in a way that I could never love the other. It has stimulated and fertilized whatever creative talent I may contain within me. A visit to Georgia last fall was the starting point of almost everything of worth that I have done. I heard folk-songs come from the lips of Negro peasants. I saw the rich

> dusk beauty that I had heard many false accents about, and of which till then, I was somewhat skeptical. And a deep part of my nature, a part that I had repressed, sprang suddenly to life and responded to them. Now, I cannot conceive of myself as aloof and separated.

Cane, the product of his visit to Georgia, is not a series of quaint sketches, but an earnest struggle toward a new identity and a vision of life. We may take as central to this vision "Song of the Son," the poem that follows "Carma."

> O land and soil, red soil and sweet-gum tree,
> So scant of grass, so profligate of pines,
> Now just before an epoch's sun declines
> Thy son, in time, I have returned to thee,
> Thy son, I have in time returned to thee.
>
> In time, for though the sun is setting on
> A song-lit race of slaves, it has not set;
> Though late, O soil, it is not too late yet
> To catch thy plaintive soul, leaving, soon gone,
> Leaving, to catch thy plaintive soul soon gone.

The sun is setting on the descendants of slaves, but one son (the narrator), seeking to make "an everlasting song," hopes that he has returned in time to share in the heritage of the soil that nurtured the "song-lit race."

Broadly speaking, *Cane* sets forth an opposition between the natural or primitive and the artificial or sophisticated. Thus the vitality of Karintha, the protagonist of the first story, is contrasted with the mechanical and the destructive, embodied in the sawmill. "At sunset, when there was no wind, and the pine-smoke from over by the sawmill hugged the earth, and you couldnt see more than a few feet in front, her sudden darting past you was a bit of vivid color, like a black bird that flashes in light." This primitive energy, even when superficially destructive, is seen as innocent and beautiful. "She stoned the cows, and beat her dog, and fought the other children. . . Even the preacher, who caught her at mischief, told himself that she was as innocently lovely as a November cotton flower."

Although the opposition of the primitive or spontaneous and the sophisticated or mechanical is persistent, it is not presented with rigid consistency, and, more important, even in the first of the three parts of the novel, where the beauty of the primitive is most evident, the primitive is not sentimentalized. We do not get pictures of happy darkies close to the soil: Karintha's infant, born "onto a bed of pine-needles in the forest," dies; Becky, a white woman who had two black sons, is banished and dies in the cabin that collapses on her; Carma's deception of her husband leads to violence even in the fertile canefield and he ends on the chain gang; and the remaining stories in the first part are similarly filled with a sense of a fertility that is not allowed to come to fruition. But suggestions of a new life, a sort of resurrection, permeate the book, often using such Christian imagery as "Bring dreams of Christ to dusky cane-lipped throngs." This sense of resurrection, or, more precisely, of the need for rebirth, is evident in the second part too. Set in Washington, D.C., the second part recounts stories of frustration among the urban blacks who have lost their roots even though "nigger life" thrusts "unconscious rhythms, black reddish blood into the white and whitewashed wood of Washington." For example, in "Box Seat," Muriel, a school teacher who is always concerned about what her landlady Mrs. Pribby will think, fears to face the pain of the past and urges her vibrant boyfriend Dan Moore to "get a good job and settle down." Dan, "born in a canefield," has "come to a sick world to heal it," but Muriel cannot respond to him ("Mrs. Pribby is right in the next room") and cannot respond with fellow-feeling toward the dwarf who gives her a rose. Against this psychologically crippled black woman, a nameless "portly Negress" is briefly juxtaposed:

> A soil-soaked fragrance comes from her. Through the cement floor her stong roots sink down. They spread under the asphalt streets. Dreaming, the streets roll over on their bellies, and suck their glossy health from them. Her strong roots sink down and spread under the river and disappear in blood lines that waver south. Her roots shoot down.

There is no need here to comment on all of the characters, but two others must be discussed, if only briefly: the narrator and the title-character of the last story, "Kabnis." The narrator is a shadowy figure of whom we are only occasionally aware, but we piece together a brief history. He cannot face the pain of the South (in "Becky," the second story, he runs away when he sees the cabin collapse on Becky); still, in Georgia — he apparently is only a visitor — he feels most receptive to invisible forces:

> I felt strange, as I always do in Georgia, particularly at dusk. I felt that things unseen to men were tangibly immediate. It would not have surprised me had I had vision. People have them in Georgia more often than you would suppose. A black woman once saw the mother of Christ and drew her in charcoal on the courthouse wall.

Kabnis, nominally a character apart from the narrator, apparently is a version of the narrator and of Jean Toomer. Like Toomer, he has come to Georgia to teach and to find his roots in a painful past. This story, too, though filled with suggestions of rebirth, does not allow Kabnis to achieve his quest. He fends off the South: the noise of the chickens bothers him; "In the church I used to go to no one ever shouted"; he fears that he will be lynched; he insists that his "ancestors were Southern blue-bloods"; and so he is "suspended a few feet above the soil whose touch would resurrect him." Most important, he rejects Father John, the ancient former slave who lives beneath the floor in quarters reminiscent of a slave ship. Kabnis is unable to return to his roots, but the book nevertheless ends with an affirmation: Carrie Kate, a child, cares for Father John, and there is the implication that unlike most of the other women in *Cane* her beauty and energy, arising from "the purpose of her present mission," will not desert her.

The last paragraph of the book, describing the rising sun, completes this "Song of the Son" who had sought to be transformed before the sun set:

> Outside, the sun arises from its cradle in the tree-tops of the forest. Shadows of pines are dreams the sun shakes from its eyes. The sun arises. Gold-glowing child, it steps into the sky and sends a birth-song slanting down gray dust streets and sleepy windows of the southern town.

THOMAS MANN

Thomas Mann (1875–1955), the son of a wealthy merchant, was born in the north German city of Lübeck, which he described as a "small and old-established city, civilized and gentle." When Mann was fifteen his father died, and after finishing school, Mann followed his mother and brother to live in Munich and to travel in Italy. After working for a few years in an insurance office and on the editorial staff of the German satiric journal *Simplicissimus,* he settled on writing as his permanent career. In 1901 he published his first novel, *Buddenbrooks,* in 1911 a short novel, *Death in Venice,* and in 1924 his portrait of European civilization, the novel *The Magic Mountain.* In 1929 he received the Nobel Prize for Literature. Because of his outspoken condemnation of totalitarianism his books were banned by the Nazis, and, after Hitler's rise to power, he left Germany, a self-exile, in 1933. Deprived of his German citizenship, in 1944 he became a naturalized citizen of the United States. He returned to Europe in 1952 to settle in Zurich, where he died. *Stories of Three Decades,* his collected stories and short novels (including *Mario and the Magician,* 1929), was published in 1931. His best-known later fiction includes a tetralogy based on the Biblical Joseph: *Joseph and His Brothers,* completed in 1943; *Doctor Faustus,* published in 1948; and his last novel, *The Confessions of Felix Krull,* published in 1955.

MARIO AND THE MAGICIAN

Translated by H. T. Lowe-Porter

The atmosphere of Torre di Venere remains unpleasant in the memory. From the first moment the air of the place made us uneasy, we felt irritable, on edge; then at the end came the shocking business of Cipolla, that dreadful being who seemed to incorporate, in so fateful and so humanly impressive a way, all the peculiar evilness of the situation as a whole. Looking back, we had the feeling that the horrible end of the affair had been preordained and lay in the nature of things; that the children had to be present at it was an added impropriety, due to the false colours in which the weird creature presented himself. Luckily for them, they did not know where the comedy left off and the tragedy began; and we let them remain in their happy belief that the whole thing had been a play up till the end.

Torre di Venere lies some fifteen kilometres from Portoclemente, one of the most popular summer resorts on the Tyrrhenian Sea. Portoclemente is urban and elegant and full to overflowing for months on end. Its gay and busy main street of shops and hotels runs down to a wide sandy beach covered with tents and pennanted sand-castles and sunburnt humanity, where at all times a lively social bustle reigns, and much noise. But this same spacious and inviting fine-sanded beach, this same border of pine grove and near, presiding mountains, continues all the way along the coast. No wonder then that some competition of a quiet kind should have sprung up further on. Torre di Venere — the tower that gave the town its name is gone long since, one looks for it in vain — is an offshoot of the larger resort, and for some years remained an idyll for the few, a refuge for more unworldly spirits. But the usual history of such places repeated itself: peace has had to retire further along the coast, to Marina Petriera and dear knows where else. We all know how the world at once seeks peace and puts her to flight — rushing upon her in the fond idea that they two will wed, and where she is, there it can be at home. It will even set up its Vanity Fair in a spot and be capable of thinking that peace is still by its side. Thus Torre — though its atmosphere so far is more modest and contemplative than that of Portoclemente — has been quite taken up, by both Italians and foreigners. It is no longer the thing to go to Portoclemente — though still so much the thing that it is as noisy and crowded as ever. One goes next door, so to speak: to Torre. So much more refined, even, and cheaper to boot. And the attractiveness of these qualities persists, though the qualities themselves long ago ceased to be evident. Torre has got a Grand Hotel. Numerous pensions[1] have sprung up, some modest, some pretentious. The people who own or rent the villas and pinetas overlooking the sea no longer have it all their own way on the beach. In July and August it looks just like the beach at Portoclemente: it swarms with a screaming, squabbling, merrymaking crowd, and the sun, blazing down like mad, peels the skin off their necks. Garish little flat-bottomed boats rock on the glittering blue, manned by children, whose mothers hover afar and fill the air with anxious cries of Nino! and Sandro! and Bice! and Maria! Pedlars step across the legs of recumbent sun-bathers, selling flowers and corals, oysters, lemonade, and *cornetti al burro,*[2] and crying their wares in the breathy, full-throated southern voice.

Such was the scene that greeted our arrival in Torre: pleasant enough, but after all, we thought, we had come too soon. It was the middle of August, the Italian season was still at its height, scarcely the moment for strangers to learn to love the special charms of the place. What an afternoon crowd in the cafés on the front! For instance, in the Esquisito, where we sometimes sat and were served by Mario, that very Mario of whom I shall have presently to tell. It is well-nigh impossible to find a table; and the various orchestras contend together in the midst of one's conversation with bewildering effect. Of course, it is in the afternoon that people come over from Portoclemente. The excursion is a favourite one for the restless denizens of that pleasure resort, and a Fiat motor-bus plies to and fro, coating inch-thick with dust the oleander and laurel hedges along the highroad — a notable if repulsive sight.

Yes, decidedly one should go to Torre in September, when the great public has left. Or else in May, before the water is warm enough to tempt the Southerner to bathe. Even in the before and after seasons Torre is not empty, but life is less national and more subdued. English, French, and German prevail under the tent-awnings and in the pension dining-rooms; whereas in August — in the Grand Hotel, at least, where, in default of private addresses, we had engaged rooms — the stranger finds the field so occupied by Florentine and Roman society that he feels quite isolated and even temporarily *déclassé.*

1 [Boarding houses. — Editors' note.]
2 [Crescent-shaped butter-rolls. — Editors' note.]

We had, rather to our annoyance, this experience on the evening we arrived, when we went in to dinner and were shown to our table by the waiter in charge. As a table, it had nothing against it, save that we had already fixed our eyes upon those on the veranda beyond, built out over the water, where little red-shaded lamps glowed — and there were still some tables empty, though it was as full as the dining-room within. The children went into raptures at the festive sight, and without more ado we announced our intention to take our meals by preference in the veranda. Our words, it appeared, were prompted by ignorance; for we were informed, with somewhat embarrassed politeness, that the cosy nook outside was reserved for the clients of the hotel: *ai nostri clienti*. Their clients? But we were their clients. We were not tourists or trippers, but boarders for a stay of some three or four weeks. However, we forbore to press for an explanation of the difference between the likes of us and that clientèle to whom it was vouchsafed to eat out there in the glow of the red lamps, and took our dinner by the prosaic common light of the dining-room chandelier — a thoroughly ordinary and monotonous hotel bill of fare, be it said. In Pensione Eleonora, a few steps landward, the table, as we were to discover, was much better.

And thither it was that we moved, three or four days later, before we had had time to settle in properly at the Grand Hotel. Not on account of the veranda and the lamps. The children, straightway on the best of terms with waiters and pages, absorbed in the joys of life on the beach, promptly forgot those colourful seductions. But now there arose, between ourselves and the veranda clientèle — or perhaps more correctly with the compliant management — one of those little unpleasantnesses which can quite spoil the pleasure of a holiday. Among the guests were some high Roman aristocracy, a Principe X and his family. These grand folk occupied rooms close to our own, and the Principessa, a great and a passionately maternal lady, was thrown into a panic by the vestiges of a whooping-cough which our little ones had lately got over, but which now and then still faintly troubled the unshatterable slumbers of our youngest-born. The nature of this illness is not clear, leaving some play for the imagination. So we took no offence at our elegant neighbour for clinging to the widely held view that whooping-cough is acoustically contagious and quite simply fearing lest her children yield to the bad example set by ours. In the fullness of her feminine self-confidence she protested to the management, which then, in the person of the proverbial frock-coated manager, hastened to represent to us, with many expressions of regret, that under the circumstances they were obliged to transfer us to the annexe. We did our best to assure him that the disease was in its very last stages, that it was actually over, and presented no danger of infection to anybody. All that we gained was permission to bring the case before the hotel physician — not one chosen by us — by whose verdict we must then abide. We agreed, convinced that thus we should at once pacify the Princess and escape the trouble of moving. The doctor appeared, and behaved like a faithful and honest servant of science. He examined the child and gave his opinion: the disease was quite over, no danger of contagion was present. We drew a long breath and considered the incident closed — until the manager announced that despite the doctor's verdict it would still be necessary for us to give up our rooms and retire to the *dépendance*. Byzantinism like this outraged us. It is not likely that the Principessa was responsible for the wilful breach of faith. Very likely the fawning management had not even dared to tell her what the physician said. Anyhow, we made it clear to his understanding that we preferred to leave the hotel altogether and at once — and packed our trunks. We could do so with a light heart, having already set up casual friendly relations with Casa Eleonora. We had noticed its pleasant exterior and formed the acquaintance of its proprietor, Signora Angiolieri, and her husband: she slender and black-haired, Tuscan in type, probably at the beginning of the thirties, with the dead ivory complexion of the southern woman, he quiet and bald and carefully dressed. They owned a larger establishment in Florence and presided only in summer and early autumn over the branch in Torre di Venere. But earlier, before her marriage, our new landlady had been companion, fellow-traveller, wardrobe mistress, yes, friend, of Eleonora Duse and manifestly regarded that period as the crown of her career. Even at our first visit she spoke of it with animation. Numerous photographs of the great actress, with affectionate inscriptions, were displayed about the drawing-room, and other souvenirs of their life together adorned the little tables and étagères. This cult of a so interesting past was calculated, of course, to heighten the advantages of the signora's present business. Nevertheless our pleasure and interest were quite genuine as we were conducted through the house by its owner and listened to her sonorous and staccato Tuscan voice relating anecdotes of that immortal mistress, depicting her suffering saintliness, her genius, her profound delicacy of feeling.

Thither, then, we moved our effects, to the dismay of the staff of the Grand Hotel, who, like all Italians, were very good to children. Our new quarters were retired and pleasant, we were within easy reach of the sea through the avenue of young plane trees that ran down to the esplanade. In the clean, cool dining-room Signora Angiolieri daily served the soup with her own hands, the service was attentive and good, the table capital. We even discovered some Viennese acquaintances, and enjoyed chatting with them after luncheon, in front of the house. They, in their turn, were the means of our finding others — in short, all seemed for the best, and we were heartily glad of the change we had made. Nothing was now wanting to a holiday of the most gratifying kind.

And yet no proper gratification ensued. Perhaps the stupid occasion of our change of quarters pursued us to the new ones we had found. Personally, I admit that I do not easily forget these collisions with ordinary humanity, the naïve misuse of power, the injustice, the sycophantic corruption. I dwelt upon the incident too much, it irritated me in retrospect — quite futilely, of course, since such phenomena are only all too natural and all too much the rule. And we had not broken off relations with the Grand Hotel. The children were as friendy as ever there, the porter mended their toys, and we sometimes took tea in the garden. We even saw the Principessa. She would come out, with her firm and delicate tread, her lips emphatically corallined, to look after her children, playing under the supervision of their English governess. She did not dream that we were anywhere near, for so soon as she appeared in the offing we sternly forbade our little one even to clear his throat.

The heat — if I may bring it in evidence — was extreme. It was African. The power of the sun, directly one left the border of the indigo-blue wave, was so frightful, so relentless, that the mere thought of the few steps between the beach and luncheon was a burden, clad though one might be only in pyjamas. Do you care for that sort of thing? Weeks on end? Yes, of course, it is proper to the south, it is classic weather, the sun of Homer, the climate wherein human culture came to flower — and all the rest of it. But after a while it is too much for me, I reach a point where I begin to find it dull. The burning void of the sky, day after day, weighs one down; the high coloration, the enormous naïveté of the unrefracted light — they do, I dare say, induce light-heartedness, a carefree mood born of immunity from downpours and other meteorological caprices. But slowly, slowly, there makes itself felt a lack: the deeper, more complex needs of the northern soul remain unsatisfied. You are left barren — even, it may be, in time, a little contemptuous. True, without that stupid business of the whooping-cough I might not have been feeling these things. I was annoyed, very likely I wanted to feel them and so half-unconsciously seized upon an idea lying ready to hand to induce, or if not to induce, at least to justify and strengthen, my attitude. Up to this point, then, if you like, let us grant some ill will on our part. But the sea; and the mornings spent extended upon the fine sand in face of its eternal splendours — no, the sea could not conceivably induce such feelings. Yet it was none the less true that, despite all previous experience, we were not at home on the beach, we were not happy.

It was too soon, too soon. The beach, as I have said, was still in the hands of the middle-class native. It is a pleasing breed to look at, and among the young we saw much shapeliness and charm. Still, we were necessarily surrounded by a great deal of very average humanity — a middle-class mob, which, you will admit, is not more charming under this sun than under one's own native sky. The voices these women have! It was sometimes hard to believe that we were in the land which is the western cradle of the art of song. *"Fuggièro!"* I can still hear that cry, as for twenty mornings long I heard it close behind me, breathy, full-throated, hideously stressed, with a harsh open *e*, uttered in accents of mechanical despair. *"Fuggièro! Rispondi almeno!"* Answer when I call you! The *sp* in *rispondi* was pronounced like *shp*, as Germans pronounce it; and this, on top of what I felt already, vexed my sensitive soul. The cry was addressed to a repulsive youngster whose sunburn had made disgusting raw sores on his shoulders. He outdid anything I have ever seen for ill-breeding, refractoriness, and temper and was a great coward to boot, putting the whole beach in an uproar, one day, because of his outrageous sensitiveness to the slightest pain. A sand-crab had pinched his toe in the water, and the minute injury made him set up a cry of heroic proportions — the shout of an antique hero in his agony — that pierced one to the marrow and called up visions of some frightful tragedy. Evidently he considered himself not only wounded, but poisoned as well; he crawled out on the sand and lay in apparently intolerable anguish, groaning *"Ohi!"* and *"Ohimè!"* and threshing about with arms and legs to ward off his mother's tragic appeals and the questions of the bystanders. An audience gathered round. A doctor was fetched — the same who had pronounced objective judgment on our whooping-cough — and here again acquitted himself like a man of science. Good-naturedly he reassured the boy, telling him that he was not hurt at all, he should simply go into the water again to relieve the smart. Instead of which, Fuggièro was borne off the beach, followed by a concourse of people. But he did not fail to appear next morning, nor did he leave off spoiling our children's sand-castles. Of course, always by accident. In short, a perfect terror.

And this twelve-year-old lad was prominent among the influences that, imperceptibly at first, combined to spoil our holiday and render it unwholesome. Somehow or other, there was a stiffness, a lack of innocent enjoyment. These people stood on their dignity — just why, and in what spirit, it was not easy at first to tell. They displayed much self-respectingness; towards each other and towards the foreigner their bearing was that of a person newly conscious of a sense of honour. And wherefore? Gradually we realized the political implications and understood that we were in the presence of a national ideal. The beach, in fact, was alive with patriotic children — a phenomenon as unnatural as it was depressing. Children are a human species and a society apart, a nation of their own, so to speak. On the basis of their common form of life, they find each other out with the greatest ease, no matter how different their small vocabularies. Ours soon played with natives and foreigners alike. Yet they were plainly both puzzled and disappointed at times. There were wounded sensibilities, displays of assertiveness — or rather hardly assertiveness, for it was too self-conscious and too didactic to deserve the name. There were quarrels over flags, disputes about authority and precedence. Grownups joined in, not so much to pacify as to render judgment and enunciate principles. Phrases were dropped about the greatness and dignity of Italy, solemn phrases that spoilt the fun. We saw our two little ones retreat, puzzled and hurt, and were put to it to explain the situation. These people, we told them, were just passing through a certain stage, something rather like an illness, perhaps; not very pleasant, but probably unavoidable.

We had only our own carelessness to thank that we came to blows in the end with this "stage" — which, after all, we had seen and sized up long before now. Yes, it came to another "cross-purposes," so evidently the earlier ones had not been sheer accident. In a word, we became an offence to the public morals. Our small daughter — eight years old, but in physical development a good year younger and thin as a chicken — had had a good long bathe and gone playing in the warm sun in her wet costume. We told her that she might take off her bathing-suit, which was stiff with sand, rinse it in the sea, and put it on again, after which she must take care to keep it cleaner. Off goes the costume and she runs down naked to the sea, rinses her little jersey, and comes back. Ought we to have foreseen the outburst of anger and resentment which her conduct, and thus our conduct, called forth? Without delivering a homily on the subject, I may say that in the last decade our attitude towards the nude body and our feelings regarding it have undergone, all over the world, a fundamental change. There are things we "never think about" any more, and among them is the freedom we had permitted to this by no means provocative little childish body. But in these parts it was taken as a challenge. The patriotic children hooted. Fuggièro whistled on his fingers. The sudden buzz of conversation among the grown people in our neighbourhood boded no good. A gentleman in city togs, with a not very apropos bowler hat on the back of his head, was assuring his outraged womenfolk that he proposed to take punitive measures; he stepped up to us, and a philippic descended on our unworthy heads, in which all the emotionalism of the sense-loving south spoke in the service of morality and discipline. The offence against decency of which we had been guilty was, he said, the more to be condemned because it was also a gross ingratitude and an insulting breach of his country's hospitality. We had criminally injured not only the letter and spirit of the public bathing regulations, but also the honour of Italy; he, the gentleman in the city togs, knew how to defend that honour and proposed to see to it that our offence against the national dignity should not go unpunished.

We did our best, bowing respectfully, to give ear to this eloquence. To contradict the man, overheated as he was, would probably be to fall from one error into another. On the tips of our tongues we had various answers: as, that the word "hospitality," in its strictest sense, was not quite the right one, taking all the circumstances into consideration. We were not literally the guests of Italy, but of Signora Angiolieri, who had assumed the rôle of dispenser of hospitality some years ago on laying down that of familiar friend to Eleonora Duse. We longed to say that surely this beautiful country had not sunk so low as to be reduced to a state of hypersensitive prudishness. But we confined ourselves to assuring the gentleman that any lack of respect, any provocation on our parts, had been the furthest from our thoughts. And as a mitigating circumstance we pointed out the tender age and physical slightness of the little culprit. In vain. Our protests were waved away, he did not believe in them; our defence would not hold water. We must be made an example of. The authorities were notified, by telephone, I believe, and their representative appeared on the beach. He said the case was *"molto grave."*[3] We had to go with him to the Municipio up in the Piazza, where a higher official confirmed the previous verdict of *"molto grave,"* launched into a stream of the usual didactic phrases — the selfsame tune and words as the man in the bowler hat — and levied a fine and ransom of fifty lire. We felt that the adventure must willy-nilly be worth to us this much of a contribution to the economy of the Italian government; paid, and left. Ought we not at this point to have left Torre as well?

If we only had! We should thus have escaped that fatal Cipolla. But circumstances combined to prevent us from making up our minds to a change. A certain poet says that it is indolence that makes us endure uncomfortable situations. The *aperçu* may serve as an explanation for our inaction. Anyhow, one dislikes voiding the field immediately upon such an event. Especially if sympathy from other quarters encourages one to defy it. And in the Villa Eleonora they pronounced as with one voice upon the injustice of our punishment. Some Italian after-dinner acquaintances found that the episode put their country in a very bad light, and proposed taking the man in the bowler hat to task, as one fellow-citizen to another. But the next day he and his party had vanished from the beach. Not on our account, of course. Though it might be that the consciousness of his impending departure had added energy to his rebuke; in any case his going was a relief. And, furthermore, we stayed because our stay had by now become remarkable in our own eyes, which is worth something in itself, quite apart from the comfort or discomfort involved. Shall we strike sail, avoid a certain experience so soon as it seems not expressly calculated to increase our enjoyment or our self-esteem? Shall we go away whenever life looks like turning in the slightest uncanny, or not quite normal, or even rather painful and morti-

3 [Very serious. — Editors' note.]

fying? No, surely not. Rather stay and look matters in the face, brave them out; perhaps precisely in so doing lies a lesson for us to learn. We stayed on and reaped as the awful reward of our constancy the unholy and staggering experience with Cipolla.

I have not mentioned that the after season had begun, almost on the very day we were disciplined by the city authorities. The worshipful gentleman in the bowler hat, our denouncer, was not the only person to leave the resort. There was a regular exodus, on every hand you saw luggage-carts on their way to the station. The beach denationalized itself. Life in Torre, in the cafés and the pinetas, became more homelike and more European. Very likely we might even have eaten at a table in the glass veranda, but we refrained, being content at Signora Angiolieri's — as content, that is, as our evil star would let us be. But at the same time with this turn for the better came a change in the weather: almost to an hour it showed itself in harmony with the holiday calendar of the general public. The sky was overcast; not that it grew any cooler, but the unclouded heat of the entire eighteen days since our arrival, and probably long before that, gave place to a stifling sirocco air, while from time to time a little ineffectual rain sprinkled the velvety surface of the beach. Add to which, that two-thirds of our intended stay at Torre had passed. The colourless, lazy sea, with sluggish jellyfish floating in its shallows, was at least a change. And it would have been silly to feel retrospective longings after a sun that had caused us so many sighs when it burned down in all its arrogant power.

At this juncture, then, it was that Cipolla announced himself. Cavaliere Cipolla he was called on the posters that appeared one day stuck up everywhere, even in the dining-room of Pensione Eleonora. A travelling virtuoso, an entertainer, *"forzatore, illusionista, prestidigatore,"*[4] as he called himself, who proposed to wait upon the highly respectable population of Torre di Venere with a display of extraordinary phenomena of a mysterious and staggering kind. A conjuror! The bare announcement was enough to turn our children's heads. They had never seen anything of the sort, and now our present holiday was to afford them this new excitement. From that moment on they besieged us with prayers to take tickets for the performance. We had doubts, from the first, on the score of the lateness of the hour, nine o'clock; but gave way, in the idea that we might see a little of what Cipolla had to offer, probably no great matter, and then go home. Besides, of course, the children could sleep late next day. We bought four tickets of Signora Angiolieri herself, she having taken a number of the stalls on commission to sell them to her guests. She could not vouch for the man's performance, and we had no great expectations. But we were conscious of a need for diversion, and the children's violent curiosity proved catching.

4 [Strongman, illusionist, magician. — Editors' note.]

The Cavaliere's performance was to take place in a hall where during the season there had been a cinema with a weekly programme. We had never been there. You reached it by following the main street under the wall of the "*palazzo,*" a ruin with a "For sale" sign, that suggested a castle and had obviously been built in lordlier days. In the same street were the chemist, the hairdresser, and all the better shops; it led, so to speak, from the feudal past the bourgeois into the proletarian, for it ended off between two rows of poor fishing-huts, where old women sat mending nets before the doors. And here, among the proletariat, was the hall, not much more, actually, than a wooden shed, though a large one, with a turreted entrance, plastered on either side with layers of gay placards. Some while after dinner, then, on the appointed evening, we wended our way thither in the dark, the children dressed in their best and blissful with the sense of so much irregularity. It was sultry, as it had been for days; there was heat lightning now and then, and a little rain; we proceeded under umbrellas. It took us a quarter of an hour.

Our tickets were collected at the entrance, our places we had to find ourselves. They were in the third row left, and as we sat down we saw that, late though the hour was for the performance, it was to be interpreted with even more laxity. Only very slowly did an audience — who seemed to be relied upon to come late — begin to fill the stalls. These comprised the whole auditorium; there were no boxes. This tardiness gave us some concern. The children's cheeks were already flushed as much with fatigue as with excitement. But even when we entered, the standing-room at the back and in the side aisles was already well occupied. There stood the manhood of Torre di Venere, all and sundry, fisherfolk, rough-and-ready youths with bare forearms crossed over their striped jerseys. We were well pleased with the presence of this native assemblage, which always adds colour and animation to occasions like the present; and the children were frankly delighted. For they had friends among these people — acquaintances picked up on afternoon strolls to the further ends of the beach. We would be turning homeward, at the hour when the sun dropped into the sea, spent with the huge effort it had made and gilding with reddish gold the oncoming surf; and we would come upon bare-legged fisherfolk standing in rows, bracing and hauling with long-drawn cries as they drew in the nets and harvested in dripping baskets their catch, often so scanty, of *frutta di mare.*[5] The children looked on, helped to pull, brought out their little stock of Italian words, made friends. So now they exchanged nods with the "standing-room" clientèle; there was Guiscardo, there Antonio, they knew them by name and waved and called across in half-whispers, getting answering nods and smiles that displayed rows of healthy white teeth. Look, there is even Mario, Mario from the Esquisito, who brings us

5 [Sea food. — Editors' note.]

the chocolate. He wants to see the conjuror, too, and he must have come early, for he is almost in front; but he does not see us, he is not paying attention; that is a way he has, even though he is a waiter. So we wave instead to the man who lets out the little boats on the beach; he is there too, standing at the back.

It had got to a quarter past nine, it got to almost half past. It was natural that we should be nervous. When would the children get to bed? It had been a mistake to bring them, for now it would be very hard to suggest breaking off their enjoyment before it had got well under way. The stalls had filled in time; all Torre, apparently, was there: the guests of the Grand Hotel, the guests of Villa Eleonora, familiar faces from the beach. We heard English and German and the sort of French that Rumanians speak with Italians. Madame Angiolieri herself sat two rows behind us, with her quiet, bald-headed spouse, who kept stroking his moustache with the two middle fingers of his right hand. Everybody had come late, but nobody too late. Cipolla made us wait for him.

He made us wait. That is probably the way to put it. He heightened the suspense by his delay in appearing. And we could see the point of this, too — only not when it was carried to extremes. Towards half past nine the audience began to clap — an amiable way of expressing justifiable impatience, evincing as it does an eagerness to applaud. For the little ones, this was a joy in itself — all children love to clap. From the popular sphere came loud cries of *"Pronti!" "Cominciamo!"*[6] And lo, it seemed now as easy to begin as before it had been hard. A gong sounded, greeted by the standing rows with a many-voiced "Ah-h!" and the curtains parted. They revealed a platform furnished more like a schoolroom than like the theatre of a conjuring performance — largely because of the blackboard in the left foreground. There was a common yellow hat-stand, a few ordinary straw-bottomed chairs, and further back a little round table holding a water carafe and glass, also a tray with a liqueur glass and a flask of pale yellow liquid. We had still a few seconds of time to let these things sink in. Then, with no darkening of the house, Cavaliere Cipolla made his entry.

He came forward with a rapid step that expressed his eagerness to appear before his public and gave rise to the illusion that he had already come a long way to put himself at their service — whereas, of course, he had only been standing in the wings. His costume supported the fiction. A man of an age hard to determine, but by no means young; with a sharp, ravaged face, piercing eyes, compressed lips, small black waxed moustache, and a so-called imperial in the curve between mouth and chin. He was dressed for the street with a sort of complicated evening elegance, in a wide black pelerine with velvet collar and satin lining; which, in the hampered state of his arms, he held together in front with his

6 [Hurry up! Let's begin! — Editors' note.]

white-gloved hands. He had a white scarf round his neck; a top hat with a curving brim sat far back on his head. Perhaps more than anywhere else the eighteenth century is still alive in Italy, and with it the charlatan and mountebank type so characteristic of the period. Only there, at any rate, does one still encounter really well-preserved specimens. Cipolla had in his whole appearance much of the historic type; his very clothes helped to conjure up the traditional figure with its blatantly, fantastically foppish air. His pretentious costume sat upon him, or rather hung upon him, most curiously, being in one place drawn too tight, in another a mass of awkward folds. There was something not quite in order about his figure, both front and back — that was plain later on. But I must emphasize the fact that there was not a trace of personal jocularity or clownishness in his pose, manner, or behaviour. On the contrary, there was complete seriousness, an absence of any humorous appeal; occasionally even a cross-grained pride, along with that curious, self-satisfied air so characteristic of the deformed. None of all this, however, prevented his appearance from being greeted with laughter from more than one quarter of the hall.

All the eagerness had left his manner. The swift entry had been merely an expression of energy, not of zeal. Standing at the footlights he negligently drew off his gloves, to display long yellow hands, one of them adorned with a seal ring with a lapis-lazuli in a high setting. As he stood there, his small hard eyes, with flabby pouches beneath them, roved appraisingly about the hall, not quickly, rather in a considered examination, pausing here and there upon a face with his lips clipped together, not speaking a word. Then with a display of skill as surprising as it was casual, he rolled his gloves into a ball and tossed them across a considerable distance into the glass on the table. Next from an inner pocket he drew forth a packet of cigarettes; you could see by the wrapper that they were the cheapest sort the government sells. With his fingertips he pulled out a cigarette and lighted it, without looking, from a quick-firing benzine lighter. He drew the smoke deep into his lungs and let it out again, tapping his foot, with both lips drawn in an arrogant grimace and the grey smoke streaming out between broken and saw-edged teeth.

With a keenness equal to his own his audience eyed him. The youths at the rear scowled as they peered at this cocksure creature to search out his secret weaknesses. He betrayed none. In fetching out and putting back the cigarettes his clothes got in his way. He had to turn back his pelerine, and in so doing revealed a riding-whip with a silver claw-handle that hung by a leather thong from his left forearm and looked decidedly out of place. You could see that he had on not evening clothes but a frock-coat, and under this, as he lifted it to get at his pocket, could be seen a striped sash worn about the body. Somebody behind me whispered that this sash went with his title of Cavaliere.

I give the information for what it may be worth — personally, I never heard that the title carried such insignia with it. Perhaps the sash was sheer pose, like the way he stood there, without a word, casually and arrogantly puffing smoke into his audience's face.

People laughed, as I said. The merriment had become almost general when somebody in the "standing seats," in a loud, dry voice, remarked: *"Buona sera."*[7]

Cipolla cocked his head. "Who was that?" asked he, as though he had been dared. "Who was that just spoke? Well? First so bold and now so modest? *Paura,*[8] eh?" He spoke with a rather high, asthmatic voice, which yet had a metallic quality. He waited.

"That was me," a youth at the rear broke into the stillness, seeing himself thus challenged. He was not far from us, a handsome fellow in a woollen shirt, with his coat hanging over one shoulder. He wore his curly, wiry hair in a high, dishevelled mop, the style affected by the youth of the awakened Fatherland; it gave him an African appearance that rather spoiled his looks. *"Bè!*[9] That was me. It was your business to say it first, but I was trying to be friendly."

More laughter. The chap had a tongue in his head. *"Ha sciolto la scilinguágnolo,"*[10] I heard near me. After all, the retort was deserved.

"Ah, bravo!" answered Cipolla. "I like you, *giovanotto.*[11] Trust me, I've had my eye on you for some time. People like you are just in my line. I can use them. And you are the pick of the lot, that's plain to see. You do what you like. Or is it possible you have ever not done what you liked — or even, maybe, what you didn't like? What somebody else liked, in short? Hark ye, my friend, that might be a pleasant change for you, to divide up the willing and the doing and stop tackling both jobs at once. Division of labour, *sistema americano, sa'!* For instance, suppose you were to show your tongue to this select and honourable audience here — your whole tongue, right down to the roots?"

"No, I won't," said the youth, hostilely. "Sticking out your tongue shows a bad bringing-up."

"Nothing of the sort," retorted Cipolla. "You would only be *doing* it. With all due respect to your bringing-up, I suggest that before I count ten, you will perform a right turn and stick out your tongue at the company here further than you knew yourself that you could stick it out."

He gazed at the youth, and his piercing eyes seemed to sink deeper into their sockets. *"Uno!"* said he. He had let his riding-whip slide down his arm and made it whistle once through the air. The boy faced about and put out his tongue, so

7 [Good evening. — Editors' note.]
8 [Afraid. — Editors' note.]
9 [Well! — Editors' note.]
10 [He has the gift of gab. — Editors' note.]
11 [Boy. — Editors' note.]

long, so extendedly, that you could see it was the very uttermost in tongue which he had to offer. Then turned back, stony-faced, to his former position.

"That was me," mocked Cipolla, with a jerk of his head towards the youth. "*Bè!* That was me." Leaving the audience to enjoy its sensations, he turned towards the little round table, lifted the bottle, poured out a small glass of what was obviously cognac, and tipped it up with a practised hand.

The children laughed with all their hearts. They had understood practically nothing of what had been said, but it pleased them hugely that something so funny should happen, straightaway, between that queer man up there and somebody out of the audience. They had no preconception of what an "evening" would be like and were quite ready to find this a priceless beginning. As for us, we exchanged a glance and I remember that involuntarily I made with my lips the sound that Cipolla's whip had made when it cut the air. For the rest, it was plain that people did not know what to make of a preposterous beginning like this to a sleight-of-hand performance. They could not see why the *giovanotto,* who after all in a way had been their spokesman, should suddenly have turned on them to vent his incivility. They felt that he had behaved like a silly ass and withdrew their countenances from him in favour of the artist, who now came back from his refreshment table and addressed them as follows:

"Ladies and gentlemen," said he, in his wheezing, metallic voice, "you saw just now that I was rather sensitive on the score of the rebuke this hopeful young linguist saw fit to give me" — *"questo linguista di belle speranze"* was what he said, and we all laughed at the pun.[12] "I am a man who sets some store by himself, you may take it from me. And I see no point in being wished a good-evening unless it is done courteously and in all seriousness. For anything else there is no occasion. When a man wishes me a good-evening he wishes himself one, for the audience will have one only if I do. So this lady-killer of Torre di Venere" (another thrust) "did well to testify that I have one tonight and that I can dispense with any wishes of his in the matter. I can boast of having good evenings almost without exception. One not so good does come my way now and again, but very seldom. My calling is hard and my health not of the best. I have a little physical defect which prevented me from doing my bit in the war for the greater glory of the Fatherland. It is perforce with my mental and spiritual parts that I conquer life — which after all only means conquering onself. And I flatter myself that my achievements have aroused interest and respect among the educated public. The leading newspapers have lauded me, the *Corriere della Sera*[13] did me the courtesy of calling me a phenomenon, and in Rome the brother of the *Duce*[14]

12 [This hopeful linguist; the pun is on *lingua* = tongue. — Editors' note.]
13 [*Evening Post.* — Editors' note.]

honoured me by his presence at one of my evenings. I should not have thought that in a relatively less important place" (laughter here, at the expense of poor little Torre) "I should have to give up the small personal habits which brilliant and elevated audiences had been ready to overlook. Nor did I think I had to stand being heckled by a person who seems to have been rather spoilt by the favours of the fair sex." All this of course at the expense of the youth whom Cipolla never tired of presenting in the guise of *donnaiuolo*[15] and rustic Don Juan. His persistent thin-skinnedness and animosity were in striking contrast to the self-confidence and the worldly success he boasted of. One might have assumed that the *giovanotto* was merely the chosen butt of Cipolla's customary professional sallies, had not the very pointed witticisms betrayed a genuine antagonism. No one looking at the physical parts of the two men need have been at a loss for the explanation, even if the deformed man had not constantly played on the other's supposed success with the fair sex. "Well," Cipolla went on, "before beginning our entertainment this evening, perhaps you will permit me to make myself comfortable."

And he went towards the hat-stand to take off his things.

"Parla benissimo,"[16] asserted somebody in our neighbourhood. So far, the man had done nothing; but what he had said was accepted as an achievement, by means of that he had made an impression. Among southern peoples speech is a constituent part of the pleasure of living, it enjoys far livelier social esteem than in the north. That national cement, the mother tongue, is paid symbolic honours down here, and there is something blithely symbolical in the pleasure people take in their respect for its forms and phonetics. They enjoy speaking, they enjoy listening; and they listen with discrimination. For the way a man speaks serves as a measure of his personal rank; carelessness and clumsiness are greeted with scorn, elegance and mastery are rewarded with social éclat. Wherefore the small man too, where it is a question of getting his effect, chooses his phrase nicely and turns it with care. On this count, then, at least, Cipolla had won his audience; though he by no means belonged to the class of men which the Italian, in a singular mixture of moral and aesthetic judgments, labels *"simpatico."*[17]

After removing his hat, scarf, and mantle he came to the front of the stage, settling his coat, pulling down his cuffs with their large cuff-buttons, adjusting his absurd sash. He had very ugly hair; the top of his head, that is, was almost bald, while a narrow, black-varnished frizz of curls ran from front to back as though stuck on; the side hair, likewise blackened, was brushed forward to the

14 [Leader, i.e., Mussolini. — Editors' note.]
15 [Ladies' man. — Editors' note.]
16 [He speaks very well. — Editors' note.]
17 [Congenial. — Editors' note.]

corners of the eyes — it was, in short, the hairdressing of an old-fashioned circus-director, fantastic, but entirely suited to his outmoded personal type and worn with so much assurance as to take the edge off the public's sense of humour. The little physical defect of which he had warned us was now all too visible, though the nature of it was even now not very clear: the chest was too high, as is usual in such cases; but the corresponding malformation of the back did not sit between the shoulders, it took the form of a sort of hips or buttocks hump, which did not indeed hinder his movements but gave him a grotesque and dipping stride at every step he took. However, by mentioning his deformity beforehand he had broken the shock of it, and a delicate propriety of feeling appeared to reign throughout the hall.

"At your service," said Cipolla. "With your kind permission, we will begin the evening with some arithmetical tests."

Arithmetic? That did not sound much like sleight-of-hand. We began to have our suspicions that the man was sailing under a false flag, only we did not yet know which was the right one. I felt sorry on the children's account; but for the moment they were content simply to be there.

The numerical test which Cipolla now introduced was as simple as it was baffling. He began by fastening a piece of paper to the upper right-hand corner of the blackboard; then lifting it up, he wrote something underneath. He talked all the while, relieving the dryness of his offering by a constant flow of words, and showed himself a practised speaker, never at a loss for conversational turns of phrase. It was in keeping with the nature of his performance, and at the same time vastly entertained the children, that he went on to eliminate the gap between stage and audience, which had already been bridged over by the curious skirmish with the fisher lad: he had representatives from the audience mount the stage, and himself descended the wooden steps to seek personal contact with his public. And again, with individuals, he fell into his former taunting tone. I do not know how far that was a deliberate feature of his system; he preserved a serious, even a peevish air, but his audience, at least the more popular section, seemed convinced that that was all part of the game. So then, after he had written something and covered the writing by the paper, he desired that two persons should come up on the platform and help to perform the calculations. They would not be difficult, even for people not clever at figures. As usual, nobody volunteered, and Cipolla took care not to molest the more select portion of his audience. He kept to the populace. Turning to two sturdy young louts standing behind us, he beckoned them to the front, encouraging and scolding by turns. They should not stand there gaping, he said, unwilling to oblige the company. Actually, he got them in motion; with clumsy tread they came down the middle aisle, climbed the steps, and stood in front of the blackboard, grinning sheepishly at their comrades' shouts and applause. Cipolla joked with them for a few minutes, praised their heroic firmness of limb and the size of their hands, so well calculated to do this service for the public. Then he handed one of them the chalk and told him to write down the numbers as they were called out. But now the creature declared that he could not write! *"Non so scrivere,"* said he in his gruff voice, and his companion added that neither did he.

God knows whether they told the truth or whether they wanted to make game of Cipolla. Anyhow, the latter was far from sharing the general merriment which their confession aroused. He was insulted and disgusted. He sat there on a straw-bottomed chair in the centre of the stage with his legs crossed, smoking a fresh cigarette out of his cheap packet; obviously it tasted the better for the cognac he had indulged in while the yokels were stumping up the steps. Again he inhaled the smoke and let it stream out between curling lips. Swinging his leg, with his gaze sternly averted from the two shamelessly chuckling creatures and from the audience as well, he stared into space as one who withdraws himself and his dignity from the contemplation of an utterly despicable phenomenon.

"Scandalous," said he, in a sort of icy snarl. "Go back to your places! In Italy everybody can write — in all her greatness there is no room for ignorance and unenlightenment. To accuse her of them, in the hearing of this international company, is a cheap joke, in which you yourselves cut a very poor figure and humiliate the government and the whole country as well. If it is true that Torre di Venere is indeed the last refuge of such ignorance, then I must blush to have visited the place — being, as I already was, aware of its inferiority to Rome in more than one respect —"

Here Cipolla was interrupted by the youth with the Nubian coiffure and his jacket across his shoulder. His fighting spirit, as we now saw, had only abdicated temporarily, and he now flung himself into the breach in defence of his native heath. "That will do," said he loudly. "That's enough jokes about Torre. We all come from the place and we won't stand strangers making fun of it. These two chaps are our friends. Maybe they are no scholars, but even so they may be straighter than some folks in the room who are so free with their boasts about Rome, though they did not build it either."

That was capital. The young man had certainly cut his eye-teeth. And this sort of spectacle was good fun, even though it still further delayed the regular performance. It is always fascinating to listen to an altercation. Some people it simply amuses, they take a sort of kill-joy pleasure in not being principals. Others feel upset and uneasy, and my sympathies are with these latter, although on the present occasion I was under the impression that all this was part of the show — the analphabetic yokels no less than the *giovanotto* with the jacket. The children listened well pleased. They understood not at all, but the sound of the voices made them hold their breath. So this was a "magic evening" — at least it was the kind they have in Italy. They expressly found it "lovely."

Cipolla had stood up and with two of his scooping strides was at the footlights.

"Well, well, see who's here!" said he with grim cordiality. "An old acquaintance! A young man with his heart at the end of his tongue" (he used the word *linguaccia,* which means a coated tongue, and gave rise to much hilarity). "That will do, my friends," he turned to the yokels. "I do not need you now, I have business with this deserving young man here, *con questo torregiano di Venere,* this tower of Venus, who no doubt expects the gratitude of the fair as a reward for his prowess —"

"*Ah, non scherziamo!*[18] We're talking earnest," cried out the youth. His eyes flashed, and he actually made as though to pull off his jacket and proceed to direct methods of settlement.

Cipolla did not take him too seriously. We had exchanged apprehensive glances; but he was dealing with a fellow-countryman and had his native soil beneath his feet. He kept quite cool and showed complete mastery of the situation. He looked at his audience, smiled, and made a sideways motion of the head towards the young cockerel as though calling the public to witness how the man's bumptiousness only served to betray the simplicity of his mind. And then, for the second time, something strange happened, which set Cipolla's calm superiority in an uncanny light, and in some mysterious and irritating way turned all the explosiveness latent in the air into matter for laughter.

Cipolla drew still nearer to the fellow, looking him in the eye with a peculiar gaze. He even came half-way down the steps that led into the auditorium on our left, so that he stood directly in front of the trouble-maker, on slightly higher ground. The riding-whip hung from his arm.

"My son, you do not feel much like joking," he said. "It is only too natural, for anyone can see that you are not feeling too well. Even your tongue, which leaves something to be desired on the score of cleanliness, indicates acute disorder of the gastric system. An evening entertainment is no place for people in your state; you yourself, I can tell, were of several minds whether you would not do better to put on a flannel bandage and go to bed. It was not good judgment to drink so much of that very sour white wine this afternoon. Now you have such a colic you would like to double up with the pain. Go ahead, don't be embarrassed. There is a distinct relief that comes from bending over, in cases of intestinal cramp."

He spoke thus, word for word, with quiet impressiveness and a kind of stern

18 [We're not kidding! — Editors' note.]

sympathy, and his eyes, plunged the while deep in the young man's, seemed to grow very tired and at the same time burning above their enlarged tear-ducts — they were the strangest eyes, you could tell that not manly pride alone was preventing the young adversary from withdrawing his gaze. And presently, indeed, all trace of its former arrogance was gone from the bronzed young face. He looked open-mouthed at the Cavaliere and the open mouth was drawn in a rueful smile.

"Double over," repeated Cipolla. "What else can you do? With a colic like that you *must* bend. Surely you will not struggle against the performance of a perfectly natural action just because somebody suggests it to you?"

Slowly the youth lifted his forearms, folded and squeezed them across his body; it turned a little sideways, then bent, lower and lower, the feet shifted, the knees turned inward, until he had become a picture of writhing pain, until he all but grovelled upon the ground. Cipolla let him stand for some seconds thus, then made a short cut through the air with his whip and went with his scooping stride back to the little table, where he poured himself out a cognac.

"Il boit beaucoup,"[19] asserted a lády behind us. Was that the only thing that struck her? We could not tell how far the audience grasped the situation. The fellow was standing upright again, with a sheepish grin — he looked as though he scarcely knew how it had all happened. The scene had been followed with tense interest and applauded at the end; there were shouts of *"Bravo, Cipolla!"* and *"Bravo, giovanotto!"* Apparently the issue of the duel was not looked upon as a personal defeat for the young man. Rather the audience encouraged him as one does an actor who succeeds in an unsympathetic rôle. Certainly his way of screwing himself up with cramp had been highly picturesque, its appeal was directly calculated to impress the gallery — in short, a fine dramatic performance. But I am not sure how far the audience were moved by that natural tactfulness in which the south excels, or how far it penetrated into the nature of what was going on.

The Cavaliere, refreshed, had lighted another cigarette. The numerical tests might now proceed. A young man was easily found in the back row who was willing to write down on the blackboard the numbers as they were dictated to him. Him too we knew; the whole entertainment had taken on an intimate character through our acquaintance with so many of the actors. This was the man who worked at the greengrocer's in the main street; he had served us several times, with neatness and dispatch. He wielded the chalk with clerkly confidence, while Cipolla descended to our level and walked with his deformed gait through the audience, collecting numbers as they were given, in two, three, and four

19 [He drinks a lot. — Editors' note.]

places, and calling them out to the grocer's assistant, who wrote them down in a column. In all this, everything on both sides was calculated to amuse, with its jokes and its oratorical asides. The artist could not fail to hit on foreigners, who were not ready with their figures, and with them he was elaborately patient and chivalrous, to the great amusement of the natives, whom he reduced to confusion in their turn, by making them translate numbers that were given in English or French. Some people gave dates concerned with great events in Italian history. Cipolla took them up at once and made patriotic comments. Somebody shouted "Number one!" The Cavaliere, incensed at this as at every attempt to make game of him, retorted over his shoulder that he could not take less than two-place figures. Whereupon another joker cried out "Number two!" and was greeted with the applause and laughter which every reference to natural functions is sure to win among southerners.

When fifteen numbers stood in a long straggling row on the board, Cipolla called for a general adding-match. Ready reckoners might add in their heads, but pencil and paper were not forbidden. Cipolla, while the work went on, sat on his chair near the blackboard, smoked and grimaced, with the complacent, pompous air cripples so often have. The five-place addition was soon done. Somebody announced the answer, somebody else confirmed it, a third had arrived at a slightly different result, but the fourth agreed with the first and second. Cipolla got up, tapped some ash from his coat, and lifted the paper at the upper right-hand corner of the board to display the writing. The correct answer, a sum close on a million, stood there; he had written it down beforehand.

Astonishment, and loud applause. The children were overwhelmed. How had he done that, they wanted to know. We told them it was a trick, not easily explainable offhand. In short, the man was a conjuror. This was what a sleight-of-hand evening was like, so now they knew. First the fisherman had cramp, and then the right answer was written down beforehand — it was all simply glorious, and we saw with dismay that despite the hot eyes and the hand of the clock at almost half past ten, it would be very hard to get them away. There would be tears. And yet it was plain that this magician did not "magick" — at least not in the accepted sense, of manual dexterity — and that the entertainment was not at all suitable for children. Again, I do not know, either, what the audience really thought. Obviously there was grave doubt whether its answers had been given of "free choice"; here and there an individual might have answered of his own motion, but on the whole Cipolla certainly selected his people and thus kept the whole procedure in his own hands and directed it towards the given result. Even so, one had to admire the quickness of his calculations, however much one felt disinclined to admire anything else about the performance. Then his patriotism, his irritable sense of dignity — the Cavaliere's own countrymen might feel in their element with all that and continue in a laughing mood; but the combination certainly gave us outsiders food for thought.

Cipolla himself saw to it — though without giving them a name — that the nature of his powers should be clear beyond a doubt to even the least-instructed person. He alluded to them, of course, in his talk — and he talked without stopping — but only in vague, boastful, self-advertising phrases. He went on awhile with experiments on the same lines as the first, merely making them more complicated by introducing operations in multiplying, subtracting, and dividing; then he simplified them to the last degree in order to bring out the method. He simply had numbers "guessed" which were previously written under the paper; and the guess was nearly always right. One guesser admitted that he had had in mind to give a certain number, when Cipolla's whip went whistling through the air, and a quite different one slipped out, which proved to be the "right" one. Cipolla's shoulders shook. He pretended admiration for the powers of the people he questioned. But in all his compliments there was something fleering and derogatory; the victims could scarcely have relished them much, although they smiled, and although they might easily have set down some part of the applause to their own credit. Moreover, I had not the impression that the artist was popular with his public. A certain ill will and reluctance were in the air, but courtesy kept such feelings in check, as did Cipolla's competency and his stern self-confidence. Even the riding-whip, I think, did much to keep rebellion from becoming overt.

From tricks with numbers he passed to tricks with cards. There were two packs, which he drew out of his pockets, and so much I still remember, that the basis of the tricks he played with them was as follows: from the first pack he drew three cards and thrust them without looking at them inside his coat. Another person then drew three out of the second pack, and these turned out to be the same as the first three — not invariably all the three, for it did happen that only two were the same. But in the majority of cases Cipolla triumphed, showing his three cards with a little bow in acknowledgment of the applause with which his audience conceded his possession of strange powers — strange whether for good or evil. A young man in the front row, to our right, an Italian, with proud, finely chiselled features, rose up and said that he intended to assert his own will in his choice and consciously to resist any influence, of whatever sort. Under these circumstances, what did Cipolla think would be the result? "You will," answered the Cavaliere, "make my task somewhat more difficult thereby. As for the result, your resistance will not alter it in the least. Freedom exists, and also the will exists; but freedom of the will does not exist, for a will that aims at its own freedom aims at the unknown. You are free to draw or not to draw. But if you draw, you will draw the right cards — the more certainly, the more wilfully obstinate your behaviour."

One must admit that he could not have chosen his words better, to trouble the waters and confuse the mind. The refractory youth hesitated before drawing. Then he pulled out a card and at once demanded to see if it was among the chosen three. "But why?" queried Cipolla. "Why do things by halves?" Then, as the other defiantly insisted, *"E servito,"*[20] said the juggler, with a gesture of exaggerated servility; and held out the three cards fan-wise, without looking at them himself. The left-hand card was the one drawn.

Amid general applause, the apostle of freedom sat down. How far Cipolla employed small tricks and manual dexterity to help out his natural talents, the deuce only knew. But even without them the result would have been the same: the curiosity of the entire audience was unbounded and universal, everybody both enjoyed the amazing character of the entertainment and unanimously conceded the professional skill of the performer. *"Lavora bene,"*[21] we heard, here and there in our neighbourhood; it signified the triumph of objective judgment over antipathy and repressed resentment.

After his last, incomplete, yet so much the more telling success, Cipolla had at once fortified himself with another cognac. Truly he did "drink a lot," and the fact made a bad impression. But obviously he needed the liquor and the cigarettes for the replenishment of his energy, upon which, as he himself said, heavy demands were made in all directions. Certainly in the intervals he looked very ill, exhausted and hollow-eyed. Then the little glassful would redress the balance, and the flow of lively, self-confident chatter run on, while the smoke he inhaled gushed out grey from his lungs. I clearly recall that he passed from the card-tricks to parlour games — the kind based on certain powers which in human nature are higher or else lower than human reason: on intuition and "magnetic" transmission; in short, upon a low type of manifestation. What I do not remember is the precise order things came in. And I will not bore you with a description of these experiments; everybody knows them, everybody has at one time or another taken part in this finding of hidden articles, this blind carrying out of a series of acts, directed by a force that proceeds from organism to organism by unexplored paths. Everybody has had his little glimpse into the equivocal, impure, inexplicable nature of the occult, has been conscious of both curiosity and contempt, has shaken his head over the human tendency of those who deal in it to help themselves out with humbuggery, though, after all, the humbuggery is no disproof whatever of the genuineness of

20 [It's all ready. — Editors' note.]
21 [He does well. — Editors' note.]

the other elements in the dubious amalgam. I can only say here that each single circumstance gains in weight and the whole greatly in impressiveness when it is a man like Cipolla who is the chief actor and guiding spirit in the sinister business. He sat smoking at the rear of the stage, his back to the audience while they conferred. The object passed from hand to hand which it was his task to find, with which he was to perform some action agreed upon beforehand. Then he would start to move zigzag through the hall, with his head thrown back and one hand outstretched, the other clasped in that of a guide who was in the secret but enjoined to keep himself perfectly passive, with his thoughts directed upon the agreed goal. Cipolla moved with the bearing typical in these experiments: now groping upon a false start, now with a quick forward thrust, now pausing as though to listen and by sudden inspiration correcting his course. The rôles seemed reversed, the stream of influence was moving in the contrary direction, as the artist himself pointed out, in his ceaseless flow of discourse. The suffering, receptive, performing part was now his, the will he had before imposed on others was shut out, he acted in obedience to a voiceless common will which was in the air. But he made it perfectly clear that it all came to the same thing. The capacity for self-surrender, he said, for becoming a tool, for the most unconditional and utter self-abnegation, was but the reverse side of that other power to will and to command. Commanding and obeying formed together one single principle, one indissoluble unity; he who knew how to obey knew also how to command, and conversely; the one idea was comprehended in the other, as people and leader were comprehended in one another. But that which was *done,* the highly exacting and exhausting performance, was in every case his, the leader's and mover's, in whom the will became obedience, the obedience will, whose person was the cradle and womb of both, and who thus suffered enormous hardship. Repeatedly he emphasized the fact that his lot was a hard one — presumably to account for his need of stimulant and his frequent recourse to the little glass.

Thus he groped his way forward, like a blind seer, led and sustained by the mysterious common will. He drew a pin set with a stone out of its hiding-place in an Englishwoman's shoe, carried it, halting and pressing on by turns, to another lady — Signora Angiolieri — and handed it to her on bended knee, with the words it had been agreed he was to utter. "I present you with this in token of my respect," was the sentence. Their sense was obvious, but the words themselves not easy to hit upon, for the reason that they had been agreed on in French; the language complication seemed to us a little malicious, implying as it did a conflict between the audience's natural interest in the success of the miracle, and their desire to witness the humiliation of this presumptuous man. It was a strange sight: Cipolla on his knees before the signora, wrestling, amid efforts at speech, after knowledge of the preordained words. "I must say something," he said, "and I feel clearly what it is I must say. But I also feel that if it passed my lips it would be wrong. Be careful not to help me unintentionally!" he cried out, though very likely that was precisely what he was hoping for. "*Pensez très fort,*"[22] he cried all at once, in bad French, and then burst out with the required words — in Italian, indeed, but with the final substantive pronounced in the sister tongue, in which he was probably far from fluent: he said *vénération* instead of *venerazione,* with an impossible nasal. And this partial success, after the complete success before it, the finding of the pin, the presentation of it on his knees to the right person — was almost more impressive than if he had got the sentence exactly right, and evoked bursts of admiring applause.

Cipolla got up from his knees and wiped the perspiration from his brow. You understand that this experiment with the pin was a single case, which I describe because it sticks in my memory. But he changed his method several times and improvised a number of variations suggested by his contact with his audience; a good deal of time thus went by. He seemed to get particular inspiration from the person of our landlady; she drew him on to the most extraordinary displays of clairvoyance. "It does not escape me, madame," he said to her, "that there is something unusual about you, some special and honourable distinction. He who has eyes to see descries about your lovely brow an aureola — if I mistake not, it once was stronger than now — a slowly paling radiance . . . hush, not a word! Don't help me. Beside you sits your husband — yes?" He turned towards the silent Signor Angiolieri. "You are the husband of this lady, and your happiness is complete. But in the midst of this happiness memories rise . . . the past, signora, so it seems to me, plays an important part in your present. You knew a king . . . has not a king crossed your path in bygone days?"

"No," breathed the dispenser of our midday soup, her golden-brown eyes gleaming in the noble pallor of her face.

"No? No, not a king; I meant that generally, I did not mean literally a king. Not a king, not a prince, and a prince after all, a king of a loftier realm; it was a great artist, at whose side you once — you would contradict me, and yet I am not wholly wrong. Well, then! It was a woman, a great, a world-renowned woman artist, whose friendship you enjoyed in your tender years, whose sacred memory overshadows and transfigures your whole existence. Her name? Need I utter it, whose fame has long been bound up with the Fatherland's, immortal as its own? Eleonora Duse," he finished, softly and with much solemnity.

The little woman bowed her head, overcome. The applause was like a patriotic demonstration. Nearly everyone there knew about Signora Angiolieri's

22 [Think very hard. — Editors' note.]

wonderful past; they were all able to confirm the Cavaliere's intuition — not least the present guests of Casa Eleonora. But we wondered how much of the truth he had learned as the result of professional inquiries made on his arrival. Yet I see no reason at all to cast doubt, on rational grounds, upon powers which, before our very eyes, became fatal to their possessor.

At this point there was an intermission. Our lord and master withdrew. Now I confess that almost ever since the beginning of my tale I have looked forward with dread to this moment in it. The thoughts of men are mostly not hard to read; in this case they are very easy. You are sure to ask why we did not choose this moment to go away — and I must continue to owe you an answer. I do not know why. I cannot defend myself. By this time it was certainly eleven, probably later. The children were asleep. The last series of tests had been too long, nature had had her way. They were sleeping in our laps, the little one on mine, the boy on his mother's. That was, in a way, a consolation; but at the same time it was also ground for compassion and a clear leading to take them home to bed. And I give you my word that we wanted to obey this touching admonition, we seriously wanted to. We roused the poor things and told them it was now high time to go. But they were no sooner conscious than they began to resist and implore — you know how horrified children are at the thought of leaving before the end of a thing. No cajoling has any effect, you have to use force. It was so lovely, they wailed. How did we know what was coming next? Surely we could not leave until after the intermission; they liked a little nap now and again — only not go home, only not go to bed, while the beautiful evening was still going on!

We yielded, but only for the moment, of course — so far as we knew — only for a little while, just a few minutes longer. I cannot excuse our staying, scarcely can I even understand it. Did we think, having once said A, we had to say B — having once brought the children hither we had to let them stay? No, it is not good enough. Were we ourselves so highly entertained? Yes, and no. Our feelings for Cavaliere Cipolla were of a very mixed kind, but so were the feelings of the whole audience, if I mistake not, and nobody left. Were we under the sway of a fascination which emanated from this man who took so strange a way to earn his bread; a fascination which he gave out independently of the programme and even between the tricks and which paralysed our resolve? Again, sheer curiosity may account for something. One was curious to know how such an evening turned out; Cipolla in his remarks having all along hinted that he had tricks in his bag stranger than any he had yet produced.

But all that is not it — or at least it is not all of it. More correct it would be to answer the first question with another. Why had we not left Torre di Venere itself before now? To me the two questions are one and the same, and in order to get out of the impasse I might simply say that I had answered it already. For, as things had been in Torre in general: queer, uncomfortable, troublesome, tense, oppressive, so precisely they were here in this hall tonight. Yes, more than precisely. For it seemed to be the fountainhead of all the uncanniness and all the strained feelings which had oppressed the atmosphere of our holiday. This man whose return to the stage we were awaiting was the personification of all that; and, as we had not gone away in general, so to speak, it would have been inconsistent to do it in the particular case. You may call this an explanation, you may call it inertia, as you see fit. Any argument more to the purpose I simply do not know how to adduce.

Well, there was an interval of ten minutes, which grew into nearly twenty. The children remained awake. They were enchanted by our compliance, and filled the break to their own satisfaction by renewing relations with the popular sphere, with Antonio, Guiscardo, and the canoe man. They put their hands to their mouths and called messages across, appealing to us for the Italian words. "Hope you have a good catch tomorrow, a whole netful!" They called to Mario, Esquisito Mario: *"Mario, una cioccolata e biscotti!"* And this time he heeded and answered with a smile: *"Subito, signorini!"*[23] Later we had reason to recall this kindly, if rather absent and pensive smile.

Thus the interval passed, the gong sounded. The audience, which had scattered in conversation, took their places again, the children sat up straight in their chairs with their hands in their laps. The curtain had not been dropped. Cipolla came forward again, with his dipping stride, and began to introduce the second half of the programme with a lecture.

Let me state once for all that this self-confident cripple was the most powerful hypnotist I have ever seen in my life. It was pretty plain now that he threw dust in the public eye and advertised himself as a prestidigitator on account of police regulations which would have prevented him from making his living by the exercise of his powers. Perhaps this eye-wash is the usual thing in Italy; it may be permitted or even connived at by the authorities. Certainly the man had from the beginning made little concealment of the actual nature of his operations; and this second half of the programme was quite frankly and exclusively devoted to one sort of experiment. While he still practised some rhetorical circumlocutions, the tests themselves were one long series of attacks upon the will-power, the loss or compulsion of volition. Comic, exciting, amazing by turns, by midnight they were still in full swing; we ran the gamut of all the phenomena this natural-unnatural field has to show, from the unimpressive at one end of the scale to the monstrous at the other. The audience laughed and applauded as they

23 [Right away, young people! — Editors' note.]

followed the grotesque details; shook their heads, clapped their knees, fell very frankly under the spell of this stern, self-assured personality. At the same time I saw signs that they were not quite complacent, not quite unconscious of the peculiar ignominy which lay, for the individual and for the general, in Cipolla's triumphs.

Two main features were constant in all the experiments: the liquor glass and the claw-handled riding-whip. The first was always invoked to add fuel to his demoniac fires; without it, apparently, they might have burned out. On this score we might even have felt pity for the man; but the whistle of his scourge, the insulting symbol of his domination, before which we all cowered, drowned out every sensation save a dazed and outbraved submission to his power. Did he then lay claim to our sympathy to boot? I was struck by a remark he made — it suggested no less. At the climax of his experiments, by stroking and breathing upon a certain young man who had offered himself as a subject and already proved himself a particularly susceptible one, he had not only put him into the condition known as deep trance and extended his insensible body by neck and feet across the backs of two chairs, but had actually sat down on the rigid form as on a bench, without making it yield. The sight of this unholy figure in a frock-coat squatted on the stiff body was horrible and incredible; the audience, convinced that the victim of this scientific diversion must be suffering, expressed its sympathy: *"Ah, poveretto!"* Poor soul, poor soul! *"Poor soul!"* Cipolla mocked them, with some bitterness. "Ladies and gentlemen, you are barking up the wrong tree. *Sono io il poveretto.* I am the person who is suffering, I am the one to be pitied." We pocketed the information. Very good. Maybe the experiment was at his expense, maybe it was he who had suffered the cramp when the *giovanotto* over there had made the faces. But appearances were all against it; and one does not feel like saying *poveretto* to a man who is suffering to bring about the humiliation of others.

I have got ahead of my story and lost sight of the sequence of events. To this day my mind is full of the Cavaliere's feats of endurance; only I do not recall them in their order — which does not matter. So much I do know: that the longer and more circumstantial tests, which got the most applause, impressed me less than some of the small ones which passed quickly over. I remember the young man whose body Cipolla converted into a board, only because of the accompanying remarks which I have quoted. An elderly lady in a cane-seated chair was lulled by Cipolla in the delusion that she was on a voyage to India and gave a voluble account of her adventures by land and sea. But I found this phenomenon less impressive than one which followed immediately after the intermission. A tall, well-built, soldierly man was unable to lift his arm, after the hunchback had told him that he could not and given a cut through the air with his whip. I can still see the face of that stately, mustachioed colonel smiling and clenching his teeth as he struggled to regain his lost freedom of action. A staggering performance! He seemed to be exerting his will, and in vain; the trouble, however, was probably simply that he could not will. There was involved here that recoil of the will upon itself which paralyses choice — as our tyrant had previously explained to the Roman gentleman.

Still less can I forget the touching scene, at once comic and horrible, with Signora Angiolieri. The Cavaliere, probably in his first bold survey of the room, had spied out her ethereal lack of resistance to his power. For actually he bewitched her, literally drew her out of her seat, out of her row, and away with him whither he willed. And in order to enhance his effect, he bade Signor Angiolieri call upon his wife by her name, to throw, as it were, all the weight of his existence and his rights in her into the scale, to rouse by the voice of her husband everything in his spouse's soul which could shield her virtue against the evil assaults of magic. And how vain it all was! Cipolla was standing at some distance from the couple, when he made a single cut with his whip through the air. It caused our landlady to shudder violently and turn her face towards him. "Sofronia!" cried Signor Angiolieri — we had not known that Signora Angiolieri's name was Sofronia. And he did well to call, everybody saw that there was no time to lose. His wife kept her face turned in the direction of the diabolical Cavaliere, who with his ten long yellow fingers was making passes at his victim, moving backwards as he did so, step by step. Then Signora Angiolieri, her pale face gleaming, rose up from her seat, turned right round, and began to glide after him. Fatal and forbidding sight! Her face as though moonstruck, stiff-armed, her lovely hands lifted a little at the wrists, the feet as it were together, she seemed to float slowly out of her row and after the tempter. "Call her, sir, keep on calling," prompted the redoubtable man. And Signor Angiolieri, in a weak voice, called: "Sofronia!" Ah, again and again he called; as his wife went further off he even curved one hand round his lips and beckoned with the other as he called. But the poor voice of love and duty echoed unheard, in vain, behind the lost one's back; the signora swayed along, moonstruck, deaf, enslaved; she glided into the middle aisle and down it towards the fingering hunchback, towards the door. We were convinced, we were driven to the conviction, that she would have followed her master, had he so willed it, to the ends of the earth.

"*Accidente!*"[24] cried out Signor Angiolieri, in genuine affright, springing up as the exit was reached. But at the same moment the Cavaliere put aside, as it were, the triumphal crown and broke off. "Enough, signora, I thank you," he

24 [Damn! — Editors' note.]

said, and offered his arm to lead her back to her husband. "Signor," he greeted the latter, "here is your wife. Unharmed, with my compliments, I give her into your hands. Cherish with all the strength of your manhood a treasure which is so wholly yours, and let your zeal be quickened by knowing that there are powers stronger than reason or virtue, and not always so magnanimously ready to relinquish their prey!"

Poor Signor Angiolieri, so quiet, so bald! He did not look as though he would know how to defend his happiness, even against powers much less demoniac than these which were now adding mockery to frightfulness. Solemnly and pompously the Cavaliere retired to the stage, amid applause to which his eloquence gave double strength. It was this particular episode, I feel sure, that set the seal upon his ascendancy. For now he made them dance, yes, literally; and the dancing lent a dissolute, abandoned, topsy-turvy air to the scene, a drunken abdication of the critical spirit which had so long resisted the spell of this man. Yes, he had had to fight to get the upper hand — for instance against the animosity of the young Roman gentleman, whose rebellious spirit threatened to serve others as a rallying-point. But it was precisely upon the importance of example that the Cavaliere was so strong. He had the wit to make his attack at the weakest point and to choose as his first victim that feeble, ecstatic youth whom he had previously made into a board. The master had but to look at him, when this young man would fling himself back as though struck by lightning, place his hands rigidly at his sides, and fall into a state of military somnambulism, in which it was plain to any eye that he was open to the most absurd suggestion that might be made to him. He seemed quite content in his abject state, quite pleased to be relieved of the burden of voluntary choice. Again and again he offered himself as a subject and gloried in the model facility he had in losing consciousness. So now he mounted the platform, and a single cut of the whip was enough to make him dance to the Cavaliere's orders, in a kind of complacent ecstasy, eyes closed, head nodding, lank limbs flying in all directions.

It looked unmistakably like enjoyment, and other recruits were not long in coming forward: two other young men, one humbly and one well dressed, were soon jigging alongside the first. But now the gentleman from Rome bobbed up again, asking defiantly if the Cavaliere would engage to make him dance too, even against his will.

"Even against your will," answered Cipolla, in unforgettable accents. That frightful *"anche se non vuole"* still rings in my ears. The struggle began. After Cipolla had taken another little glass and lighted a fresh cigarette he stationed the Roman at a point in the middle aisle and himself took up a position some distance behind him, making his whip whistle through the air as he gave the order: *"Balla!"*[25] His opponent did not stir. *"Balla!"* repeated the Cavaliere incisively, and snapped his whip. You saw the young man move his neck round in his collar; at the same time one hand lifted slightly at the wrist, one ankle turned outward. But that was all, for the time at least; merely a tendency to twitch, now sternly repressed, now seeming about to get the upper hand. It escaped nobody that here a heroic obstinacy, a fixed resolve to resist, must needs be conquered; we were beholding a gallant effort to strike out and save the honour of the human race. He twitched but danced not; and the struggle was so prolonged that the Cavaliere had to divide his attention between it and the stage, turning now and then to make his riding-whip whistle in the direction of the dancers, as it were to keep them in leash. At the same time he advised the audience that no fatigue was involved in such activities, however long they went on, since it was not the automatons up there who danced, but himself. Then once more his eye would bore itself into the back of the Roman's neck and lay siege to the strength of purpose which defied him.

One saw it waver, that strength of purpose, beneath the repeated summons and whip-crackings. Saw with an objective interest which yet was not quite free from traces of sympathetic emotion — from pity, even from a cruel kind of pleasure. If I understand what was going on, it was the negative character of the young man's fighting position which was his undoing. It is likely that *not* willing is not a practicable state of mind; *not* to want to do something may be in the long run a mental content impossible to subsist on. Between not willing a certain thing and not willing at all — in other words, yielding to another person's will — there may lie too small a space for the idea of freedom to squeeze into. Again, there were the Cavaliere's persuasive words, woven in among the whip-crackings and commands, as he mingled effects that were his own secret with others of a bewilderingly psychological kind. *"Balla!"* said he. "Who wants to torture himself like that? Is forcing yourself your idea of freedom? *Una ballatina!* Why, your arms and legs are aching for it. What a relief to give way to them — there, you are dancing already! That is no struggle any more, it is a pleasure!" And so it was. The jerking and twitching of the refractory youth's limbs had at last got the upper hand; he lifted his arms, then his knees, his joints quite suddenly relaxed, he flung his legs and danced, and amid bursts of applause the Cavaliere led him to join the row of puppets on the stage. Up there we could see his face as he "enjoyed" himself; it was clothed in a broad grin and the eyes were half-shut. In a way, it was consoling to see that he was having a better time than he had had in the hour of his pride.

25 [Dance! — Editors' note.]

His "fall" was, I may say, an epoch. The ice was completely broken, Cipolla's triumph had reached its height. The Circe's wand, that whistling leather whip with the claw handle, held absolute sway. At one time — it must have been well after midnight — not only were there eight or ten persons dancing on the little stage, but in the hall below a varied animation reigned, and a long-toothed Anglo-Saxoness in a pince-nez left her seat of her own motion to perform a tarantella in the centre aisle. Cipolla was lounging in a cane-seated chair at the left of the stage, gulping down the smoke of a cigarette and breathing it impudently out through his bad teeth. He tapped his foot and shrugged his shoulders, looking down upon the abandoned scene in the hall; now and then he snapped his whip backwards at a laggard upon the stage. The children were awake at the moment. With shame I speak of them. For it was not good to be here, least of all for them; that we had not taken them away can only be explained by saying that we had caught the general devil-may-careness of the hour. By that time it was all one. Anyhow, thank goodness, they lacked understanding for the disreputable side of the entertainment, and in their innocence were perpetually charmed by the unheard-of indulgence which permitted them to be present at such a thing as a magician's "evening." Whole quarter-hours at a time they drowsed on our laps, waking refreshed and rosy-cheeked, with sleep-drunken eyes, to laugh to bursting at the leaps and jumps the magician made those people up there make. They had not thought it would be so jolly; they joined with their clumsy little hands in every round of applause. And jumped for joy upon their chairs, as was their wont, when Cipolla beckoned to their friend Mario from the Esquisito, beckoned to him just like a picture in a book, holding his hand in front of his nose and bending and straightening the forefinger by turns.

Mario obeyed. I can see him now going up the stairs to Cipolla, who continued to beckon him, in that droll, picture-book sort of way. He hesitated for a moment at first; that, too, I recall quite clearly. During the whole evening he had lounged against a wooden pillar at the side entrance, with his arms folded, or else with his hands thrust into his jacket pockets. He was on our left, near the youth with the militant hair, and had followed the performance attentively, so far as we had seen, if with no particular animation and God knows how much comprehension. He could not much relish being summoned thus, at the end of the evening. But it was only too easy to see why he obeyed. After all, obedience was his calling in life; and then, how should a simple lad like him find it within his human capacity to refuse compliance to a man so throned and crowned as Cipolla at that hour? Willy-nilly he left his column and with a word of thanks to those making way for him he mounted the steps with a doubtful smile on his full lips.

Picture a thickset youth of twenty years, with clipt hair, a low forehead, and heavy-lidded eyes of an indefinite grey, shot with green and yellow. These things I knew from having spoken with him, as we often had. There was a saddle of freckles on the flat nose, the whole upper half of the face retreated behind the lower, and that again was dominated by thick lips that parted to show the salivated teeth. These thick lips and the veiled look of the eyes lent the whole face a primitive melancholy — it was that which had drawn us to him from the first. In it was not the faintest trace of brutality — indeed, his hands would have given the lie to such an idea, being unusually slender and delicate even for a southerner. They were hands by which one liked being served.

We knew him humanly without knowing him personally, if I may make that distinction. We saw him nearly every day, and felt a certain kindness for his dreamy ways, which might at times be actual inattentiveness, suddenly transformed into a redeeming zeal to serve. His mien was serious, only the children could bring a smile to his face. It was not sulky, but uningratiating, without intentional effort to please — or, rather, it seemed to give up being pleasant in the conviction that it could not succeed. We should have remembered Mario in any case, as one of those homely recollections of travel which often stick in the mind better than more important ones. But of his circumstances we knew no more than that his father was a petty clerk in the Municipio and his mother took in washing.

His white waiter's-coat became him better than the faded striped suit he wore, with a gay coloured scarf instead of a collar, the ends tucked into his jacket. He neared Cipolla, who however did not leave off that motion of his finger before his nose, so that Mario had to come still closer, right up to the chair-seat and the master's legs. Whereupon the latter spread out his elbows and seized the lad, turning him so that we had a view of his face. Then gazed him briskly up and down, with a careless, commanding eye.

"Well, *ragazzo mio,*[26] how comes it we make acquaintance so late in the day? But believe me, I made yours long ago. Yes, yes, I've had you in my eye this long while and known what good stuff you were made of. How could I go and forget you again? Well, I've had a good deal to think about. . . . Now tell me, what is your name? The first name, that's all I want."

"My name is Mario," the young man answered, in a low voice.

"Ah, Mario. Very good. Yes, yes, there is such a name, quite a common name, a classic name too, one of those which preserve the heroic traditions of the Fatherland. *Bravo! Salve!*" And he flung up his arm slantingly above his crooked shoulder, palm outward, in the Roman salute. He may have been

26 [My boy. — Editors' note.]

slightly tipsy by now, and no wonder; but he spoke as before, clearly, fluently, and with emphasis. Though about this time there had crept into his voice a gross, autocratic note, and a kind of arrogance was in his sprawl.

"Well, now, Mario *mio*," he went on, "it's a good thing you came this evening, and that's a pretty scarf you've got on; it is becoming to your style of beauty. It must stand you in good stead with the girls, the pretty pretty girls of Torre — "

From the row of youths, close by the place where Mario had been standing, sounded a laugh. It came from the youth with the militant hair. He stood there, his jacket over his shoulder, and laughed outright, rudely and scornfully.

Mario gave a start. I think it was a shrug, but he may have started and then hastened to cover the movement by shrugging his shoulders, as much as to say that the neckerchief and the fair sex were matters of equal indifference to him.

The Cavaliere gave a downward glance.

"We needn't trouble about him," he said. "He is jealous, because your scarf is so popular with the girls, maybe partly because you and I are so friendly up here. Perhaps he'd like me to put him in mind of his colic — I could do it free of charge. Tell me, Mario. You've come here this evening for a bit of fun — and in the daytime you work in an ironmonger's shop?"

"In a café," corrected the youth.

"Oh, in a café. That's where Cipolla nearly came a cropper! What you are is a cup-bearer, a Ganymede — I like that, it is another classical allusion — *Salvietta!*"[27] Again the Cavaliere saluted, to the huge gratification of his audience.

Mario smiled too. "But before that," he interpolated, in the interest of accuracy, "I worked for a while in a shop in Portoclemente." He seemed visited by a natural desire to assist the prophecy by dredging out its essential features.

"There, didn't I say so? In an ironmonger's shop?"

"They kept combs and brushes," Mario got round it.

"Didn't I say that you were not always a Ganymede? Not always at the sign of the serviette? Even when Cipolla makes a mistake, it is a kind that makes you believe in him. Now tell me: Do you believe in me?"

An indefinite gesture.

"A half-way answer," commented the Cavaliere. "Probably it is not easy to win your confidence. Even for me, I can see, it is not so easy. I see in your features a reserve, a sadness, *un tratto di malinconia*[28] . . . tell me" (he seized Mario's hand persuasively) "have you troubles?"

"*Nossignore,*"[29] answered Mario, promptly and decidedly.

27 [Napkin! — Editors' note.]
28 [A bit of melancholy. — Editors' note.]
29 [No, sir. — Editors' note.]

"You *have* troubles," insisted the Cavaliere, bearing down the denial by the weight of his authority. "Can't I see? Trying to pull the wool over Cipolla's eyes, are you? Of course, about the girls — it is a girl, isn't it? You have love troubles?"

Mario gave a vigorous head-shake. And again the *giovanotto*'s brutal laugh rang out. The Cavalicre gave heed. His eyes were roving about somewhere in the air; but he cocked an ear to the sound, then swung his whip backwards, as he had once or twice before in his conversation with Mario, that none of his puppets might flag in their zeal. The gesture had nearly cost him his new prey: Mario gave a sudden start in the direction of the steps. But Cipolla had him in his clutch.

"Not so fast," said he. "That would be fine, wouldn't it? So you want to skip, do you, Ganymede, right in the middle of the fun, or, rather, when it is just beginning? Stay with me, I'll show you something nice. I'll convince you. You have no reason to worry, I promise you. This girl — you know her and others know her too — what's her name? Wait! I read the name in your eyes, it is on the tip of my tongue and yours too — "

"Silvestra!" shouted the *giovanotto* from below.

The Cavaliere's face did not change.

"Aren't there the forward people?" he asked, not looking down, more as in undisturbed converse with Mario. "Aren't there the young fighting-cocks that crow in season and out? Takes the word out of your mouth, the conceited fool, and seems to think he has some special right to it. Let him be. But Silvestra, your Silvestra — ah, what a girl that is! What a prize! Brings your heart into your mouth to see her walk or laugh or breathe, she is so lovely. And her round arms when she washes, and tosses her head back to get the hair out of her eyes! An angel from paradise!"

Mario stared at him, his head thrust forward. He seemed to have forgotten the audience, forgotten where he was. The red rings round his eyes had got larger, they looked as though they were painted on. His thick lips parted.

"And she makes you suffer, this angel," went on Cipolla, "or, rather, you make yourself suffer for her — there is a difference, my lad, a most important difference, let me tell you. There are misunderstandings in love, maybe nowhere else in the world are there so many. I know what you are thinking: what does this Cipolla, with his little physical defect, know about love? Wrong, all wrong, he knows a lot. He has a wide and powerful understanding of its workings, and it pays to listen to his advice. But let's leave Cipolla out, cut him out altogether and think only of Silvestra, your peerless Silvestra! What! Is she to give any young gamecock the preference, so that he can laugh while you cry? To prefer him to a chap like you, so full of feeling and so sympathetic? Not very likely, is it? It is impossible — we know better, Cipolla and she. If I were to put myself in her place and choose between the two of you, a tarry lout like that — a codfish, a sea-urchin — and a Mario, a knight of the serviette, who moves among gentlefolk and hands round refreshments with an air — my word, but my heart would speak in no uncertain tones — it knows to whom I gave it long ago. It is time that he should see and understand, my chosen one! It is time that you see me and recognize me, Mario, my beloved! Tell me, who am I?"

It was grisly, the way the betrayer made himself irresistible, wreathed and coquetted with his crooked shoulder, languished with the puffy eyes, and showed his splintered teeth in a sickly smile. And alas, at his beguiling words, what was come of our Mario? It is hard for me to tell, hard as it was for me to see; for here was nothing less than an utter abandonment of the inmost soul, a public exposure of timid and deluded passion and rapture. He put his hands across his mouth, his shoulders rose and fell with his pantings. He could not, it was plain, trust his eyes and ears for joy, and the one thing he forgot was precisely that he could not trust them. "Silvestra!" he breathed, from the very depths of his vanquished heart.

"Kiss me!" said the hunchback. "Trust me, I love thee. Kiss me here." And with the tip of his index finger, hand, arm, and little finger outspread, he pointed to his cheek, near the mouth. And Mario bent and kissed him.

It had grown very still in the room. That was a monstrous moment, grotesque and thrilling, the moment of Mario's bliss. In that evil span of time, crowded with a sense of the illusiveness of all joy, one sound became audible, and that not quite at once, but on the instant of the melancholy and ribald meeting between Mario's lips and the repulsive flesh which thrust itself forward for his caress. It was the sound of a laugh, from the *giovanotto* on our left. It broke into the dramatic suspense of the moment, coarse, mocking, and yet — or I must have been grossly mistaken — with an undertone of compassion for the poor bewildered, victimized creature. It had a faint ring of that "*Poveretto*" which Cipolla had declared was wasted on the wrong person, when he claimed the pity for his own.

The laugh still rang in the air when the recipient of the caress gave his whip a little swish, low down, close to his chair-leg, and Mario started up and flung himself back. He stood in that posture staring, his hands one over the other on those desecrated lips. Then he beat his temples with his clenched fists, over and over; turned and staggered down the steps, while the audience applauded, and Cipolla sat there with his hands in his lap, his shoulders shaking. Once below, and even while in full retreat, Mario hurled himself round with legs flung wide apart; one arm flew up, and two flat shattering detonations crashed through applause and laughter.

There was instant silence. Even the dancers came to a full stop and stared about, struck dumb. Cipolla bounded from his seat. He stood with his arms spread out, slanting as though to ward everybody off, as though next moment he would cry out: "Stop! Keep back! Silence! What was that?" Then, in that instant, he sank back in his seat, his head rolling on his chest; in the next he had fallen sideways to the floor, where he lay motionless, a huddled heap of clothing, with limbs awry.

The commotion was indescribable. Ladies hid their faces, shuddering, on the breasts of their escorts. There were shouts for a doctor, for the police. People flung themselves on Mario in a mob, to disarm him, to take away the weapon that hung from his fingers — that small, dull-metal, scarcely pistol-shaped tool with hardly any barrel — in how strange and unexpected a direction had fate levelled it!

And now — now finally, at last — we took the children and led them towards the exit, past the pair of *carabinieri*[30] just entering. Was that the end, they wanted to know, that they might go in peace? Yes, we assured them, that was the end. An end of horror, a fatal end. And yet a liberation — for I could not, and I cannot, but find it so!

AFTERWORD

Johann Wolfgang von Goethe, in a conversation in 1827, tossed off a definition of a literary form, the *Novelle*, that he himself had employed and that Germans have been especially adept at and fond of. The *Novelle*, he said, is "the narration of an extraordinary event that has taken place" (*eine ereignete unerhörte Begebenheit*). Goethe's apparent suggestion that the event must really have occurred is perhaps odd, for how can a reader necessarily know whether or not a given story really took place? But perhaps Goethe meant (in accordance with most German theories of the *Novelle*) that the story must be set in a world that seems real rather than in a world that is evidently fanciful. In any case, that the story of a *Novelle* be *unerhört* — extraordinary, unheard of — is generally regarded as essential. And since in a fanciful world the extraordinary is not unusual, we come back to the idea that the story must seem rooted in our world and at the same time must suggest the strange possibilities of this world. And so the *Novelle* has something of the quality of an anecdote — the narration of an interesting happening. Although a *Novelle* is much longer than an anecdote (it can be classified as a kind of short novel), it preserves the anecdote's concentration on a single

30 [Policemen. — Editors' note.]

unusual happening, especially a happening with an unexpected twist. Mann's first paragraph, with its reference to "the shocking business of Cipolla" and "the horrible end of the affair" makes it pretty clear to the reader that he is beginning a *Novelle*.

Interestingly enough, the idea for *Mario and the Magician* came to Mann from a real event. In a letter to a friend he says that "the 'magician' existed and behaved exactly as I have described. Only the lethal outcome is invented. In reality, after the kiss Mario ran away in foolish embarrassment and next day, when he waited on us at tea again, was extremely well pleased with himself and full of matter-of-fact appreciation for 'Cipolla's' work. . . . Not even the shots are my own invention. Back here, when I described the evening, my eldest daughter said: 'I wouldn't have been surprised if he had shot him down.' It was only from this moment that the experience became a novella."

Mann, then, took a real experience but altered it to make a work of art. This work of art is, first of all, an entertaining story. It entertains partly because its subject matter is interesting (not merely a strange magician, hypnosis, and death, but psychological probings and political implications) but partly too because this subject matter is skillfully narrated. The first paragraph immediately arouses our keen interest by its mysterious references to an "unpleasant" memory, a "fateful" experience, "the shocking business of Cipolla," "the horrible end of the affair," and the "tragedy." The first quarter of the story, describing the atmosphere at Torre di Venere, narrates numerous little disturbing episodes and is permeated by the narrator's sense of discomfort and his feeling that his persistence in tolerating this discomfort remains mysterious even to him. He ends a paragraph, "Ought we not at this point to have left Torre . . . ?" The next paragraph (by that white space between the end of one paragraph and the beginning of the next, the storyteller has held us in suspense by a second of pregnant silence) begins, "If only we had!" Suspense is generated, too, by the title, for in the early part of the story Mario is mentioned only briefly ("that very Mario of whom I shall have presently to tell"), and yet we know from the title that he must play an important role and so we are kept on edge. These few examples are enough to suggest what every reader of the story knows — that Mann tells his extraordinary tale extraordinarily well. (By the way, we should not fail to note that part of the telling of the tale is the revelation of the narrator's personality. He is cultivated, sensitive, and given to irony: when the magician asks if the proprietor of the boarding house had not been associated with "a king," the narrator reports, " 'No,' breathed the dispenser of our midday soup, her golden-brown eyes gleaming in the noble pallor of her face." But for all his irony and the poise that this irony suggests, he is disconcerted by the mysterious tale he narrates.)

The story, like any good story however distressing, is entertaining, and we know from his letters and essays that Mann considered an artist as an entertainer.

(That the magician Cipolla is an entertainer and therefore a symbol of the artist — a man who manipulates emotions — is a topic that deserves consideration.) He added, however, that "what counts is how high one carries the entertainment: the higher it goes, the more absorbing the story becomes." In an essay on Chekhov, Mann suggests that there is a connection between the esthetic and the ethical, and that Chekhov's increasing mastery of form was connected with his deepening ethical perceptions. And so Mann says in this essay (he is of course thinking of himself as well as of Chekhov), "One goes on working, telling stories, giving form to truth, hoping darkly, sometimes almost confidently, that truth and serene form will avail to set free the human spirit and prepare mankind for a better, lovelier, worthier life." We are not surprised, then, to find that although Mann considered himself an entertainer and must have considered *Mario and the Magician* an entertaining story, he also considered it (he tells us in the preface to his *Stories of Three Decades*) "a tale with moral and political implications." The "political implications," on the most obvious level, are evident in the references to renewed Italian patriotism stimulated by Mussolini and in the brief reference to Il Duce himself; the story is certainly in part about a particular national state of mind at a particular time, and the introductory portion of the story is of course related to the Cipolla episode by its description of incipient fascist behavior. And if the magician Cipolla is an entertainer and therefore in part symbolic of an artist, he is also in part symbolic of the politician, whose job is to persuade people to accept his politics. But the story is "about" early fascist Italy in only a very limited sense, because for Mann, and for any thoughtful person, politics is a part of ethics, and the story, though set in a particular country and period, goes on to study principles of human behavior, especially involving the imposition of one person's will on others.

Beyond (or, rather, within) the entertaining tale (a strange happening), and the political implications (a sketch of the state of mind of early Fascist Italy) is a study of the nature of the human will and its possibilities for freedom. The narrator tells us, quite simply, that the evening with Cipolla was "one long series of attacks upon the will power." We are continually shown Cipolla's energy, his aggressiveness, and his arrogance, and we are continually told of his whip that seems to force people to perform his will. Cipolla himself explicitly discusses the question of freedom of will: "Freedom exists, and also the will exists; but freedom of the will does not exist, for a will that aims at its own freedom aims at the unknown." Later the narrator offers a somewhat different opinion but one that also calls into question our usually easy assumption that the will is free and that's that. Commenting on the heroic but unsuccessful effort of the Roman to resist Cipolla's will, the narrator says: "It is likely that *not* willing is not a practicable state of mind; *not* to want to do something may be in the long run a mental content impossible to subsist on."

This question of the freedom of the will, then, is explicitly discussed, and it is also dramatized, as it were, in the events narrated. We notice, among other things, that if at times Cipolla seems to impose his will on others, they at times impose theirs on him, "but he made it perfectly clear that it all came to the same thing. The capacity for self-surrender, he said, for becoming a tool, for the most unconditional and utter self-abnegation, was but the reverse side of that other power to will and to command." We notice, too, that Cipolla picks his victims carefully. To one man he says, "I've had my eye on you for some time. People like you are just in my line. I can use them." Inevitably we ask ourselves, Exactly what quality in people is Cipolla looking for? and (another question) For what does he use these people? Perhaps part of the answer to the first question is that he looks for people who in fact *wish* to surrender their will. Of one entranced man the narrator comments, "He seemed quite content in his abject state, quite pleased to be relieved of the burden of voluntary choice." In a sense, then, what seems to *happen to* this man is really *done by* him; Cipolla provides him with the opportunity to do what he really wishes to do — to surrender. (Mann discusses this relationship between "happening" and "doing" in an essay, "Freud and the Future," in *Essays of Three Decades*, where he begins with the point that although in our dreams things seem to happen to us, really "each of us is the secret theatre-manager of our own dreams.") And so in *Mario and the Magician*, although the narrator says that "Cipolla made us wait for him," it is evident too that for some mysterious reason the spectators want to wait for Cipolla; what is happening to them is something they themselves are doing. This, of course, is not the whole of the matter, as is indicated, for example, by the narrator's discussion of one heroic man's "gallant effort to strike out and save the honour of the human race." But this gallant effort is unsuccessful; if there is any effort that saves the honor of the human race it is Mario's, and his success is ambiguous because although he brings "a liberation" (so the narrator says), the last we hear of him is that he is set upon by a mob. Still, it is suggested that resistance to the tyrannical will — whether that will imposes itself on others or allows others to express their inmost desires for submission — can effectively come not from the conscious efforts of willful people but from a primitive sense of dignity that is somehow related to love. For apparently it is love that the deformed Cipolla craves, and Mario's bestowal of a kiss is to be Cipolla's final achievement. But in his quest for love Cipolla so deeply violates humanity, seeking to compel what can only be freely bestowed, that Mario, the least demanding, the least willful, of men and therefore perhaps in closest contact with something finally more elemental and more powerful than will, is the instrument of liberation and the savior of the honor of the human race.

WILLIAM FAULKNER

William Faulkner (1897–1962) was born in New Albany, Mississippi, and for the greater part of his life continued to live in the South, mainly in Oxford, Mississippi. Without having completed high school, he joined the Canadian Air Force during World War I and was eventually wounded in action in France. After the war he returned to Oxford, enrolled in the University of Mississippi there, but soon left it to do odd jobs around the town, to farm, and to write. He drifted to New Orleans, where he became friends with Sherwood Anderson, on to New York, and to Europe, where he spent a year touring on foot. He began to publish poems, short stories, and novels, and for a short period he worked as a scriptwriter in Hollywood. His most notable novels, centering for the most part on the mythical Yoknapatawpha County, include *The Sound and the Fury* (1929), *As I Lay Dying* (1929), *Light in August* (1932), *Absalom, Absalom!* (1936), *The Wild Palms* — which includes *Old Man* in chapters alternating with the title story (1939) — and *The Hamlet* (1940). *The Collected Stories of William Faulkner* (three volumes) was published in 1950. In the same year he won the Nobel Prize for Literature, and in 1955 the Pulitzer Prize. He died in Charlottesville, Virginia, where he lived after being Writer-in-Residence at the University of Virginia in 1957–58.

OLD MAN

I

Once (it was in Mississippi, in May, in the flood year 1927) there were two convicts. One of them was about twenty-five, tall, lean, flat-stomached, with a sunburned face and Indian-black hair and pale, china-colored outraged eyes — an outrage directed not at the men who had foiled his crime, not even at the lawyers and judges who had sent him here, but at the writers, the uncorporeal names attached to the stories, the paper novels — the Diamond Dicks and Jesse James and such — whom he believed had led him into his present predicament through their own ignorance and gullibility regarding the medium in which they dealt and took money for, in accepting information on which they placed the stamp of verisimilitude and authenticity (this so much the more criminal since there was no sworn notarized statement attached and hence so much the quicker would the information be accepted by one who expected the same unspoken good faith, demanding, asking, expecting no certification, which he extended along with the dime or fifteen cents to pay for it) and retailed for money and which on actual application proved to be impractical and (to the convict) criminally false; there would be times when he would halt his mule and plow in midfurrow (there is no walled penitentiary in Mississippi; it is a cotton plantation which the convicts work under the rifles and shotguns of guards and trusties) and muse with a kind of enraged impotence, fumbling among the rubbish left him by his one and only experience with courts and law, fumbling until the meaningless and verbose shibboleth took form at last (himself seeking justice at the same blind fount where he had met justice and been hurled back and down): Using the mails to defraud: who felt that he had been defrauded by the third-class mail system not of crass and stupid money which he did not particularly want anyway, but of liberty and honor and pride.

He was in for fifteen years (he had arrived shortly after his nineteenth birthday) for attempted train robbery. He had laid his plans in advance, he had followed his printed (and false) authority to the letter; he had saved the paper-backs for two years, reading and re-reading them, memorizing them, comparing and weighing story and method against story and method, taking the good from each and discarding the dross as his workable plan emerged, keeping his mind open to make the subtle last-minute changes, without haste and without impatience, as the newer pamphlets appeared on their appointed days as a conscientious dressmaker makes the subtle alterations in a court presentation costume as the newer bulletins appear. And then when the day came, he did not even have a chance to go through the coaches and collect the watches and the rings, the brooches and the hidden money-belts, because he had been captured as soon as he entered the express car where the safe and the gold would be. He had shot no one because the pistol which they took away from him was not that kind of a pistol although it was loaded; later he admitted to the District Attorney that he had got it, as well as the dark lantern in which a candle burned and the black handkerchief to wear over the face, by peddling among his pinehill neighbors subscriptions to the *Detectives' Gazette*. So now from time to time (he had ample leisure for it) he mused with that raging impotence, because there was something else he could not tell them at the trial, did not know how to tell them. It was not the money he had wanted. It was not riches, not the crass loot; that would have been merely a bangle to wear upon the breast of his pride like the Olympic runner's amateur medal — a symbol, a badge to show that he too was the best at his chosen gambit in the living and fluid world of his time. So that at times as he trod the richly shearing black earth behind his plow or with a hoe thinned the sprouting cotton and corn or lay on his sullen back in his bunk after supper, he cursed in a harsh steady unrepetitive stream, not at the living men who had put him where he was but at what he did not even know were pennames, did not even know were not actual men but merely the designations of shades who had written about shades.

The second convict was short and plump. Almost hairless, he was quite white. He looked like something exposed to light by turning over rotting logs or planks and he too carried (though not in his eyes like the first convict) a sense of burning and impotent outrage. So it did not show on him and hence none knew it was there. But then nobody knew very much about him, including the people who had sent him here. His outrage was directed at no printed word but at the paradoxical fact that he had been forced to come here of his own free choice and will. He had been forced to choose between the Mississippi State penal farm and the Federal Penitentiary at Atlanta, and the fact that he, who resembled a hairless and pallid slug, had chosen the out-of-doors and the sunlight was merely another manifestation of the close-guarded and solitary enigma of his character, as something recognizable roils momentarily into view from beneath stagnant and opaque water, then sinks again. None of his fellow prisoners knew what his crime had been, save that he was in for a hundred and ninety-nine years — this incredible and impossible period of punishment or restraint itself carrying a vicious and fabulous quality which indicated that his reason for being here was such that the very men, the paladins and pillars of justice and equity who had sent him here had during that moment become blind apostles not of mere justice but of all human decency, blind instruments not of equity but of all human outrage and vengeance, acting in a savage personal concert, judge, lawyer and jury, which certainly abrogated justice and possibly even law. Possibly only the Federal and State's Attorneys knew what the crime actually was. There had been a woman in it and a stolen automobile transported across a State line, a filling station robbed and the attendant shot to death. There had been a second man in the car at the time and anyone could have looked once at the convict (as the two attorneys did) and known he would not even have had the synthetic courage of alcohol to pull a trigger on anyone. But he and the woman and the stolen car had been captured while the second man, doubtless the actual murderer, had escaped, so that, brought to bay at last in the State's Attorney's office, harried, dishevelled and snarling, the two grimly implacable and viciously gleeful attorneys in his front and the now raging woman held by two policemen in the anteroom in his rear, he was given his choice. He could be tried in Federal Court under the Mann Act and for the automobile, that is, by electing to pass through the anteroom where the woman raged he could take his chances on the lesser crime in Federal Court, or by accepting a sentence for manslaughter in the State Court he would be permitted to quit the room by a back entrance, without having to pass the woman. He had chosen; he stood at the bar and heard a judge (who looked down at him as if the District Attorney actually had turned over a rotten plank with his toe and exposed him) sentence him to a hundred and ninety-nine years at the State Farm. Thus (he had ample leisure too; they had tried to teach him to plow and had failed, they had put him in the blacksmith shop and the foreman trusty himself had asked to have him removed: so that now, in a long apron like a woman, he cooked and swept and dusted in the deputy wardens' barracks) he too mused at times with that sense of impotence and outrage though it did not show on him as on the first convict since he leaned on no halted broom to do it and so none knew it was there.

It was this second convict who, toward the end of April, began to read aloud to the others from the daily newspapers when, chained ankle to ankle and herded by armed guards, they had come up from the fields and had eaten supper and were gathered in the bunkhouse. It was the Memphis newspaper which the deputy wardens had read at breakfast; the convict read aloud from it to his companions who could have had but little active interest in the outside world, some of whom could not have read it for themselves at all and did not even know where the Ohio and Missouri river basins were, some of whom had never seen the Mississippi River although for past periods ranging from a few days to ten and twenty and thirty years (and for future periods ranging from a few months to life) they had plowed and planted and eaten and slept beneath the shadow of the levee itself, knowing only that there was water beyond it from hearsay and because now and then they heard the whistles of steamboats from beyond it and, during the last week or so had seen the stacks and pilot houses moving along the sky sixty feet above their heads.

But they listened, and soon even those who like the taller convict had probably never before seen more water than a horse pond would hold knew what thirty feet on a river gauge at Cairo or Memphis meant and could (and did) talk glibly of sandboils. Perhaps what actually moved them were the accounts of the conscripted levee gangs, mixed blacks and whites working in double shifts against the steadily rising water; stories of men, even though they were Negroes, being forced like themselves to do work for which they received no other pay than coarse food and a place in a mudfloored tent to sleep on — stories, pictures, which emerged from the shorter convict's reading voice; the mudsplashed white men with the inevitable shotguns, the antlike lines of Negroes carrying sandbags, slipping and crawling up the steep face of the revetment to hurl their futile ammunition into the face of a flood and return for more. Or perhaps it was more than this. Perhaps they watched the approach of the disaster with that same amazed and incredulous hope of the slaves — the lions and bears and elephants, the grooms and bathmen and pastrycooks — who watched the mounting flames of Rome from Ahenobarbus' gardens. But listen they did and presently it was May and the wardens' newspaper began to talk in headlines two inches tall — those black staccato slashes of ink which, it would almost seem, even the illiterate should be able to read: *Crest Passes Memphis at Midnight 4000 Homeless in White River Basin Governor Calls out National Guard Martial Law Declared in Following Counties Red Cross Train with President Hoover Leaves Washington Tonight;* then, three evenings later (It had been raining all day — not the vivid brief thunderous downpours of April and May, but the slow steady gray rain of November and December before a cold north wind. The men had not gone to the fields at all during the day, and the very second-hand optimism of the almost twenty-four-hour-old news seemed to contain its own refutation.): *Crest Now Below Memphis 22,000 Refugees Safe at Vicksburg Army Engineers Say Levees Will Hold.*

"I reckon that means it will bust tonight," one convict said.

"Well, maybe this rain will hold on until the water gets here," a second said. They all agreed to this because what they meant, the living unspoken thought among them, was that if the weather cleared, even though the levees broke and the flood moved in upon the Farm itself, they would have to return to the fields and work, which they would have had to do. There was nothing paradoxical in this, although they could not have expressed the reason for it which they instinctively perceived: that the land they farmed and the substance they produced from it belonged neither to them who worked it nor to those who forced them at guns' point to do so, that as far as either — convicts or guards — were concerned, it could have been pebbles they put into the ground and papier-mâché cotton- and corn-sprouts which they thinned. So it was that, what between the sudden wild hoping and the idle day and the evening's headlines, they were sleeping restlessly beneath the sound of the rain on the tin roof when at midnight the sudden glare of the electric bulbs and the guards' voices waked them and they heard the throbbing of the waiting trucks.

"Turn out of there!" the deputy shouted. He was fully dressed — rubber boots, slicker and shotgun. "The levee went out at Mound's Landing an hour ago. Get up out of it!"

II

When the belated and streaming dawn broke the two convicts, along with twenty others, were in a truck. A trusty drove, two armed guards sat in the cab with him. Inside the high, stall-like topless body the convicts stood, packed like matches in an upright box or like the pencil-shaped ranks of cordite in a shell, shackled by the ankles to a single chain which wove among the motionless feet and swaying legs and a clutter of picks and shovels among which they stood, and was riveted by both ends to the steel body of the truck.

Then and without warning they saw the flood about which the plump convict had been reading for two weeks or more. The road ran south. It was built on a raised levee, known locally as a dump, about eight feet above the flat surrounding land, bordered on both sides by the barrow pits from which the earth of the levee had been excavated. These barrow pits had held water all winter from the fall rains, not to speak of the rain of yesterday, but now they saw that the pit on either side of the road had vanished and instead there lay a flat still sheet of brown water which extended into the fields beyond the pits, ravelled out into long motionless shreds in the bottom of the plow furrows and gleaming faintly in the gray light like the bars of a prone and enormous grating. And then (the truck was moving at good speed) as they watched quietly (they had not been talking much anyway but now they were all silent and quite grave, shifting and craning as one to look soberly off to the west side of the road) the crests of the furrows vanished too and they now looked at a single perfectly flat and motionless steel-colored sheet in which the telephone poles and the straight hedgerows which marked section lines seemed to be fixed and rigid as though set in concrete.

It was perfectly motionless, perfectly flat. It looked, not innocent, but bland. It looked almost demure. It looked as if you could walk on it. It looked so still that they did not realize it possessed motion until they came to the first bridge. There was a ditch under the bridge, a small stream, but ditch and stream were both invisible now, indicated only by the rows of cypress and bramble which marked its course. Here they both saw and heard movement — the slow profound eastward and upstream ("It's running backward," one convict said quietly) set of the still rigid surface, from beneath which came a deep faint subaquean rumble which (though none in the truck could have made the comparison) sounded like a subway train passing far beneath the street and which inferred a terrific and secret speed. It was as if the water itself were in three strata, separate and distinct, the bland and unhurried surface bearing a frothy scum and a miniature flotsam of twigs and screening as though by vicious calculation the rush and fury of the flood itself, and beneath this in turn the original stream, trickle, murmuring along in the opposite direction, following undisturbed and unaware its appointed course and serving its Lilliputian end, like a thread of ants between the rails on which an express train passes, they (the ants) as unaware of the power and fury as if it were a cyclone crossing Saturn.

Now there was water on both sides of the road and now, as if once they had become aware of movement in the water the water seemed to have given over deception and concealment, they seemed to be able to watch it rising up the flanks of the dump; trees which a few miles back had stood on tall trunks above the water now seemed to burst from the surface at the level of the lower branches like decorative shrubs on barbered lawns. The truck passed a Negro cabin. The water was up to the window ledges. A woman clutching two children squatted on the ridgepole, a man and a halfgrown youth, standing waist-deep, were hoisting a squealing pig onto the slanting roof of a barn, on the ridgepole of which sat a row of chickens and a turkey. Near the barn was a haystack on which a cow stood tied by a rope to the center pole and bawling steadily; a yelling Negro boy on a saddleless mule which he flogged steadily, his legs clutching the mule's barrel and his body leaned to the drag of a rope attached to a second mule, approached the haystack, splashing and floundering. The woman on the housetop began to shriek at the passing truck, her voice carrying faint and melodious across the brown water, becoming fainter and fainter as the truck passed and went on, ceasing at last, whether because of distance or because she had stopped screaming those in the truck did not know.

Then the road vanished. There was no perceptible slant to it yet it had slipped abruptly beneath the brown surface with no ripple, no ridgy demarcation, like a flat thin blade slipped obliquely into flesh by a delicate hand, annealed into the water without disturbance, as if it had existed so for years, had been built that way. The truck stopped. The trusty descended from the cab and came back and dragged two shovels from among their feet, the blades clashing against the serpentining of the chain about their ankles. "What is it?" one said. "What are you fixing to do?" The trusty didn't answer. He returned to the cab, from which one of the guards had descended, without his shotgun. He and the trusty, both in hip boots and each carrying a shovel, advanced into the water, gingerly, probing and feeling ahead with the shovel handles. The same convict spoke again. He was a middle-aged man with a wild thatch of iron-gray hair and a slightly mad face. "What the hell are they doing?" he said. Again nobody answered him. The truck moved, on into the water, behind the guard and the trusty, beginning to push ahead of itself a thick slow viscid ridge of chocolate water. Then the gray-haired convict began to scream. "God damn it, unlock the chain!" He began to struggle, thrashing violently about him, striking at the men nearest him until he reached the cab, the roof of which he now hammered on with his fists, screaming. "God damn it, unlock us! Unlock us! Son of a bitch!" he screamed, addressing no one. "They're going to drown us! Unlock the chain!" But for all the answer he got the men within radius of his voice might have been dead. The truck crawled on, the guard and the trusty feeling out the road ahead with the reversed shovels, the second guard at the wheel, the twenty-two convicts packed like sardines into the truck itself. They crossed another bridge — two delicate and paradoxical iron railings slanting out of the water, travelling parallel to it for a distance, then slanting down into it again with an outrageous quality almost significant yet apparently meaningless like something in a dream not quite nightmare. The truck crawled on.

Along toward noon they came to a town, their destination. The streets were paved; now the wheels of the truck made a sound like tearing silk. Moving faster now, the guard and the trusty in the cab again, the truck even had a slight bone in its teeth, its bow-wave spreading beyond the submerged sidewalks and across the adjacent lawns, lapping against the stoops and porches of houses where people stood among piles of furniture. They passed through the business district; a man in hip boots, emerged knee-deep in water from a store, dragging a flat-bottomed skiff containing a steel safe.

At last they reached the railroad. It crossed the street at right angles, cutting the town in two. It was on a dump, a levee, also, eight or ten feet above the town itself; the street ran blankly into it and turned at right angles beside a cotton compress and a loading platform on stilts at the level of a freight car door. On this platform was a khaki army tent and a uniformed National Guard sentry with a rifle and bandolier.

The truck turned and crawled out of the water and up the ramp which cotton wagons used and where trucks and private cars filled with household goods came and unloaded onto the platform. They were unlocked from the chain in the truck and shackled ankle to ankle in pairs they mounted the platform and into an apparently inextricable jumble of beds and trunks, gas and electric stoves, radios and tables and chairs and framed pictures which a chain of Negroes under the eye of an unshaven white man in muddy corduroy and hip boots carried piece by piece into the compress, at the door of which another guardsman stood with his rifle, they (the convicts) not stopping here but herded on by the two guards with their shotguns, into the dim and cavernous building where among the piled heterogeneous furniture the ends of cotton bales and the mirrors on dressers and sideboards gleamed with an identical mute and unreflecting concentration of pallid light.

They passed on through, onto the loading platform where the army tent and the first sentry were. They waited here. Nobody told them for what nor why. While the two guards talked with the sentry before the tent the convicts sat in a line along the edge of the platform like buzzards on a fence, their shackled feet dangling above the brown motionless flood out of which the railroad embankment rose, pristine and intact, in a kind of paradoxical denial and repudiation of change and portent, not talking, just looking quietly across the track to where the other half of the amputated town seemed to float, house shrub and tree, ordered and pageant-like and without motion, upon the limitless liquid plain beneath the thick gray sky.

After a while the other four trucks from the Farm arrived. They came up, bunched closely, radiator to tail light, with their four separate sounds of tearing silk and vanished beyond the compress. Presently the ones on the platform heard the feet, the mute clashing of the shackles, the first truckload emerged from the compress, the second, the third; there were more than a hundred of them now in their bed-ticking overalls and jumpers and fifteen or twenty guards with rifles and shotguns. The first lot rose and they mingled, paired, twinned by their clanking and clashing umbilicals; then it began to rain, a slow steady drizzle like November instead of May. Yet not one of them made any move toward the open door of the compress. They did not even look toward it, with longing or hope or without it. If they thought at all, they doubtless knew that the available space in it would be needed for furniture, even if it were not already filled. Or perhaps they knew that, even if there were room in it, it would not be for them, not that the guards would wish them to get wet but that the guards would not think about getting them out of the rain. So they just stopped talking and with their jumper collars turned up and shackled in braces like dogs at a field trial they stood, immobile, patient, almost ruminant, their backs turned to the rain as sheep and cattle do.

After another while they became aware that the number of soldiers had increased to a dozen or more, warm and dry beneath rubberized ponchos, there was an officer with a pistol at his belt, then and without making any move toward it, they began to smell food and, turning to look, saw an army field kitchen set up just inside the compress door. But they made no move, they waited until they were herded into line, they inched forward, their heads lowered and patient in the rain, and received each a bowl of stew, a mug of coffee, two slices of bread. They ate this in the rain. They did not sit down because the platform was wet, they squatted on their heels as country men do, hunching forward, trying to shield the bowls and mugs into which nevertheless the rain splashed steadily as into miniature ponds and soaked, invisible and soundless, into the bread.

After they had stood on the platform for three hours, a train came for them. Those nearest the edge saw it, watched it — a passenger coach apparently running under its own power and trailing a cloud of smoke from no visible stack, a cloud which did not rise but instead shifted slowly and heavily aside and lay upon the surface of the aqueous earth with a quality at once weightless and completely spent. It came up and stopped, a single old fashioned open-ended wooden car coupled to the nose of a pushing switch engine considerably smaller. They were herded into it, crowding forward to the other end where there was a small cast iron stove. There was no fire in it, nevetheless they crowded about it — the cold and voiceless lump of iron stained with fading tobacco and hovered about by the ghosts of a thousand Sunday excursions to Memphis or Moorhead and return — the peanuts, the bananas, the soiled garments of infants — huddling, shoving for places near it. "Come on, come on," one of the guards shouted. "Sit down, now." At last three of the guards, laying aside their guns, came among them and broke up the huddle, driving them back into seats.

There were not enough seats for all. The others stood in the aisle, they stood braced, they heard the air hiss out of the released brakes, the engine whistled four blasts, the car came into motion with a snapping jerk; the platform, the compress fled violently as the train seemed to transpose from immobility to full speed with that same quality of unreality with which it had appeared, running backward now though with the engine in front where before it had moved forward but with the engine behind.

When the railroad in its turn ran beneath the surface of the water, the convicts did not even know it. They felt the train stop, they heard the engine blow a long blast which wailed away unechoed across the waste, wild and forlorn, and they were not even curious; they sat or stood behind the rain-streaming windows as the train crawled on again, feeling its way as the truck had while the brown water swirled between the trucks and among the spokes of the driving wheels and lapped in cloudy steam against the dragging fire-filled belly of the engine; again it blew four short harsh blasts filled with the wild triumph and defiance yet also with repudiation and even farewell, as if the articulated steel itself knew it did not dare stop and would not be able to return. Two hours later in the twilight they saw through the streaming windows a burning plantation house. Juxtaposed to nowhere and neighbored by nothing it stood, a clear steady pyre-like flame rigidly fleeing its own reflection, burning in the dusk above the watery desolation with a quality paradoxical, outrageous and bizarre.

Sometime after dark the train stopped. The convicts did not know where they were. They did not ask. They would no more have thought of asking where they were than they would have asked why and what for. They couldn't even see, since the car was unlighted and the windows fogged on the outside by rain and on the inside by the engendered heat of the packed bodies. All they could see was a milky and sourceless flick and glare of flashlights. They could hear shouts and commands, then the guards inside the car began to shout; they were herded to their feet and toward the exit, the ankle chains clashing and clanking. They descended into a fierce hissing of steam, through ragged wisps of it blowing past the car. Laid-to alongside the train and resembling a train itself was a thick blunt motor launch to which was attached a string of skiffs and flat boats. There were more soldiers; the flashlights played on the rifle barrels and bandolier buckles and flicked and glinted on the ankle chains of the convicts as they stepped gingerly down into knee-deep water and entered the boats; now car and engine both vanished completely in steam as the crew began dumping the fire from the firebox.

After another hour they began to see lights ahead — a faint wavering row of red pin-pricks extending along the horizon and apparently hanging low in the sky. But it took almost another hour to reach them while the convicts squatted in the skiffs, huddled into the soaked garments (they no longer felt the rain any more at all as separate drops) and watched the lights draw nearer and nearer until at last the crest of the levee defined itself; now they could discern a row of army tents stretching along it and people squatting about the fires, the wavering reflections from which, stretching across the water, revealed an involved mass of other skiffs tied against the flank of the levee which now stood high and dark overhead. Flashlights glared and winked along the base, among the tethered skiffs; the launch, silent now, drifted in.

When they reached the top of the levee they could see the long line of khaki tents, interspersed with fires about which people — men, women and children, Negro and white — crouched or stood among shapeless bales of clothing, their heads turning, their eyeballs glinting in the firelight as they looked quietly at the striped garments and the chains; further down the levee, huddled together too though untethered, was a drove of mules and two or three cows. Then the taller convict became conscious of another sound. He did not begin to hear it all at once, he suddenly became aware that he had been hearing it all the time, a sound so much beyond all his experience and his powers of assimilation that up to this point he had been as oblivious of it as an ant or a flea might be of the sound of the avalanche on which it rides, he had been travelling upon water since early afternoon and for seven years now he had run his plow and harrow and planter within the very shadow of the levee on which he now stood, but this profound deep whisper which came from the further side of it he did not at once recognize. He stopped. The line of convicts behind jolted into him like a line of freight cars stopping, with an iron clashing like cars. "Get on!" a guard shouted.

"What's that?" the convict said. A Negro man squatting before the nearest fire answered him:

"Dat's him. Dat's de Ole Man."

"The old man?" the convict said.

"Get on! Get on up there!" the guard shouted. They went on; they passed another huddle of mules, the eyeballs rolling too, the long morose faces turning into and out of the firelight; they passed them and reached a section of empty tents, the light pup tents of a military campaign, made to hold two men. The guards herded the convicts into them, three brace of shackled men to each tent.

They crawled in on all fours, like dogs into cramped kennels, and settled down. Presently the tent became warm from their bodies. Then they became quiet and then all of them could hear it, they lay listening to the bass whisper deep, strong and powerful. "The old man?" the train-robber convict said.

"Yah," another said. "He don't have to brag."

At dawn the guards waked them by kicking the soles of the projecting feet. Opposite the muddy landing and the huddle of skiffs an army field kitchen was set up, already they could smell the coffee. But the taller convict at least, even though he had had but one meal yesterday and that at noon in the rain, did not move at once toward the food. Instead and for the first time he looked at the River within whose shadow he had spent the last seven years of his life but had never seen before; he stood in quiet and amazed surmise and looked at the rigid steel-colored surface not broken into waves but merely slightly undulant. It stretched from the levee on which he stood, further than he could see — a slowly and heavily roiling chocolate-frothy expanse broken only by a thin line a mile away as fragile in appearance as a single hair, which after a moment he recognized. *It's another levee,* he thought quietly. *That's what we look like from there. That's what I am standing on looks like from there.* He was prodded from the rear; a guard's voice carried forward: "Go on! Go on! You'll have plenty of time to look at that!"

They received the same stew and coffee and bread as the day before; they squatted again with their bowls and mugs as yesterday, though it was not raining yet. During the night an intact wooden barn had floated up. It now lay jammed by the current against the levee while a crowd of Negroes swarmed over it, ripping off the shingles and planks and carrying them up the bank; eating steadily and without haste, the taller convict watched the barn dissolve rapidly down to the very water-line exactly as a dead fly vanished beneath the moiling industry of a swarm of ants.

They finished eating. Then it began to rain again, as upon a signal, while they stood or squatted in their harsh garments which had not dried out during the night but had merely become slightly warmer than the air. Presently they were haled to their feet and told off into two groups, one of which was armed from a stack of mud-clogged picks and shovels nearby, and marched away up the levee. A little later the motor launch with its train of skiffs came up across what was, fifteen feet beneath its keel, probably a cotton field, the skiffs loaded to the gunwales with Negroes and a scattering of white people nursing bundles on their laps. When the engine shut off the faint plinking of a guitar came across the water. The skiffs warped in and unloaded; the convicts watched the men and women and children struggle up the muddy slope, carrying heavy towsacks and bundles wrapped in quilts. The sound of the guitar had not ceased and now the convicts saw him — a young, black, lean-hipped man, the guitar slung by a piece of cotton plow line about his neck. He mounted the levee, still picking it. He carried nothing else, no food, no change of clothes, not even a coat.

The taller convict was so busy watching this that he did not hear the guard until the guard stood directly beside him shouting his name. "Wake up!" the guard shouted. "Can you fellows paddle a boat?"

"Paddle a boat where?" the taller convict said.

"In the water," the guard said. "Where in hell do you think?"

"I ain't going to paddle no boat nowhere out yonder," the tall convict said, jerking his head toward the invisible river beyond the levee behind him.

"No, it's on this side," the guard said. He stooped swiftly and unlocked the chain which joined the tall convict and the plump hairless one. "It's just down the road a piece." He rose. The two convicts followed him down to the boats. "Follow them telephone poles until you come to a filling station. You can tell it, the roof is still above water. It's on a bayou and you can tell the bayou because the tops of the trees are sticking up. Follow the bayou until you come to a cypress snag with a woman in it. Pick her up and then cut straight back west until you come to a cottonhouse with a fellow sitting on the ridgepole —" He turned, looking at the two convicts, who stood perfectly still, looking first at the skiff and then at the water with intense sobriety. "Well? What are you waiting for?"

"I can't row a boat," the plump convict said.

"Then it's high time you learned," the guard said. "Get in."

The tall convict shoved the other forward. "Get in," he said. "That water ain't going to hurt you. Ain't nobody going to make you take a bath."

As, the plump one in the bow and the other in the stern, they shoved away from the levee, they saw other pairs being unshackled and manning the other skiffs. "I wonder how many more of them fellows are seeing this much water for the first time in their lives too," the tall convict said. The other did not answer. He knelt in the bottom of the skiff, pecking gingerly at the water now and then with his paddle. The very shape of his thick soft back seemed to wear that expression of wary and tense concern.

Some time after midnight a rescue boat filled to the guard rail with homeless men and women and children docked at Vicksburg. It was a steamer, shallow of draft; all day long it had poked up and down cypress- and gum-choked bayous and across cottonfields (where at times instead of swimming it waded) gathering its sorry cargo from the tops of houses and barns and even out of trees, and now it warped into that mushroom city of the forlorn and despairing where kerosene flares smoked in the drizzle and hurriedly strung electrics glared upon the bayonets of martial policemen and the red cross brassards and doctors and nurses and canteen-workers. The bluff overhead was almost solid with tents, yet still there were more people than shelter for them; they sat or lay, single and by the whole families, under what shelter they could find or sometimes under the rain itself, in the little death of profound exhaustion while the doctors and the nurses and the soldiers stepped over and around and among them.

Among the first to disembark was one of the penitentiary deputy wardens, followed closely by the plump convict and another white man — a small man with a gaunt unshaven wan face still wearing an expression of incredulous outrage. The deputy warden seemed to know exactly where he wished to go. Followed closely by his two companions he threaded his way swiftly among the piled furniture and the sleeping bodies and stood presently in a fiercely lighted and hastily established temporary office, almost a military post of command in fact, where the Warden of the Penitentiary sat with two army officers wearing majors' leaves. The deputy warden spoke without preamble. "We lost a man," he said. He called the tall convict's name.

"Lost him?" the Warden said.

"Yah. Drowned." Without turning his head he spoke to the plump convict. "Tell him," he said.

"He was the one that said he could row a boat," the plump convict said. "I never. I told him myself —" he indicated the deputy warden with a jerk of his head "— I couldn't. So when we got to the bayou —"

"What's this?" the Warden said.

"The launch brought word in," the deputy warden said. "Woman in a cypress snag on the bayou, then this fellow —" he indicated the third man; the Warden and the two officers looked at the third man "— on a cotton house. Never had room in the launch to pick them up. Go on."

"So we come to where the bayou was," the plump convict continued in a voice perfectly flat, without any inflection whatever. "Then the boat got away from him. I don't know what happened. I was just sitting there because he was so positive he could row a boat. I never saw any current. Just all of a sudden the boat whirled clean around and began to run fast backward like it was hitched to a train and it whirled around again and I happened to look up and there was a limb right over my head and I grabbed it just in time and that boat was snatched out from under me like you'd snatch off a sock and I saw it one time more upside down and that fellow that said he knew all about rowing holding to it with one hand and still holding the paddle in the other —" He ceased. There was no dying fall to his voice, it just ceased and the convict stood looking quietly at a half-full quart of whiskey sitting on the table.

"How do you know he's drowned?" the Warden said to the deputy. "How do you know he didn't just see his chance to escape, and took it?"

"Escape where?" the other said. "The whole Delta's flooded. There's fifteen foot of water for fifty miles, clean back to the hills. And that boat was upside down."

"That fellow's drowned," the plump convict said. "You don't need to worry about him. He's got his pardon; it won't cramp nobody's hand signing it, neither."

"And nobody else saw him?" the Warden said. "What about the woman in the tree?"

"I don't know," the deputy said. "I ain't found her yet. I reckon some other boat picked her up. But this is the fellow on the cotton house."

Again the Warden and the two officers looked at the third man, at the gaunt, unshaven wild face in which an old terror, an old blending of fear and impotence and rage still lingered. "He never came for you?" the Warden said. "You never saw him?"

"Never nobody came for me," the refugee said. He began to tremble though at first he spoke quietly enough. "I set there on that sonabitching cotton house, expecting hit to go any minute. I saw that launch and them boats come up and they never had no room for me. Full of bastard niggers and one of them setting there playing a guitar but there wasn't no room for me. A guitar!" he cried; now he began to scream, trembling, slavering, his face twitching and jerking. "Room for a bastard nigger guitar but not for me —"

"Steady now," the Warden said. "Steady now."

"Give him a drink," one of the officers said. The Warden poured the drink. The deputy handed it to the refugee, who took the glass in both jerking hands and tried to raise it to his mouth. They watched him for perhaps twenty seconds, then the deputy took the glass from him and held it to his lips while he gulped, though even then a thin trickle ran from each corner of his mouth, into the stubble on his chin.

"So we picked him and —" the deputy called the plump convict's name now "— both up just before dark and come on in. But that other fellow is gone."

"Yes," the Warden said. "Well. Here I haven't lost a prisoner in ten years, and now, like this — I'm sending you back to the Farm tomorrow. Have his family notified, and his discharge papers filled out at once."

"All right," the deputy said. "And listen, chief. He wasn't a bad fellow and maybe he never had no business in that boat. Only he did say he could paddle one. Listen. Suppose I write on his discharge, Drowned while trying to save lives in the great flood of nineteen twenty-seven, and send it down for the Governor to sign it. It will be something nice for his folks to have, to hang on the wall when neighbors come in or something. Maybe they will even give his folks a cash bonus because after all they sent him to the Farm to raise cotton, not to fool around in a boat in a flood."

"All right," the Warden said. "I'll see about it. The main thing is to get his name off the books as dead before some politician tries to collect his food allowance."

"All right," the deputy said. He turned and herded his companions out. In the drizzling darkness again he said to the plump convict: "Well, your partner beat you. He's free. He's done served his time out but you've got a right far piece to go yet."

"Yah," the plump convict said. "Free. He can have it."

III

As the short convict had testified, the tall one, when he returned to the surface, still retained what the short one called the paddle. He clung to it, not instinctively against the time when he would be back inside the boat and would need it, because for a time he did not believe he would ever regain the skiff or anything else that would support him, but because he did not have time to think about turning it loose. Things had moved too fast for him. He had not been warned, he had felt the first snatching tug of the current, he had seen the skiff begin to spin and his companion vanish violently upward like in a translation out of Isaiah, then he himself was in the water, struggling against the drag of the paddle which he did not know he still held each time he fought back to the surface and grasped at the spinning skiff which at one instant was ten feet away and the next poised above his head as though about to brain him, until at last he grasped the stern, the drag of his body becoming a rudder to the skiff, the two of them, man and boat and with the paddle perpendicular above them like a jackstaff, vanishing from the view of the short convict (who had vanished from that of the tall one with the same celerity though in a vertical direction) like a tableau snatched offstage intact with violent and incredible speed.

He was now in the channel of a slough, a bayou, in which until today no current had run probably since the old subterranean outrage which had created the country. There was plenty of current in it now though; from his trough behind the stern he seemed to see the trees and sky rushing past with vertiginous speed, looking down at him between the gouts of cold yellow in lugubrious and mournful amazement. But they were fixed and secure in something; he thought of that, he remembered in an instant of despairing rage the firm earth fixed and founded strong and cemented fast and stable forever by the generations of laborious sweat, somewhere beneath him, beyond the reach of his feet, when, and again without warning, the stern of the skiff struck him a stunning blow across the bridge of his nose. The instinct which had caused him to cling to it now caused him to fling the paddle into the boat in order to grasp the gunwale with both hands just as the skiff pivoted and spun away again. With both hands free he now dragged himself over the stern and lay prone on his face, streaming with blood and water and panting, not with exhaustion but with that furious rage which is terror's aftermath.

But he had to get up at once because he believed he had come much faster (and so farther) than he had. So he rose, out of the watery scarlet puddle in which he had lain, streaming, the soaked denim heavy as iron on his limbs, the black hair plastered to his skull, the blood-infused water streaking his jumper, and dragged his forearm gingerly and hurriedly across his lower face and glanced at it then grasped the paddle and began to try to swing the skiff back upstream. It did not even occur to him that he did not know where his companion was, in which tree among all which he had passed or might pass. He did not even speculate on that for the reason that he knew so incontestably that the other was upstream from him, and after his recent experience the mere connotation of the term upstream carried a sense of such violence and force and speed that the conception of it as other than a straight line was something which the intelligence, reason, simply refused to harbor, like the notion of a rifle bullet the width of a cottonfield.

The bow began to swing back upstream. It turned readily, it outpaced the aghast and outraged instant in which he realized it was swinging far too easily, it had swung on over the arc and lay broadside to the current and began again that vicious spinning while he sat, his teeth bared in his bloody streaming face while his spent arms flailed the impotent paddle at the water, that innocent-appearing medium which at one time had held him in iron-like and shifting convolutions like an anaconda yet which now seemed to offer no more resistance to the thrust of his urge and need than so much air, like air; the boat which had threatened him and at last actually struck him in the face with the shocking violence of a mule's hoof now seemed to poise weightless upon it like a thistle bloom, spinning like a wind vane while he flailed at the water and thought of, envisioned, his companion safe, inactive and at ease in the tree with nothing to do but wait, musing with impotent and terrified fury upon that arbitrariness of human affairs which had abrogated to the one the secure tree and to the other the hysterical and unmanageable boat for the very reason that it knew that he alone of the two of them would make any attempt to return and rescue his companion.

The skiff had paid off and now ran with the current again. It seemed again to spring from immobility into incredible speed, and he thought he must already be miles away from where his companion had quitted him, though actually he had merely described a big circle since getting back into the skiff, and the object (a clump of cypress trees choked by floating logs and debris) which the skiff was now about to strike was the same one it had careened into before when the stern had struck him. He didn't know this because he had not yet ever looked higher than the bow of the boat. He didn't look higher now, he just saw that he was going to strike; he seemed to feel run through the very insentient fabric of the skiff a current of eager gleeful vicious incorrigible wilfulness; and he who had never ceased to flail at the bland treacherous water with what he had believed to be the limit of his strength now from somewhere, some ultimate absolute reserve, produced a final measure of endurance, will to endure which adumbrated mere muscle and nerves, continuing to flail the paddle right up to the instant of striking, completing one last reach thrust and recover out of pure desperate reflex, as a man slipping on ice reaches for his hat and money-pocket, as the skiff struck and hurled him once more flat on his face in the bottom of it.

This time he did not get up at once. He lay flat on his face, slightly spread-eagled and in an attitude almost peaceful, a kind of abject meditation. He would have to get up sometime, he knew that, just as all life consists of having to get up sooner or later and then having to lie down again sooner or later after a while. And he was not exactly exhausted and he was not particularly without hope and he did not especially dread getting up. It merely seemed to him that he had accidentally been caught in a situation in which time and environment, not himself, was mesmerized; he was being toyed with by a current of water going nowhere, beneath a day which would wane toward no evening; when it was done with him it would spew him back into the comparatively safe world he had been snatched violently out of and in the meantime it did not much matter just what he did or did not do. So he lay on his face, now not only feeling but hearing the strong quiet rustling of the current on the underside of the planks, for a while longer. Then he raised his head and this time touched his palm gingerly to his face and looked at the blood again, then he sat up onto his heels and leaning over the gunwale he pinched his nostrils between thumb and finger and expelled a gout of blood and was in the act of wiping his fingers on his thigh when a voice slightly above his line of sight said quietly, "It's taken you a while," and he who up to this moment had had neither reason nor time to raise his eyes higher than the bows looked up and saw, sitting in a tree and looking at him, a woman. She was not ten feet away. She sat on the lowest limb of one of the trees holding the jam he had grounded on, in a calico wrapper and an army private's tunic and a sunbonnet, a woman whom he did not even bother to examine since that first startled glance had been ample to reveal to him all the generations of her life and background, who could have been his sister if he had a sister, his wife if he had not entered the penitentiary at an age scarcely out of adolescence and some years younger than that at which even his prolific and monogamous kind married — a woman who sat clutching the trunk of the tree, her stockingless feet in a pair of man's unlaced brogans less than a yard from the water, who was very probably somebody's sister and quite certainly (or certainly should have been) somebody's wife, though this too he had entered the penitentiary too young to have had more than mere theoretical female experience to discover yet. "I thought for a minute you wasn't aiming to come back."

"Come back?"

"After the first time. After you run into this brush pile the first time and got into the boat and went on." He looked about, touching his face tenderly again; it could very well be the same place where the boat had hit him in the face.

"Yah," he said. "I'm here now though."

"Could you maybe get the boat a little closer? I taken a right sharp strain getting up here; maybe I better. . . ." He was not listening; he had just discovered that the paddle was gone; this time when the skiff hurled him forward he had flung the paddle not into it but beyond it. "It's right there in them brush tops," the woman said. "You can get it. Here. Catch a holt of this." It was a grapevine. It had grown up into the tree and the flood had torn the roots loose. She had taken a turn with it about her upper body; she now loosed it and swung it out until he could grasp it. Holding to the end of the vine he warped the skiff around the end of the jam, picking up the paddle, and warped the skiff on beneath the limb and held it and now he watched her move, gather herself heavily and carefully to descend — that heaviness which was not painful but just excruciatingly careful, that profound and almost lethargic awkwardness which added nothing to the sum of that first aghast amazement which had served already for the catafalque of invincible dream since even in durance he had continued (and even with the old avidity, even though they had caused his downfall) to consume the impossible pulp-printed fables carefully censored and as carefully smuggled into the penitentiary; and who to say what Helen, what living Garbo, he had not dreamed of rescuing from what craggy pinnacle or dragoned keep when he and his companion embarked in the skiff. He watched her, he made no further effort to help her beyond holding the skiff savagely steady while she lowered herself from the limb — the entire body, the deformed swell of belly bulging the calico, suspended by its arms, thinking, *And this is what I get. This, out of all the female meat that walks, is what I have to be caught in a runaway boat with.*

"Where's that cottonhouse?" he said.

"Cottonhouse?"

"With that fellow on it. The other one."

"I don't know. It's a right smart of cottonhouses down here. With folks on them too, I reckon." She was examining him. "You're bloody as a hog," she said. "You look like a convict."

"Yah," he snarled. "I feel like I done already been hung. Well, I got to pick up my pardner and then find that cottonhouse." He cast off. That is, he released his hold on the vine. That was all he had to do, for even while the bow of the skiff hung high on the log jam and even while he held it by the vine in the comparatively dead water behind the jam, he felt steadily and constantly the whisper, the strong purring power of the water just one inch beyond the frail planks on which he squatted and which, as soon as he released the vine, took charge of the skiff not with one powerful clutch but in a series of touches light, tentative, and catlike; he realized now that he had entertained a sort of foundationless hope that the added weight might make the skiff more controllable. During the first moment or two he had a wild (and still foundationless) belief that it had; he had got the head upstream and managed to hold it so by terrific exertion continued even after he discovered that they were travelling straight enough but stern-first and continued somehow even after the bow began to wear away and swing: the old irresistible movement which he knew well by now, too well to fight against it, so that he let the bow swing on downstream with the hope of utilizing the skiff's own momentum to bring it through the full circle and so upstream again, the skiff travelling broadside then bow-first then broadside again, diagonally across the channel, toward the other wall of submerged trees; it began to flee beneath him with terrific speed, they were in an eddy but did not know it; he had no time to draw conclusions or even wonder; he crouched, his teeth bared in his blood-caked and swollen face, his lungs bursting, flailing at the water while the trees stooped hugely down at him. The skiff struck, spun, struck again; the woman half lay in the bow, clutching the gunwales, as if she were trying to crouch behind her own pregnancy; he banged now not at the water but at living sapblooded wood with the paddle, his desire now not to go anywhere, reach any destination, but just to keep the skiff from beating itself to fragments against the tree trunks. Then something exploded, this time against the back of his head, and stooping trees and dizzy water, the woman's face and all, fled together and vanished in bright soundless flash and glare.

An hour later the skiff came slowly up an old logging road and so out of the bottom, the forest, and into (or onto) a cottonfield — a gray and limitless desolation now free of turmoil, broken only by a thin line of telephone poles like a wading millipede. The woman was now paddling, steadily and deliberately, with that curious lethargic care, while the convict squatted, his head between his knees, trying to stanch the fresh and apparently inexhaustible flow of blood from his nose with handfuls of water. The woman ceased paddling, the skiff drifted on, slowly, while she looked about. "We're done out," she said.

The convict raised his head and also looked about. "Out where?"

"I thought maybe you might know."

"I don't even know where I used to be. Even if I knowed which way was north, I wouldn't know if that was where I wanted to go." He cupped another handful of water to his face and lowered his hand and regarded the resulting crimson marbling on his palm, not with dejection, not with concern, but with a kind of sardonic and vicious bemusement. The woman watched the back of his head.

"We got to get somewhere."

"Don't I know it? A fellow on a cottonhouse. Another in a tree. And now that thing in your lap."

"It wasn't due yet. Maybe it was having to climb that tree quick yesterday, and having to set in it all night. I'm doing the best I can. But we better get somewhere soon."

"Yah," the convict said. "I thought I wanted to get somewhere too and I ain't had no luck at it. You pick out a place to get to now and we'll try yours. Gimme that oar." The woman passed him the paddle. The boat was a double-ender; he had only to turn around.

"Which way you fixing to go?" the woman said.

"Never mind that. You just keep on holding on." He began to paddle, on across the cottonfield. It began to rain again, though not hard at first. "Yah," he said. "Ask the boat. I been in it since breakfast and I ain't never knowed, where I aimed to go or where I was going either."

That was about one o'clock. Toward the end of the afternoon the skiff (they were in a channel of some sort again, they had been in it for some time; they had got into it before they knew it and too late to get out again, granted there had been any reason to get out, as, to the convict anyway, there was certainly none and the fact that their speed had increased again was reason enough to stay in it) shot out upon a broad expanse of debris-filled water which the convict recognized as a river and, from its size, the Yazoo River though it was little enough he had seen of this country which he had not quitted for so much as one single day in the last seven years of his life. What he did not know was that it was now running backward. So as soon as the drift of the skiff indicated the set of the current, he began to paddle in that direction which he believed to be downstream, where he knew there were towns — Yazoo City, and as a last resort, Vicksburg, if his luck was that bad, if not smaller towns whose names he did not know but where there would be people, houses, something, anything he might reach and surrender his charge to and turn his back on her forever, on all pregnant and female life forever and return to that monastic existence of shotguns and shackles where he would be secure from it. Now, with the imminence of habitations, release from her, he did not even hate her. When he looked upon the swelling and unmanageable body before him it seemed to him that it was not the woman at all but rather a separate demanding threatening inert yet living mass of which both he and she were equally victims; thinking, as he had been for the last three or four hours, of that minute's — nay, second's — aberration of eye or hand which would suffice to precipitate her into the water to be dragged down to death by that senseless millstone which in its turn would not even have to feel agony, he no longer felt any glow of revenge toward her as its custodian, he felt sorry for her as he would for the living timber in a barn which had to be burned to rid itself of vermin.

He paddled on, helping the current, steadily and strongly, with a calculated husbandry of effort, toward what he believed was downstream, towns, people, something to stand upon, while from time to time the woman raised herself to bail the accumulated rain from the skiff. It was raining steadily now though still not hard, still without passion, the sky, the day itself dissolving without grief;

the skiff moved in a nimbus, an aura of gray gauze which merged almost without demarcation with the roiling spittle-frothed debris-choked water. Now the day, the light, definitely began to end and the convict permitted himself an extra notch or two of effort because it suddenly seemed to him that the speed of the skiff had lessened. This was actually the case though the convict did not know it. He merely took it as a phenomenon of the increasing obfuscation, or at most as a result of the long day's continuous effort with no food, complicated by the ebbing and fluxing phases of anxiety and impotent rage at his absolutely gratuitous predicament. So he stepped up his stroke a beat or so, not from alarm but on the contrary, since he too had received that lift from the mere presence of a known stream, a river known by its ineradicable name to generations of men who had been drawn to live beside it as man always has been drawn to dwell beside water, even before he had a name for water and fire, drawn to the living water, the course of his destiny and his actual physical appearance rigidly coerced and postulated by it. So he was not alarmed. He paddled on, upstream without knowing it, unaware that all the water which for forty hours now had been pouring through the levee break to the north was somewhere ahead of him, on its way back to the River.

It was full dark now. That is, night had completely come, the gray dissolving sky had vanished, yet as though in perverse ratio surface visibility had sharpened, as though the light which the rain of the afternoon had washed out of the air had gathered upon the water as the rain itself had done, so that the yellow flood spread on before him now with a quality almost phosphorescent, right up to the instant where vision ceased. The darkness in fact had its advantages; he could now stop seeing the rain. He and his garments had been wet for more than twenty-four hours now so he had long since stopped feeling it, and now that he could no longer see it either it had in a certain sense ceased for him. Also, he now had to make no effort even not to see the swell of his passenger's belly. So he was paddling on, strongly and steadily, not alarmed and not concerned but just exasperated because he had not yet begun to see any reflection on the clouds which would indicate the city or cities which he believed he was approaching but which were actually now miles behind him, when he heard a sound. He did not know what it was because he had never heard it before and he would never be expected to hear such again since it is not given to every man to hear such at all and to none to hear it more than once in his life. And he was not alarmed now either because there was not time, for although the visibility ahead, for all its clarity, did not extend very far, yet in the next instant to the hearing he was also seeing something such as he had never seen before. This was that the sharp line where the phosphorescent water met the darkness was now about ten feet higher than it had been an instant before and that it was curled forward upon itself like a sheet of dough being rolled out for a pudding. It reared, stooping; the crest of it swirled like the mane of a galloping horse and, phosphorescent too, fretted and flickered like fire. And while the woman huddled in the bows, aware or not aware the convict did not know which, he (the convict), his swollen and blood-streaked face gaped in an expression of aghast and incredulous amazement, continued to paddle directly into it. Again he simply had not had time to order his rhythm-hypnotized muscles to cease. He continued to paddle though the skiff had ceased to move forward at all but seemed to be hanging in space while the paddle still reached thrust recovered and reached again; now instead of space the skiff became abruptly surrounded by a welter of fleeing debris — planks, small buildings, the bodies of drowned yet antic animals, entire trees leaping and diving like porpoises above which the skiff seemed to hover in weightless and airy indecision like a bird above a fleeing countryside, undecided where to light or whether to light at all, while the convict squatted in it still going through the motions of paddling, waiting for an opportunity to scream. He never found it. For an instant the skiff seemed to stand erect on its stern and then shoot scrabbling and scrambling up the curling wall of water like a cat, and soared on above the licking crest itself and hung cradled into the high actual air in the limbs of a tree, from which bower of new-leafed boughs and branches the convict, like a bird in its nest and still waiting his chance to scream and still going through the motions of paddling though he no longer even had the paddle now, looked down upon a world turned to furious motion and in incredible retrograde.

Some time about midnight, accompanied by a rolling cannonade of thunder and lightning like a battery going into action, as though some forty hours' constipation of the elements, the firmament itself, were discharging in clapping and glaring salute to the ultimate acquiescence to desperate and furious motion, and still leading its charging welter of dead cows and mules and outhouses and cabins and hencoops, the skiff passed Vicksburg. The convict didn't know it. He wasn't looking high enough above the water; he still squatted, clutching the gunwales and glaring at the yellow turmoil about him out of which entire trees, the sharp gables of houses, the long mournful heads of mules which he fended off with a splintered length of plank snatched from he knew not where in passing (and which seemed to glare reproachfully back at him with sightless eyes, in limber-lipped and incredulous amazement) rolled up and then down again, the skiff now travelling forward now sideways now sternward, sometimes in the water, sometimes riding for yards upon the roofs of houses and trees and even upon the backs of the mules as though even in death they were not to escape that burden-bearing doom with which their eunuch race was cursed. But he didn't see Vicksburg; the skiff, travelling at express speed, was in a seething gut between soaring and dizzy banks with a glare of light above them but he did not see it; he saw the flotsam ahead of him divide violently and begin to climb upon itself, mounting, and he was sucked through the resulting gap too fast to recognize it as the trestling of a railroad bridge; for a horrible moment the skiff seemed to hang in static indecision before the looming flank of a steamboat as though undecided whether to climb over it or dive under it, then a hard icy wind filled with the smell and taste and sense of wet and boundless desolation blew upon him; the skiff made one long bounding lunge as the convict's native state, in a final paroxysm, regurgitated him onto the wild bosom of the Father of Waters.

This is how he told about it seven weeks later, sitting in new bedticking garments, shaved and with his hair cut again, on his bunk in the barracks:

During the next three or four hours after the thunder and lightning had spent itself the skiff ran in pitch streaming darkness upon a roiling expanse which, even if he could have seen, apparently had no boundaries. Wild and invisible, it tossed and heaved about and beneath the boat, ridged with dirty phosphorescent foam and filled with a debris of destruction — objects nameless and enormous and invisible which struck and slashed at the skiff and whirled on. He did not know he was now upon the River. At that time he would have refused to believe it, even if he had known. Yesterday he had known he was in a channel by the regularity of the spacing between the bordering trees. Now, since even by daylight he could have seen no boundaries, the last place under the sun (or the streaming sky rather) he would have suspected himself to be would have been a river; if he had pondered at all about his present whereabouts, about the geography beneath him, he would merely have taken himself to be travelling at dizzy and inexplicable speed above the largest cottonfield in the world; if he who yesterday had known he was in a river, had accepted that fact in good faith and earnest, then had seen that river turn without warning and rush back upon him with furious and deadly intent like a frenzied stallion in a lane — if he had suspected for one second that the wild and limitless expanse on which he now found himself was a river, consciousness would simply have refused; he would have fainted.

When daylight — a gray and ragged dawn filled with driving scud between icy rain-squalls — came and he could see again, he knew he was in no cottonfield. He knew that the wild water on which the skiff tossed and fled flowed above no soil tamely trod by man, behind the straining and surging buttocks of a mule. That was when it occurred to him that its present condition was no phenomenon of a decade, but that the intervening years during which it consented to bear upon its placid and sleepy bosom the frail mechanicals of man's clumsy contriving was the phenomenon and this the norm and the river was now doing what it liked to do, had waited patiently the ten years in order to do, as a mule will work for you ten years for the privilege of kicking you once. And he also learned something else about fear too, something he had even failed to discover on that other occasion when he was really afraid — that three or four seconds of that night in his youth while he looked down the twice-flashing pistol barrel of the terrified mail clerk before the clerk could be persuaded that his (the convict's) pistol would not shoot: that if you just held on long enough a time would come in fear after which it would no longer be agony at all but merely a kind of horrible outrageous itching, as after you have been burned bad.

He did not have to paddle now, he just steered (who had been without food for twenty-four hours now and without any sleep to speak of for fifty) while the skiff sped on across that boiling desolation where he had long since begun to not dare believe he could possibly be where he could not doubt he was, trying with his fragment of splintered plank merely to keep the skiff intact and afloat among the houses and trees and dead animals (the entire towns, stores, residences, parks and farmyards, which leaped and played about him like fish), not trying to reach any destination, just trying to keep the skiff afloat until he did. He wanted so little. He wanted nothing for himself. He just wanted to get rid of the woman, the belly, and he was trying to do that in the right way, not for himself, but for her. He could have put her back into another tree at any time —

"Or you could have jumped out of the boat and let her and it drown," the plump convict said. "Then they could have given you the ten years for escaping and then hung you for the murder and charged the boat to your folks."

"Yah," the tall convict said. — But he had not done that. He wanted to do it the right way, find somebody, anybody he could surrender her to, something solid he could set her down on and then jump back into the river, if that would please anyone. That was all he wanted — just to come to something, anything. That didn't seem like a great deal to ask. And he couldn't do it. He told how the skiff fled on —

"Didn't you pass nobody?" the plump convict said. "No steamboat, nothing?"

"I don't know," the tall one said. — while he tried merely to keep it afloat, until the darkness thinned and lifted and revealed —

"Darkness?" the plump convict said. "I thought you said it was already daylight."

"Yah," the tall one said. He was rolling a cigarette, pouring the tobacco carefully from a new sack, into the creased paper. "This was another one. They had several while I was gone." — the skiff to be moving still rapidly up a winding corridor bordered by drowned trees which the convict recognized again to be a river running again in the direction that, until two days ago, had been upstream. He was not exactly warned through instinct that this one, like that of two days ago, was in reverse. He would not say that he now believed himself to be in the same river, though he would not have been surprised to find that he did believe this, existing now, as he did and had and apparently was to continue for an unnamed period, in a state in which he was toy and pawn on a vicious and inflammable geography. He merely realized that he was in a river again, with all the subsequent inferences of a comprehensible, even if not familiar, portion of the earth's surface. Now he believed that all he had to do would be to paddle far enough and he would come to something horizontal and above water even if not dry and perhaps even populated; and, if fast enough, in time, and that his only other crying urgency was to refrain from looking at the woman who, as vision, the incontrovertible and apparently inescapable presence of his passenger, returned with dawn, had ceased to be a human being and (you could add twenty-four more hours to the first twenty-four and the first fifty now, even counting the hen. It was dead, drowned, caught by one wing under a shingle on a roof which had rolled momentarily up beside the skiff yesterday and he had eaten some of it raw though the woman would not) had become instead one single inert monstrous sentient womb from which, he now believed, if he would only turn his gaze away and keep it away, would disappear, and if he could only keep his gaze from pausing again at the spot it occupied, would not return. That's what he was doing this time when he discovered the wave was coming.

He didn't know how he discovered it was coming back. He heard no sound, it was nothing felt nor seen. He did not even believe that finding the skiff to be now in slack water — that is, that the motion of the current which, whether right or wrong, had at least been horizontal, had now stopped that and assumed a vertical direction — was sufficient to warn him. Perhaps it was just an invincible and almost fanatic faith in the inventiveness and innate viciousness of that medium on which his destiny was now cast, apparently forever; a sudden conviction far beyond either horror or surprise that now was none too soon for it to prepare to do whatever it was it intended doing. So he whirled the skiff, spun it on its heel like a running horse, whereupon, reversed, he could not even distinguish the very channel he had come up. He did not know whether he simply could not see it or if it had vanished some time ago and he not aware at the time; whether the river had become lost in a drowned world or if the world had become drowned in one limitless river. So now he could not tell if he were running directly before the wave or quartering across its line of charge; all he could do was keep that sense of swiftly accumulating ferocity behind him and paddle as fast as his spent and now numb muscles could be driven, and try not to look at the woman, to wrench his gaze from her and keep it away until he reached something flat and above water. So, gaunt, hollow-eyed, striving and wrenching almost physically at his eyes as if they were two of those suction-tipped rubber arrows shot from the toy gun of a child, his spent muscles obeying not will now but that attenuation beyond mere exhaustion which, mesmeric, can continue easier than cease, he once more drove the skiff full tilt into something it could not pass and, once more hurled violently forward onto his hands and knees, crouching, he glared with his wild swollen face up at the man with the shotgun and said in a harsh, croaking voice: "Vicksburg? Where's Vicksburg?"

Even when he tried to tell it, even after the seven weeks and he safe, secure, riveted warranted and doubly guaranteed by the ten years they had added to his sentence for attempted escape, something of the old hysteric incredulous outrage came back into his face, his voice, his speech. He never did even get on the other boat. He told how he clung to a strake (it was a dirty unpainted shanty boat with a drunken rake of tin stove pipe, it had been moving when he struck it and apparently it had not even changed course even though the three people on it must have been watching him all the while — a second man, barefoot and with matted hair and beard also at the steering sweep, and then — he did not know how long — a woman leaning in the door, in a filthy assortment of men's garments, watching him too with the same cold speculation) being dragged violently along, trying to state and explain his simple (and to him at least) reasonable desire and need; telling it, trying to tell it, he could feel again the old unforgettable affronting like an ague fit as he watched the abortive tobacco rain steadily and faintly from between his shaking hands and then the paper itself part with a thin dry snapping report:

"Burn my clothes?" the convict cried. "Burn them?"

"How in hell do you expect to escape in them billboards?" the man with the shotgun said. He (the convict) tried to tell it, tried to explain as he had tried to explain not to the three people on the boat alone but to the entire circumambience — desolate water and forlorn trees and sky — not for justification because he needed none and knew that his hearers, the other convicts, required none from him, but rather as, on the point of exhaustion, he might have picked dreamily and incredulously at a suffocation. He told the man with the gun how he and his partner had been given the boat and told to pick up a man and a woman, how he had lost his partner and failed to find the man, and now all in the world he wanted was something flat to leave the woman on until he could find an officer, a sheriff. He thought of home, the place where he had lived almost since childhood, his friends of years whose ways he knew and who knew his ways, the familiar fields where he did work he had learned to do well and to like, the mules with characters he knew and respected as he knew and respected the characters of certain men; he thought of the barracks at night, with screens against the bugs in summer and good stoves in winter and someone to supply the fuel and the food too; the Sunday ball games and the picture shows — things which, with the exception of the ball games, he had never known before. But most of all, his own character (Two years ago they had offered to make a trusty of him. He would not longer need to plow or feed stock, he would only follow those who did with a loaded gun, but he declined. "I reckon I'll stick to plowing," he said, absolutely without humor. "I done already tried to use a gun one time too many.") his good name, his responsibility not only toward those who were responsible toward him but to himself, his own honor in the doing of what was asked of him, his pride in being able to do it, no matter what it was. He thought of this and listened to the man with the gun talking about escape and it seemed to him that, hanging there, being dragged violently along (it was here he said that he first noticed the goats' beards of moss in the trees, though it could have been there for several days so far as he knew. It just happened that he first noticed it here.) that he would simply burst.

"Can't you get it into your head that the last thing I want to do is run away?" he cried. "You can set there with that gun and watch me; I give you fair lief. All I want is to put this woman —"

"And I told you she could come aboard," the man with the gun said in his level voice. "But there ain't no room on no boat of mine for nobody hunting a sheriff in no kind of clothes, let alone a penitentiary suit."

"When he steps aboard, knock him in the head with the gun barrel," the man at the sweep said. "He's drunk."

"He ain't coming aboard," the man with the gun said. "He's crazy."

Then the woman spoke. She didn't move, leaning in the door, in a pair of faded and patched and filthy overalls like the two men: "Give them some grub and tell them to get out of here." She moved, she crossed the deck and looked down at the convict's companion with her cold sullen face. "How much more time have you got?"

"It wasn't due till next month," the woman in the boat said. "But I —" The woman in overalls turned to the man with the gun.

"Give them some grub," she said. But the man with the gun was still looking down at the woman in the boat.

"Come on," he said to the convict. "Put her aboard, and beat it."

"And what'll happen to you," the woman in overalls said, "when you try to turn her over to an officer. When you lay alongside a sheriff and the sheriff asks you who you are?" Still the man with the gun didn't even look at her. He hardly even shifted the gun across his arm as he struck the woman across the face with the back of his other hand, hard. "You son of a bitch," she said. Still the man with the gun did not even look at her.

"Well?" he said to the convict.

"Don't you see I can't?" the convict cried. "Can't you see that?"

Now, he said, he gave up. He was doomed. That is, he knew now that he had been doomed from the very start never to get rid of her, just as the ones who sent him out with the skiff knew that he never would actually give up; when he recognized one of the objects which the woman in overalls was hurling into the skiff to be a can of condensed milk, he believed it to be a presage, gratuitous and irrevocable as a death-notice over the telegraph, that he was not even to find a flat stationary surface in time for the child to be born on it. So he told how he held the skiff alongside the shanty boat while the first tentative toying of the second wave made up beneath him, while the woman in overalls passed back and forth between house and rail, flinging the food — the hunk of salt meat, the ragged and filthy quilt, the scorched lumps of cold bread which she poured into the skiff from a heaped dishpan like so much garbage — while he clung to the strake against the mounting pull of the current, the new wave which for the moment he had forgotten because he was still trying to state the incredible simplicity of his desire and need until the man with the gun (the only one of the three who wore shoes) began to stamp at his hands, he snatching his hands away one at a time to avoid the heavy shoes, then grasping the rail again until the man with the gun kicked at his face, he flinging himself sideways to avoid the shoe and so breaking his hold on the rail, his weight canting the skiff off at a tangent on the increasing current so that it began to leave the shanty boat behind and he paddling again now, violently, as a man hurries toward the precipice for which he knows at last he is doomed, looking back at the other boat, the three faces sullen derisive and grim and rapidly diminishing across the widening water and at last, apoplectic, suffocating with the intolerable fact not that he had been refused but that he had been refused so little, had wanted so little, asked for so little, yet there had been demanded of him in return the one price out of all breath which (they must have known) if he could have paid it, he would not have been where he was, asking what he asked, raising the paddle and shaking it and screaming curses back at them even after the shotgun flashed and the charge went scuttering past along the water to one side.

So he hung there, he said, shaking the paddle and howling, when suddenly he remembered that other wave, the second wall of water full of houses and dead mules building up behind him back in the swamp. So he quit yelling then and went back to paddling. He was not trying to outrun it. He just knew from experience that when it overtook him, he would have to travel in the same direction it was moving in anyway, whether he wanted to or not, and when it did overtake him, he would begin to move too fast to stop, no matter what places he might come to where he could leave the woman, land her in time. Time: that was his itch now, so his only chance was to stay ahead of it as long as he could and hope to reach something before it struck. So he went on, driving the skiff with muscles which had been too tired so long they had quit feeling it, as when a man has had bad luck for so long that he ceases to believe it is even bad, let alone luck. Even when he ate — the scorched lumps the size of baseballs and the weight and durability of cannel coal even after having lain in the skiff's bilge where the shanty boat woman had thrown them — the iron-like lead-heavy objects which no man would have called bread outside of the crusted and scorched pan in which they had cooked — it was with one hand, begrudging even that from the paddle.

He tried to tell that too — that day while the skiff fled on among the bearded trees while every now and then small quiet tentative exploratory feelers would come up from the wave behind and toy for a moment at the skiff, light and curious, then go on with a faint hissing sighing, almost a chuckling, sound, the skiff going on, driving on with nothing to see but trees and water and solitude: until after a while it no longer seemed to him that he was trying to put space and distance behind him or shorten space and distance ahead but that both he and the wave were now hanging suspended simultaneous and unprogressing in pure time, upon a dreamy desolation in which he paddled on not from any hope even to reach anything at all but merely to keep intact what little of distance the length of the skiff provided between himself and the inert and inescapable mass of female meat before him; then night and the skiff rushing on, fast since any speed over anything unknown and invisible is too fast, with nothing before him and behind him the outrageous idea of a volume of moving water toppling forward, its crest frothed and shredded like fangs, and then dawn again (another of those dreamlike alterations day to dark then back to day again with that quality truncated, anachronic and unreal as the waxing and waning of lights in a theatre scene) and the skiff emerging now with the woman no longer supine beneath the shrunken soaked private's coat but sitting bolt upright, gripping the gunwales with both hands, her eyes closed and her lower lip caught between her teeth and he driving the splintered board furiously now, glaring at her out of his wild swollen sleepless face and crying, croaking, "Hold on! For God's sake hold on!"

"I'm trying to," she said. "But hurry! Hurry!" He told it, the unbelievable: hurry, hasten: the man falling from a cliff being told to catch onto something and save himself; the very telling of it emerging shadowy and burlesque, ludicrous, comic and mad, from the ague of unbearable forgetting with a quality more dreamily furious than any fable behind proscenium lights:

He was in a basin now — "A basin?" the plump convict said. "That's what you wash in."

"All right," the tall one said harshly, above his hands. "I did." With a supreme effort he stilled them long enough to release the two bits of cigarette paper and watched them waft in light fluttering indecision to the floor between his feet, holding his hands motionless even for a moment longer — a basin, a broad peaceful yellow sea which had an abruptly and curiously ordered air, giving him, even at that moment, the impression that it was accustomed to water even if not total submersion; he even remembered the name of it, told to him two or three weeks later by someone: Atchafalaya —

"Louisiana?" the plump convict said. "You mean you were clean out of Mississippi? Hell fire." He stared at the tall one. "Shucks," he said. "That ain't but just across from Vicksburg."

"They never named any Vicksburg across from where I was," the tall one said. "It was Baton Rouge they named." And now he began to talk about a town, a little neat white portrait town nestling among enormous very green trees, appearing suddenly in the telling as it probably appeared in actuality, abrupt and airy and mirage-like and incredibly serene before him behind a scattering of boats moored to a line of freight cars standing flush to the doors in water. And now he tried to tell that too: how he stood waist-deep in water for a moment looking back and down at the skiff in which the woman half lay, her eyes still closed, her knuckles white on the gunwales and a tiny thread of blood creeping down her chin from her chewed lip, and he looking down at her in a kind of furious desperation.

"How far will I have to walk?" she said.

"I don't know, I tell you!" he cried. "But it's land somewhere yonder! It's land, houses."

"If I try to move, it won't even be born inside a boat," she said. "You'll have to get closer."

"Yes," he cried, wild, desperate, incredulous. "Wait. I'll go surrender, then they will have —" He didn't finish, wait to finish; he told that too: himself splashing, stumbling, trying to run, sobbing and grasping; now he saw it — another loading platform standing above the yellow flood, the khaki figures on it as before, identical, the same; he said how the intervening days since that first innocent morning telescoped, vanished as if they had never been, the two contiguous succeeding instants (succeeding? simultaneous) and he transported across no intervening space but merely turned in his own footsteps, plunging, splashing, his arms raised, croaking harshly. He heard the startled shout, "There's one of them!", the command, the clash of equipment, the alarmed cry: "There he goes! There he goes!"

"Yes!" he cried, running, plunging, "here I am! Here! Here!" running on, into the first scattered volley, stopping among the bullets, waving his arms, shrieking, "I want to surrender! I want to surrender!" watching not in terror but in amazed and absolutely unbearable outrage as a squatting clump of the khaki figures parted and he saw the machine gun, the blunt thick muzzle slant and drop and probe toward him and he still screaming in his hoarse crow's voice, "I want to surrender! Can't you hear me?" continuing to scream even as he whirled and plunged splashing, ducking, went completely under and heard the bullets going thuck-thuck-thuck on the water above him and he scrabbling still on the bottom, still trying to scream even before he regained his feet and still all submerged save his plunging unmistakable buttocks, the outraged screaming bubbling from his mouth and about his face since he merely wanted to surrender. Then he was comparatively screened, out of range, though not for long. That is (he didn't tell how nor where) there was a moment in which he paused, breathed for a second before running again, the course back to the skiff open for the time being though he could still hear the shouts behind him and now and then a shot, and he panting, sobbing, a long savage tear in the flesh of one hand, got when and how he did not know, and he wasting precious breath, speaking to no one now any more than the scream of the dying rabbit is addressed to any mortal ear but rather an indictment of all breath and its folly and suffering, its infinite capacity for folly and pain, which seems to be its only immortality: "All in the world I want is just to surrender."

He returned to the skiff and got in and took up his splintered plank. And now when he told this, despite the fury of element which climaxed it, it (the telling) became quite simple; he now even creased another cigarette paper between fingers which did not tremble at all and filled the paper from the tobacco sack without spilling a flake, as though he had passed from the machine-gun's barrage into a bourne beyond any more amazement: so that the subsequent part of his narrative seemed to reach his listeners as though from beyond a sheet of slightly milky though still transparent glass, as something not heard but seen — a series of shadows, edgeless yet distinct, and smoothly flowing, logical and unfrantic and making no sound: They were in the skiff, in the center of the broad placid trough which had no boundaries and down which the tiny forlorn skiff flew to the irresistible coercion of a current going once more he knew not where, the neat small liveoak-bowered towns unattainable and miragelike and apparently attached to nothing upon the airy and unchanging horizon. He did not believe them, they did not matter, he was doomed; they were less than the figments of smoke or of delirium, and he driving his unceasing paddle without destination or even hope now, looking now and then at the woman sitting with her knees drawn up and locked and her entire body one terrific clench while the threads of bloody saliva crept from her teeth-clenched lower lip. He was going nowhere and fleeing from nothing, he merely continued to paddle because he had paddled so long now that he believed if he stopped his muscles would scream in agony. So when it happened he was not surprised. He heard the sound which he knew well (he had heard it but once before, true enough, but no man needed hear it but once) and he had been expecting it; he looked back, still driving the paddle, and saw it, curled, crested with its strawlike flotsam of trees and debris and dead beasts and he glared over his shoulder at it for a full minute out of that attenuation far beyond the point of outragement where even suffering, the capability of being further affronted, had ceased, from which he now contemplated with savage and invulnerable curiosity the further extent to which his now anesthetized nerves could bear, what next could be invented for them to bear, until the wave actually began to rear above his head into its thunderous climax. Then only did he turn his head. His stroke did not falter, it neither slowed nor increased; still paddling with that spent hypnotic steadiness, he saw the swimming deer. He did not know what it was nor that he had altered the skiff's course to follow it, he just watched the swimming head before him as the wave boiled down and the skiff rose bodily in the old familiar fashion on a welter of tossing trees and houses and bridges and fences, he still paddling even while the paddle found no purchase save air and still paddled even as he and the deer shot forward side by side at arm's length, he watching the deer now, watching the deer begin to rise out of the water bodily until it was actually running along upon the surface, rising still, soaring clear of the water altogether, vanishing upward in a dying crescendo of splashings and snapping branches, its damp scut flashing upward, the entire animal vanishing upward as smoke vanishes. And now the skiff struck and canted and he was out of it too, standing knee-deep, springing out and falling to his knees, scrambling up, glaring after the vanished deer. "Land!" he croaked. "Land! Hold on! Just hold on!" He caught the woman beneath the arms, dragging her out of the boat, plunging and panting after the vanished deer. Now earth actually appeared — an acclivity smooth and swift and steep, bizarre, solid and unbelievable; an Indian mound, and he plunging at the muddy slope, slipping back, the woman struggling in his muddy hands.

"Let me down!" she cried. "Let me down!" But he held her, panting, sobbing, and rushed again at the muddy slope; he had almost reached the flat crest with his now violently unmanageable burden when a stick under his foot gathered itself with thick convulsive speed. *It was a snake,* he thought as his feet fled beneath him and with the indubitable last of his strength he half pushed and half flung the woman up the bank as he shot feet first and face down back into that medium upon which he had lived for more days and nights than he could remember and from which he himself had never completely emerged, as if his own failed and spent flesh were attempting to carry out his furious unflagging will for severance at any price, even that of drowning, from the burden with which, unwitting and without choice, he had been doomed. Later it seemed to him that he had carried back beneath the surface with him the sound of the infant's first mewling cry.

IV

When the woman asked him if he had a knife, standing there in the streaming bed-ticking garments which had got him shot at, the second time by a machine gun, on the two occasions when he had seen any human life after leaving the levee four days ago, the convict felt exactly as he had in the fleeing skiff when the woman suggested that they had better hurry. He felt the same outrageous affronting of a condition purely moral, the same raging impotence to find any answer to it; so that, standing above her, spent suffocating and inarticulate, it was a full minute before he comprehended that she was now crying, "The can! The can in the boat!" He did not anticipate what she could want with it; he did not even wonder nor stop to ask. He turned running; this time he thought, *It's another moccasin* as the thick body truncated in that awkward reflex which had nothing of alarm in it but only alertness, he not even shifting his stride though he knew his running foot would fall within a yard of the flat head. The bow of the skiff was well up the slope now where the wave had set it and there was another snake just crawling over the stern into it and as he stooped for the bailing can he saw something else swimming toward the mound, he didn't know what — a head, a face at the apex of a vee of ripples. He snatched up the can; by pure juxtaposition of it and water he scooped it full, already turning. He saw the deer again, or another one. That is, he saw a deer — a side glance, the light smoke-colored phantom in a cypress vista then gone, vanished, he not pausing to look after it, galloping back to the woman and kneeling with the can to her lips until she told him better.

It had contained a pint of beans or tomatoes, something, hermetically sealed and opened by four blows of an axe heel, the metal flap turned back, the jagged edges razor-sharp. She told him how, and he used this in lieu of a knife, he removed one of his shoelaces and cut it in two with the sharp tin. Then she wanted warm water — "If I just had a little hot water," she said in a weak serene voice without particular hope; only when he thought of matches it was again a good deal like when she had asked him if he had a knife, until she fumbled in the pocket of the shrunken tunic (it had a darker double vee on one cuff and a darker blotch on the shoulder where service stripes and a divisional emblem had been ripped off but this meant nothing to him) and produced a match-box contrived by telescoping two shotgun shells. So he drew her back a little from the water and went to hunt wood dry enough to burn, thinking this time, *It's just another snake,* only, he said, he should have thought *ten thousand other snakes:* and now he knew it was not the same deer because he saw three at one time, does or bucks he did not know which since they were all antlerless in May and besides he had never seen one of any kind anywhere before except on a Christmas card; and then the rabbit, drowned, dead anyway, already torn open, the bird, the hawk, standing upon it — the erected crest, the hard, vicious, patrician nose, the intolerant omnivorous yellow eye — and he kicking at it, kicking it lurching and broad-winged into the actual air.

When he returned with the wood and the dead rabbit, the baby, wrapped in the tunic, lay wedged between two cypress-knees and the woman was not in sight, though while the convict knelt in the mud, blowing and nursing his meagre flame, she came slowly and weakly from the direction of the water. Then, the water heated at last and there produced from somewhere he was never to know, she herself perhaps never to know until the need comes, no woman perhaps ever to know, only no woman will even wonder, that square of something somewhere between sackcloth and silk — squatting, his own wet garments steaming in the fire's heat, he watched her bathe the child with a savage curiosity and interest that became amazed unbelief, so that at last he stood above them both, looking down at the tiny terra-cotta colored creature resembling nothing, and thought, *And this is all. This is what severed me violently from all I ever knew and did not wish to leave and cast me upon a medium I was born to fear, to fetch up at last in a place I never saw before and where I do not even know where I am.*

Then he returned to the water and refilled the bailing can. It was drawing toward sunset now (or what would have been sunset save for the high prevailing overcast) of this day whose beginning he could not even remember; when he returned to where the fire burned in the interlaced gloom of the cypresses, even after this short absence, evening had definitely come, as though darkness too had taken refuge upon that quarter-acre mound, that earthen Ark out of Genesis, that dim wet cypress-choked life-teeming constricted desolation in what direction and how far from what and where he had no more idea than of the day of the month, and had now with the setting of the sun crept forth again to spread upon the waters. He stewed the rabbit in sections while the fire burned redder and redder in the darkness where the shy wild eyes of small animals — once the tall mild almost plate-sized stare of one of the deer — glowed and vanished and glowed again, the broth hot and rank after the four days; he seemed to hear the roar of his own saliva as he watched the woman sip the first canful. Then he drank too; they ate the other fragments which had been charring and scorching on willow twigs; it was full night now. "You and him better sleep in the boat," the convict said. "We want to get an early start tomorrow." He shoved the bow of the skiff off the land so it would lie level, he lengthened the painter with a piece of grapevine and returned to the fire and tied the grapevine about his wrist and lay down. It was mud he lay upon, but it was solid underneath, it was earth, it did not move; if you fell upon it you broke your bones against its incontrovertible passivity sometimes but it did not accept you substanceless and enveloping and suffocating, down and down and down; it was hard at times to drive a plow through, it sent you spent, weary, and cursing its light-long insatiable demands back to your bunk at sunset at times but it did not snatch you violently out of all familiar knowing and sweep you thrall and impotent for days against any returning. *I don't know where I am and I don't reckon I know the way back to where I want to go,* he thought. *But at least the boat has stopped long enough to give me a chance to turn it around.*

He waked at dawn, the light faint, the sky jonquil-colored; the day would be fine. The fire had burned out; on the opposite side of the cold ashes lay three snakes motionless and parallel as underscoring, and in the swiftly making light others seemed to materialize: earth which an instant before had been mere earth broke up into motionless coils and loops, branches which a moment before had been mere branches now become immobile ophidian festoons even as the convict stood thinking about food, about something hot before they started. But he decided against this, against wasting this much time, since there still remained in the skiff quite a few of the rocklike objects which the shanty woman had flung into it, besides (thinking this) no matter how fast nor successfully he hunted, he would never be able to lay up enough food to get them back to where they wanted to go. So he returned to the skiff, paying himself back to it by his vine-spliced painter, back to the water on which a low mist thick as cotton batting (though apparently not very tall, deep), lay, into which the stern of the skiff was already beginning to disappear although it lay with its prow almost touching the mound. The woman waked, stirred. "We fixing to start now?" she said.

"Yah," the convict said. "You ain't aiming to have another one this morning, are you?" He got in and shoved the skiff clear of the land, which immediately began to dissolve into the mist. "Hand me the oar," he said over his shoulder, not turning yet.

"The oar?"

He turned his head. "The oar. You're laying on it." But she was not, and for an instant during which the mound, the island continued to fade slowly into the mist which seemed to enclose the skiff in weightless and impalpable wool like a precious or fragile bauble or jewel, the convict squatted not in dismay but in that frantic and astonished outrage of a man who, having just escaped a falling safe, is struck by the following two-ounce paper weight which was sitting on it: this the more unbearable because he knew that never in his life had he less time to give way to it. He did not hesitate. Grasping the grapevine end he sprang into the water, vanishing in the violent action of climbing and reappeared still climbing and (who had never learned to swim) plunged and threshed on toward the almost-vanished mound, moving through the water then upon it as the deer had done yesterday and scrabbled up the muddy slope and lay gasping and panting, still clutching the grapevine end.

Now the first thing he did was to choose what he believed to be the most suitable tree (for an instant in which he knew he was insane he thought of trying to saw it down with the flange of the bailing can) and build a fire against the butt of it. Then he went to seek food. He spent the next six days seeking it while the tree burned through and fell and burned through again at the proper length and he nursing little constant cunning flames along the flanks of the log to make it paddle-shaped, nursing them at night too while the woman and the baby (it was eating, nursing now, he turning his back or even returning into the woods each time she prepared to open the faded tunic) slept in the skiff. He learned to watch for stooping hawks and so found more rabbits and twice possums; they ate some drowned fish which gave them both a rash and then a violent flux and one snake which the woman thought was turtle and which did them no harm, and one night it rained and he got up and dragged brush, shaking the snakes (he no longer thought, *It ain't nothing but another moccasin*, he just stepped aside for them as they, when there was time, telescoped sullenly aside for him) out of it with the older former feeling of personal invulnerability and built a shelter and the rain stopped at once and did not recommence and the woman went back to the skiff.

Then one night — the slow tedious charring log was almost a paddle now — one night and he was in bed, in his bed in the bunkhouse and it was cold, he was trying to pull the covers up only his mule wouldn't let him, prodding and bumping heavily at him, trying to get into the narrow bed with him and now the bed was cold too and wet and he was trying to get out of it only the mule would not let him, holding him by his belt in its teeth, jerking and bumping him back into the cold wet bed and, leaning, gave him a long swipe across the face with its cold limber musculated tongue and he walked to no fire, no coal even beneath where the almost-finished paddle had been charring and something else prolonged and coldly limber passed swiftly across his body where he lay in four inches of water while the nose of the skiff alternately tugged at the grapevine tied about his waist and bumped and shoved him back into the water again. Then something else came up and began to nudge at his ankle (the log, the oar, it was) even as he groped frantically for the skiff, hearing the swift rustling going to and fro inside the hull as the woman began to thrash about and scream. "Rats!" she cried. "It's full of rats!"

"Lay still!" he cried. "It's just snakes. Can't you hold still long enough for me to find the boat?" Then he found it, he got into it with the unfinished paddle; again the thick muscular body convulsed under his foot; it did not strike; he would not have cared, glaring astern where he could see a little — the faint outer luminosity of the open water. He poled toward it, thrusting aside the snake-looped branches, the bottom of the skiff resounding faintly to thick solid plops, the woman shrieking steadily. Then the skiff was clear of the trees, the mound, and now he could feel the bodies whipping about his ankles and hear the rasp of them as they went over the gunwale. He drew the log in and scooped it forward along the bottom of the boat and up and out; against the pallid water he could see three more of them in lashing convolutions before they vanished. "Shut up!" he cried. "Hush! I wish I was a snake so I could get out too!"

When once more the pale and heatless wafer disc of the early sun stared down at the skiff (whether they were moving or not the convict did not know) in its nimbus of fine cotton batting, the convict was hearing again that sound which he had heard twice before and would never forget — that sound of deliberate and irresistible and monstrously disturbed water. But this time he could not tell from what direction it came. It seemed to be everywhere, waxing and fading; it was like a phantom behind the mist, at one instant miles away, the next on the point of overwhelming the skiff within the next second; suddenly, in the instant he would believe (his whole weary body would spring and scream) that he was about to drive the skiff point-blank into it and with the unfinished paddle of the color and texture of sooty bricks, like something gnawed out of an old chimney by beavers and weighing twenty-five pounds, he would whirl the skiff frantically and find the sound dead ahead of him again. Then something bellowed tremendously above his head, he heard human voices, a bell jangled and the sound ceased and the mist vanished as when you draw your hand across a frosted pane, and the skiff now lay upon a sunny glitter of brown water flank to flank with, and about thirty yards away from, a steamboat. The decks were crowded and packed with men and women and children sitting or standing beside and among a homely conglomeration of hurried furniture, who looked mournfully and silently down into the skiff while the convict and the man with a megaphone in the pilot house talked to each other in alternate puny shouts and roars above the chuffing of the reversed engines:

"What in hell are you trying to do? Commit suicide?"

"Which is the way to Vicksburg?"

"Vicksburg? Vicksburg? Lay alongside and come aboard."

"Will you take the boat too?"

"Boat? Boat?" Now the megaphone cursed, the roaring waves of blasphemy and biological supposition empty cavernous and bodiless in turn, as if the water, the air, the mist had spoken it, roaring the words then taking them back to itself and no harm done, no scar, no insult left anywhere. "If I took aboard every floating sardine can you sonabitchin mushrats want me to I wouldn't even have room forrard for a leadsman. Come aboard! Do you expect me to hang here on stern engines till hell freezes?"

"I ain't coming without the boat," the convict said. Now another voice spoke, so calm and mild and sensible that for a moment it sounded more foreign and out of place than even the megaphone's bellowing and bodiless profanity:

"Where is it you are trying to go?"

"I ain't trying," the convict said. "I'm going. Parchman." The man who had spoken last turned and appeared to converse with a third man in the pilot house. Then he looked down at the skiff again.

"Carnarvon?"

"What?" the convict said. "Parchman?"

"All right. We're going that way. We'll put you off where you can get home. Come aboard."

"The boat too?"

"Yes, yes. Come along. We're burning coal just to talk to you." So the convict came alongside then and watched them help the woman and baby over the rail and he came aboard himself, though he still held to the end of the vine-spliced painter until the skiff was hoisted onto the boiler deck. "My God," the man, the gentle one, said, "is that what you have been using for a paddle?"

"Yah," the convict said. "I lost the plank."

"The plank," the mild man (the convict told how he seemed to whisper it), "the plank. Well. Come along and get something to eat. Your boat is all right now."

"I reckon I'll wait here," the convict said. Because now, he told them, he began to notice for the first time that the other people, the other refugees who crowded the deck, who had gathered in a quiet circle about the upturned skiff on which he and the woman sat, the grapevine painter wrapped several times about his wrist and clutched in his hand, staring at him and the woman with queer hot mournful intensity, were not white people —

"You mean niggers?" the plump convict said.

"No. Not Americans."

"Not Americans? You was clean out of *America* even?"

"I don't know," the tall one said. "They called it Atchafalaya." — Because after a while he said, "What?" to the man and the man did it again, gobble-gobble —

"Gobble-gobble?" the plump convict said.

"That's the way they talked," the tall one said. "Gobble-gobble, whang, caw-caw-to-to." — And he sat there and watched them gobbling at one another and then looking at him again, then they fell back and the mild man (he wore a Red Cross brassard) entered, followed by a waiter with a tray of food. The mild man carried two glasses of whiskey.

"Drink this," the mild man said. "This will warm you." The woman took hers and drank it but the convict told how he looked at his and thought, *I ain't tasted whiskey in seven years.* He had not tasted it but once before that; it was at the still itself back in a pine hollow; he was seventeen, he had gone there with four companions, two of whom were grown men, one of twenty-two or -three, the other about forty; he remembered it. That is, he remembered perhaps a third of that evening — a fierce turmoil in the hell-colored firelight, the shock of blows about his head (and likewise of his own fists on other hard bone), then the waking to a splitting and blinding sun in a place, a cowshed, he had never seen before and which later turned out to be twenty miles from his home. He said he thought of this and he looked about at the faces watching him and he said,

"I reckon not."

"Come, come," the mild man said. "Drink it."

"I don't want it."

"Nonsense," the mild man said. "I'm a doctor. Here. Then you can eat." So he took the glass and even then he hesitated but again the mild man said, "Come along, down with it; you're still holding us up," in that voice still calm and sensible but a little sharp too — the voice of a man who could keep calm and affable because he wasn't used to being crossed — and he drank the whiskey and even in the second between the sweet full fire in his belly and when it began to happen he was trying to say, "I tried to tell you! I tried to!" But it was too late now in the pallid sunglare of the tenth day of terror and hopelessness and despair and impotence and rage and outrage and it was himself and the mule, his mule (they had let him name it — John Henry) which no man save he had plowed for five years now and whose ways and habits he knew and respected and who knew his ways and habits so well that each of them could anticipate the other's very movements and intentions; it was himself and the mule, the little gobbling faces flying before them, the familiar hard skullbones shocking against his fists, his voice shouting, "Come on, John Henry! Plow them down! Gobble them down, boy!" even as the bright hot red wave turned back, meeting it joyously, happily, lifted, poised, then hurling through space, triumphant and yelling, then again the old shocking blow at the back of his head: he lay on the deck, flat on his back and pinned arm and leg and cold sober again, his nostrils gushing again, the mild man stooping over him with behind the thin rimless glasses the coldest eyes the convict had ever seen — eyes which the convict said were not looking at him but at the gushing blood with nothing in the world in them but complete impersonal interest.

"Good man," the mild man said. "Plenty of life in the old carcass yet, eh? Plenty of good red blood too. Anyone ever suggest to you that you were hemophilic?" ("What?" the plump convict said. "Hemophilic? You know what that means?" The tall convict had his cigarette going now, his body jackknifed backward into the coffinlike space between the upper and lower bunks, lean, clean, motionless, the blue smoke wreathing across his lean dark aquiline shaven face. "That's a calf that's a bull and a cow at the same time."

"No, it ain't," a third convict said. "It's a calf or a colt that ain't neither one."

"Hell fire," the plump one said. "He's got to be one or the other to keep from drounding." He had never ceased to look at the tall one in the bunk; now he spoke to him again: "You let him call you that?") The tall one had done so. He did not answer the doctor (this was where he stopped thinking of him as the mild man) at all. He could not move either, though he felt fine, he felt better than he had in ten days. So they helped him to his feet and steadied him over and lowered him onto the upturned skiff beside the woman, where he sat bent forward, elbows on knees in the immemorial attitude, watching his own bright crimson staining the mud-trodden deck, until the doctor's clean clipped hand appeared under his nose with a phial.

"Smell," the doctor said. "Deep." The convict inhaled, the sharp ammoniac sensation burned up his nostrils and into his throat. "Again," the doctor said. The convict inhaled obediently. This time he choked and spat a gout of blood, his nose now had no more feeling than a toenail, other than it felt about the size of a ten-inch shovel, and as cold.

"I ask you to excuse me," he said. "I never meant —"

"Why?" the doctor said. "You put up as pretty a scrap against forty or fifty men as I ever saw. You lasted a good two seconds. Now you can eat something. Or do you think that will send you haywire again?"

They both ate, sitting on the skiff, the gobbling faces no longer watching them now, the convict gnawing slowly and painfully at the thick sandwich, hunched, his face laid sideways to the food and parallel to the earth as a dog chews; the steamboat went on. At noon there were bowls of hot soup and bread and more coffee; they ate this, too, sitting side by side on the skiff, the grapevine still wrapped about the convict's wrist. The baby waked and nursed and slept again and they talked quietly:

"Was it Parchman he said he was going to take us?"

"That's where I told him I wanted to go."

"It never sounded exactly like Parchman to me. It sounded like he said something else." The convict had thought that too. He had been thinking about that fairly soberly ever since they boarded the steamboat and soberly indeed ever since he had remarked the nature of the other passengers, those men and women definitely a little shorter than he and with skin a little different in pigmentation from any sunburn, even though the eyes were sometimes blue or gray, who talked to one another in a tongue he had never heard before and who apparently did not understand his own, people the like of whom he had never seen about Parchman nor anywhere else and whom he did not believe were going there or beyond there either. But after his hill-billy country fashion and kind he would not ask, because to his raising asking information was asking a favor and you did not ask favors of strangers; if they offered them perhaps you accepted and you expressed gratitude almost tediously recapitulant, but you did not ask. So he would watch and wait, as he had done before, and do or try to do to the best of his ability what the best of his judgment dictated.

So he waited, and in midafternoon the steamboat chuffed and thrust through a willow-choked gorge and emerged from it, and now the convict knew it was the River. He could believe it now — the tremendous reach, yellow and sleepy in the afternoon — ("Because it's too big," he told them soberly. "Ain't no flood in the world big enough to make it do more than stand a little higher so it can look back and see just where the flea is, just exactly where to scratch. It's the little ones, the little piddling creeks that run backward one day and forward the next and come busting down on a man full of dead mules and hen houses.") — and the steamboat moving up this now (*like a ant crossing a plate,* the convict thought, sitting beside the woman on the upturned skiff, the baby nursing again, apparently looking too out across the water where, a mile away on either hand, the twin lines of levee resembled parallel unbroken floating thread) and then it was nearing sunset and he began to hear, to notice, the voices of the doctor and of the man who had first bawled at him through the megaphone now bawling again from the pilot house overhead:

"Stop? Stop? Am I running a street car?"

"Stop for the novelty then," the doctor's pleasant voice said. "I don't know how many trips back and forth you have made in yonder nor how many of what you call mushrats you have fetched out. But this is the first time you ever had two people — no, three — who not only knew the name of some place they wished to go to but were actually trying to get there." So the convict waited while the sun slanted more and more and the steamboat-ant crawled steadily on across its vacant and gigantic plate turning more and more to copper. But he did not ask, he just waited. *Maybe it was Carrollton he said,* he thought. *It begun with a C.* But he did not believe that either. He did not know where he was, but he did not know that this was not anywhere near the Carrollton he remembered from that day seven years ago when, shackled wrist to wrist with the deputy sheriff, he had passed through it on the train — the slow spaced repeated shattering banging of trucks where two railroads crossed, a random scattering of white houses tranquil among trees on green hills lush with summer, a pointing spire, the finger of the hand of God. But there was no river there. *And you ain't never close to this river without knowing it,* he thought. *I don't care who you are nor where you have been all your life.* Then the head of the steamboat began to swing across the stream, its shadow swinging too, travelling long before it across the water, toward the vacant ridge of willow-massed earth empty of all life. There was nothing there at all, the convict could not even see either earth or water beyond it; it was as though the steamboat were about to crash slowly through the thin low frail willow barrier and embark into space, or lacking this, slow and back and fill and disembark him into space, granted it was about to disembark him, granted this was that place which was not near Parchman and was not Carrollton either, even though it did begin with c. Then he turned his head and saw the doctor stooping over the woman, pushing the baby's eyelid up with his forefinger, peering at it.

"Who else was there when he came?" the doctor said.

"Nobody," the convict said.

"Did it all yourselves, eh?"

"Yes," the convict said. Now the doctor stood up and looked at the convict.

"This is Carnarvon," he said.

"Carnarvon?" the convict said. "That ain't —" Then he stopped, ceased. And now he told about that — the intent eyes as dispassionate as ice behind the rimless glasses, the clipped quick-tempered face that was not accustomed to being crossed or lied to either. ("Yes," the plump convict said. "That's what I was aiming to ask. Them clothes. Anybody would know them. How if this doctor was as smart as you claim he was —"

"I had slept in them for ten nights, mostly in the mud," the tall one said. "I had been rowing since midnight with that sapling oar I had tried to burn out that I never had time to scrape the soot off. But it's being scared and worried and then scared and then worried again in clothes for days and days and days that changes the way they look. I don't mean just your pants." He did not laugh. "Your face too. That doctor knowed."

"All right," the plump one said. "Go on.")

"I know it," the doctor said. "I discovered that while you were lying on the deck yonder sobering up again. Now don't lie to me. I don't like lying. This boat is going to New Orleans."

"No," the convict said immediately, quietly, with absolute finality. He could hear them again — the thuck-thuck-thuck on the water where an instant before he had been. But he was not thinking of the bullets. He had forgotten them, forgiven them. He was thinking of himself crouching, sobbing, panting before running again — the voice, the indictment, the cry of final and irrevocable repudiation of the old primal faithless Manipulator of all the lust and folly and injustice: *All in the world I wanted was just to surrender;* thinking of it, remembering it but without heat now, without passion now and briefer than an epitaph: *No. I tried that once. They shot at me.*

"So you don't want to go to New Orleans. And you didn't exactly plan to go to Carnarvon. But you will take Carnarvon in preference to New Orleans." The convict said nothing. The doctor looked at him, the magnified pupils like the heads of two bridge nails. "What were you in for? Hit him harder than you thought, eh?"

"No. I tried to rob a train."

"Say that again." The convict said it again. "Well? Go on. You don't say that in the year 1927 and just stop, man." So the convict told it, dispassionately too — about the magazines, the pistol which would not shoot, the mask and the dark lantern in which no draft had been arranged to keep the candle burning so that it died almost with the match but even then left the metal too hot to carry, won with subscriptions. *Only it ain't my eyes or my mouth either he's watching,* he thought. *It's like he is watching the way my hair grows on my head.* "I see," the doctor said. "But something went wrong. But you've had plenty of time to think about it since. To decide what was wrong, what you failed to do."

"Yes," the convict said. "I've thought about it a right smart since."

"So next time you are not going to make that mistake."

"I don't know," the convict said. "There ain't going to be a next time."

"Why? If you know what you did wrong, they won't catch you next time."

The convict looked at the doctor steadily. They looked at each other steadily; the two sets of eyes were not so different after all. "I reckon I see what you mean," the convict said presently. "I was eighteen then. I'm twenty-five now."

"Oh," the doctor said. Now (the convict tried to tell it) the doctor did not move, he just simply quit looking at the convict. He produced a pack of cheap cigarettes from his coat. "Smoke?" he said.

"I wouldn't care for none," the convict said.

"Quite," the doctor said in that affable clipped voice. He put the cigarettes away. "There has been conferred upon my race (the Medical race) also the power to bind and to loose, if not by Jehovah perhaps, certainly by the American Medical Association — on which incidentally, in this day of Our Lord, I would put my money, at any odds, at any amount, at any time. I don't know just how far out of bounds I am on this specific occasion but I think we'll put it to the touch." He cupped his hands to his mouth, toward the pilot house overhead. "Captain!" he shouted. "We'll put these three passengers ashore here." He turned to the convict again. "Yes," he said, "I think I shall let your native State lick its own vomit. Here." Again his hand emerged from his pocket, this time with a bill in it.

"No," the convict said.

"Come, come; I don't like to be disputed either."

"No," the convict said. "I ain't got any way to pay it back."

"Did I ask you to pay it back?"

"No," the convict said. "I never asked to borrow it either."

So once more he stood on dry land, who had already been toyed with twice by that risible and concentrated power of water, once more than should have fallen to the lot of any one man, any one lifetime, yet for whom there was reserved still another unbelievable recapitulation, he and the woman standing on the empty levee, the sleeping child wrapped in the faded tunic and the grapevine painter still wrapped about the convict's wrist, watching the steamboat back away and turn and once more crawl onward up the platter-like reach of vacant water burnished more and more to copper, its trailing smoke roiling in slow copper-edged gouts, thinning out along the water, fading, stinking away across the vast serene desolation, the boat growing smaller and smaller until it did not seem to crawl at all but to hang stationary in the airy substanceless sunset, dissolving into nothing like a pellet of floating mud.

Then he turned and for the first time looked about him, behind him, recoiling, not through fear but through pure reflex and not physically but the soul, the spirit, that profound sober alert attentiveness of the hillman who will not ask anything of strangers, not even information, thinking quietly, *No. This ain't Carrollton neither.* Because he now looked down the almost perpendicular landward slope of the levee through sixty feet of absolute space, upon a surface, a terrain flat as a waffle and of the color of a waffle or perhaps of the summer coat of a claybank horse and possessing that same piled density of a rug or peltry, spreading away without undulation yet with that curious appearance of imponderable solidity like fluid, broken here and there by thick humps of arsenical green which nevertheless still seemed to possess no height and by writhen veins of the color of ink which he began to suspect to be actual water but with judgment reserved, with judgment still reserved even when presently he was walking in it. That's what he said, told: So they went on. He didn't tell how he got the skiff single-handed up the revetment and across the crown and down the opposite sixty-foot drop, he just said he went on, in a swirling cloud of mosquitoes like hot cinders, thrusting and plunging through the saw-edged grass which grew taller than his head and which whipped back at his arms and face like limber knives, dragging by the vine-spliced painter the skiff in which the woman sat, slogging and stumbling knee-deep in something less of earth than water, along one of those black winding channels less of water than earth: and then (he was in the skiff too now, paddling with the charred log, what footing there had been having given away beneath him without warning thirty minutes ago, leaving only the air-filled bubble of his jumperback ballooning lightly on the twilit water until he rose to the surface and scrambled into the skiff) the house, the cabin a little larger than a horse-box, of cypress boards and an iron roof, rising on ten-foot stilts slender as spider's legs, like a shabby and death-stricken (and probably poisonous) wading creature which had got that far into that flat waste and died with nothing nowhere in reach or sight to lie down upon, a pirogue tied to the foot of a crude ladder, a man standing in the open door holding a lantern (it was that dark now) above his head, gobbling down at them.

He told it — of the next eight or nine or ten days, he did not remember which, while the four of them — himself and the woman and baby and the little wiry man with rotting teeth and soft wild bright eyes like a rat or a chipmunk, whose language neither of them could understand — lived in the room and a half. He did not tell it that way, just as he apparently did not consider it worth the breath to tell how he had got the hundred-and-sixty-pound skiff single-handed up and across and down the sixty-foot levee. He just said, "After a while we come to a house and we stayed there eight or nine days then they blew up the levee with dynamite so we had to leave." That was all. But he remembered it, but quietly now, with the cigar now, the good one the Warden had given him (though not lighted yet) in his peaceful and steadfast hand, remembering that first morning when he waked on the thin pallet beside his host (the woman and baby had the one bed) with the fierce sun already latticed through the warped rough planking of the wall, and stood on the rickety porch looking out upon that flat fecund waste neither earth nor water, where even the senses doubted which was which, which rich and massy air and which mazy and impalpable vegetation, and thought quietly. *He must do something here to eat and live. But I don't know what. And until I can go on again, until I can find where I am and how to pass that town without them seeing me I will have to help him do it so we can eat and live too, and I don't know what.* And he had a change of clothing too, almost at once on that first morning, not telling any more than he had about the skiff and the levee how he had begged borrowed or bought from the man whom he had not laid eyes on twelve hours ago and with whom on the day he saw him for the last time he still could exchange no word, the pair of dungaree pants which even the Cajan had discarded as no longer wearable, filthy, buttonless, the legs slashed and frayed into fringe like that on an 1890 hammock, in which he stood naked from the waist up and holding out to her the mud-caked and soot-stained jumper and overall when the woman waked on that first morning in the crude bunk nailed into one corner and filled with dried grass, saying, "Wash them. Good. I want all them stains out. All of them."

"But the jumper," she said. "Ain't he got ere old shirt too? That sun and them mosquitoes —" But he did not even answer, and she said no more either, though when he and the Cajan returned at dark the garments were clean, stained a little still with the old mud and soot, but clean, resembling again what they were supposed to resemble as (his arms and back already a fiery red which would be blisters by tomorrow) he spread the garments out and examined them and then rolled them up carefully in a six-months-old New Orleans paper and thrust the bundle behind a rafter, where it remained while day followed day and the blisters on his back broke and suppurated and he would sit with his face expressionless as a wooden mask beneath the sweat while the Cajan doped his back with something on a filthy rag from a filthy saucer, she still saying nothing since she too doubtless knew what his reason was, not from that rapport of the wedded conferred upon her by the two weeks during which they had jointly suffered all the crises emotional social economic and even moral which do not always occur even in the ordinary fifty married years (the old married: you have seen them, the electroplate reproductions, the thousand identical coupled faces with only a collarless stud or a fichu out of Louisa Alcott to denote the sex, looking in pairs like the winning braces of dogs after a field trial, out from among the packed columns of disaster and alarm and baseless assurance and hope and incredible insensitivity and insulation from tomorrow propped by a thousand morning sugar bowls or coffee urns; or singly, rocking on porches or sitting in the sun beneath the tobacco-stained porticoes of a thousand county courthouses, as though with the death of the other having inherited a sort of rejuvenescence, immortality; relict, they take a new lease on breath and seem to live forever, as though that flesh which the old ceremony or ritual had morally purified and made legally one had actually become so with long tedious habit and he or she who entered the ground first took all of it with him or her, leaving only the old permanent enduring bone, free and trammelless) — not because of this but because she too had stemmed at some point from the same dim hill-bred Abraham.

So the bundle remained behind the rafter and day followed day while he and his partner (he was in partnership now with his host, hunting alligators on shares, on the halvers he called it — "Halvers?" the plump convict said. "How could you make a business agreement with a man you claim you couldn't even talk to?"

"I never had to talk to him," the tall one said. "Money ain't got but one language.") departed at dawn each day, at first together in the pirogue but later singly, the one in the pirogue and the other in the skiff, the one with the battered and pitted rifle, the other with the knife and a piece of knotted rope and a lightwood club the size and weight and shape of a Thuringian mace, stalking their pleistocene nightmares up and down the secret inky channels which writhed the flat brass-colored land. He remembered that too: that first morning when turning in the sunrise from the rickety platform he saw the hide nailed drying to the wall and stopped dead, looking at it quietly, thinking quietly and soberly, *So that's it. That's what he does in order to eat and live,* knowing it was a hide, a skin, but from what animal, by association, ratiocination or even memory of any picture out of his dead youth, he did not know but knowing that it was the reason, the explanation, for the little lost spider-legged house (which had already begun to die, to rot from the legs upward almost before the roof was nailed on) set in that teeming and myriad desolation, enclosed and lost within the furious embrace of flowing mare earth and stallion sun, divining through pure rapport of kind for kind, hill-billy and bayou-rat the two one and identical because of the same grudged dispensation and niggard fate of hard and unceasing travail not to gain future security, a balance in the bank or even in a buried soda can for slothful and easy old age, but just permission to endure and endure to buy air to feel and sun to drink for each's little while, thinking (the convict), *Well, anyway I am going to find out what it is sooner than I expected to,* and did so, re-entered the house where the woman was just waking in the one sorry built-in straw-filled bunk which the Cajan had surrendered to her, and ate the breakfast (the rice, a semi-liquid mess violent with pepper and mostly fish considerably high, the chicory-thickened coffee) and, shirtless, followed the little scuttling bobbing bright-eyed rotten-toothed man down the crude ladder and into the pirogue. He had never seen a pirogue either and he believed that it would not remain upright — not that it was light and precariously balanced with its open side upward but that there was inherent in the wood, the very log, some dynamic and unsleeping natural law, almost will, which its present position outraged and violated — yet accepting this too as he had the fact that that hide had belonged to something larger than any calf or hog and that anything which looked like that on the outside would be more than likely to have teeth and claws too, accepting this, squatting in the pirogue, clutching both gunwales, rigidly immobile as though he had an egg filled with nitroglycerin in his mouth and scarcely breathing, thinking, *If that's it, then I can do it too and even if he can't tell me how I reckon I can watch him and find out.* And he did this too, he remembered it, quietly even yet, thinking, *I thought that was how to do it and I reckon I would still think that even if I had it to do again now for the first time* — the brazen day already fierce upon his naked back, the crooked channel like a voluted thread of ink, the pirogue moving steadily to the paddle which both entered and left the water without a sound; then the sudden cessation of the paddle behind him and the fierce hissing gobble of the Cajan at his back and he squatting bate-breathed and with that intense immobility of complete sobriety of a blind man listening while the frail wooden shell stole on at the dying apex of its own parted water. Afterward he remembered the rifle too — the rust-pitted single-shot weapon with a clumsily wired stock and a muzzle you could have driven a whiskey cork into, which the Cajan had brought into the boat — but not now; now he just squatted, crouched, immobile, breathing with infinitesimal care, his sober unceasing gaze going here and there constantly as he thought, *What? What? I not only don't know what I am looking for, I don't even know where to look for it.* Then he felt the motion of the pirogue as the Cajan moved and then the tense gobbling hissing actually, hot rapid and repressed, against his neck and ear, and glancing downward saw projecting between his own arm and body from behind the Cajan's hand holding the knife, and glaring again saw the flat thick spit of mud which as he looked at it divided and became a thick mud-colored log which in turn seemed, still immobile, to leap suddenly against his retinae in three — no, four — dimensions: volume, solidity, shape, and another: not fear but pure and intense speculation and he looking at the scaled motionless shape, thinking not, *It looks dangerous* but *It looks big,* thinking, *Well, maybe a mule standing in a lot looks big to a man that never walked up to one with a halter before,* thinking, *Only if he could just tell me what to do it would save time,* the pirogue drawing nearer now, creeping now, with no ripple now even and it seemed to him that he could even hear his companion's held breath and he taking the knife from the other's hand now and not even thinking this since it was too fast, a flash; it was not a surrender, not a resignation, it was too calm, it was a part of him, he had drunk it with his mother's milk and lived with it all his life: *After all a man can't only do what he has to do, with what he has to do it with, with what he has learned, to the best of his judgment. And I reckon a hog is still a hog, no matter what it looks like. So here goes,* sitting still for an instant longer until the bow of the pirogue grounded lighter than the falling of a leaf and stepped out of it and paused just for one instant while the words *It does look big* stood for just a second, unemphatic and trivial, somewhere where some fragment of his attention could see them and vanished, and stooped straddling, the knife driving even as he grasped the near foreleg, this all in the same instant when the lashing tail struck him a terrific blow upon the back. But the knife was home, he knew that even on his back in the mud, the weight of the thrashing beast longwise upon him, its ridged back clutched to his stomach, his arm about its throat, the hissing head clamped against his jaw, the furious tail lashing and flailing, the knife in his other hand probing for the life and finding it, the hot fierce gush: and now sitting beside the profound upbellied carcass, his head again between his knees in the old attitude while his own blood freshened the other which drenched him, thinking, *It's my durn nose again.*

So he sat there, his head, his streaming face, bowed between his knees in an attitude not of dejection but profoundly bemused, contemplative, while the shrill voice of the Cajan seemed to buzz at him from an enormous distance; after a time he even looked up at the antic wiry figure bouncing hysterically about him, the face wild and grimacing, the voice gobbling and high; while the convict, holding his face carefully slanted so the blood would run free looked at him with the cold intentness of a curator or custodian paused before one of his own glass cases, the Cajan threw up the rifle, cried "Boom-boom-boom!" flung it down and in pantomime re-enacted the recent scene then whirled his hands again, crying "Magnifique! Magnifique! Cent d'argent! mille d'argent! Tout l'argent sous le ciel de Dieu!" But the convict was already looking down again, cupping the coffee-colored water to his face, watching the constant bright carmine marble it, thinking, *It's a little late to be telling me that now,* and not even thinking this long because presently they were in the pirogue again, the convict squatting again with that unbreathing rigidity as though he were trying by holding his breath to decrease his very weight, the bloody skin in the bows before him and he looking at it, thinking, *And I can't even ask him how much my half will be.*

But this not for long either, because as he was to tell the plump convict later, money has but one language. He remembered that too (they were at home now, the skin spread on the platform, where for the woman's benefit now the Cajan once more went through the pantomime — the gun which was not used, the hand-to-hand battle; for the second time the invisible alligator was slain and amid cries, the victor rose and found this time that not even the woman was watching him. She was looking at the once more swollen and inflamed face of the convict. "You mean it kicked you right in the face?" she said.

"Nah," the convict said harshly, savagely. "It never had to. I done seem to got to where if that boy was to shoot me in the tail with a bean blower my nose would bleed.") — remembered that too but he did not try to tell it. Perhaps he could not have — how two people who could not even talk to one another made an agreement which both not only understood but which each knew the other would hold true and protect (perhaps for this reason) better than any written and witnessed contract. They even discussed and agreed somehow that they should hunt separately, each in his own vessel, to double the chances of finding prey. But this was easy: the convict could almost understand the words in which the Cajan said, "You do not need me and the rifle; we will only hinder you, be in your way." And more than this, they even agreed about the second time the invisible alligator was slain amid who — friend, neighbor, perhaps one in business in that line — from whom they could rent a second rifle; in their two patois, the one bastard English, the other bastard French — the one volatile, with his wild bright eyes and his voluble mouth full of stumps of teeth, the other sober, almost grim, swollen-faced and with his naked back blistered and scoriated like so much beef — they discussed this, squatting on either side of the pegged-out hide like two members of a corporation facing each other across a mahogany board table, and decided against it, the convict deciding: "I reckon not," he said. "I reckon if I had knowed enough to wait to start out with a gun, I still would. But since I done already started out without one, I don't reckon I'll change." Because it was a question of the money in terms of time, days. (Strange to say, that was the one thing which the Cajan could not tell him: how much the half would be. But the convict knew it was half.) He had so little of them. He would have to move on soon, thinking (the convict), *All this durn foolishness will stop soon and I can get on back,* and then suddenly he found he was thinking, *Will have to get on back,* and he became quite still and looked about at the rich strange desert which surrounded him, in which he was temporarily lost in peace and hope and into which the last seven years had sunk like so many trivial pebbles into a pool, leaving no ripple, and he thought quietly, with a kind of bemused amazement, *Yes. I reckon I had done forgot how good making money was. Being let to make it.*

So he used no gun, his the knotted rope and the Thuringian mace, and each morning he and the Cajan took their separate ways in the two boats to comb and creep the secret channels about the lost land from (or out of) which now and then still other pint-sized dark men appeared gobbling, abruptly and as though by magic from nowhere, in other hollowed logs, to follow quietly and watched him at his single combats — men named Tine and Toto and Theule, who were not much larger than and looked a good deal like the muskrats which the Cajan (the host did this too, supplied the kitchen too, he expressed this too like the rifle business, in his own tongue, the convict comprehending this too as though it had been English. "Do not concern yourself about food, O Hercules. Catch alligators; I will supply the pot.") took now and then from traps as you take a shoat pig at need from a pen, and varied the eternal rice and fish (the convict did tell this: how at night, in the cabin, the door and one sashless window battened against mosquitoes — a form, a ritual, as empty as crossing the finger or knocking on wood — sitting beside the bug-swirled lantern on the plank table in a temperature close to blood heat he would look down at the swimming segment of meat on his sweating plate and think, *It must be Theule. He was the fat one.*) — day following day, unemphatic and identical, each like the one before and the one which would follow while his theoretical half of a sum to be reckoned in pennies, dollars, or tens of dollars he did not know, mounted — the mornings when he set forth to find waiting for him like the *matador* his *aficionados* the small clump of constant and deferential pirogues, the hard noons when ringed half about by little motionless shells he fought his solitary combats, the evenings, the return, the pirogues departing one by one into inlets and passages which during the first few days he could not even distinguish, then the platform in the twilight where before the static woman and the usually nursing infant and the one or two bloody hides of the day's take the Cajan would perform his ritualistic victorious pantomime before the two growing rows of knifemarks in one of the boards of the wall; then the nights when, the woman and child in the single bunk and the Cajan already snoring on the pallet and the reeking lantern set close, he (the convict) would sit on his naked heels, sweating steadily, his face worn and calm, immersed and indomitable, his bowed back raw and savage as beef beneath the suppurant old blisters and the fierce welts of tails, and scrape and chip at the charred sapling which was almost a paddle now, pausing now and then to raise his head while the cloud of mosquitoes about it whined and whirled, to stare at the wall before him until after a while the crude boards themselves must have dissolved away and let his blank unseeing gaze go on and on unhampered, through the rich oblivious darkness, beyond it even perhaps, even perhaps beyond the seven wasted years during which, so he had just realized, he had been permitted to toil but not to work. Then he would retire himself, he would take a last look at the rolled bundle behind the rafter and blow out the lantern and lie down as he was beside his snoring partner, to lie sweating (on his stomach, he could not bear the touch of anything to his back) in the whining ovenlike darkness filled with the forlorn bellowing of alligators, thinking not, *They never gave me time to learn* but *I had forgot how good it is to work.*

Then on the tenth day it happened. It happened for the third time. At first he refused to believe it, not that he felt that now he had served out and discharged his apprenticeship to mischance, had with the birth of the child reached and crossed the crest of his Golgotha and would now be, possibly not permitted so much as ignored, to descend the opposite slope free-wheeling. That was not his feeling at all. What he declined to accept was the fact that a power, a force such as that which had been consistent enough to concentrate upon him with deadly undeviation for weeks, should with all the wealth of cosmic violence and disaster to draw from, have been so barren of invention and imagination, so lacking in pride of artistry and craftsmanship, as to repeat itself twice. Once he had accepted, twice he even forgave, but three times he simply declined to believe, particularly when he was at last persuaded to realize that this third time was to be instigated not by the blind potency of volume and motion but by human direction and hands: that now the cosmic joker, foiled twice, had stooped in its vindictive concentration to the employing of dynamite.

He did not tell that. Doubtless he did not know himself how it happened, what was happening. But he doubtless remembered it (but quietly above the thick rich-colored pristine cigar in his clean steady hand), what he knew, divined of it. It would be evening, the ninth evening, he and the woman on either side of their host's empty place at the evening meal, he hearing the voices from without but not ceasing to eat, still chewing steadily, because it would be the same as though he was seeing them anyway — the two or three or four pirogues floating on the dark water beneath the platform on which the host stood, the voices gobbling and jabbering, incomprehensible and filled not with alarm and not exactly with rage or ever perhaps absolute surprise but rather just cacophony like those of disturbed marsh fowl, he (the convict) not ceasing to chew but just looking up quietly and maybe without a great deal of interrogation or surprise too as the Cajan burst in and stood before them, wild-faced, glaring, his blackened teeth gaped against the inky orifice of his distended mouth, watching (the convict) while the Cajan went through his violent pantomime of violent evacuation, ejection, scooping something invisible into his arms and hurling it out and downward and in the instant of completing the gesture changing from instigator to victim of that which he had sent into pantomimic motion, clasping his head and, bowed over and not otherwise moving, seeming to be swept on and away before it, crying "Boom! Boom! Boom!", the convict watching him, his jaw not chewing now, for just that moment, thinking, *What? What is it he is trying to tell me?* thinking (this a flash too, since he could not have expressed this, and hence did not even know that he had ever thought it) that though his life had been cast here, circumscribed by this environment, accepted by this environment and accepting it in turn (and he had done well here — this quietly, soberly indeed, if he had been able to phrase it, thinking it instead of merely knowing it — better than he had ever done, who had not even known until now how good work, making money, could be) yet it was not his life, he still and would ever be no more than the water bug upon the surface of the pond, the plumbless and lurking depths of which he would never know, his only actual contact with it being the instants when on lonely and glaring mudspits under the pitiless sun and amphitheatred by his motionless and riveted semicircle of watching pirogues, he accepted the gambit which he had not elected, entered the lashing radius of the armed tail and beat at the thrashing and hissing head with his lightwood club, or this failing, embraced without hesitation the armored body itself with the frail web of flesh and bone in which he walked and lived and sought the raging life with an eight-inch knife-blade.

So he and the woman merely watched the Cajan as he acted out the whole charade of eviction — the little wiry man gesticulant and wild, his hysterical shadow leaping and falling upon the rough wall as he went through the pantomime of abandoning the cabin, gathering in pantomime his meagre belongings from the walls and corners — objects which no other man would want and only some power or force like blind water or earthquake or fire would ever dispossess him of, the woman watching too, her mouth slightly open upon a mass of chewed food, on her face an expression of placid astonishment, saying, "What? What's he saying?"

"I don't know," the convict said. "But I reckon if it's something we ought to know we will find it out when it's ready for us to." Because he was not alarmed, though by now he had read the other's meaning plainly enough. *He's fixing to leave,* he thought. *He's telling me to leave too* — this later, after they had quitted the table and the Cajan and the woman had gone to bed and the Cajan had risen from the pallet and approached the convict and once more went through the pantomime of abandoning the cabin, this time as one repeats a speech which may have been misunderstood, tediously, carefully repetitional as to a child, seeming to hold the convict with one hand while he gestured, talked, with the other, gesturing as though in single syllables, the convict (squatting, the knife open and the almost-finished paddle across his lap) watching, nodding his head, even speaking in English: "Yah; sure. You bet. I got you." — trimming again at the paddle but no faster, with no more haste than on any other night, serene in his belief that when the time came for him to know whatever it was, that would take care of itself, having already and without even knowing it, even before the possibility, the question, ever arose, declined, refused to accept even the thought of moving also, thinking about the hides, thinking, *If there was just some way he could tell me where to carry my share to get the money* but thinking this only for an instant between two delicate strokes of the blade because almost at once he thought, *I reckon as long as I can catch them I won't have no big trouble finding whoever it is that will buy them.*

So the next morning he helped the Cajan load his few belongings — the pitted rifle, a small bundle of clothing (again they traded, who could not even converse with one another, this time the few cooking vessels, a few rusty traps by definite allocation, and something embracing and abstractional which included the stove, the crude bunk, the house or its occupancy — something — in exchange for one alligator hide) — into the pirogue, then, squatting and as two children divide sticks they divided the hides, separating them into two piles, one-for-me-and-one-for-you, two-for-me-and-two-for-you, and the Cajan loaded his share and shoved away from the platform and paused again, though this time he only put the paddle down, gathered something invisibly into his two hands and flung it violently upward, crying "Boom? Boom?" on a rising inflection, nodding violently to the half-naked and savagely scoriated man on the platform who stared with a sort of grim equability back at him and said, "Sure. Boom. Boom." Then the Cajan went on. He did not look back. They watched him, already paddling rapidly, or the woman did; the convict had already turned.

"Maybe he was trying to tell us to leave too," she said.

"Yah," the convict said. "I thought of that last night. Hand me the paddle." She fetched it to him — the sapling, the one he had been trimming at nightly, not quite finished yet though one more evening would do it (he had been using a spare one of the Cajan's. The other had offered to let him keep it, to include it perhaps with the stove and the bunk and the cabin's freehold, but the convict had declined. Perhaps he had computed it by volume against so much alligator hide, this weighed against one more evening with the tedious and careful blade.) and he departed too with his knotted rope and mace, in the opposite direction, as though not only not content with refusing to quit the place he had been warned against, he must establish and affirm the irrevocable finality of his refusal by penetrating even further and deeper into it. And then and without warning the high fierce drowsing of his solitude gathered itself and struck at him.

He could not have told this if he had tried — this not yet midmorning and he going on, alone for the first time, no pirogue emerging anywhere to fall in behind him, but he had not expected this anyway, he knew that the others would have departed too; it was not this, it was his very solitude, his desolation which was now his alone and in full since he had elected to remain; the sudden cessation of the paddle, the skiff shooting on for a moment yet while he thought, *What? What?* Then, *No. No. No,* as the silence and solitude and emptiness roared down upon him in a jeering bellow: and now reversed, the skiff spun violently on its heel, he the betrayed driving furiously back toward the platform where he knew it was already too late, that citadel where the very crux and dear breath of his life — the being allowed to work and earn money, that right and privilege which he believed he had earned to himself unaided, asking no favor of anyone or anything save the right to be let alone to pit his will and strength against the sauric protagonist of a land, a region, which he had not asked to be projected into — was being threatened, driving the home-made paddle in grim fury, coming in sight of the platform at last and seeing the motor launch lying alongside it with no surprise at all but actually with a kind of pleasure as though at a visible justification of his outrage and fear, the privilege of saying *I told you so* to his own affronting, driving on toward it in a dream-like state in which there seemed to be no progress at all, in which, unimpeded and suffocating, he strove dreamily with a weightless oar, with muscles without strength or resiliency, at a medium without resistance, seeming to watch the skiff creep infinitesimally across the sunny water and up to the platform while a man in the launch (there were five of them in all) gobbled at him in that same tongue he had been hearing constantly now for ten days and still knew no word of, just as a second man, followed by the woman carrying the baby and dressed again for departure in the faded tunic and the sunbonnet, emerged from the house, carrying (the man carried several other things but the convict saw nothing else) the paper-wrapped bundle which the convict had put behind the rafter ten days ago and no other hand had touched since, he (the convict) on the platform too now, holding the skiff's painter in one hand and the bludgeon-like paddle in the other, contriving to speak to the woman at last in a voice dreamy and suffocating and incredibly calm: "Take it away from him and carry it back into the house."

"So you can talk English, can you?" the man in the launch said. "Why didn't you come out like they told you to last night?"

"Out?" the convict said. Again he even looked, glared, at the man in the launch, contriving even again to control his voice: "I ain't got time to take trips. I'm busy," already turning to the woman again, his mouth already open to repeat as the dreamy buzzing voice of the man came to him and he turning once more, in a terrific and absolutely unbearable exasperation, crying, "Flood? What flood? Hell a mile, it's done passed me twice months ago! It's gone! What flood? and then (he did not think this in actual words either but he knew it, suffered that flashing insight into his own character or destiny: how there was a peculiar quality of repetitiveness about his present fate, how not only the almost seminal crises recurred with a certain monotony, but the very physical circumstances followed a stupidly unimaginative pattern) the man in the launch said, "Take him" and he was on his feet for a few minutes, yet, lashing and striking in panting fury, then once more on his back on hard unyielding planks while the four men swarmed over him in a fierce wave of hard bones and panting curses and at last the thin dry vicious snapping of handcuffs.

"Damn it, are you mad?" the man in the launch said. "Can't you understand they are going to dynamite that levee at noon today — Come on," he said to the others. "Get him aboard. Let's get out of here."

"I want my hides and boat," the convict said.

"Damn your hides," the man in the launch said. "If they don't get that levee blowed pretty soon you can hunt plenty more of them on the capitol steps at Baton Rouge. And this is all the boat you will need and you can say your prayers about it."

"I ain't going without my boat," the convict said. He said it calmly and with complete finality, so calm, so final that for almost a minute nobody answered him, they just stood looking quietly down at him as he lay, half-naked, blistered and scarred, helpless and manacled hand and foot, on his back, delivering his ultimatum in a voice peaceful and quiet as that in which you talk to your bedfellow before going to sleep. Then the man in the launch moved; he spat quietly over the side and said in a voice as calm and quiet as the convict's:

"All right. Bring his boat." They helped the woman, carrying the baby and the paper-wrapped parcel, into the launch. Then they helped the convict to his feet and into the launch too, the shackles on his wrists and ankles clashing. "I'd unlock you if you'd promise to behave yourself," the man said. The convict did not answer this at all.

"I want to hold the rope," he said.

"The rope?"

"Yes," the convict said. "The rope." So they lowered him into the stern and gave him the end of the painter after it had passed the towing cleat, and they went on. The convict did not look back. But then, he did not look forward either, he lay half sprawled, his shackled legs before him, the end of the skiff's painter in one shackled hand. The launch made two other stops; when the hazy wafer of the intolerable sun began to stand once more directly overhead there were fifteen people in the launch; and then the convict, sprawled and motionless, saw the flat brazen land begin to rise and become a greenish-black mass of swamp, bearded and convoluted, this in turn stopping short off and there spread before him an expanse of water embraced by a blue dissolution of shore line and glittering thinly under the noon, larger than he had ever seen before, the sound of the launch's engine ceasing, the hull sliding on behind its fading bow-wave. "What are you doing?" the leader said.

"It's noon," the helmsman said. "I thought we might hear the dynamite." So they all listened, the launch lost of all forward motion, rocking slightly, the glitter-broken small waves slapping and whispering at the hull, but no sound, no tremble even, came anywhere under the fierce hazy sky; the long moment gathered itself and turned on and noon was past. "All right," the leader said. "Let's go." The engine started again, the hull began to gather speed. The leader came aft and stooped over the convict, key in hand. "I guess you'll have to behave now, whether you want to or not," he said, unlocking the manacles. "Won't you?"

"Yes," the convict said. They went on; after a time the shore vanished completely and a little sea got up. The convict was free now but he lay as before, the end of the skiff's painter in his hand, bent now with three or four turns about his wrist; he turned his head now and then to look back at the towing skiff as it slewed and bounced in the launch's wake; now and then he even looked out over the lake, the eyes alone moving, the face grave and expressionless, thinking, *This is a greater immensity of water, of waste and desolation, than I have ever seen before;* perhaps not; thinking three or four hours later, the shoreline raised again and broken into a clutter of sailing sloops and power cruisers, *These are more boats than I believed existed, a maritime race of which I also had no cognizance* or perhaps not thinking it but just watching as the launch opened the shored gut of the ship canal, the low smoke of the city beyond it, then a wharf, the launch slowing in; a quiet crowd of people watching with that same forlorn passivity he had seen before and whose race he did recognize even though he had not seen Vicksburg when he passed it — the brand, the unmistakable hallmark of the violently homeless, he more so than any, who would have permitted no man to call him one of them.

"All right," the leader said to him. "Here you are."

"The boat," the convict said.

"You've got it. What do you want me to do — give you a receipt for it?"

"No," the convict said. "I just want the boat."

"Take it. Only you ought to have a bookstrap or something to carry it in." ("Carry it in?" the plump convict said. "Carry it where? Where would you have to carry it?")

He (the tall one) told that: how he and the woman disembarked and how one of the men helped him haul the skiff up out of the water and how he stood there with the end of the painter wrapped around his wrist and the man bustled up, saying, "All right. Next load! Next load!" and how he told this man too about the boat and the man cried, "Boat? Boat?" and how he (the convict) went with them when they carried the skiff over and racked, berthed, it with the others and how he lined himself up by a coca-cola sign and the arch of a draw bridge so he could find the skiff again quick when he returned, and how he and the woman (he carrying the paper-wrapped parcel) were herded into a truck and after a while the truck began to run in traffic, between close houses, then there was a big building, an armory —

"Armory?" the plump one said. "You mean a jail."

"No. It was a kind of warehouse, with people with bundles laying on the floor." And how he thought maybe his partner might be there and how he even looked about for the Cajan while waiting for a chance to get back to the door again, where the soldier was and how he got back to the door at last, the woman behind him and his chest actually against the dropped rifle.

"Gwan, gwan," the soldier said. "Get back. They'll give you some clothes in a minute. You can't walk around the streets that way. And something to eat too. Maybe your kinfolks will come for you by that time." And he told that too: how the woman said,

"Maybe if you told him you had some kinfolks here he would let us out." And how he did not; he could not have expressed this either, it was too deep, too ingrained; he had never yet had to think it into words through all the long generations of himself — his hillman's sober and jealous respect not for truth but for the power, the strength, of lying — not to be niggard with lying but rather to use it with respect and even care, delicate quick and strong, like a fine and fatal blade. And how they fetched him clothes — a blue jumper and overalls, and then food too (a brisk starched young woman saying, "But the baby must be bathed, cleaned. It will die if you don't" and the woman saying, "Yessum. He might holler some, he ain't never been bathed before. But he's a good baby.") and now it was night, the unshaded bulbs harsh and savage and forlorn above the snorers and he rising, gripping the woman awake, and then the window. He told that: how there were doors in plenty, leading he did not know where, but he had a hard time finding a window they could use but he found one at last, he carrying the parcel and the baby too while he climbed through first — "You ought to tore up a sheet and slid down it," the plump convict said. But he needed no sheet, there were cobbles under his feet now, in the rich darkness. The city was there too but he had not seen it yet and would not — the low constant glare; Bienville had stood there too, it had been the figment of an emasculate also calling himself Napoleon but no more, Andrew Jackson had found it one step from Pennsylvania Avenue. But the convict found it considerably further than one step back to the ship canal and the skiff, the coca-cola sign dim now, the draw bridge arching spidery against the jonquil sky at dawn: nor did he tell, any more than about the sixty-foot levee, how he got the skiff back into the water. The lake was behind him now; there was but one direction he could go. When he saw the River again he knew it at once. He should have; it was now ineradicably a part of his past, his life; it would be a part of what he would bequeath, if that were in store for him. But four weeks later it would look different from what it did now, and did: he (the old man) had recovered from his debauch, back in banks again, the Old Man, rippling placidly toward the sea, brown and rich as chocolate between levees whose inner faces were wrinkled as though in a frozen and aghast amazement, crowned wth the rich green of summer in the willows; beyond them, sixty feet below, slick mules squatted against the broad pull of middle-busters in the richened soil which would not need to be planted, which would need only to be shown a cotton seed to sprout and make, there would be the symmetric miles of strong stalks by July, purple bloom in August, in September the black fields snowed over, spilled, the middles dragged smooth by the long sacks, the long black limber hands plucking, the hot air filled with the whine of gins, the September air then but now June air heavy with locust and (the towns) the smell of new paint and the sour smell of the paste which holds wall paper — the towns, the villages, the little lost wood landings on stilts on the inner face of the levee, the lower storeys bright and rank under the new paint and paper and even the marks on spile and post and tree of May's raging water-height fading beneath each bright silver gust of summer's loud and inconstant rain; there was a store at the levee's lip, a few saddled and rope-bridled mules in the sleepy dust, a few dogs, a handful of Negroes sitting on the steps beneath the chewing tobacco and malaria medicine signs, and three white men, one of them a deputy sheriff canvassing for votes to beat his superior (who had given him his job) in the August primary, all pausing to watch the skiff emerge from the glitter-glare of the afternoon water and approach and land, a woman carrying a child stepping out, then a man, a tall man who, approaching, proved to be dressed in a faded but recently washed and quite clean suit of penitentiary clothing, stopping in the dust where the mules dozed and watching with pale cold humorless eyes while the deputy sheriff was still making toward his armpit that gesture which everyone present realized was to have produced a pistol in one flashing motion for a considerable time while still nothing came of it. It was apparently enough for the newcomer, however.

"You a officer?" he said.

"You damn right I am," the deputy said. "Just let me get this damn gun —"

"All right," the other said. "Yonder's your boat, and here's the woman. But I never did find that bastard on the cottonhouse."

V

One of the Governor's young men arrived at the Penitentiary the next morning. That is, he was fairly young (he would not see thirty again though without doubt he did not want to, there being that about him which indicated a character which never had and never would want anything it did not, or was not about to, possess), a Phi Beta Kappa out of an Eastern university, a colonel on the Governor's staff who did not buy it with a campaign contribution, who had stood in his negligent Eastern-cut clothes and his arched nose and lazy contemptuous eyes on the galleries of any number of little lost backwoods stores and told his stories and received the guffaws of his overalled and spitting hearers and with the same look in his eyes fondled infants named in memory of the last administration and in honor (or hope) of the next and (it was said of him and doubtless not true) by lazy accident the behinds of some who were not infants any longer though still not old enough to vote. He was in the Warden's office with a briefcase, and presently the deputy warden of the levee was there too. He would have been sent for presently though not yet, but he came anyhow, without knocking, with his hat on, calling the Governor's young man loudly by a nickname and striking him with a flat hand on the back and lifted one thigh to the Warden's desk, almost between the Warden and the caller, the emissary. Or the vizier[1] with the command, the knotted cord, as began to appear immediately.

1 ["When the Sultan decided he was tired of a courtier he would send his Prime Minister with a knotted cord to suggest that he choke himself to death" (Faulkner in an interview). — Editors' note.]

"Well," the Governor's young man said, "you've played the devil, haven't you?" The Warden had a cigar. He had offered the caller one. It had been refused, though presently, while the Warden looked at the back of his neck with hard immobility even a little grim, the deputy leaned and reached back and opened the desk drawer and took one.

"Seems straight enough to me," the Warden said. "He got swept away against his will. He came back as soon as he could and surrendered."

"He even brought that damn boat back," the deputy said. "If he'd a throwed the boat away he could a walked back in three days. But no sir. He's got to bring the boat back. 'Here's your boat and here's the woman but I never found no bastard on no cottonhouse.' " He slapped his knee, guffawing. "Them convicts. A mule's got twice as much sense."

"A mule's got twice as much sense as anything except a rat," the emissary said in his pleasant voice. "But that's not the trouble."

"What is the trouble?" the Warden said.

"This man is dead."

"Hell fire, he ain't dead," the deputy said. "He's up yonder in that bunkhouse right now, lying his head off probly. I'll take you up there and you can see him." The Warden was looking at the deputy.

"Look," he said. "Bledsoe was trying to tell me something about that Kate mule's leg. You better go up to the stable and —"

"I done tended to it," the deputy said. He didn't even look at the Warden. He was watching, talking to, the emissary. "No sir. He ain't —"

"But he has received an official discharge as being dead. Not a pardon nor a parole either: a discharge. He's either dead, or free. In either case he doesn't belong here." Now both the Warden and the deputy looked at the emissary, the deputy's mouth open a little, the cigar poised in his hand to have its tip bitten off. The emissary spoke pleasantly, extremely distinctly: "On a report of death forwarded to the Governor by the Warden of the Penitentiary." The deputy closed his mouth, though otherwise he didn't move. "On the official evidence of the officer delegated at the time to the charge and returning of the body of the prisoner to the Penitentiary." Now the deputy put the cigar into his mouth and got slowly off the desk, the cigar rolling across his lip as he spoke:

"So that's it. I'm to be it, am I?" He laughed shortly, a stage laugh, two notes. "When I done been right three times running through three separate administrations? That's on a book somewhere too. Somebody in Jackson can find that too. And if they can't, I can show —"

"Three administrations?" the emissary said. "Well, well. That's pretty good."

"You damn right it's good," the deputy said. "The woods are full of folks that didn't." The Warden was again watching the back of the deputy's neck.

"Look," he said. "Why don't you step up to my house and get that bottle of whiskey out of the sideboard and bring it down here?"

"All right," the deputy said. "But I think we better settle this first. I'll tell you what we'll do —"

"We can settle it quicker with a drink or two," the Warden said. "You better step on up to your place and get a coat so the bottle —"

"That'll take too long," the deputy said. "I won't need no coat." He moved to the door, where he stopped and turned. "I'll tell you what to do. Just call twelve men in here and tell him it's a jury — he never seen but one before and he won't know no better — and try him over for robbing that train. Hamp can be the judge."

"You can't try a man twice for the same crime," the emissary said. "He might know that even if he doesn't know a jury when he sees one."

"Look," the Warden said.

"All right. Just call it a new train robbery. Tell him it happened yesterday, tell him he robbed another train while he was gone and just forgot it. He couldn't help himself. Besides, he won't care. He'd just as lief be here as out. He wouldn't have nowhere to go if he was out. None of them do. Turn one loose and be damned if he ain't right back here by Christmas like it was a reunion or something, for doing the very same thing they caught him at before." He guffawed again. "Them convicts."

"Look," the Warden said. "While you're there, why don't you open the bottle and see if the liquor's any good. Take a drink or two. Give yourself time to feel it. If it's not good, no use in bringing it."

"O. K.," the deputy said. He went out this time.

"Couldn't you lock the door?" the emissary said. The Warden squirmed faintly. That is, he shifted his position in his chair.

"After all, he's right," he said. "He's guessed right three times now. And he's kin to all the folks in Pittman County except the niggers."

"Maybe we can work fast then." The emissary opened the briefcase and took out a sheaf of papers. "So there you are," he said.

"There what are?"

"He escaped."

"But he came back voluntarily and surrendered."

"But he escaped."

"All right," the Warden said. "He escaped. Then what?" Now the emissary said look. That is, he said,

"Listen. I'm on per diem. That's tax-payers, votes. And if there's any possible chance for it to occur to anyone to hold an investigation about this, there'll be ten senators and twenty-five representatives here on a special train maybe. On per diem. And it will be mighty hard to keep some of them from going back to Jackson by way of Memphis or New Orleans — on per diem."

"All right," the Warden said. "What does he say to do?"

"This. That man left here in charge of one specific officer. But he was delivered back here by a different one."

"But he surren —" This time the Warden stopped of his own accord. He looked, stared almost, at the emissary. "All right. Go on."

"In specific charge of an appointed and delegated officer, who returned here and reported that the body of the prisoner was no longer in his possession; that, in fact, he did not know where the prisoner was. That's correct, isn't it?" The Warden said nothing. "Isn't that correct?" the emissary said, pleasantly, insistently.

"But you can't do that to him. I tell you he's kin to half the — "

"That's taken care of. The Chief has made a place for him on the highway patrol."

"Hell," the Warden said. "He can't ride a motorcycle. I don't even let him try to drive a truck."

"He won't have to. Surely an amazed and grateful State can supply the man who guessed right three times in succession in Mississippi general elections with a car to ride in and somebody to run it if necessary. He won't even have to stay in it all the time. Just so he's near enough so when an inspector sees the car and stops and blows the horn of it he can hear it and come out."

"I still don't like it," the Warden said.

"Neither do I. Your man could have saved all of this if he had just gone on and drowned himself, as he seems to have led everybody to believe he had. But he didn't. And the Chief says do. Can you think of anything better?" The Warden sighed.

"No," he said.

"All right." The emissary opened the papers and uncapped a pen and began to write. "Attempted escape from the Penitentiary, ten years' additional sentence," he said. "Deputy Warden Buckworth transferred to Highway Patrol. Call it for meritorious service even if you want to. It won't matter now. Done?"

"Done," the Warden said.

"Then suppose you send for him. Get it over with." So the Warden sent for the tall convict and he arrived presently, saturnine and grave, in his new bed-ticking, his jowls blue and close under the sunburn, his hair recently cut and neatly parted and smelling faintly of the prison barber's (the barber was in for life, for murdering his wife, still a barber) pomade. The Warden called him by name.

"You had bad luck, didn't you?" The convict said nothing. "They are going to have to add ten years to your time."

"All right," the convict said.

"It's hard luck. I'm sorry."

"All right," the convict said. "If that's the rule." So they gave him the ten years more and the Warden gave him the cigar and now he sat, jackknifed backward into the space between the upper and lower bunks, the unlighted cigar in his hand while the plump convict and four others listened to him. Or questioned him, that is, since it was all done, finished, now and he was safe again, so maybe it wasn't even worth talking about any more.

"All right," the plump one said. "So you come back into the River. Then what?"

"Nothing. I rowed."

"Wasn't it pretty hard rowing coming back?"

"The water was still high. It was running pretty hard still. I never made much speed for the first week or two. After that it got better." Then, suddenly and quietly, something — the inarticulateness, the innate and inherited reluctance for speech, dissolved and he found himself listening to himself, telling it quietly, the words coming not fast but easily to the tongue as he required them: How he paddled on (he found out by trying it that he could make better speed, if you could call it speed, next the bank — this after he had been carried suddenly and violently out to midstream before he could prevent it and found himself, the skiff, travelling back toward the region from which he had just escaped and he spent the better part of the morning getting back inshore and up to the canal again from which he had emerged at dawn) until night came and they tied up to the bank and ate some of the food he had secreted in his jumper before leaving the armory in New Orleans and the woman and the infant slept in the boat as usual and when daylight came they went on and tied up again that night too and the next day the food gave out and he came to a landing, a town, he didn't notice the name of it, and he got a job. It was a cane farm —

"Cane?" one of the other convicts said. "What does anybody want to raise cane for? You cut cane. You have to fight it where I come from. You burn it just to get shut of it."

"It was sorghum," the tall convict said.

"Sorghum?" another said. "A whole farm just raising sorghum? *Sorghum?* What did they do with it?" The tall one didn't know. He didn't ask, he just came up the levee and there was a truck waiting full of niggers and a white man said, "You there. Can you run a shovel plow?" and the convict said,

"Yes," and the man said, "Jump in then," and the convict said, "Only I've got a —"

"Yes," the plump one said. "That's what I been aiming to ask. What did —" The tall convict's face was grave, his voice was calm, just a little short:

"They had tents for the folks to live in. They were behind." The plump one blinked at him.

"Did they think she was your wife?"

"I don't know. I reckon so." The plump one blinked at him.

"Wasn't she your wife? Just from time to time kind of, you might say?" The tall one didn't answer this at all. After a moment he raised the cigar and appeared to examine a loosening of the wrapper because after another moment he licked the cigar carefully near the end. "All right," the plump one said. "Then what?" So he worked there four days. He didn't like it. Maybe that was why: that he too could not quite put credence in that much of what he believed to be sorghum. So when they told him it was Saturday and paid him and the white man told him about somebody who was going to Baton Rouge the next day in a motor boat, he went to see the man and took the six dollars he had earned and bought food with it and tied the skiff behind the motor boat and went to Baton Rouge. It didn't take long and even after they left the motor boat at Baton Rouge and he was paddling again it seemed to the convict that the River was lower and the current not so fast, so hard, so they made fair speed, tying up to the bank at night among the willows, the woman and baby sleeping in the skiff as of old. Then the food gave out again. This time it was a wood landing, the wood stacked and waiting, a wagon and team being unladen of another load. The men with the wagon told him about the sawmill and helped him drag the skiff up the levee; they wanted to leave it there but he would not so they loaded it onto the wagon too and he and the woman got on the wagon too and they went to the sawmill. They gave them one room in a house to live in here. They paid two dollars a day and furnish. The work was hard. He liked it. He stayed there eight days.

"If you liked it so well, why did you quit?" the plump one said. The tall convict examined the cigar again, holding it up where the light fell upon the rich chocolate-colored flank.

"I got in trouble," he said.

"What trouble?"

"Woman. It was a fellow's wife."

"You mean you had been toting one piece up and down the country day and night for over a month, and now the first time you have a chance to stop and catch your breath almost you got to get in trouble over another one?" The tall convict had thought of that. He remembered it: how there were times, seconds, at first when if it had not been for the baby he might have, might have tried. But they were just seconds because in the next instant his whole being would seem to flee the very idea in a kind of savage and horrified revulsion; he would find himself looking from a distance at this millstone which the force and power of blind and risible Motion had fastened upon him, thinking, saying aloud actually, with harsh and savage outrage even though it had been two years since he had had a woman and that a nameless and not young Negress, a casual, a straggler whom he had caught more or less by chance on one of the fifth-Sunday visiting days, the man — husband or sweetheart — whom she had come to see having been shot by a trusty a week or so previous and she had not heard about it: "She ain't even no good to me for that."

"But you got this one, didn't you?" the plump convict said.

"Yah," the tall one said. The plump one blinked at him.

"Was it good?"

"It's all good," one of the others said. "Well? Go on. How many more did you have on the way back? Sometimes when a fellow starts getting it it looks like he just can't miss even if —" That was all, the convict told them. They left the sawmill fast, he had no time to buy food until they reached the next landing. There he spent the whole sixteen dollars he had earned and they went on. The River was lower now, there was no doubt of it, and sixteen dollars' worth looked like a lot of food and he thought maybe it would do, would be enough. But maybe there was more current in the River still than it looked like. But this time it was Mississippi, it was cotton; the plow handles felt right to his palms again, the strain and squat of the slick buttocks against the middle buster's blade was what he knew, even though they paid but a dollar a day here. But that did it. He told it: they told him it was Saturday again and paid him and he told about it — night, a smoked lantern and a disc of worn and barren earth as smooth as silver, a circle of crouching figures, the importunate murmurs and ejaculations, the meagre piles of worn bills beneath the crouching knees, the dotted cubes clicking and scuttering in the dust; that did it. "How much did you win?" the second convict said.

"Enough," the tall one said.

"But how much?"

"Enough," the tall one said. It was enough exactly; he gave it all to the man who owned the second motor boat (he would not need food now), he and the woman in the launch now and the skiff towing behind, the woman with the baby and the paper-wrapped parcel beneath his peaceful hand, on his lap; almost at once he recognized, not Vicksburg because he had never seen Vicksburg, but the trestle beneath which on his roaring wave of trees and houses and dead animals he had shot, accompanied by thunder and lightning, a month and three weeks ago; he looked at it once without heat, even without interest as the launch went on. But now he began to watch the bank, the levee. He didn't know how he would know but he knew he would, and then it was early afternoon and sure enough the moment came and he said to the launch owner: "I reckon this will do."

"Here?" the launch owner said. "This don't look like anywhere to me."

"I reckon this is it," the convict said. So the launch put inshore, the engine ceased, it drifted up and lay against the levee and the owner cast the skiff loose.

"You better let me take you on until we come to something," he said. "That was what I promised."

"I reckon this will do," the convict said. So they got out and he stood with the grapevine painter in his hand while the launch purred again and drew away, already curving; he did not watch it. He laid the bundle down and made the painter fast to a willow root and picked up the bundle and turned. He said no word, he mounted the levee, passing the mark, the tide-line of the old raging, dry now and lined, traversed by shallow and empty cracks like foolish and deprecatory senile grins, and entered a willow clump and removed the overalls and shirt they had given him in New Orleans and dropped them without even looking to see where they fell and opened the parcel and took out the other, the known, the desired, faded a little, stained and worn, but clean, recognizable, and put them on and returned to the skiff and took up the paddle. The woman was already in it.

The plump convict stood blinking at him. "So you come back," he said. "Well well." Now they all watched the tall convict as he bit the end from the cigar neatly and with complete deliberation and spat it out and licked the bite smooth and damp and took a match from his pocket and examined the match for a moment as though to be sure it was a good one, worthy of the cigar perhaps, and raked it up his thigh with the same deliberation — a motion almost too slow to set fire to it, it would seem — and held it until the flame burned clear and free of sulphur, then put it to the cigar. The plump one watched him, blinking rapidly and steadily. "And they give you ten years more for running. That's bad. A fellow can get used to what they give him at first, to start off with, I don't care how much it is, even a hundred and ninety-nine years. But ten more years. Ten years more, on top of that. When you never expect it. Ten more years to have to do without no society, no female companionship —" He blinked steadily at the tall convict. But he (the tall convict) had thought of that too. He had had a sweetheart. That is, he had gone to church singings and picnics with her — a girl a year or so younger than he, short-legged, with ripe breasts and a heavy mouth and dull eyes like ripe muscadines, who owned a baking-powder can almost full of ear-rings and brooches and rings bought (or presented at suggestion) from ten-cent stores. Presently he had divulged his plan to her, and there were times later when, musing, the thought occurred to him that possibly if it had not been for her he would not actually have attempted it — this a mere feeling, unworded, since he could not have phrased this either: that who to know what Capone's uncandled bridehood she might not have dreamed to be her destiny and fate, what fast car filled with authentic colored glass and machine guns, running traffic lights. But that was all past and done when the notion first occurred to him, and in the third month of his incarceration she came to see him. She wore ear-rings and a bracelet or so which he had never seen before and it never became quite clear how she had got that far from home, and she cried violently for the first three minutes though presently (and without his ever knowing either exactly how they had got separated or how she had made the acquaintance) he saw her in animated conversation with one of the guards. But she kissed him before she left that evening and said she would return the first chance she got, clinging to him, sweating a little, smelling of scent and soft young female flesh, slightly pneumatic. But she didn't come back though he continued to write to her, and seven months later he got an answer. It was a postcard, a colored lithograph of a Birmingham hotel, a childish X inked heavily across one window, the heavy writing on the reverse slanted and primer-like too: *This is where were honnymonning at. Your friend (Mrs) Vernon Waldrip*

The plump convict stood blinking at the tall one, rapidly and steadily. "Yes, sir," he said. "It's them ten more years that hurt. Ten more years to do without a woman, no woman a tall a fellow wants —" He blinked steadily and rapidly, watching the tall one. The other did not move, jackknifed backward between the two bunks, grave and clean, the cigar burning smoothly and richly in his clean steady hand, the smoke wreathing upward across his face saturnine, humorless, and calm. "Ten more years —"

"Women — !" the tall convict said.

AFTERWORD

It would be pushing things only a bit to say that most of the short novels in this collection deal with freedom. It would not be pushing things at all to say that most of them deal with the intimately related topic, the development of a self; without a self or coherent personality the individual can have no freedom, but is at the mercy of every fleeting emotion and momentary circumstance, and thus (in words already quoted in the afterword to *Notes from Underground*) is in "bondage to the passing moment." And the way in which a human being truly becomes an individual, a coherent personality, is by establishing a code, a conception of virtue, which shapes his daily actions. Faulkner's story is about a man with an unusual code.

The story is almost a fable or parable, a (seemingly) simple tale that allows a moral to be drawn. The directness of the opening sentence, for example, puts us in mind of such tales, or perhaps of a bedtime story: "Once (it was in Mississippi, in May, in the flood year 1927) there were two convicts." We notice also that the protagonist remains nameless, a sort of type; he doggedly persists in his task through almost insuperable obstacles; his character does not develop any more than that of a handsome prince in a fairy tale. We notice that the narrative concerns a journey on water (compare Conrad's *Heart of Darkness*) which takes him to an Indian burial ground, an "earthern Ark out of Genesis," and then takes him back into a sort of prehistoric world where he encounters what seem to be grunting savages, and where armed with only a club and a knife he fights monstrous reptiles. Such matters quite properly alert us to the fact that if this is a tale about a particular man, it is also a highly resonant tale. The fable-like suggestions are only part of what is in fact an extremely complicated study of what we might consider a rather simple man's mind. Faulkner himself, in a conversation with students at the University of Virginia, remarked that *Old Man* was the story of a man "just stupid and ignorant enough to bull right on. . . . To accept anything the gods threw at him without even knowing that he was being tried." This is a genial simplification, refuted by almost any page of the novel, but it can serve as a useful beginning. The long second sentence of the story can — very crudely — be reduced to the idea that the convict was so stupid that he believed he could learn how to perform a successful train robbery by reading pulp magazines, but when we read or reread this sentence, we see that this apparently simple idea in fact presupposes an impressive moral code: people who collect money for their writings ought to write truthfully, especially since their writings are not accompanied by a sworn claim to truth, for such a claim would alert one to the likelihood of untruths. That is not at all stupid or simple. On several occasions elsewhere in *Old Man,* after describing detailed and complicated trains of thought, Faulkner tells us that the convict did *not* think such thoughts, but this does not mean he is simple; it means that he has an intuitive knowledge and a deeply cherished code that make unnecessary the complicated cogitations of such thought-bound people as we.

If asked what this code was, the convict would be able to reply only that "he wanted to do it the right way"; what "the right way" is, is implicit throughout the story. If the code can be summed up in one word, possibly the word is "selflessness," or possibly "magnanimity." We can, for example, contrast the convict's behavior with that of the law-officers near the end. Here we meet people who are adept in the art of getting ahead — people who are able to hatch plans far beyond the thoughts of the convict. There is a deputy sheriff "canvassing for votes to beat his superior (who had given him his job) in the August primary." There is a deputy whose political power forces a governor's aide and a warden to get him out of a mess and into a job on the highway patrol although he "can't ride a motorcycle" ("He won't have to. Surely an amazed and grateful State can supply the man who guessed right three times in succession in Mississippi general elections with a car to ride in and somebody to run it if necessary").

These officers hear voices — the voices of others, and the voice that tells them how to take care of themselves, but the convict hears different voices, a voice of duty, and (much the same thing) the voice of the Mississippi River, the Old Man, who makes it clear that although for the most part men confidently move on a "placid and sleepy" surface, nature is never tamed and may at any time overturn their puny creations and test them to the uttermost.

> He did not begin to hear it all at once, he suddenly became aware that he had been hearing it all the time, a sound so much beyond all his experience and his powers of assimilation that up to this point he had been as oblivious of it as an ant or a flea might be of the sound of the avalanche on which it rides, he had been travelling upon water since early afternoon and for seven years now he had run his plow and harrow and planter within the very shadow of the levee on which he now stood, but this profound deep whisper which came from the further side of it he did not at once recognize.

In prison he had established a way of life that, though lacking in physical freedom, was satisfactory to him: he renounced the "fluid world of his time." But then, during the flood, the fluid world quite literally breaks in on him, and he finds himself in utterly different circumstances, ordered to rescue a pregnant woman. He does so, and he assists at childbirth, and finally after weeks of being battered by nature and by men (twice he is shot at, and once he is dynamited out of security) he gets the mother and child safely home and himself restored to prison where he can again, paradoxically, find freedom in the routine.

These comments have been rather solemn, and it would be unfair to the story to fail to mention that in many ways it is comic, having affinities with humorous tall tales of the frontier: a man survives a flood, fights alligators, drags a skiff with him wherever he goes, and finally — after making strenuous efforts to return to prison — is given an additional ten years for attempting to escape. The series of mishaps on the flooded river — for example, against his will he is swept from the Mississippi River to the Yazoo River and then back onto the Mississippi — bears some resemblance, too, to silent comedies, where a Buster Keaton is comically whirled hither and thither but partly through good luck and partly through resourcefulness comes out unhurt and where he wants to be. Consider, too, some of the ludicrous situations in *Old Man*: a man bases a train robbery on what he has read in pulp magazines; in prison he enjoys the absence of women (a woman got him into prison) but he is thrust out of this comfortable seclusion and assigned to rescue a pregnant woman in a tree. His boat capsizes, he nearly drowns, and he finds her quite by accident when the boat, at the mercy of the flood, crashes into a snag; then from her tree she laconically observes, "It's taken you a while," and (since the current had swept him past her once before), "I thought for a minute you wasn't aiming to come back." He can be laconic himself: summarizing the seven-week ordeal that ensued after he set out in a skiff to rescue a woman from a tree and a man from a cottonhouse (the man, we know but the convict does not, was rescued by others on the first day), he says, "Yonder's your boat, and here's the woman. But I never did find that bastard on the cottonhouse."

One additional quotation may help to show this fusion of comedy and simple dignity in *Old Man*. The convict is preparing to fight an alligator, and at this stage, having seen an alligator's hide nailed to a wall he knows only two relevant things: one is that alligators are bigger than hogs and "anything which looked like that on the outside would be more than likely to have teeth and claws too"; the second is that *"After all a man can't only do what he has to do, with what he has to do it with, with what he has learned, to the best of his judgment. And I reckon a hog is still a hog, no matter what it looks like."*

Most of the best literature of the twentieth century has concerned itself with the unconscious, especially the irrational, usually exploring in detail (as Dostoevsky already had done) the neurotic and anarchic impulses in man. Faulkner too is concerned with the unconscious or irrational, but in a most unusual way: he sees in the convict's unreasoned and unreasoning code a primitive way of life that, if it sometimes amuses, also compels our respect.

ALEXANDER SOLZHENITSYN

Alexander Solzhenitsyn (b. 1918) was born in Kislovodsk in the Caucasus in southern Russia. In 1938 he studied mathematics and physics at Rostov University; eventually he married and taught in a secondary school in Rostov-on-Don. He joined the Soviet Army in 1941, and became an artillery officer, twice decorated for valor. In 1945, arrested for having criticized Stalin in a letter to a friend, he was sentenced to eight years in a slave labor camp. Freed in 1953, he was exiled to Kazakhstan. He was stricken with cancer of the stomach and was sent to Tashkent where, after treatment, he recovered. In 1956 he was released from exile and rehabilitated in the post-Stalin era a year later. He settled in Ryazan where he once more taught mathematics in a local school. *One Day in the Life of Ivan Denisovich,* personally authorized by Khrushchev, was published in the official Soviet publication *Novy Mir (New World)* in 1962. It was followed in 1963 by several short stories, but with Khrushchev's fall from power Solzhenitsyn was once more denounced and in 1969 expelled from the Soviet Writers Union. His works are still officially banned in Russia. Two novels, *The First Circle* and *Cancer Ward,* were published outside Russia in 1968, and another novel, *August 1914,* was published outside Russia in 1972. He was awarded the Nobel Prize for Literature in 1970 but was not allowed to leave Russia to accept the citation. A movie version of *One Day* was released in 1971.

ONE DAY IN THE LIFE OF IVAN DENISOVICH

Translated by Thomas P. Whitney

At five, as always, reveille was sounded — a hammer pounded on a rail at headquarters barracks. The clanging crept faintly, sporadically, through the window glass and the inch-thick coating of ice that covered it. It ended soon. That morning was cold and the guard didn't feel like hammering very long.

Outside the window deep darkness lay everywhere, just as it had in the middle of the night when Shukhov had waked to go to the latrine barrel. Only the gleam of lamplight fell on the window from two yellow lamps out in the zone and one inside the camp.

For some reason they hadn't come to open the barracks yet. And Shukhov didn't hear the usual noises of the orderlies lifting the latrine barrel on poles to carry it out.

Shukhov never slept past the rising gong. He always got up when he heard it. Until lineup there was an hour and a half of one's own time, not the government's. Anyone who knew camp life could always earn a bit then. He could sew a mitten-cover out of an old lining. He could run to deliver the dry *valenki* — felt boots — of some rich fellow-member of the work brigade to his bunk so he wouldn't have to hop barefoot around the pile to find them himself. A man could busy himself in the storerooms doing odd chores, sweeping or carrying. Or he could go to the mess hall to gather bowls from the tables and carry them in piles to the dishwasher. For that job he'd be fed, but many others were playing that game, too. Too many in fact. But the dangerous thing about that job was that if a bowl had something left in it, one couldn't restrain oneself and would lick it clean. Shukhov remembered the warning words of his first-brigade foreman, Kuzyemin. An old camp wolf who had served time for twelve years by 1943. Kuzyemin once said, at a bonfire in a clearing in the woods, to reinforcements brought from the front, "It's the law of the jungle here. But even so, people live. The men who die in camp are the ones who lick bowls, the ones who pin hopes on the medical department, and the ones who play stool-pigeon."

About the stool-pigeon bit — there, of course, he overdid it. That kind took good care of themselves, though it cost the blood of others.

Shukhov always got up at rising gong. But not today. Since the evening before, he'd felt ill: at times he felt feverish, at times he ached all over. And he hadn't been able to get warm. During the night, even in his sleep, he felt as though he had really fallen seriously ill. Then a while later he seemed better. He kept wishing morning wouldn't come.

But the morning came on schedule.

Where could he get warm? There was ice an inch thick on the window, white spiderwebs of frost high up on the walls. What a barracks!

Shukhov didn't get up. He stayed in his bunk, his head covered with blanket and coat. Both feet were pushed down together into one turned-under sleeve of his cotton-padded underjacket. With his head covered he couldn't see, but he knew exactly what was going on by the sounds in the barracks and in the corner of it occupied by his own brigade. There now, moving clumsily along the corridor, came the orderlies carrying one of the eight-bucket latrine barrels. That's considered light work, you invalid! But just try to haul it out without slopping it over! In the section occupied by the 75th brigade, the bundle of valenki returned from the dryer was slammed down on the floor. Now: the same sound in our section. It was our turn, too, to dry out valenki today. The brigade foreman and assistant foreman were pulling on their boots in silence, but their bunks creaked. The assistant foreman would be going off to the bread rationing office: the foreman to headquarters barracks, to the planning-production section.

Yes, and today the foreman was not just going to the work assignment officers as he did every day. Today the brigade's fate was being decided. There were plans afoot to shift the 104th from the construction of workshops to a new project, the "Socialist Life Town." The Socialist Life Town was now just a bare open field, all snow ridges and drifts. Before anything could be built there, the prisoners would have to dig holes, set in posts, and put up barbed wire — fencing themselves in so they couldn't escape. Only when that was done could they start to build. For at least a month there'd be no place to get warm out there. No bonfires either — nothing to build them with. Working like hell would be the only salvation.

The brigade foreman was worried about that project and he'd gone to try to fix things so that some other brigade would get sent there, instead of his own. Of course, he couldn't manage this empty-handed. He had to take a pound of fat bacon for the senior work-assignment officer. Maybe even two pounds. It was worth trying, anyway.

Maybe Shukhov should have a try at the infirmary, see if he could get out of work today. Really, his whole body felt as if it was coming apart.

He tried to recall which of the guards was on duty that day.

He remembered — it was One-and-a-Half Ivan, a thin, tall sergeant with black eyes. The first time you saw him he seemed terrifying. But actually he was the easiest to get along with of all the duty guards. He didn't put people in solitary, didn't drag them off to the chief of discipline. So it was all right for Shukhov to lie there awhile — even till barracks nine went to the mess hall.

His bunk shook and shuddered. Two men were getting out of bed at the same time: the Baptist, Alyesha, who was next to Shukhov in a top bunk, and Buinovsky, who had the bunk under Shukhov. Buinovsky was a navy captain, second rank — that is, he used to be.

Now the orderlies, having carried out the latrine barrel, were squabbling about who would go for the hot water. They sounded like a couple of old women. The electric welder from the 20th brigade yelled at them:

"Hey, you old good-for-nothings!" He threw a boot at them. "I'll shut you up!"

The fat boot whammed hollowly against a post. They shut up.

In the neighboring brigade the assistant foreman growled, just audibly:

"Vasil Fedorych! They cheated again at the ration counter, the bastards: there were four two-pound loaves, and now there are only three. Who gets short rations?"

He said this in a low voice, but, of course, that whole brigade was listening with bated breath. Some of them were going to be missing part of their bread that evening.

Shukhov just kept lying there on the hard-packed sawdust. He wished that he would either come down with a fever or else that the ache would go away. This way he was neither sick nor well.

Meanwhile, the Baptist whispered his prayers and Buinovsky returned from the latrine and announced to no one in particular, but in a gloating tone: "Brace yourselves, Red Navy men! It's twenty below for certain!"

Shukhov decided to go to the infirmary.

And right at that moment an authoritative hand jerked his blanket and underjacket off him. Shukhov pushed his coat off his face and lifted his head. Beneath him, his head level with the upper edge of the bunk, stood the lean Tartar.

So the Tartar was on duty, though it wasn't his turn — and had sneaked up on Shukhov silently.

"S-854!" the Tartar read the numbered label on the back of the black coat. "Three days penalty — with outside work!"

And hardly had his lowered voice sounded, than throughout the still-dim half of the barracks, where not all the bulbs were burning, where on fifty bedbug-infested bunks two hundred men slept, a buzz of activity began and everyone who was not up hurriedly started dressing.

"Why, citizen chief?" Shukhov asked, putting into his voice a more imploring-pitiful tone than he really felt. Because work outside was only semi-solitary. There was hot food and there was no time to brood. Total solitary was when they didn't take you out to work.

"Why didn't you get up at the signal? Let's get going to the commandant," the Tartar explained carelessly, because he and Shukhov and everyone else knew what the penalty was for.

The hairless, worn face of the Tartar was an expressionless blank. He turned to look for another victim, but in half-darkness, under lamps, on lower bunks and upper, everyone was pushing his legs down into the black quilted trousers, or else, already dressed, was bundling up and hurrying off to the exit in order to wait outside till the Tartar left.

If Shukhov had received solitary for something else, something that really rated solitary, he wouldn't have been so put out. He was angry because he was always one of the first to get up. But he knew he couldn't beg off. Not from the Tartar. And though he continued for appearance' sake to ask to be let off, Shukhov pulled on his quilted trousers (on the left knee there was a ragged, dirty patch, with a black number in faded ink — S-854) and then his quilted under-jacket (there were two numbers on the jacket — one in front and the other on the back), then went and picked out his valenki from the pile on the floor, put on his cap (with the same kind of patch and number in front) and followed the Tartar.

All the 104th saw Shukhov led out, but no one said a word. It was useless. What was there to say? The foreman might have defended him, but he wasn't in the barracks. And Shukhov didn't say a word to his bunkmates. They'd look after his breakfast without his asking.

The two went outside.

The cold, combined with mist, made one gasp. Two big searchlights swept the zone in a crisscross starting from the two corner watchtowers. Lamps were lit in the zone and inside the camp itself. There were so many of them they shut out the stars with their light.

With valenki crunching in the snow, *zeks* — prisoners — ran quickly about their affairs: some to latrines, some to storerooms, one to the warehouse for package from home, another to the individual kitchen to turn in cereals to be cooked for him. All of them had their shoulders hunched, heads down, coats buttoned up. All were cold, not so much from the low temperature itself, as from the realization that they were going to be spending the whole day out in that low temperature. But the Tartar, in his old army coat with its bedraggled blue tabs, walked erect as if he didn't feel the cold one bit.

They went past the high board fence that surrounded the BUR — the internal camp punishment prison — then past the barbed wire that protected the camp bakery from the prisoners, past the corner of the headquarters barracks where the frost-covered length of track hung suspended from its post by a thick wire, past another post where the frost-covered thermometer hung in a sheltered corner so it didn't show too low a temperature. Shukhov hopefully sneaked a glance at its milky-white tube. If it were to show 42° below they would not drive the zeks out to work. But today it wasn't anywhere near 40° below.

They went into headquarters barracks and straight into the guards' room. There it quickly became clear (as Shukhov had begun to sense on the way) that he was not going to be given solitary at all, but simply ordered to scrub the dirty floor in the guards' room. At this point the Tartar announced that he had forgiven Shukhov and ordered him to wash the floor.

Washing the floor in the guards' room was the assignment of a special zek who was not sent out in the zone to work. He was the barracks orderly and this was his own particular job. But, having made himself at home in the headquarters barracks, he had access to the offices of the major, the chief of discipline, and the "Godfather" too — the security chief. He waited on them, and now and then heard things even the guards did not know. As a result, he had come to consider it beneath his dignity to wash floors for ordinary guards. These called for him once or twice, then understood what the score was, and began to grab men from among the camp working stiffs to wash their floors.

In the guards' room the stove was vigorously radiating heat. Stripped down to dirty undershirts, two guards were playing checkers. The third slept on a narrow bench in his belted sheepskin and valenki. In a corner stood a bucket with a rag.

Shukhov was pleased to be let off. He said to the Tartar:

"Thank you, citizen chief. I'll never sleep too late again."

The rule here was simple: finish and get out. Now that Shukhov had work to do it seemed his aches had stopped. He took the pail. He had no mittens — in his hurry he had left them under his pillow. He went out to the well.

Several brigade foremen on their way to the planning and production section were gathered around the pole where the thermometer was hung. And one, younger than the rest, a former Hero of the Soviet Union, had climbed up the pole to read the thermometer. From below came words of advice:

"Be careful to breathe to one side — otherwise it will rise."

"Like your prick it will! Rise! Not a chance!"

Tyurin, Shukhov's brigade foreman, was not there. Having put down his bucket and shoved his hands in his sleeves, Shukhov watched, curious.

Then the one up the pole said hoarsely:

"Seventeen below! Oh, the hell with it!"

And taking one more look to be sure, he dropped down.

"Well, it's never right, it's always wrong," someone said. "Unlikely they'd hang an accurate one here!"

The brigade foremen went their ways. Shukhov ran on to the well. Beneath his untied earflaps the frost bit at his ears.

The log well-housing was coated with a thick layer of ice. The bucket hardly fit through the opening in it. The rope was as stiff as a stick.

With his full bucket giving off a frosty mist, Shukhov returned to the guardroom. His hands were numb: he shoved them into the cold water. They seemed to get warmer.

The Tartar was no longer there. But there were four guards now. They had given up checkers and sleep and were quarreling about how much millet they were going to be given in January. In the nearby settlement food was short, and the guards, even though rationing had long since come to an end, were being sold certain food products outside the general distribution system for the locals, at cut rate.

As Shukhov came in, one shouted, "Shut that door, you *shit!* There's a draft!"

It was very bad to get valenki wet in the morning. There were no other shoes even had he been able to run back to the barracks. Shukhov had seen various deals with footwear in his eight years of sitting in camps. Once he had gone a whole winter without either valenki or leather shoes, at all, just with *lapty* — sandals of bark — and C-T-Zs — from the initials of the Chelysbinsk Tractor Factory — made out of pieces of tires. Now things had improved: in October Shukhov had trailed along behind the assistant foreman to the storerooms, and received a pair of tough leather boots. They had hard toes, with room for two warm footcloths. For a week he had gone about as gaily as if he were celebrating his birthday and he kept clapping his heels. And then in December the felt valenki had come. What a good life! No need to die after all! But then some devil in the bookkeeping department had whispered to the chief: let them have the valenki and turn the leather shoes in. It seemed it was out of order for a zek to have two pairs of shoes at once. And so Shukhov had to choose: either go out in leather shoes all winter long, or keep the valenki even for the thaws, when they would get soaked through. He turned in the shoes. He had taken loving care of them, softened their leather with oil, new shoes, oh my! He hadn't been so regretful about anything in all eight years as those shoes. They were thrown on a big pile. There was no chance that he'd find his own again in the spring.

Now Shukhov deftly slipped off his valenki, put them in a corner, and threw his footcloths after them. His spoon fell out of his valenki, and rang out as it hit the floor. No matter how hurriedly he had dressed for solitary, he never forgot his spoon. He retrieved it: then, barefoot; generously sloshing water on the floor with the rag, he went to work right under the feet of the guards.

"You! Bastard! Careful!" one of the guards noticed the water, lifting his feet onto a chair.

"Rice? Rice is in another category," another guard went on. "Don't try to draw comparison with rice!"

"Listen, fool, how much water are you going to slop around? Who washes that way?"

"Citizen chief! You can't wash it off otherwise. The dirt has eaten its way in."

"Haven't you ever seen how your old woman washed floors, pig?"

Shukhov drew himself up straight, holding in his hand the dripping rag. He smiled simple-mindedly, showing where teeth were missing which he'd lost when he had had scurvy at Ust-Izhma[1] in the far north, in 1943. He had nearly been done for then: he had come so close that bleeding diarrhea had just about emptied him of his insides and his exhausted stomach hadn't wanted to hold a thing. But now all he had left of that was missing teeth and a lisp.

"From my old woman, citizen chief, they gave me a discharge in 1941. I can't even remember what kind of an old woman she was."

"That's the way they wash. . . . The bastards don't know how to do anything and don't want to do anything. They aren't worth the bread they are given. They should get shit to eat."

"Fuck it! Why should the floor be washed every day! The damp won't go away. Listen here, 854! You wipe it off easy, so it's a little wet, and then get out."

"Rice! Don't compare millet and rice."

Shukhov quickly dealt with the task.

Work — it's like a stick. It has two ends. If you do it for humans then you give quality. If you do it for idiots then it's just for show.

1 [A labor camp. — Editors' note.]

Otherwise everyone would have dropped dead long since. Everyone knew that.

Shukhov wiped the floor boards just so no dry spots were left. He threw the unwrung rag behind the stove. At the threshold he pulled on his valenki, splashed the pail of water out along the path that the chiefs used, and hurried out past the bath, past the dark, cold club building, taking a short cut to the mess hall.

He still had to get to the infirmary. He was aching all over again. And he had to be careful not to run into guards in front of the mess hall. There was a strict order from the camp chief: catch lone zeks who lagged behind their brigades and put them in solitary.

In front of the mess hall today — it was a miracle — there was no crowd milling about, no line. He could just go in.

Inside there was as much steam as a bath house. Gusts of frost from the door and steam from the thin camp soup. Brigades were sitting at the tables or crowding about in the aisles, waiting for room to sit down. Yelling to each other through the mob, two or three workers from each brigade were carrying wooden trays with bowls of thin soup and *kasha* — cooked porridge: usually oats, buckwheat or grits. They were looking for room on the tables.

That guy blocking the aisle doesn't hear, the stupid ass. There you go, you've bumped a tray! Slip, slop! Give it to him good with your free hand, on the neck! That's right! Get out of the way! Don't stand there looking for a bowl to lick.

At a nearby table, a young chap crossed himself before he began to eat. That meant he was Western Ukrainian, and a newcomer. The Russians have even forgotten what hand to cross themselves with.

It was cold in the mess hall. Most of the men ate with their caps on but without hurrying, catching the boiled chunks of disintegrated fish out from under the leaves of black cabbage and spitting the bones on the table. When a whole pile of bones accumulated someone brushed them off the table and they crunched beneath the boots on the floor. But spitting them straight onto the floor was considered to be sort of improper.

In the center of the barracks were two rows of things which weren't quite pillars and not quite supports either. And at one of these posts sat Shukhov's fellow-brigade member, Fetyukov, guarding Shukhov's breakfast. He was one of the lowest-ranking members of the brigade, lower than Shukhov. From outside the brigade everyone seemed alike in their black three-quarter length coats, in their similar numbers, but on the inside it was very unequal — it went by steps. Buinovsky would not be asked to sit guarding a bowl, and even Shukhov would not undertake just any kind of work. There were steps beneath him.

Fetyukov noticed Shukhov and sighed, yielding his seat.

"Everything is cold. I was just about to eat your portion. I thought you were in solitary."

He didn't hang around because he knew Shukhov wouldn't leave a thing, that he would clean out both bowls.

Shukhov pulled his spoon from one of his valenki. That spoon was dear to him. It had travelled with him through the whole north country. He had cast it himself out of aluminum wire in sand. On it was etched in dots: "Ust-Izhma, 1944."

Then Shukhov took his cap off his shaved head. He didn't eat with his cap on, no matter what the temperature. He stirred the cooled-off soup and studied it to see what he had in the bowl. What he had received was from the middle. It wasn't from the top of the pot nor from the bottom either. And he knew Fetyukov: it could well be that while guarding the bowl he might have picked out a potato or two.

The one pleasure in that thin camp soup was that it was hot. Shukhov's was quite cold by now. However, he began to eat it as slowly, as attentively, as usual. He wouldn't have hurried if the building were burning. Not taking sleep into account, a camp inmate lives for himself only ten minutes in the morning at breakfast, five at lunch, and another five at dinner.

The camp soup didn't change from day to day. It depended on what vegetable had been procured for the winter. The year before they had had only salted carrots. And so the soup had been made of plain carrots from September to June. This year it was black cabbage. The most nourishing time of the year for the camp inmates was June. All the vegetables were finished and were replaced by grits. The most meagre time was July: the cooks cut up nettles for the pot.

They got mostly the bones of the little fish. The meat boiled off the bones, fell apart, and clung only to the head and tail. Shukhov chewed and sucked away on the brittle network of the fish skeleton, which bore no trace of flesh or scale — then spat it out on the table. In any fish he ate everything, even gills and tail. Even the eyes, when they were still in their place in the head. But when they boiled out and swam about in the bowl separately — big fish eyes — he wouldn't eat them. The other zeks laughed at him for this.

Today Shukhov had saved up a bit of food. Since he hadn't gone back to the barracks and had not received his bread ration he was now eating without bread. Bread — that could be eaten later by itself. Even more satisfying.

For his second course there was kasha made from *magara*. It came in one chunk. Shukhov broke pieces off it. Even when it was hot it was without any taste or feeling of nourishment: grains like grass, only yellow, looking like millet. It was said to come from the Chinese. In boiled weight it ran to maybe ten ounces a portion: kasha which wasn't kasha but given out instead of kasha.

Having licked off his spoon and shoved it down in its former place in one of his valenki, Shukhov put on his cap and went off to the infirmary.

It was still just as dark in the sky. The two searchlights still cut with the same powerful beams across the camp zone. When they had originally set up that camp, a Special Camp, the guards had had a lot of rocket illuminating flares on hand left from the war. Whenever the electricity failed they showered rockets over the zone — white, green, red. Just like a real war. Then they stopped shooting off rockets. Maybe it was too costly?

It was just as dark outside as it had been when the rising gong had rung, but to an experienced eye various small details would easily have indicated that lineup was soon to be called. The assistant to that mess hall orderly named Khromoi — whom Khromoi supported on his own — went to call to breakfast the sixth barracks, which was filled with invalids — those who did not go out to work in the zone. An old artist with a little beard made his way slowly to the cultural and educational section to get paints and a brush to paint prisoner numbers. Then the Tartar strode hurriedly through the lineup ground in the direction of headquarters barracks. There were few people out — that meant nearly everyone had taken shelter to be warm for those last lovely minutes.

Shukhov adroitly hid from the Tartar behind the corner of the barracks. If he caught Shukhov once more he'd come at him again. The fact was, one couldn't even afford to yawn: stay alert! One had to keep from being caught alone by any guard. A guard might be looking for someone for some work, or he might be looking for someone on whom to vent his meanness. For instance, take that order that had been read off in the barracks — remove your cap five steps in front of a guard, and two steps beyond him put it on. Some guards didn't look and didn't care — but for others this was sugar candy. How many zeks had been dragged off to solitary because of that cap deal! Still it was always better to hide around a corner.

The Tartar went by. Shukhov was about to go on to the infirmary when he suddenly remembered that he had planned to go before lineup, this morning to the seventh barracks to buy two glassfuls of home-grown tobacco from that tall Latvian. But Shukhov had been so rushed it had completely slipped his mind. The tall Latvian had received a package last night. It was possible that tomorrow he'd have no more of that tobacco left. Then Shukhov would have to wait a whole month before more arrived. The Latvian had good tobacco, just strong and pungent enough. Brownish.

Shukhov tapped a foot in annoyance — should he go to the seventh barracks? But he was very close to the infirmary now so he trotted over to the building. The snow crunched loudly beneath his feet.

In the infirmary, as always, the hallway was so clean he was almost afraid to walk on the floor. The walls painted in white enamel. All the furniture white, too.

But the doors of all the receiving rooms were shut. The doctors, he supposed, weren't up yet. The medical assistant was on duty, a young chap named Kolya Vdovushkin. He was sitting behind a clean table, in a fresh white coat, writing.

No one else was about.

Shukhov took off his cap, as if the young man were a camp official, and with the camp habit of noticing everything he shouldn't, he saw that Kolya was writing level, even lines and every line was indented from the edge and began with a capital letter. Shukhov understood immediately, of course, that this was not official work, but something of his own. But that wasn't Shukhov's affair.

"Listen, Nikolai Semenych," he said to Kolya, "I am kind of . . . sick. . . ." Shukhov spoke guiltily as if he had designs on something that didn't belong to him.

Vdovushkin lifted his calm, big eyes from his work. He had on a white cap, as well as the white coat. His numbers were not visible.

"Why are you so late? And why didn't you come last night? You know that we don't receive patients in the morning. The list of those excused from work today has been sent to the planning and production section already."

Shukhov knew all that. He also knew that it wasn't any easier to get excused from work in the evening.

"Look Kolya. . . . In the evenings, when I need it, it doesn't ache. . . ."

"What is *it?* What aches?"

"Well, if I try to pin it down then nothing aches. But I hurt all over."

Shukhov was not one of the men who made pests of themselves at the infirmary and Vdovushkin knew that. But he only had the right to excuse two men in the morning. He had already given permission to two, and their names were written beneath the greenish glass on the desk.

"Well, you should have done something about it before. What are you thinking of — right before lineup! Here, take this!"

Vdovushkin pulled a thermometer from the jar in which several were stuck through cuts in gauze, wiped off the solution, and gave it to Shukhov to take his temperature.

Shukhov sat on the bench next to the wall, on its farthest edge, so that he almost but not quite tipped over with it. He picked this uncomfortable position not on purpose — but involuntarily showing he was not at home in the infirmary and wasn't there for anything of major importance.

Vdovushkin went on writing.

The infirmary was in the quietest, most distant corner of the zone and no sounds at all reached here. No wall clock ticking away. (The prisoners were not allowed watches or clocks: the administration was supposed to know the time for them.) And not even a mouse scratching. The hospital cat had caught all of them. That was his function.

Shukhov felt delighted to be sitting in such a clean room, in such stillness, under a bright lamp, doing nothing for five whole minutes. He looked over the walls, but there was nothing on them. He inspected his underjacket — the number on his chest was worn and should be touched up; otherwise they might get him for that. He felt his beard with his free hand. It had grown out a lot. Been growing ever since the last visit to the bath house, more than ten days ago. But it didn't matter anyway. In another three days there'd be another visit to the bath house and then he would be shaved. Why stand in the barber shop line for nothing? Shukhov had nobody to pretty up for.

Then, looking at Vdovushkin's white cap, Shukhov remembered the field hospital on the Lovat River, how he had arrived there with a wounded jaw and then — what a stupid jackass he'd been — of his own will he had returned to the front, though he could have spent at least five days in bed.

And now he even had dreams about getting sick for a week or two, not mortally ill, of course, and nothing that required operations, but just sick enough so they'd put him in the hospital, where he could lie still for three weeks, not moving. They would feed him only clear broth. That was all right too.

But then Shukhov remembered that even in the hospital they no longer allowed a stay in bed. A new doctor had appeared among a new load of prisoners. Stepan Grigorich, noisy and active, never kept still himself, and wouldn't allow the patients to rest, either. He thought up the idea of forcing all the patients who could move to work around the hospital: to put up a fence around the garden, to make little paths, to carry soil for flower beds, and in the winter to pile snow for soil moisture. He declared work was the best medicine for sickness.

But even horses die from overwork; he ought to know that. If *he* had to work his tail off laying cement blocks, he might quiet down for a change.

Vdovushkin went on writing. It was true that he was busy working for himself, but what he was doing would have been incomprehensible to Shukhov even if Shukhov had known what it was. He was copying out a long new poem he had finished the night before and had promised to show to Stepan Grigorich, that same doctor who was a supporter of work therapy.

It was one of those things that happens only in camps. Stepan Grigorich had advised Vdovushkin to declare himself to be a medical assistant, and had put him to work as a medical assistant. He had begun to teach Vdovushkin to give intravenous injections to unenlightened working stiffs whose decent honest minds would never suspect that a medical assistant might not really be a medical assistant at all. Actually Kolya had been a student in a university literary department and was arrested in his second year. Stepan Grigorevich wanted him to have the chance to write in prison what he would not have been allowed to write in freedom.

Through the double windows covered over with translucent white ice, the lineup gong was barely audible. Shukhov sighed and stood up when he heard it. He felt as feverish as before, but it didn't look as if he had much chance to get out of working. Vdovushkin reached for the thermometer and read it:

"Well, it's neither one thing nor the other — just 99. If it were 100.4 then the whole thing would be quite clear. As it is I can't free you from work. If you want, you can wait here at your own risk. If the doctor believes you're ill, you'll be excused from work. If he thinks you're healthy and malingering — off to solitary. You'd be smarter to go out to the zone."

Shukhov didn't answer. Without even nodding he pulled on his cap and went out.

Will a warm man ever understand one who's cold?

The cold pinched. The cold, and a biting little fog, made Shukhov cough. Out in the cold it was 17° below. Inside Shukhov it was 99° above. Now it was a question of who would do in whom.

Shukhov trotted to the barracks. The lineup grounds were completely empty. The whole camp was empty. It was that short minute, relaxed, when though all retreat has been cut off people were pretending that there wouldn't be any lineup. The convoy of escort guards sat in their warm barracks, sleepy heads leaning on rifles — it wasn't sweet butter for them either to stamp up and down in guard towers in such a cold. The guards on duty in the main watch house shovelled some coal in the stove. The guards in the guards' room smoked their last hand-rolled cigarette. The zeks, dressed in all their tatters, all belted with ropes, all wrapped from chin to eyes with pieces of cloth to protect them against the cold, were lying on their bunks on top of their blankets, eyes closed, hearts sinking. Waiting for the foreman to shout, "Let's go!"

With the rest of the ninth barracks, the 104th brigade dozed. Only the assistant foreman, Pavlo, with silently moving lips, was adding something with a pencil, yes, and up on the upper bunk the Baptist, Alyesha, Shukhov's neighbor, clean, well-washed, was reading the notebook in which he had copied half of the Gospels.

Shukhov ran in fast but quiet and went straight to the assistant foreman's bunk.

Pavlo raised his head.

"So they didn't put you in solitary, Ivan Denisych? You're alive?"

Those Western Ukrainians, no matter how they tried to teach them better in the camps, addressed people politely and decently.

And taking Shukhov's bread ration from the table he handed it over to him. On the bread there was, in a little white mound, a scoop of sugar.

Shukhov was in a great hurry but nevertheless he replied politely. For the assistant foreman was also a chief and in fact was even more important to Shukhov than the chief of the camp. As he hurried, he licked the sugar off the bread and, with one foot on the bracket — he had to climb up to make his bunk — managed to look over the bread ration and weigh it with his hand to see whether it was really the eighteen ounces it was supposed to be. He had received thousands of these rations in prisons and camps. Though he had never had the chance to check any of them on a scale, and though he, shy as he was, did not dare to make a fuss and yell about his rights, nevertheless to Shukhov (and to every prisoner) it had long been evident that anyone who weighed bread out honestly wouldn't keep his job long in the bread-cutting room. There was something missing in every ration. The only question was how much. A lot? And so every day you look, to ease your soul — maybe today they didn't cheat me badly? Maybe it's close to the correct weight.

"One ounce missing," Shukhov decided. He broke the ration in two. One half he shoved down inside his clothes, beneath his underjacket, where he had sewed a special white pocket — underjackets for zeks were made without pockets. The other half he almost ate right then and there, but food is not food if eaten in a hurry. It goes down for nothing, without satisfying the appetite. He started to push the half-ration into his locker but thought better of that idea too. He remembered that the orderlies had been beaten up twice for stealing. It was a big barracks and accessible to anyone who wanted to come in.

And therefore, without letting go of the bread, Ivan Denisovich pulled his feet out of his valenki, adroitly leaving inside both his footcloths and his spoon, and climbed up barefoot. He then set to widening a little tear in his mattress, and he hid there, in the sawdust, his half-ration. He pulled his cap off, pulled out his needle and thread. They were also hidden deeply. At inspection caps were examined, and once a guard had pricked himself on the needle and almost broke Shukhov's head in fury. Stitch, stitch again, and stitch a third time, and he had sewn shut the little hole behind which the ration was hidden. By this time the suger in his mouth had melted. Shukhov was tense as he could be. Any second the duty detail guard was going to start shouting at the door. Shukhov's fingers worked nimbly and his brain, running ahead, figured what to do next.

The Baptist was reading the Gospels, not in silence, but softly under his breath. Perhaps this was for Shukhov's benefit. Those Baptists liked to hand out a little propaganda.

"But let none of you suffer as a murderer, or a thief, or a wrongdoer, or as a mischief-maker; yet if one suffers as a Christian, let him not be ashamed, but under that name let him glorify God."

Alyesha had managed to hide his little book in a cranny in the wall so well that they hadn't found it during any search yet. He deserved a pat on the back.

Shukhov, with the same quick movements, hung his coat up on a crossbar, pulled his mittens out from under his mattress, and a second pair of footcloths — thin ones — a piece of rope and a piece of cloth with ribbons on its ends.

He smoothed out the sawdust in the mattress — it was hard and bumpy. He pushed the edges of the blanket under and tossed the pillow to its place. Then he climbed down and began to put on his footwear, first his good footcloths, then the thin ones over those.

Then the foreman coughed, got up and barked emphatically:

"Off the beds, 104th, get outside!"

Immediately the whole brigade, those dozing, those not dozing, got up, yawning, and headed for the door. The foreman had been sitting in camps for nineteen years. He wasn't likely to drive the men out for lineup one minute earlier than necessary. When he said "Get outside!" It meant get out as fast as you can.

And during the brief interval while the brigade members tramped out without a word, in file, into the corridor and then into the covered entry and out to the porch, and the foreman of the 20th, imitating Tyurin, had also declared, "Get outside!" Shukhov had succeeded in pulling on his valenki over two sets of footcloths, pulling on his coat over his underjacket and tightly belting himself with rope. (Leather belts had been taken away from any who had them — no belts in Special Camps.)

So Shukhov succeeded in getting everything done and in the covered entry he caught up with his last fellow brigade members as they hurried through the door onto the porch. Thick with layers of clothing, wearing everything they owned, the brigade members, moving in single file far enough apart to keep off each other's heels, tramped to the lineup ground. The only sound they made was the noise of feet crunching on snow.

It was still dark, though the sky in the east was becoming greenish and light. A thin mean little wind was blowing from the east, too.

There is no moment more bitter than this — to go out to lineup in the morning, in the darkness, in the cold, with hungry stomachs for a whole day. Your tongue is bitten off. You don't want to talk with each other.

Out on the lineup ground a junior work assignment officer was rushing back and forth. He snapped:

"Well, Tyurin, how long are we supposed to wait? You dragging things out again?"

Shukhov was afraid of the junior assignment officer but Tyurin certainly wasn't. He wouldn't even waste one breath on the officer this cold morning, just strode on in silence. And the whole brigade right behind him: tramp-tramp, crunch-crunch.

The two pounds of bacon evidently had worked as a bribe because the 104th was still in its old place. Some poorer and more stupid outfit was being driven out to the Socialist Life Town. Oh, but it would be ferocious out there today — a windy 17° below and no shelter, no fire!

The brigade foreman had to have a great deal of bacon. He had to have some to take to the planning and production section and some to satisfy his own stomach. The foreman, even though he didn't receive any parcels himself, ate bacon all the time. Everyone in the brigade who got any took it to him right away.

Otherwise you wouldn't last.

The senior work assignment officer noted on his board:

"One sick for you today, Tyurin, and twenty-three at work?"

Who is missing? Panteleyev is missing. Is he supposed to be sick? Immediately there were whispers in the brigade. Panteleyev, the dog, had remained in camp again. Not very likely he's sick! The security section had been asking for him. He was probably denouncing someone right now.

During the day the security section could send for him without hindrance. Hold him for three hours or more if they felt like it. No one saw. No one heard. They processed him through the medical department.

The whole lineup ground was dark with black coats. The brigades slowly pushed and shoved forward to body inspection. Shukhov remembered he had wanted to have the number on his underjacket touched up and pushed his way through the lineup ground to the far side. Two or three zeks were standing in line waiting for the artist. Shukhov got in line too. For the zeks, the number was one big pain in the neck. By your number a guard could spot you at a distance and the convoy guard could write it down, but if you let it fade, then solitary for you — why don't you take care of your number?

Three artists in the camp. They painted free pictures for the officers and in addition to that took turns at painting numbers at lineup. Today it was the old man with the little gray beard. When he painted the number on a cap with his brush he seemed like the priest anointing foreheads with oil.

He painted away and painted away and breathed into his glove. He wore thin knit gloves. His hand was stiff, didn't make the numbers clear. The artist touched up the S-854 on his underjacket. Shukhov, without buttoning his coat, because it was only a few minutes to body search, rushed off and caught up with his brigade, the rope belt in his hand. Right away he noticed that his fellow brigade member, Tsezar, was smoking. And smoking not a pipe but a cigarette. That meant he might be able to bum a butt-end. Shukhov didn't ask directly, but he moved right next to Tsezar and his face, half-turned, looked over past him.

He looked past him, pretending to be indifferent, but saw how after every puff — and they were infrequent because Tsezar was buried in thought — the red ember moved along the cigarette, and approached the cigarette holder.

Right then Fetyukov, the jackal, appeared opposite Tsezar and stared right at his mouth, his eyes burning.

Shukhov didn't have a shred of tobacco left and he didn't foresee any chance of getting any till evening. He was strained in expectation, and, it seemed at that moment that he wanted that cigarette butt more than he wanted freedom. But even so, he wouldn't humiliate himself like Fetyukov, by staring at Tsezar's lips.

All nations were mingled in Tsezar. Whether he was a Greek, Jew, or Gypsy was hard to say. He was still young. He had been a motion picture cameraman, but he hadn't even finished his own first film before he was arrested. He had a moustache, black, thick, dense as if sculptured. They were not shaved off because in his official record he had been photographed with them on.

"Tsezar Markovich!" Losing restraint, Fetyukov slobbered. "Let me have a drag!" His face was twisted with hunger and greed.

Tsezar barely raised his eyelids, which half covered his black eyes, and looked at Fetyukov. Lately Tsezar had begun to smoke a pipe so that the zeks wouldn't interrupt him while he was smoking, with a plea for a drag. It wasn't the tobacco he regretted but the interrupted thought. He smoked and gave himself over to contemplation: he got ideas that way. But he was able to hardly light a cigarette before he read in several eyes: "Let me finish it off!"

Now Tsezar turned to Shukhov and said:

"Take it, Ivan Denisych!"

And with his thumb he twisted the burning butt out of his short amber mouthpiece. Shukhov roused himself and hurriedly and gratefully took the butt end, holding a hand on guard underneath so he wouldn't drop it. He had waited for Tsezar himself to offer it. He was not offended that Tsezar was squeamish about giving him the mouthpiece along with the cigarette. After all some people have clean mouths and others have putrid mouths. And his calloused fingers were not burned, even touching the burning end. The main thing was that he had beat out the jackal, Fetyukov, and was now inhaling smoke while his lips began to burn from the fire. Yummmmmm! The smoke went all through his hungry body. He felt it in his feet and in his head.

And hardly had that bliss poured through his body than he heard the roar:

"They're taking away our undershirts!"

Trouble was a zek's whole life. Shukhov was used to it. Just watch out or they'll tear out your throats.

Why undershirts? The undershirts had been given out by the chief himself! No, it couldn't be. . . .

There were two brigades ahead of them before body search. The 104th watched as the chief of camp discipline, Lieutenant Volkovoi, came out of headquarters barracks and shouted to the guards. The guards, who without Volkovoi around had been carrying out the body searches haphazardly and inactively, immediately got a real move on, went for the men like beasts. And their supervisor shouted:

"Unnnnnbutttttton undershirts!"

Not just the zeks and the guards but, it was said, the chief of the camp feared Volkovoi too. His name meant "wolf." God certainly had marked that rascal well — gave him a name that belonged to him. He even glared like a wolf. Dark, tall, frowning — fast on his feet. Jumped out at people from behind barracks: "What's going on here?" No hiding from him. At first he carried a short whip, made of braided leather. They said he flogged prisoners with it, in solitary. Sometimes when the zeks were too crowded and unruly during the evening count at the barracks, he might sneak up from behind and: whop! Whip on the neck! "Why didn't you fall in, shit?" Then the men would retreat from him in a wave. The burned one grabbed his neck, wiped off the blood, kept his mouth shut — to keep from getting solitary.

Now for some reason Volkovoi had stopped carrying the whip.

In extreme cold the system of body search was relaxed in the mornings, though not in the evenings. Each zek unbuttoned his three-quarter length coat and pulled it open. Then they advanced in rows of five. Five guards stood opposite. The guards slapped the zek up the sides of his belted underjacket, clapped him on his only permitted pocket on his right knee, remaining gloved themselves. And if they felt something unusual, instead of going right after it, they asked lazily:

"What's that?"

In the mornings, what was there to look for on a zek? Knives? They don't get carried out of camp, just into camp. Mornings they just had to discover if a zek might be carrying six pounds or so of food, in order to escape. There was even a time when they were so afraid of a piece of bread, a six-ounce chunk for lunch, that they issued an order that every brigade should make a wooden case and carry in it all the brigade's bread for the midday meal. Just exactly what they expected to accomplish by this it was hard to imagine. Probably they did it just to cause trouble and extra bother. A zek had to take a bite out of his own ration to try to mark it when he put it in the case. But all those pieces were the same, just like each other, all from the same bread. So then all the way to work a zek worried whether someone else was going to get his piece. And there were quarrels between brigade members, sometimes even to the point of fights. But then three zeks ran away from the work zone in an automobile and took with them one of the wooden cases full of bread. At that point the chiefs came to their senses and all the cases were chopped up in the watch house. Everyone carry his own chunk, they said.

Another thing they were supposed to check on in the mornings was whether there might not be civilian clothes on under prison clothes. But, after all, civilian things had long since been taken away from all of them and they had been told they would not be given back till the end of their sentences. And no one had finished a term in this camp yet.

Also the guards were supposed to check to see if letters were being carried out to be passed on through a free person. But if they really looked for letters on everyone then they'd have to mess around until lunch time.

But Volkovoi shouted something, and the guards quickly took off their gloves, ordered that underjackets be opened, where everyone had stored a bit of barracks warmth, shirts be unbuttoned. Then they went on to see if something extra was being worn, against the rules. A zek was supposed to have two shirts — an undershirt and an outer shirt. The rest to be removed! That's how the zeks passed Volkovoi's order from row to row. Whatever brigades had gone through already — they were lucky. Some brigades were already outside the gates. But these men still here — open up. Whoever had something extra on, toss it down, right there in the cold.

That's the way they began, but things got in a mess. The gates had been cleared out and the convoy guards from the watch house were yelling: come on! come on! Volkovoi relaxed his rule for the 104th. He ordered that instead of removing unauthorized garments on the spot, the guards write down the names of any zek who was wearing extra clothing. In the evening the zeks must turn in the extra garments at the storeroom and with a note explaining how and why they hid them.

Everything on Shukhov was government issue. Here I am, so to speak, feel me over body and soul. But Tsezar Markovich had an extra flannelette vest which they listed and Buinovsky, too, some kind of a vest or wrap around. Buinovsky let out a bellow. On his destroyers he had been used to shouting. And he had only been in camp three months:

"You don't have the right to undress people in the cold! You don't know the ninth clause of the criminal code!"

They have and they know. You're the one, brother, who doesn't know yet.

"You aren't Soviet people!" the captain hammered away. "You aren't Communists!"

Volkovoi let the one about the ninth clause pass, but at the next remark, like lightning, he flashed:

"Ten days of strict solitary!"

And aside to the senior guard:

"Document it for tonight."

They don't like to take men to solitary in the morning. Man-hours lost on the job. So let him break his back during the day and go to solitary in the evening.

The camp punishment prison was right next to the lineup ground. It was made of masonry, in two wings. The second wing had been added that fall. There wasn't enough room in the first. It was a prison of eighteen cells, and those cells had been partitioned off into smaller solitary confinement cells. The whole camp was built of wood: only the prison was built of concrete block.

The cold had crept under Shukhov's shirt and now he couldn't drive it out. The zeks had wrapped themselves up for nothing. Shukhov's back was bothering him again. Oh, how he'd like to be lying on a hospital cot right now — asleep. He didn't want anything more than that. And the heavier the blanket, the better.

The zeks stood in front of the gates, buttoning up, tying themselves together. Outside the gates the convoy guards waited.

"Get a move on! Get a move on!"

The work assignment officer pushed them from the rear:

"Get a move on! Get a move on!"

The first gates. The pre-zone area. The second gates. And a rail on both sides next to the watch house.

"Stop!" shouted the guard on watch. Like a herd of sheep. "Divide into fives."

It was growing light. The convoy's bonfire was burning out beyond the watch house. Before lineup they always lit a bonfire to get warm and to have more light for counting.

One watch guard counted out loudly, sharply:

"One! Two! Three!"

And the groups of five separated out into columns so that from ahead and behind there could be seen five heads, five backs, ten feet.

And a second watch guard — a count checker — stood silently at the other railing. His only job was to verify whether or not the count was correct. In addition a lieutenant was standing, watching.

He was from the camp.

A man was more precious than gold to the guards. If one head was missing behind the barbed wire, a guard would take his place.

Once more the brigade was together again.

And now the sergeant from the convoy was counting:

"One! Two! Three!"

And again the five separated and marched in individual columns.

And the assistant chief of the convoy guard was on the other side, checking.

And another lieutenant.

This one was from the convoy.

The guards could not afford to make a mistake. If they signed for an extra head their own heads were forfeit.

The place was full of convoy guards. They surrounded the column of zeks in a semicircle, sub-machineguns at the ready, stuck right in your snout. And the dog-leaders were there with their gray dogs. One of the dogs bared his fangs as if he were laughing at the zeks. The convoy guards were all in short sheepskins, except for six who wore full length sheepskin coats. The long coats were assigned by the day, only to those who had to stay up in the watch towers.

And once more mingling brigades, the convoy counted the whole power station column by fives again.

"It's coldest of all at the dawn!" explained the captain. "Because that's the last point of night-time heat reduction."

The captain loved to explain things. He could tell you what phase of the moon it was, new, old, for any day of any year.

The captain himself was waning right in front of everyone. His cheeks were sunken, but his spirit hadn't collapsed.

The wind bit sharply in the open zone. Even Shukhov's face, which was used to everything, felt frostbitten. Realizing that the wind would be blowing in his teeth all the way to the project, Shukhov decided to put on his head rag. The rag, that he kept for just such cases of head wind, had a long ribbon at each end. Many zeks had such rags: they considered them helpful. He bound the cloth over his face to the very eyes, drew the tapes beneath his ears, tied them behind his head. Then he covered the back of his neck with the flap of his cap and raised the collar of his coat. Then he dropped the front flap of his cap over his forehead. Finally, only his eyes were exposed to the weather. He bound his coat tightly at the waist with his length of rope. Everything was tight by this point, and snug, except that his mittens were thin and his hands were chilled already. He rubbed and clapped them, knowing that he would have to put them behind his back and hold them there the entire march.

Every day the chief of the guard read the prisoners' "prayer." Everyone was sick and tired of it:

"Attention, prisoners! Observe strict column order. Do not stretch out; do not run; do not move from one five to another; do not talk; do not look to the sides; hold your hands behind your backs only. One step to the right or left is considered an attempt to escape and the convoy will open fire *without* warning! Leader, forward march!"

At that point, the two lead guards stepped forward on the road. The column swayed forward, shoulders rocking, and the convoy guards were arrayed twenty steps to the right and left of the column, ten steps apart from each other, marching, holding sub-machineguns at the ready.

There had been no snow for a week. The road was worn down, packed hard. They passed the camp and the wind hit them obliquely in the face. Hands behind their back, heads down, the column marched as if to a funeral. And there were visible only the feet of the preceding two or three men, yes and a piece of trampled earth where you were setting down your own feet. From time to time some convoy guard would shout out: "U-47! Hands Back!" "B-502! Catch up!" And then they began to shout less often. The wind was cutting at them, and it hindered them from seeing clearly. They weren't allowed to wear face rags. Their jobs weren't too pleasant, either!

When the weather was warmer everyone in the column would talk no matter how much the guards shouted. But today everyone was huddled up. Everyone was burying himself behind the back of the man in front — and deep in his own thoughts.

Even a prisoner's thoughts are not free. Shukhov's thoughts kept coming back to the same thing over and over again. Would they find the ration in the mattress? Would the infirmary let him off work in the evening? Would they put the captain in solitary or not? And how had Tsezar gotten hold of his warm underwear? Probably he had bribed someone in the storeroom for personal belongings. Where else?

Because he had breakfasted without his bread ration and eaten everything cold Shukhov felt unfed today. So that his stomach wouldn't gnaw, so that it would not beg for food, he stopped thinking about the camp and began thinking how he would soon be writing a letter home.

The column moved past the woodworking enterprise built by the zeks, past the apartment block built by the zeks in which free workers lived, past the new club built by the zeks in which only the free workers watched the movies. Then the column moved out onto the open plain, directly against the wind, facing the rosy dawn. Naked white snow lay right and left to the horizon and there wasn't a single tree on the whole steppe.

A new year had begun, '51, and Shukhov would have the right to send and receive two letters sometime during the year. He had sent his last letter off in July, and he had received an answer to it in October. In Ust-Izhma there had been a different system — write every month if you want. But what could you write about? Shukhov hadn't written home any oftener than he did now.

Shukhov had left home on June 23, 1941. That Sunday, the day before, people had come from mass at church in Polomnya and said there's a war. The post office in Polomnya had heard, but in Temgenyevo no one had a radio before the war. Now, his wife wrote, there was a radio making a racket in every house — a wired loudspeaker.

Writing letters nowadays was like tossing a pebble into a deep dense pool. It sank and disappeared without a trace. You hardly felt like writing about your brigade, about what sort of a foreman Andrei Prokofyevich Tyurin was for you. Right now you had more in common with that Latvian, Kilgas, than with your family at home.

Yes, and they would write to you twice a year themselves, but you couldn't make head or tails of their lives. There was a new chairman of the collective farm, Shukhov's wife said. But there was a new one every year. The collective farm had been merged and enlarged — well they had enlarged it before and then later made it smaller again. Yes, and those who didn't fulfill their work quota on the collective farm had had their garden plots cut down to less than half an acre, some of them to practically nothing.

Shukhov couldn't understand at all what his wife had written about the collective farm. She said that since the war the collective farm had not increased by even one living soul. All the young people, and whoever else could manage it, were departing in crowds for factories in the city or for the peat workings. Half of the men hadn't come back from the war at all. Those who had returned didn't pay any attention to the collective farm. They lived at home and worked on the side. The only men left in the collective farm were the foreman, Zakhar Vasilich, and the 84-year-old carpenter, Tikhon. Tikhon got married not long ago and already has children. The collective farm was still being dragged along by those same women who'd been there since 1930 when it was formed.

Shukhov couldn't understand that at all. "They live at home and work on the side." Shukhov had seen life as an individual peasant farmer as well as life as a member of the collective farm. But he couldn't understand how peasants would not work in their own village — that he couldn't accept. Did they have something like a seasonal trade away from home? And what about the haying season?

Seasonal trades away from home, his wife wrote, had long since disappeared. The men didn't get work as carpenters, though that was a craft for which their district had been famous, nor did they weave baskets, because no one wanted them any more. But there was some sort of jolly new trade — painting rugs. Someone had brought stencils back from the war, and ever since then more and more painters had appeared. They weren't attached to anything, didn't work in any one place. They helped the collective farm for a month — at haying or harvest, to get a document from the farm: collective farmer so-and-so has permission to leave on his personal business and owes the farm no back payments. And then they can travel around the whole country. They even travel by plane to save time and they rake in money by the thousands. Everywhere they go they paint those rugs. For fifty rubles they paint a rug on any old wornout sheet or blanket you give them. And it takes no more than an hour. Ivan's wife cherishes the hope that he too will come home and become such a painter. Then they'll rise out of the poverty in which she is struggling, send the children to technical schools, and build a new house instead of the rotting old hut. All the rug painters are building themselves new houses. Homes near the railroad now cost, not 5,000 rubles, as they used to, but 25,000.

So he wrote and asked his wife — how could he become a painter if as long as he could remember he'd never even been able to draw? And what kind of miraculous rugs were they anyway, what do they have on them? His wife answered that only a fool couldn't draw these: put down the stencil and brush through the holes. There were types: One rug was called "Troika" — a beautiful troika in full regalia carrying a Hussar officer. The second was called "Reindeer" and the third was an imitation of a Persian rug. And that was all the designs there were. But everywhere in the country people were glad to get them and would say thank you and practically grab them out of your hands. Because they were only fifty rubles, while a real rug cost several thousand.

Shukhov just wished he could get a look at one of those rugs.

During his many years in camps and prisons Ivan Denisovich had lost the habit of thinking about tomorrow, about what might happen in a year's time, and planning how to feed his family. The camp administration did all his thinking for him, and in a way that was simpler. Besides he still had two full years to serve. But that rug deal really had him bothered.

Earnings there, obviously, as easy as spitting. And one wouldn't want to be behind all one's fellow-villagers. That would hurt. . . . But, really, Ivan Denisovich didn't want to get involved with those rugs. One had to have impertinence, insolence, for that sort of thing. One had to grease someone's extended hand. Shukhov had been tramping the earth for forty years. Half his teeth were gone already. There was a bald spot on his head. But he'd never given a bribe to anyone, never taken one. He hadn't learned that bit even in camp.

Easy money has no weight, no feeling that you've earned it. The old folks were right when they said that what you don't pay for in full you don't take all the way home. Shukhov's hands were still skilled, capable. Was it possible that when he got free he wouldn't find work as a stove-builder, carpenter, tinsmith?

But then, perhaps he wouldn't be allowed to work, because he had been in prison. Maybe they wouldn't let him go home either. Then maybe he'd be ready to try the rug deal.

By this time the column had reached its destination and was standing in front of the watch house of the outer zone of the *project*. Even before that, from the corner of the zone, two convoy guards in long sheepskin coats had separated from the others and made their way across the field to their distant watch towers. Until all the watch towers were manned they wouldn't let the prisoners inside the zone. The chief of convoy guards, sub-machinegun hung over his shoulder, went into the watch house. Smoke kept pouring out of the watch house chimney. They kept a civilian watchman there all night long to prevent pilferage of cement and planks.

Through the wire gates, across the construction zone, and through the wire away over on the far side, a big red sun was rising through a mist. Standing next to Shukhov, Alyesha looked happily at the sun, a smile curving his lips. Sunken cheeks, lives on his ration, doesn't earn an extra penny — what's he so happy about? On Sundays he whispers and mumbles with the other Baptists. Camp life rolls off them like water off a duck's back.

Shukhov's muzzle for the wind, his face rag, had become all wet from his breath. And here and there the frost had caught it, so it had a crust of ice. Shukhov shifted it from face to neck, turned to stand with his back to the wind. The cold hadn't gotten inside his clothes very much, but his hands had grown chilled in his thin mittens, and so had the toes on his left foot. They were numb. That left felt boot of his was worn out. It had been mended twice already.

He ached from the small of his back all the way up to his shoulders. How was he supposed to work?

He looked around and noticed his brigade foreman, Tyurin. He was in the last five. The foreman was wide in the shoulders and broad in the face. With a scowl. He permitted his brigade no nonsense, but he fed them pretty well. He worried about getting them a better bread ration. He was in camp for the second term, a real son of GULAG, the agency that administered concentration camps for the whole country. He knew camp life and customs from beginning to end.

In camp a foreman is everything to the zek. A good foreman can give you a second life. A bad foreman will drive you into a wooden overcoat — underground. Andrei Prokofyevich knew Shukhov from Ust-Izhma, the general camp where they had met. But in that camp Ivan hadn't been in Andrei's brigade. And when they had driven all of those sentenced under the 58th clause of the code — the clause dealing with counter-revolutionary crimes and activities —

from Ust-Izhma to this hard-labor camp, Tyurin had picked him up here. Shukhov had nothing to do with the chief of the camp, with the planning and production section, with the work bosses, with the engineers. His foreman stood up for him as if he were made of iron. And in return if Tyurin frowned or raised his finger, Shukhov ran fast, did whatever he wanted. Deceive whoever you feel like deceiving in the camp — but not Andrei Prokofyevich. That way you stay alive.

Shukhov wanted to ask the foreman whether they would work where they had the day before or move on to another place — but he hesitated to interrupt Tyurin's weighty thoughts. He had just settled the business of that Socialist Life Town and now was thinking about the problem of "exceeding the quota." This meant the food for the whole brigade for the next five days.

The foreman's face was marked by big red pits, from smallpox. He stood facing the wind without squinting. The skin on his face was like oak bark.

The zeks slapped their hands together, stamped up and down, throughout the column. A mean wind. Well, it looked as if the birds were now perched in all six of the watch towers. But they still weren't admitting prisoners to the zone. More vigilance.

At last the chief of escort guard and the checking officer came out of the watch house, stopped at the gates and opened them.

"Sseppparrrattte by ffffivvvves! Onnne! Twooo!"

The prisoners marched as if on parade, almost in step. If only they could get inside the zone! You don't need to teach them what to do there.

Right behind the watch house was the office shed. Next to the office, the project construction supervisor was calling all the brigade foremen to him. They were hurrying over. Der was going, too. He was a junior work supervisor who had been a zek. He was a real swine, who drove his brother zeks worse than any dog.

It was eight o'clock, five minutes after eight — that generator train had just blown its whistle — and the officers were afraid that the zeks might waste time, might scatter around to warm themselves. But the zeks had a long day ahead of them. There was time for everything. The ones already inside the zone were bending over, searching. Here a stick. There a stick. Kindling for the stove. They shoved the pieces of wood into hiding places in their ragged clothes.

Tyurin ordered Pavlo, his assistant, to accompany him to the office. Tsezar headed that way too. Tsezar was rich. He got parcels twice a month and made presents wherever it was necessary. He was employed in the office in a soft job as assistant to the work norms officer.

And the rest of the 104th moved to the side right away — stay out of sight, out of sight.

The sun rose red, foggy, over the empty zone. Over the section where the panels for prefab houses were piled up, covered with snow. Over the place where a foundation had been dug and some cement blocks had been laid. Over the spot where an excavator lay abandoned, along with a scoop and a mass of iron scrap. There were ditches, trenches, and holes all about. There were the auto repair shops ready to be roofed over. And on a ridge stood the power station under construction, with the second floor already started.

All the men had hidden. The only people outside were the six guards up in the towers — and the big to-do going on next to the office. Now this is our chance! The senior work supervisor had threatened many times to give out the brigade assignments the night before, but he never managed to do it because between evening and morning everything had always been turned upside down.

So this moment is ours. While the bosses are settling the assignments, hide. Hide wherever it's warmer. Sit down, sit. Don't break your back. If you're near a stove, it's a good idea to turn your footcloths about and warm them a bit. Then your feet will be warm the rest of the day. And even with no stove handy — not bad then, either!

The 104th went into a big hall in the auto repair shops that had been glassed in since fall, where the 38th brigade was pouring concrete panels. Some panels were lying in their forms and others were set upright. On one side there was reinforcement netting. Earthen floor and high ceiling. It wasn't possible to keep that building very warm, nevertheless they heated the place. They don't mind using coal. Of course they don't use it so that people can get warm, but so that the panels will dry better. There was even a thermometer hanging in there. And on Sundays, if the zeks didn't go out there to work, there was a civilian to keep the stove going.

The 38th, of course, didn't permit anyone from another brigade near the stove. They monopolized it themselves. Well, that's all right! We can sit in the corner. That's not so bad either.

Shukhov rested the backside of his cotton-padded trousers, which had rested on almost everything, on the edge of a wooden form. He leaned back against the wall. As he leaned back, his coat and underjacket stretched out and on the left side of his chest, next to his heart, he felt a sudden pressure. This hard object was the piece of bread, his morning ration which he had taken with him for lunch. He always took half his ration to work with him and didn't touch it till lunch. But other days he ate half at breakfast, and today he hadn't. And Shukhov understood at last that he wasn't really ahead. He wanted to eat that half ration right now, while he was warm. Five hours to lunch. A long time!

The pain in his back had now settled into his legs. They felt very weak. Oh, if only he could get to a stove.

Shukhov put his mittens on his knees, unbuttoned his coat, untied his frozen face rag, bent it across several times to snap off the ice, and dropped it in his pocket. Then he got out his bread, wrapped in a white cloth, and, holding the cloth so that not a crumb could escape, he started to bite slowly into the bread and chew it. Since the bread had been carried beneath two layers of clothing, warmed with his body, it wasn't the least bit frozen.

In camps Shukhov had often remembered how they ate at home in the village; potatoes by the frying-panful, kasha by the cast-iron potful, and long ago, meat in big chunks. And then they had swilled milk till their stomachs were ready to burst. Shukhov had learned in camp that it shouldn't have been that way. One should eat so that one's mind focuses on what one is eating. Like now, these little pieces that you bite off and mill about with your tongue and suck with your cheeks. How tasty that wet black bread is. What has Shukhov been eating for eight-years-going-on-nine? Nothing. But work he's done! Ho-ho! Not so bad!

So Shukhov was occupied with his six ounces, and near him sat the whole 104th.

Two Estonians, who were as close as brothers, sat on a low concrete panel and took turns smoking half a cigarette from one cigarette holder. Both of them were blonds, both tall, both spare, with long noses, big eyes. They stayed so close that it seemed as if one couldn't breathe the blue air without the other. The foreman never separated them. They shared all their food and slept on an upper bunk together. And they talked with each other all the time, softly and slowly when they stood in the column, or waited at lineup, or went to bed at night. But they weren't brothers at all and had met right there in the 104th. One was a sailor who had been raised at the coast; the other, when Soviet power had been established, had been taken to Sweden as a child. He had grown up and on his own had returned to Estonia for his education.

They say nationality doesn't mean anything, that in every nation there are men who are no good. But no matter how many Estonians Shukhov met, he never came across a bad one.

So the prisoners all sat, some on panels, some on casing for panels, some on the ground. The tongue won't wag in the morning; everyone concentrated on his own thoughts, everyone was silent. Fetyukov, the jackal, had somehow collected some cigarette butts. He would even forage butts out of a spittoon — he didn't care. Now he had them out on his knee where he was unrolling them and pouring the unburned tobacco into one paper. Fetyukov had three children on the outside, but when he had been arrested all of them renounced him, and his wife married again. So he got no help from them.

Buinovsky kept looking sideways at Fetyukov and finally barked at him.

"Why are you picking up all kinds of crap? You'll end up with syphilis of the lip! Get rid of that!"

The naval captain was used to giving orders: he spoke to everyone that way. But Buinovsky had no hold on Fetyukov. The captain got no parcels either. Laughing maliciously Fetyukov said:

"Wait a while, captain. You just serve for eight years — and you'll be picking things up, too. Prouder people than you have come to camp. . . ."

Fetyukov was judging by his own standards, but the captain might just make it in his own way. . . .

"What, what?" The deaf Senka Klevshin hadn't heard what was said: he thought the conversation was about Buinovsky's trouble at lineup. He said, "You shouldn't have stuck your neck out!" He shook his head in distress. "Everything would have worked out all right."

Senka Klevshin was a quiet, unfortunate man. One of his eardrums had been broken in 1941. Then he had been taken prisoner, escaped, been recaptured and shoved into Buchenwald. By a miracle he had escaped death in Buchenwald. Now he was serving his sentence quietly. "Stick your neck out," he said, "and you're done for."

That was right. Groan and bend. If you fight back you'll be broken.

Alyesha was silent, his face in his hands. He was praying.

Shukhov ate his bread ration right down to the last crumb, leaving only a round piece of crust from the top of the bread. No spoon in the world is as good at cleaning the last bit of kasha from your bowl as a piece of bread. He rewrapped that piece of crust in the white cloth to save it for lunch, put the cloth in his inside pocket beneath the underjacket, fastened himself up against the cold, and was ready. Let them send him out to work now. Though it would be nicer if they took a while longer.

The 38th got up and separated. Some went to the cement mixer, some for water, some over to the reinforcing rods. Neither Tyurin nor his assistant Pavlo came to the 104th. And even though the brigade had been waiting hardly twenty minutes, and the working day (shortened for winter) lasted until six, this pause seemed to all of them great good luck, as if the hours to evening had really been cut shorter.

The red-faced, well-fed Latvian, Kilgas, sighed. "Well, we haven't had any snowstorms for a long time! The whole winter long — not one snowstorm! What kind of a winter is that?"

"Yes — no snowstorms, no snowstorms," the rest of the brigade sighed in turn.

When one of the local snowstorms started blowing in that area, it wasn't just a question of not going out to work. They were not even let out of barracks. Between the barracks and the mess hall you could get lost if you didn't hold on to the guide rope. If a prisoner got frozen in the snow, let a dog eat him — who cared. But if he ran away? There had been cases. During the snowstorms the snow was very fine and if it lodged in a drift it became as hard as if someone had packed it down. A few men had escaped over the barbed wire on such a drift. True, they didn't get far.

If one really considered it, there wasn't any advantage to a snowstorm. The zeks were under lock and key. Coal wasn't sent on time. The warmth was blown out of the barracks. Flour wasn't delivered, so there was no bread. They didn't get things done in the kitchen. And no matter how long the storm lasted — three days or a week — those days were counted as if they were rest days, and afterwards for that many Sundays in a row they marched you out to work.

Just the same the zeks loved snowstorms and prayed for them. If the wind rose a bit, everyone watched the sky. *Come on stuff! Come on stuff!*

They meant snow.

Someone tried to move up close to the stove of the 38th to get warm, but he was pushed away.

Tyurin came in. He was gloomy. The brigade members understood that there was work to be done, quickly.

"Sssooo!" Tyurin looked around. "Everyone here, 104?"

And then without checking and counting them, because no one could have gone anywhere, he handed out assignments swiftly. He sent the two Estonians and Klevshin and Gopchik to get the big mortar mixing box nearby, to bring it into the power station building. It was clear that the brigade was moving over to work on the power station building which was incomplete and which had been untouched since autumn. He sent another two men to the tool room where Pavlo was getting the tools. He ordered four men to clear the snow next to the power station building, at the entrance to the generator room, in the generator room itself, and off the ladders. Two others he told to start a fire in the stove in the generator room with coal and with whatever wood they could swipe. He sent one to take cement to the building on a sled, two to bring water, two to get sand, and one more to help clean the snow off that sand and break it up with a crowbar.

And after all this only Shukhov and Kilgas — the most highly skilled workers in the brigade — remained unassigned. Calling them over, the foreman said:

"Listen here, boys!" Even though he was no older than they were, he called all of them boys. "After lunch you'll lay cement blocks on the second-story wall, up there where the sixth brigade left off last fall. Right now the problem is to heat up the generator room. There are three big windows there. Cover them with something. I'll give you men some others to help; just figure out what we can use to cover the windows. The generator room is going to be used both for mixing and for warming ourselves. And if we don't have a place to warm ourselves we're going to freeze like dogs."

Maybe he would have said something else but Gopchik rushed up to complain. He was a boy of sixteen, rosy as a piglet. The other brigade wouldn't hand over the mixing box, was fighting over it. Tyurin ran right out there.

No matter how hard it was to begin the working day in such cold, the only important thing was to cross over that beginning, just that.

Shukhov and Kilgas looked at one another. They had worked together often and respected each other's skills both as carpenter and mason. To scrounge around and come up with something, out there in the naked snow, something practical to cover the window openings, was not going to be easy. But Kilgas said:

"Vanya, where the prefabricated panels are stored I know there's a big roll of roofing paper. I hid it myself. Shall we go get it?"

Kilgas, though a Latvian, knew Russian as if it were his own tongue. Next to his home was a village of Old Believers,[2] and he'd learned Russian in his childhood. He had only been in camps for two years, but he already understood the important thing: if you don't bite it off yourself you won't get it at all. His name was Johann. Shukhov called him Vanya, as he called Shukhov Vanya.

They decided to go for the roofing. But first Shukhov ran into the auto repair shop, which was under construction, to get his mason's trowel. A well-balanced trowel is important to a mason especially if it's light and fits the hand. But at the construction projects tools were handed out every morning and turned in every evening. Whatever you got the next day was just a matter of luck. But Shukhov once managed to give the tool clerk a short count and thus grab off the best trowel. Every day he hid it again. And every morning if he was laying brick or block he went to get it. Of course, if they had driven the 104th out to the Socialist Life Town today he would have been left without his trowel. But now he moved some stones, stuck his fingers into a cranny, and pulled it out.

Shukhov and Kilgas went out of the auto repair shop toward the prefabricated houses. Their breath formed thick steam. The sun had already risen but it was without rays as if in a fog, and along the sides of the sun there rose streaks almost like poles of light.

"Are they poles?" Shukhov asked, gesturing at the sun with his head.

2 [A sect that refused to accept liturgical reforms introduced into the Russian Orthodox Church in the seventeenth century. — Editors' note.]

"Poles don't bother us," Kilgas brushed the remark aside, laughing. "Just so they don't have barbed wire on them. That's the kind to watch out for."

Kilgas could hardly talk without joking. The whole brigade liked him for that. And other Latvians in the camp all esteemed him a great deal. Well, Kilgas ate normally. Got two packages a month. Rosy-cheeked as if he weren't in the camp at all. He could afford to joke.

The zone for their construction project was big. It was a long way across. On the way they ran into the boys from the 82nd. They had been ordered again to try to dig holes in the frozen ground. Not very big holes, a foot and a half wide by a foot and a half long and a foot and a half deep. But the ground was like stone here, even in summer, and now, frozen solid, just try to chew it up. Pound it with a pick and the pick merely slides off. Sparks — but no loosened dirt, not a crumb. Each of the men was standing over his little hole, and looked around as Shukhov and Kilgas went by. No place to get warm, and they were not permitted to leave their posts. Back to the pick — the only warmth there came from using it.

Shukhov saw an acquaintance among them, a fellow from Vyatka, and advised him, "Listen here, you earth-cutters, what you ought to do is build a fire over every hole. That way the earth would thaw out."

"They don't permit it," said the fellow from Vyatka. "They don't give us any firewood."

"You have to find it."

Kilgas just spat.

"Well, now, tell me, Vanya, if the bosses were smart — would they really put men hammering at the ground with picks in such cold?"

Kilgas swore several times indistinctly and shut up. You don't talk much in that kind of cold. They went further and came to the place where the panels of the prefabs were piled beneath the snow.

Shukhov liked working with Kilgas. Just one disappointment about Kilgas. He didn't smoke and got no tobacco in his parcels.

This was really the right spot. Kilgas was an observing sort. Together they raised one plank, then another. Under the planks was a roll of roofing.

They pulled it out. Now, how to carry it? If the guards saw them from the watch towers that didn't matter. The birds perched up there had just one concern — that the zeks did not escape. And the guards inside the working zone? Well, for all they cared you could chop up all the panels for firewood. Even if a camp guard ran smack into you, that was all right, too. He would be looking around himself for something he could use at home. And so far as the ordinary zeks were concerned, they spit on those prefabs. And the brigade foremen, too. The only men who cared about them were, first, the civilian (in other words, free) work supervisor; second, the junior work supervisor, Der (a zek); and then, third, the tall, thin Shkuropatenko. He was a nobody, Shkuropatenko, just another zek. He'd been given a work assignment at time rates for just one thing — to keep the zeks from walking off with the prefabs. That Shkuropatenko was the type who would be most likely to catch them out in the open.

"Here's what, Vanya, we can't carry it lengthwise," said Shukhov. "Let's carry it upright, holding it up from both sides and move along with it quickly, covering it with our bodies. From a distance no one will be able to make it out."

Shukhov's idea was not so bad. It wouldn't be smart to carry the roll lengthwise, so they didn't carry it that way, but held it up between them like a third man, and hurried away with it. From the side the only thing that could be seen was two men walking close together.

"But the work supervisor is going to see that roofing on the windows. He'll figure it out," said Shukhov.

"What's that got to do with us?" Kilgas asked, surprised. "So they come to the power station and it's already there. So, it *was* there before. Do you think they're going to tear it down?"

That made sense.

His fingers had grown numb in his thin mittens, he could hardly feel them. But his left felt boot was holding up. The valenki — they were the main thing. Hands would get warm in work.

They made their way on virgin snow. Then they came to a sled track that led from the tool storeroom to the power station. Evidently the cement had been carted along ahead.

The power station stood on a ridge. Behind it the zone came to an end. It had been a long time since anyone had worked on the power station, and all the approaches to it were covered with snow. The sled tracks and the fresh deep trail seemed really clear by contrast. Brigade members had passed that way, clearing off the snow with wooden shovels near the power station and the auto road.

It would be very pleasant if the elevator at the power station were working. But the motor had burned out, and it had not been fixed. Everything would have to be hauled by hand up to the second story. Mortar. Cement blocks.

For two months the power station had stood there like a gray skeleton abandoned in the snow. And then the 104th had come along. And what was there to hold the men of the 104th together? Empty stomachs tied about with canvas belts? Crackling cold? No cover, and no spark of a fire. Nevertheless the 104th arrived, and life began again in the building.

At the very entrance to the generator room the mortar mixing box had fallen apart. The box was rotten. Shukhov hadn't even believed that it would arrive in one piece. The foreman swore a whole series of oaths, just for appearance's sake, but he could see that no one was to blame. And at that moment Shukhov and Kilgas came in with the roofing between them. The foreman was pleased. Immediately he rearranged his men. Shukhov to fix the stovepipe, so that the stove could be lit as soon as possible. Kilgas to fix the mixing box, with the two Estonians to help him. And for Senka Klevshin there's an axe, cut up some long planks so we have something to fasten the roofing to. Two widths of roofing would cover the window. Where should the planks come from? The work supervisor won't allot boards just for shelter. The foreman looked around and so did the rest of them. One way to get planks was to knock off a pair of boards that served as handrails on the ladder to the second floor. What else was there to do? When you climb up don't be careless or you'll fall off.

One might wonder why a zek in for ten years should break his back working hard in a camp. I don't feel like it — and that's that, so to speak. Fool away the time during the day till evening. The night is mine.

Well, it didn't work that way. That was the reason the work brigades were organized. Not the same kind of brigade as in freedom, where Ivan Ivanych receives separate pay and Petr Petrovich separate pay. In camps the brigade is a kind of system to make the zeks watch each other so the administration doesn't have to. Here's the way it goes: either everyone gets *additional* food or everyone goes hungry. If you don't work, you viper, I will be hungry because of you. Get a move on, you shit!

A set-up like this put the screws on. Very unlikely that you could sit around on your ass. Want to or not you jump, hop, get moving. If we haven't built shelter for ourselves in two hours, then we're all screwed. But good.

Pavlo had brought the tools. Just pick out what you need. And some stovepipe. No tinsmith's tools, true, but there's a metal-worker's hammer and a small axe. We'll manage one way or another.

Shukhov was clapping his hands together to warm them, and matching stovepipes and pounding the joints together. Clap again and pound again. He had hidden his trowel close by. Even though they were all from his own brigade they might switch it on him. Even Kilgas.

All thought whisked out of his head. Shukhov didn't recollect anything or concern himself with anything at all. He kept in mind just one thing — how to place and arrange the stovepipe elbows in such a way that the stove wouldn't smoke. Gopchik was sent to look for wire — to fasten the stovepipe at the window where it emerged to the outside.

In the corner there was another stove, a low-slung one with a brick chimney. It had a cast-iron plate atop it which grew hot and on which sand was thawed and dried. The brigade had already built a fire in that stove and the captain and Fetyukov were hauling barrows of sand to it. No intelligence needed to push hand barrows. So the foreman put the former bosses on that job. Fetyukov, they said, had been a big chief in some office or other, and used to go about in a car.

Fetyukov at first had tried to bully the captain, yelled at him. But the captain whacked him in the teeth just once. After that they made peace.

The zeks were pushing their way to that stove to warm themselves, but the foreman warned them.

"I'll warm you — on the head! Do your work first!"

Show the whip to the whipped dog, and that's enough. The cold was fierce but the foreman fiercer! The men moved off to their jobs.

Shukhov heard the foreman say softly to Pavlo:

"You stay here. Hold tight. I have to go and exceed the quota."

More depended on surpassing the quota than on the work itself. A smart foreman was one who worked hard on the paper work involved in reporting plan fulfillment — on "surpassing the quota." That was how one got fed. Whatever hadn't been done — prove that it had been done. Whatever was classified at cheap rates — manipulate it so that it was classified at higher rates. For this maneuvering a foreman needed a quick mind. Plus some pull with the quota-setters. The quota-setters had to be handed gifts, too. And if one thought about it — who were those quotas for? For the camp. The camp raked in thousands of extra rubles from the construction organizations and gave bonuses to its officers. To Volkovoi for his whip. While the zeks got six extra ounces of bread in the evening. Six ounces of bread rules life.

The men carried in two buckets of water which had frozen on the way. Pavlo decided that there was no point to getting any more. Better to melt snow right in the building. They put the buckets on the stove.

Gopchik swiped some new aluminum wire, the kind the electricians were putting up. He said: "Ivan Denisych! Here's good wire to make a spoon. Will you teach me to cast a spoon?"

Ivan Denisych loved that little rogue Gopchik. His own son had died in childhood and he had two grown daughters at home. Gopchik had been imprisoned because he carried some milk to the woods for the Western Ukrainian Bendera partisans.[3] He had been sentenced as if he were an adult. He was a gentle little calf and played up to all the men. But he'd already acquired some slyness. He ate what was in his food parcels all by himself, alone. Sometimes he was even chewing away at night.

Well, after all, he couldn't feed everyone.

3 [Stepan Bendera, a Western Ukrainian, led a group that for a while collaborated with the Germans. — Editors' note.]

They broke off a piece of wire for the spoon and hid it in a corner. Shukhov used two boards to hammer together a makeshift stepladder and sent Gopchik climbing up to hang the stovepipe. Gopchik was as quick as a squirrel. He made his way up the crosspieces, hammered in a nail, hung the wire on it and slung it around the pipe. Shukhov wasn't idling, either. He made the outlet for the stovepipe, using one extra elbow. Even if there wasn't much wind today there might be some tomorrow, and he didn't want the smoke backing up, not when this stove was for themselves.

Senka Klevshin had already split some long planks. They told Gopchik-Klopchik to nail them in place. The imp clambered about and yelled down at them from above.

The sun rose higher and chased away the mist. There were no more of those sunrays that resembled poles. Crimson sparkled inside the building. Right then they lit the second stove with the stolen firewood. A lot happier!

"In January the sun warms the cow's ass!" announced Shukhov.

Kilgas finished fixing the mixing box, gave it one last whack with the axe and shouted:

"Listen, Pavlo, I won't take less than one hundred rubles from the foreman for that work!"

Pavlo laughed:

"You'll get one hundred grams." That would be about three ounces of vodka.

"The prosecutor will add something to it," shouted Gopchik from up above.

"Don't touch that, don't touch that!" Shukhov yelled to the boy. That wasn't the right way to cut the roofing.

Shukhov showed him how it ought to be done.

The men crowded up to the iron stove; Pavlo chased them away. He gave Kilgas some helpers, and ordered him to make hand barrows for carrying the cement. He set a few more men to hauling sand, and sent some up above to clean the snow off the scaffolding and off the section where new blocks were to be laid. One more man was assigned to move the heated sand from the stove top to the mixing box.

Outside a motor sputtered; the concrete blocks were being delivered. A truck was making its way through the snow. Pavlo went out to wave it in and point out where to dump the blocks.

They nailed up one sheet of roofing, and another. What protection would it be? It's just paper. But it looked as if a real wall was there. Inside it became darker. In the dimness the stove seemed brighter.

Alyesha brought coal. Some shouted at him, "Pour it on!" Others, "Don't pour it on! At least with firewood we can warm up." He just stood there, confused.

Fetyukov got up to the stove and, like an idiot, stuck his valenki right in the fire. The captain lifted him by the scruff of his neck and shoved him at the barrows:

"Go and haul sand, scum!"

The captain regarded camp work like naval service. If you're told to do something, do it! His cheeks had sunken fast in the last month but he pulled his load.

Finally all three windows had been closed in. The only light came from the doors now. And the cold came in that way, too. Pavlo ordered the top parts of the doors shut off and the bottoms left as they were, so a man could walk in if he stooped. They boarded them off as he directed.

By this time three truckloads of blocks had been delivered. The problem now was how to get the blocks up without any elevator.

"Masons! Let's go up!" Pavlo shouted in his customary broad Ukrainian.

That was a matter of honor. Shukhov, Kilgas and Pavlo climbed up. The ladder was narrow enough anyway but now that Senka had knocked the railing off it you had to press close to the wall so you didn't fall. Worse, snow had stuck to the treads and made them rounded. No footing. How would they carry up the mortar?

They looked at the place they were to lay blocks. The snow was being shovelled off. Right here. They'd have to hammer the ice off the top layer of the last rungs and then sweep with a twig broom.

They studied the layout for the best way to get the blocks up to the second story. After looking down they decided that instead of having the men climb up that long ladder carrying blocks, they would put four men on the ground to toss blocks up to the scaffolding stage. From there another two men could pass the blocks up. On the second floor another two could deliver them to the masons. That would be the fastest way.

Up on the second floor the wind wasn't strong, but it cut. As soon as they started to lay blocks it would get hold of them all right. But if they could get behind the rows already done, there'd be some protection; not too bad, much warmer.

Shukhov looked at the sky, surprised. In the clear sky the sun had almost reached lunch time. Miracle of miracles. That's the way time passes at work. Many times Shukhov had noticed that the days in the camp just rolled by. There was no time to look around. But his term didn't seem to change; as if it wasn't getting shorter at all.

They went down and found the rest of the men were sitting around the stove. Only the captain and Fetyukov were carrying sand. Pavlo, furious, sent eight men to fetch blocks, two to pouring cement into the mixing box where they were to mix it dry with the sand. Another for water. Another for coal. Kilgas said to his crew:

"Come on, boys, get those barrows finished."

"Should I help them?" Shukhov asked Pavlo.

"Go ahead," Pavlo nodded.

Then they brought a tank in which to melt snow for the cement. Someone announced it was noon.

"Right," declared Shukhov. "The sun's at its peak."

"If it's at its peak," retorted the captain, "then that means it's not noon but one o'clock."

"Why is that?" Shukhov was surprised. "Every grandfather knows that the sun is highest of all at noon."

"*That* for the grandfathers!" the captain shot back. "Since their time a new decree has been passed. The sun is highest at one o'clock."

"Whose decree?"

"Soviet authority."

The captain went out with the barrows. But Shukhov wouldn't have argued with him anyway. Was it possible that the sun was subject to government decrees, too?

They hammered, pounded, and finished four barrows.

"All right — let's sit down and warm up," Pavlo said to the two masons. "You too, Senka. After lunch you're going to lay blocks with them."

So they had a right to sit by the stove. There wasn't time to begin laying blocks before the meal break and if the cement were mixed too soon it would freeze.

The coal had finally begun to burn and was now throwing off heat steadily. But you could only feel it if you were right beside the stove. The rest of the room was just as cold as ever.

All four took off their mittens and held their hands near the warmth.

But feet in boots or shoes should never be put near a fire. You have to learn that. If you're wearing boots, then the leather will crack in the heat. Valenki grow damp, steam rises from them, and you won't be the slightest bit warmer. And if you try getting even closer to the fire, you'll burn them. That means you wear them with a hole till spring. Don't expect another pair.

"What's it to Shukhov?" Kilgas teased. "Shukhov, brothers, has one foot out of here already."

"That one there — the barefoot one," someone added. They all laughed. Shukhov had taken off his mended felt boot and was warming up the footcloths.

"Shukhov's finishing up his term."

Kilgas was in for twenty-five years. In the good old days, everyone got the same haircut — ten years. But from 1949 a new era had begun — twenty-five years to everyone, no matter what. One might manage to last ten years without kicking the bucket, but just try and stick it for twenty-five.

Shukhov enjoyed having everyone point at him. Actually, he *was* finishing up his term, but he didn't seriously believe it would end. After all, during the war everyone whose sentence ended was held until a special order was issued in 1946. So the ones who had had a basic sentence of three years got five more. Law — that was something the government turned inside out as it pleased. So your ten is ended. Then they'll say, here you are, take ten more. Or go into exile.

Still, once in a while you'd think about it and it would take your breath away. In spite of everything the term is coming to an end. The spool unwinds . . . good God! To step outside a free man. Free!?

However, it wasn't right for an old camp veteran to talk about that out loud. And so Shukhov said to Kilgas:

"Just don't bother to count your twenty-five. To sit for twenty-five years is like trying to paddle a canoe with a pitchfork. But I have sat out eight full ones — that's the truth."

You live with your head in the sand, like an ostrich, and you don't have time to think how you got into prison and how you'll get out.

According to his record, Shukhov had been sentenced for treason and he had testified to it himself. That he had surrendered to the Germans in order to be a traitor to the motherland, and had returned to the Russian army because he was carrying out assignments for German intelligence. What kind of assignments these were neither Shukhov nor the investigator could invent. So that's the way it was left — just assignments.

Shukhov had simply figured: If you don't sign it means a wooden overcoat. If you sign, you live a little longer. So he signed.

Actually here's what happened. In February '42 on the Northwest front the Russian forces were encircled. No food was dropped to them: there weren't any planes. It got so bad that they were cutting hooves off dead horses, soaking them and eating them. No ammunition. And so the Germans captured them a few at a time. In one such group, Shukhov spent a couple of days as a prisoner, in the woods. Then five men escaped. They slunk through woods, waded through swamps and by a miracle got back to their own lines. But two were shot down by a machine gunner, a third died from wounds. Only two survived. They would have been smarter to have explained that they were lost in the forest. That would have been all right. But they said that they had escaped.

The interrogators shouted, "Escaped from the Germans? Palm that off on your mother!" If all five had been alive maybe they'd have compared the stories and believed the evidence. But they didn't believe two. The interrogators shouted, "You bastards fixed up your 'escape' stories together."

Senka Klevshin heard through his deafness the talk about escape from the Germans and said loudly:

"I escaped from them three times and three times they caught me."

Senka, long-sufferer, was usually silent. He couldn't hear much of what people said, so he didn't talk much. They didn't know a great deal about him except that he had been in Buchenwald, was a member of the underground there, and had smuggled in weapons for the mutiny there. The Germans had hung him up by the arms and beat him with sticks.

"Vanya, you've sat eight years — in what camps?" Kilgas argued. "You were in ordinary camps, living with women. You didn't wear any numbers. Just try and sit eight years in a hard-labor camp! No one yet has sat them out to the end."

"With women? With logs, not with women. . . ."

Shukhov stared into the fire and remembered his seven years in the north. For three years he had hauled logs for crating material and railway ties. And the bonfires had flamed there too — at the timber cuttings at night. The chief had ordered that a brigade which didn't fulfill the day's quota must remain in the forest at night. They didn't get back to the camp till after midnight and were out in the woods in the morning again.

"Nnoo, brothers. . . . It's quieter here, I'd say," he said. "Here whether quotas have been fulfilled or not, it's back to the camp. And the rock-bottom minimum ration is three ounces more than it was there. You can live here. So it's a Special Camp, so what! Do the numbers bother you? They don't weigh anything, those numbers."

"Quieter here," Fetyukov hissed. Everyone was near the stove now, since the lunch break was close. "They knife people in their beds. Quieter."

"Not people but stool-pigeons!" Pavlo pointed his finger threateningly at Fetyukov.

It was true that something new had started in camp. Two well-known stool-pigeons had been knifed in their bunks at the rising gong. Then one innocent working stiff. Had they confused the bunk? One stool-pigeon had run to the officers in the camp punishment prison, and they had hidden him there, in the stone prison. Strange. Nothing like that in ordinary camps. Yes, and it hadn't happened here before this either.

Suddenly the power train whistle blew. Not a full blast at first but a hoarse one as if it were clearing its throat.

Half a day out of the way. Lunch break.

Whew, they'd been slow. They should have gone to the mess-hall long since and taken a place in line. There were eleven brigades at the project and no more than two could get in the mess hall at the same time.

But the foreman still hadn't come. Pavlo looked around quickly.

"Shukhov and Gopchik — with me. Kilgas! When I send Gopchik to you bring the whole brigade."

Their places at the stove were taken immediately. Men surrounded the stove as if it were a woman and they were getting close to embrace her.

"Move off it," some shouted. "Let's have a smoke!"

They all looked at each other to see who would light up. But no one had anything to smoke. Either there was no tobacco or whoever had any was hiding it.

Shukhov and Gopchik went out with Pavlo. Gopchik trailed after them like a little rabbit.

"It's warmer," Shukhov immediately decided. "No more than zero, now. It won't be so bad laying blocks."

They looked back at the blocks. The men had thrown a pile up on the scaffolding. Some blocks were already piled on the second floor.

Shukhov also squinted up at the sun, testing to see if the captain was right about that decree.

Out in the open the wind was still biting. It still smarted as if to say, don't forget it's January.

The work kitchen was just a small shed of planks hammered together around a stove, with rusty sheet metal nailed on to close the cracks. Inside the shed a partition divided it in two, kitchen and mess hall. There were no floorboards, the earth was packed down by feet and that's the way it was left, holes and bumps and all. The entire kitchen equipment consisted of a pot cemented into a square stove.

Two men worked in the kitchen, a cook and a sanitary instructor. In the morning before they left camp, the cook was given the day's ration of grits at the big camp kitchen. Probably not quite two ounces for each working man, two pounds a brigade, less than thirty-six pounds for the whole project. The cook wouldn't haul that bag for nearly two miles. He gave it to a helper. Better to give the helper an extra portion out of the working stiffs' share than to break his own back. Getting water, gathering firewood, or lighting the stove were chores the cook didn't do either. He found other zeks, working stiffs, even some poor fellows on their last legs, to do them and gave them an extra portion. Who cares about what belongs to someone else.

The rule was that they ate without leaving the mess shed. Bowls had to be brought from the camp and couldn't be left out overnight because the free workers made off with them. So they carried fifty to the mess hall, no more, washed them on the spot and put them back into use. The man who carried the bowls got an extra portion. So that the bowls wouldn't be taken out of the mess hall, another helper was put at the door to watch. But no matter how carefully he watched the zeks they still got the bowls out, either by persuading him or distracting his attention. So another helper had to be sent all over the project grounds to collect the dirty bowls and cart them back to the kitchen. One more extra portion, and then another.

The only thing the cook did was to put the meal in the pot, add salt, and divide the fat between himself and the pot. Good fat did not get to the working stiffs, but rancid fat all went into the pot. So when rancid fat was handed out at the warehouse the zeks had a bonus. Then the cook mixed the cereal as it cooked. The sanitary instructor didn't even do that. He just sat and watched. When the kasha was ready, the sanitary instructor tried it first, a bellyful for him. A bellyful for the cook, too. Then the duty foreman came — they changed every day — to try it and see if this kasha could be given to the working stiffs. A double portion for the duty foreman.

Right then the whistle sounded. Then the other foremen came in, and the cook handed the filled bowls out through a window, and only the bottom of those bowls was covered with the thin kasha, and you weren't going to weigh or ask how much there was of your own kasha allotment. You'd get a hundred horseradishes in your mouth if you so much as opened it.

The wind whistled over the naked steppe. In summer the wind was dry and parching; in winter it was cold. Nothing ever grew on that steppe, especially between barbed wire. The only grain that grew around there was in the bread storeroom. Oats ripened only in the food warehouse. And even if you broke your back with work and lay on your stomach, you couldn't suck any food from that earth. You couldn't get more than the chief handed out. And you wouldn't even get the right amount because of the cooks, the helpers, and the zeks in soft jobs. Out here they steal. In the zone they steal. Before that, they steal at the warehouse. And the ones who steal are not usually the ones who swing picks. But as for you, swing away and then take what they give you. And get away from that serving window.

It was every man for himself.

Pavlo, Shukhov and Gopchik went into the mess hall. The men were so crowded in there they couldn't see the tables or the benches. A few ate sitting down but more were standing. The men of the 82nd, who had been digging holes outside without fires for half a day, had grabbed the first places. And now, though they had eaten, they wouldn't leave. Where else could they get warm? Others cursed them but the curses bounced off their backs. It was still better inside than out in the cold.

Pavlo and Shukhov elbowed their way in. They had arrived just at the right time. One brigade was getting its share. Only one group waited in line. Only the assistant foremen at the window. The rest came after us.

"Bowls, bowls!" the cook shouted out of the window, and they shoved them at him. Shukhov himself picked some up and shoved them at him. Not for an extra portion, but so things would move faster.

Helpers were washing the bowls. Extra portions for them too.

The assistant foreman in front of Pavlo began to get his, and Pavlo shouted over his shoulder:

"Gopchik!"

"Me!" from the door. A thin little voice like a small goat.

"Call the brigade!"

Gopchik ran off.

The important thing was that today the cereal was good, the best. Oatmeal. They didn't get it often. Usually it was that *magara* twice a day or waste from the flour mills. In oatmeal the broth between the grains is satisfying—and rich, too.

Shukhov, who in his youth had fed oats so often to his horses, had never thought then that he would long for a handful someday.

"Bowls, bowls!" they shouted from the window.

The turn of the 104th came. The assistant foreman got a double "foreman's portion" and retreated from the window.

That, too, came out of the stomachs of the working stiffs, but no one protested. For every foreman there was one such extra portion, and either he could eat it himself or give it to his assistant. Tyurin gave his to Pavlo.

Shukhov now had the task of pushing his way through to a table. He booted out two men on their last legs, asked one working stiff politely to get out of his way, and cleared part of a table. He would put twelve bowls close together, six on top of them, and another two on top of those. Now he had to take the bowls from Pavlo, repeat his count and watch carefully that no one swiped a bowl. Watch, too, that no one pushed them with their elbows or knocked them over. Close by some were getting up from the benches, others were climbing in, beginning to eat. He had to watch the table boundary. Are you eating from your own bowl or have you gotten into ours?

"Two, four, six!" the cook counted from behind the window. He handed out two at a time. That way he stood less chance of losing count.

"Two, four, six," Pavlo repeated softly in Ukrainian. He gave Shukhov two bowls at once and Shukhov put them on the table. Shukhov said nothing out loud but counted them all the more carefully.

"Eight, ten."

Why wasn't Gopchik bringing in the brigade?

"Twelve, fourteen," went the count.

No bowls in the kitchen. Over Pavlo's head and shoulder Shukhov could see the cook's hands put two bowls in the window and, holding on to them, hesitate. He must have turned about to swear at the dishwasher. Just then another pile of empty bowls was shoved at him through the window. He let go of the two bowls and handed the pile of empties back.

Shukhov left his bowls at the table, and hopped on over a bench, grabbed both bowls in the window, and, as if he were not talking to the cook, but to Pavlo he repeated not very loud:

"Fourteen."

"Stop! Where are you taking them?" hollered the cook.

"He's from ours, ours," Pavlo said.

"Yours, yours, but don't make me miscount."

"Fourteen," Pavlo shrugged his shoulders. He himself would not have gone to the lengths of swiping oatmeal. He, as assistant foreman, had to maintain his dignity, but he had just repeated what Shukhov said. He could blame it on Shukhov.

"I already said 'fourteen'!" screamed the cook.

"Well, what about it! But you didn't hand them over. You held on to them!" Shukhov yelled. "Go and count them if you don't believe me. They're all on the table over there!"

As Shukhov shouted at the cook, he noticed the two Estonians coming towards him. He quickly shoved the two bowls at them. And then he managed to get back to the table and count to make sure that all the bowls were still there, that no one had swiped any though they could have gotten away with it.

Out of the window peered the cook's red face:

"Where are the bowls?" he asked stiffly.

"Right here, if you please," shouted Shukhov. "Move over, don't block the view!" he pushed someone out of the way. "Here are two!" he lifted the two dishes on top. "And here are three rows of four each, exactly — count them."

"And the brigade hasn't come yet?" the cook looked suspiciously through the small opening of the window which was narrow so that the zeks couldn't peer into the kitchen from the mess hall to see how much was left in the pot.

"The brigade hasn't arrived yet," Pavlo shook his head.

"Then what the hell are you taking bowls for if the brigade isn't here?" the cook raged.

"Here's the brigade, right here!" yelled Pavlo.

And everyone heard the captain shouting as he came through the doorway, just as if he were still on the bridge of his destroyer:

"What are you crowding around for? You've eaten — so get out of here. Give the rest of us some room!"

The cook muttered a bit more, straightened up, and again his hands appeared in the window.

"Sixteen, eighteen. . . ."

And, having poured out the last one, a double portion:

"Twenty-three, that's all! Next!"

The men of the brigade made their way through the room and Pavlo handed out the bowls. He passed the bowls over the heads of those already seated to some at a second table.

In the summer, five men would have sat at each bench, but now when all were dressed in thick clothes four could hardly fit. Even then it was difficult to eat.

Calculating that at least one of the two extra portions would be his, Shukhov quickly set to devouring his rightful one. He raised his right knee to his stomach, removed from the top of his boot his spoon, "Ust-Izhma, 1944," removed his cap and put it in his left armpit. Then he stirred his spoon in his kasha bowl, around the edge.

At that moment one should concentrate entirely on eating, on removing that thin layer of kasha from the bowl, putting it neatly in one's mouth and rolling it over one's tongue. But he had to hurry so that Pavlo could see that he had already finished and would offer him a second portion. Fetyukov, who had come in with the Estonians and watched Shukhov swipe the two bowls for them, ate standing up opposite Pavlo. He kept looking at the extra portions, trying to convince Pavlo that he should be given another portion or at least another half-portion.

The swarthy young Pavlo, however, calmly ate his own double portion and by his face no one could tell whether or not he saw who was next to him, or even if he remembered that there were two extra portions.

Shukhov finished his kasha. Because he had set his heart on two portions, the single bowl left him feeling empty. He reached into his inside pocket, took out the white cloth, unwrapped the piece of bread crust and began to wipe all the remnants of the oatmeal carefully from the bottom and sides of the bowl. He licked the kasha from the crust with his tongue and then wiped the bowl again. Finally it was as clean as if it had been washed, just a little dull on the surface. He handed it back to the bowl-collector and continued to sit for a moment with his cap off.

Even though it was Shukhov who had swiped the two bowls the assistant foreman was their owncr. Pavlo kept him in suspense a while longer, till he finished his own bowl. He didn't lick it out; he licked off the spoon, put it away, crossed himself. Then he lightly touched two bowls of the four.

"Ivan Denisovich. Take one for yourself and give one to Tsezar."

Shukhov realized that he was to take one bowl to Tsezar. Tsezar never lowered himself to go to the mess hall, neither here nor in the camp. He remembered that, but when Pavlo had touched two of the bowls at the same time his heart had nearly stopped: was it possible that Pavlo was going to give him both? Then his heart resumed beating as before.

He bent over his lawful prize and began to eat with deliberation, not feeling the new brigades pushing against him. Shukhov was worried only that the other extra kasha might be given to Fetyukov. He was an expert at scavenging, that Fetyukov, though he never had the boldness to swipe anything.

Nearby, across the table, sat Captain Buinovsky. He had long since finished his kasha and didn't even know that there were some extras. He was relaxing, warming himself. He didn't have the strength to get up and go out into the cold or back to the unwarmed shelter. He was unlawfully keeping a place, hindering the newly arrived brigades, just like the people he had hounded out with his metallic voice a few minutes before. He hadn't been long in camp, not long at the common work. Such minutes as these, though he didn't know it, were especially important for him, transforming him from an authoritative brassy naval officer into a slow-moving, quick-eyed zek. Only by virtue of that slow movement would he be able to live through twenty-five years of prison.

People were already shouting at him and pushing him from behind so that he would leave his place.

Pavlo said, "Captain! Hey, captain!"

Buinovsky jumped as if he was just awakening and turned around.

Pavlo handed him another portion of kasha without asking whether he wanted it.

Buinovsky's eyebrows rose. He looked at the kasha as if it were a miracle.

"Take it, take it," Pavlo reassured him and, picking up the last portion for the foreman, left.

A guilty smile crept over the cracked lips of the captain who had often sailed around Europe and over the North Sea route. He bent down, happy, over a half-full scoop of thin oatmeal gruel, no fat in it, just oats and water.

Fetyukov looked hastily at Shukhov and the captain before he went out.

But as far as Shukhov was concerned, he thought it was right to give it to the captain. The time would come when the captain would learn the way to survive, but so far he didn't know how.

Shukhov even had some small hope that Tsezar might give him his portion of kasha. But probably not, because Tsezar hadn't received a parcel from home for two weeks.

After the second kasha, he wiped off the bottom and side of the bowl as carefully as the first time and licked off his crust the same way. Finally he ate the crust. Then he picked up Tsezar's cooled-off kasha and went out.

"To the office!" He elbowed aside the helper at the door who didn't want to let him out with the bowl. The office was a log hut near the watch house. As in the morning, smoke was pouring out of the chimney. An orderly kept the fire going. He was a messenger, too, and was given time rates. And they weren't stingy about kindling and logs for the office fire.

The vestibule door creaked behind Shukhov. There was one more door, completely covered with rope insulation. Clouds of steam from the frost billowed as Shukhov entered. He pulled the door shut behind himself quickly, hurrying so they wouldn't yell: "Hey, fathead, close the door."

It seemed as hot inside the office as a steam bath. Through the melting ice of the window the sun was playing, not maliciously as it did on top of the power station, but gaily. In its rays the smoke from Tsezar's pipe drifted like incense in a church. The stove was red hot all the way through, they had fired it so fiercely, heartless bastards. The stovepipe was red hot, too. In such heat if you sat down for just a moment you'd fall asleep.

There were two rooms in the office. The second, belonging to the construction supervisor, had a door which wasn't quite shut, and from inside the voice of the construction supervisor rang out.

"We're overspending the wage funds and overspending for construction materials. Valuable boards, to say nothing of panels, are being cut up by your prisoners for firewood and burned in their shelters. And you don't see a thing! Cement was unloaded near the warehouse recently in a strong wind: then the prisoners carried it loose in hand barrows for ten yards. The whole area was ankle deep with cement and the workers went out of there not black but gray. What waste."

Obviously a meeting with the construction supervisor. It must be for the junior work supervisors.

In the corner near the door an orderly sat on a stool, resting. Beyond him stood Shkuropatenko, zek B-219, like a crooked beanpole. He was watching out the window to be sure that no one ran off with his prefabs. You sure missed seeing that roofing walk off, uncle.

Two bookkeepers, also zeks, were toasting bread on the stove. They had made a wire holder so it wouldn't burn.

Tsezar smoked his pipe, sprawled at his desk. His back was to Shukhov; he didn't see him. Opposite Tsezar sat K-123, who had been sentenced to twenty years at hard-labor by a court verdict. He was a sinewy old man. Eating kasha.

"No, old fellow," Tsezar said softly, casually. "Objectivity demands you recognize that Eisenstein is a genius. *Ivan the Terrible* — isn't that a work of genius? The dance of the *oprichniks!*[4] The scene in the cathedral!"

"Affectation!" K-123 grew angry, holding his spoon in front of his mouth.

4 [The Czar's special soldiers. — Editors' note.]

"So much art it isn't art any longer. Pepper and poppy seed instead of our daily bread! And then, too, it's the most repulsive political idea — justification of one-man tyranny. Mockery at the memory of three generations of the Russian intelligentsia."

Eating his kasha absentmindedly — losing all the good of it.

"But what other treatment would they have passed?"

"Ah, *passed?* Then don't talk about genius! Say simply that he's a bootlicker, that he executed a dog's order. Genius doesn't fit its treatment to the taste of tyrants."

"Hmm, hmm," coughed Shukhov, too shy to break into the intellectual conversation. But there wasn't any reason for him just to go on standing there, either.

Tsezar turned around, reached out his hand for his kasha, didn't even look at Shukhov, as if the kasha had floated in through the air on its own.

"But listen to me — art is not *what* but *how.*"

K-123 hit the table with the edge of his hand, once, again. He retorted:

"No sir, to the devil's mother with your 'how' if it doesn't arouse good feelings in me!"

Shukhov stood there just exactly as long as it was dignified for him to stand there after having delivered the kasha. He was waiting to see whether Tsezar might not offer him a smoke. But Tsezar didn't even notice him. So Shukhov turned on his heel and left quietly.

Not too bad, not so very cold outside. They could lay blocks, all right.

Shukhov went along the path. He noticed a piece of steel blade on the snow, a broken piece of a strip. Though he hadn't any particular use for such a piece, you can't foresee all your needs ahead of time. He picked it up, shoved it into his trouser pocket. Hide it at the power station. Thrifty is better than rich.

At the power station first thing he did was get the hidden trowel. He stuck it behind his rope belt. Only then did he duck down into the mortar-mixing room.

In there after being out in the sunlight it seemed dark and not any warmer than outside. Damp too.

Everyone was crowded up next to the round stove that Shukhov had installed, or was close to the one where the sand was heating and steaming a little as it dried. Whoever could find no room there was sitting on the edge of the mixing box. The foreman was at the stove, finishing his kasha. Pavlo had warmed it up for him on the stove.

Buzz buzz among the men. They were in a good mood. And they passed the word to Ivan Denisych quietly. The foreman had surpassed the quota well. He had come back pleased.

Where he'd found the work they were supposed to have done and what kind it was — that was his business. So far today, for instance, what had they accomplished? Nothing. There's no pay for installing a stove or for making a shelter. That was for themselves, not for production. But something had to be written in the work sheet. Maybe Tsezar was helping the foreman with the work sheets. The foreman was quite respectful toward Tsezar, and he wouldn't act that way for nothing.

He had surpassed the quota well — that meant five days of good rations. Well, not quite five, only four. The officers would grab one for themselves by putting the whole camp on the guaranteed minimum ration, both the competent and the incompetent workers. Probably it shouldn't cause bad feelings, everyone equal. But they economize on our stomachs. Well, all right, a zek's stomach can stand anything. Somehow or other we'll get through today, and tomorrow we'll eat. The whole camp goes to sleep with that dream on days of the guaranteed minimum.

But then you figure it out — you worked five days and ate four.

The brigade was quiet. Anyone who had anything to smoke was smoking silently. They were gathered close in the dark, looking into the fire. Like a big family. For the zek the brigade is a family. They listened to the foreman telling a story to a few men at the stove. He never talked a lot, so if he had started a story, it meant he was in a good mood.

Andrei Prokofych, too, had never learned to eat with cap on. Without a cap his head looked old. It was shaved short, like all the others, but even in the dim light from the stove you could see how much white was scattered among the gray.

". . . I even trembled in front of the battalion commander, and there in front of me was the commander of the regiment. 'Red Army man, Tyurin, awaits your orders.'

"He stared at me from under his wild brows. 'Your patronymic?'

"I told him.

" 'Year of birth?' I told him. That was in '30 and I was just 22 — just a kid.

" 'Well, and how do you serve,[5] Tyurin?'

" 'I serve the working people!'[5] How he boiled, banged his two fists on the table — whop!

" 'You serve the working people! And who are *you*, you scoundrel?'

"I was boiling inside me! But I kept control. 'Infantryman-machine gunner, first class. Distinguished battle and political. . . .'

"And he interrupted: 'What class, you bastard? Your father's a *kulak*.[6]

5 [Standard forms of address in the Soviet army. — Editors' note.]
6 [A rich peasant who opposed collectivization of the land. — Editors' note.]

Here's a paper from Kamen. Your father's a kulak and you ran away from there. They've been looking for you for two years!'

"I went pale, kept quiet. I hadn't written letters home for a year so they wouldn't get on the trail. I didn't know whether my folks were alive and they didn't know about me either.

" 'What kind of conscience do you have,' he yelled and all the four bars on his uniform danced, 'to deceive the Soviet authority?'

"I thought he was going to beat me. But he didn't. He signed an order — in six hours out the gate with me. . . . And outside it was November. They tore the winter uniform off my back, handed me a three-year-old summer uniform for raw recruits. I had been given a real screwing. I didn't know that I didn't have to turn in the winter uniform, that I could have told them where to go. And they gave me a fierce document in my hands. 'Dismissed from the ranks . . . as the son of a kulak.' Only try to find work with a reference like that. Four days' train ride to get home and they didn't give me a ticket and not even one day's dry ration. Fed me with lunch the last time and shoved me out of the camp.

"Incidentally in '38 at the Kotlas transit center I met my former squad commander. He'd also been given ten. I found out from him that both the regimental commander and his political commissar were shot in '37. No difference then whether they were proletarians or kulaks, whether they had a conscience or none. . . . When I heard that I crossed myself and I said 'Nevertheless, Creator, Thou art in heaven. You bide your time but you deal a wicked blow.' "

After two bowls of kasha Shukhov wanted a smoke desperately. Since he counted on buying two mugsful of tobacco from the Latvian in the seventh barracks, he could repay a loan, so he quietly said to the Estonian fisherman, "Listen, Eino, lend me the makings for one smoke till tomorrow. You know I won't cheat you."

Eino looked Shukhov straight in the eyes, then without hurrying he shifted his eyes to his adopted brother. They shared everything fifty-fifty. One of them wouldn't hand out even a bit of tobacco by himself. They muttered something to each other and Eino got out a tobacco pouch decorated with a rose-colored pull string. He took out a pinch of factory-cut tobacco, put it on Shukhov's palm, measured it and added a few more shreds. Just enough for one, that's all.

Shukhov had a piece of newspaper. He tore it off, rolled it, picked up an ember from between Tyurin's feet — and inhaled. He inhaled again. Dizziness flowed through his whole being. It was almost as if he were drunk from head to toe.

He had just started to smoke but already from across the whole mixing room green eyes flashed — Fetyukov. Shukhov might have relented and given the jackal a puff, but he had scrounged once today already. Shukhov had seen that. Better leave it for Senka Klevshin. Senka couldn't hear what the foreman was saying, just sat there, unlucky guy, in front of the fire, head inclined to one side.

The foreman's pocked face was lighted by the fire. He was talking without any self-pity as if it weren't about himself at all:

"All the trash I had with me I sold to a dealer for a quarter of what it was worth. I bought two loaves of bread from under the counter — there were ration cards. I thought I'd make it on freight trains but there were strict new laws against that. And as anyone can remember you couldn't get tickets even for money, let alone without money — only with travel orders or travel passes. No admission to the station platform either. Militiamen at the doors, guards on the tracks on both sides of the station. The sun cold and sinking. Puddles with coats of ice. Where to spend the night? I managed to get up on top of a smooth brick wall, went right on over with my two loaves. Into the station toilet. Stood there, waited. No one was after me. I went out like a passenger, a soldier. And right there on the track stood the train — Vladivostok-Moscow. A mob was going for hot water, banging each other over the head with their pots. A girl in a dark blue sweater holding a two-quart teapot was wandering about in a circle, afraid to try to get near the hot water heater. Her small feet might get scalded or trampled.

" 'Here,' I said to her, 'take my loaves and I'll get you your hot water.' While I got up to the heater, the train had started to pull out. She was holding my loaves and crying because she didn't know what to do with them. Would have been glad to lose the teapot. 'Run,' I yelled. 'Run, I'll catch up!' She in front and me behind. I caught up. With one hand I lifted her onto the train — the train was gathering speed. I also jumped on the step. The conductor didn't beat me across the knuckles or push against me in the chest. Other soldiers were in the car, he confused me with them."

Shukhov gave Senka a nudge in the side. "Here, take the cigarette, finish it up, unlucky one." Gave it to him with his wooden mouthpiece, let him pull on it, he's all right. Senka was a strange one: like an actor he pressed his hand to his heart and nodded his head. Well, what can you expect from a deaf man.

The foreman went on. "Six girls travelling in a compartment, Leningrad students returning from practice work. On their little table there was nice fresh butter and fancy clutter, raincoats hanging on hooks, pretty little suitcases in covers. They were travelling right past life with green lights. . . . They talked, they joked, we drank tea together. 'And you,' they asked, 'from what car are you?' I sighed and I confessed: 'I'm from the car, girls, that's life for you but death for me. . . .' "

Quiet in the mortar mixing room. The oven crackled.

"They said 'ah' and they said 'oh' and had a conference. . . . They kept me covered with a raincoat on the top shelf. They hid me all the way to Novosibirsk, got me there.... Incidentally, I had a chance to thank one of those girls in Pechora. In '35 she got caught in the Kirov round-up,[7] was just about dead of hard labor, and I managed to get her a spot in the tailor shop."

"Maybe we should mix the cement?" Pavlo asked the foreman in a whisper.

The foreman didn't hear him.

"I came home at night through the vegetable gardens and left the same night. I took along my little brother and took him down to the warm country, to Frunze. I had nothing to feed him with, or myself either. In Frunze they were melting asphalt in a pot while some young hoodlums sat around and watched. I sat down with them: 'Listen, you gentlemen without britches! Take my little brother on as an apprentice, teach him how to live!' They took him.... Sorry I didn't join the thieves myself...."

"And you never saw your brother again?" the captain asked.

Tyurin yawned.

"No, never saw him again." He yawned once more and said: "Well, boys, don't cry! We'll settle in, even here at the power station. Whoever is mixing mortar, get going. Don't wait for the whistle."

And that's what it's like in the brigade. The chiefs up above can't get a working stiff to move, even in working time. But at rest time the foreman says work, and it means work. Because he feeds you, the foreman does. And he doesn't compel you to work for nothing.

While they're mixing mortar what will the masons be doing when work is supposed to begin? Just stand there? Shukhov sighed and got up.

"Going to clear off ice."

He took a small axe and a brush. For laying the blocks he had a mason's hammer, a measuring rod, mason's twine, and a plumb line.

The ruddy Kilgas looked at Shukhov and made a face as if he was asking, why are you jumping for the foreman? But, after all Kilgas didn't care how the brigade got fed: the baldhead could get along on seven ounces a day or less. He lived on his parcels.

Nevertheless he got up, too. He understood. He wasn't going to hold back the brigade.

"Wait, Vanya, I'm coming too!" he called.

No doubt, no doubt, fatface. If you'd been working for yourself you'd have been up at it faster.

Shukhov had hurried for another reason too — in order to grab off the plumb line before Kilgas got it. They'd taken only one plumb from the tool shop.

Pavlo asked the foreman, "Can we make it with three men laying block?

7 [The assassination of Sergei Kirov, in 1934, was followed by mass arrests. — Editors' note.]

What about adding one more? Or don't we have enough mortar?" As usual he spoke in Ukrainian.

The foreman scowled in thought. "I'll be the fourth, Pavlo. You stay here with the mortar. It's a big box — put six on it. Work it so that the ready mortar is taken from one end while new mortar is being mixed in the other half. No interruptions."

"Whew," Pavlo jumped up, a young chap, fresh-blooded, not yet worn down by the camps, his face round from eating Ukrainian dumplings. "If you're going to lay blocks yourself — then I'll mix mortar myself. We'll see who gets the most done. Where's the longest shovel?"

Now that's a brigade for you. Pavlo had been a forest partisan, had carried out night raids on provincial towns. Why should he break his back here? But doing it for the foreman, that's something else again.

Shukhov and Kilgas climbed up on the roof and heard Senka creaking up the ladder behind them. The deaf man had guessed what was up without being told.

On the second floor the laying of the walls had barely been started. Three rows all the way around and in a few places, more. They were going to be working with the easiest rows today — from knee to chest and no scaffolding to bother with.

The scaffolding and trestles which had been there previously had been all hauled away by zeks to other buildings, or chopped up for firewood just so another brigade wouldn't get them. Now, they would have to put some trestles together the next day in order to operate efficiently unless they wanted to halt work entirely.

From the top of the power station Shukhov could see a long way. The whole zone was snowy and empty. The zeks were under shelter, warming themselves until the work whistle. Black watch towers and sharpened poles for the barbed wire were sharply outlined. The wire itself could be seen on the sun side — but not in the other direction. The sun was gleaming fiercely. You couldn't keep your eyes wide open.

And then nearby — the power train. Smoking, dirtying up the sky. It puffed heavily, always with a sick hoarse wheeze just before the whistle. There, it blew. They hadn't really gone to work very much ahead of time.

"Hey, you Stakhanovite. Don't waste time with that plumb!" Kilgas hurried him.

"Look at your wall — how much ice there is! Can you get it off before night? You brought your trowel up with you for nothing," Shukhov made fun of him too.

They were about to stand at the respective walls allotted them before lunch, but then and there the foreman shouted from beneath:

"Hey, boys. We're going to work in pairs so the mortar won't freeze on us. Shukhov! You take Klevshin for your wall, and I'll work with Kilgas. And till I get there Gopchik can work at cleaning ice off the wall with Kilgas."

Shukhov and Kilgas exchanged looks. True. That was the most effective way. They took up their axes. Then Shukhov no longer had time to look at the distant view where the sun shone on the snow, or to see how the working stiffs clambered out of their shelters throughout the zone, some to pound away at the little holes which they hadn't managed to complete during that whole morning, some to fasten reinforcement rods in place, some to raise rafters in the plant workshops. Shukhov saw only his own wall, from the joint on the left where the blocks rose higher than his waist to the right where his section met that where Kilgas was working. He showed Senka where to knock ice off and himself whacked zestfully away with both heel and cutting edge of the axe so ice chips flew all about, even right into his face. He worked away recklessly, not a thought in his head. And his imagination and eyes sculptured out from under the ice the wall of the power station, two concrete blocks thick. At this section the wall had been laid by an unknown mason who either didn't know how or didn't give a damn. But now Shukhov studied the wall as if it was his. Right there, a depression. That can't be leveled off in one row. It will take three rows, each time making the mortar layer a little thicker at that point. Right there the external wall bellies out a bit. That can be straightened two rows later. He divided the wall in his mind's eye into the part he would lay himself from the joint where the blocks rose in steps above the general level on the left, and from Senka's sector between him and Kilgas on the right. There on the corner, he calculated, Kilgas could not help but put down a few blocks for Senka since that would make things easier for himself. And while they were messing around in the corner, he would lay down more than half a run so that his pair didn't fall behind the other two. He made notes where the cement blocks should be set down. And no sooner had the blocks appeared on top than he yelled at Alyesha:

"Bring them over here to me! Put them here. And here."

Senka was still chopping away at the ice. Shukhov gripped the wire brush with two hands and hither-thither, hither-thither, brushed along the wall, cleaning off the top row of cement blocks. Though they were not completely clean, the ice was down to a light touch of gray mainly between the seams.

The foreman clambered up, too, and while Shukhov was still working with his brush, Tyurin put up his measuring rod at the corner. On the edges Shukhov and Kilgas had put theirs up before.

"Hey!" shouted Pavlo from below. "Who's still alive up there? Take the mortar!"

Shukhov started to sweat; his mason's twine hadn't been stretched out yet.

He hurried. He decided to stretch the twine for three rows right away leaving space for adjustment. Also to make it easier for Senka he would take another part of the outside row and help him a bit with the inside row, too.

He set up the twine along the top edge and explained to Senka both with words and signs where to lay block. The deaf man understood. He bit his lips, crossed his eyes, nodded in the direction of the foreman's wall as if he were saying, 'let's build a fire under them, what do you say? We won't fall behind.' Shukhov laughed.

Already the mortar was being carried up the ladder. Eight men were to be engaged in mortar hauling. The foreman decided not to put mortar boxes near the masons — the mortar would only freeze. Instead they put the barrows close by so the two masons could take it directly from a barrow and slap it onto the wall, then lay the blocks. During that interval the barrow men were to carry blocks so they wouldn't freeze standing around up there. As soon as the mortar was out of the barrows, new barrow men came to replace them and the first men carried down the empties. Down below they thawed the frozen mortar out of the barrows and warmed themselves a bit, too.

Two barrows at once — one for Kilgas's wall and one for Shukhov's. Mortar steaming out in the cold — smoking, but only the least bit of warmth in it. With trowel slap it onto the wall and if you stop to yawn it will be stiff. Frozen, you have to chip it off with the heel of the axe — the trowel won't chip it. And if you put the block just a little out of line, it freezes into place crooked. You must knock it off with the heel of the axe and then chip off the mortar.

But Shukhov made no mistakes. The blocks were not all exactly the same dimensions. Some had a knocked-off corner, uneven edge, or other defect. Shukhov spotted them right away and spotted the side on which that block wanted to sit, and spotted also the place in the wall that was waiting for that block.

Shukhov scooped up smoking mortar with his trowel and threw it into that place. He remembered where the lower seam went — that seam had to be in the center of the upper block. He laid on mortar evenly, just enough for one block. And then he picked up one block — but carefully so as not to tear his mitten, because cement blocks scratch painfully. And, once more smoothing the mortar with his trowel, plop into place went the block. And right away, right away, even it up, hit it on the side with the trowel if it wasn't quite right. So the outside wall should be exactly straight to the plumb, so the block lay exactly level both length and width.

And then if some of the mortar had been forced out into its sides, that mortar had to be knocked off with the edge of the trowel right away and thrown over the wall. In summer it would have gone under the next block but don't even think of trying that now. Then the lower seams had to be examined. The block might have crumbled. And then you'd put mortar down again, so that it was thicker on the left side. And then you wouldn't just put the block in place but you'd slide it in from the right to the left since otherwise it would press out that excess of mortar between itself and the next on the left. Eye on the plumb line. Eye on the level. It's set. Next.

The work went right along. When two rows are down, the old mistakes will be straightened out. Then it will move along smoothly. But right now — look closely.

And he kept pushing along and pushing along the outside row toward Senka. And Senka there at the corner had moved away from the foreman, and was working toward Shukhov.

Shukhov winked at the barrow men — mortar, mortar, bring it over faster. The work was going so fast there wasn't even time to wipe his nose. When he and Senka met up and took mortar from the same barrow, they quickly scraped bottom.

"Mortar!" yelled Shukhov over the wall.

"Commmming!" Pavlo shouted.

They brought up a barrow and the two finished that off too, all of it that was liquid. On the sides it had frozen. Scratch it off yourselves. If you let a crust form there, you're the ones who haul it up and down. Move along. Next.

Shukhov and the other masons stopped feeling the cold. From the fast and all-absorbing work they felt at first the initial surge of heat — that heat surge that brings dampness underneath the coat, underneath the underjacket, underneath the outer and inner undershirts. But they didn't stop for a minute. They pushed the block-laying further and further. And an hour later came the second heat surge. In this one the sweat dries out. The cold did not get into their feet and that was the main thing. Nothing else, including the biting light wind, could distract their thoughts from the work. Only Klevshin was knocking his feet together. He, poor fellow, a foot size 11, had been given unmatched valenki which were too tight.

The foreman from time to time shouted: "Morrtarr!" And Shukhov too: "Morrrttarr!" Anyone who pushes his work along fast becomes something like a foreman over his fellows. Shukhov wasn't going to fall behind that pair. He would have chased his own blood brother up and down that ladder with barrows.

Buinovsky, from lunch-time on, hauled mortar with Fetyukov. The ladder was both steep and difficult, and at first he wasn't quite pulling his load. Shukhov urged him on quietly. "Captain, faster. Captain, more blocks."

But with every barrow the captain became quicker and Fetyukov slower. Along he went, the bitch's tit, tipping the barrow and slopping mortar out of it so it was lighter to carry.

Shukhov gave him a punch in the back: "Oh, you snake shit. So you were a director, Fetyukov! I'll bet you drove your workers!"

"Foreman," yelled the captain. "Put me with a human being. I'm not going to haul mortar with this piece of shit."

The foreman reshuffled the men. Fetyukov was sent down to throw blocks up to the scaffolding, but his work was set up so that there could be a separate count of how many blocks he had moved. The foreman put Alyesha with the captain. Alyesha was quiet. Anyone at all could order him around.

"Man the pumps, you lubbers," the captain shouted. "Look how fast they're laying blocks there!"

Alyesha smiled submissively:

"If it must be faster then it will be faster — let it be faster. Whatever you say."

And he clumped on down.

A mild man is a treasure for the brigade.

Someone called to the foreman from below. Another truck had arrived with blocks. None for half a year and now a flood. While they were delivering them was the time to work. First day. After that there'd be delays and you couldn't do any rushing along.

The foreman was cursing. Something about the elevator. Shukhov wanted to know what, but there wasn't time. He was levelling the wall. The barrow carriers told him the repairman had come to fix the motor on the elevator and with him came the construction supervisor for electricians, a free worker. The repairman fiddled around and the supervisor watched.

By the book: one works, one watches.

If they could fix the elevator both blocks and mortar could go up on it.

Shukhov had laid his third row and Kilgas had begun his when up the ladder came another one of the snoopers, one more boss; the junior supervisor, Der. A Muscovite they said. Used to work in a ministry.

Shukhov, who was near Kilgas, pointed at Der.

"Bahhh!" Kilgas brushed the warning away. "I don't have anything to do with the bosses. Call me if he falls off the ladder."

Now Der would hover behind the masons and look over their shoulders. These observers were the hardest of all for Shukhov to take. This one acts as if he were an engineer, the pig's ass. Once when he was demonstrating how to lay brick, Shukhov laughed out loud. The way he looked at it was build a house with your own hands and then maybe you'll be a craftsman.

Back in Temgenyevo they didn't have "stone" buildings — brick or block. The huts were of logs. So was the school. Forty-foot tree trunks were brought in from the forest reserve. Here in camp Shukhov had had to become a mason. And so, if you please, he became a mason. Anyone who has two manual skills can pick up another ten.

Der didn't fall. He just stumbled once. He went up the ladder almost at a run. He yelled,

"Tyurin!" His eyes were bulging: "Tyurin!"

On his heels came Pavlo still holding the shovel he'd had in his hand.

Der's coat was camp issue, but new and clean. A nice leather cap, but like everyone else's it had a number on it — B-731.

"Well?" Tyurin went to meet him, trowel in hand, foreman's cap crooked, down over one eye.

Something unusual. Shukhov couldn't ignore it even though the mortar was cooling off in the barrow. Shukhov kept laying blocks, laying and listening.

"What are you up to?" Der shouted, spit flying as he yelled. "That's not just a question of solitary. That smells of a criminal offense. Tyurin, you'll get a third term!"

Only then did Shukhov get what was up. He looked at Kilgas. Kilgas understood too. The roofing. They had seen the roofing on the windows.

Shukhov didn't worry about himself at all. The foreman would never turn him in. He was afraid for the foreman. For us the foreman is a father. For them — he's a pawn. They could really paste another term on to the foreman's sentence.

How the foreman's face had twisted. And how he threw down the trowel. And right toward Der — one step. Der looked behind — Pavlo had his shovel raised high. Pavlo hadn't dragged the shovel along with him for nothing.

And Senka had understood in spite of his deafness. He approached, hands on hips. He was big and rough-looking.

Der blinked, shuddered, looked for a "fifth corner" — a way out.

The foreman bent toward Der and said very, very quietly but distinctly, "Your time to hand out prison terms, you rat, has passed. If you say one word, you bloodsucker, it will be your last day on earth, remember!"

Tyurin's whole body shook. It shook and he couldn't control it. And sharp-faced Pavlo was glaring at Der, really glaring.

"Boys, boys, please!" Der was pale. He edged away from the ladder.

The foreman said nothing more. He adjusted his cap, picked up his trowel, and went to his wall.

And Pavlo, holding his shovel, went slowly down.

Slllllowly. . . .

Der was terrified to stay and terrified to descend. He edged behind Kilgas, and just stood there. Kilgas kept on laying block, the way they weigh out drugs at a pharmacy, a druggist who would not be hurried at all. He stood with his back to Der as if he hadn't noticed him.

Then Der moved toward the foreman. Where had all his arrogance gone?

"What am I going to tell the construction supervisor, Tyurin?"

The foreman continued laying block without turning around.

"You'll tell him that's the way it *was*. We came here and that's the way it *was*."

Der stayed a while longer. He saw they weren't going to finish him off right then. He went about quietly, hands in his pockets.

"Hey, S-854," he muttered. "Why is it you're putting mortar on in such thin layers?"

He had to take it out on someone. He couldn't pick on Shukhov for either his joints or his level.

"Please let me inform you," Shukhov said, with a little laugh, "that if I lay down a thick layer now, the whole power station is going to leak in the spring."

"You are a mason — so listen to what I say," Der frowned and blew out his cheeks, as was his habit.

Well, in places maybe the mortar was thin and could have been thicker. But that was if it were laid under human conditions: not here, in winter. One had to have pity for people. Here there had to be results, work accomplished. But why explain if the man couldn't understand it himself?

Der went down the ladder quietly.

"You get that elevator fixed!" Tyurin hollered after him from the wall. "What do you think we are, donkeys? Moving concrete blocks up to the second story by hand."

"You'll be paid for the lifting work," Der replied from the ladder, submissively.

"At 'wheel barrow' rates? You just take a wheel barrow and try to roll it up the ladder. Pay at 'hand barrow' rates."

"Personally it's all right with me; why not? But the bookkeeping office won't pass it at 'hand barrow' rates."

"The bookkeeping office! And my whole brigade is working to keep four masons busy. How much can we earn that way?"

The foreman kept shouting but didn't stop laying block.

"Mortar!" he shouted down.

"Mortar!" Shukhov caught up the cry. Everything was evened up on the third row and they were ready to get moving on the fourth. The mason's twine had to be raised a row — oh well, he could go for one row without the twine.

Der went out by himself, and through the field, all hunched up. Off to the office to get warm. Not too cosy for him maybe. But he should have thought twice before he attacked a wolf like Tyurin. If he'd managed to get along with such foremen he'd have no trouble. He doesn't have to break his back at work, gets a big bread ration, lives in a separate shack. What more does he want? If he sticks his neck out that way he's just playing the smart aleck.

Some of the zeks came up and said the construction supervisor for electrical repairs had gone and the repairman too. The elevator could not be fixed.

And so donkeys it was.

No matter how much construction work Shukhov had seen, all of the equipment either broke down by itself or else the zeks broke it up. He'd once seen a log conveyor wrecked — the zeks pushed a big stick in the chain and pried till they broke it off. They wanted a rest. The bosses had had them piling on one log after another. They couldn't keep that up.

"Blocks, blocks!" shouted the foreman, annoyed. And he cursed them out with curses and more curses, all of them, the men carrying mortar and the men carrying blocks.

"Pavlo is asking how's it to be with the mortar?" they shouted from below.

"Mix it!"

"There is half a box mixed!"

"So make one more box."

Well they were really cooking now. They were pushing the fifth row. At the beginning they'd had to bend way over to lay the first, and now it was all the way up to chest height, look. Well, and why not push it along — no window nor door spaces to worry about, just two blank walls joining together and plenty of blocks. And he should have put up the mason's twine, but it was too late for that.

"The 82nd went to turn in its tools," Gopchik reported.

The foreman turned on him, eyes snapping.

"You mind your own business, shrimp. More blocks."

Shukhov looked outside. Yes, the sun was sinking. It was going down in a red glow that seemed grayish in the fog. They had really pushed along — you couldn't have asked for more. They had already begun the fifth row. They'd end with the fifth, making it level all the way across.

The mortar carriers were, like overworked horses, short of wind. The captain's face was gray with fatigue. After all, he wasn't so young, that captain second rank. Forty. Not forty, but almost.

Degree by degree the temperature went down. Hands work on but fingers ache through the thin mittens. And the frost had moved into that left felt boot. Tap, tap, went Shukhov with his foot, tap, tap.

They didn't have to bend down over the wall any longer — but they were struggling over every block and every spoonful of mortar.

"Boys, boys." Shukhov fussed. "Just bring the blocks close to the wall. Up to the wall."

The captain was willing but he no longer had the strength. He wasn't used to exhaustion.

But Alyesha said, "Good, Ivan Denisych. Show me where to put them."

That Alyesha was always willing, no matter what he was asked to do. If everyone in the world had been like that then Shukhov would have been like that too. If a man asks for help, why not help him? That was the way it ought to be.

Through the whole zone and sounding clear in the power station came the pounding on the rail. Quitting time. And there they were, caught with fresh mortar on their hands. Ah, they had tried too hard!

"Bring up the mortar! Bring up the mortar!" shouted the foreman. There was a new box of it mixed, so they'd have to keep going — no way out. If the mortar box wasn't emptied they might as well break it up for firewood tomorrow. The mortar would be like rock and even a pickaxe wouldn't get it out.

"Come on, brothers, don't slow down." Shukhov cried.

Kilgas became angry. He hated alarms and emergencies. But he was keeping up the pace too. What else was there to do?

Pavlo came running up the ladder, pulling a barrow, trowel in his belt. And then he set to laying block. Five trowels flying. Now just finish up the joints. Shukhov studied what block to use for the joint. He handed Alyesha a hammer.

"Come on, smooth it off for me, smooth it down!"

Things done fast are not done well. And now, when everyone was hurrying, Shukhov slowed down to examine the wall carefully. He moved Senka toward the left and he himself moved to the right, to the main corner. If they messed up the corner now — that was a catastrophe. It would take a half day's work tomorrow to fix things up.

"Stop!" He pushed Pavlo away from a block and fixed it himself. And in the corner, look. Senka's line was uneven. Shukhov dashed to Senka, corrected the error with two blocks.

Like a good gelding, the captain brought up another barrow of mortar.

"Two more coming," he shouted.

The captain was staggering, but he was pulling his share of the load. Shukhov had once owned a hard-working gelding like the captain. Shukhov had taken good care of him, too. But eventually he had slaughtered the horse. And skinned him.

The sun was sinking to the horizon. Now, even without Gopchik to point things out, one could see that not only had all the brigades turned in their tools, but the men were moving in a wave to the watch house. After the gong sounds no one goes out, no one's fool enough to stand outside and freeze. They were all in their shelters. But then the moment would come when the foremen agreed it was time to leave and all the brigades would pour out at once. If the foremen didn't get together on the time, these convicts were so mean and stubborn they would try to outsit each other, even if it meant staying in their shelters till midnight.

Finally Tyurin came to his senses, saw he had over-stayed. Probably the tool clerk was cursing him out already.

"Hey!" he shouted. "Why worry about that shit. Mortar carriers! Get down and scrape out the big mixing box. Whatever you get out of it bury in that hole in the ground and cover it with snow so it can't be seen. And you, Pavlo, take two men, collect the tools and turn them in. After we've finished the mortar up here, I'll send Gopchik over with these three trowels."

The men scurried. They took Shukhov's hammer and unwound his mason's twine. The mortar carriers and the block haulers, all of them, ran into the mortar-mixing room since there was nothing more for them to do. The three masons remained — Kilgas, Klevshin and Shukhov. The foreman was checking to see how much had been done. Satisfied.

"We laid it out well, eh? In half a day without any elevator, without any other fucking thing, too."

Shukhov saw that Kilgas had very little mortar left. He was worried that the foreman might be cursed out in the tool room because of the trowels.

"Listen, you guys," Shukhov said. "Take the trowels to Gopchik. Because mine isn't on the list, and doesn't have to be turned in, I'll finish up."

The foreman laughed. "How are we ever going to let you go out into freedom? The whole prison will weep for you!"

Shukhov laughed too, and kept laying blocks.

Kilgas took the trowels away. Senka pushed blocks to Shukhov and poured Kilgas's mortar into their barrow.

Gopchik ran all the way to the tool room to catch up with Pavlo. The 104th marched across the field without Tyurin. The foreman was a power, but the convoy was a greater power. The guards wrote down the names of those who were late and into solitary with them.

It was getting too crowded at the watch house. All the men had assembled. It even seemed as if the convoy had arrived and had started to take the count.

They count twice at exit. It's done once inside the closed gates to be sure it's all right to open the gates, and the second count is taken as the men go through the open gates. If the count goes wrong, then they count outside the gates too.

"The hell with the mortar," the foreman waved his arm. "Toss it over the wall."

"Get along with you, foreman. Get along with you — they need you over there!"

Shukhov ordinarily called him Andrei Prokofievich — but right now by virtue of his work he had made himself equal with the foreman. Not that he announced to himself: "Now I have become equal," but he simply had the feeling that this was so. And he tossed a joke in the wake of the foreman who was taking big steps down the ladder. "Why the hell is the working day so short? Just as you get going — it's over."

Shukhov was alone with the deaf man. You couldn't talk much with him and there was nothing to talk to him about, for that matter, since he was smarter than all of them; understood everything without words.

Plop went the mortar. Plop went the block. They pushed it into place. They checked on it. Mortar. Block. Mortar. Block.

The foreman had ordered him not to worry about the mortar — to toss it over the wall. And they had all run off, left him. But Shukhov had such an idiotic character that even eight years in camp hadn't changed him. He couldn't bear to see anything, or any kind of work, go to waste.

Mortar. Block. Mortar. Block.

"We've finished it. Do it to your mother by the leg." Senka shouted. "Let's beat it."

They grabbed the hand barrows. Down the ladder.

But Shukhov ran back to have a look at the work. The guards could have sicked the convoy dogs on him, but even that wouldn't have stopped him. Not so bad! And now he ran up and looked the wall over from right to left. He had an eye like a mason's level. It was straight. His hands had skill in them yet.

He ran down the ladder.

Senka was out of the mortar-mixing room and running along the slope.

"Come on, come on." He turned around.

"Go ahead. I'll be there right away!" Shukhov waved him on. Then he went into the mortar-mixing room. He wasn't going to throw away his trowel just like that. Maybe tomorrow he wouldn't be at work. Maybe they'd shove the brigade over to the Socialist Life Town after all, maybe he wouldn't get back here for half a year. Why let that trowel be lost? If you *swipe* something, keep it swiped.

In the mortar-mixing room all the stoves were cold. Dark. Terrifying. Not so terrifying because of the dark but because everyone had left, because only he would be missing at the watch house, because the convoy guards would beat him.

Nevertheless, peek and seek, he noticed a big stone in the corner, rolled it back, shoved the trowel underneath and moved it back again. Everything in order!

Now he had to catch up with Senka. But Senka had only gone a short way, and was waiting for him. Klevshin would never let a man down. If there was trouble then they would face it together.

They ran along side by side, the big man and the little one. Senka was a head and a half taller than Shukhov, and his head was an enormous one.

There are some loafers who willingly run races at a stadium. He'd like to see how they'd run, the devils, after a long day's work, with their backs still bent, and wet mittens, and patched valenki. Yes, and in the cold.

The two ran till they were afire like mad dogs and the only thing they heard was their own panting, in — out, in — out. Anyway, the foreman was at the watch house. He'd explain. Now they were running right into the crowd.

Suddenly hundreds of voices were screaming at them at once. Do that to their mothers, do that to their fathers, do that to them in the mouth, do that to them up their nose and in the ribs. It's terrifying when five hundred men are raging at you at once. But even more important, what about the convoy guards? How about them?

But the convoy guards paid no attention and the foreman was right there in the last row. That meant he had explained, taken the blame himself.

But the zeks yelled and screamed a river of curses. They yelled so loud even Senka could hear. He drew in his breath and whirled on them, big and tall. All his life he had been a quiet man. Now, suddenly, he roared. Lifted his fists and was all set to fight. The zeks quieted down. One of them laughed:

"Hey, 104th! So he isn't deaf after all?" Others shouted, "We found out."

Everyone laughed, even the convoy guards.

"Count off by fives!"

But the guards didn't open the gates. They didn't even trust themselves. They shoved the crowd back from the gate. The crowd had pushed up there, idiotically, as if that would hurry things.

"Count off by fives. One! Two! Three. . . ."

As they called out, each five stepped forward several yards.

Shukhov was catching his breath, looking around. The moon, the little father, wore a crimson frown and already showed its full face in the sky. But it was starting to wane. Last night at this time it had been higher.

Shukhov was in a gay mood because everything had come out all right. He poked the captain in the ribs.

"Listen, captain second rank, and what does your science have to say — where does the old moon disappear to?"

"What do you mean, where? Ignoramus! It's simply not visible."

Shukhov twisted his head and laughed.

"If it's not visible how do you know that it's there?"

"What's your idea about it?" asked the captain in dismay. "That every month there's a new moon?"

"What's so miraculous about that? Every day in the year people are born, so why can't the moon do it, too; every four weeks?"

"Tfoo!" spat the captain. "I've never even met a sailor who was as ignorant as you. Where do you think the old moon goes?"

"That's what I'm asking you. Where?" Shukhov grinned widely.

"Well, where?"

Shukhov sighed, and reminisced. "They used to say in our village that God crumbles up the old moon for stars."

"That's savages for you." The captain laughed. "I never heard that before! Do you believe in God, Shukhov?"

"Sure, so what?" Shukhov was surprised. "When it thunders try not believing!"

"And why does God do that?"

"What?"

"Crumble up the moon for stars — why?"

"How come you don't understand? Shukhov shrugged his shoulders. "The stars in time fall down. More have to be made to replace those that fall."

"Turn around!" A convoy guard cursed them with an oath. "Line up!"

The count had already come to them. The twelfth five of the fifth hundred had counted off, and there were two at the end — Buinovsky and Shukhov.

The convoy guards were troubled. They were busily conferring over their count boards. Short count! Again they were missing someone. If only they were able to count right!

They counted 462 and there had to be 463, they said.

Again they pushed everyone back from the gates for the zeks were crowding the gates again. And then once more.

"Count off by fives! One! Two!"

These recounts were unfortunate because the time wasted on them was no longer the government's but the zeks' own time. In addition there was still the march across the steppe to the camp, and then standing in line for body inspection in front of the camp. The groups of zeks from all the different projects usually ran on the double trying to get ahead of each other in order to be first at body inspection and thus sooner into camp. Whichever of the groups got into camp first was king. The mess hall was ready; it would be first in line at the parcels' room, first at the check room and at the kitchen, first at the cultural-educational section to receive letters, or at censorship to hand in letters, or the infirmary, the barber shop, the bath house — first everywhere!

And the convoy guards would hurry to turn them over to the camp, so they could get to their own quarters in camp sooner. Soldiers don't just wander around. They have much to do and little time.

But the count was short.

As the last fives began to count off Shukhov thought for an instant that at the end there would be three. But, no, two again.

The counters went to the chief of convoy guards with their count boards. They talked. The chief of convoy guards shouted:

"Foreman of the 104th!"

Tyurin stepped out half a pace:

"Here."

"No one of yours stayed behind at the power station? Think."

"No."

"Think twice — I'll tear your head off!"

"No, I'm telling the exact truth."

But he glared at Pavlo — had anyone gone to sleep in the mortar-mixing room?

"Count off by brigades!" shouted the chief of convoy guards.

They had been standing by fives as they happened to be, at random. Now they jostled and began to buzz. Shouts rang out: "Seventy-sixth — to me!" "Thirteenth! Here!" And then somewhere else, "Thirty-second!"

The 104th came after all the others. Shukhov saw that the brigade members were empty-handed. They had been worked so hard they hadn't had time to gather kindling for the stove. Only two of them had bundles.

The same game went on every day. Before the end of the work day the working stiffs gathered up chips, sticks, broken lathes, tied them up with pieces of cloth or thin twine and carried them back to camp. But there were traps. The first was at the watch house. If the construction supervisor or one of the junior supervisors was there he ordered them to drop all bundles. The officials had already sent millions of rubles up in smoke through waste, so they tried mean economies like using the zeks' kindling.

But the working stiffs had their own way of figuring things. If every man in a brigade brought back a few sticks, it would be warmer in the barracks. Otherwise, the barracks orderlies got only ten pounds of coal dust for each stove. Don't expect any warmth from that! That's why the men broke up the sticks, or sawed them shorter, and hid them under their coats, so that the construction supervisor wouldn't see the bundles.

The convoy guard at the construction project would never order the bundles of wood dropped. The convoy guards wanted firewood, too. But they couldn't carry it themselves. For one thing, the prestige of the service didn't permit it. For another their hands were busy holding their sub-machine guns, in order to be able to shoot. However, as soon as they got to the camp the convoy guards would order: "From such and such a row to such and such a row, throw your firewood down over here." But they took with Godlike mercy — after all they had to leave some for the camp guards and for the zeks themselves. Otherwise the zeks wouldn't carry any at all.

And that's the way it worked out: every zek carried wood every day. Didn't know which day he'd get it there or which day they'd grab it from him.

Shukhov looked around to see if he couldn't find some chips underfoot. Meanwhile the foreman had counted the lot of them and reported to the chief of the guard.

"One hundred fourth — all present and accounted for."

And Tsezar had come up to his own brigade from the group of office workers. He puffed away so that a red glow came from his pipe, while his black moustaches were covered with frost.

"Well, how are things, captain?" he asked.

A warm man can't understand a frozen man. Empty question — how are things?

"Well, how?" the captain shrugged his shoulders. "I worked so hard I can hardly straighten my back."

You might at least understand enough to give him a smoke.

Tsezar did give him a smoke. It was only with the captain that he maintained a relationship. There wasn't anyone else with whom he could talk.

"One man missing in the 32nd! In the 32nd!" Everyone was buzzing.

The assistant foreman of the 32nd and another chap ran back to the auto repair shop to look for the missing man. And the crowd kept asking: Who? What? They wanted to know. The story got to Shukhov. The missing man was a swarthy little Moldavian. Which Moldavian was that. Not the one who, they said, was a Romanian spy — a real spy?

There were five spies to every brigade but they were made-to-order, artificial spies: their cases had been processed as if they were the real thing, but they were only former P.O.W.s. Shukhov himself was that kind of spy.

But that Moldavian — he was a real spy.

The chief of guard looked at the list and got black in the face. If a spy escaped, what would happen to the chief of convoy guard?

And the crowd, including Shukhov, grew furious. What kind of piece of stinking shit, goddam bastard was that spy? Here it was, getting dark. The only light came from the moon. The stars were out, the cold was working up to its night-time strength. And that wet-behind-the-ears runt was missing. Didn't you have enough work, swine? Is the government's day too short for you, from dawn to dusk, eleven hours? Never mind, the prosecutor will add some.

It seemed queer to Shukhov that someone could work without noticing the stop-work whistle. Shukhov forgot that he had just been working that way himself — and that he had been sorry when he had to start out for the watch house so soon. But now he was frozen like everyone else. Probably there would be a half-hour delay because of that Moldavian. If the convoy could have turned him over to the mob the zeks would have torn him apart the way a wolf tears a calf.

Now the cold really began to gather strength. No one was able to stand still. They either stamped up and down or else moved two steps forward and two steps back.

Could the Moldavian have escaped? The men argued about that. Well, if he got out during the daytime that was one thing. But if he was hidden now and was waiting for the guards to come out of the towers he'd never be able to wait long enough for that. If there was no trail under the barbed wire to show that he had crawled through, then the guards would have to stay in the towers, watching, for as long as it took to find him, if it took three days, four days, even a week. That was the rule, and the old convicts knew it. In general if someone escaped life became hell for the convoy guards, and they were worked day and night without food or sleep. Sometimes the guards were driven so hard they became insane with rage. Then they wouldn't bring the escapee back alive.

Tsezar was trying to persuade the captain:

"For example, that pince-nez hanging on the ship's rigging, do you remember that?"[8]

"Mmmm . . . yes." The captain was smoking his tobacco.

"Or that baby carriage rolling down the long stairway, rolling and rolling down."

"Yes . . . but shipboard life in that film was somehow artificial, doll-like."

"We have been spoiled by contemporary techniques of movie photography."

"And the worms in the meat were just like the kind that come out of the ground after a rain. Could it really be the same kind?"

"But you couldn't show any any smaller than that for motion pictures!"

"Well, I think if that meat were brought to us in camp right now instead of the fish we get, and if it were dumped in the pot without being washed or scraped, we would be. . . ."

"Aaaaaaaaah!" roared the zeks. "Ooooooo!"

They had seen three men hurry out of the auto repair shop. That meant they had found the Moldavian.

"Booooooo!" The crowd bellowed from the gates. And then as the three ran up: "Bastard! Stinking son of a bitch! Shithead!" Even Shukhov shouted:

"Rat!"

After all, it was a serious matter to take more than half an hour of their time from five hundred men.

With his lowered head, the Moldavian ran like a little mouse.

8 [The discussion is of Sergei Eisenstein's film *Potemkin* (1925). — Editors' note.]

"Stop!" the guard yelled. He wrote as he talked: "K-460 — where were you?" He strode over to the Moldavian and turned the butt of his rifle toward him.

Some in the crowd shouted:

"Swine! Puke! Bastard!"

But the rest fell silent when the sergeant raised his rifle butt.

The Moldavian said nothing. His head bent, he drew back from the guard. The assistant foreman of the 32nd stepped forward:

"This scum climbed up on the scaffolding for plaster work, hid, got warm up there and fell asleep."

And he suddenly cracked him in the face with a fist, then slammed him in the center of his back. And in this way he pushed the Moldavian away from the guard. The Moldavian staggered. Then a Hungarian from the same 32nd kicked him in the rear, and kicked him in the rear again.

This isn't spying for you. Even a fool can be a spy. A spy has a clean, jolly life. But just try to survive ten years in a hard-labor camp.

The guard dropped his rifle.

The chief of guard shouted, "Get back from the gates! Count off by fives!"

The dogs are taking the count again. Why count now when it's all clear? The zeks growled. All their hate for the Moldavian shifted to the convoy guard. They hooted and wouldn't move back from the gate.

"What?" the chief of guard began to roar. "Do you want me to sit you down in the snow? Is that it? I'll do it too! I'll hold you here till morning!"

He would too — wouldn't think twice about it either. He'd do it. Many times the guards sat them down, even made them lie down. "Lie down! Weapons ready to fire!" The zeks knew those things had happened. So they began to move away from the gates.

"Get back! Get back!" the convoy guard pushed at them.

"Well, why are you pushing at the gates, idiots?" The zeks in the rear grew angry at those ahead. They moved back under pressure.

"Count off by fives! One! Two! Three!"

Now the moon was in full glory, it had grown bright and the crimson tinge had disappeared. It had risen a quarter of its way up the sky. The whole evening was lost. That damned Moldavian! That damned convoy guard. This damned life!

The men up front who had been counted turned around and stood on tiptoe to see if the last row had two or three men. Their lives depended on it right now.

For a moment Shukhov imagined he saw four in the last row, and he was numb with fear. An extra man! Another count. But it turned out that Fetyukov, the jackal, had been begging the butt from the captain and hadn't switched back to his own group on time, had been left at the end like an extra.

The assistant to the chief of convoy guard angrily whacked Fetyukov on the neck.

That's right.

There were three in the last line. It tallied, thank the Lord!

"Back from the gates!" Again the convoy pushed them.

But this time the zeks did not growl. They saw soldiers emerging from the watch house and forming a cordon on the other side of the gates.

That meant they would be let out.

The junior construction supervisors were not in sight, nor was the construction supervisor. The zeks still had their firewood. The gates were opened. On the other side, behind timber barriers, waited the chief of convoy guard and the count checker.

"One! Two! Three!"

If the count jibed once more they would call down the watch tower guards.

And it was such a long hike from the distant watch towers along the zone edge. Only when the last zek had been led out of the zone and the count tallied did they telephone the towers: "Come down." If the chief of guard was intelligent he'd move toward camp immediately knowing that there was nowhere for the zeks to escape and that the tower guards would catch up with the columns quickly. But sometimes the chief of guard was a fool, and feared his armed guards were not enough to deal with the zeks. Then the zeks would have to wait.

They had one of those blockheads this evening as chief of guard. He waited.

The zeks had been freezing for a whole day out in the cold. Pure death. And since the end of work they'd been standing outside freezing another hour. But right now the anger hurt even more than the cold. The whole evening gone. No chance to do anything in camp.

"And how is it that you know so much about the English navy?" someone in the next five asked.

"Well, you see, I lived almost a month on an English cruiser, had my own cabin there. I travelled in a naval convoy. I was liaison officer. And then, after the war, can you imagine, the English admiral, the devil take him, sent me a gift inscribed, 'A token of gratitude.' That did it! So here I am, lumped together with everyone else. Not much satisfaction to sit here with Ukrainian Benderov partisans."

Queer. Queer to look around and see naked steppe, empty zone, snow gleaming beneath the moon. The convoy already in formation, ten steps apart, guns at the ready. A black herd of zeks. And in the midst of all this, in the identical kind of coat was a man to whom life without gold shoulder boards would once have seemed unthinkable, a man who had rubbed elbows with an English admiral, who was now hauling hand barrows with Fetyukov. S-311.

Things can happen one way — or another. . . .

Well, the convoy guard was assuming formation. Take off, without the "prayer." "Forward march! Faster!"

Oh, no, the hell with you. Why faster? We're behind all the other projects, so why hurry now. The zeks, without talking it over, had come to the same conclusion: you kept us there — now we're going to keep you. Probably you want to get warm, too.

"Longer steps!" shouted the chief of guard. "Longer steps, leader!"

The hell with you, "longer steps!" The zeks went along evenly, dragging their heels as if trudging to a funeral. Nothing more for us to lose. We're going to be last into camp anyway. You didn't want to deal with us like humans so now you can shout till you burst.

The chief of guard shouted and shouted: "Longer steps!" Finally he understood the zeks wouldn't move faster. He couldn't shoot, either. They were marching in fives, in a column, in proper order. He didn't have the power to drive the zeks faster. In the morning on the way to work it's their dragging heels that saves the zeks. Whoever runs fast won't finish his term in camp. He'll drop from exhaustion.

So they marched along evenly and neatly. Their boots creaked on the snow. Some talked quietly, some didn't. Shukhov tried to recall what it was he hadn't finished in camp that morning. He remembered — the infirmary! Well, it was practically miraculous, but at work he had completely forgotten about the infirmary.

Right now it was receiving time in the infirmary. He could still get there if he didn't eat. But his aches were gone. And likely they wouldn't even take his temperature, wouldn't take the time for that. He'd gotten over his sickness without the doctors. Those doctors cured their patients right into wooden overcoats.

It wasn't the infirmary that attracted him now, but figuring how he could add a little something to his dinner. His hopes were pinned on Tsezar's receiving a parcel. It was a long time since one had arrived.

Suddenly there was a change in the zeks' column. A flutter. The even step was broken. The column jerked. It buzzed and buzzed. And now the tail-end fives, among them Shukhov, were no longer right on the heels of those ahead but had to run after them. They walked several steps and then ran.

As the tail end of the column came to the crest of the hill, Shukhov saw at their right, far out on the steppe, another column looming black. It was moving diagonally toward his column and it was also hurrying.

That column could only be the zeks from the machine factory. There were three hundred men in it. Evidently they'd had bad luck, too, and had been held up. What for? It happened that now and then they were kept at their work because they hadn't finished repairing some piece of machinery or other. Of course it didn't make much difference to them, since they were inside all day where it was warm.

Now it was a question of who would beat out whom. The zeks were running, really running. And the convoy guards took up the trot.

But the chief of guards shouted, "Don't stretch out! Rear, close ranks! Close ranks!"

We'll rap you in the head, what are you hollering about? Can't you see we're keeping up?

And the men who had been talking or thinking forgot about it. There was just one thought in the whole column, "Beat them out, head them off!"

And now everything was so mixed up, that the convoy guards no longer seemed to be enemies of the zeks, but friends. The enemy was that other column.

The men got cheerful. The anger was gone.

"Get a move on, get a move on!" the ones in the rear called out to those ahead.

The column rushed onto the road while the machine factory men were hidden behind an apartment block. The race was on in the dark. Hurrying was easier for the column in the middle of the road. And things were smoother for the convoy guards on the sides, too.

Shukhov's column had to head them off right there because the machine factory men were submitted to a particularly long body search. Since the first incident of knifing in the camp, the officers suspected that the knives were made at the machine factory and moved from there to camp. Therefore at the camp entrance the machine factory men were searched especially carefully.

In late fall, when the earth was already frozen, the guards shouted at them, "Take off your boots, machine factory. Take your boots in your hands."

And then they searched them barefoot.

And even now, despite the cold, they'd poke a man at random. "Come on there, get off your right felt boot. And you there, take off your left boot."

The zek would take off his felt boot and hop about on one foot, empty out the boot and shake out his foot cloths to show there was no knife there.

Shukhov had heard — he didn't know whether it was true or not — that the machine factory men had brought two volleyball posts into camp in summer and had hidden knives in those posts. Ten long ones in each post. Even now, once in a long while they'd find one of the knives in the camp here, there, another place.

At a half-run they passed the new clubhouse and the block of apartment houses, then the wood-carving factory, and poured out onto the road that crossed to the camp watch house.

"Ho! Ho!" the column roared with one voice.

It was this road crossing on which they were so intent. And now the machine factory men were one hundred fifty yards off to the right — in the rear.

Now all the rows in the column could move along quietly. Like the rabbit in the old story who was glad that at least the frogs were afraid of him, now they too had someone to look down on.

The camp loomed up before them. It was just as light now as it had been when they left in the morning. Night lamps shone in the zone over the solid board fence, and were placed close together in front of the watch house. The entire area for body inspection was so brightly lit it was as though the sun were out.

Then, before they got to the watch house, "Stop!" shouted the assistant chief guard. He handed his sub-machine gun to a soldier, and ran right up to the column. He wasn't permitted to come close to them with his sub-machine gun. "All those standing at the right who have firewood — throw the firewood down to the right."

On the outside row they were carrying the bundles openly — he could see all of them. One . . . two . . . and a third bundle flew. Some tried to hide theirs inside the column but their neighbors objected:

"Because of you they'll take it away from the rest of us! Do what you're told!"

A convict's worst enemy is another convict. If the convicts weren't always at each other's throats, life would be something very different.

"Forward march!" shouted the assistant chief guard.

And they moved on to the watch house.

At the watch house five roads came together. An hour earlier, the groups from the different projects had been milling about. If these roads were made into streets someday then instead of this watch house and yard for body inspection there would be a main square. And in the same way that the columns marching from all the projects converged here now, perhaps holiday demonstration parades would merge here in that future city.

The search guards had already managed to warm themselves at the watch house. They came out and waited across the road.

"Unbutton coats! Unfasten underjackets!"

They extended their arms. During body inspection they'd embrace you. Slap you on the sides. In general, it was just like the morning.

It wasn't so terrifying to unfasten clothes now — the zeks were close to home.

That's the way they all talked — "home." No time to think about any other home during the day.

They had already inspected the head of the column when Shukhov went up to Tsezar and said:

"Tsezar Markovich! From here I'll run to the parcel room and hold a place in line for you."

Tsezar turned to Shukhov, the tips of his sculptured black moustaches now white:

"Why should you take a place in line, Ivan Denisych? Maybe there won't be a parcel."

"Well, if there's none — what have I lost? I'll wait ten minutes and if you don't come, I'll be off to the barracks."

Shukhov figured that even if Tsezar didn't show up, perhaps he could sell his turn in the line to someone else.

It seemed Tsezar was longing for a package.

"Well, all right, Ivan Denisych, run along and hold a spot. Wait ten minutes, no more."

The body inspection was moving closer. Today Shukhov had nothing to hide, and he could move up toward it fearlessly. He unbuttoned his coat, without hurrying, and unfastened the underjacket beneath his canvas sash.

Even though he didn't remember having anything on himself which was forbidden, nevertheless the wariness of eight years of sitting had become a habit. He shoved his hand into his pants knee pocket to prove it was empty — as he knew it was.

But he found the little steel blade, that piece of blade strip! The steel blade he had so thriftily picked up today in the working zone, which he hadn't intended to take into camp at all.

He hadn't intended to take it in, but now when he had it there he just didn't want to throw it away! After all it might be sharpened into a little knife, good enough for shoemaker's work, maybe for tailoring.

If he had planned to take it through body inspection with him, he would have figured out how to hide it well. But now there were only two rows in front of him, and the first had already separated and gone forward to inspection.

He had to decide quicker than the wind. There was a choice. Screened by the five men in front of him, he could throw it down on the snow where it would be found later, but no one would know whose it was. Or, he could try to take it in with him.

They could give him ten days of solitary for that little steel blade if they considered it a knife.

But a shoemaker's knife was earnings, it was bread.

He didn't want to throw it down.

So Shukhov shoved it into his cotton mitten.

Right then the order was issued for the next five to step up for body inspection.

Now, in the glare, just the three of them were left: Senka, Shukhov, and the lad from the 32nd who had run to find the Moldavian.

Because there were three of them and five guards stood facing them, it was possible to play it cleverly — to choose which one of the guards to approach. Shukhov chose not the young, ruddy-faced one, but the old one with the gray moustache. The old one was, of course, experienced and could easily have found it if he had wanted to, but just because he was old it was a sure thing that he was more sick and tired of the service than of hell.

By that time Shukhov had removed both mittens, the one with the blade and the empty one, and was holding them in one hand. The empty mitten was shoved forward. In that same hand he held the rope belt, unfastened his underjacket completely, obsequiously held up the flaps of both his coat and underjacket. Never had he been so obsequious at the inspection but now he wanted to show that he was all open, as if to say, 'go ahead, take me!' And at the order he went up to gray-moustaches.

Gray-moustaches clapped Shukhov on sides and back, slapped him on the knee pocket. Nothing there. He pressed the flaps of the underjacket and coat in his hands. Nothing. And, letting him through, for insurance he grasped the mitten Shukhov had shoved forward — the empty one.

The guard pressed the mitten and pincers clamped on Shukhov's insides. One more grasp; on the second mitten, and he would have had it. In solitary on ten ounces a day and warm food every third day. Immediately he imagined how he would weaken there, how he would hunger and how difficult it would be for him to return to that wiry, neither famished nor well-fed state in which he lived now.

At that moment he prayed with real fervor, "God! Save me! Don't give me solitary!"

All those thoughts raced through his mind in the instant that the guard touched the first mitten and moved his hand to grab the second one. He would have pressed them both at once if Shukhov had held them out separately, not together. But right then a voice rang out. The senior noncom who was in command at body search shouted at the convoy:

"Bring up the machine factory men!"

And gray-moustaches, instead of going on to Shukhov's second mitten, waved his hand as if to say: 'Get on with you.' He let him go.

Shukhov ran to catch up with his fellows. They were already lined up by fives between the two long log barriers which were like horse stalls at a market, and formed a kind of pen for the column. He ran quickly, not feeling the ground. He didn't pray to give thanks because there wasn't any time.

The convoy guards who had led their column went to the side now, clearing the road for the guards from the machine factory. They were waiting for the chief. The convoy guards had picked up for themselves the firewood thrown down before inspection. The firewood taken away at inspection time by the camp guards was collected in a pile at the watch house.

The moon rolled up higher. In the white, bright night the cold intensified.

The chief of convoy, going into the watch house to get back his receipt for 463 heads, spoke with Priakha, assistant to Volkovoi, and the latter shouted, "K-460!"

The Moldavian who had buried himself in the depths of the column, sighed and went up to the right barrier. He held his head down and drawn into his shoulders in the same way.

"Come here!" Priakha pointed him around the barrier.

The Moldavian went around. He was ordered to hold his hands behind his back and stand there.

That meant they were going to slap on charges of attempting to escape. Into solitary he would go.

At the gates, right and left, beyond the pen, stood two guards. The gates, three times a man's height, opened slowly and the order was heard:

"Count off by fives!" No necessity to shout "Away from the gates!" at this point, since all the gates opened into the zone. Even if the zeks mobbed them from inside they couldn't break these gates open. "One! Two! Three!"

At that evening count, returning through the camp gates, the zek was exposed to the wind, frozen, hungrier than at any other time during the day. The evening meal, a ladle of scalding hot thin cabbage soup was as welcome as rain on thirsty dry ground. He'd drain the bowl with one gulp. That ladleful was at that moment dearer than freedom, dearer than all his former life and all his life to come.

The zeks poured through the camp gates like soldiers returning from a campaign — loud, tough, rough. Clear the way! That rushing wave of zeks looked frightening to a man with a soft job in headquarters barracks.

After that last count, the zek was a free man for the first time since morning when they rang the six-thirty gong for lineup. He had gone through the big gates of the zone, the smaller gates of the pre-zone sector, and crossed the lineup ground. Now scatter where you please!

Scatter where you please, but the work assignment clerk caught the foremen:

"Foremen! Go to the planning production section!"

Shukhov ran past the camp punishment prison, between the barracks, to the parcel room. And Tsezar went at a dignified, leisurely pace in the other direction, to where a crowd was swarming. A plywood board was nailed to a post and on it were written in indelible pencil the names of all those who had received parcels today.

In camp they rarely wrote on paper, more often on plywood. Everything seemed firmer, more reliable, on a board. The assignment clerks and the guards kept count on boards. The next day they would scrape the boards clean — and write on them again. Economy.

Whoever stayed in camp during the day could scavenge a bit. They could see on the board who'd received a package, meet him at lineup ground as he came in and give him the parcel number right then. They couldn't get much for that, but it was worth at least a cigarette.

Shukhov ran to the parcel room, a shed with a big vestibule built onto a barracks. The vestibule had no outside door to close, so the cold entered freely. But it was better than waiting in the open. After all there was a roof overhead.

Inside the vestibule the line stretched along the wall. Shukhov took a place. There were fifteen ahead of him. This meant more than an hour of waiting, right up to curfew. Nevertheless the men from the power station column who went to look at the list first would all be behind Shukhov, as well as all the machine factory men. Likely many would have to come for their parcels a second time, tomorrow morning.

They all stood in line holding bags or sacks. There, behind that door (Shukhov himself had never received a parcel in this camp, but he knew about it from the talk) they opened the packages with a small axe and the guard took everything out and inspected it. Some things he cut open, others he broke open or spilled out. If there was a liquid, the guards would not hand it over in a glass or metal container. They would unbottle it and pour it out for you, hold your hands out for it if that was the best you could do, or wipe it up with a towel or cloth. They would not give out cans. If there was something like a pie, some interesting candy, or sausage, or fish, the guard would eat some. And just try to object. Right away he'd insist that it was a forbidden item. And he wouldn't give it out. Any man who received a package had to give, beginning with that guard, then give some more and keep giving. And when they finished inspecting the package, they wouldn't give the zeks the box the parcel had arrived in. Just pile everything loose into your sack, or even in a fold of your coat. And move along. Next! They were hurried through so fast that now and then a zek would forget something on the counter. Don't go back for it. It isn't there.

Back in Ust-Izhma, Shukhov had received a pair of parcels from home. But after that he wrote to his wife that it was no use. "Don't send them," he told her, "don't take things from the children."

Even though Shukhov had found it easier to feed his whole family when he was free than it was just to feed himself in this camp, he knew exactly how much those packages cost. You couldn't squeeze them out of the family for ten years. Better to go without.

But even though he had decided that, still, whenever someone nearby in the barracks or in the brigade received a parcel — just about every day — he felt unhappy that there was none for him. And though he had strictly forbidden his wife to send him anything, even for Easter, and he never went to the post with the list except on behalf of some rich fellow brigade member, he often longed for someone to run up to him and say:

"Shukhov, what are you waiting for? There's a parcel for you."

But no one ever ran up.

And there was ever less and less reason to remember Temgenyvo and his hut. The life here wore him out from waking to sleep, leaving no time for empty recollections.

Now, standing among those who were comfortably anticipating the first bite of bacon, or spreading butter on their bread, or sweetening their mug with sugar, Shukhov kept himself together with one idea and one only, to get to the mess hall with his brigade and eat thin soup that was hot and not cold. Cold soup wasn't half as good as hot soup.

He calculated that if Tsezar's name was not on the list he had long since gone back to barracks to wash. And if the name was there, then he was right now gathering bags, plastic mugs, and other permitted containers. That was why Shukhov had promised to wait ten minutes.

Standing in line, Shukhov heard some news. The zeks would work this Sunday. Again the camp was taking away their Sunday. He had expected that. The others had expected it too. If there were five Sundays in the month then they let the zeks have three, the other two they drove the zeks out to work. But even though he had expected it, when he heard the news his whole soul ached. Who wouldn't grieve for the loss of that dear day? What they were saying in the line was true, of course; the camp bosses could ruin a rest day even when the zeks were allowed to stay inside the camp. They could invent work. Build a bath house. Or build a wall to close a passageway. Or clean up the yard. Or else change your mattresses, shake them out, and catch bedbugs on the bunks. Or there might be verification of identity by identity cards. Or inventory. That meant take all your things outside and sit in the yard half a day.

The bosses couldn't bear it if a zek went to sleep after breakfast.

The line moved along slowly. Several came in and got into line out of turn, silently pushing aside the person in front, one barber, one bookkeeper and one man from the cultural educational section. These people were not just ordinary gray zeks but firmly ensconced camp trusties who had jobs inside the camp. Complete rats. The working stiffs thought them worse than shit. And they looked at the working stiffs in exactly the same way. But it was useless to quarrel with them. The trusties had a gang all their own and were in with the guards, too.

Ahead of Shukhov there were ten men now, behind him seven. At that point Tsezar entered the doorway, ducking down, in his new fur cap sent from freedom. Look at that cap. Tsezar had bribed someone and he was permitted to wear that clean, new, city cap. Most of the others had had even their worn old army caps snatched away, and they'd been handed camp pigskins instead.

Tsezar smiled at Shukhov and greeted a strange fellow in glasses who was reading a newspaper in line, "Ah! Petr Mikhalych."

And they blossomed out at each other like poppies. The stranger said, "I have a new *Evening Moscow* here. Look at it! I got it by mail."

"Well, well." Tsezar stuck his nose in that paper. And beneath the ceiling the lamp was dim. How could they read the small print here?

"Here's a most interesting review of Zavadsky's[9] premiere!"

The Muscovites smell each other out from a long ways away, like dogs. And when they get together they sniff around and sniff around at each other in their own peculiar way. And they mutter quick-quick to see who can say the most words. And when they mutter that way it's rarely that real Russian words are heard. Listening to them talk is like listening to a Latvian or Romanian.

However, Tsezar was holding the sacks he had collected.

"So I . . . Tsezar Markovich. . . ." Shukhov lisped. "Maybe, I can go now?"

"Of course, of course," Tsezar raised his black moustaches from his newspaper. "Who's ahead of me? And who is behind me?"

Shukhov explained who came after whom, and without waiting for Tsezar to remember about dinner he asked:

"Shall I bring you your dinner?"

That meant carrying it from the mess hall to the barracks in a mess tin. It was not permitted to take meals out of the mess hall, and there were many rules on the subject. If they caught you they would pour the food on the ground and put you in solitary. But just the same the zeks took meals out and would continue to take them out because when a man had business to do he could not manage to get into mess hall with his own brigade.

Shukhov asked whether to bring dinner but thought to himself, 'Well, can you possibly be stingy and not give me your dinner? After all there's no kasha at dinner, just bare thin soup.'

"No, no," Tsezar smiled. "You eat my dinner yourself, Ivan Denisych!"

Shukhov was waiting for just that. Now he was like a bird uncaged. He

9 [A Soviet theatrical producer. — Editors' note.]

rushed out from under the vestibule roof and on through the camp, right through the camp.

The zeks were coming from all directions. At one time the chief of the camp had issued an order that no prisoners were to go about camp alone. Whenever possible the whole brigade must go in formation. And wherever the whole brigade could not go at the same time, say to the infirmary or the latrine, groups of four and five persons should be formed with a man in charge to accompany the group to its destination and then take them back, still in formation.

The chief of camp put much stock in this order. No one dared contradict him. The guards caught men alone and wrote down their numbers and put them in solitary. Yet the order broke down. Quietly, the way many noisy orders break down. Let's say if they called a man by himself to the security section, you wouldn't be likely to send a whole squad with him. Or if you had to go for your food in the parcel check room, why should I go there with you? And if one man wanted to go to the cultural educational section to read newspapers, who was going to go along with him? Or if someone else took his felt boots to be repaired, or someone went to the drying room, or someone simply headed from one barracks to another — though going from barracks to barracks was the most strictly forbidden of all. Still, how could you stop them?

With that order the chief of camp — old potbelly — wanted to take their last bit of freedom. But it didn't work.

On the way to the barracks Shukhov met a guard and raised his cap, just in case. He ran on into the barracks. A row was going on. Someone's bread ration had been stolen during the day. Zeks were screaming at the orderlies, and the orderlies were screaming, too. The 104th's corner was empty.

Shukhov had come to think it a lucky evening when he returned to camp and did not find mattresses overturned or the barracks searched.

He dashed to his cot, pulling his coat off on the run. Shoved the coat on top, felt the mattress, his morning piece of bread was still there. He was glad he had sewn it in.

And on the run, outside. To the mess hall.

He dodged to the mess hall without running into a guard. Met only zeks, arguing about rations.

Moonlight lit everything in the courtyard. The lamps were pale, and the barracks cast black shadows. The mess hall was entered through a broad porch with four steps. That porch was in shadow right now, though a hanging lamp bobbed over it, whining in the cold. The lamp bulbs shed rainbows, perhaps from cold, perhaps from dirt.

There used to be another strict order from the camp chief. Brigades were to enter the mess hall in formation, by twos. The order went on: on arriving at the mess hall the brigades were not to go up on the porch but to line up in fives and wait till the mess hall orderly let them in.

The post of mess hall orderly was firmly held in the grip of Khromoi, the "cripple." He had managed to elevate his limp into a formal status as an invalid. He was a big mean son-of-a-bitch. Got himself a birch cane and from the porch he'd lam anyone who tried to get up there against his orders. But not quite everyone. The quick-eyed Khromoi could recognize every man; even in the dark, even by his back. He never hit anyone who was able to give him a crack in the teeth. He beat those who were already beaten. He had nailed Shukhov once.

He was called "orderly." But if you figured it out he was really a prince! A friend of the cook.

Today either all the brigades had piled up at once, or else it had taken a long time to get things organized, but the porch was densely crowded. Khromoi was up there with his helper and the head of mess hall. The fat dogs were running the show without the help of a guard.

The head of mess hall was a well-fed bastard! Head like a pumpkin, shoulders a yard wide. He had so much excess power that when he walked he seemed to be bouncing, as if his legs and arms were made of springs. Wore a white fur cap without a number. No one else — not even any of the free civilians — had a cap like that. And he wore a fur lambskin vest. There was a number on the vest — but only about the size of a postage stamp. That was a concession to Volkovoi. But on his back, no number. The head of mess hall bowed to no one and all the zeks were afraid of him. He held thousands of lives in his hand. Once they started to beat him up, but all the cooks jumped out to his defense, and a real collection of plug-uglies they were too.

It would be bad if the 104th had gone in already. Khromoi knew everyone in the camp, and with the head of mess hall present he would never permit anyone to enter out of turn. He'd be mean just for the fun of it.

Sometimes it was possible to climb the porch railings behind Khromoi's back. Shukhov had done it himself. But not today with the mess hall head standing there. He'd fix you so you'd be carted off to the hospital.

Quick, quick, up on the porch for a look at the black coats, all alike, for those of the 104th.

Right at that minute the brigades moved confusedly ahead, kept moving ahead. Curfew coming soon. As if storming a fortress, they rushed the first, second, third, fourth step and piled onto the porch.

"Stop it, you whores." Khromoi shouted and lifted his cane against those in front. "Get back! I'll smash your heads!"

"Not our fault!" the ones in front shouted at him. "They're pushing from behind."

True enough, they were being pushed from behind. But the men in front were not resisting very energetically, hoping to fly right on into the mess hall.

Then Khromoi held his cane across his chest like a closed railway gate, and with all his weight fell right on those in front. And Khromoi's helper grabbed one end of the long cane. The mess hall head wasn't squeamish about using his hands, either.

They moved fast and they were strong — they ate meat. The zeks fell back. The ones up front fell back on the men behind them, mowed them down like sheaves. "Fuck you, Khromoi . . . in your face, Khromoi!" Voices, well hidden in the crowd, yelled at him. Others fell in silence and silently got up fast before they were trampled.

The steps were cleared. The mess hall head left, and Khromoi stood on the top step.

"Form up by fives, you dumbheads, how many times do I have to tell you? When it's necessary, I'll let you in."

Shukhov spotted someone who looked like Senka Klevshin, was delighted, tried to elbow his way closer. He pushed past a few people but no, not enough strength. You couldn't get through there.

Khromoi shouted: "Twenty-seven! Come on up!"

The 27th jumped up the steps and to the doors. The rest of the crowd started pushing up the steps again. Shukhov pushed with might and main. The porch was shaking. The porch lamp was whining again.

"Again, you shits?" Khromoi became enraged. Whack went his cane on someone's head, on someone's backside. He pushed against the crowd and knocked some down. He cleared the steps again.

Shukhov could see that Pavlo had risen to Khromoi's level. He was taking the brigade in. Tyurin wouldn't come to dirty himself in that mob scene.

"Count off by fives, 104th!" Pavlo shouted from above. "Let them through, friends."

Like hell those friends were going to let them through.

"Let me through. I'm from that brigade!" Shukhov trembled.

The men in front would have been glad to let him through but he was being crushed from every side.

The crowd heaved and suffocated to get its soup. Its rightful soup.

Then Shukhov tried another tack. He grabbed the railings at the left, gripped the porch post with his hands and — hung there. He was off the ground. His legs were kicking someone in the knees. Whoever it was gave it to him in the side, let fly a pair of oaths at him. But he managed to pull himself up. He stood with one foot on the porch cornice at the upper step and waited. His friends saw him, reached out for him.

The head of mess hall looked out of the door. "All right, Khromoi, two more brigades."

"One hundred and fourth!" Khromoi shouted. "And you, bastard, where do you think you're climbing to?" Whack with his stave across the neck of an interloper.

"One hundred and fourth!" Pavlo shouted, letting his own men move past him.

"Phhooo!" Shukhov broke through into the mess hall. And without waiting till Pavlo gave orders, he went to look for empty trays.

In the mess hall as always steam rolled in clouds from the doors. The zeks were sitting at tables, packed as close to each other as seeds in a sunflower. Between tables zeks were wandering, pushing about, some making their way through with full trays. But after so many years Shukhov was used to this. His eyes were sharp and he saw S-208 carrying five bowls on his tray, meaning that was the last tray in his brigade; otherwise there would have been more bowls.

Shukhov caught up with him and whispered in his ear:

"Brother. Let me have the tray after you."

"I promised it to a fellow over there at the window."

"To hell with him. Let him wait. He shouldn't dawdle."

They came to agreement.

That zek unloaded the tray at his table. Shukhov took the tray. The one to whom it had been promised hurried up and grabbed one end. But he was not as big as Shukhov. Shukhov poked him with the tray just as he pulled on it and the zek flew backward as his hands lost their grip. Shukhov tucked the tray under his arm and ran to the window.

Pavlo stood in line at the window, waiting for trays. Happily, "Ivan Denisovich!" And he pushed away the assistant foreman of the 27th.

"Let us through. Don't just stand there. I have a tray."

And look there. Gopchik, the rogue, with another tray.

"They were slow," he was laughing. "And I got it."

Gopchik was going to become a good camp dweller in another three years. He would grow up a bit and then he'd really make good — nothing lower than bread cutter at the very least.

Pavlo ordered the second tray taken by Yermolayev, a husky Siberian who had also received ten as a P.O.W. Pavlo sent Gopchik to look for a table where the men were almost finished. Shukhov leaned his tray on the serving window and waited.

"One hundred and fourth." Pavlo reported into the window.

There were five service windows in all — three for serving, one for those fed a special diet (ten were sick with ulcers, and, because they had influence, the entire bookkeeping office got the same diet), and one more for returning dishes.

At that window they fought for the right to lick plates. The windows were low, little more than waist high. Couldn't see the cooks; only their arms and ladles.

This cook had white arms, sleek, hairy, big. More like a boxer, not a cook. He took his pencil and on a list on the wall he noted:

"One hundred fourth — 24!"

Panteleyev had dragged himself along to the mess hall. Of course he wasn't sick, the hound.

The cook took a big ladle that held three quarts and mixed, mixed, mixed it in the tank. The pot in front of him was newly filled, nearly to the top, and steam was rising from it. And then, picking up a ladle less than a quart in size he began, hardly dipping it in, to fill bowls with it:

"One, two, three, four. . . ."

Shukhov noted what bowls were filled before the thick stuff had settled to the bottom, and which were the thinner portions — just liquid. He put ten bowls on his tray, and moved on. Gopchik waved at him from the second row of posts:

"Over here, Ivan Denisych, over here!"

You have to have a steady hand to carry bowls. Shukhov walked smoothly so the tray was steady and he talked as he walked:

"Hey, you, K-920. Look out there, uncle. Get out of the way, fellow."

It wasn't easy to carry even one bowl in this crowd without spilling it — let alone ten. Nevertheless, when he put the tray down carefully at the table end freed by Gopchik there were no fresh splashes on it. And he had even figured out how to put it down so that the two thickest bowls were at the corner of the tray where he would sit.

Yermolayev brought ten. Gopchik ran off and with Pavlo brought the last four by hand.

Kilgas brought bread on a tray. Today they got fed according to their work. Some seven ounces, some ten and Shukhov fourteen. He took his fourteen from the crust, and another seven as Tsezar's share from the center.

Right then the brigade members arrived from all parts of the hall to get their dinner. Just gulp it down wherever you find a place. Shukhov handed out the bowls, remembering who had already eaten, while keeping his eye on his own corner of the tray. He put his spoon into one of the bowls with thick soup. That meant it was taken. Fetyukov took his bowl early and went off. He calculated there'd be nothing to scavenge in his own brigade, so he'd better cover the whole hall. Maybe someone would leave a bit and he could scrounge it. If anyone pushed his bowl away unfinished, several men would grab for it, like vultures.

Shukhov and Pavlo counted the portions. It seemed there were enough. Shukhov put aside one of the bowls with thick soup for Tyurin. Pavlo poured it into a narrow little German mess kit with a top. It would be taken out under his coat, pressed to his chest.

They gave up the trays. Pavlo sat down with his double portion, Shukhov with his two. And no more conversation. The sacred minutes had come.

Shukhov took off his cap, put it on his knees. He examined one bowlful, stirring it with his spoon, and then the other. Not too bad. Even a few little fish. In general the soup was much thinner than in the mornings. Mornings the zeks had to be fed so they'd work, but evenings they'd go to sleep anyway.

He began to eat. First he drank the thin liquid. The warmth poured into him and flooded through his whole body. His innards were palpitating to greet that soup. Goooood. That's it, that fleeting moment for which a zek lives.

Then Shukhov began to eat the cabbage together with the bit of liquid remaining.

At that moment Shukhov was not angry about anything, not even that his term was long, not even that the day was long, not even that Sunday would be a work day. Instead, he was thinking, we'll live through it. We'll live through it all. And if God wills, it will end someday.

Having drunk down the liquid from both the first and second bowls, he poured remains of the second into the first, turned the bowl upside down, and cleaned it out with his spoon. That way it was more relaxed. He didn't have to think about the second bowl, or keep guarding it with his eyes or hand.

Now he could look around at his neighbors' bowls. On his left his neighbor had nothing but water. That's what they do, the vipers, to their own zeks!

Shukhov began to eat the cabbage and the rest of the soup. He'd found one potato in Tsezar's bowl. A middle-sized potato, frozen, of course, but with some firmness and on the sweet side. Hardly any fish, now and then a fleshless bit of bone. But he had to chew every bit of fish bone and fin, and suck the marrow from them because the marrow was beneficial. To do all this, of course, he needed time. But Shukhov was not in a hurry now. Today was a holiday. At lunch he had managed to snag two portions and now two at dinner. Because of this he could afford to forget about his other affairs.

Except, of course, he must go to the Latvian for tobacco. Maybe there wouldn't be any left by morning.

Shukhov dined without bread. Two portions plus bread would be too much. The bread would hold for the next day. One's stomach was a scoundrel, didn't remember old good turns and would make demands again tomorrow.

Shukhov finished his soup and didn't try very hard to notice who was near him because it wasn't necessary. He wasn't on the lookout for anything extra and was eating what was rightfully his. Yet he did notice that right across the table from him a tall old man — Y-81 — sat down when a spot was freed. He was, as Shukhov knew, from the 64th brigade. In line at the parcel room Shukhov had heard that the 64th had gone to the Socialist Life Town instead of the 104th and had been stretching barbed wire a whole day without getting warm, building a new zone for itself.

Shukhov had heard that this old man had been sitting in camps and prisons for years without end, that not one amnesty had touched him. Whenever one ten-year term came to an end they gave him another right away.

Shukhov looked at him closely. Among all the stooped backs in camp, the old man's was notable for its straightness. At the table he sat so tall it seemed he was sitting on something. He hadn't needed a barber in years: his hair had all fallen out from the good life. The old man's eyes did not examine the goings-on in the mess hall, but were fixed on something private, focussed absently over Shukhov's head. He ate his thin soup slowly with a worn-down wooden spoon. He did not bend to the bowl like the others but carried his spoon high up to his mouth. He hadn't a tooth in his head. His bony gums chewed the bread instead of teeth. His face was worn down, not to the weakness of a helpless invalid, but to dark hewn rock. And by his hands, large, wrinkled, work-stained, it was clear that for all his years of sitting he hadn't had much time at soft jobs. There was something in him that refused to compromise. He didn't put his ten ounces of bread on the dirty splotched table as the others did. He put it on a clean-washed piece of cloth.

However, Shukhov didn't have more time to study him. He finished eating, licked off his spoon and shoved it down into his felt boot, pulled his cap down over his forehead, got up, took his bread ration — his own and Tsezar's — and went out. The exit from the mess hall was through another porch. Out there stood two orderlies whose only job was to take off the door hook, let people out, then hang the hook in place.

Shukhov went out with a full stomach, satisfied with himself, and decided that he would run over to see the Latvian though it would be curfew soon. Without taking his bread back to the ninth he marched toward the seventh barracks.

The moon was high, as if sculptured in the heavens, clean, white. The sky was clear. And brilliant stars dotted the darkness. But Shukhov didn't have time to study the heavens. He understood just one thing — the cold was not lessening. Some of the free civilians had heard, and repeated, that by night it would be less than 20° below and toward morning down to 40° below.

A long way off he could hear a tractor humming in the settlement, in the direction of the highway an excavator shrilling. And a crunch and a creak from every pair of valenki walking or running.

But there was no wind.

The homegrown tobacco Shukhov was going to get would cost him one ruble for each small glassful. Outside of camp the same glassful would cost three rubles and maybe more, depending on grade. In a hard-labor camp all the prices were special, not like anywhere else, because there was not supposed to be any money there. Few had any, and it was hard to come by. Zeks were not paid one kopeck in this camp. In Ust-Izhma Shukhov had received thirty rubles or more a month. If relatives sent any here by mail, the officials didn't hand it over but credited it to an account. The money from such an account could be used to buy toilet soap once a month, moldy cake, *Prima* brand cigarettes. You had to order the merchandise from the chief at their prices, and whether you liked it or not, you kept it. If you didn't buy, the money was gone anyway, withdrawn from the account.

Shukhov got money only by doing private work. Slippers made from material given him by the purchaser — two rubles. Patching an underjacket — by agreement.

The seventh barracks was not like the ninth, which had two large halves. In the seventh there was a long corridor, ten doors in it, and a brigade crowded into seven bunks in each room. Yes, and a cabin for the latrine barrel, also a separate room for the barracks' senior orderly. The artists had their own rooms too.

Shukhov went into the room where his Latvian lived. The Latvian was lying on a lower bunk, feet up on the edge, and he was joking with his neighbor in Latvian.

Shukhov sat down beside him. "Hello, so to speak."

"Hello," the Latvian answered and kept his leg up. A small room and everyone would hear everything right away. They both understood that. Therefore, Shukhov sat and waited.

"Well, so to speak, how's everything?"

"All right."

"Cold today?"

"Yes."

Shukhov waited till the men all around had begun to talk again about their own affairs. They were arguing about the war in Korea, whether, because the Chinese had gone into it, there would be a world war or not. Shukhov bent over the Latvian.

"You have some tobacco?"

"I have."

"Show it to me."

The Latvian took his feet off the edge, put them out in the passageway, got up. That Latvian was a skinflint. When he poured out a glassful he was always afraid he'd give one smoke more than he had to.

He showed Shukhov the pouch and opened it.

Shukhov took a pinch of it on his palm, saw that it was the same as the last time, brown and pungent. He lifted it to his nose: smelled. Yes, it was. He said to the Latvian:

"It doesn't seem to be the same."

"The same. The same." The Latvian grew angry. "I don't have any other sort, ever, always the same."

"Well, all right," Shukhov agreed. "You pack down a glassful. I'll have a smoke and maybe buy another, too."

He had said "pack down" because the Latvian liked to fill it loosely.

The Latvian got another pouch from under his pillow, fuller than the first one, and took his small glass out of his locker. Though it was a plastic glass Shukhov had measured it and knew it was equal to a standard one of real glass.

He poured tobacco out.

"Come on, press it down, press it down!" Shukhov poked with his finger himself.

"I know how!" the Latvian angrily grabbed the glass and pressed the tobacco down but more gently. He poured in some more.

Shukhov by that time had unfastened his underjacket and poked the cotton filling until he felt the paper. Using two hands he moved it along the cotton to a small hole that had been torn in another part of the lining and barely sewn with two threads. Having pushed it up to that hole he tore off the threads with his fingernails and folded the paper lengthwise twice. He pulled it out of the hole. Two rubles, so old they didn't even crackle.

And in the room someone shouted, "Just wait for the old boy with the moustaches to take pity on you. He wouldn't believe his own blood brother, let alone you, you jackass."

The good thing about hard-labor camps was that there was plenty of freedom in them. In Ust-Izhma if you whispered that there was a shortage of matches outside they put you in a cell and gave you another ten years. But here — shout whatever you please from the upper bunks — even the stool-pigeons didn't report such stuff, the security section didn't give a damn.

It was free, but there wasn't any time to talk about things.

"Hey, you're putting it in loose," Shukhov complained.

"Well, there, there." The Latvian added a pinch on top.

Shukhov pulled his pouch out of his inner pocket and poured the tobacco into it.

"All right," he decided, not wanting to smoke the first sweet cigarette on the run. "Pat down another."

After some more wrangling the second was poured out. Shukhov handed over two rubles, nodded to the Latvian and left.

Once outside he ran off to his own barracks, not wanting to miss Tsezar when he got back with his package.

But Tsezar was already sitting on a lower bunk and gloating over his package. The things he had were all out on his cot and locker, but the light from the lamp didn't fall there directly, since Shukhov's upper bunk shadowed it.

Shukhov walked down the aisle between the captain's bunk and Tsezar's, and bent to hand over the evening bread ration.

"Your bread, Tsezar Markovich."

He didn't say, "So you got it?" because that would be a hint he had taken a place in line and now had a right to a share in the parcel. He knew, without saying it, that he had such right. But he wasn't a jackal, not even after eight years of general work in camps, and the longer he lived the firmer he became in his resolve not to be one.

However, he couldn't control his eyes. His eyes, eagle eyes of an old camp dweller, swiftly glanced over the contents of Tsezar's package as they were spread on the cot and the locker. And even though the things were not entirely unwrapped from their paper and bags, and some of them were still closed, with this swift glance and the confirmation of his sense of smell Shukhov knew that Tsezar had received a sausage, condensed milk, a fat smoked fish, fat bacon, some rusks with a sweet smell, baked goods with a different spicy smell, two pounds of lump sugar, and — besides all that — butter, cigarettes, and pipe tobacco; and that wasn't all.

And he had succeeded in scanning all that during the moment he had said, "Your bread, Tsezar Markovich."

And Tsezar, rumpled, excited, as if he were intoxicated — after receiving a food parcel everyone became that way — waved at the bread with his hand:

"Take it for yourself, Ivan Denisych."

Soup plus seven ounces of bread! That was a full dinner and, obviously, it was to be Shukhov's total share of Tsezar's foodstuffs. Well, there was absolutely nothing worse than to lick your chops in expectation and then get nothing.

Anyway he had fourteen ounces of bread in one ration, seven in another, and at least seven in the mattress. That was enough. Seven ounces right now. Tomorrow morning he could devour another pound or more. Take nearly a pound with him to work, too. To work — what a life! Let the portion in the mattress stay there. Good that he had had the chance to sew it in. Rations had been stolen from a locker in the 75th today. Just complain and see how far it gets you.

Some people think that because a man has a package he's got plenty, so they grab whatever they can get. And yet, if you think about it, easy come, easy go. It often happens that before his next parcel arrives a man is glad to work for an extra kasha, and wait to get a butt. The guard, the foreman, the guy with the soft job in the package room — how can you refuse to give them something? If you refuse, he'll hide your package, so it won't be listed for a week. And what about the man in the checkroom where the packages have to be turned in, where that same Tsezar is going to deliver his bag containing his package, to keep it from thieves, and from inspection. The chief of camp ordered that. If you don't give something to the checkroom man he's going to get his anyway — and more — crumb by crumb. He sits there the whole livelong day, the rat, locked up with other peoples' foodstuffs. And just try to catch him stealing! What about services rendered, like the things Shukhov had done? And what about the man at the bath house so that he will give clean linen, not much for him, but something? And for the barber who uses a paper to wipe the razor on instead of wiping it on a zek's naked leg. Not much either, but at least three or four cigarettes. And then something in the cultural educational section so that letters will be saved, so that they don't get lost. And suppose you want to stay in bed for a day or two, something for the doctor too. And what about your next-door neighbor who shares one locker with you — like the captain with Tsezar — can you avoid giving him something? After all he counts every piece you have. Even a man without conscience can't hold out, has to give.

So let someone else be envious of the man with a package, someone who always thinks the turnip in another man's hand is bigger. But Shukhov understood life and didn't expect much from anyone.

By that time he had taken off his boots and climbed to his bunk. He pulled out the piece of blade, looked it over and decided that tomorrow he'd find a good stone to sharpen that blade into a shoemaker's knife. In four days, if he worked on it morning and evenings, he could turn it into a fine little knife with a curved sharp blade.

But for the time being, till morning, he had to hide it. In the wall. And while the captain wasn't in the bunk below — Shukhov didn't want anything to drop on his face — he pulled back his heavy sawdust-filled mattress and proceeded to hide his blade.

His neighbors on other top bunks noticed what he was doing. Alyesha, the Baptist, and, across the passageway on the neighboring bunk, the two brother-Estonians. But Shukhov wasn't worried about them.

Fetyukov came through the barracks, sobbing. Humped over. Blood-smeared lip. He had been beaten up again for plate-licking. Without looking at anyone, not hiding his tears, he went past the entire brigade, climbed up to his bunk, hid his face in his mattress.

If you stopped to think, you felt sorry for him. He wouldn't live through his term. He couldn't adjust.

Then the captain appeared, pleased, carrying a pot of very special tea. In the barracks there were two barrels full of tea — but what kind of tea? Just warm, colored water. Flat tasting. The only fragrance it gave off was the steamy wood and mold smell of the barrels. That was tea fit only for ordinary working stiffs. But the captain must have accepted a handful of real tea from Tsezar, thrown it into a kettle, and run off to the hot water faucet.

"I nearly scalded my fingers at the hot water faucet!" he bragged in satisfaction as he set the tea up at his locker.

Below Shukhov, Tsezar unfolded a sheet of paper and began to write one thing or another. Shukhov moved back on his mattress so as not to see him and not become unhappy. But then Tsezar proved that they couldn't get along without Shukhov. Tsezar stood erect in the aisle, looked up at Shukhov and winked at him:

"Denisych! Give me your *ten days!*"

That meant he wanted the knife, the folding knife, the small one. The one Shukhov owned. He had that hidden in the partition, too. The folding knife was half the size of a finger, but the little so-and-so could easily cut bacon five fingers thick. Shukhov had made that knife; made it and sharpened it, too.

He reached for it, got it out, handed it down. Tsezar nodded and disappeared into his bunk.

So that knife would be income, too. After all, the penalty for owning it was solitary. Only someone totally without conscience could say: 'Lend me the knife, I'm cutting up a sausage, but there's nothing in it for you.'

It was all right if Tsezar borrowed from Shukhov.

Having taken care of bread and blade, Shukhov's next piece of business was the tobacco pouch. He took out a pinch, the same size as the one he had borrowed, and handed it across to the Estonian; well, after all, thank you!

The Estonian opened his lips as if he was trying to smile. He muttered something to his neighbor-brother and they rolled the pinch into a cigarette — 'let's try Shukhov's tobacco, so to speak.'

Well it's no worse than yours — try it as much as you like. Shukhov would have tried it himself but a kind of internal wristwatch kept telling him there were only a few seconds till check. Right now was the time the guards wandered around the barracks. To smoke right now meant going out into the corridor, but Shukhov was too cosy on his bunk. It wasn't warm at all in the barracks. Frost was on the ceiling, but for the time being it seemed bearable. It was at night that he shivered.

Now he began to break off small pieces of his seven ounce ration. But unwillingly he overheard the captain talking with Tsezar down below, as they drank tea.

"Come on, captain, eat, don't be shy! Take some smoked fish. Take some sausage."

"Thank you, I will."

"Come on, spread some butter on that bread! It's a real Moscow loaf!"

"Ai, yai, yai! I can't believe that somewhere they are still baking real bread. You know, this sudden abundance reminds me of a situation I was in once, in Archangel. . . ."

There was the racket and din of two hundred voices in that half of the barracks, but despite the noise Shukhov thought he heard the curfew gong hammered out on the rail. No one else heard it. Shukhov also noticed the guard, Pugnose, had entered the barracks. He was a short fellow with a red face. He held a piece of paper in one hand, and because of that, and by his bearing, Shukhov knew he wasn't trying to catch smokers after hours, or chase anyone out for the nightly check. No he was coming for *someone*.

Pugnose looked at his sheet of paper and asked:

"Where is 104?"

"Here," he was answered. The Estonians hid their cigarette and waved away the smoke.

"Where is the foreman?"

"Well?" Tyurin asked, from his cot, hardly moving.

"Have the men written explanatory notes, as ordered?"

"They'll write!" Tyurin answered with conviction.

"It should have been done already."

"My men are illiterates; it's not an easy thing." (That for Tsezar and the captain, second rank. Well, good boy, that foreman, never slow on the uptake.) "No pens. No ink."

"You should have them."

"They take them away."

"Now, look here, foreman, if you keep talking back, I can put you in prison, too!" Pugnose declared, but he wasn't very angry. "I want those explanations to be in the guards' room! And there must be a statement that the illegal items have been turned in to the personal belongings check room. Do you understand?"

"I understand."

(Shukhov thought to himself: 'The captain has had it.' But the captain had heard nothing, was sitting there eating sausage.)

"And now," the guard asked. "Do you have a S-311?"

"I have to look in my list," the foreman began to fumble around. "Should

I remember those dogs' numbers?" The foreman was stalling to save Buinovsky for one night, or at least until check time.

"Is there a Buinovsky?"

"What? Me!" the captain replied from beneath Shukhov's bunk where he was sheltered from view.

Well, that's the way it goes. A quick flea always gets caught first on the comb.

"You? Right. S-311, get ready."

"Where?"

"You already know."

The captain just sighed and grunted. And, no doubt, it had been easier for him to lead his squadron of destroyers into the dark and stormy night than to break away from the friendly conversation and go off to icy solitary.

"How many days?" he asked, in a lowered voice.

"Ten. Come on, come on. Faster!"

Right then the orderlies shouted:

"Check! Check! Come on out for check!"

That meant the guard ordered to carry out the check was in the barracks.

The captain looked around. Should he take his coat? But it would be torn off him there anyway, and he'd be left in his underjacket all the same. He concluded he should go as he was. The captain had hoped that Volkovoi would forget — but Volkovoi never forgot anything about anybody. The captain hadn't prepared himself. Hadn't even hidden a bit of tobacco in his underjacket. And to take it now — no good. Probably they'd take it away from him at body inspection anyway. Nevertheless, while he was putting on his cap Tsezar shoved a pair of cigarettes in his hand.

"Well, so long, brothers," the captain absentmindedly called out to the brigade members, and he followed the guard out.

Several voices shouted to him. One — "Buck up." Another — "Don't lose heart." But what was there to say? The brigade had built the camp punishment prison. The 104th knew what it was like. Stone walls, cement floor, no window, stove barely heated, just enough so the ice melted off the wall and formed icy puddles on the floor. Sleep on bare boards. If you didn't shiver the teeth out of your head, you ate ten ounces of bread a day, with hot soup on the third, sixth and ninth days.

Ten days. Ten days of solitary in that place, if sat out strictly to the very end, meant loss of health for life. If it became TB, you'd never get out of hospitals. The men who had gone through fifteen days of strict solitary were in the cold, cold ground.

While you live in the barracks, be happy and grateful and keep your nose clean.

"Come on, get outside, I'm counting to three," the senior barracks orderly yelled. "If anyone isn't out by the count of three, I'll write his number down and give it to the citizen guard."

The senior barracks orderly was also a senior swine. After all, they lock him up in the barracks with us every night, yet he works for the officers, isn't afraid of any zek. On the contrary, everyone is afraid of him. Whenever he betrays a zek to the guards he also hits him in the face. He's classified as an invalid because he lost one of his fingers in a fight. He has the mug of a professional criminal, and he is a criminal, too, sent up on criminal rather than political counts. Though among all the other charges against him they hung a political charge, too — section 58 clause 14 of the code. That's how he got into this camp.

Easy does it — or he writes your number down, passes it to the guard, and there you are with two days in solitary with work outside.

The zeks had been dragging slowly to the doors but when he began to yell they crowded together, immediately piled right to top of each other to get out. The men in upper bunks leaped down like monkeys, and everyone tried to push through the narrow doors at once.

Shukhov, holding the home-rolled, long-desired cigarette, jumped down deftly. He shoved his feet into his felt boots and started out. Then he felt sorry for Tsezar. Not that Shukhov wanted to get anything else from him, but he sincerely pitied him. It was as if he thought too highly of himself, Tsezar, and didn't understand life one little bit. For instance, he got a parcel, but the thing to do was not to gloat over it but to haul it quickly to the checkroom before the check. He could have put part of it aside to eat. And now what could he do with the package? If he took the whole bagful out to the check he'd be the laughingstock of the camp. Five hundred throats roaring. But if he left it inside there was a good chance that whoever ran back into the barracks first would swipe it.

In Ust-Izhma, Shukhov remembered that things had been even rougher. There, when you got back from work, the criminal elements would be in barracks first, and by the time those in the rear had come up their lockers had been cleaned out.

Shukhov saw Tsezar was shoving things here, hiding things there, but he was too late. He was pushing the sausage and bacon down his jacket front — he was going to take them out to check and at least save them.

Shukhov took pity on him and gave him some instructions:

"Sit there, Tsezar Markovich. Sit there hidden in the shadow, and wait till the last second. When the guard and orderlies start around the barracks examining all the corners, then go on out. Act as if you're sick! And I'll go out and hurry back inside first. That's how. . . ."

Then Shukhov ran out.

First he pushed his way swiftly ahead — careful of the home-made cigarette in his hand. In the corridor that was used by both halves of the barracks, and in the entries, no one was going out. Prisoners had animal-cunning. They pressed against the wall in double rows on both sides. That left an empty passageway in the middle, wide enough for one man. Anybody stupid enough can go out into the cold, but as for us, we're going to stay right here. As it is we spend the whole day in the cold, so why should we freeze for an extra ten minutes? No, we're not such fools. You drop dead today — but we'll wait till tomorrow!

Any other night Shukhov would have been huddling against that wall, too. But on this occasion he walked through with long strides and even exposed his teeth in a big grin.

"What are you afraid of, softies? Haven't you seen Siberian cold yet? Go on out and warm yourselves under that wolf's sun up there! How about a light, uncle?"

He lit up out in the entry and went on out on the porch. "Wolf's sun" was what they jokingly called the moon in Shukhov's village.

The moon was high; a little bit more and it would be at its zenith. White sky, touched with green, brilliant stars scattered far apart, glistening white snow. Barracks walls white, too, so that the lamps seemed ineffectual.

Over at another barracks there loomed a black mass — the zeks had come out and were forming up. Over there another group. And from barracks to barracks the buzz of the chatter was not as loud as the creaking of the snow underfoot.

Five men walked down the steps and turned to face the door. Three more came behind them. Shukhov joined the three in the second row. He could stand there and munch bread and hold a cigarette in his teeth. Good tobacco. The Latvian hadn't cheated — it was both biting and pungent.

Other zeks came out slowly and fell in. Soon there were two, three, lines of fives behind Shukhov. Now the men outside got furious at the ones indoors. Why are those snakes jammed in the corridor? Why aren't they out here? We're freezing for their sakes.

None of the zeks ever saw a watch or clock. What was the use of them anyway? A zek only needed to know: When is the rising gong? How long to lineup? To lunch? To curfew?

Despite that, they declared the evening check was held at nine. But it never ended at nine. Often they'd call a second check, even a third one. Prisoners never go to sleep before ten, and the rising gong sounded at five. It wasn't astonishing that the Moldavian fell asleep during work. Wherever a zek got warm he fell asleep in that spot, immediately. During the week so much sleep was lost that on

Sunday the entire barracks slept through the whole day. If they were not driven out, that is.

"Hey, get out there. Get down off the porch." The senior barracks orderly and the guard were flushing them out, barking at their backs. Good for them, the sheep!

The first rows shouted at the laggards: "Playing tricks, you vipers? Trying to lick sour cream off shit, is that it? Should have been out here long ago — they'd have counted you off long ago."

The entire barracks piled out. There were four hundred in the barracks; eighty groups of five. They lined up at the rear, at first strictly by fives, and then farther on — in a mess.

"Line up in fives out there in back!" the senior barracks orderly yelled from the steps.

The pricks aren't separating out; bastards.

Tsezar came out of the door, all huddled up and shivering, pretending to be sick. Two orderlies from that half of the barracks, two from the other half, and one cripple came out too. They made up a first five in front of the rest — making Shukhov's line the third. Tsezar was chased to the end of the line.

And the guard came out on the porch.

"Count off by fives!" He yelled at the tail end. He had a loud voice.

"Count off by fives." The senior barracks orderly yelled. His voice was even louder.

Still hadn't formed up, the pricks!

The senior barracks orderly rushed down from the porch to the back of the crowd. Oaths, and kicks in the ass.

But he looked first: to see whom he kicked. He beat only the ones who wouldn't fight back.

They separated. He returned. Then, together with the guard, "One! Two! Three!"

When they called out a five, it dashed off to the barracks at full speed. For this day they were finally finished with the chief.

That is, they were finished, if there wasn't a second count. Those parasites, those lame brains, counted worse than any herdboy. A herdboy is illiterate, but he drives his herd, and knows without stopping whether all the calves are there. But these types — they train them and what good does it do?

Last winter in this camp there were no dryers: footwear was left in the barracks at night for everyone. So for second, third, fourth count the zeks were driven out of doors. Finally the zeks hadn't even bothered to get dressed, just put on valenki, wrapped themselves in blankets, and went out that way. This year they had built dryers, not for all the shoes at once, but so that after two days every brigade would have a turn to dry its valenki on the third. So now they had begun the practice of conducting second counts inside the barracks: the zeks were chased from one half into the other.

Shukhov ran in. He wasn't exactly first but close enough so he didn't let the first ones in out of his sight. He ran to Tsezar's cot and sat down there. He tore off his valenki, scrambled on the bunk near the stove, and set his valenki on the stove. It was a question of who got his valenki to the stove first. Back to Tsezar's cot. Sat there, legs folded, one eye alert to see that Tsezar's bag didn't get jerked out from under the head of the bed, and another eye peeled to make sure that the men rushing the stove didn't move his valenki.

"Hey!" He had to shout. "You, redhead! How'd you like a boot in the kisser? Put yours down and leave mine alone."

The zeks kept pouring and pouring into the barracks. Over in the 20th a guard yelled:

"Turn in valenki!"

So those zeks would be allowed out of the barracks with their valenki. The barracks would be locked. Then the zeks would return:

"Citizen chief! Let us in the barracks."

And the guards would meet in headquarters barracks and do their bookkeeping with their count boards: had someone run away or were all present and accounted for?

Well, Shukhov wasn't concerned with that today. Here came Tsezar diving along between the bunks.

"Thank you, Ivan Denisych!"

Shukhov nodded and climbed up to his bunk as fast as a squirrel. Now he could eat that six-ounce piece, smoke a second cigarette, go to sleep.

Except that he'd had such a good day he didn't feel like sleeping.

Making his bed was a simple matter for Shukhov. Black blanket off the mattress. Lie down on the mattress. (Shukhov had not slept on sheets since 1941 when he had left home. Now it even seemed strange to him that women would bother with sheets and all that extra washing.) His head on his pillow, which was stuffed with shavings. Feet in his underjacket. Coat on top of the blanket. Thank You, good Lord, one more day has passed! Thanks, too, that he was not sleeping in solitary. Here in the barracks, he could manage.

Shukhov lay with his head to the window. Across a ledge from Shukhov Alyesha was nearby on a similar top bunk. Alyesha was leaning back so that light reached him from the lamp bulb. He was reading the Gospels again. The lamp bulb was not far from them. One could read and even sew.

Alyesha heard how Shukhov praised God aloud, and turned.

"You see, Ivan Denisovich, your soul begs to pray to God. Why don't you let it have its way?"

Shukhov looked sideways at Alyesha. The Baptist's eyes were shining like two candles. Shukhov sighed. "Because, Alyesha, those prayers, like official petitions, either don't get there at all or else bear the imprint 'Complaint rejected.' "

In front of headquarters barracks there were four petition boxes, sealed. Once a month a specially empowered officer emptied them. Many zeks slipped declarations and petitions into those boxes. They waited, counting the time, hoping, after two months, for an answer, hoping that in another month a reply would come.

But it doesn't come. Or it does, "Rejected."

"Because, Ivan Denisych, you pray little, poorly, without enthusiasm, that's why things haven't come true from your prayers. Prayer must be incessant. And if you have faith, and you say to that mountain, 'Move!' It will move."

Shukhov laughed and rolled himself one more cigarette. He got a light from the Estonian.

"Stop your chatter, Alyesha! I haven't seen that mountain moved. Well, to be honest, I've never seen any mountains at all. You used to pray in the Caucasus with your Baptist group. Did even one mountain move?"

Those Baptists were unfortunates, too. They prayed to God. Whom did they bother? Yet the whole lot of them got twenty-five years. Because it's that kind of a time now. Twenty-five years, one measure for everything.

"But we didn't pray for that, Denisych," Alyesha said persuasively. He moved closer to Shukhov, close to his face. "Of all that belongs to this earth, all that is transient, the Lord willed only that we would pray for our daily bread, 'Give us this day our daily bread!' "

"The bread ration, you mean?" Shukhov asked.

But Alyesha kept at it. His eyes said more than words, and he took Shukhov's hand in his and stroked it.

"Ivan Denisych! You shouldn't pray to get a package or an extra portion of soup. What people value highly is merely foulness to God. You must pray about spiritual things, ask God to take the scum of evil from your heart. . . ."

"Listen to me instead. In our church in Polomnya the priest. . . ."

"Don't talk to me about your priest!" Alyesha begged, his forehead wrinkled with pain.

"No, you listen to me." Shukhov raised himself up on his elbow. "In Polomnya, our parish, no one is richer than the priest. There, let's say they call me to fix a roof — I get thirty-five rubles a day, but get one hundred from the priest.

And he doesn't even squawk about it. That Polomnya priest has three women in three towns to whom he pays alimony. He lives with the fourth family. And the provincial bishop is caught on his hook. He shoves a well-greased paw at the bishop. No matter how many other priests are sent to our town, he forces them out, refuses to divide up with anyone. . . ."

"Why do you talk to me about a priest? The Orthodox Church has departed from the Gospels. That's why the government doesn't put them in prison. Because they have no firm faith."

Smoking, Shukhov looked calmly at Alyesha's excitement.

"Alyesha," he took his hand away, blew smoke in the Baptist's face. "I'm not against God, you understand. I willingly believe in God. Only I don't believe in Heaven and Hell. Why do you take us for fools, keep pushing Heaven and Hell at us? That's what I don't like."

Shukhov lay on his back, threw the ash carefully over his head, between bunk and window, in order not to burn the captain's things. Lost in his thoughts, he didn't hear what Alyesha was muttering.

"In general," Shukhov decided, "no matter how much you pray they aren't going to shorten your term. And so you'll keep sitting from gong to gong."

"Don't pray for that either!" Alyesha was horrified. "What's freedom for? In freedom your last particle of faith will be suffocated. Be glad you are in prison. Here you have time to think about your soul. This is what the apostle Paul said: 'What are you doing, weeping and breaking my heart? For I am ready not only to be imprisoned but even to die for the name of the Lord Jesus.' "

In silence Shukhov looked up at the ceiling. He just didn't know whether he still wanted freedom or not. At first he had wanted it very much and each night had counted how many days of his term had passed and how many were left. Then he got tired of counting. And then it became clear that men in his boots weren't allowed to go home. They were shipped into exile. And he didn't know where he could live better, here or in exile.

He only wanted one thing out of freedom — to go home.

But they don't let people go home.

Alyesha wasn't lying. His voice and his eyes showed that he was glad to sit in prison.

"See here, Alyesha," Shukhov explained to him. "Somehow or other things have worked out for you. Because your Christ ordered you to sit, you are sitting for Christ. But what am I sitting for? Because in 1941 they weren't prepared for the war. What's that got to do with me?"

Kilgas muttered from his cot, "Doesn't seem as if there'll be a second check."

"Yesss!" Shukhov replied. "Well, we'll have to write that in the stovepipe with a piece of coal, no second count." He yawned: "Guess I'll sleep."

And at that moment, the men in the quieted-down, pacified barracks heard the rattle of the bolt on the outside door. Two of the zeks who had taken valenki to the dryer ran in and shouted:

"Second check!"

Right then the guard came in after them, commanded, "Go out to the other half."

Some of the men had been asleep. They snarled, began to move, shoved their feet into their valenki. No one took off the padded trousers at night. Without them you'd freeze under the blanket.

"God damn them!" Shukhov swore. But he wasn't very angry, because he hadn't been asleep yet.

Tsezar shoved his hand up, holding out two cookies for him, two pieces of sugar and one round slice of sausage.

"Thank you, Tsezar Markovich," Shukhov bent over the edge of the bunk. "Come on, give me your bag. I'll put it under my mattress head for safety." No one could swipe on the run from an upper, and anyway who would look for anything in Shukhov's bunk?

Tsezar handed up his tied white sack. Shukhov shoved it under his mattress. He waited till the guards had chased more zeks out so he wouldn't have to stand barefoot on the floor too long. But the guard showed his teeth. "Well, how about it, you there in the corner?"

So Shukhov jumped down softly, barefoot, onto the floor. His valenki and footcloths were set so well on the stove that he just didn't want to take them off. And no matter how many slippers he had sewn for others he never left any for himself. Well, after all, he was used to the cold and it wouldn't be for very long.

Anyway they take slippers away when they find them in searches during the day.

As for those brigades that turned their valenki in to the dryer — it's all right for those who have slippers, but the others have to walk on the cold floor either in footcloths or else barefoot.

"Well, well," growled the guard.

"You want me to beat you up, you bastard?" the senior barracks orderly was right there with him.

They pushed the zeks into the other half of the barracks and the last ones into the corridor. Shukhov stood at the partition next to the latrine barrel. Beneath his feet the floor was damp, and there was an icy draft from under the door.

They chased them all out and the guard and the senior barracks orderly went back to see if anyone had hidden, or was in a corner, sleeping. Because if the count was short, it was a catastrophe. And if the count was long, that was a catastrophe. Another recheck either way. They went over the empty half of the barracks, once, twice, and then returned to the doors.

"One, two, three, four. . . ." This time they were readmitting quickly one by one. Shukhov managed to get in as the eighteenth. Ran to his berth, had his foot on the support — whoosh — already up on top.

All right. Feet in the underjacket sleeve, blanket on top of him and on top of that his coat. Sleep. They'd order the other half of the barracks into our half now. No skin off our ass.

Tsezar returned. Shukhov handed down his bag.

Alyesha returned. He was such an incompetent. He helped everyone, but couldn't manage to earn anything extra.

"Here, Alyesha!" Shukhov gave him one cookie.

Alyesha smiled.

"Thank you. You don't have anything yourself."

"Eat."

We don't have any, so we always earn a little something.

Shukhov shoved a little piece of sausage into his mouth. Bite with his teeth. Bite again. Meat fragrance. And real meat juice. It flowed down to his stomach.

No more sausage.

He'd eat everything else, Shukhov calculated, in the morning before lineup.

He pulled his thin, unwashed blanket over his head without listening to the zeks from the other half of the barracks who were filling the spaces between the bunks, waiting till their half was checked.

Shukhov went to sleep, quite content. He had had many successes that day. They hadn't put him in solitary, the brigade had not been driven to the Socialist Life Town, at lunch he had made off with an extra kasha, the foreman had surpassed their quota, Shukhov had had a damn good time laying that wall, he hadn't been caught with that piece of blade at body inspection, he had earned something from Tsezar at evening, and bought himself some tobacco. And he hadn't become really sick. He had managed to recover.

A day had passed that was not darkened by anything. Almost a happy day.

Of such days from gong to gong in his term there were three thousand six hundred and fifty-three.

Three days extra due to leap year.

AFTERWORD

Before the publication of *One Day in the Life of Ivan Denisovich* it was widely known that at last the Russian government would allow the publication of a work that depicted the brutality of the slave labor camps during Stalin's regime. A public, doubtless partly just curious to see if the rumor was true but also doubtless hungry for the depiction of the truth that many of them had in one way or another experienced, bought in a single day all 95,000 copies of the magazine in which *One Day* was published. Some idea of the enormous desire to read this novel may be gained from one of the numerous letters that its author received: "In Kharkov I have seen all kinds of lines — for the film *Tarzan,* butter, women's drawers, chicken giblets and horse-meat sausage. But I cannot remember a line as long as the one for your book in the libraries." Behind this letter, and behind the popularity that it represents, we sense a hunger for truth (as well as for chicken giblets and horse-meat sausage) that had long gone unsatisfied.

Roughly speaking, Soviet publication since the early 1930's had been guided by a critical doctrine called "socialist realism," which was epitomized in the 1934 statute of the Union of Soviet Writers:

> Socialist Realism is the fundamental method of Soviet literature and criticism: it demands of the artist a true, historically concrete representation of reality in its revolutionary development. Further, it ought to contribute to the ideological transformation and education of the workers in the spirit of socialism.

There are two points here which might seem to be in opposition: first, a demand for truth, a "concrete representation of reality," and, second, a demand — to put it bluntly — for propaganda, for a literature that would "contribute to the ideological transformation and education of the workers in the spirit of socialism [i.e., communism]." There need not, however, be a contradiction if due attention is paid to the words "a true, historically concrete representation of reality *in its revolutionary development.*" That is, the writer depicts not merely external details but also the direction in which political and economic forces are inevitably moving. To depict merely the surface, the argument goes, is not really to be realistic for it is to miss the underlying reality and produce a misleading work. A true work of art, in this view, gives us an accurate picture of life *and* a guide for our own action. That in the Soviet Union writers were expected to do something socially useful is evident from Stalin's assertion that writers are "engineers of the human soul." Stalin's words seem a bit cold-blooded, but at least he paid the arts the compliment of assuming that they were more than the trivial amusements of idle hours. And his metaphor of engineering helps to indicate the connection between the two criteria of socialist realism: just as an engineer cannot produce a valuable work (1) if he does not take account of the underlying principles of mechanics, chemistry, and electricity, and (2) if he does not have some goal in view, so (the argument goes) a writer must take into account the real facts, and must write with the aim of assisting his readers to see them so that they can then live in better accord with the needs of their times.

This doctrine for some thirty years shaped the production of what seem to Western readers to be shallow books, naive depictions of unhappy people who finally achieve happiness when they learn to put aside their personal ambitions and work harder in the factory or on the farm to bring about Russia's new destiny. The implication regularly was that the system is right, and that once the individual understands and accepts it he will achieve happiness. To a nation wherein scarcely a family did not have some member in a concentration camp, it all must have seemed grotesquely unreal. And so it is not surprising that the public eagerly devoured a novel that at last told the truth about the stupidity and the brutality in the camps.

In an interview Solzhenitsyn said, "While still in the camp I made up my mind to describe one day of prison life. Tolstoy once said that a novel can deal with either centuries of European history or a day in one man's life." Now, it is obvious — from any point of view, including socialist realism — that a single day if properly studied can give us a vision of life. And a single day need not be too brief a period for a story, a plot, a happening, an action (if we may for the moment use these words as synonyms). The traditional "well-made plot" begins with the protagonist in a situation of equilibrium; then the equilibrium is disturbed (think of Faulkner's *Old Man,* which begins with a convict cozily in jail, then routed out of it to fight a flood); and finally, after responses and further disturbances there is a resolution, in which a new equilibrium is established. In some fiction, detective novels for example, plot dominates, and the reader's interest is held by a chain of surprising happenings. In such fiction character usually counts for very little; indeed detective fiction customarily works on the premise that at the end people are not at all what they seemed to be throughout the book. But in books that make a more serious claim, plot (or "incident") and character usually work together. As Henry James said, "What is character but the determination of incident? What is incident but the illustration of character?"

If we agree that the books of most permanent interest are those that tell us about living (rather than those that, on reflection, offer only suspenseful actions), one day can be enough, especially one day in the life of a man who lives under extremely demanding circumstances. Another Russian novelist, Boris Pasternak, in *Doctor Zhivago* mentions a Russian proverb, "To live your life is not as simple as to cross a field," but Solzhenitsyn gives us a book in which even crossing a field — in a sub-zero winter, under the eyes of guards — is a matter of life and death; a book, in short, in which the routine events of a single day test a man to his limits and fully reveal his nature.

In one sense, almost nothing happens in *One Day in the Life of Ivan Denisovich;* prisoner S-854, a member of brigade 104, gets up, helps to build a brick wall on the second story of a building, and finally goes to bed. If we contrast this short novel with Faulkner's *Old Man,* also about a convict's labors, we find a striking difference, Faulkner's convict being swept by the flood from one adventure to another. But in both stories life is precarious, lived under intense pressures, and a more accurate description of Solzhenitsyn's novel would, in a list of "what happens," include the ordeal of getting out of the bunk, attempting to get on the sick list, watching out for informers, getting a bit of tobacco or some extra food, smuggling a piece of metal past the guards, for in this elemental situation all of these activities require enormous effort and severely test one's physique, one's wits, and one's principles.

By the end of the novel, we know a great deal not only about labor camps in Stalin's day, but also about Ivan Denisovich. In many ways he must be like Solzhenitsyn, since Denisovich's behavior gives us an idea of what one must be like to survive such a camp. But Solzhenitsyn, probably wisely, chose to invent a man whose background is very different from his own; Ivan Denisovich is a peasant-carpenter, not an intellectual, and we thus get none of the thought processes (or rationalizations) that a better-educated or more thoughtful prisoner might comfort himself with. About the closest we come to a discussion is the brief conversation on Eisenstein's film *Ivan the Terrible* that Ivan Denisovich overhears, and brief as it is, a reader almost feels that such talk about the role of the artist in a dictatorship is intrusive in a world in which merely to keep alive is both an art and a craft. Ivan Denisovich survives, one feels, partly because he is a peasant, not given to reasoning but to getting along in difficult circumstances. He is resourceful and strong; his earth-bound mind protects him from thinking too much about how things ought to be and keeps him in contact with how things are. He knows that "A warm man can't understand a frozen man." But most of all, perhaps, he is sustained by a sense of craftsmanship. He must build a wall; all right, let it be a good wall: "Shukhov made no mistakes. The blocks were not all exactly the same dimensions. Some had a knocked-off corner, uneven edge, or other defect. Shukhov spotted them right away and spotted the side on which that block wanted to sit, and spotted also the place in the wall that was waiting for that block." And a little later: "Shukhov ran back to have a look at the work. The guards could have sicked the convoy dogs on him, but even that wouldn't have stopped him. Not so bad! And now he ran up and looked the wall over from right to left. He had an eye like a mason's level. It was straight. His hands had skill in them yet." These passages (many similar ones could be quoted) owe something to the happy workers in earlier novels prescribed by socialist realism, but Ivan Denisovich Shukhov is infinitely more believable and more attractive. True, he shoves a weaker fellow prisoner out of the way in the mess hall, lies when he thinks it necessary, breaks as many prison rules as he can get away with; but that he has a compelling dignity we can easily see when, for example, we compare his efforts to get a smoke with Fetyukov's: "Shukhov . . . was strained in expectation, and, it seemed at that moment that he wanted that cigarette butt more than he wanted freedom. But even so, he wouldn't humiliate himself like Fetyukov, by staring at Tsezar's lips." And later we hear, "He was an expert at scavenging, that Fetyukov, though he never had the boldness to swipe anything."

To a Western reader the book is not (except in quality) the radical break with socialist realism that many Soviet readers say it is; rather, since Shukhov is a hard worker ("What has Shukhov been eating for eight-years-going-on-nine? Nothing. But work he's done!") and, moreover, a contented worker ("he'd had such a good day — he didn't feel like sleeping"), the book seems like a belated fulfillment of the ideals of the socialist realist critics of the thirties. We notice, too, that there is no criticism of the Communist Party, only of Stalin. It is not really surprising that Khrushchev saw no threat in the book.

Or is it? We see *One Day,* first, as a story about prison life in Russia under Stalin. But we can easily go a little further, and see the prison — like the cancer ward in Solzhenitsyn's later novel — as a metaphor for Soviet society, a world of people deprived of freedom. Solzhenitsyn apparently occasionally hints at such an interpretation, for example when he says that "there were plans afoot to shift the 104th from the construction of workshops to a new project, the 'Socialist Life Town.' The Socialist Life Town was now just a bare open field, all snow ridges and drifts. Before anything could be built there, the prisoners would have to dig holes, set in posts, and put up barbed wire — fencing themselves in so they couldn't escape." The new society, that is, will begin with people imprisoning themselves. Moreover, references throughout the book suggest that Soviet life outside the camp is characterized by the same waste of energy and suppression of creativity that are found inside the camp. Whether a reader may go yet further, and see in the novel something of a representation of life itself as a condition of imprisonment but not without its victories, is a question not so much to be asked as to be experienced.

GLOSSARY

allegory. A work with a system of equivalents, so that, for example, the characters action, and setting not only tell a coherent story but also refer to another story. George Orwell's *Animal Farm* is on the surface a story intelligible to children about the activities of animals on a farm, but the story repeatedly corresponds to historical events, and the initiated reader understands that he is reading about the Russian Revolution.

archetype. The common meaning, "the original pattern or model from which all other things of the same kind are made," is somewhat broader than its meaning in literary criticism. Carl G. Jung, the Swiss psychologist, in *Contributions to Analytical Psychology,* postulates the existence of a "collective unconscious" in men's minds, an inheritance in the brain consisting of "countless typical experiences [such as birth, escape from danger, selection of a mate] of our ancestors." These experiences, such as perception of the perpetual rising and setting (birth and death, one might say) of the sun, manifest themselves in dreams, myths, and literature (see *motif*). Among the archetypes are the Hero (savior, deliverer), the Terrible Mother (witch, cruel stepmother — even the wolf "grandmother" in the tale of Little Red Ridinghood), and the Wise Old Man (magician). Because (the theory holds) both writer and reader share unconscious memories, the tale an author tells, derived from the collective unconscious, may strangely move the reader, stirring his collective unconscious.

atmosphere. The air (calm, sinister, oppressive, etc.) breathed by the reader as he enters into the world of a literary work. For example, an atmosphere of child-like simplicity or of mystery may be set up, partly by the objects described and partly by the style of the description.

Bildungsroman, or **Erziehungsroman** (German for "novel of development"). A novel dealing with maturation, wherein the hero becomes "civilized" — i.e., becomes aware of himself as he relates to the objective world outside of his subjective consciousness. Notable examples are Goethe's *Wilhelm Meister* and Thomas Mann's *The Magic Mountain.* When the *Bildungsroman* is concerned specifically with the development of the artist, as are Samuel Butler's *The Way of All Flesh* and James Joyce's *A Portrait of the Artist as a Young Man,* it is sometimes termed a **Künstlerroman** (German for "novel of the artist").

character. A figure in a work of fiction, or the personality (traits) of such a figure. Characters are sometimes divided into **flat** and **round characters.** The former (common in Dickens) have only one "side," representing a single trait (e.g., the faithful wife, the genial drunkard), whereas the latter have many traits and are seen, as it were, from all sides, in the round. The behavior of flat characters is thoroughly predictable; that of round characters is sometimes unexpected though always credible. The term "flat" is not necessarily pejorative, for it is sometimes desirable to show only one aspect of a single character.

epiphany. Literally, a "showing-forth," especially of a deity. James Joyce first made the word current in literary criticism. A person may make a gesture — say, a sudden movement of the hand — which shows his state of mind. An epiphany is such a sudden revelation of the inner essence or "whatness" of an object, character, situation, or experience, usually manifested by physical details.

episode. In a plot, a portion having some unity of its own, an incident.

flashback. An interruption in the chronological arrangement, presenting an earlier episode than the one that has just been presented.

Gothic novel. A long prose narrative of horror, often involving eerie medieval castles with secret passageways, ghosts, and a virgin harried by a villain who himself is tortured by mysterious guilt. Horace Walpole's *Castle of Otranto, a Gothic Story* (1764) was the first of a line which has stressed horror; William Faulkner's *Absalom, Absalom!* is not the last. Notable Gothic novels written between these are Matthew Lewis's *The Monk* and Mary Shelley's *Frankenstein;* Dickens's *Great Expectations,* with Miss Havisham's cobwebbed and rat-infested chamber, also belongs in part to this tradition.

irony. In **verbal irony** there is a contrast between what is stated and what is more or less wryly suggested. As Robert Frost puts it, "In irony, the tone indicated contradicts the words." **Dramatic irony,** designating a condition of affairs that is different from what the participants think, is almost always present in some degree because the reader of a novel has a fuller view of the network of relationships between the characters than any of the characters has; he is aware of the discrepancy between what a character says or thinks or does and the real state of affairs in the book.

motif. A recurrent word, phrase, situation, object, or idea. Most frequently, "motif" is applied to a situation that recurs in various literary works, e.g., the rags-to-riches motif. But a motif (in the following sense sometimes called a **leitmotif,** from the German "leading-motif") can occur within a single work: it is any repetition that helps unify a work by potently recalling its earlier occurrence and all that surrounded it. Examples are the periodic striking of Big Ben in Virginia Woolf's *Mrs. Dalloway* and the ubiquitous discarded circular in James Joyce's *Ulysses.*

motivation. Grounds in character for action. Although in some works a god or equivalent (Fortune, Chance) intervenes and determines the happenings, most often what happens is in part the plausible outcome of a character's personality. If a character does things that seem inappropriate to his personality and his situation, he is said to be poorly motivated, and poor motivation in realistic fiction is usually regarded as a fault.

myth. (1) Sometimes "myth" is synonymous with plot, denoting the fictional happening in a narrative or drama. (2) Mark Schorer (in his *William Blake*) defines "myth" as "a large, controlling image that gives philosophic meaning to the facts of ordinary life. . . . All real convictions involve a mythology. . . . Wars may be described as the clash of mythologies." A myth, then, in the broadest usage is any idea, true or false, to which people subscribe. Thus, one can speak of the "myth" of democracy or of totalitarianism.

new novel (**nouveau roman**). A form produced in reaction, beginning in France in the 1950's, to the traditional novel. Writers of the new novel (such as Alain Robbe-Grillet, Nathalie Sarraute, and Claude Simon) argue that the traditional novel is utterly false, for it presents characters (whereas people are not psychologically consistent creatures, but a complex series of appearances), plots (whereas plots do not exist in nature), cause and effect (a naive assumption), and it assumes that there is a connection between people and the objects of the world they move in (another naive assumption). The new novel, instead of presenting a story of coherent characters acting in a context, offers a sort of dreamlike series of perceptions; the identities of the perceivers are usually unclear, and so is the chronology, and, of course, the story has no conclusion.

non-fiction novel. A term apparently coined by Truman Capote to describe his *In Cold Blood,* an account of a multiple murder committed in Kansas in 1959. The details are all true, but the book is written with a novelist's sense of irony and of symbolic details; in short, it is history written by a novelist — but this form is not to be confused with the "historical novel," which by its usual emphasis on plot and on the exotic is a kind of romance. Another example of the non-fiction novel: Norman Mailer's *The Armies of the Night,* describing the anti–Vietnam War march of 1967 and subsequent related events, in which Mailer writes of himself in the third person.

novelle. See pp. 487–88.

novelette. See p. 8.

parable. A short narrative from which a lesson can be drawn, such as Christ's tale of the Good Samaritan (Luke 10:30–7).

picaresque novel. The picaresque novel is usually a detailed satiric picture of middle-class life, in which a roguish but engaging fellow (Spanish *pícaro,* "rogue") from the lower fringes of society tells of the shrewd shifts by which he triumphs over the less bright members of the bourgeois whom he encounters. Because the form originated (in sixteenth-century Spain) as a kind of burlesque of tales of chivalric adventures, the *pícaro* wins in one situation after another, and the novel has an episodic structure. Examples are Smollett's *The Adventures of Roderick Ransom,* Mark Twain's *Adventures of Huckleberry Finn,* and Thomas Mann's *The Confessions of Felix Krull.*

plot and **story.** Distinctions between "plot" and "story" vary widely, but for many critics "story" is the chronological sequence in which events occur as parts of a happening, and "plot" is the sequence in which the author arranges (narrates) them. The plot thus is the narrative structure, consisting of smaller units, called episodes. This meaning of "plot," implying construction, has the virtue of being very old, for in the Middle Ages a plot was a groundplan for a building (by extension of the meaning of a patch of earth).

point of view. A piece of literature is told or recorded by someone, and this narrator has a particular identity. The story is rarely told by the artist speaking in his own personality; usually it is told through an assumed "point of view," an assumed eye and mind.

Points of view can be divided into first and third person. The teller of a first-person point of view can be a **first-person observer** of a tale about Jones ("I last met Jones in 1922") or a **first-person participant** — Jones or his wife ("I had just got married, and was looking for a house"). If the first-person narrator is naive (a child, a not-too-bright adult, an idiot) and the tale is filtered through his uncomprehending mind, the point of view is usually called the **innocent eye** (e.g., Benjy, the thirty-three-year-old idiot who narrates the first part of Faulkner's *The Sound and the Fury*). A first-person point of view normally involves some degree of ironic distance between the narrator and the author. **Third-person** points of view are commonly divided into omniscient, selective omniscient, and objective. In the **omniscient point of view,** the voice narrating the tale can record the thoughts of all the characters ("John was lonely, but didn't perceive that Mary was lonely too"). If the voice comments on the story ("Loneliness has its pleasures as well as its pains," or "But, dear readers, we must not be upset by the loneliness of these puppets"), it exemplifies **editorial omniscience.** Many modern critics are distressed by such editorializing; they tend to identify the narrator with the author, and they feel that the author should be less in evidence and more willing to let us interpret the story for ourselves. If the voice abstains from editorializing and merely records, it exemplifies **neutral omniscience.** If the voice enters into the mind of only one character, or very few, the point of view exemplifies **selective omniscience** (also called **limited omniscience).** If the voice does not editorialize and does not enter into the minds of any of the characters, but simply records what is visible ("John looked at Mary. She looked away"), it is an **objective point of view,** sometimes called "fly-on-the-wall," or "the camera."

roman à clef (French for "novel with a key"). A novel using as its chief characters contemporary historical figures who are disguised with fictitious names. In Aldous Huxley's *Point Counter Point* Mark Rampion is modeled on D. H. Lawrence.

romance. The Greek romance may go back to the second century B.C., but most of the extant ones are from the second and third centuries A.D. It is usually concerned with chaste young royal lovers who undergo innumerable misfortunes such as abduction and shipwreck, and who finally are united in marriage. The emphasis is on plot (the characters are merely virtuous or merely vicious), and there are stories within stories as the lovers seek each other, sometimes in disguise, often in exotic lands. (See p. 3.)

setting. Environment, including locale and historical time. The setting may work oppressively against the character, conditioning his behavior, but often the setting is metaphoric (especially when it is a domestic interior), expressing something of the personality of the individual who moves within it.

stream of consciousness. (A metaphor coined in 1890 by William James in *Principles of Psychology* to describe the flux of thought.) A stream of consciousness novel records mental activity ranging from complete consciousness to unconsciousness. Its most prominent technique is the **interior monologue,** which reveals the minds of characters and presents not overt actions and speech or even thoughts in logical and grammatical order; rather, it attempts to present what has been called the mind's "pre-speech levels of consciousness" in such a manner (commonly without punctuation, logical transitions, or conventional syntax, and with little or no intervention by the author) as to suggest the fluid and unending activity of the mind, with all its apparent irrelevant associations. Joyce's *Ulysses* is a stream of consciousness novel; its last forty-six pages, an uninterrupted flow of Molly Bloom's thoughts, are an interior monologue. But words printed one after the other on a page cannot, of course, precisely duplicate the welter of thoughts which — without even being verbalized — pass through the mind.

symbolism. Derived from Greek *symballein,* "to throw together," which thus suggests the essential quality of symbolism: the drawing together of two worlds, the revelation of an otherwise invisible world through the presentation of the concrete material world of roses, toads, caves, stars, etc. As a noun, the original Greek word denoted half of something broken in two, and thus the word suggests not something that stands for something else, but something that is part of a larger unit.

Symbolism is also distinguished from allegory. Whereas the allegorist commonly invents a world (Bunyan's man named Christian, in *The Pilgrim's Progress,* meets a Giant named Despair) in order to talk about the real world, the symbolist commonly presents the phenomena of what we usually call the real world, and he uses them to reveal a "higher," eternal world of which the symbol is a part. In allegory there is a system of equations, but in symbolism there is an extension. The allegorist is free to invent any number of imaginary worlds to talk about the real world, but the symbolist feels that there is only one way by which he can present the "higher" real world he envisions. An allegory can with relative ease be paraphrased, but a symbol, because it not only stands for something else which cannot otherwise be expressed, but also is *part of something else* and *is itself too,* cannot be clearly explained. As Carlyle says in *Sartor Resartus,* in a symbol "the Infinite is made to blend itself with the Finite, to stand visible, and as it were, attainable there." Henry James says that symbolism is the presentation "of objects casting . . . far behind them a shadow more curious . . . than the apparent figure." Having said all this, it must be mentioned that there is an increasing tendency to blur the distinction between symbol and allegory, especially when the writer's invented world (usually associated with allegory) has no clear equations.

unity. Generally means something like "coherence" or "congruence"; in a unified piece the parts work together and jointly contribute to the whole. Unity suggests "completeness" or "pattern" resulting from a controlling intelligence. Robert Louis Stevenson, complaining about arbitrary unhappy endings, explained to James Barrie: "If you are going to make a book end badly, it must end badly from the beginning."

To the student:

We, as publishers, realize that one way to improve education is to improve textbooks. We also realize that you, the student, have a large role in the success or failure of textbooks. Although teachers choose books to be used in the classroom, if the students do not buy and use books, those books are failures.

Usually only the teacher is asked about the quality of a text; his opinion alone is considered as revisions are written or as new books are planned. Now, Little, Brown would like to ask you about this book: how you liked or disliked it; why it was successful or dull; if it taught you anything. Would you fill in this form and return it to us at: Little, Brown and Co., College Division, 34 Beacon St., Boston, Mass. 02106. It is your chance to directly affect the publication of future textbooks.

Book title:__________ School:__________

Course title:__________ Course enrollment:__________

1. Did you like the book?__________

2. CONTENT: Was it too easy?__________

   Did you read all the selections?__________

   Which did you like most?__________

   Which did you like least?__________

3. FORMAT: Did you like the cover?__________

   Did you like the size?__________

   Did you like the margins?__________

   Did you like the illustrations?__________

   Did you like the type size?__________

(over)

4. Were the study questions, review summaries, or other pedagogical apparatus useful? ____________

How should they be changed? ____________

____

5. INT ____________

Hov ____________

____

6. Do this book next year?

____

7. Wil ____________

8. Plea might improve this boo

____

9. May k, or in future pub-
lishi

____

date signature